WEALTH...POWER...PASSION...
AND THREE SISTERS WHO
WANTED IT ALL

HONORA. The eldest ... the gentlest ... Her all-consuming love for one man would make her an outcast — and ignite a bitter family feud.

CRYSTAL. Sexy ... ruthless ... She would stop at nothing in her quest for wealth and position. Including seducing her sister's husband in an act of revenge.

JOSCELYN. The youngest ... the smartest ... She sacrificed her brilliant career to further her husband's — only to have her marriage shattered in a brutal act of violence.

TOO MUCH TOO SOON
Jacqueline Briskin

"First there was Jacqueline Susann. Then came Jackie Collins. And now a third Jackie must be added... Jacqueline Briskin."
— *People* magazine

"Picturesque ... surprising." — *Los Angeles* magazine

"A spellbinding tale." — *Forecast*

Books by Jacqueline Briskin

Too Much Too Soon

Jacqueline Briskin

BERKLEY BOOKS, NEW YORK

FOR BERT

This Berkley book contains the complete
text of the original hardcover edition.
It has been completely reset in a typeface
designed for easy reading and was printed
from new film.

TOO MUCH TOO SOON

A Berkley Book / published by arrangement with
G. P. Putnam's Sons

PRINTING HISTORY
G. P. Putnam's edition / August 1985
Berkley edition / June 1986

ISBN: 0-425-08783-2

A BERKLEY BOOK ® TM 757,375
Berkley Books are published by The Berkley Publishing Group,
200 Madison Avenue, New York, NY 10016.
The name "BERKLEY" and the stylized "B" with design
are trademarks belonging to Berkley Publishing Corporation.

PRINTED IN THE UNITED STATES OF AMERICA

CONTENTS

INTRODUCTION

The swarthy man had positioned himself three feet or so to their left. He looked utterly commonplace. So why should her attention be drawn to him? Because, she realized, surrounding him was an aura of wildness that set him apart from the rest of the journalists. His muscles were flexed tautly, moisture gleamed on his Levantine flesh. The pupils of his eyes were wary pinpoints fixed on Alexander.

She gripped her son's arm, feeling the lean muscles, wanting to draw him away from the feral gaze, yet unable to speak.

Did I have time to warn him?

This fine point would haunt her the rest of her life.

She saw the man's hand reach under the Dacron jacket. A movement swift, yet also incredibly predictable. And she was not surprised at the gun, a smallish pistol, the familiar and accoutrement of countless television shows. So much for all the metal detectors and security, she thought.

He wants to kill Alexander....

Later, later she would wonder why, if her thoughts drifted so leisurely, she didn't have time to scream a warning.

A body hurled between the gun and Alexander, moving so swiftly that in the blur she didn't realize immediately that it was Curt. Simultaneously there was a sound like a twig cracking. Curt's mouth opened, he swayed from side to side and back and forth. Hands reached out to break his fall.

The frenzied crowd trapped the Captol police near the doorway, and had the assailant intended to escape he would have had a good chance in the confusion. Instead, his feet planted apart, he raised his left hand to steady his right wrist as he aimed again.

The second shot cracked just before the screaming filled the universe.

"A-a-l-e-e-x-a-a-n-d-e-e-e-r...."

ONE

1949

The Sylvander Sisters

1

The wind can be sharp in San Francisco. On this afternoon
in early March of 1949 the prevailing westerly had swept
the air so that in Pacific Heights, where turn-of-the-century
nabobs had raised their architectural fantasies, the spectacular view of the city was razor-sharp. The undiluted sunlight dramatically shaded the plunging hills, the great
swags of Golden Gate Bridge gleamed like molten strands
of caramelized sugar, skipping little whitecaps intensified
the flag blue of San Francisco Bay—in this clarity one felt
capable of reaching across the immense bay to touch
mountainous Berkeley.

Two young girls climbed the steep grade of Clay Street.
They wore identical heavy, shabby navy coats that had a
foreign cut and polished brown oxfords that were too
sturdy to find favor locally. The hats that they clutched
against the wind, however, had an inexpensive smartness
that was uniquely American.

Honora and Crystal Sylvander were sisters and English.

Crystal, who wore the creamy felt pillbox, possessed an
astonishing amalgam of Saxon attributes. Blond hair,
bright as polished brass, framed delicate features. Her
peerless white complexion was enlivened by dimpled
cheeks that seemed rouged but were not. The clear blue
irises of her eyes were ringed with a darker cobalt. Crystal's
one flaw, if you could call it that, was a lack of height; however, the clumsy coat couldn't hide the voluptuous curves
of her diminutive body.

Honora, the elder sister, wearing the russet velvet hat
with the turned-down brim, lacked her sister's blatantly
provocative beauty, yet her charms grew on you. Her glossy
black pageboy was wind ruffled, her dark eyes large and
memorable. Tall, with the long, fragile Sylvander bone
structure, she moved with a fine, unconscious grace.

Reaching the crest of the hill, they could see twin lines of large cars edged into the curb around a red sandstone Victorian mansion that crouched between its round Norman towers.

Honora halted, her upper lip rising in dismay. "Do you suppose that's Uncle Gideon's house?" she asked in her soft, well-bred English accent.

"We're close to his address," Crystal replied airily.

"But he has other visitors."

"Did you expect we'd be the only ones? Uncle Gideon's only the top engineer in San Francisco!"

"So many people . . ." Honora's voice faltered. "We can't just barge in."

Crystal set her pretty chin firmly. At seventeen, younger by almost an exact calendar year than Honora, she had maneuvered her sister into making this condolence call on their wealthy, as yet unknown American uncle by marriage. "You're the end, Honora, the living end!" she said. "Our aunt has just died, and you let a few motorcars frighten you off."

"This isn't the right way for us to get to know Uncle Gideon." Honora heard her own pleading tone. A gust of wind tugged at the wide brim of her hat and she reached for it. She was overly conscious that despite the new hat, bought in Macy's basement with the dollar and a half Crystal had wheedled from their father, money that the family could ill afford, she did not look American. *What's so wrong with that?* she asked herself. The English have always been passionately if offhandedly proud of their origins, and Honora, whose patriotism had been further honed by wartime hardships, was not a girl who changed her loyalties easily. These past two months, though, her natural shyness had been increased by Crystal's unceasing endeavors to make the two of them "fit in with everyone else here."

Crystal was saying, "We've been in San Francisco since Christmas and we haven't met him yet."

"Yes, but—"

"This is the perfect opportunity to introduce ourselves."

"I'm not sure that American girls make visits alone."

"Oh, for goodness sake, Honora, stop talking absolute rot! You know as well as I do they're much less stiff here. And we're doing the decent thing."

"Uncle Gideon's never shown the least interest in us."

Crystal's pretty, penciled brows drew together sharply at this truth. Aunt Matilda was their blood kin. Birthdays and Christmas she had dispatched practical mufflers and jumpers to her motherless nieces. The enclosed card invariably said, *With love from Uncle Gideon and Aunt Matilda*, but they knew his name was included as form.

Gideon's first correspondence had arrived last November, a reply to Langley Sylvander's painfully composed request for a loan to pay his daughters' tuition.

Re your request of September 1. I consider it morally wrong to either borrow or lend. However, I can offer you aid if you move to San Francisco.

Even though you have no engineering background, I can guarantee that Talbott's will take you on and train you as a specifications writer. In this country your expenses will be more sensible as we have an excellent free educational system for the two younger girls. Your oldest, Matilda informs me, is eighteen. I consider it my duty to see that she gets working papers. She should have no difficulty locating some sort of a job. Matilda, who is in ill health, sends her best.

                                        Yours
                                        Gideon Talbott

"Then it's time he does pay attention," Crystal snapped. "With Aunt Matilda gone, he's our only family."

"But what if, well, if our coming reflects badly on Daddy?" Honora murmured.

Another burst of wind made Crystal squash her new hat to her head. "I'm being blown to bits," she said. "And since you're so worried about Daddy's job, he's the one who told us to come."

"You know he doesn't mean what he says when he has . . . one of his headaches."

"Oh, do whatever you want. After tramping up and down hills for hours, I'm not going home."

Honora stood for a moment of worried indecision, then hurried after her younger sister, who was clipping smartly toward the large, ugly house.

The waiting chauffeurs sheltered in the porte cochere turned admiring red faces to watch the girls ascend four shallow marble steps. Crystal pressed the bell. After a long minute, the black-sprayed wreath bounced dryly against Honduran mahogany and the front door opened. An elderly Filipino peered at them with an unsmiling, unblinking gaze.

With a spontaneous movement Honora and Crystal clasped hands. Faced with any hostility, they rose as if in a helium balloon above minor jealousies and sibling squabbles.

"Yes?" the servant asked coldly.

Each family has its assigned ritual roles, and Honora, as the oldest daughter, had become surrogate for her dead mother, tacitly being assigned the more onerous responsibilities of the impecunious Sylvanders. "The Misses Sylvander to see Mr. Talbott," she replied with a slight tremor.

The unpleasant scrutiny lasted another few seconds, then the Filipino said, "Please come in."

Leaving them by the door, he limped arthritically toward the hum of a gathering in the rear of the house. Voices rose briefly then were muted as an unseen door opened and closed.

After the roiling, windswept brilliance of the afternoon, the gloom and stillness in the house seemed eerie, and the girls stood mute and immobilized. They had never entered a private house this large. Crystal peered around, familiarizing herself with the stamping grounds of the wealthy. Honora clasped her shaking hands. The entry, with its opulent paneling and grandiose, three-story stairwell from which hung a massive ormolu chandelier, had been designed for this exact purpose, to unnerve visitors.

The servant returned. "Mr. Talbott will see you," he said. He took their coats, folding them over his arm in a purposeful manner to show the long, embarrassing frays in the worn blue rayon lining before leading them into the interior of one of the turrets. The room's circular shape, pierced metalwork and the enormous fringed hassock placed in the center gave it the look of a Turkish alcove.

Crystal went directly to the brass mirror, standing on tiptoe to adjust her hat and smooth her yellow hair. Almost immediately, the sound of heavy footsteps rang on the parquet.

The Sylvanders' photographic portrait of their American relations, taken many years before, showed that Gideon Talbott's sternly aggressive jaw was balanced by a full head of dark hair. Judging from his thick neck and burly shoulders, the girls had deduced him to be tall. Seeing him in the flesh, standing on his stumpy legs, they realized that the picture had misled them. He was under 5′5″. His youthful thatch had deserted him and the last few faithful strands had been combed across his flattish head to meet his virile, bushy brown sideburns.

Gideon's broad features were knotted into an expression of stern righteousness that added to his aura of masculine command. *The grand Napoleon,* thought Honora.

Closing the door with a sharp bang, Gideon moved briskly to the Moorish fireplace, where he continued his examination of his late wife's nieces.

"Good afternoon, Uncle Gideon," Honora murmured, flushing.

"I'm surprised your father's not with you." His voice had a peculiar grittiness, distinctive and compelling.

"D-Daddy's resting . . ." Honora's soft little stammer trapped her tongue. "He's ill. . . ."

"Sylvander was at work yesterday," retorted Gideon. "And which one are you?"

"I'm—" Honora started.

Gideon cut in. "Besides, aren't there three of you?"

"Yes. Joss—Joscelyn—is only n-nine, nearly ten. We didn't bring her along. Uncle Gideon, I'm Honora, and this is Crystal. We came to tell you how sorry we are about Aunt M-Matilda . . ." Honora floundered on. "We never met her, but she was always most awfully kind to us."

"Your aunt was in poor health for many years. For the last year and a half she was bedridden and in constant pain."

Honora swallowed miserably.

Crystal took a step toward her sister. Her lashes had descended over the angry blue glint in her eyes, yet her voice was rich with sympathy as she said, "It must have been a terrible time for her, Uncle Gideon—and for you, too."

Gideon's gaze lingered a moment on the lovely downcast face with its windwhipped, crimson cheeks. "I have other callers," he said, assuming a kindlier tone. "Come on in and have some coffee with us."

2

The sliding doors were open between the three elaborately paneled, high-ceilinged rooms, and fires burned in all three of the massive black marble fireplaces. The prune-colored velvet drapes were drawn in the rear room, blocking what was a magnificent panorama of San Francisco and the Bay. Yet other than the dun light cast by the wall sconces and the black clothing of the twenty or so people gathered, there was no sign of bereavement, not a red-tinged eye, no discreet blowing of a nose.

Propelling the two sisters in front of him, Gideon stamped up to three matrons who were engaged in affable conversation while deftly balancing Imari cups and plates.

"Matilda's nieces, just arrived from England," he introduced. "Mrs. Indge, Mrs. Carstairs, Mrs. Burdetts, may I present Carol and Monica Sylvander."

Having performed his obligation as host, albeit with the wrong names for his nieces, he marched off to join a group of middle-aged men who were talking loudly.

After a momentary pause, the stoutest lady—she was Mrs. Burdetts—offered condolences and inquired about their dear aunt's private services, which had been held the previous day.

Honora's slender shoulders hunched. "We weren't at the funeral."

"But, dear, surely Gideon had the family?"

"I . . . uhh, we . . . never met Aunt Matilda," Honora whispered.

At this admission, the triumvirate eyed the carefully ironed pastel frocks and new bargain-basement hats, gave the girls vague smiles and returned to their criticism of the previous night's symphony.

The girls listened and when the subject changed to the windy weather, Crystal joined in politely.

Honora smiled until her mouth felt stiff. After a few minutes she drifted away, pretending interest in the bric-a-brac that sprang from every flat surface. Self-conscious about being the only person unattached to a grouping, she wandered through the central drawing room into an empty room whose velvet draperies were open. It was furnished with a gilded harp and a full-size Steinway—Honora suspected the piano's purpose was not musical, but to hold bric-a-brac. Above the open keyboard was a miniature copy of the Michelangelo *Pietà*. She ran a tentative fingertip over the cool, smooth marble.

"Hideous, isn't it?" asked a nearby masculine voice.

Jumping, Honora looked up. Her first confused thought about the man who had addressed her was: *So that's what they mean, leonine.* His powerfully built body managed to appear both relaxed and alert. His cheekbones were broad and high, his hair thick and tawny. The eyebrows were very fair at the outer edges, darkening toward the bridge of his nose like markings. As Californians went, he wasn't tall, but he had the requisite deep tan. Honora knew that he had just arrived, for she certainly would have noticed him in the lugubriously clad gathering. Not only was he the youngest man present—Honora placed him in his mid-twenties—but he was dressed in a pearl gray suit with a handsome maroon tie.

The statuette teetered under her touch and with a gasp she saved it from toppling over.

"Why look so worried? Don't you know that sort of junk is indestructible?" The man's lopsided, very white grin managed to be attractive and unpleasant at the same time. "Haven't you heard? It's the survival of the ugliest."

The stranger's casual snideness had somehow released Honora from the constraint that she normally experienced with strangers, especially the overattractive male ones, and her confidence surged. "I never heard of that particular law. *I* happen to think the carving's rather nicely done." A smile showed at the corner of her soft, full mouth. "But then I've never seen the original, so maybe you have the advantage?"

"Never been near Rome," he replied.

"Then how do you know that the artist wasn't successful?"

"Never in a million years. Anything worthwhile is original."

"Another of your laws?" she parried.

"Come on, you know as well as I do that any halfway good sculptor would refuse to make copies," he said. "I'm an engineer, but I'd give it up in a minute if I had to mimic other people's projects."

"Then you're original."

"Creative is the word we use here. And I am. *Very.*"

"Lucky me, talking to you." Her body had taken on a peculiar will of its own. Without any consciousness on her part, her neck had tilted to better display the shining dark hair, and her shoulders had pulled back to show her small, pretty breasts.

"You English underplay everything, but I can't see any reason to downgrade my good points."

"Modesty isn't among them, I see."

Honora's repartee came as a surprise to her, and she could feel her heart beating. In the past her nonthreatening gentleness had drawn the awkward boys and humorless swots—grinds they were called in America. It seemed that all one needed to be witty was a lively partner. She wondered whether the hair on his chest was the same flaxen shade of his outer eyebrows or the darker shade of his hair. Her eyelashes fluttered and she flushed at thinking of his nakedness.

Smiling, he was giving her the once-over, a leisurely examination that made her skin tingle and the blood rise up to her face. He looked again into her eyes, which were the warm, dark shade of good sherry. ("My Portuguese," her father had fancifully nicknamed her.)

"Tell me," he asked, "since you don't consider originality part of success, how do you define it?" He glanced down the long vista to the somberly dressed group in the rear drawing room. "Of course they'd all deny it to the death, but their yardstick is cold cash."

"I dare say that's a jolly good ingredient, being comfortably off," she retorted.

"Bull. You don't have an avaricious bone in your body."

"Oh don't I just! How lovely it would be not to have to go out looking for work."

He gave her a quick glance. "Looking for work? You hardly seem the career girl type."

"I'm trying." Her low, soft voice wavered. Never in a life not overly abundant in self-confidence had she felt more inadequate than when facing across the desk of the Golden Gate Job Placement Agency.

"What's your field?"

She recovered. "Woolgathering."

"Try putting that on an application," he chuckled. "Anyway, you can't convince me you're interested in money, not with those dark, nonacquisitive eyes, Monica Sylvander."

He knew who she was! Her blinding sense of betrayal must have shown.

"I should have introduced myself first," he said with a small, mocking bow. "I'm Curt Ivory." He ran his finger on the keyboard, a rippling of sound. "Ivory, like these."

"It's Honora," she murmured.

"What?"

"It's not Monica, it's Honora."

"Honora, I work for Mr. Talbott. He asked me to let you know that his car'll be around in a few minutes to take you and your sister home."

Filled with shame at her mistaken assumption of his interest, she replied in a clipped tone, "That's most unnecessary."

"You're angry."

"I didn't mean to chatter on."

He was peering at her. "No, you're not mad. You're embarrassed."

She guessed her face was crimson. "It's most kind of Uncle Gideon, but my sister and I planned to walk home."

"There's no point arguing. He wants you driven home. And what Mr. Talbott wants, Mr. Talbott gets." There was irony in Curt's tone, and also deep affection. He touched a harp string, drawing a long, plangent note. "I figured Langley was laying it on a bit thick about his daughters, but now I see he wasn't."

"You know Dad—you know my father?"

"I told you I'm an engineer."

"I'm sorry. How silly of me. Naturally you know him."

"He's a peacock about his girls, calls you his three graces—"

"Curt," interrupted a female drawl. "Oh, Curt."

An exceptionally thin young woman was leaning against the jamb of the sliding door. Her long-sleeved gray silk dress fitted her narrow, near breastless torso, flaring out in a gored skirt that reached to just above her sharply boned ankles. Her brown hair was swept back into a severe knot and she held a cigarette between two long fingers. She wasn't pretty at all—indeed, with her hollow cheeks and visible jawbones, she resembled a young Duchess of Windsor. And like the Duchess, she possessed a unique chic.

"Well, well," Curt drawled. "So you finally made it."

"I had a tea, darling, *another* tea. What a bore. But Mother informs me *you* only put in an appearance a few minutes ago." Her voice was magically American, especially when she emphasized certain words. Honora felt herself dwindle.

"I was at the Oakland field office," Curt said. "Imogene, this is Mrs. Talbott's niece. Honora Sylvander, Imogene Burdetts."

"I'm so *terribly* sorry about your aunt," Imogene Burdetts said rapidly.

"Thank you."

"Honora just arrived from jolly old England," Curt said.

"Yes, I can tell by the accent." Imogene didn't look at Honora. "Curt, Mother wants to talk to you. It's an invitation, so don't say I didn't *warn* you."

"Duty calls, then," he said. He turned toward Honora with one of his satirical grins. "The odds are we'll be bumping into each other."

Honora watched the couple cross the length of the rooms to the couch where the three ladies still sat, then move to stand alone by the prune-colored drapes. Curt's back was to Honora, but she could see by the expression on Imogene's face that he was engaged in the same kind of insulting banter that she had found exhilarating.

She was bleakly staring at them when a gray-haired maid clumped in to tell her that the car was waiting.

3

As the limousine eased from under the glass-encased porte cochere, Crystal rubbed a hand across the luxurious seat. "Oh, lovely, lovely, the leather's like silk. Honora, how good of Uncle Gideon to send us home in style—though I must say I don't see generosity as his line."

"Crystal!" Honora murmured, staring meaningfully at the opened glass between them and the elderly Filipino, who had donned a peaked cap for his role as chauffeur.

"He's all business." Crystal refused to be silenced, but she did lower her voice. "Talk about being overcome by grief! I found out that Aunt Matilda was housebound for ages. I'm positive Uncle Gideon has a mistress."

Honora, praying that the hum of the motor covered their voices, pinched Crystal's wrist.

Crystal rubbed at the skin, too pleased with herself to pinch back. "He was married to an invalid," she continued. "And everybody knows rich men need 'it' more. The drive."

"He's not the type at all." Honora whispered her defense of her uncle.

"He does have a poker up his bottom, doesn't he?" Crystal stroked the seat again, her beautiful mouth smug. "If he was angry that we showed up, he's obviously forgiven us."

"He just doesn't want his friends to see us tramping about San Francisco. Mr. Ivory as much as said so."

Crystal turned in surprise. "Mr. Ivory?"

"Curt Ivory. He works for Uncle Gideon."

"That most fearfully divine man in the gorgeous pale gray suit that you snagged off alone into the music room, is Curt Ivory? Of course he's at Talbott's. He's Uncle Gideon's right-hand man. That skinny Imogene was playing up to him like mad. Her dress, it's the New Look. Maybe a Dior original—can you imagine how divine it'd be to wear originals? Well, why not? With her family."

"Are they so important?"

"Oh, honestly, Honora. How you can be so clever at literature and books and such an idiot at remembering every single thing that counts in real life? Remember? Daddy told us that Mr. Burdetts and Uncle Gideon are involved in something called a joint venture to build that freeway in Oakland. What's he like, Curt Ivory?"

"He's Imogene Burdett's young man."

"You sound disappointed. I'll bet anything she's not a virgin."

"Crystal, this whole conversation is so—"

"I know, I know. Daddy would say it's common and Sylvanders don't giggle over young men like scullery maids. But what's so wonderful about being a Sylvander? Do you suppose any of those rich old cows has an attractive, eligible son?"

"You're only seventeen."

"They get serious much younger here. Remember what they said in the war? Yanks are oversexed."

"We're going home to England the minute Daddy's on his feet again."

"Which means, Honora dear, that we're staying here forever and ever, amen."

Honora forgot the aged chauffeur and her voice rose, shaking. "What a filthy thing to say!"

"I love Daddy as much as you do, Honora, but you're just not realistic about him. He's not cut out to be a business success. So we have to look out for ourselves." The energy and determination in Crystal's expression, rather than tarnishing her beauty, made her yet more irresistible. "We have to find rich husbands."

"I could never get married like that, for money."

Shrugging, Crystal said, "At least we have Uncle Gideon behind us."

"Now who isn't being realistic? He didn't even remember our names."

"Well, we've met him and that's the first step." Crystal's eyes turned a darker blue. "He *has* to take an interest in us. I'll be meeting the right kind of young men. And if you aren't so keen on marriage, at least you won't have to grub at some filthy job, you'll be at university. Joscelyn can go to a decent school where everyone isn't Chinese or Italian. Daddy won't drink so much—"

"Crystal!" Honora's whisper trembled with intensity.

Crystal, glancing at the chauffeur, nodded, and said no more.

The car had left the fine homes behind. As they glided up Lombard Street between drab apartment buildings toward the steep hill topped by the gray, upraised finger of Coit Tower, Honora bent forward to tap the separating pane of glass. "This is our number," she called politely.

The big sedan braked, passing a nearly invisible entry, a narrow arch that led below a block of flats. The brilliant afternoon sunlight exposed the leprous flaking of gray Navy-surplus paint.

A third-story window was flung open, and a man leaned on the window ledge, his thinning brown hair blowing around his long, pale features, his unknotted old school tie flapping.

"Oh God, look at Daddy," Crystal whispered.

"You two deserve a good hiding!" Langley Sylvander shouted. "Where in the devil have you been, all tarted up?"

"He's really blotto," Crystal muttered.

Honora, not waiting for the chauffeur to open the door, jumped from the car with a mumbled thank you. Crystal was right after her.

They dashed through the dark, narrow tunnel with its line of mailboxes, emerging in a sloping, cracked cement courtyard. Sheets and clothes billowed overhead on lines crisscrossing between two barrackslike frame structures.

They raced up three flights of exterior steps. Before Honora could use her key, the door swung open and Langley blocked their way.

The upper part of his face was strong and handsome, with a broad brow and deep-set eyes nearly as vivid a blue as Crystal's. With his muscles loosened by drinking, however, the weakness of his chin and the self-indulgent petulance of his full, well-chiseled mouth showed.

"I won't have the pair of you getting into trouble," he bawled.

"Daddy, please let us in," Honora said. "We can explain it all."

"What were you doing, parading around in that gaudy American motorcar?"

Crystal raised her chin. "It belongs to Uncle Gideon."

"That common upstart! What were you doing with *him?*"

"You told us to go to his house."

Langley gave her a look of surprise. "I did? Ahh yes, that was to offer your condolences on your aunt's death. Not to use his big, vulgar possessions!" His light-timbred voice had taken on resonance.

Honora pushed him inside and Crystal yanked the front door shut.

They were in a very narrow corridor. The door to their left opened to a small bedroom crowded by a Queen Anne-style double bed and a high-legged nightstand on which stood a glass and a whiskey bottle.

"Where's my motherless babe? Is she out bagging for coins? Joscelyn. *Joss.*"

"Isn't she in our room?" Honora asked, worried.

"Joss-e-lynnn!" bawled Langley.

The door to their right opened. A short, thin child wearing an English schoolgirl's tunic stood clutching a book to her skinny chest. Her mousy brown hair was skinned back from her narrow face into one long braid—in England the girls had called it a plait—her pale blue eyes appeared watery behind thick lensed glasses, her upper teeth bucked out. Joscelyn Sylvander, a remarkably homely child, was an unlikely postscript to the handsome Sylvander family.

"What's all the shouting about?" she asked with purposeful ignorance. "Is anything wrong?"

"As if you didn't know," Crystal interjected—she was not too old to bicker with her little sister.

"If I call, you're to answer," Langley shouted.

"Oh, when you're inebriated you're a hopeless case," Joscelyn cried.

"You're being cheeky, miss."

Joscelyn barged back into the room, the brown-painted, plywood walls shivering as she slammed the door.

"These scenes!" Crystal stalked down the slit into the square room that served as kitchen and dining room, leaving Honora to soothe their father.

Honora took his arm. "Daddy, I'll make a nice pot of tea."

Langley shook off her hand, asking plaintively, "How could you have let that bounder do you a favor?"

"It was wrong of us—me. Daddy, it's nearly four. Tea'll buck you up." Honora's tone was pleading.

"You girls were reared to be ladies. It's my fault, I never

should have brought you to this insufferable country!" The
thin walls shivered again as the second door slammed.

Honora's full upper lip quivered. Practical Crystal and
clever Joscelyn were able to handle Langley's atypical out-
bursts, but his drunken rages always shook his oldest
daughter to the depth of her vulnerable soul. She not only
loved him—all three girls did—but she idolized him as
well. She took a few deep, slow breaths, then went into the
other bedroom, which had every inch of space jammed
with a large fumed oak chest of drawers and three iron
beds.

"I get blamed for everything," Joscelyn whimpered. She
was hunched on the farthest bed.

"Joss, you know how most dreadfully unhappy he is,
having to work for Uncle."

Joscelyn's left eye blinked rapidly as she struck out. "Do
you suppose I'm in a state of bliss? You're lucky, you're not
in school! All those dreadful boys mimicking every word I
say. I hate them—I wish I was back in Edinthorpe, where
there's only girls. Not that the girls here are any better.
They're absolute imbeciles." Joscelyn, placed with children
two years her senior, excelled them in almost every subject,
and with her blind, intellectual arrogance let them know
the full extent of her superiority. She had no more idea how
to get along with her peers in San Francisco than she had in
England.

Honora sighed. "On job interviews they always seem to
be poking fun at me, too." She edged along the narrow
space to sit next to her little sister, kissing the top of the
mousy hair, which gave off a faint odor of homemade tof-
fee and Castile soap. "Still, it's not all that terrible. We're
together. And we generally have a happy time, don't we?"

"I suppose." Joscelyn snuggled closer to her sister's side,
a nearly sly expression of contentment on her narrow face
as she let her oldest sister, her surrogate mother, comfort
her.

Later, while Honora stood at the sagging sink, inexpertly
putting together the parts of the old-fashioned meat grinder
to make a shepherd's pie from pieces of gristly leftover
lamb and leftover mashed potatoes, Crystal turned on the
little radio that the previous tenants had left because the
bakelite was cracked. After a moment, a swinging Tommy
Dorsey version of "Buttons and Bows" filled the kitchen.

When the shepherd's pie gave off savory aromas and the table was laid, they peered down the corridor, glancing apprehensively at one another. Honora went to give Langley's door a tentative tap. "Daddy, supper's ready."

"I'm not hungry." His reply was slurred. "Go ahead without me."

The girls ate quickly and went to bed early, even Crystal, who generally stayed up until all hours on the weekend.

Sunday morning, Honora woke first. She tiptoed from the bedroom so as not to disturb her sisters and went to the kitchen.

Langley sat at the table behind a white earthenware teapot with a brown scar.

He gave his favorite daughter a helpless little grin. "I couldn't find the biscuits," he said sheepishly.

She smiled back, padding in her slippers to the open shelves above the stove. "Here, Daddy," she said, opening the tin.

The other two girls straggled out.

"Well, Joss," said Langley, patting his youngest's cheek. "What do you say to a visit to the Fleishhacker Zoo? Maybe we can persuade your sister to make a picnic."

The Sylvanders readied themselves for the outing, laughing and teasing.

In spite of Langley's profound selfishness and susceptibility to the bottle, Crystal's vanity and ambitions, Joscelyn's studied insolence and complete lack of beguilement, they had always been a happy family. In this transitional period, while they dangled like chrysalides in their shabby clothes between the old life and the new, they clung together yet closer.

At the zoo people smiled at the English group, the two charming older girls laughing as they lugged the brown bags, the handsome man wearing a derby and tapping his unnecessary umbrella on the cage bars as he pointed out an animal's peculiarities to a thin, pigtailed child, a family obviously delighted in each other's company.

4

The Sylvander family tree, while not as illustrious as Langley believed, had irrefutably sprung from gentlemanly soil: his spindly branch, however, was rotted through with poverty. His father, a humorless bank clerk, had scrimped to the meanest degree to send Langley to a mediocre public school although the London County Council gave a far better education gratis.

After matriculation he gravitated to the underpaid thoroughly respectable profession of publishing and was a junior editor at Cullomton House when he met Doris Kinnon. Six years his senior, on her first visit to Europe, Doris tumbled for Langley's accent, his handsome profile, his whimsical charm. On Langley's part, he fell for Doris's wholehearted adoration of him and—though his conscious mind could never admit to this—for the ease she could bring him.

Doris and Matilda's father, a successful San Francisco attorney, had left each daughter fifty thousand dollars. Ten thousand pounds! In those years between the wars it was a fortune. Langley's touchstone of a true gentleman was one who stood aloof from commerce, and now he cultivated his ignorance of financial matters. The eight-room flat in Kensington, the staff of three, the fine old port, the occasional trips to the continent, tunneled deep into their capital. That, however, was the concern of Lloyd's Bank. Langley was a happy man. Then, on September 2, 1939, the day after Hitler's troops invaded Poland, Doris died giving birth to their third daughter. Langley, in his grief, made the grand gesture, enlisting in His Majesty's Navy. Honora and Crystal were evacuated with the Edinthorpe boarders to a crenellated Victorian country house near Exeter, and the Head Mistress, a kindly, bewhiskered spinster, ensconced Joscelyn with her decrepit nanny in the school's wartime quarters. Honora passed her free time cuddling the wailing, colicky baby in her thin arms.

Langley spent the duration at the British naval installation in Reykjavik. After the war, in 1947, the last block of Doris's stocks had to be sold. The wind of impending poverty chilled Langley more than had the Icelandic blizzards. In rapid succession he lost three positions.

In extremis, Langley composed that hortatory letter to his unknown brother-in-law.

Gideon Talbott's terse reply sent him on a three-day bender. Bad enough that the family's bread and butter would be dependent on his kowtowing to this common, *common* American swine, but what made Langley thirst for the bottle was the suggestion that Honora, his heart's child, Honora with her Sylvander blood, should become a menial wageslave.

The Monday after the condolence call to the Talbott house, Honora rose before six, scurrying in her dressing gown to the big trash barrels at the bottom of the steps, rummaging for the previous day's *Chronicle.* At the kitchen table, she ran a pencil down the Help Wanted column, her dark eyes bleak as she checked two advertisements. She then bent to light the broiler, jumping back from the bursting blue flame. Today's breakfast was toast and drippings. This week, all meals would be variations on the bread theme—mayonnaise or margarine sandwiches for lunch, suppers of fried bread with ketchup, or eggybread, which was called French toast in America.

Just like during the war, Crystal or Joscelyn would remark, and Langley would beg with whimsical testiness, *What about a nice bit of chicken tomorrow, Honora?*

There would be no chicken. Less than a dollar in change was in the bottom of the jam jar that served as her bank. No replenishment would be dropped in until Friday—Talbott's employees were paid every other Friday afternoon. Langley had had a little left from the money he'd borrowed for their passage, but yesterday, ashamed of his binge and desperate to make it up to his girls, he had topped off the warm, heavenly wad of their day at the zoo by spending his last two crumpled dollar bills to take them to an exotic Basque restaurant where they had crowded together with other people at a long table to laugh over a vast eight-course supper.

At exactly seven thirty Langley and Joscelyn left the flat.

Honora dressed slowly and carefully. Crystal primped at
the bathroom mirror.

Crystal was enrolled at City College. Unlike her older
and younger sisters, she had no interest in academics but
being ineligible for a green work card until her eighteenth
birthday she spent her time at this free, two-year campus,
routinely cutting class to join her new friends at the big corner booth of the Treat Shop. Usually some adoring-eyed
boy treated her to a sundae, a long glass dish with three
plump scoops melting richly under their burden of hot
fudge and real whipped cream, such a delight after that
whale-fat ersatz they were still using in England. When a
youth dredged up the courage to ask her for a date, she did
not accept until ascertaining he owned a car and had a
friend for Honora.

As the sisters emerged onto Lombard Street, they could
see no farther than the corner: from the Bay foghorns
lowed like primitive, mating creatures.

Honora wore a sweater that nearly matched her new
russet hat—for job interviews she never wore her shabby
old coat. Shivering, she held her arms close to her body. "If
only we'd learned typing and shorthand at Edinthorpe,"
she sighed.

"As if you could be a secretary!" An awareness of class
barriers had been inoculated into the Sylvander girls from
birth on, and each in her own way was an innocently artless
snob. "The very least you can take is Debutante Dresses at
I. Magnin's, or a receptionist at a good law firm. Was there
anything like that in the paper?"

"A two-line advert for saleslady at Shreve's. It's a silver
shop on Post Street."

"I know the place and it's perfect for you," Crystal said
enthusiastically. Shreve's had the same prestige as Gump's.
"Any other possibilities?"

They were on their way to the cable car and had reached
Washington Square; Honora looked up at the misty, ornate
spires atop the Church of St. Peter and St. Paul. "Stroud's,"
she said.

"Stroud's?" Crystal asked. "Is that a firm or a shop?"

"It's, uhh, a cafe."

"A hostess? If you want my opinion don't even bother.
It's not good enough."

"They need a waitress." Honora's face was crimson.

"A waitress!" Crystal cried.

"We don't have a dollar between us until Friday."

"Honora, you mustn't take everything to heart so," Crystal said, her voice sympathetic. "We've eaten bread before."

"The hole in Joscelyn's shoe wore through and this morning I had to put in cardboard. She has that toothache on and off. There'll never be enough for a dentist unless I find work." Honora was speaking doggedly, as if justifying a major crime. "Our stockings are going; American men don't wear shirts with detachable collars like Daddy's—oh, you know we can't keep on in this hand-to-mouth way."

"Suppose somebody *sees* you?"

"We don't know anybody here," Honora said, immediately thinking of Curt Ivory.

"But a waitress?"

"Crystal, you know how many places I've tried."

"Poor thing," Crystal said, reaching for her sister's cold, slim hand.

"I *must* find a job." Honora's soft voice was hollow with despair. "If I have to take that one, will you promise never to tell Daddy?"

"Of course I wouldn't tell him. It'd kill him. But don't you see? We must really get to work on Uncle Gideon."

"Not a ghost of a chance—"

"There it is!"

A crowded cable car was clanging toward them.

"Crystal, we can't afford—"

"Stop worrying. Don't I always swizz the conductor? Come on! *Hurry!"*

The sisters ran, jumping onto the ledge, clinging to an outside post. Crystal's bus pass for school didn't cover the cable car, and the small, wizened conductor bemusedly watched the extraordinarily lovely little English blonde search through her bag, growing more charmingly agitated as she discovered her change purse was missing. "Okay, okay. Put this ride down to international goodwill," he said with a cheerful wink.

Honora hopped off at Union Square.

It was ten, and freshly painted shop doors were being unlocked for waiting little clusters of well-dressed matrons. Reaching Shreve's, Honora closed her eyes as if praying before she went inside.

When she emerged three minutes later, her luminous skin was drained of its glow.

She stood shivering on the corner for two full minutes, then turned, trotting toward the financial district.

Stroud's turned out to be across the street from the gray granite, pillared Pacific Coast Stock Exchange. Not waiting to catch her breath, Honora darted inside.

A colored Tiffany-glass screen partially hid long rows of tray-sized, linen-draped tables where a few businessmen smoked over coffee cups. Behind the brass cash register sat a waitress. Her starched Dutch cap perched atop her too-vivid red upsweep, her tight, blue-checked uniform exposed the rounds of big, bra-bound breasts whose heavily scented cleavage disappeared into the V-neck.

Honora inquired politely, "Miss, can you please tell me where I inquire about the advertisement—the one in yesterday's *Chronicle*?"

The waitress looked up from the leather menu folder into which she was clipping a mimeographed sheet of Daily Specials. Her small greenish eyes were alert yet noncommittal. "That's quite an accent," she said.

"I'm from England." Honora attempted a smile. "Is the manager in?"

"Al's the owner. Right now he's over to the bakery, hassling about the bill. Ever wait table?"

"At Edinthorpe."

"That's a new one on me. Is it here in Frisco?"

"London," Honora asserted, then couldn't brazen out the half lie. "Actually it's a school, miss."

"The name's Vi Knodler," the waitress said, suddenly cold.

"I'm Honora Sylvander, Miss Knodler. Could you tell me what will be required?"

"Nope."

"Then the position's been filled?" Honora asked.

"You kids! You're all alike no matter where you come from. The minute you're up against it, you figure you'll condescend to wait tables. Well, let me tell you, slinging hash ain't no breeze, no breeze at all."

Vi's outburst was Honora's first indication that, having thrown herself into the sea of "common" occupations, she might not be able to swim.

"I appreciate that, Miss Knodler," she said, then added, "I'll try very hard."

"It takes a darn sight more than trying. Stroud's does the biggest lunch business in the financial district. And me, I make more dough than a lot of the brokers I serve. The tips, Honora, are big tips. And you know why? Because the girls who work here are tops. Take me, I'm smiling at 'em as soon as they sit down, I take orders and when the plates come out of the kitchen, I rush them to the table, hot. I never let a coffee cup stay half empty. I treat 'em all like they was President Truman. I remember names, I remember them good. Nothing makes 'em drop a real tip like hearing, 'Hello, Mr. Jerkface, how are you today, Mr. Jerkface.' The shift starts at six and there's a breakfast rush before the Exchange opens. Lunch is a regular zoo. You gotta be fast and good around here."

"I'm positive I could learn." Close to weeping, Honora clipped her words.

"Stroud's ain't a school." Vi leaned back in her stool, surveying Honora. "Listen, I gotta get these specials stuck in the menus," she said in a kindlier tone. "I like listening to that cute accent of yours, so why not keep me company? Have some java on the house."

At this about-face kindness, Honora felt tears well in her eyes. "No, thank you . . . most kind."

She ran around the stained-glass screen and onto Pine Street.

The job of waitress at Stroud's that until a few minutes ago had seemed the ultimate plunge had become shining, desirable, a holy grail of which she was unworthy.

She walked blindly away from the Stock Exchange. The fog had lifted, and she wished it would return, pea-soup thick. Her strongest desire at the moment was invisibility in which to regain some small semblance of equilibrium. Without realizing it, she was heading toward the Ferry Building with its square clock tower—a copy of the Giralda in Seville, Langley had told them. He had also told them that this neighborhood, the Embarcadero, was "much too rough for my girls." Honora wasn't thinking of his warning.

A short, slight man in a black sweater with a wool cap pulled down over his ears lurched out of a beer joint. Swaying on his feet, he grinned at her. "Hiya, babe. Swell hat you're wearing . . . always was my favorite color, red."

Is this the next step? Is there any other choice? She stared at him.

Taking this as encouragement, he reached for her arm.
He smelled of stale sweat and beer, and had a wart above
his lip. Quite literally she was paralyzed.

"Come in and have yourself a drink, babe."

His fingers on her upper arm moved, nuzzling like small,
nursing rodents against the sides of her breast. The touch
was somehow far more intimate than the groping caresses
of the boys she went out with. "Let's you and me get acquainted, huhh?"

She stared at him in horrified disgust, not seeing a wiry,
tipsy little merchant seaman but a photograph printed on
thin wartime paper that one of the older girls had shown
around when she was ten. It showed a naked man with a
monstrous, engorged penis standing over a terrified
woman.

Jerking from the loose grasp, she ran all the way back to
Stroud's.

Vi was propping menu folders on the tables. "Hey,
what's chasing you?" she asked.

Honora panted, "Miss Knodler—"

"Vi."

"Vi, listen—I simply must find work. At least give me a
try. They don't have to pay unless I'm worth paying. Whatever's decided, I promise I won't argue."

"Well, I'll say this for you British, you don't give up easy.
That's why there'll always be an England, ehh?" Vi's small
eyes were twinkling. "As a matter of fact it's luck you're
back. Carrie, she's the girl who's quitting, just called in
sick. Tell that to Ripley's *Believe It or Not.*"

"You mean you'll let me have the job?"

"For the rest of today. A tryout."

"I can't tell you how . . . grateful I am . . ."

"No violins necessary. There's a uniform that oughta fit
hanging in the help's john."

"John? Who is John?"

Vi laughed. "First thing you gotta do, kid, is learn the
English language."

The blue-checked uniform was permeated with a mixture of cheap rose perfume and acid sweat. Honora's flesh
rose in goosebumps. She reminded herself of the little merchant seaman and pulled it over her head. The waist was
enormous on her. After she cinched it in with the beruffled
rayon apron she surveyed herself in the wavy mirror. The
bustline was darted, and though her small, round breasts

did not fill out the fabric, the seaming accentuated her nipples. The short skirt barely covered the top of her stockings. She turned away quickly.

Scotch-taped onto the restroom door was a diagram of the cafe with the tables numbered and divided into five stations.

Vi came in. "Like I figured, it's a darn good fit."

"But not quite long enough."

Vi grinned. "Exactly what the customers like."

Stroud's clientele was made up almost exclusively of men in dark business suits who, had they met Honora in other circumstances, would have been politely, jovially condescending—in other words, they would have treated her like a lady. In her cologne doused uniform, however, she was exposed to another masculine side.

Her first two parties were seated at the same time. The benign, heavily accented grandfather type, while inquiring how the lamb stew was today, patted her exposed thigh, his little finger stroking the bared flesh around her garter snap. She edged away as far as the narrow space between the tables permitted. A tactical mistake. Turning to light his cigar, he mumbled his order. Timidly she asked him to repeat. He glared at her. "Zee zalat vit oil 'n' vinegar, the zpenzer zteak pink, and no peaz, iz dat clear enough, Limey? You unnerztand dat?"

She clipped her orders to the revolving wheel but forgot the lingo used by the help to call them out. The other waitresses rushing from the service area were balancing incredible numbers of plates on their arms, using napkins below the hot foods, but when Honora attempted to carry more than two starters the salad would slide or the clam chowder slop over to scald her forearm.

By twenty to twelve every table was filled and the waiting crowd spilled around the Tiffany-glass screen. In the uproar Honora often missed her signal and one of the waitresses would rush past telling her that her order was getting cold.

She felt like a poor, stupid donkey in a stable of racehorses.

Finally, after what seemed a decade, it was three o'clock. After her last table had paid she stood in the service corridor raising her thick, damp black hair from the wet nape of her neck.

"Some snap job, ehh?" Vi chuckled as she served two

wedges of French apple pie, generously dousing them with whipped cream. "Come on, get a load off." At the corner table, she began wolfing down her pie.

"Vi, I can't tell you how much I appreciate the help," Honora said. Vi had taken over two tables of her station and had refilled all the coffee cups.

"Forget it. How much did you take in?"

"Tips? I don't know."

"What's wrong with finding out?"

Honora fished the jingling change from the pocket below her apron and began stacking the coins.

Before she could finish, Vi said, "Ten forty."

"So much?"

"Quick-eye Vi, they call me. Not bad, not bad at all considering you weren't here all day. The big brown eyes and fancy talk must do it, kid." Vi smiled. "Tomorrow won't be as rough."

"Mr. Stroud won't be keeping me." She glanced toward the cash register, which was manned by the overweight ex-GI who was the owner. His thick black brows had drawn together as he corrected most of Honora's checks. The currency was not yet familiar and with the customers yelling at her on all sides she forgot even simple addition.

"Who says? Al told *me* he's giving you another day's trial."

Honora leaned back in the chair, too weary to hide her flood of shamed relief.

Vi chuckled. "Kid, it's as plain as the nose on your face that this job ain't for you. You're class, pure class. But what the hell, it's a good living. Now go ahead and dig into the pie."

"It's with a firm in the financial district," Honora replied, her cheeks hot, when Langley queried about her new job. They were eating roast chicken and the first asparagus of the season, a celebratory dinner for which she had counted out small change from her tips. "Near the Pacific Coast Stock Exchange."

"A brokerage office?" Langley asked.

"Umm." Honora stared down at the wishbone. "They're only trying me out."

"These brokers need a delightful young thing to liven up their offices," Langley said. "A receptionist's hardly what I had in mind for my Portuguese, but it's only temporary. Before you know it things will pick up for me and you'll be at the University over in Berkeley."

Honora couldn't look at him.

"Tell me about it," Crystal demanded.

It was an hour later and the sisters were at Fisherman's Wharf, sitting on a bench that faced the ghostly, bobbing shapes of mist-veiled boats. After they had washed the dishes, Crystal had suggested she and Honora take a walk: these few blocks were as far as Honora's blisters would permit.

"The others are quite amazing—you should see them dashing about with hundreds of plates."

"Honora, no stiff upper lip. This is just us."

Just us, a phrase they had used since they were very little. The words meant that they were in a special, twinlike state, almost one person, and innermost thoughts could be shared.

Honora's sigh trembled. "It's odious. Nasty old men pat your legs and expect you to play up to them. Each time I picked up a tip I felt like a beggar. And there's the smells—bacon, frying, cigars. Are they in my hair?"

"No." Crystal sniffed. "Yes, a little."

"How awful. Crys, the very worst part is I feel so rotten about being ashamed of doing the work. The others were very kind. Especially the one I told you about—Vi."

Crystal got up, moving the few feet to the railing. The lamppost's misty light turned her bright yellow hair to a blurred silver halo. "Tomorrow I'll meet you—"

"Crys," Honora interrupted unsteadily, "I couldn't bear you coming there."

"Not at the cafe. On Maiden Lane."

Honora drew a sharp breath. G.D. Talbott's was on Maiden Lane, and Langley had repeatedly informed his daughters that no visitors were admitted. "You know Uncle Gideon's rule," she said.

"About not getting in? I've never believed in that rule."

"Daddy doesn't lie!"

"It wouldn't exactly be a lie. He never did like us seeing him at work. *You* should understand that."

Honora stirred uneasily on the hard bench. "Anyway, why should we go?"

"Because I say so. Or do you want me to tell Daddy about that wonderful job of yours?"

"Oh, go ahead and tell him." Honora's voice shook in the fish-scented darkness. "What's the difference? He'll have to find out sooner or later."

"Not unless somebody tells him point-blank. He always prefers to keep the unpleasant details vague." Crystal peered at her. "Well? Are you coming?"

A gull landed on a nearby stanchion, a cab pulled up to let off diners at Tarantino's. After a long pause, Honora nodded.

"Good," Crystal said. "Quarter to four on the corner of Maiden Lane and Union Square."

5

Crystal normally contrived to appear sophisticated, but today she wore bobby socks and her Peter Pan dickey with her favorite sweater, a pale blue cloud of angora from Harvey Nichols, one of Langley's final London extravagances. She had tied back that fresh-minted hair in a girlish pony-tail, but a few tendrils had escaped—either by design or chance—to blow about her exquisite features. As she crossed Union Square men and women alike turned to smile at her.

Honora waved. She often found imponderables in Crystal's behavior, and as Crystal saw her and waved back she was asking herself for the thousandth time what her sister was up to with this visit. The truth was uncomplicated. Crystal had a talent for going directly after what she wanted.

"Don't you look a dream," Crystal said in greeting. Secure in her own looks, she dispensed compliments with careless generosity. "That blouse always did do something for you—is the top button undone for Curt Ivory?"

Sisterly teasing.

"I still say we shouldn't risk Daddy's situation," Honora said, hastily changing the subject.

Crystal's eyes glittered like faceted sapphires. "Let's not start that again," she snapped, turning down Maiden Lane.

After the brightness, bustling pedestrians and honking cars of Union Square, they might have entered another universe. Maiden Lane, which ran two short blocks, once had been a street of knifings and prostitutes exposing their wares at every window, but the 1906 earthquake and ensuing fire had scattered the revelers and now the narrow, tree-lined little alley was highly respectable, with a few quietly exclusive shops tucked under the office buildings.

Talbott's occupied a lavishly bulbous wood edifice. The girls ascended the steps and entered a large, uncarpeted hall that echoed with masculine voices coming from open-doored offices. To the left of the stairwell was a switchboard.

"Talbott Engineering," said the operator. "Yes sir, he is. I'll connect you right away." Plugging in the wire, pressing down the mouthpiece, she looked up at Crystal and Honora. "Can I help you?"

Honora murmured, "We're here to see Mr. Sylvander."

"Yes, sure." The switchboard operator's smile revealed her pink gums. "The spec writers are in the furthest office to your right."

A specification writer, Langley had explained to his daughters, was an editor whose task was to translate the engineers' incomprehensible jargon into language that a prospective client could comprehend—and buy. The work, he emphasized, demanded a rare and unique skill. Honora had accepted this version of his importance. Now, as they went into the dingy, smoke-filled cubicle, filial pity clutched her throat, and she couldn't look at him.

The typing had ceased and the three other men, all extremely young, lounged back in their metal typist's chairs, removing the cigarettes from their mouths as a form of reverent courtesy as they gawked at the visitors.

"What are you doing here?" Langley barked.

"We were looking through City of Paris, Daddy," Crystal said, going to plant a gay little kiss on his forehead. "On the spur of the moment we decided to drop in to see you."

Langley turned to Honora, who remained frozen in the doorway.

She stammered her support of Crystal's lie. "I . . . yes, it seemed a good idea."

One of the other writers inquired, "Are these your daughters, Mr. Sylvander?"

Langley rose, making the introductions with overly much of his whimsy—"Two of my three graces." Crystal cast radiant smiles. Honora, burning with contrite empathy for her father, could barely nod toward each typewriter.

"Daddy," Crystal said earnestly, "while we're here, we really must thank Uncle Gideon. It was so thoughtful of him to send us home in his car."

"He's out in the field today."

"He was at the Oakland freeway project, but I'm pretty sure he came back after lunch," said the spec writer who sported a carrot-red crew cut—he looked no older than Crystal. "A few minutes ago I heard footsteps."

"Is that where Uncle Gideon's office is?" Crystal asked, pointing upward.

"I'll show you the way," volunteered the crew cut.

"There's no necessity," Langley said.

While at the same instant Crystal was saying, "What a sweetie you are, Brian."

The upstairs hall was crowded with a half dozen large, tilt-topped drafting tables where men were busy with India ink, T squares, triangles, protractors, linear scales, compasses.

"The new draftsmen," their guide informed them. "They've got no place else to work. The scuttlebutt is that we're renting a floor in the next building, but your uncle knows more about that than I do."

Gideon's antechamber was Spartan, especially when compared with the Clay Street mansion. A short, equally undecorative secretary was retrieving a manila file from the top drawer of one of the gray metal filing cabinets.

Looking up, she said, "Yes?"

Before Crystal could reply, the door to the inner office opened. Curt stood there, looking the classic young American executive in his broad-shouldered charcoal suit and beautiful blue tie with the small crest below the knot. The discreet motif matched the extraordinary golden topaz of the amused eyes smiling at Honora.

An almost unbearable joy suffused her chest and she looked away.

He raised an eyebrow. "Well, Honora, didn't I say we'd bump into each other?"

"Prescient of you," she heard herself answer. "Do you know my sister Crystal?"

Gideon's voice rasped from the interior of the office, "Curt, who's out there?"

"It's us, Uncle Gideon," called Crystal. "Honora and Crystal."

Gideon stumped to the doorway. "So you dropped in to see your father? I'm surprised you haven't sooner."

"We really came to see you, Uncle," Crystal chirped. "We never had a chance to thank you for the ride home." It was impossible not to respond to the girlish magic of her smile.

And Gideon's answering smile proved that he was not the ancient that the girls saw him as. "It was my pleasure, Crystal." This time he got the name right.

"Uncle Gideon," Crystal said softly, "I've brought something that you should have."

Honora could not control her sharp intake of breath as Crystal drew from her purse a small jade Kwan Yin. This exquisite little goddess of mercy carved during the Ming dynasty had been prized by their mother and for this sentimental reason Langley had not taken it to the London pawnshops during the past penurious year.

"A Christmas ago Aunt Matilda sent me this," Crystal lied with downcast lashes. "She wrote on the card that she'd owned it ever since she and Mother were little girls."

"It's very generous of you," Gideon said. "But if your aunt sent it to you, she wanted you to have it."

"I never really knew her. You were married such a long time, Uncle, so her special things must mean everything to you." Crystal clasped the figurine briefly, as if she could not bear to part with an object so drenched with sentiment, then she dropped the dark green jade, warm from her small hand, into Gideon's thick, deeply grooved palm.

The white smile lines showed in the tan at the corners of Curt's eyes.

"Come on, Crystal," Honora said, her hand clamping on her sister's arm. "We've taken up enough of Uncle Gideon's time."

"No need for thanks or giving me your things, girls," said Gideon, but he slipped the Kwan Yin into his pocket. "Run along now."

"I'm on the way down, too," Curt said.

Crystal, glancing at Honora, lagged back a bit as they moved along the crowded hallway.

"So now you've been at Talbott's," Curt said. He moved easily, as if he had spent his life on the tennis court.

"What's everybody so busy doing?"

"Next time you stop by, I'll explain the principles and practices of engineering."

Crystal caught up as he opened the front door for them. "Nice meeting you, Crystal. Honora, goodbye for now."

Crystal pranced along Maiden Lane, her golden ponytail abounce on her angora sweater, a hum rising from her throat. Mmm, mmm, *mmm.* "He's not really my type, Curt. Too cocksure of himself. But if that Imogene's sleeping with him, I don't blame her."

Honora's bubble of pure joy broke. "That was really rotten!" she burst out. "Giving away Mother's jade. It doesn't even belong to you—it's Daddy's, remember?"

"How do you suppose Uncle's going to rescue us from our Lombard Street rattrap if he doesn't know we exist? Glare all you want. To get something, you have to give something."

"All that saccharine—don't you have any pride?"

"Pride? Look who's picking up tips."

"You took the money to buy stockings."

Crystal's step faltered. It was as if her mature strength of will had deserted her.

"I'm sorry, Crys." Honora took her sister's hand. "Please. I'm a monster to throw that at you. I didn't mean it. I'm tired, that's all." She walked a few steps in silence. "Crys, we're happy, our family."

"Yes, we're happy. But there's so much more." They had reached Union Square and Crystal looked around at the sunlit, marble-façaded shops where uniformed doormen admitted elegantly dressed women. "And I intend to have it all."

6

That Friday when Crystal unlocked the Sylvander mail slot, she found a stiff envelope addressed to *The Sylvander Family.* Inside was a creamy engraved card:

SATURDAY OPEN HOUSE
Three to five
Mr. and Mrs. Gideon Talbott II

Obviously Gideon had not yet had time to order new invitations.

"Whoopeeeeee!" Her exultancy echoed through the narrow, drafty tunnel as she offered up her devout gratitude to the small, ancient jade goddess.

This time Gideon introduced the four Sylvanders as "my English family," giving his dry, gravelly chuckle and extending a large, thick hand toward them in an attempt to be convivial.

Joscelyn, the only child present, stationed herself on a large, squashy, brown velvet chair near the mammoth tea and coffee set, her hand shooting out each time the heavy-footed maid, Mrs. Wartobe, or Juan—the Filipino—passed with a silver tray of frosted cake or tiny tarts. Joscelyn's insatiable sweet tooth showed no effects on her meager frame: all evidence lay packed with silver within her molars. Her plain little face solemn with curiosity, her heavy eyeglasses glinting, she peered around.

This was her first meeting with their American uncle. He was ugly, but everyone spoke respectfully to him, so he must have more than money, he must have power. Joscelyn, a wretched outsider on two continents, had the deepest respect for power.

Crystal was tossing her head like a bright-crested tropical

bird as she flittered between various groups, including
Uncle Gideon's.

Honora chatted animatedly with a younger man who
grinned at her with exactly the right amount of amused
sarcasm. Seeing this sister, almost a mother figure, so flirtatiously vivacious struck Joscelyn as a desecration.

Her father held his hands in his pockets, lounging with
aristocratic nonchalance. The men present, obviously too
common to realize his good breeding, did not include him
in their conversations.

When they were ready to leave, Uncle Gideon insisted
on having Juan drive them home. Escorting them through
the huge front hall, he said with a stiffly warm smile,
"We—I—have Open House every other Saturday afternoon. And I expect all of you."

Joscelyn perched proudly on the limousine's jumpseat.

Langley remained silent in the car. As they emerged, he
said, "Your daddy has a matter of business to attend to, my
pets. Eat your suppers without me." He raised his derby,
executing a little dance, his charade of a vaudeville actor
exiting from the stage. "Adieu, adieu."

"Daddy, you're being an ass," Joscelyn called in a thin,
high voice, praying her father would not leave.

But he, typically, paid no attention to her prayer.

She moped around the flat, refusing to go to bed until
her sisters did. Soon the sound of regular breathing came
from their beds. Joscelyn was desperate to use the lavatory
but she could not face the sinister hall, the evil shadows in
the living room, the dread song of the pipes in the bathroom.

She had always been a terrible coward, a cowardice that
she disguised with truculent bravado and a sharp, mean
tongue, and her fears had been freighted to this side of the
Atlantic. Let the least thing go wrong, and she was like
Pavlov's dog, secreting terror. Where was her father? San
Francisco was earthquake territory. Could one part of the
city fall in ruins while another section remained stable and
unscathed?

Why didn't he come home? Just when she was positive
she would wet the bed, she heard the loud creak of uneven
footsteps on the exterior staircase, her father's voice muttering oaths as his key jabbed against the lock. Stumbling
into his room with a sob, he slammed the door.

Joscelyn darted into the lavatory. She was back in bed and asleep within five minutes.

That was Langley's first and last Open House.

The next few weeks Honora learned her trade, or rather, Vi instructed her in it. She and the pepper-tempered older woman were bound in an unarticulated yet genuine friendship that excluded outside lives—Honora knew almost nothing about Vi except that she had two exes, had "been around" and had worked five years at the Hollywood Pig'n'Whistle.

Although Honora refused to submit to the lightfingered sexual reconnoitering that Vi insisted led to much silver being left on the table, her youth, her prettiness, her soft-voiced accent earned her excellent tips. A good thing. Langley was depositing less and less in the housekeeping jam jar so the money was urgently needed for the household as well as Joscelyn's dentistry and new clothing.

Dior's New Look also proved an expenditure. Skirts had plummeted. She and Crystal could no longer wear their English clothes, which they both thoroughly detested anyway. After work Honora would meet Crystal at the nearby Mode o'Day: they consulted anxiously over each blouse, dress, skirt, but in the end Honora relied on Crystal's keen eye to select the smartest from endless racks of inexpensive rayon clothing. They both would have preferred quality, but it was essential that they own several outfits for the Open Houses.

The three Sylvander sisters had become part of the Clay Street regulars. With Curt Ivory and Imogene Burdetts, they were the only guests under forty.

"You'll fit in better if you drop the Uncle," said their host, his gravel-voice awkward with warmth. "We aren't blood kin anyway. Just call me Gideon."

To all three it seemed a daring American departure to address a forty-five-year-old man by his Christian name, and Joscelyn especially felt a thrill of pride each time she obeyed him.

Curt invariably bantered with Honora, spending nearly as much time with her as with Imogene, whom he escorted to the Opera Ball, and to dinner dances given by their friends.

("Do you honestly think he's sleeping with her, Crys?"

"He's rich, Honora, she's rich."

"But is he *sleeping* with her?"

"If he enjoyed it madly, she'd have hooked him by now.")

Honora always left Clay Street with a deep feeling of inferiority. What good did it do to remind herself that she was a Sylvander when maybe Curt could smell the fry cook's Crisco on her just-shampooed hair?

Curt wore gorgeous clothes, he drove a large yellow convertible, he smelled of a tangy after-shave. He belonged with Imogene. They knew all the same people, they spoke the same slang with the same accent, they had been graced since birth by the same good fortune. Honora would imagine him in dinner clothes—how handsome he must be in the gleaming black and white—waltzing with Imogene, the skirt of her honest Dior swirling around them as they circled and dipped, Ginger Rogers and Fred Astaire. She would imagine his mouth kissing Imogene's, she would imagine him undressing the enviably angular body.

Each week she swore never to return. *He doesn't really know I exist so why torture myself?* But of course she could no more stay away than stop breathing.

On June 29, at the height of the breakfast rush, Honora left the service area holding three orders while expertly nudging open the Out door with her left hip.

Easing into the crowded cafe, she saw Curt at the table near the cash register.

Instinctively she tottered backward. Vi was a step behind her. They collided.

Honora's orders seemed to move in slow motion. Eggs and bacon lifted upward from the plate, waffle with hash slid downward and two poached eggs slithered in a tango-like dance. Then, abruptly, blue willow pattern crashed. Honora was left gripping two toast plates in precise horizontal position.

"Oh crap!" Vi yelled as her arm contorted to maintain balance of her plates. She was so experienced that only the oatmeal fell, splattering on her ankle. "You dumb English cunt. Ain't I taught you nothing?"

The soprano fury soared above the breakfast clatter and boom of male voices. Heads swiveled.

For a heartbeat Curt's gaze met Honora's. So intense was

her focus across the distance that she could see his pupils contract with shocked surprise. *Revulsion, too?*

She barged through the In door. Panting and quivering, she stood on the raised-up, slatted floor of the service area. She could hear Vi on the other side shouting for a busboy, then heard her bark, "You can't go in back, sir, it's employees only."

But the door swung open and Curt stood there, a handsomely dressed anomaly. Honora's heart was thudding so hard that she thought she would faint.

"So it *was* you," Curt said.

"Coming through!" shouted Salvador, the new busboy, wielding a broom and handled scuttle.

Curt asked, "What was that about a brokerage firm's receptionist?"

She had studiously avoided compounding her lie, so the information must have been passed on to him by her father or Crystal—or was it Joscelyn? "Obviously misinformation," she said, attempting a light yet haughty tone. "A false rumor. This is how I earn my daily bread."

"Rye, toasted," he said, referring to the triangularly cut slices on the two plates she still gripped, keeping his tone as light as hers. But his eyes weren't fanning into the smile creases as he peered at her tight, short uniform, the cap with its idiotic little points, the awful rubber-soled, laced-up white oxfords.

Vi darted into the service area, a whirl of blue checks. She glared at Honora. "Listen, ain't it bad enough you dropped your order and mosta mine, do you have to stand here jawing at rush hour?"

"What time are you off?" Curt asked quietly.

"Three thirty," Vi replied. "Now beat it, mister. Even if you're above obeying the rules, Honora works here."

He turned and left without speaking. As the door swung in decreasing arcs, Honora's little smile crumpled.

"Come on, don't look like that," Vi said, her voice less cantankerous. "Whatever the handsome bozo said to you, it ain't the end of the world."

Not the demise of the planet Earth, maybe, but Honora's pride and her dreams lay dead in the service area. Her body convulsed, her mouth opened, releasing a gasping whimper that cascaded into a torrent of harsh, wracking sobs. She pressed her forehead against the shelf with the blue and white sugar and creamers, unable to halt the disgrace of public tears.

"What the hell's going on around here?" Al's furious voice.

"The flu, she shouldn't of come," Vi muttered.

"Honora, you get on home." Al, quieter.

"I'll ... be ... all ... right. . . ." she gasped, escaping to the waitresses' washroom.

She stood with her arms pressed across her breasts, her fingernails digging into her upper arms as she tried to get hold of herself. Each time she quieted down a bit, she would conjure up Curt's pale, horror-struck face. The hoarse, unwilled sobs would start afresh. When finally she had no more tears and she could neither think nor feel, she sat torpidly in the toilet cubicle.

"Everything all right, Honora?" Vi called on the other side of the stall.

"Yes," Honora said weakly, and came out.

"Go home and get some rest, kid. It's okay with Al."

From the depth of her blankness, Honora fished up the information that this was Friday and Joscelyn had a four o'clock dental appointment. The two-dollar fee was payable at Dr. Brady's office, so she had arranged to meet her little sister with the money—money which must come from today's tips. "I'll be all right," she said with more strength.

"You sure look like hell."

"A bit of lipstick'll do wonders."

"In case you're interested, your friend left right away." Vi was surveying her with worry. "Listen, you ain't in trouble, are you?"

Trouble? Honora looked blankly at the powdered, sympathetic face.

"Sitting on the nest," Vi added.

"You mean having a baby?"

"Don't let it throw you, kid." Vi glanced around, then whispered, "I know a doctor."

"It's nothing like that," Honora protested.

Vi's sympathetic disbelief showed. "Kid, I'm on your side."

"Honestly, Vi, he's not even exactly a friend."

"Whatever he is, he ain't worth an hour and a half's crying. No man is."

* * *

Honora plodded through the day, blocking out the scene with an effort that brought on a monster of a headache. She finished Vi's aspirin while she changed to go home.

As she went out the door she glimpsed Curt lounging against one of the Tuscan pillars of the Stock Exchange. Seeing her, he waved. She hurried around the corner, each step jolting inside her head. He must have run across the busy intersection of Pine and Sansome. She heard a horn blare behind her.

Catching up, he said, "How about a lift home."

"I'm not going home," she said stiffly.

"Why not? You look beat."

"Joss has a four o'clock appointment at the dentist's and I'm meeting her."

"I'll drop you off there."

"No thank you." She headed in the direction of Telegraph Hill.

He kept up with her. "My car's up the block."

"What do you want?" she asked in a low, fierce voice.

"I'm offering you transportation, Honora."

"Why aren't you at Talbott's? Why should you take me anywhere? You never have before. Now you know I'm a waitress d'you think I'm easy?"

Their hurrying steps faltered and they turned to each other, wary as fencing duelists. A muscle moved in his eyelid, an intimation of hurt. Curt Ivory hurt?

She made an inarticulate sound in her throat. "I'm sorry. I have a rotten headache."

"I get them, too," he said.

His yellow Buick convertible was parked just ahead of them. He opened the door.

"It's really not—"

"Honora, will you just shut up and get in."

Unable to look at him, she obeyed. When he was behind the wheel, she murmured the address on Washington Square so quietly that he had to ask her to repeat it.

Maneuvering through the traffic, he didn't attempt conversation. She held two fingers to her left temple. Her lack of experience with men and her fastidiousness about sex had protected her, but now she wondered if she had blurted out the truth. It hardly seemed Curt's style to hang around like a stage-door Johnny, but on the other hand, why had he waited for her? She glanced at his profile. Mouth folded tight, high cheekbones raised so that his eye was narrowed, aloof. Not the look of a man intent on seduction. Beyond that she could not read his expression. He might have been angry, resentful, bored or simply concentrating on driving.

Dr. Brady practiced above the drugstore in Washington Square. Curt drew up and glanced at his watch. "On the dot," he said.

"This was most kind of you," she said, then blurted, "Listen, Curt, Daddy and Joscelyn don't know where I work, they *do* think it's at a brokerage . . ." Her voice trailed away and she knew her face was crimson.

"I understand," he said quietly.

In the waiting room, Joscelyn was frowning over an il- lustrated history book: American History was her one weak subject. "You look like the wrath of God," she said.

"Headache. Joss, I'm sorry, I can't stay with you."

After paying the nurse, Honora trudged home, swal- lowed three more aspirin and filled the yellow-stained tub, washing her hair under the long-necked faucet, sitting until the soap-scummed water was cold. Crawling into bed, she tried to read but the library novel couldn't raise her from the slough of despond. She shivered under the eiderdown. Life stretched ahead of her, a bleak cement track of hateful work.

She used her headache to beg off making supper and coming to the table.

It was after eight when the telephone rang. Honora didn't open her eyes. The calls were mostly for Crystal.

The door opened, and Crystal popped her head in. "For you, Honora. Want me to say you're under the weather?"

"Who is it?"

"The masculine gender."

"Gerry?" One of the San Francisco City College blind dates had become enamored of Honora. His loud, droning voice irritated her—and besides he wasn't Curt. She in- vented previous engagements when he called.

Crystal shook her head. "Deeper, more witty voice. This is wild, and of course it couldn't be him, he'd have said something to me—but it sounded like Curt Ivory."

Honora leaped out of bed, pulling on her plaid dressing gown, which was so old it only reached to her knees.

The telephone was in the kitchen, where Langley, Josce- lyn and Crystal were playing Monopoly.

Honora picked up the receiver. "H-hello."

"Headache better?" Curt asked.

At the sound of his voice, she sank into a rush-bottomed kitchen chair. "Much, thank you."

"Good. Then you can come out."

She drew a sharp breath. She wanted nothing more than the reassurance of being with him, but a resistant wall—pride, maybe—made his invitation unthinkable.

"It's late," she hedged.

"Not exactly the witching hour yet."

"I get up very early."

"Stroud's is closed on the weekend."

"I mean, I got up early this morning."

"I know a place where the weary gather to rest. Pick you up at nine." The phone went dead.

She stood holding the buzzing instrument, wondering how she had lost the argument. Then she realized Curt Ivory had invited her on a date!

Crystal, as banker, counted out hundred-pound notes. "Well, you look more human," she said. "Who cheered you up?"

"It *was* Curt. He's picking me up at nine."

"You can't mean you're going out?" Langley threw down the dice cup and a die rattled to the floor. "I forbid it. Not with that nasty headache."

"The rest cured me, Daddy. Honestly, I'm well now."

Langley hesitated. He trod warily when it came to discussions of health with his older daughters, fearing such conversations might intrude on the tabu of menses. Then he peered at her. "Curt? You can't mean *Curt Ivory?*"

She nodded with that blatantly joyous smile.

"You're not going anywhere with him!" Langley cried. "You're just a baby. He should be thoroughly ashamed!"

"Daddy, it's only for a soda water. . . ." Honora was pleading.

The other two girls casually ignored their father's regulations, but Honora treated his commands with balmful respect. Poor child, her face was quite white. He relented. "Since you've already accepted, you may go. But I don't want him hanging around you." At the thought of Curt, so coolly debonair, hanging around any girl, Crystal and Joscelyn tittered. Langley barked sternly. "I'll not stand for any nonsense from him."

"Good grief, Daddy, let her get dressed," Crystal said. "It's twenty-five to nine. Come on, Honora, I'll help you."

7

Descending the worn wooden steps, Honora bit back a nervous giggle. If it hadn't been for the cold dampness penetrating her thin coat and the odor of rotting oranges rising from the big trash barrels below, she would have imagined herself asleep, suspended between a euphoric dream of being on a date with Curt Ivory and the humiliating nightmare of their earlier encounters today.

"Vilma's Place isn't far," Curt said. "On Columbus. Feel up to walking?"

"Absolutely. But you do realize they won't serve me? I'm nineteen." Last week the family had celebrated her birthday with a rose-decorated cake that Langley had brought home in a cellophane-topped box, and paper chains that Joscelyn and Crystal had festooned around the kitchen. Stating her age still surprised and pleased her—nineteen had a ring of maturity.

"We don't need to advertise you're under legal age."

Vilma's Place was dimly lit by the dripping candles at each table. In the rear, a crowded bar surrounded the dais where a woman in flowing white swayed over a piano, rippling out a wondrously convoluted version of "September Song."

A colored waiter wove through the crush of small tables to stand attentively at theirs. "Evening, Mr. Ivory. Good to see you."

"Hey, Martin, how's it going? Honora, what'll you have?"

She had already decided on a ginger ale, but since she was with Curt Ivory, a regular patron, no IDs would be demanded of her. "I'd adore a sloe gin fizz," she said, picking a name that had always intrigued her.

Curt repeated her order. "The usual for me, Martin."

After the waiter left, Curt sat back. "Now you know where I come when I have in mind to debauch underage waitresses."

The remark, rather than embarrassing her, put them back on their old jocular footing.

"Is the mood often upon you?" she asked.

"Each time the new moon rises."

She was luxuriously aware of his legs near hers under the tiny round of table. Her drink was frothy and extraordinarily delicious, and she sipped it rapidly through the short pink straw. The badinage that passed between them was as light as a breeze-tossed shuttlecock. Honora had not eaten since her breakfast at five thirty, and her father had never spoken of the swift depredations of alcohol on an empty stomach, so she decided that her wit was entirely due to the sophisticated ambience at Vilma's Place and the wry amusement that tugged one side of Curt's mouth.

"Something I've always wanted to know," she said, "is what, exactly, an engineer does."

"Good Lord! Is this Gideon Talbott's niece?"

"I've never truly understood."

"Well, I'll tell you, Honora. It's not a complicated line of work at all. The client tells an engineer the impossibility that he wants done or built and the engineer makes the necessary designs and watches over the construction of everything from dams and highways to pyramids and rockets and land reclamation. He calculates the strength of material necessary. It's up to the engineer to insure every structure will remain standing for a good long time under the most extreme conditions that it will be used."

"One time Daddy took us to see Hadrian's wall."

"Ahh, those Romans, they built to last. I'm a civil engineer. As far as civil engineering goes, the Romans were the greatest. Their roads are still in use, and some of their aqueducts and bridges." His voice went lower. "That's my definition of immortality, having one of my projects still in use two thousand years from now."

"I'm sure that it will be," she said.

"Honora, I hate to break the news to you," he said dryly, "but I'm Mr. Talbott's assistant. Thus far I haven't headed up a single project."

"You will. Curt, explain about Talbott's. I'm confused. You don't only do engineering, do you?"

"We're also in construction. Talbott's will either bid on the plans and supervision for a client or take over the entire project." Curt caught Martin's eye and pointed at their table, a signal to bring another round. "Now it's your turn. Tell me about *your* career."

"What can I say about it?"

"For openers, what attracted you?"

"MGM begged me to come to Hollywood, but I said no, I need much more of a challenge. And it's crass, but a lot of the brokers who eat at Stroud's make less than I do." Was she quoting Vi's wisdom? No matter.

"So it's the money?"

"The bare truth is, wonderfully qualified as I am, for some reason nobody else saw fit to hire me."

"Waitresses there *do* pull down good tips, don't they?"

Was Curt obliquely pointing out that her father was derelict in his fiscal responsibilities? Her high-voltage glow dimmed a trifle. "There's a lot of expenses when you're getting on your feet in a new country, you know."

"You're very different," he said.

"How?"

"Beats me."

"Is it being English?"

"You're just different. Not like other girls."

"Is that good or bad?"

"Bad, very. Honora, you're up the creek unless you manage to find some pervert with a taste for classy females who are hopelessly altruistic—and have dark, velvety eyes with little lights behind them."

Warm with delight, she made her honest, routine disclaimer. "Crystal has the looks in our family."

"She's stunning all right," he said. "Me, I go for tall brunettes."

"Like Imogene Burdetts?" The overly candid question jumped from her lips.

"Jealous?" The candlelight shone on his mocking grin. "Why should I be?"

"Come on, Honora, we both know you're mad about me."

In her inviolable security, she laughed. "True, true," she said. "It's your turn again. Are you ready to confess about those terrible rumors?" A frivolous question.

His smile faded. "No truth at all," he said. "I do assure

you on the best authority that I am not the illegitimate scion of my boss."

Gideon? Curt? She knew her mouth had opened in surprise.

"You hadn't heard that bilgewater?" he asked.

She shook her head.

"I jumped in unnecessarily, didn't I? It's hardly a tale that a veddy, veddy proper Englishman takes home to his nubile fold."

She realized then that envy brewed ugly explanations for Curt's success at Talbott's and that this malice was as painful to him as her job was to her. The revelation that they shared similar mortal weaknesses brought a peculiar ache to her heart, and she reached out in consolation. When she touched the warm, hard flesh of the back of his hand, her fingers trembled. She withdrew hastily.

He said, "First of all, Mr. Talbott—"

"Why don't you call him Gideon, like we do?"

"He hasn't made the request. I am not family. Repeat. I—am—not—family. Mr. Talbott is a man of rare and unique carnal rectitude—as opposed to me, Honora dear. To my knowledge he never cheated on that dreary woman, your aunt."

"You're very fond of him, aren't you?"

"I am," Curt said, crushing out his cigarette. "I ought to be."

"Why?"

He stared at her somberly. "You should be very fond of him, too. There's not many employers in this republic who'd put up with your father's pathetic ritual snobbery."

She realized he was paying her back for what he considered prying, but how could she let the insult pass unanswered? "Daddy's a wonderful editor," she said with quiet intensity. "He's not a snob. Not at all. He's a gentleman."

"Gentleman? Is that a synonym for a guy who gets his back up at every little remark that hits him the wrong way?"

Loyalty to her father stung her into opinions that sober she might have kept to herself. "And why do you think Gideon's so wonderful? Being faithful to his wife? Decent men are. He's pompous and conceited, he lords it over people, bossing them around. Good? Do you consider it good or generous or kind to leave your family out in the cold?"

"I gather what you're saying incoherently is that it isn't enough for Mr. Talbott to employ your father, who though a wonderful editor and etcetera, has a tendency to take off an extra hour for lunch and then show up smelling of booze. You believe that it's Mr. Talbott's duty to shower the lovely Sylvander sisters with all the luxuries their father cannot provide."

His vehemence had blown out the candle. While he struck a match to relight it, Honora stared down at her glass.

Curt said quietly, "Now we each know where our loyalties lie, don't we?"

"I suppose," she said listlessly.

"Make you a deal. You lay off Mr. Talbott and I won't attack your father, who incidentally doesn't have a mean bone in his body." He raised his hand again for the waiter. "What we need is another drink."

The third drink restored her. Now they were no longer bantering, but gazing at each other. His mouth had an unfamiliar softness; she wanted to ever so lightly trace his lips, a tactile urge so strong that she reached for her pearls instead—Crystal, selecting the strand at Woolworth's, had taken ages to find the deepest luster.

All at once the heat and noise engulfed her like a bone-crushing demon, spinning her amid the crowded tables. A sourness rose in her throat. She stumbled to her feet, peering around. "Curt, will you excuse me . . ."

Curt was standing too. "The restrooms are back there," he said, giving her a gentle push.

She tottered dizzily past the piano bar. Mercifully the toilet was free. She crouched over the bowl, throwing up stringy, pinkish liquid. The great heaves reminded her of this morning's weeping. *What a day,* she thought, leaning back on her heels, wiping her hand over her cold, sweaty forehead.

When she emerged, a woman was repainting her mouth at the rococo mirror. Honora could see their two reflections, her own apparently raised from a crypt.

"Had one too many?" the woman asked nonjudgmentally. She fished through her beaded bag for a half-finished round of Life Savers. "Here, this'll take the taste away."

Honora thanked her, washing her face and cupping handfuls of water to her mouth before she chewed the candy.

At the table a cup of black coffee waited. Unable to look Curt in the eye, she stared down at the steaming liquid, her hands circling the thick, hot china. "I didn't have dinner," she said. "Do you suppose that was my trouble?"

"Christ, why didn't you tell me? I'd never have let you have three. I shouldn't have, anyway. We'll get you a burger."

"Just fresh air, please," she said.

She could not resist a professional glance at the tip he dropped. It was outrageously large.

Fog had rolled in, and the lighted windows of the closed Italian food stores shimmered hazily and there were no hard-edged shapes, no distances. Headlights and an occasional pedestrian came out of nowhere. She took deep, restorative breaths of the moisture-laden air. Curt didn't speak, but after they had climbed a hilly block he took her hand. He pressed his hard, warm palm against hers, and their fingers clasped. In the touch of their bare flesh there was a sense of preordained intimacy.

In the entry tunnel to her building, he turned her toward him, holding her loosely with his hands linked behind her waist. "Better?"

"Yes," she whispered. It was very dark in here and the usual smell of urine was overcome by his after-shave, his cigarette, a very faint odor of masculine sweat, the whiskey on his warm breath. She blessed the woman who had given her the Lifesavers that had taken the horrible sourness from her mouth.

"Sure?" He was whispering, too.

Nodding, she leaned forward, touching her lips to his— later she would wonder at her audacity, but at the time it seemed the most natural thing in the world.

His arms tightened around her and she pressed against the solid warmth she had conjured up so often in her dreams. His mouth was softer than she had imagined, and she touched it with her tongue. When her dates had French-kissed her, she had fought the lingual intrusion, but now she was initiating it, and Curt's tongue roused exquisite sensations throughout her body. Her nipples had always been sensitive, and the tissue seemed to expand to cover her breasts. His quivering arms were lifting her high above the dark, mist-drenched city, and if she let go she would plummet to earth, so she clung to him with all her strength, arching her pelvis against that coiled strength in his trousers.

The kiss ended and he pressed his cheek against hers. "I'd made up my mind not to do that," he said, his breath filling her ear.

"I kissed you. . . ."

"You're too damn trusting and tender. You don't know the first thing about me, who I am, where I came from, where I intend going."

"I love you."

He moved his head back to look at her. In the dim light that seeped into the entry tunnel, she could see that his eyes had a puffiness under them, as if he'd just awoken, and his mouth, dark with her lipstick, was soft, sensual, vulnerable.

"You shouldn't say that."

Her metabolism altered and she felt heavy, despairing, gauche. "I didn't mean to embarrass you," she mumbled.

"Look, Honora, by now you've realized I'm an ambitious bastard, driven to succeed and red-hot for the big money, haven't you?"

"There's a lot more to you than that."

"Yes, I'm a helluva fine engineer. That's where the ambition fits. I have it in me to plan and build miracles never before seen on this earth." His voice rumbled with seriousness.

"Is that the attraction to Imogene?"

"You're asking if I use her? So I come across as that much of an SOB, do I?"

"No, but . . ."

"Honora, I like her. She's a good time, a kick."

"And Mr. Burdetts could help you."

"Sure. I'd get my pick of projects if I married her."

Married her. The words reverberated inside Honora's head, and she tried to pull away.

His palms remained stationed firmly above and below the small of her back. "I told you I haven't been in charge of projects at Talbott's. And I won't be until I'm forty. Honora, even though it hurts you, I am not Sir Galahad."

"Why did you pick me up at Stroud's?"

"Seeing you there threw me for a loop," he said. "You

were so out of place with those other tough-looking broads. There's a fairy-tale quality about you, and I had this overwhelming urge to *be* Sir Galahad, to gallop up on my white horse to rescue you."

"You truly felt like that?"

"Why not? A guy could drown in your eyes." He kissed her eyelids, then her lips.

8

When the phone rang at ten in the morning, Honora was dreamily rinsing breakfast dishes: she straightened with an instantaneous flash of hope that it was Curt. Last night when he had climbed the stairs with her, he had made no mention of another date. Twisting off the faucet, she reached for the dishcloth to dry her hands.

Crystal had already darted from the bathroom, blond ringlets streaming on her luminous, bare shoulders, the towel she was wrapping sarong style around her shapely torso transforming her into the ultimate movie-style seductive South Sea Islander. "I'll get it!" she cried. Lowering her voice, which she knew tended toward the higher soprano register, she cooed, "Hello?"

"Crystal? Gideon here," said the familiar gravelly notes. "I'd like you and your family to come for dinner tonight."

Crystal's eyes were a vivid, shining blue. This was Gideon's first important overture since the engraved Open House invitation. How she had chafed through those Saturday afternoons with the old fogies, waiting, hoping against hope that some young man other than Curt would show up! Crystal's strong sense of family loyalty precluded making a play for a man her sister liked, and besides she didn't go for Curt's caustic sense of humor—however, had he been the sole property of Imogene she wouldn't have let that stop her. The phone call, a move toward a Sylvander-

Talbott entente, would substantially advance her toward
the kind of life she had in mind.

Already dreaming up an excuse for Bobby Dupre, who
thought he was taking her to see *The Bells of St. Mary's*
with Bing Crosby tonight, she said, "How nice of you,
Gideon. It sounds lovely." Der Bingle wasn't one of her fa-
vorites anyway.

"I'm expecting your father, too, Crystal."

"Of course, Gideon. Daddy'll be delighted."

"My car'll be there at seven." He hung up.

Crystal stared down at the buzzing instrument in her
hand. "You'll never guess who that was."

"Wouldn't I just!" Joscelyn, at the kitchen table, raised
her head from a special geometry project for summer
school. "Gideon has a loud voice."

"Gideon?" A soapy cup slithered dangerously in Honora's grasp.

"He's invited all of us to dinner."

"To dinner? Why?"

"Stop tying everything in the world to your date last
night," said Crystal with mock severity.

"Oh, who can work with all of this going on?" Joscelyn
demanded.

Crystal ignored the remark. "Finally he's acting like a
real uncle. I'll bet he'll see to it that we're launched. Of
course he couldn't before now, because of Aunt Matilda,
but now he's coming out of deep mourning—"

"I never noticed him dissolved in the depths," Joscelyn
interjected.

"—and he'll be able to give parties for us to meet the
right people. Honora, it's a bit late for you, but he could
give me a debut. Imogene told me that Mrs. Burdetts hired
somebody called Mrs. Ekberg when she had hers. They had
three hundred people, including the Hearsts and the
Knowlands. Governor Warren showed up with Honeybear,
and she was asked back to 'the most *divinely* wild parties
where everyone got absolutely smashed on French bubbly.'" Crystal mimicked Imogene's exaggerated intonations.

During this effusion, Joscelyn's face had become pinched
and sullen. If Gideon were entertaining for Honora and
Crystal, he'd do the same for her. Parties terrified Joscelyn—not that she had been invited to many, either here or

in England. Her old crepe de chine party dress made her look even more spidery, and out of sickish anxiety she invariably spilled something down it. If she could have one of Crystal's attributes she would not choose the obvious, beauty, but Crystal's ability to glide through every function.

"Didn't I hear Gideon include Daddy in the invitation?" Joscelyn asked.

"So you finally rinsed the wax out of your ears," Crystal retorted.

"Crystal, Joss," Honora soothed.

"Daddy won't go," Joscelyn said flatly.

"Of course he will," Crystal said. "Gideon especially asked for him."

"Either you're more cretinous than I thought. Or blind. Haven't you noticed that he always has an excuse for the Open House? I'll bet anything he won't go tonight."

Crystal tightened the knot in her sarong towel. To her it was crucial that the entire Sylvander clan ingratiate itself with Gideon: she wanted the best of everything for all of them. "He'll be there," she snapped. Her sharp slam of the difficult bathroom door succeeded in shutting it.

"Oh, Joss," Honora sighed. "Why must you go out of your way to upset her?"

"You've been washing that same cup for hours." Joscelyn's eye twitched. It cut like broken glass whenever Honora sided with Crystal. "Are you pretending it's Curt Ivory's feet?"

Reddening, Honora set the cup on the drainboard.

Joscelyn nearly won her bet.

Langley indeed attempted to squirm out of this dinner. "I have an engagement with a very important chap," he said. "Somebody interested in starting a publishing house. With a snap of his fingers he could appoint me editor in chief." (Langley retained an endearing perennial hopefulness that every stranger who proclaimed himself rich in some way would pilot the good ship Sylvander into safe harbor.)

Crystal retorted that he couldn't let them down and shed a few becoming tears. But it was Honora, mindful of what Curt had told her the previous evening, who quietly pointed out that Gideon, after all his employer, might be

offended if he didn't show up. Langley, muttering something about delaying his arrangements with the possible
patron, left the apartment at four, returning a few minutes
after six with a sheepish little smile and a strong aroma of
whiskey and peppermint breath mints.

It turned out that Curt was the only other guest.

Mrs. Wartobe stood at the heavy Gothic sideboard, la-
dling rich cream of vegetable soup. Then came a plump leg
of lamb that Gideon carved, his broad red hands expertly
wielding the long, flashing knife and two-pronged fork,
jovially going around the table to inquire of each of them
which slice they preferred. Creamed potatoes, pearl onions,
fresh peas glazed with butter, golden hot yeast biscuits
completed the main course. At the Open Houses Juan
never offered the girls sherry. Tonight he tilted the wine
basket for Crystal and would have filled Honora's goblet,
too, but the vinous odors of burgundy brought a sour taste
to her mouth, and she said hastily, "None for me, thank
you."

Curt raised an amused eyebrow.

Limp with desire, she forced herself not to look at him
except when he spoke. Fortunately he and Gideon talked a
lot, discussing a cost projection for a refinery project in
Oxnard that they were bidding on. (The strong lines of affection between the two showed during this debate.) She
found it near impossible to reconcile this forceful Curt and
the man who had last night held her with shaking arms and
covered her face with small, nibbling kisses.

Gideon was saying, "Sylvander, you know about the refinery. You're writing up the proposal."

"I suppose I am." Langley's words slurred together.

Honora emerged from her bemusement to turn to her
father, who sat next to her. His nose was red at its narrow
tip, the blue eyes bloodshot. He had been at the Crowned
Head two hours, and at Gideon's table he had emptied
glass after glass of the burgundy, then the dessert Château
d'Yquem that came with the peach pie: she didn't need her
newfound knowledge of alcohol to know he was well in
his cups.

Gideon noticed, too. "Mrs. Wartobe, we're ready for the
coffee," he said.

After coffee was poured, the two servants retired with
trayloads of dishes through the green baize door.

Gideon sat straighter in his chair, a portentous expression on his heavy features. He cleared his throat. "I wanted you girls here because what I have to say concerns the three of you as well as your father." His gaze lingered on Crystal. "I've grown quite fond of you, and I hope the feeling is mutual."

The three sisters replied quite honestly that it was.

"This house is very large, seven family bedrooms upstairs. What I have in mind is for you Sylvanders to move in with me."

The ensuing silence was punctuated by Curt's cracking of a walnut. Honora, in her confusion, looked directly at him. He evinced no surprise.

"You mean *live* here?" Crystal asked. During her months in San Francisco her voice had undergone a metamorphosis to the looser American dipthongs, but now she spoke with her precise English intonation.

"More than that. This would be your home, but also I'd take care of your clothes, bills, tuitions, allowances, items like that."

Langley had lurched to his feet, a vein beating at his temple. "We might be associated in business, Talbott," he cried, "but I'll thank you to remember that my daughters are my concern!"

Gideon glared up at his tall, swaying brother-in-law. Gratitude for his generosities might embarrass him, still, he wasn't accustomed to having his good deeds flung back at him. "What's gotten into you?"

Langley's clenched fist slammed on the table. The small silver baskets of the epergne bobbled and an almond fell. "Having been married to poor Matilda gives you no entrée to my family concerns!"

"You should lay off the bottle, Sylvander," Gideon said sternly. "You've had far too much."

"What else could I do? You Americans!"

"Daddy," Honora murmured. "Please?"

Langley ignored her. "Money, money, money, that's all you talk about, even at the dinner table."

Gideon's shoulders hunched like a bull's. The light from the enormous chandelier picked out the sweat beading on his forehead. "I have no intention of letting Crystal follow her sister's footsteps. *She* will not be a waitress."

Honora wished that the inlaid parquet would part beneath her straight-backed Gothic chair to hurtle her into the basement. She shot a look of anguished reproach at Curt. He, a study in ironic control, gazed back. So this was his method of playing Sir Galahad! Honora twined her napkin in her lap, her hands shaking. *Oh God,* she thought. *How I've let poor Daddy down.*

"A waitress?" Joscelyn, beyond Langley, twisted in her chair to get a better view of her idolized sister. "Gideon, you have it all wrong."

"Absolutely the most ridiculous lie I ever heard." Langley turned to Honora, his full mouth oddly petulant. "Honora, kindly tell this man that you work at a highly respected brokerage house."

"I . . . Daddy, I, well, I was ashamed, so I, well . . . I invented the receptionist job."

"A Sylvander a waitress?" His mouth opened as if he had been shot in the chest by his tender favorite.

Honora looked down at her cup, afraid yesterday's devastating tears would return.

"Honora works at Stroud's," Curt put in smoothly. "As I told Mr. Talbott, the place is no dive. The flower of the financial district eat at Stroud's. Working there's hardly a reason to put on sackcloth and ashes. Honora told me you need the money. But you yourself agree she's college material. She ought to be at Berkeley—"

"She will be," Langley broke in.

"When?" Curt asked.

"This autumn."

"I'll be American and bring up the subject of money again," Curt said. "Have you enough put away?"

"You know which side your bread is buttered on, don't you, Ivory?"

"No need to see insult where there is none," Gideon said. "Curt is only trying to point out that she won't be working and she will have minor tuition fees and other expenses."

"Hahh!"

"I want what's best for the girls. Here in San Francisco there's a woman, Mrs. Ekberg, she handled Imogene Burdetts' coming out party. She's promised to move in."

"I'll never live in this damn house!"

Crystal's eyes had gleamed at the mention of Mrs. Ekberg, facilitator of debuts. "Daddy," she said sweetly, "Gideon's offer is something the family should discuss privately."

9

Curt volunteered to drive them home.

Langley slumped in the back seat, not speaking. The convertible was a two door and when they reached Lombard Street, he hauled himself out with difficulty, ignoring Curt's outstretched hand, staggering from the running board.

Crystal and Joscelyn had scurried through the entry tunnel, but Honora waited on the sidewalk for her father.

"You," he snarled at her. "A Sylvander selling yourself for a few filthy pennies."

"Daddy, please. . . ."

"How could you?" His ranting voice was almost unrecognizable.

"Daddy, the work isn't really so awful . . . it was the only job I could get . . ."

"You're common!" He repeated it like the foulest curse, a few flecks of saliva flying. *"Common!"*

"I never meant to hurt you."

Muttering, "Common . . . common . . . liar," he lurched toward the entry.

She started to follow, but Curt took her arm. "Honora, hold on a minute. We have to talk."

"What about?" she asked leadenly.

"It's freezing," he said. "Come on back in the car."

She sat with her arm pressed against the door.

"Okay," Curt said, lighting a cigarette. "You're ready to throw me off the Golden Gate Bridge."

"You promised to keep Stroud's between us."

"Look, I knew Mr. Talbott wanted to make life easier for you girls and couldn't figure out how to do it."

"So he insulted Daddy."

"He's trying to help," Curt said, adding in a low voice,

"Take it from one who knows, my boss is a very generous guy."

"All right," she said dully.

"He's told me quite a few times that having a family brings light into the old house—and he does get in fine fettle when the Sylvander sisters arrive."

Honora rested the back of her head against the comfortless glass.

"He didn't know exactly how rough things've been since you came over, but he's discussed ways to set you up more comfortably. He considered giving your father a raise, but then decided against it because it might encourage his drinking."

"I don't see what all of this has to do with you breaking your word." Her voice rose.

"That's better. Now you're mad."

"Of course I am. Can you imagine how it was for Daddy, finding out this way? Or don't you care?"

"Honora, a couple of minutes ago I cared so much I could happily have throttled him. Christ, who does he think he is, King George? He flubs the dub supporting his family and then flays you because you do it for him."

"I do not support the family," she said. "I help out a bit, that's all."

"Like hell. I know his takehome, I know what it costs to get loaded in a bar."

"We were managing before I got the job."

"I'll bet. What does he do, wear blinkers? Or hasn't he noticed that his family's eating, wearing new clothes—going to the dentist?"

It was the same brutal anger as the previous night.

She could scarcely whisper. "It was an awful thing for him to have my job thrown at him. He's very sensitive."

"I've a pet theory that sensitive people are only sensitive about their own thin skins. Look at the way he just lashed out at you."

"He's had a bit too much wine—"

"Wine, hell. He was potted before he got to the house." Curt pulled out the ashtray, crushing his unsmoked cigarette slowly, as if grinding out his anger. "Honora," he said quietly, "I know you won't believe this, but when he's sober, and doesn't have a sliver up his ass, I find him a very likable guy. If it's any comfort, breaking the promise hurt me more than it did him. Or do you suppose I get my kicks seeing that kind of betrayal on your face?"

She needed Curt to admit that her father hadn't been at fault. "To support us he took a job that's beneath him, and he's always been so proud—"

Curt placed a silencing finger across her lips. "Let's not talk about it. You're too gentle for the world, and I don't care to see the people you love screw you."

He was rubbing his fingertip on the tiny ridge that divided the sides of her full upper lip, and she could feel herself melting. With a fleeting sense of filial disloyalty, she abandoned her arguments. He tuned the radio, halting the luminous line at the number that played classical music.

"Tchaikovsky's Fifth," she whispered.

"I think you've got me witched," he said, his arm drawing her to his side, breathing against her ear, "Why else would I make up my mind definitely not to do this, then keep doing it." He kissed her lightly.

"Curt. . . ."

"What, sweet?"

"Curt. . . . I just like saying your name. . . ."

"I like the way you say it. Your uncle won't approve of us dating."

"Why not?"

"Because I don't share his moral standards."

"You sleep with girls?"

"And do other things with them, yes."

"I hate them all."

He kissed her properly. She felt a languorous underwater creature, as if the Buick were submerged in the depths of the Bay, her body liquid, pressing against his, his tongue in its element of her mouth, and when he unbuttoned her coat and lightly rubbed his thumb on the rayon over her nipple, she felt an exquisite, drowning surge of wetness between her legs.

"Curt . . . I love you . . ."

"This is called the hots."

"Not for me."

"These are so pretty," he said, cupping his hands around her breasts.

She was caressing the musculature of his shoulders, the deep indentation of his spine. "I do love you."

"Good, because it's not just the hots for me, either."

"Darling. . . ."

*   *   *

Neither of them saw Langley emerge. He glanced at the car, saw his daughter hugging and making up to that smirking, insufferable Ivory who everybody at Talbott's knew was Don Juan in modern dress, treating women as his private preserves of prostitution. That Honora, his dreamy heart's child, not only had disgraced the Sylvander line but was also in the man's clutches reached into the deep pocket of Langley's despair.

He trudged unevenly down Lombard Street on his way to the Crowned Head.

"Wake up, Honora." Crystal was shaking her shoulder.

Honora, who had been dreaming vividly of Curt, blinked at the thin line of sunlight coming through the lengthwise rip in the ecru canvas blind.

Crystal said worriedly, "Daddy's bed hasn't been slept in."

"And it's half past nine," Joscelyn wailed.

Honora pushed up on her elbow. "You mean he's been gone all night?" This was an unprecedented occurrence.

"That's what we're trying to tell you." Joscelyn jumped on Honora's narrow bed, burying her head in the softness of her older sister's pajama top. "Something dreadful's happened."

"Joss, let me get dressed," Honora said. "We must go to the police."

The child gripped both sisters' hands, jabbering constantly as they trotted to the wooden station house near Fisherman's Wharf. The desk sergeant, a large-nosed man in his thirties, smiled indulgently as Honora explained their father's disappearance.

"Listen, girls, I was over in your country during the war, and I can tell you it's the same here as there. If you put out a missing person on every man who stayed out all night, us Dick Tracys'd never have time to chase criminals." He winked at Crystal.

"But our father's never done this before," Honora said.

"Maybe your kid sister doesn't understand things like this, but you know how it is. Sometimes us men have a special lady we like spending time with."

"I hardly think our father would do that, especially without warning us," Honora said.

"Sometimes these things just happen."

"We don't live far from Chinatown. How do you know he hasn't been hurt in some tong violence?" Joscelyn demanded.

The cop shrugged. "If he's still missing after a couple of days, check back."

They usually attended church, but that Sunday they searched the neighborhood. When Langley hadn't returned by midnight, they went to bed, each dozing fitfully, listening for his step outside the window.

Black guilt engulfed Honora as she trudged to work. When Al saw the delicate smudges under her eyes, he ordered her home. "You're still sick, Honora."

Back at the flat, Joscelyn was dithering whether or not to go to summer school—in the end she decided that she couldn't ruin her perfect attendance record. Crystal telephoned Talbott's with an excuse of illness for Langley. She and Honora stayed home.

"It was a terrible mistake, not telling him," Honora said.

They had gone over this ground a hundred times.

"Honora, what's the use of blaming yourself?"

"Maybe I could have stopped him. If only I hadn't stayed out in the car!"

"Is Curt a good neck?"

"Oh, Crystal."

"I know, I know, Honorable Honora wouldn't discuss her loverboy's lusts and lewdnesses." Crystal began walking up and down the kitchen, her small, high arched feet hitting the worn linoleum sharply.

"Do sit down, Crys."

"I wanted what was best for all of us—I never dreamed it would turn out so hideously."

"Now who's blaming herself?"

"It's not like me, is it?"

Honora drew a long, shuddery breath. "Where do you think San Francisco's morgue is?"

"Stop it, stop it!" Crystal resumed her pacing.

When the hands of the clock with the cracked face—the glass had broken in shipping—pointed to ten to two, Crystal said, "It's time for the Crowned Head to open. I'll go on over and ask if anybody's seen him."

Thus, Honora was alone at the kitchen table when Langley unlocked the front door.

In her swelling rush of relief, she could not speak. Pushing to her feet, she stared down the corridor. Her father's derby was gone and also his tie, his collar button was undone and a long, brownish stain ran down his rumpled trousers. What disturbed her most, though, was the graying stubble on his cheeks and jaw—in her life she had never seen her father with more than a day's growth of beard.

"Hello." He gave her a rueful little smile and came unsteadily into the kitchen.

"Oh, Daddy, thank heavens you're here." She hugged him. He smelled vile, but there was no hint of perfume. "We've been so crazy."

"I should have telephoned," he said, playing the silver link up and down in his soiled cuff. "That chap, remember, I told you about him, the fellow who wants to make an investment, he kept me discussing the ins and outs of publishing. I lost track of time."

Two interminable days and nights.

An idol had fallen in Honora's mind, and from the shards was rising a sweet, vulnerable, middle-aged child whom she must love and protect.

"He sounds very keen," she said, entering into a complicity to protect his pride.

"You don't know that half of it," said Langley with pathetic eagerness. "He's going to start his own press—small publishing houses are quite the thing in San Francisco, you know. He wants yours truly on his payroll, as of now."

He spoke too quickly and Honora wasn't sure whether she believed him or not, but she cried, "Daddy, how marvelous! You'll be working in your own line again."

"More than that. I'll be editor in chief."

"It's like a dream! Daddy, why don't you have a bath while I put the kettle on? We'll celebrate with a cup of tea."

Langley, shaved and wearing a fresh shirt under his old cardigan, hungrily devoured anchovy paste sandwiches. Between bites he expounded on the trust placed in him by his new employer, avoiding any mention of the work that his job would entail.

Joscelyn came up the steps with Crystal—they had met on Columbus and Lombard.

Before they could blurt out questions, Honora cried, "Daddy has some wonderful news. He's back in publishing."

Kissing his younger daughters, he explained about his new job in that rapid staccato.

Congratulations all around.

"Crystal, Honora, you sit here," he said, pointing at the chairs to his left and right. "Joss, get on my lap." When the thin little body was snuggled against his, he said, "We have something important to go over."

"It's all right, Daddy," Crystal said. "It's obvious why you were gone so long. You were all tied up."

"Yes," Joscelyn said, taking off her glasses to rub them on his sweater. "Let's not get boring about it, Daddy."

"It's your uncle's offer we need to discuss." A tension showed around Langley's mouth. "I've been giving it serious thought."

"You want us all to move into the mausoleum?" Joscelyn asked.

"No, pet, I meant that your pater needs to put his total energy behind his new position. Starting a top-notch publishing house is quite tricky. Until it's safely on its feet, you three will stay with your uncle."

"Without you?" Joscelyn whimpered.

"I'll need all my wits about me," Langley said.

"Daddy, we won't be a drain." Honora paused. "I'll keep on working."

Langley shuddered. "University's the job for you."

"But we'll be separated." Joscelyn's eye was twitching.

"How I loathed it during the war," Crystal burst out. "Please, Daddy, don't break up the family. I can get a green card."

"Why're you girls carrying on so? I won't be in Reykjavik. My pets, I'll see you every Sunday. But it's of the utmost importance to me to know you're being taken care of properly. Otherwise how will I keep my mind on my great adventure?" Although his long, thin-featured face was very pale he spoke humorously.

"Daddy, we're not going to Gideon's without you and that's that." Crystal's eyes were glittering with tears. She had schemed for Gideon and his wealth to do great things for her family: now confusion and self-recrimination filled her.

"For once Crystal's dead right," Joscelyn said. "In this family it's all for one and one for all."

"Now, chickens, no more arguments. Not one. My mind is made up." Langley's voice broke miserably.

After a brief silence, Crystal asked, "How long until this publishing deal is on the way?"

Joscelyn pressed her homely little face against his cardigan. "Yes, Daddy, give us an idea of the time we'll be staying at Gideon's."

"A couple of months at the most," Langley said.

"Then what're we arguing about?" Crystal asked. The separation would run its course, and each of the Sylvanders would be incalculably better off. "By autumn we'll be together."

"Precisely. Think of it as an extended summer holiday," Langley said. "Now come here, all of you."

A family ritual. They put their arms around one another's shoulders and the gray head, the glossy black, the vivid gold and the mouse-brown touched.

10

Life in the big ugly house on Clay Street did not remotely resemble Crystal's brightly colored anticipations.

Her vision of Gideon being an open sesame to the free-wheeling excitement of San Francisco's *jeunesse dorée* had proved utterly false. Langley, in his feckless need for love, had overlooked his children's disciplinary breaches, allowing them an inordinate amount of freedom. Gideon, however, was made of sterner stuff. With executive precision he wrote out rules for his charges, giving the list to Mrs. Ekberg. (It turned out that Mrs. Ekberg, a nervous, thin little widow who chewed Tums continuously, had not facilitated Imogene's debut but had served as Mrs. Burdetts' temporary social secretary.) Needing this job desperately, the widow enforced her employer's regulations to her utmost. And as for Crystal's hopes of rich young men, Gideon did not introduce her to any. When he met Crystal's dates he narrowed his small brown eyes, inquiring how they were planning to transport and entertain his aristocratic charge. The City College boys, already overextended by Crystal's beauty and the gloomy, anachronistic mansion, crumpled under the strain. The phone rang fewer and fewer times for Crystal.

On the other hand, Gideon was boundlessly generous. He gave Crystal *carte blanche* to refurnish her spacious bedroom, which had been Aunt Matilda's, and she turned it into a girl's dream room, ordering the reluctant painter to quadruple-coat powder-blue paint over the original walnut paneling, covering the hand-etched parquet with shaggy blue carpet, replacing the thick-legged, turn-of-the-century bedroom suite with a bed canopied with dotted Swiss, a huge, beruffled, kidney-shaped vanity, a flock of little blue velvet slipper chairs.

He allowed all three sisters to use his Chargaplate to buy new wardrobes, he splurged on a spiffy new car, he installed one of those new televisions in the music room.

On the second Saturday night in a row that Crystal stayed home dateless he surprised her with genuine cultured pearls. As she excitedly fastened the graduated strand around her smooth white throat, she wondered briefly whether Gideon, like a doting, elderly father, nursed a subconscious jealousy of her boyfriends.

But wasn't that silly?

He was just as strict with Honora.

On a hot Friday afternoon in early September, Curt and Honora drove along the broad, unpaved swathe that topped a wall of dirt. In theory, Curt was taking the day off: in actuality he had been going over a revision of the plans for the East Oakland freeway project and now was delivering them to the resident engineer. Distance turned workers into pins with red tops while a line of earthmovers became double-bodied toys—Honora could just make out the tiny lettering, G.D. TALBOTT'S. Headquarters was the one remaining structure on the cleared site, an old frame bungalow surrounded by a survey truck, a Jeep and several dust-thick cars parked higgledy-piggledy.

Curt pulled up next to a battered Onyx. "We're here," he said. "Come on in."

"I'll wait," Honora said.

"In this heat?"

"I'm working on a tan."

In reality she was prickling with anxiety. Gideon was away for a few days, but if he heard that she had come here with Curt it might be the final straw. When she had moved to Clay Street, her uncle had clearly stated his objections to Curt—too sophisticated, meaning too sexy—then glared his disapproval each time Curt picked her up. If Curt was concerned, he never showed it: he always popped into his employer's downstairs office or the drawing room to say a few words, seemingly oblivious to the stern wrinkling and blue veins standing out at the bald temples. Whenever plausible, she arranged that they meet elsewhere.

"Tan?" Curt was laughing. "Sunstroke, more like it."

"Are you going to be *that long?*"

"Just a couple of minutes," he said, reaching in the back seat for two thick scrolls, then jogging onto the narrow porch. In homage to the day-off theory, he wore madras Bermudas. She watched the muscles work in the tanned calves with the thick, curling pale hairs, then flushed and turned away.

The house-studded hills nestled at the foot of the long, maternal mountains. Afternoon sun ruddied the tall downtown buildings of Oakland, glinting a window here and there into a faceted ruby. She gazed at the sunstruck vista, her eyes growing rapt as her thoughts turned to Curt.

He often told her he loved her, playing with a strand of her blue-black hair as he said the words, or breathing endearments into her ear when they were "involved," and although in rational moments she warned herself that a man nearing thirty with his experience doubtless possessed a well-thumbed lexicon of amatory phrases, intuitively she divined he meant what he said—at the time, anyway. He had never mentioned marriage—or even going steady. Last month he had escorted Imogene to the Burdetts Company's annual picnic, and a couple of weeks ago they had attended a charity gala together. For all Honora knew, he saw her far more frequently. Curt, being Curt, never offered explanation of how he spent his time. *Is he making love to that skinny clotheshorse?* Honora thought, and shivered with despair.

Yet in a perverse way his independence pleased her: her love was no tamed, domestic creature.

"Honora?"

Jerking, she blinked up at the object of her reverie.

"I brought out a friend to meet you," Curt said.

For a moment the figure behind Curt was a blob, then he took form, a stout man in his late thirties wearing dark trousers and a short-sleeved shirt that was loudly patterned. His ample nose—bent toward the right as if once broken—presided over a thick black mustache and big smile. Sweat burnished his skin, which had a rich, dark tan, as if the pigmentation were genetically adapted for too strong sun. *Jewish,* Honora thought with a trace of envious admiration. Having been reared amid Church of England pallor in a country where there were few Jews, no Negroes or Chinese, and therefore correspondingly little prejudice, she saw members of these groups as emissaries of exotic and superior cultures.

Curt said, "Honora, this is an old school buddy of mine—"

"I guided him through Math One in Durant Hall," said the stranger in an unplaceably soft, guttural accent.

"You helped me? As I recall, you were flunking until I came along," Curt said. "Honora Sylvander, this is Fuad Abdulrahman."

Honora hastily converted her new acquaintance's religion to Islam. But how could he have been at Berkeley with Curt? He was at least a decade older. "How do you do, Mr. Abdulrahman," she said.

"So you're one of the gorgeous Talbott nieces we've heard so much of," said Fuad. "You really are an exquisite creature. Could I convince you to become part of a well-ordered harem in Lalarhein?"

"Lalarhein?"

"You have to clear your throat as you say the *r,*" Fuad said. "Lala *ch*rain."

"It's a barren patch of desert near the Persian Gulf," Curt said.

"Curt speaks from envy and ignorance—he's never been to our paradise." Fuad wiped his forehead, scattering a few iridescent drops into the car. "I can see by your eyes, so dark and soulful, that you would respond well to our roses and fountains."

"It does sound lovely."

"I promise you a thousand and one nights of fleshly delights."

"Do you always make this offer when you meet a girl?" Honora asked, smiling.

"Only when he's positive he won't be taken up," Curt said.

"Ahh, so there's a Mrs. Abdulrahman," Honora said.

Fuad gestured expansively, indicating numerous wives. "But you would be the favorite," he said, leaning his arms on her window. "Miss Sylvander, this is a serious offer."

"And I assure you I'm giving it serious consideration."

Dust clouded around the convertible as they drove away. Curt lapsed into silence. Occasionally and unaccountably he sank into moods that excluded her.

She didn't say anything until they had halted to pay at one of the tollbooths of the Oakland Bay Bridge and joined the traffic flowing toward San Francisco. (In October, when the Berkeley semester began, she would make the round trip on this bridge every weekday.)

"Did you and Fuad start out on a sweat gang?" she asked in a low, tentative voice. She knew from Gideon that a college engineering student's first job was generally chopping weeds and digging ditches with a sweat gang.

"Nope. As a matter of fact my first job is right under us," he said. "I was a Talbott's messenger boy on the bridge project."

"How old were you?"

"Twelve."

What about that privileged American boyhood? "Isn't that very young?"

He shrugged. The wind blew his tawny hair back.

She shifted her legs, which were sweating lightly. "Gideon's proud that he was on both the Bay Bridge projects, but he's never explained how they were built."

"They're entirely different. Golden Gate's a single span, and this bridge has a permanent pier structure under water." They were nearing Yerba Buena Island, and he pointed downward. "Right here, Pier E4, is the world's deepest pier. It goes down to minus 247 feet." He explained how they had floated the caissons from the Oakland docks and then sunk them at the piers. His pitch was lower, and she could swear he was grateful she had roused him from his brooding.

The car bounced with small, hollow clicks as they drove over the bridge sections.

"Fuad's very nice," she said. "He's a bit corny, but I did like him tremendously."

"He's a terrific, warm guy."

"Isn't he a bit old to have been at university with you?"

"When he came to Berkeley he was married with two kids."

"Does he live here and work for Talbott's?"

"Neither. He's here to observe the job. In Lalarhein they're planning to build a road system. Incidentally, it's not just plain Fuad, it's Prince Fuad."

She bit her lip in embarrassment. "And I called him Mr. Abdulrahman—and his wife Mrs. Abdulrahman."

"He's used to that. In Lalarhein, or so he says, being a prince means you're middle class. The country's got a population of under two million." They were coming off the bridge. "Listen, are you really dying to see the Palace of Fine Arts?" He had planned to show her the small park with the classical remnants of the 1915 Panama-Pacific Exposition.

"No," she whispered.

"My place, then," he said.

11

There was a parking space on Telegraph Hill outside the tall stucco apartment building. When Curt opened the car door for Honora, she tilted her head up at him.

"When you look at me like this," he said, "all's right with the world. Did I ever tell you what unusual eyes you have?"

"Often," she said.

"I never saw irises so deep and dark—or whites so clear that they have an almost bluish tinge, like a baby's."

Just at that moment the Talbott Cadillac was moving

down the hill. Both Juan and Mrs. Ekberg saw them go inside.

The first time Honora had come here with Curt was on their third date. Her crimson-faced awkwardness as she'd passed the doorman had been so intense that she'd stumbled, and even now it was difficult for her to smile at the wizened man who tipped his dark green cap to them as he pushed open the etched glass door.

Curt's apartment was on the tenth floor.

The furnishings, though obviously expensive, were agreeably sparse. A long, sleek, gray tweed couch took full advantage of the magnificent view of the Bay. A handsome birch drafting table was neatly arranged with graph paper, T-square, triangle, compass, a bottle of Higgins India ink. The built-in modern bookcase held college texts, stacked copies of *American Engineering*, and fat volumes on structural problems—the lack of a single novel had initially caused Honora a serious pang.

Curt closed the door and reached his arms around her, resting his cheek against hers as if their embrace had nothing to do with carnality but was consolation for some unbearable loss.

Her eyes squeezed shut, and she encircled his waist, drawing his warmth yet closer. The same ungovernable reactions she always experienced flooded over her, the trembling, the racing of her heart, the weakness, the mysterious epidermal receptiveness—she was all tactile sensation. Her lips traced the moist, shaven skin and fine bones of his Adam's apple.

"Sweet, look at me," he said in her ear.

She blinked, pulling her head back, so that all she saw was his eyes, eyes which she always thought of as lion-colored, lion-sure. They were moist, vulnerable.

"What is it, darling?"

He shook his head, searching her face.

It flashed through her mind that he was questioning whether she wanted to go into his bedroom—but why would he question that? He hadn't asked her the first time.

"I love you." Her whisper was breathy.

"You are love," he said, and, arms wound around one another, they went into the rear room which held only the huge, custom covered bed.

He pushed back the box-cornered spread and the blanket

while she threw off her sundress and underwear. When they were lying naked on the bottom sheet, he kissed her sensitive breasts, his hands tenderly caressing her hips, her slender, tremulous thighs. The sumptuous melting physical desire that he invoked was tied to her profoundest emotions, her strivings toward beauty, her sense of honor, her need to nurture and cherish and love. At his entry, she floated in a miraculous stillness, then great spasms of ecstasy bucked through her body uncontrollably and she gasped out rhythmic cries of his name. After this initial craziness, her orgasms would be gentler, and she would caress him in the ways that gave him joy until he could no longer control his climax.

They lay entwined, her heart calming, her fingers and ears still tingling.

He pulled the sheet and blanket over them, taking an ashtray onto his chest and lighting a cigarette. He inhaled deeply. "I was born in Austria."

She raised her head, looking at him. "You're American," she denied.

"Sure, but not native born. Like you, an immigrant."

"Austria?"

"Maybe, but I'm not even sure of that. Maybe Germany. It's the same language. The truth is, I have remarkably few facts about myself." His sigh shook the ashtray.

She kissed his shoulder, inhaling the acrid odors of his coital sweat.

"My earliest memory is of a soft-armed, pale-haired woman feeding me a rusk soaked in something sweet. I can't remember another thing about her, but it pleases me to suppose the soft, pale lady my mama. Then I'm living with an old woman. She told me she and I were no kin—she was a loathsome old crone, so it didn't exactly destroy me. Vaguely—and again I'm not at all sure—I think she'd been some kind of servant in my family's home. She and I shared a root cellar near an outhouse. Not an esthetic or hygienic location, but then we weren't exactly royalty. The old woman had hard, pinching fingers and she coughed all night loud enough to wake the dead. But she was all I had, so when I came up with anything edible I brought it home to share with her. I worked the garbage cans behind the Ringstrasse restaurants, where the rich ate. Sometimes I unearthed treasures, a fragment of whipped cream pastry, the carcass of a game bird. I learned to move fast, to scratch and hit—the competition was keen. The reparations that the allies had wreaked on the Austro-Hungarian Empire had spawned an entire class privileged to scrounge in garbage cans."

Her flesh had gone cold. She kept wiping her eyes, aching to comfort him, yet knowing she mustn't halt his purgative flow of words. The sky outside grew dark, and the only light in the room was the glowing red circle from Curt's cigarette. Chain-smoking, he dredged up incidents. A tiny girl he had seen sucking off a fat-bellied old man for one chocolate, boys his age who did the same thing, the "adult" whores, who in retrospect must have been eleven or twelve. "No, I never peddled my bony little ass," he said. "Don't ask why not, I just never did. To get my food I scavenged or went in for juvenile assault and battery."

The old woman's coughing and blood-spitting worsened. One morning he dreamed of snow and awakening to feel her icy rigid body curled around his. After her death he had deserted the root cellar and taken shelter under a bridge.

"Weren't there orphanages?" Honora asked.

"Too overcrowded to seek recruits. But don't think we received no benefits under our bridge. Every night a municipal trolley came around and the sanitation department lugged away the corpses. The old woman had told me I was born in 1921, three years after the final shot. This was 1927, nine years after the war, and the dying hadn't ended."

One winter day he had heard a rumor of bread being given out by the Quakers, who were always engaged in such ridiculous enterprises. "I would have set out to China for a crust, so the miles to the Gürtel were nothing. It was dark, and as I charged around a corner, I butted into this solid, well-dressed American."

"Gideon?" Honora whispered incredulously.

"Mr. Talbott, yes. He asked where I was rushing, and when I told him he took me into a bakery. Since I had no last name, he gave me one—he said after a good scrub I'd be white as ivory. So Curt Ivory I became. A meal, a bath and one thing led to another. He arranged to bring me to California. He found a couple in Oakland, the Howells, to take care of me. They were cold, joyless people, but respectable. They must have figured they were sheltering some crazy sort of animal. The old woman had taught me to bow and click my heels like a little gentleman, so I bowed and clicked while I stole from their ice box. It was months before I left the table without a roll or a hunk of meat hidden in my pocket. I lived for the times Mr. Talbott dropped by to visit. He inspired me to become an engineer; he lent me the money for college. Honora, I know he has faults. He's self-righteous, a puritanical dictator, but he's also generous, kind, decent. And if you sometimes think I have too much of a soft spot for him, remember he not only saved my life, he gave me a new country, my name. He gave me my identity. I owe everything to him."

"Curt, darling, I bless him."

"One of the reasons I love you is whenever I look into your eyes, I'm healed of my childhood."

"It's over," she said, hugging him fiercely.

"Things like that are never over." He switched on the light. "Honora, you must always remember that starving boy lives inside me. He'll always go for the jugular. He'll always prod me to grab and scratch for the kind of luxuries those rich bastards who ate in the Ringstrasse cafes had, he'll do whatever he must to push ahead."

"You're not ruthless."

"Face it, Honora, my dominant trait's ambition. I intend to make it to the top." He forced a smile. "Come on, all this talk of starving's made me ravenous. Let's scramble some eggs."

She watched the strong, well-knit body cross the room before she got out of bed.

Joscelyn lay immobile in the center of the big, soft bed, carefully simulating the deep, modulated breath of sleep. Her ears were alert, though, and her eyes staring into the governing darkness. She was a mess when either of her sisters went out at night; especially when Honora was absent a gamut of terrors prowled. Tonight, with Gideon away too, the flesh of her enforcedly still body was covered with goosebumps. Joscelyn was keenly intelligent, and certainly old enough to understand that her fears were irrational . . . yet, mightn't that creak herald an intruder, couldn't that shadow in the corner be a lurking kidnapper, wouldn't an old house with this much paneling burst into instant conflagration?

Mrs. Ekberg believed that Honora was out with a friend—Vi Knodler, that waitress at Stroud's she still sometimes saw—but Joscelyn knew that Honora was spending the afternoon and evening with Curt and was with him now. Joscelyn accepted that her sister was sticky in love.

Joscelyn's prepubescent heart, too, had an icon shrine lit by smoky candles for Curt. He had it all: style, brains, a gorgeous convertible, an impervious, sarcastic smile. The thing she couldn't understand was why Gideon, whom she admired, didn't want Honora going out with this flower of manhood.

The sound of a car grew louder, and Joscelyn, an outspoken agnostic, found her mind teeming with infantile prayers. *Please, God, let it be Honora, I'll be nice to everyone tomorrow if it's her.*

A light blossomed behind her curtains, abruptly extinguishing when the motor was cut.

Only when the side door opened and closed, and Honora's light footsteps ran up the staircase, did she roll over and breathe normally.

"Honora," she called. "That you?"

Honora came in, switching on a light. "You're still up, Joss?"

"I *was* asleep until you came in."

"I tried not to make a racket." Honora came to press her night-cool cheek on Joscelyn's forehead.

Joscelyn inhaled the unique body fragrance that was dewy and sweet. There was a smell of soap, too, as if she'd recently showered. Another reason to envy both sisters: neither ever had the odor of smelly feet, as Joscelyn was positive she did. "I'll never get back to sleep."

"If you were in my bed would it help?" Honora asked.

Was that a trace of hesitancy in the soft voice? Joscelyn's face burned. Was Honora remembering the first week they were in this house, when every morning this bed had an ignominiously sunken damp splotch? "Your snoring's hardly the cure for insomnia."

"Do I snore?" Honora asked in a hurt little voice.

Remorse flooded through Joscelyn. Her pride halted her from confessing her lie.

"Sometimes, but not too very loud," she said, adding aggrievedly, "Oh well, if you insist, I'll give it a try in your room."

12

It was an inviolable commitment for the four Sylvanders to spend Sunday together. Gideon had bought a luxurious wood-bodied Chrysler Town and Country (because it had been delivered on Crystal's birthday, he referred to it with stilted jests as Crystal's convertible) and enrolled the two older girls at Ace Driving School. In sporty magnificence, the top down, they would pick up their father. Langley had moved from Lombard Street to Stockton Street, a better class of flat, he said, but the exterior of the building was yet more shabby, and they never glimpsed his apartment. He was always waiting on the pavement for them.

The weather had remained hot over the weekend. Honora had told her father they were bringing a picnic, but as they drove up Stockton, he was waiting on the shady side, his long, weedy body encased in his narrow, three-piece black pin-striped suit. His white flannels, made for him on Savile Row in his halcyon honeymoon days, had turned an uneven, sulfuric yellow, and he owned no American sport clothes. They drove across the bridge, winding up to a piny park in the Berkeley hills. The heat is more intense on the inland side of the Bay, yet Langley, ever the gentleman, did not shed his jacket. He mopped his brow while making the whimsical remarks that kept laughter bubbling at their redwood picnic table.

The only awkward note of the afternoon rang when Langley raised a Dixie cup of Mrs. Wartobe's lemonade. "Here's to being in our own climate next summer," he toasted.

"I'm staying here, Daddy," Honora said softly.

"What's that?" Langley peered in surprise at his pet, his steadfast English girl.

Her creamy skin was flushed, and the faint sheen of

sweat made her radiant. "I like California," she murmured.

"Face it, Daddy," Crystal said, fanning her wide-brimmed straw hat in the hot, still, pine-odored air. "We're Americans."

"It takes five years to get citizenship," Joscelyn corrected, but didn't refute her sisters' main point.

Langley drank his lemonade in silence. After a minute, he rose to his feet, mimicking an aged, crablike walk. "Girls, who am I?"

By the time Honora guessed Lear, he had them laughing so hard she could hardly get out the name.

They dropped him off at six.

When they drove up Clay Street they saw the Cadillac parked in the porte cochere with Juan hauling Gideon's small suitcase from the trunk. Gideon, on the steps to the side entry with the larger valise, set down his briefcase to lift his arm in greeting.

"The return of the native," Crystal called flirtatiously from the Town and Country's driver's seat.

"It's swell to have you back, Gideon," called Joscelyn, who never passed up a chance to use his first name.

"Welcome home," Honora cried warmly.

"The-ere's n-oooo pu-lace like ho-o-ome." Gideon's gravelly, toneless voice raised in song.

It was so unlike him that Honora stared. The virile auburn sideburns were freshly barbered, his suit jacket was jauntily open, displaying a spritely red tie. Being in love herself, she speculated whether Gideon, too, had fallen into the tender trap. Though Matilda Talbott had died only a little over a half year ago, she had been an invalid a very long time. It would not be surprising if Gideon had found some sympathetic widow—his high standards of morality would prevent his wooing a divorcée. And with a little jolt, she accepted that though he was short-legged, bald, with strong, ugly features, he had vigorous presence—and more than enough wealth—to attract older women in their thirties and forties.

The girls piled out of the convertible, leaving it for Juan to drive down to the garage, which had been the carriage house.

Joscelyn took Gideon's thick, reddish hand, and Honora picked up his attaché case.

Crystal kissed near his cheek. "How was Oxnard?" she asked.

"The refinery's going well, but you can't imagine how I missed you girls," he said with a hearty, jocular laugh. "Now go get washed up. Curt's coming to dinner."

Mrs. Ekberg was waiting in a dark corner of the immense hall. Coming forward, she nervously fingered her swirled gray French knot. "Mr. Talbott, may I have a word?"

"After dinner."

"This is important," Mrs. Ekberg twittered.

"Have your charges been harassing you?" he asked, winking at Crystal.

Mrs. Ekberg's narrow features contorted into beseeching desperation.

"Come on in the office, then," Gideon said, setting his valise on the parquet.

The girls clattered upstairs. "What do you suppose Ekberg's so het up about?" Crystal said.

"You got home late Thursday night," Joscelyn retorted.

"Even she's not idiotically prissy enough to let that get to her. Maybe the principal phoned that our Jossie's being expelled after one week."

"Ha-ha," Joscelyn said.

Honora said nothing, but ran into her room.

"That's right," Crystal called. "Go make yourself bee-oot-eous for Curt."

Mrs. Wartobe, who took off Sundays, had left a cold supper that Juan served. Mrs. Ekberg was not at the table—she often excused herself from meals when her colitis was acting up. Gideon had plunged from his homecoming pleasure. Head hunched between his thick shoulders, he silently forked up cold cuts and potato salad, glaring at a big, lazy fly as it buzzed through the room.

Though Honora normally reacted like mercury to the emotional temperature, she paid little attention to Gideon's mood shift. Her efforts were expended on not gazing at Curt. He and Crystal were carrying on a meaningless banter, artificial notes ringing too loudly in the strained atmosphere. Joscelyn, always unnerved by anger, spilled her chocolate milk on the cutwork cloth. Mopping up created a welcome diversion. They were toying with Mrs. Wartobe's meltingly rich devil's food cake when Gideon got to his feet, dropping his napkin on the table. "Come into my office, Ivory," he said, and stalked from the room.

Honora's tingle of anxiety came not so much from Gideon's tone—he often was abrupt when it came to business matters—but by his use of the patronym he had bestowed. She glanced at Curt. He raised an eyebrow, indicating he was as mystified as she.

"Another scintillating Sunday evening watching 'Show of Shows,' " Crystal sighed.

Honora paid no attention to Sid Caesar and Imogene Coca's preenings on the ten-inch screen. Her attention was fixed on any sounds that might come from Gideon's small office across the hall.

Once, over the televised laughter, she heard Gideon's raised voice. A web of her sympathy went out to Curt. How immeasurably difficult it must be for him to be dressed down by the man to whom he had given his most profound loyalty and affection. But what on earth was Gideon yelling about?

Me, she thought. *Gideon's telling him to stay away from me.*

She could no longer bear the idiocies on the black and white screen. "I'm going upstairs," she said, laying two fingers to her brow. "A headache."

Crystal stopped chuckling. "Honora, didn't I warn you this afternoon? We just aren't used to this strong a sun."

Honora closed the music room door quietly and stood in the vast hall. She heard nothing except the faraway burbling of "Your Show of Shows," then Gideon's gravelly voice rose in a crescendo. She couldn't make out the words, but the anger vibrated.

She retreated to the staircase, sitting halfway up the bottom flight, where the last of the afternoon sun came through the stained-glass windows in dusty shafts of ruby, azure and amethyst light that stained her pale pink dress and white face in unearthly colors.

After what seemed hours, Curt emerged. He halted, peering about as if he had blundered into some alien place.

Getting to her feet, she called softly, "Curt?"

He jerked. "Oh, Honora. I didn't see you."

She crossed the hall, poised to put a reassuring hand on his arm, but his flat, expressionless eyes halted the consoling gesture.

"What happened?" she whispered. "Curt, I heard Gideon shouting."

"He handed me my walking papers," Curt said, his face contorting with misery.

"I don't understand. You mean he gave you the sack?"

"If the translation is that I'm fired, yes."

"Because of me?"

"Mrs. Ekberg saw us going into my place."

Honora flinched.

"He called me a considerable number of names. I've never heard him use obscenities, but he sure as hell knows the whole vocabulary."

"I never meant to make trouble ... between you. . . ." She bit her inner lip in an unsuccessful attempt to regain her composure. "Oh, Curt. It must have been torture for you. But he'll get over it, he'll come to his senses. He relies on you, he needs you. He likes you."

"Relied, needed. Liked. Past tense. Honora, he kept it up even after I told him if it'd cleanse us of our grievous fall into depravity, we'd fly to Reno tonight and get married."

The dark wood whirled around her, and she gripped his arm to keep from falling. "Married?"

"Oh, for Christ's sake, Honora, why the shocked look?"

"But you never asked ... mentioned."

"After telling you so many times how wild I am about you, I figured you also took marriage as a given."

The door of Gideon's office opened and he stood gripping the jamb. The light shining behind him had the effect of making his short, thick body appear swollen with strength. "Why are you still here?" he barked.

Curt said, "How can I let it end on a sour note like this? You've done everything for me." His voice was low, pleading.

Gideon took a tentative step toward Curt and for a few seconds stood with his hands at his sides, his fingers rubbing his trousers uncertainly. Then he noticed Honora. "Ivory, I want you out of this house immediately. And if your things are still at Talbott's tomorrow morning I'll have them shoved into a trash barrel."

"Please, Gideon," Honora murmured shakily. "Don't be angry with Curt. You've told us he's your right hand."

"He doesn't run Talbott's, whatever line he might have given you."

"You've been wonderful to me," Honora said. "And I've returned your generosity and trust despicably. But we'll be married right away—"

"Do you think you're the first foolish girl to be taken in by his flashy car and flashy white smile and talk of marriage? Before you he was talking engagement to Imogene Burdetts."

"That's absolute crap," Curt said harshly. "There's nothing serious between me and Imogene."

"*She* thinks there is." Fixing his glittering little eyes on Honora, Gideon said, "It goes against my grain to allow you to stay under my roof with your innocent sisters. But I've told myself that you're not to blame if I brought you into contact with a man with the moral decency of a sewer rat." Gideon's coarse features twisted in a tormented expression, and his forehead gleamed. "Seducing you under my own roof—exactly what I should've expected from a nameless nobody."

The thin lines around Curt's mouth tautened. Without a word, he turned, his footsteps echoing across the beautifully inlaid parquet. He let himself out the front door.

Honora wanted to weep for him. Her hands clenched as if to throttle Gideon's thick neck—how unfair his attack was—yet she doggedly continued her attempts at reconciliation. "Gideon, I'm positive he didn't make Imogene any promises," she said. "And as for his seducing me, I was in love with him from the beginning. I chased after him, I threw myself at him. It's my fault, not Curt's."

Gideon's jaw quivered and against her will Honora felt a dart of pity. "I've always wanted a son and sometimes I felt he was one. It was a mistake, a terrible mistake to care." He blinked, as if recollecting her presence, and his voice rose vehemently. "I picked him out of a gutter in Vienna—I doubt he's mentioned that—"

"He's told me everything, Gideon." Honora spoke through a dry throat. "You mean so much to him, he reveres you."

"He was so thin you could see every bone. He didn't even know his name, so I gave him one like any starving mongrel I'd take in. God knows what kind of criminals spawned him. And let me tell you, Vienna had some pretty types running around between the wars, yes, there were some mighty pretty types." Gideon's voice had turned to gravel. "I shouldn't be surprised if he's diseased."

Honora's body was shaking with fury. "You horrible, horrible man," she cried, searching for answering insults. "You're . . . you're common!" The inadequacy of this response added to her rage. She rushed to the front door.

"Go, you little tramp, I did my best with you. If you've got the bastard of a bastard in your belly that's Sylvander's problem, not mine."

She wrenched the heavy brass knob, hurling the door shut after her.

Joscelyn and Crystal both looked up as they heard the reverberating slam.

"God, what was that?" Crystal said, fiddling with the knob—the picture was showing ghosts.

"Either Curt leaving or a second San Francisco earthquake," Joscelyn replied.

The door opened and Gideon stood there, his sparse remnants of hair raised up as if he had been passing his hands over his scalp.

"Turn that off," he ordered.

The low, gravelly timbre of his voice brought an automatic response to Crystal's fingers. As the picture dwindled into a dot, Gideon walked across the music room and through to the main drawing room. Normally he strode briskly, master of all surrounding space. Now he moved to the black marble fireplace almost shufflingly, as if he had recently undergone surgery. He sank into a chair.

Crystal and Joscelyn followed him.

"What is it?" Crystal asked timidly.

"Yes, what's happened, Gideon?" Joscelyn asked.

"Honora," he said.

"Honora?" Joscelyn's voice rose. That headache, could it have been the onset of some galloping disease?

"She won't be living here anymore." Gideon's voice was flat.

"What?" Crystal cried.

"Where is she?" Joscelyn wailed. A brain tumor. Yes. Honora had been taken to the hospital—no. There would have been sirens.

"She's not staying in *my* house." Gideon's hands were clenched.

"Gideon, nothing you're saying makes sense." Crystal stood over him. "Honora had a bit much sun today, and fifteen minutes ago she went upstairs."

"First thing tomorrow morning I want you to pack her things. Juan will drive the boxes over to her father's."

"Why can't she do her own packing?" Joscelyn took off her glasses to rub her twitching eye.

"She left the house a minute ago."

"I don't believe it."

"*She* slammed the door?" Crystal asked incredulously.

"Honora never slams doors." Joscelyn's reddened eye fluttered.

Mrs. Ekberg stuck her carefully coiffed head into the room. "Is there anything I can do, Mr. Talbott?" she asked with quavery brightness.

"Take Joscelyn on upstairs," Gideon said.

"It's not my bedtime—"

"Go!"

At the command in his voice, Joscelyn shrank toward the chaperon, blinking violently. "I want Honora!"

Mrs. Ekberg put her arms around the child's thin shoulders. "Come on, Mrs. Ekberg will fix you some nice hot Ovaltine with marshmallows."

The door closed, and Crystal put both hands on her beguilingly rounded hips. Determination carved away the pouting, movie-starlet prettiness so that her vitality and beauty blazed with near terrifying intensity. "I want to know what's what," she said in the loud, blunt tone that she used when intent on getting her way with the Sylvanders.

Gideon sighed. "You know how it's disturbed me, Ivory chasing after your sister."

"I never understood why. Honora's nutty about him."

"She's been going to his apartment."

Light-headed with shock, Crystal sank into the brocade love seat. She wasn't surprised that Honora had tumbled, not with the lariat of chemistry between the two of them— but how could Honora have kept it from *her?* They shared everything. Honora was too guileless to lie. Yet on the other hand, hadn't she been known at Edinthorpe as the safest custodian of a secret?

"I didn't mean to upset you," Gideon said.

"How do you know?" Crystal asked in a subdued voice.

"Ivory didn't deny it. And she, poor girl, was quite open when I confronted her." Gideon paused. "Now you see why I can't have her living here."

Separated from Honora?

It was bad enough to live apart from their father. But she

and Honora were indivisible. To exist without Honora steadfastly backing her up and admiring her and giving in to her? To live without her other?

"I'm not at all sure," Crystal said slowly, "whether Joss and I can stay. Without her."

The wrinkles in Gideon's brow deepened and his expression turned dark. "Is that an ultimatum?"

"Gideon, the three of us have always been together."

"Try to understand how difficult this is for me. I cared deeply for Ivory." Gideon's chin sank onto the new, bright tie. "I always wanted a son, and Matilda was a sickly woman from the first. She lost three babies and after that, well, we gave up." He sighed heavily. "Curt was more or less in my care.... I paid for his keep and education and tried to guide him. He has the highest ethics—except when it comes to the opposite sex. He can't restrain himself when it comes to girls."

"Poor Honora, she's crazy in love with him."

"She was under my roof, my responsibility. It hurts that he had to seduce her. It hurts."

"She isn't having a baby?" Crystal asked anxiously.

"Not that I know of. But, Crystal, Curt flagrantly abused my trust." Gideon looked up. There were odd-shaped tears below his small brown eyes.

His unexpected misery caught at her. "Why not let it rest for tonight?" she asked sympathetically.

"It's not going to be any less painful in the morning."

"Gideon, tonight's not the time to make any permanent decisions. I'm positive this whole business won't seem as bleak tomorrow."

"You've got so much common sense, Crystal. You're right. I'll sleep on this unpleasant mess and settle it in my mind before we have our talk."

She left him hunched in the huge, shadow-rimmed room.

Upstairs, she sank into one of her slipper chairs, her delicate, carefully manicured hands covering her face as her sobs began.

She pitied Honora profoundly. Honora adored Curt, but he would never marry her. He hungered after large-scale opulence—Crystal recognized the same passion in herself—and would marry Imogene or somebody rich like her. *The bastard*, Crystal thought. *Taking Imogene to big galas and sneaking Honora into his apartment.*

Joscelyn crept in, her cotton pajamas buttoned awry.

"What's going on?" she whimpered.

"Gideon found out Honora's been going to Curt's apartment. She's been sleeping with him."

"What a lie!"

"She admitted it to Gideon. That's why he's sending her away."

Joscelyn rushed out.

In her room the child stood peering around, then turned, running full speed into Honora's room, climbing onto the high bed, flopping down on her stomach. She sniffed at the pillowcases, the tender, sweet odor of Honora. But soon the stale smell of her own tears erased all the other smells. It was impossible to believe that Curt had forced her sister into that obscene tangle of execratory organs. It was equally impossible that Honora had left her without a goodbye, a desertion incomparably more bitter than her unknown mother's death.

13

At nineteen past seven Honora was sitting on Curt's bed, the phone clamped between her shoulder and her ear as she gazed blankly at the hard morning sun slanting through the window.

Last night when Curt had pulled up outside the tall apartment house he had detached his door key from his chain. "You go on up," he had said. "It shouldn't take more than an hour to clean up the office." This was the umpteenth time that she had phoned Talbott's, and with the identical results: a constant ring. *It's a switchboard*, she told herself. But if Curt were in the silent building, wouldn't he have heard and gone downstairs to discover who kept calling so relentlessly?

Almost nine hours, she thought. *Nine hours!*

Images had paraded through her mind. His car colliding

with a huge oil truck and the combined wreckage bursting into orange flames. A robber with the flash of gunfire in the darkness of Maiden Lane. A body plummeting from the Golden Gate Bridge—of her mental dioramas, this image, the body hurtling and disappearing into the black, heaving waves, was by far the most vivid.

A single tap sounded. Dropping the receiver, she rushed to the front door, struggling with the unfamiliar catch.

Curt stood there grasping a large carton filled with rolls of construction drawings. He was pale, but his left eyebrow rose in its usual sardonic arc of greeting.

Her relief was so intense that her legs turned to water. "That's the longest hour on record!"

"Packing—there's three more of these in the car," he said, dropping the carton with a thud. "Not to mention my *auf Wiedersehens* to the old stamping grounds."

"You might have let me know!" Her fury astonished her. Who was this shrew? "It's almost eight."

"If you'll notice, there's no time clock to punch in this apartment." He was grinning.

Drawing back her hand, she hit his cheek with all her strength.

At the sharp retort of her slap, her preposterous rage dissolved. She touched her lips tenderly to the reddening mark. "Darling, darling. I've been a lunatic. Didn't you hear the phone?"

"It often rings at night." He put his arms around her and his sigh shuddered through her body. "When I got there I couldn't pull myself together. Rejection hurts. Christ, all these years I've hero-worshiped him."

"Oh, Curt. . . ." She was stroking her fingers up the crisply clipped hairs on the tendons of his neck.

"One thing's for certain. We can't live in the same town with my former boss. How does Los Angeles sound to you?"

"I've always wanted to see Hollywood," she murmured.

She was caressing his shoulders, his arms, his buttocks. She felt the vigilante instinct to protect him and use her body as a barricade between him and all misery, yet her eyes and vagina were wet with the saline moistures of lust.

She led him to his rumpled, still-made bed, yanking off the tailored spread: it was the first time she had taken the initiative for sex, and her breasts felt enormous, engorged.

Pulling off her blouse and bra, she brought his face down to her, whimpering as he kissed the erect nipples, her fingers impatiently working his fly.

"You're like hot silk," he muttered.

She raised up, kissing his chest, his belly, taking him in her mouth, hearing his faraway groans.

He came, more salt on her, then fell asleep almost immediately, sprawling on his back, his clothes awry. She rested her cheek on his hard thighs, after a few minutes hearing a small, constant buzzing. She had not hung up the phone properly. Replacing the receiver, she put on his paisley silk robe and went into the galley-size kitchen to make herself a cup of tea. Almost immediately the phone sounded. She picked it up before the ring completed itself, not wanting the bedroom extension to awaken Curt.

"Hello?" she said.

"Honora?" Gideon's surprised voice grated against her ear. "Is that you?"

Idiotically, she pulled Curt's robe tighter around her bare breasts. "Yes. Curt's sleeping." To her own ears the words sounded like an open confession of the act she had performed to make him sleep. "I'll ask him to call you back."

"That's not necessary. You can give him the message. It's for you, too. From here on in there is to be no communication between either you or him with anyone in my household. That includes your sisters."

It took a moment for the dimensions of this to sink in. Not to comfort dear, anxiety-ridden little Joscelyn whom she had held as an infant in her child's arms? To be severed from Crystal? Never to see them?

"Did you hear me?"

"Isn't that up to Joss and Crystal?" It was as if the words were disconnected from her.

"I won't have them corrupted. You are not to hang around them."

"That's very hard, Gideon."

"It won't be so difficult if you remember this." The loud, bullying voice vibrated through the telephone wires. "I have a great many friends in the engineering profession up and down the state. Come creeping around my back door and I'll see to it that Ivory doesn't get a job planning a backyard privy."

She shivered at the threat.

"Did you hear me?" he asked.

"I heard you."

"And I don't want you at your father's place when they're visiting. No letters. No communication. *Nothing.*"

"I won't bother them," she said levelly.

"Good. Now we understand each other."

After she hung up she stared at her reflection in the distorting curved steel of the Revere kettle, considering the numerous ways that Gideon Talbott could destroy Curt's future.

Curt came in, stretching.

"Who was that?"

"Gideon."

He halted in midyawn; a sophisticated pulley produced his wry smile. "What's with him?"

"He called to remind us that we are persona non grata on Clay Street," she said lightly enough, then, finding it impossible to repeat the final vituperative threat, she began to cry.

He put his arms around her. "Hey, hey."

"He's like a family to you ... I've pushed you apart."

"Let's not start that." He stroked between her shoulder blades.

"You've lost your job."

"Big fucking deal. I'll get another."

She pulled away from him. "Just because we've been to bed together is no reason for us to get married. I know Gideon pushed you into saying that and—"

"Honora," he interrupted. "You don't know me very well if you figure I can be shoved into doing what I don't want. I've screwed other girls, and not married them."

"Did you with Imogene?"

"Sure, why not? She goes in for it heavily. From now on, though, I'm going to be dull and faithful."

"I've brought you bad luck."

"Like hell. Look, I'm not going to lie and tell you I'm overjoyed how it turned out with Gideon, but wasn't it clear from what I told you the other night? I make my own luck."

"Maybe he'd forgive and forget if we broke up."

"Stop it, Honora, just stop it." He gripped her hands, compressing the knuckles. She grimaced in pain, but he didn't relax his hold. "The past is the past. We're moving toward the future. I am going to be a success, I am going to build highways and dams and bridges and cities, I am going to the goddamn top. And you're going to be with me. I'll probably wear you out because I am so hot for your smooth, smooth body and the innocent way you give a blow job. We're going to fight, and we're going to disagree, and we're going to be very happy. You're going to have my children—and I want three."

She had stopped crying. "Maybe four?"

"Three's the starting point."

"Honora Ivory . . . what an awful mouthful. Too many vowels."

"That's more like it. Now blow your nose and make us some breakfast. Today's our wedding day."

No matter how deep Curt's misery, he always managed to function. He ate a half dozen scrambled eggs surrounded by bacon, smeared his toast with strawberry jam, between mouthfuls laying out their plans. "We'll go talk to your father. Maybe he'll come up to Lake Tahoe with us. We can be married on the Nevada side without the three-day wait for blood tests." They would honeymoon overnight at the lake, then drive down to Los Angeles. "We've joint-ventured with various companies down there, and several have hinted I could have a job if I ever decided to leave Talbott's."

He set her to packing his clothes while he went down to talk to the manager about subleasing this apartment. He rounded up cartons for the books and papers in his built-in shelves, tipping the janitor to lug these boxes plus the two in his car to the storage basement.

By eleven thirty the apartment was bare of personal belongings. While Curt showered the phone rang.

"Ivory residence," she murmured, tentative after the last call.

"So you *are* there."

"Daddy," she said. "We were just coming to see you."

"And I didn't believe Talbott."

"He *told* you?"

"His man brought your things around, no message, nothing, and of course I couldn't discuss it with a servant, and it's hardly the sort of matter to go into with your sisters. So I had to call Talbott. He told me I could reach you at Ivory's number." Langley's voice was clipped, unpleasant. He had bolstered himself with a full pint of whiskey before dialing Talbott's.

"Daddy, we're getting married."

Silence at the other end.

"I know this is a big shock to you, but we're coming over to explain."

"That's quite unnecessary. You've made your plans and there's nothing I could add."

The door to the bathroom opened, and Curt stood there, wrapping a towel around his waist. His wet hair hung over his forehead and water dripped down his strong, hirsute legs onto the plushy gray carpet—this was the first carpeted bathroom Honora had seen.

Tendrils of steam curled into the bedroom as he took in her dismayed expression.

"Who is it now?" he asked.

She pressed the phone to her breasts. "Daddy. Gideon told him."

Curt took a step into the small bedroom, reaching for the phone. "Hello, Langley," he said easily. "Has Honora explained our plans? We'd like you to come to Tahoe to give the bride away."

Honora couldn't hear Langley's reply because Curt pressed the receiver close to his ear.

"Langley, you found out in a rotten way, and I can understand you're not brimming with goodwill, but it would mean a lot to Honora—and to me—if you'd drive up with us."

Another pause.

"I'm sorry that's how you feel. No, don't worry about the clothes, she'll buy what she needs in Los Angeles. Yes, we're leaving right away."

He hung up. "I'll make it up to you, love," he said, putting his arms around her, holding her to his wet body, stroking back her hair. His deep gentleness always came as a surprise to her: it seemed completely misplaced in a man who regarded life with detached amusement.

They drove on Highway 40 across the hot heart of California, near Sacramento switching to a narrow road which wound through the old gold-mining towns. When they stopped for hamburgers at Placerville, they found a dim little store that sold souvenirs and jewelry. There was only one wedding band small enough to fit her finger, sterling silver electroplated with gold.

It was dark by the time they arrived in Tahoe and the lopsided moon was reflected in the immense dark glass of the lake. The first thing they saw in Stateline was a blinking neon sign: TAHOE WEDDING CHAPEL. The false front was V-pointed like a church, and above the door, multicolored paint masqueraded as a stained-glass window.

"Welcome to beautiful Nevada," Curt said, sarcasm cutting through the weariness in his voice.

Honora touched his cheek. "It looks lovely to me."

Curt swerved into the gravel.

The bell was answered by a man with a napkin tucked into his open shirt. Large splotches marked his skin, and his cheeks were hollow so that he appeared whittled from the surrounding sugar pines. "You folks want to tie the knot?" he asked with a practiced glance at the large convertible. "Ten bucks."

"Fine," Curt said.

Not bothering to remove his napkin, the justice of the peace called in his buxom daughter and shapeless wife, who both exuded underarm odors and the aroma of fried chicken. Hastily he gabbled the minimum questions required by the State of Nevada to legitimize a union, everybody scrawled on the wedding certificate and the threesome returned to the kitchen to finish their chicken before it got cold.

"Christ," Curt said as they walked through the pine-scented night to the Buick convertible. "Well, one thing's for certain. The marriage has got to go uphill from here."

"Unless you kiss the bride it's not legal and binding," Honora murmured, her arm reaching around him.

He halted. The near-full moon and a glitter of mountain stars looked down as he cupped her face in his hands, and kissed her eyes, the tip of her nose, and her lips.

14

Earlier that same day, at around eleven thirty, Crystal was in her dressing room trying on the mist-blue silk faille suit that she'd had sent home on approval from Ransohoff's, dispiritedly turning to gauge her reflection in the mirrored closet doors. A long, almost sleepless night had laid siege to her pragmatism. Certainly she was frayed with misery about poor Honora's banishment—and would do all in her power to remind Gideon of the Christian virtues of charity and forgiveness—but she would have to be a mental case to sacrifice a Pacific Heights mansion and Chargaplate privileges in the best Debutante departments in San Francisco for the abstraction of sisterly unity.

"Crystal?" Mrs. Ekberg was a narrow sliver of darkness in the sunlit doorway between bedroom and dressing room. "Mr. Talbott would like a word with you, dear. He's downstairs in the Turkish room."

"Gideon? Home? On a Monday morning?"

"It is odd, isn't it? But then everything's topsy-turvy today. Honora back with your father. And little Joss refusing to go to school." Mrs. Ekberg buried a nervous belch in her hand. She was maintaining a façade of chirpy ignorance that she hoped would allow her to remain employed in the Talbott ménage. "Poor mite, she's beside herself."

"Tell Gideon I'll be right down."

Crystal folded the suit and carefully placed it back in its tissue before turning to her appearance. Her hair took forever. Last night, in her unhappy emotional chaos, she had not put it up in pin curls, and two recalcitrant wisps kept escaping from the shining golden mass.

It was thirty minutes before she went into the round little room.

Gideon showed no sign of the previous night's disintegrating grief. As he set down his *Wall Street Journal,* his hard mouth was clamped in a tight line.

Crystal seldom gave much thought to those who awaited her spectacular, perennially tardy entrances, but now a tiny shiver of anxiety went down her spine. "Sorry I took so long." She formed her most winsome smile. "You caught me in my bath. But what's going on? Has Talbott's declared a national holiday?"

At the glint of affectionate amusement in his eyes, she sat.

"Have you forgotten last night?" he asked. "Remember what I said about our talking?"

"Gideon, you darling, you've changed your mind about Honora, haven't you?" She leaned forward eagerly. As a small child she had learned that it was best to attack, thus placing the burden of nay-saying on the opponent.

His lips again pressed into that line. "I followed your advice. This morning I gave Ivory a buzz to hear his side. The phone was answered by your sister."

Crystal had never felt more protective of Honora—or more irritated with her. This was her sister to a T, the same unreasoning generosity as taking that waitress job. After last night couldn't she have had the sense to let Curt wallow in his own unhappiness, to stay out of his apartment? Now Gideon was her disapproving enemy.

"I shouldn't have been so blunt," Gideon said gently.

"Gideon, I know how her mind works. Sometimes she's so tenderhearted that she's wacky. She felt sorry for Curt, losing his job, and didn't like leaving him alone. . . ." The tightening around Gideon's small brown eyes told Crystal she wasn't helping her sister, and she was rousing his bonnetful of ridiculous, antiquated bees. "At least that's how I see it."

"You're the one with the tender heart."

"Gideon, whatever she's done she's our sister."

"That's exactly what I expected you to think," he said. "But she's proved herself no fit companion for a girl like you or little Joscelyn."

"Maybe Curt'll marry her."

"Him?" Gideon gave a negating snort. "Crystal, I told her in no uncertain terms that she's not to bother you or Joscelyn. And to make sure of it I've hired a detective agency."

"A detective agency!" Crystal couldn't control her outburst. "How rotten!"

Gideon's fists clenched. "She's already pulled the wool over my eyes once."

"You've been so fabulous to us, Gideon, and I certainly do see how we've disappointed you. But isn't this going a bit far? A detective agency?"

"The very last thing I care to do, ever, is hurt you," he said. "I want the world to be a paradise for you. Crystal, surely you realize that."

The heavy, deep-lined face softened into an incongruous, boyishly adoring smile.

Crystal's shock was so overwhelming that she felt as if an enormous rock were squashing the breath from her lungs. *I don't believe it,* she thought wildly. *Gideon making a pass?*

A fraction of a moment later it hit her.

Lord God Jesus, she thought. *He's talking about marriage! Marrying me!*

A strange, breathy giggle escaped her.

He was saying, "You're so very young, but you have extraordinary astuteness about people. My feelings can't come as a complete surprise."

"Gideon, how could I guess?" Another peculiar giggle. "You're my uncle."

"I was married to your aunt. You and I aren't related by blood. But certainly I am aware—overly aware—of the huge age difference between us." He pulled back his thick shoulders, sitting at attention. "You're the dearest, loveliest, daintiest girl alive, and you can have any younger man you want. But there's nobody who could give you more of a true and loving heart."

He made this Victorian speech with awkward bluffness, yet there was no escaping his sincerity. He was staring tenderly at her. Incapable of speech, Crystal clasped her shaking hands together.

"While I know that the financial angle isn't important to you, Crystal, still it's part of marriage. You've probably seen that old photograph of my father in my office?"

She nodded. Gideon Talbott Number One had a wen above his nose and the bushy white beard of an Old Testament prophet.

"Dad came out to California with a team of ten mules and went into business hauling fill for the Southern Pacific

Railroad. He wasn't a graduate engineer, yet after a year he was awarded subcontracts to drill the railroad's tunnels. He earned himself a top-notch reputation in the state, then in the west. I was his only child, but I started at the bottom. Summers I worked in the construction camps. After I graduated from MIT he put me in charge of a project for the Oregon Irrigation District. While I was there, he died. Crystal, I was twenty-two, and I had inherited Talbott's. It was a tremendous responsibility. But I've built on what Dad started. Talbott's was part of the Six Companies in thirty-one—we built the Hoover–Boulder Dam. Though we didn't make much on the job, it means a lot to me. And so does my part in the two San Francisco bridges."

Gideon, even in the throes of love for a gorgeous teenager, was no fool. Like a wily merchant at an Oriental bazaar, he was spreading the glitter of his assets—power, an impeccable reputation, great wealth.

"And Talbott's has been profitable, especially since the war." The sad brooding lines around his lips made Crystal guess he was thinking of Curt's contributions. "My personal fortune is well over ten million."

Crystal couldn't prevent her gasp. "Ten million!"

"Even before her illness it was Matilda's inclination to live quietly, so I've never really enjoyed my money. But you, dearest girl, you have the joy in life, the expansiveness. We could share a great many good years."

He reached for her hands to pull her to her feet. The slightly damp toughness of his large palms sent unpleasant tingles up Crystal's arms.

She jerked away, retreating to the door. "You brought us to live in your house," she panted.

"So you wouldn't have to do menial work, like *her.*"

"I trusted you as if you were my father!"

"Crystal—"

"You're old, old, old!"

She fled from the dim, Moorish room and the thick-shouldered, short-legged man inadequately hiding his hurt.

She locked her door and fell facedown on her canopied bed, for once careless of lipstick and Maybelline mascara on the pristine, dotted Swiss spread.

"Old, old," she whispered.

Memories jumped simultaneously. Gideon putting her poor, sweating City College dates through the grinder,

Gideon's increasing generosity as her phone calls ceased, Gideon popping for the convertible after she had admired it, Gideon's unquestioning payment of charge accounts.

That first Saturday she had come to Clay Street she had speculated to Honora about the possibility of his having a mistress: coming to know him better, though, she had concluded him far too stuffy. Since then she had seen Gideon Talbott as a venerable banking institution, not a man.

She heard the purr of the Cadillac pulling away from the driveway. Gideon was returning to Maiden Lane.

"Old," she muttered. "Never, never, never."

After a while there was a timorous rap on the locked door. "Lunchtime, Crystal dear," Mrs. Ekberg trilled. "It's that delicious chicken salad you like so much."

"I'm not hungry," Crystal said in a subdued voice.

"Yes, it's awfully hot."

"Go ahead without me."

Mrs. Ekberg coughed anxiously. "I've brought up a package for you."

Crystal wiped her tear-streaked face. Maybe Gideon had seen how ridiculous he was being and sent her long-stemmed roses as an apology. She unlocked the door.

Mrs. Ekberg handed her a brown-and-beige-striped Magnin's box. In it was the black velvet she'd sent home to size up against the mist-blue faille.

Seeing the two boxes, she was returned to everyday reality.

Gideon setting the detectives on Honora was ominous proof that the opposite side of his coin of generosity was a cold, uncharitable head. If she left this house there would be an end to such delightful choice in clothing, an end to elegantly served lunches, there would only be marriage to some boy going to school on the GI bill.

. . . my personal fortune is well over ten million. . . .

At six, when the Cadillac parked under the porte co-chere, Crystal squeezed the bulb of her cologne bottle, spraying Tabu over her throat and behind her ears, then leaned forward into the mirror, peering at her eyes to make certain that the witch hazel had erased the puffiness caused by the weeping jag.

She ran downstairs. Gideon was setting his bulging

briefcase on the hall table. His face was red and sweat-glossed.

"It's broiling out, isn't it?" she said with a charmingly pert smile. "Let me fix your drink for you."

Gideon nodded and without comment strode across the hall to the rear living room, where a long silver cocktail tray was routinely set on the sofa table.

Crystal, suddenly fearing that her painful decision had been reached tardily—Gideon never gave second chances—poured the jigger of J&B that Gideon enjoyed before dinner, dropping in two ice cubes, spraying in the soda water, carrying the gold-etched bar glass to him in both hands like a chalice, returning to splash a few companionable drops of sherry for herself.

"Gideon, you took me by surprise, I must say." Her voice was pitched high, her English accent had reappeared.

He gave her a long, unreadable look then raised his glass to his mouth.

Crystal's alarm increased. What a mortally tough business opponent he must be, concealed behind this patina of emotionlessness! Yet despite this—or maybe because of it—she experienced a genuine leap of esteem for him.

And out of this newfound admiration came an unsettling realization. Cold cash was not her only motive in accepting his proposal.

True, her frivolous instincts hungered for mink, sable, diamonds, French designer clothes, mansions, servants, lavish entertaining, the fat life, but there was another side that paid homage to the strength of this ugly, elderly multimillionaire. Overcome by this unexpected revelation, she was unable to give the sticky little recitative she had rehearsed.

"I'm very fond of you, Gideon," she said, wishing it didn't sound so lame.

"Fond?"

"You gave Daddy a job when he had nowhere else to turn, you took us in and treated us like princesses."

"Then you're grateful, is that it?" he asked gruffly.

She knew a flattering prevarication was called for, yet she heard herself speak with slow candor. "I'm not sure what I do feel for you beyond gratitude and tremendous admiration. But that's more than I've ever felt for any other man."

"Will you make me a promise?"

"Promise?"

"That no matter what, you'll always be this honest with me."

An exquisite relief drenched her and she smiled. "Oh, I will, Gideon, I will."

Ice cubes rattled as he set down his drink. As he came to the window where she stood, she saw that he was shaking.

"Crystal, don't worry about love. I have more than enough for both of us," he said thickly. "I worship you."

This time her body did not recoil when he took her hands in his. She kissed his cheek, and then his dry, chapped mouth.

The light pressure of his lips roused nothing whatsoever in her.

15

At five past five in the rain-hushed predawn of December 12, Crystal's wedding day, Joscelyn was already awake.

The umber glow of the night-light, which quelled the fiercest of her terrors, showed the pale blur of her bridesmaid's gown hanging on the closet door. She loathed the powder blue concoction and was positive that the dearly beloved assembled today at Grace Cathedral would snicker openly at the contrasting sisters, gorgeous-bride-Crystal and ugly-Joscelyn submerged in a tide of tulle ruffles.

Even after three months Joscelyn found the engagement unsettling and unnerving. That her sister was going to do "it" with somebody older than their father stirred unpleasant sensations in the pit of her stomach. Gideon, formerly reliable in his decorous, broad-shouldered business suits, had turned into a flightless penguin, executing an elaborate mating ritual, preening on his short, tuxedo-clad legs before whisking Crystal off to the parties given in their honor. To avoid unpleasant gossip he had moved into the Pacific Union Club, and a tall, overperfumed Parisian with the un-

likely name of Madame McCloskey had taken over his
downstairs office, strewing the broad expanse of his desk
with creamy invitations, fabric swatches, manila files.
Madame McCloskey consulted by the hour with a stream
of shrill-voiced florists and caterers, she kept track of the
gifts that United Parcel trucks disgorged, she entered Crystal's engagements on the large calendar that hung on the
window wall, and in general behaved with the controlled
hysteria that befitted staging a production at the Comédie-
Française rather than a wedding.

Crystal still bickered with Joscelyn, but otherwise had
moved into a new pattern, sleeping until eleven, breakfast-
ing in bed before disappearing in a cloud of perfume and
vivacious laughter. She whirled between luncheons, teas,
showers, cocktail parties and shopping expeditions with
Imogene Burdetts. One of the guest rooms was inundated
with her purchases, which included a silvery gray mink
coat.

The rain was coming down harder and Joscelyn began
worrying about puddles outside the cathedral. What if she
slipped as she went in? What if her skirt blotted up mud?
What if the car skidded on the way?

Her alarms swelled until she felt itchy all over.

Fumbling for her glasses, she tiptoed to the door, peering
both ways into the silent, graveyard darkness of the hall.
Closing the door, panting softly, she dived for the bedside
light. At the bureau, she shoved aside her no longer used
English underwear, fraying Liberty bodices and yellowed
combinations, uncovering a scuffed, red morocco jewelry
case. Darting back to bed with it, she reached in the bedside table drawer for a tiny, round key. The case held a
grubby envelope addressed to Miss J Sylvander, c/o Mr L
Sylvander, Esq, with the return address of Mrs Curt Ivory/
Apt 12/ 1415 Cherokee Avenue/ Hollywood/ California.

Joscelyn extracted the three sheets. Not that she needed
them; she had committed Honora's loosely flowing handwriting to memory. Her thumb rubbed the cheap, dog-
eared paper as if it were a rabbit's foot.

September 10

Dearest Joss,

*I would give the world to be saying this in person, but Gid-
eon warned me not to communicate with you and Crystal.
(What a way to start a letter with such momentous news.)*

Curt and I are married.

The day after I left Clay Street we drove up to Lake Tahoe to a Nevada town called Stateline. The wedding chapel had the funniest painted-on front, like at an amusement park. Joss, how I wished that you and Crystal and Daddy could have been there—but then it wouldn't have been an elopement. We live in Hollywood. It's warmer down here, and outside our window is a grapefruit tree that smells wondrously Californian. Every night we move the coffee table to let down the bed from the wall—a Murphy bed it's called.

Has Gideon mentioned the slump in engineering? Nobody is starting any projects and the important firms that used to have a hundred people are suddenly down to eight or ten, so I don't need to tell you the difficulties Curt's having. The minute he finds something, though, we both hope that you'll come and live with us. (Joss, I miss you so.)

You will adore Hollywood. Sometimes there are premieres on Hollywood Boulevard and everyone cheers at the film stars when they drive up—I've seen Joan Fontaine and Clark Gable and Rain Fairburn. Yesterday I strolled up to the Grauman's Chinese Theater and behaved like a perfect fool, fitting my hands and feet into the prints—my feet are the same size as Bette Davis's, my hands are like Norma Shearer's.

I really have become a trueblue resident of lotusland. As I said, the weather is quite warm, so sometimes I rest under the grapefruit tree holding a book, but really just daydreaming.

Curt sends you his top-notch, grade A love.

Jossie, Gideon really was quite nasty about telling me not to get in touch, so please don't let anybody know about this letter, please.

The second *please* was underlined twice, and the signature was exed around with kisses.

Joscelyn sighed, wishing with all her heart that she could be drowsing under the grapefruit tree, or standing on Hollywood Boulevard with Curt and Honora while people cheered at movie stars.

She replaced the letter and key in their separate hidey-holes.

The windows were paler rectangles now, and over the sound of the rain she heard the faint hum of a vacuum cleaner.

She fell back asleep.

* * *

At three fifteen Crystal was still upstairs, ignoring the combined prodding of Mrs. Ekberg and Madame McCloskey that they should be at the church. So it was beside the point that Langley had not yet arrived. Joscelyn squirmed impatiently on the landing window seat, which had the house's best view of rainswept Clay Street. A Yellow cab drove slowly down the hill and she pressed her nose against the window, her breath steaming on the glass. The taxi turned in and was hidden by the roof of the porte cochere. Holding her dress above her bony knees, Joscelyn raced down the stairs, on the bottom step colliding with a caterer. Muttering her apologies, she flung open the side door.

"Daddy—finally!"

Langley removed his top hat, bowing low to her. "How like a princess," he said.

Although her mirror informed her she looked totally ridiculous, the paternal compliment delighted her. "Oh, Daddy," she said irritably. "At this late hour I can't bear anything cute."

"The words sprang from here," he said, tapping the left side of his chest. "Where's the bride in her finery?"

Joscelyn rolled her eyes toward the upper floors. "Crystal ready on time?"

"What a day for a wedding." Langley took off his rain-spotted, twenty-five-year-old Burberry raincoat and draped it over a hall chair. His rented gray striped trousers and cutaway coat fit his long, slight body to perfection: he had always worn clothes well.

Joscelyn said admiringly, "Is that a morning suit?"

His smile faded and the slackness below his jaw showed. "Mourning with a *u*. There's no way around it, the Sylvanders have gone to the dogs. My poor Portuguese running off like a scullery maid." (He had forgiven his older daughter her sins, and letters traveled frequently between northern and southern California.) "Crystal marrying a man as old as her pater. Joscelyn, this is what I deserve for putting my career first and coming over here. If we were home in England the Sylvanders never would have gone so common."

"Elizabeth Barrett Browning eloped, and numberless princesses have married aged kings."

He kissed her cheek, giving her a whiff of medicinal

mouthwash. So he'd been drinking. "Nevertheless," he said, "I need something to buck me up."

"There's coffee in the kitchen."

"Joss, this is the day I bury my dreams," he said, his mouth twisting.

She went to the butler's pantry. A dozen or so enormous copper washtubs were filled with ice and bottles of Moët et Chandon champagne.

Langley was on his second glass when Madame McCloskey trotted downstairs, her face agitated below her enormous, bobbling cerise hat.

"We're *en retard*—we should be already at zee church a half hour ago!" she cried heatedly. "And Crystal, she has locked herself in zee bathroom."

Crystal gripped the Limoges washbowl. The pearl-trimmed sweetheart neckline of her white velvet wedding gown revealed the sumptuous curves of her breasts, which rose and fell convulsively, as if she were sobbing. Yet there were no tears in her vivid blue eyes.

The intervening months since the hot September evening when she had agreed to marry Gideon had proved the logic of her decision in an unequivocally material manner—the five-carat emerald cut diamond which glittered on her right hand to leave her ring finger free for the diamond and platinum wedding band, the diamond and emerald watch bracelet, the Silver Blue mink stroller.

Her hands tensed yet tighter on the antique procelain sink as she rocked backward and forward in an unsuccessful attempt to halt the dry sobs.

I can't stand his smell.

The thought burst inside her mind like a rocket.

He smells of age.

How can I sleep the rest of my nights with a man who has the mousy odor of old people?

There was a series of raps on the door.

"Crystal?" It was Joscelyn. "Crys?"

At her sister's voice, Crystal's heaves lessened.

"Let me in?" Joscelyn pleaded. "I want to help."

Crystal darted to the door, loosing the old-fashioned bolt, shooting it home again as her sister slid inside.

Joscelyn surveyed the bride. The sad blotchiness of the perfect English complexion, the puffy redness of the blue eyes, the mussed strands of bright, freshly set hair. All her life Joscelyn had longed for the moment when exquisite, unflappable Crystal got her comeuppance, but now, seeing her sister shrunk within her custom-designed wedding gown, she was overwhelmed by suffocating pity.

She held out her arms and Crystal took a step. The two Sylvander sisters hugged, the emotional charge of the embrace smoothing the sandpaper abrasiveness that lay between them.

"I can't, Joss, I can't," Crystal gasped. "I don't know what's wrong, but I just can't go through with it. . . ."

"Shhh."

". . . If only Honora were here, she'd tell me. . . ."

Joscelyn patted the bent, shuddering shoulders. "Don't, Crys."

"Honora'd say, 'If you don't love Gideon you sh-shouldn't marry him.' What do . . . you think?"

"I'm ten, Crys." Joscelyn continued her patting and pressed her kiss on the moist, perfumed cheek. "But if you don't want to marry Gideon, it's not too late. Don't worry about the other things." Another kiss. "I'm on your side."

Crystal moved away, crouching on the curved rim of the claw-footed tub, burying her face in her hands. "Maybe it's right to do what she did, run off for love, and give herself . . ."

Joscelyn, hovering ineffectually beside the desolate, quaking bride, forgot the pleas of her beloved oldest sister. "Crys, you're wrong about their not being married. They are. And you'd hate having no money and living in a one-room flat with a bed that lets down from the wall."

Crystal looked at her sharply with those dry, terrible eyes. "How do you know about everything?"

"She sent me a letter. She's deliriously happy, but it sounded quite tacky to me."

Crystal's heart beat arhythmically and the skin of her chest seemed to tingle. She got jerkily to her feet.

Prenuptial hysteria was replaced by sibling jealousy, a far deeper, more ancient wound. *So she's written to Joscelyn!* Crystal pulled aside a net curtain and watched rain beat against the mullions. When she spoke her voice was calm and cold. "She is *not* married."

"They are," Joscelyn said, modulating her combativeness for fear she might set Crystal off again.

"Why do you think Gideon's so furious? He's had a detective on them. No marriage is registered for Honora Sylvander and Curt Ivory. That letter she sent you was a total lie." Crystal was a shade pale but otherwise had recovered. "God, wasn't that a case of bride's nerves."

"Maybe you should postpone—"

"Why? I'm not sneaking into any one-room love nest." Crystal took a Kleenex from a box, delicately patting under her eyes to remove the faintest trace of brown mascara. She pinched color into her cheeks, smoothed her hair, adjusted her sweetheart neckline. The swift, miraculous transformation from pathetic child to exquisitely splendid bride! "Come on, let's toot."

A red canvas awning reached from the open door of the chapel of the not-yet-completed cathedral to the curb, and a small crowd, mainly women, stood under this protection, watching intently as Juan handed Joscelyn and Langley from the Cadillac, moving closer as the veiled bride emerged. It was four twenty-five.

Imogene Burdetts, the maid of honor in powder blue velvet and a smart turban, met them in the vestibule. "Crystal, darling! You're a dream!" she cried. "I've passed the word that it's very *you* to be late, so the mob's been waiting like lambs. I must say though, poor Gideon's been a *mite* pale."

The organ, which had been wandering above the surflike roar of church-discreet voices, slowed to the portentous notes of the wedding march from *Lohengrin*. Madame McCloskey nodded to Joscelyn, who clasped her bouquet so tightly that the baby's breath trembled and began her slow pace down the aisle.

Back at the flower-fragrant mansion, the guests inched forward to the receiving line. Langley rapidly downed Moët et Chandon, and Madame McCloskey helped him upstairs, where he passed out to snore gustily on Honora's onetime bed. Joscelyn spilled a cheese puff down her gown and was excused. One of the ushers swept Imogene to the bar. Guests continued to clap Gideon's thick shoulders and kiss the second Mrs. Talbott's exquisitely pink cheeks.

At six thirty sharp, two of the caterer's footmen wheeled the five-tiered cake into the dining room. Joscelyn, her bridesmaid's gown redolent with the Energine vigorously applied by Madame McCloskey, watched Crystal cut the first slice.

Which was the real face of her sister? This gorgeous, happy glow or that gasping mask of misery?

An hour later, Juan brought around the Cadillac. Tomorrow the couple would board the *Lurline* for a honeymoon cruise to Hawaii, but their first night would be spent in the bridal suite of the Fairmont Hotel. The night was cold and wet: nobody ventured out to throw the traditional rice. Besides, the guests were successful contractors, engineers, or politicians with wives on the boards of every charity in San Francisco, a crowd too staunchly middle aged for such foolishness.

Only Joscelyn slipped a little white box of wedding cake under her pillow to ensure a glimpse of her future husband. So much for superstition. She dreamed, as she did most nights, of Honora—and Curt Ivory.

16

Crystal stared down at the flowered carpet of the suite's sitting room, listening as Gideon, in the little foyer, tipped the bellboy. She had the jitters. Nothing like this afternoon's carnivorous attack, but certainly mild trepidations. She didn't know exactly what to expect tonight. She clasped her fingers, reassuring herself that Gideon, a widower, was an expert, and could be counted on to be tender of her in his own, awkwardly fond way.

The outer door closed, and he came over to help her off with her mink. "I've ordered a bite of supper," he said.

"Fine. Today went off very well, didn't you think?"

"After the late start. I'll have to learn patience, won't I, Mrs. Talbott?"

The peculiar warmth in his smile increased her restlessness, and she moved into the bedroom, unsnapping her brand new overnight case—the matching suitcases and steamer trunk were at the *Lurline*'s dock. He followed, watching her hang her sheer, white silk negligee set in the empty closet. Again his smile disturbed her and she took her cosmetic bag into the bathroom.

It seemed ages until a young, stout-bellied waiter wheeled in a cart that became a square table. He moved chairs, flourished silver lids from medium rare filets and steaming baked potatoes. He popped open a bottle of champagne. "Compliments of the Fairmont."

The rain had ceased, and as they ate, the sound of silverware and Gideon's chewing resonated like great chords. Crystal sipped the bubbly and forked up a nibble or two of potato.

"No appetite?" he asked. "Dear?"

The mild endearment hung like a ghost between them.

"I had too many hors d'oeuvres," she lied. "You know something, Gideon. I've never stayed in a real hotel before. If we went away for the summer holidays, we rented houses. Once a place in Bognor—that's a seaside resort— and another time a farm cottage near Great Missenden. And the first couple of days we were in San Francisco we stayed in a sort of boarding house. . . ." Her spate of words trailed off.

Gideon was crumpling his napkin on the table, his hand tensed so that the heavy brown hairs stood out like antennae on the knuckles. "It's time," he muttered. "Time."

He strode into the bedroom.

Crystal bore her trousseau lingerie into the bathroom, turning on the heater, yet as she perfumed her naked self she was shivering. The hand-stitched silk chilled her yet more.

Determined not to show her nervousness, she emerged, and leaned against the doorjamb, a humorously intended parody of a thirties' film siren.

Gideon lay on top of the blanket, his arms crossed behind his neck, the top of his pajamas unbuttoned to show a mat of dark brown hair that was thicker down the central line. His heavy brows beatled together as he stared at her, and the crotch of his paisley pajama bottoms tented up, the fly parting to show ominous, shadowy darkness. For an instant she thought of pleading illness. Crystal's heart, however, kept a meticulous set of books. Now was the time to pay for the blue-white diamond, the mutation mink, the parties, the respect that would be given to Mrs. Gideon Talbott.

"Are you ready for lights out?" she asked.

"No. Take off those things."

"Here? My negligee?"

"And the nightdress."

"Don't you want to unwrap me in bed?"

"I said take off your clothes." The terse command lacked every trace of his goofy adoration when he kissed her goodnight.

Slowly she untied the embroidered satin ribbons, letting the negligee rustle to the carpet so that her small, pedicured feet seemed embedded in snow.

"Finish," he said hoarsely.

Her fingers on the straps of her gown clenched, incapable of movement.

"Take off the nightdress, Crystal," he ordered hoarsely.

This time she managed to slip the fabric down over the lush globes of her breasts, past the curves of her hips, halting at the pale pubic fuzz before letting it drop to the floor with the negligee.

She had anticipated hosannas for her beauty, but her bridegroom neither moved nor spoke.

She scorned cowardice. "That's enough peeking," she said in an unwavering voice, and stepped across the trousseau finery.

On the Fairmont's large, bridal suite bed her torment began. He did not kiss her or caress her breasts. Instead, untying his pajama strings, he rolled on top of her, plunging into the dryness. Encountering the indisputable proof of her virginity, he battered his entry. She screamed. The pain was crueler than when, aged ten, she had fallen from her cantering mare, rolling over and breaking both an ankle and a wrist.

"Gideon, you're hurting me," she cried.

The heavy, demonic weight never shifted, the machine of masculinity continued to pound her into the firm mattress. The sound of his pelvis thumping against hers coordinated with the creaking of the bed in much the same way that her whimpering groans joined with the wail of sirens in Chinatown, which this room overlooked. She was hurtfully wet down there now, and drenched with his sweat, a thick odor, like malt vinegar.

After what seemed an hour but was probably no longer than fifteen minutes, he gave a shout, thrust violently, shouted again, and collapsed gasping on top of her.

She saw that the bed was copiously drenched with blood. When she rose to go to the bathroom, her torn thigh muscles protested. She staggered.

"My poor little Crystal," he said, lifting her effortlessly. He set her down on the towel-covered stool, soaking a washcloth to rinse her thighs, his big hands gentle. He filled a glass and gave her two aspirin. "Here, dear."

Yet the minute they returned to bed, he once more climbed atop her, spearing her under his incessant assault, which lasted yet longer this time.

During the five-day cruise, the *Lurline*'s passengers saw a middle-aged, dotingly uxorious bridegroom running to get his exquisite bride her midmorning boullion and afternoon tea, buying out the best items in the gift shop to indulge her; crew and passengers alike caught their breath at the new young wife's hauntingly lovely smiles of gratitude. They were witnessing the bright, daytime side of the Talbott marriage.

Behind the locked stateroom door, and later in their suite at the Royal Hawaiian on Waikiki Beach, the baleful intercourse continued. They never discussed their nights. Neither had the words to explain the endlessly, malevolently copulating goat and the fragile, molested girl who lay unmoving under him.

Crystal, though not given to fruitless introspection, sometimes would find herself brooding about "it." Had Gideon during those years of righteous fidelity inflicted his male violence on Aunt Matilda; was this why the poor lady had retreated into illness? Or was this sweaty warfare between the sheets a vast, ugly communal secret shared by all wives?

The most unfathomable part of the Talbotts' marriage was that outside of the bedroom, Gideon was unfailingly generous, considerate, worshipful, adoring, and on Crystal's part she felt both respect and affection for him.

By the time they returned to the mainland, she had suffered an irreversible loss. She felt nothing but a revulsed loathing for sex.

TWO

1950

Honora

17

At four on the afternoon of January 2, Honora emerged from the tall office building at the corner of Hollywood and Vine. She didn't feel the ninety-degree heat or smell the exhaust from the traffic; she barely saw the pedestrians.

A baby. The thought coursed through her like electricity through a light filament. *A baby.* She looked up at the aluminum Christmas tree that still topped the lamppost, and suddenly clasped the warm, grooved steel, whirling around: this being Hollywood, magnet for pretty girls and nuts, the passersby glanced at her with absentminded indulgence.

She still couldn't believe it.

"You're at the end of your first trimester," Dr. Capwell had said with the bombast common to medical men precarious in their professional skill.

Honora had stared across his cluttered desk disbelievingly. Her periods hadn't stopped. Last week Curt, worried about her lassitude and excessive need for sleep, had insisted she see a doctor. The apartment house manageress had recommended Dr. Capwell, who had sent blood and urine samples to the lab.

"But what about my periods?" she had mumbled, flushing.

His long, flabby cheeks had wobbled. "My dear young woman, spotting is quite common when the menses would occur." Opening and closing his drawers, he came up with a dog-eared pamphlet. A female profile, yellow lines ballooning from breasts and stomach, showed various stages of pregnancy. "This will answer any of your prepartum questions. And here is my fee schedule."

She released the lamppost and started west on Hollywood Boulevard. At Van Vliet's supermarket she bought an inexpensive cellophane bag of salad vegetables, four oranges with withered skin that would be good for juice, a quarter pound of sliced ham, a quart of milk. She stared into the bakery showcase for several minutes then splurged on a chocolate cream pie. Today's news called for a celebration.

As she replaced her wallet in her purse, she saw the pamphlet, and suddenly thought of Dr. Capwell's three-hundred-dollar fee. She had no idea of what was charged for prenatal visits and delivery, but it seemed very high—or was this in contrast with the Ivorys' bank balance, which was very low?

At Talbott's Curt had earned a top salary: secure in his abilities, insecure about his early privations, he had saved very little. A week after their arrival, he had received a cashier's check for two hundred dollars from the subleasor for his gorgeous decorator furnishings.

His Los Angeles contacts had taken him to lunch. Over martinis and porterhouses he heard the same story: private and government contracts had dried up, engineers were not being taken on but laid off by the hundreds.

Secretly Honora brooded that his inability to connect was part of a punitive conspiracy. In her scenario Gideon had discovered her letter to Joscelyn and blacklisted him.

Curt took his professional rejections with an outward jauntiness. He mailed résumés to every engineering company in the area. On the days that he had no interviews, they explored Los Angeles or went to the beach or played tennis on the cracking courts at De Longpre Park. At the beginning of December he had traded in his yellow Buick on a square, ugly prewar Ford coupe plus three hundred dollars. He made no secret of his preference for sharp convertibles, top restaurants, private clubs. Honora, dazed with love, considered southern California heaven. The one cloud was being separated from her family—she often woke from dreams of them with tears on her cheeks. About Curt's future she was incurably optimistic. Two weeks ago, when a builder had offered him a job carving an Encino lemon grove into tract-size lots, she had urged him to refuse. "When something good comes along, you'll be tied up."

This morning he had driven off to yet another appointment.

She turned at the corner of Cherokee, halting to rearrange the awkward bakery box in the heavy brown grocery bag before starting up the street's incline.

The Ivorys lived in a one-story stucco. Quite a few of the red roof tiles were missing, and a thick blanket of bougainvillea hid the peeling paint. The long, dingy hallway was cool and smelled of an unknown spice.

At her door, she called, "Curt?"

He opened the door. "What're you selling today, lady?"

"This," she said, leaning forward to kiss his mouth.

Pulling away, he took the grocery bag, asking, "Anything spoilable?"

"Milk and a pie."

"You put them away. I'll let down the bed."

Late afternoon saffron light sifted through the closed venetian blinds to cast a quadrangle across their entwined, naked bodies. They were smiling at each other.

"Now we can talk," she said. "What happened at your meeting?"

"Nothing much. I have a job."

She clutched his bicep. "Curt!"

"That surprise shows a definite lack of wifely confidence."

"You really got the job?"

"Not at the appointment." His tone was casual, but his excitement gave off vibrations against her skin.

"Will you stop being so irritating and mysterious?"

"This morning I got a letter from Fuad Abdulrahman—"

"Fuad?" She could feel the postcoital warmth drain from her. "Then it's in Lalarhein?"

"Yes. He's offered me the job of project manager on this road they're building."

How could she go to a backwater Arabian country? Now? *Stop being idiotic,* she told herself. *Women have babies there.* Her expression must have flickered. His topaz eyes were suddenly watchful. She looked down. Her breasts were definitely larger, the nipples no longer pink but light toast. She covered herself with the sheet.

"Now what about you?" he said. "What did the doctor say?"

If I tell him, she thought, *he'll turn Fuad down.* Those periods were pure serendipity—like her, Curt had never once considered pregnancy. *Time enough to let him know once we're in Lalarhein.*

Honora took a deep breath. "It turns out," she said, "that I'm as healthy as they come."

"Then why've you been sleeping twenty-three hours a day?"

"The laziness of a well-loved woman," she said.

He raised an eyebrow. "Honora?"

"Also a slight iron deficiency," she covered hastily. Dr. Capwell had prescribed something called Feosal pills.

"That's all, *iron* deficiency?"

"Nothing like a little anemia to drag a girl down." Finding wifely duplicity more than she could handle, she changed the subject. "When do we leave?"

He took her hand, playing with the narrow, electroplated gold band. "The road's going to cut from Daralam, that's the capital, to the Persian Gulf, an area generously described as primitive."

"I'll stay in my tent, then, pistol at hand."

"We're talking about heat, flies, sandstorms, lack of water, not cannibals," he said, pausing before he finished. "Sweet, Fuad says one of the conditions for the chief engineer is that he can't bring his family."

The light was gone and gray shadows filled the room.

"How long will you be gone?" she asked, attempting to keep her voice steady.

"They want me to leave right away—Lalarhein's not exactly on the flight path, it takes close to a week to get there. I'll be on the project until March, or at the longest, the beginning of April. They've offered an exorbitant salary with two months up front. I'll deposit it in the account for you."

At the mention of cold cash her throat clogged with childish tears. How could she live without him?

If she told him the truth he would never leave her. *Without his work he's dying. The baby's not due until the beginning of June, and he'll be back long before then.* Choking back the tears, she said. "There's just one thing."

Again he was alert. "What's that?"

"No lolling under the date palms with any of Fuad's concubines."

His laughter held a note of relief. "Only on my days off." He caught her hand, pressing the wrist to his lips, his breath warming her pulse.

On Janurary 4 she saw him off at the Burbank Airport, the first leg of his journey. She waited on the observation deck ten minutes after the speck that was his plane had disappeared into the cloudless blue of the eastern sky. As

she left the parking lot she turned left not right, and didn't
notice the frame shacks and citrus groves had given way to
uncultivated land, dwarfed shrubbery, then dun-colored
foothills. The only movement was a fringe-winged hawk
circling above the tumble of rocks. She was hopelessly lost.
Speeding up curves, she reached a gas station with
old-fashioned pumps. Breathlessly she explained to the
sun-dried, grizzly attendant that she was trying to get to
Hollywood. "Girlie," he said, "you're heading dead in the
wrong direction."

18

Intimidated by the way Dr. Capwell wrote in his cramped
hand across three by five cards during her visit as well as by
his convoluted medical jargon, Honora seldom questioned
him. Instead, she settled into the regimen outlined in the
pamphlet. Every morning she walked two miles, she drank
her daily quart of milk, ate bland food, showered rather
than taking a long, relaxing bath. She felt incredibly carnal,
and maybe in a way it was just as well that Curt wasn't
around since the pamphlet stated: *sexual intercourse should
be restricted as much as possible.* Fresh air being a must, she
spent a lot of time in the apartment building's narrow,
mossy backyard where hummingbirds hovered at citrus
blossoms and tangled vines. Here, she wrote voluminously
to Curt. She did not tell him about the baby. Her secrecy
lay behind an amorphous cloud of reasons. There was no
point worrying him when he was so far away. She eagerly,
gleefully, anticipated his expression of incredulous delight
when he saw her condition—hadn't he informed her they
would have a minimum of three children?

Lalarheini mail service was rotten. From Curt's comments she knew he had never received certain of her fat
letters, and assuredly some of his were missing. A clump of

finger-smeared, multistamped envelopes would arrive in one day's delivery, then she would wait for weeks on tenterhooks dreaming up disasters that had stopped him from writing.

She and Langley exchanged frequent letters, but her fingers cramped whenever she tried to mention her condition.

In her cumulative loneliness she often wept. These were the easy tears of pregnancy, but Honora didn't realize it.

Her breasts were tender and growing large—nearly as big as Crystal's, she would think proudly—but her abdomen bulged very slightly and her loose sweaters hid the straining zippers. At the end of January she felt a peculiar liquid thrusting. Though maternity clothes were not yet a must-have, she bought two smocks and a brown rayon-gabardine skirt with a cutout stomach.

One nippy evening in mid-February she was lounging on the couch listening to the Gas Company's Evening Concert while eating a green pippin and reading *The House of Mirth*. At a tentative rap on the door, she looked up bewildered. Dropping the apple core in a saucer, holding her place open in the library book, she went to answer.

Next to the familiar battered suitcase checkered with ancient, classy travel stickers stood Langley.

"Daddy. . . ." she whispered.

"I say, looks as though it'll be Grandpa before long."

Her father's whimsical tone reached back into her earliest childhood and her novel thumped to the floor as she flung herself into his arms.

He admitted he hadn't eaten dinner and while she cooked for him, he sat companionably at the aluminum tube breakfast set which crowded the miniature kitchen. Pouring himself a drink from the nearly full scotch bottle that Curt had left, he told her the family news: Joscelyn had been advanced a full year in her new school and was having orthodontia, Crystal was brightening up the Clay Street mansion with the aid of a firm of Union Street decorators—"very lavender young men," Langley called them.

He ate the lamb chop planned for her tomorrow night's dinner in two bites, swiftly cleaning his plate, confessing he would enjoy more of the peas and her excellent chips. Peeling the potatoes, she asked, "How's the publishing house doing? You've never mentioned it in your letters."

"Let business wait. I'm on holiday. But I do want the latest on Curt's project."

Honora fried the chips, explaining at length about the stabilized shoulders, the sand that must be graded, compacted and covered with layers of asphalt, the right drainage for the occasional desert flash flood.

"The sands of Araby! It's always been a dream of mine to go there. But I must say I'm a bit surprised Curt left you. Now."

"He doesn't know about the baby."

Langley poured himself a refill. "Dead soldier," he said, setting the empty bottle on the window ledge. "Honora, this isn't the sort of thing you keep from your husband."

"He'd have stayed home, and this job is terrifically important for his career."

"But still you must let him know." Langley's blue eyes grew bleak and she knew he was remembering her mother's fatal hemorrhage at Joscelyn's birth.

Sighing, she turned the potatoes. "I'll tell him soon," she said. "Daddy, you're staying here, of course."

"It's rather tight quarters."

"We'll shift the couch in here for me and you can take the Murphy bed."

"Surely there's a smallish hotel nearby." He spoke uncertainly.

Glancing up from the sizzling frying pan, she noticed that his collar was wrinkled, as if ironed by an inexperienced hand.

"Daddy, you've come nearly five hundred miles to see me," she said firmly. "No more talk about hotels."

The next two days she took Langley on sightseeing tours, chattering happily as she drove. She was a prisoner released from solitary confinement. Occasionally Langley would grow silent, a temporary brooding that she attributed to their financial discrepancies—he had explained that since he was from out of town no bank would cash his checks.

She splurged on three bottles of Black and White. Though he never reached any degree of inebriation, two of them disappeared in two days.

The sofa on which she slept crowded the kitchen and they shifted the table and chairs into the main room, mak-

ing every meal seem festive. His third day was Sunday, and
they had the traditional English midday sabbath feast of
roast beef, potatoes browned in the drippings and York-
shire pudding followed by a trifle topped with whipped
cream, mandarin orange slices and glazed violets.

After the coffee, Langley patted his lean stomach. "The
best meal I've had since we left home."

"Home? Is that any way to talk when your grandson's
going to be president?"

"*He'll* be a proper American like you and your sisters.
But me? Over here I make a hash of everything."

"Daddy, that's not true. Gideon never appreciated you.
But your new employer has every faith in you."

Beads of moisture appeared on Langley's long, clean-
shaven upper lip. "Honora, it's time we have everything out
in the open between us. There never was going to be a
publishing house."

She let out a little sigh, although from the first she had
nursed uncertainties about this job.

Langley went on quickly, "This chap hired me to ghost-
write his book. He gave me half my fee in advance. His
outline was idiotic schoolboy trash, a yarn of derring-do in
the Boer War. I made the plot less ridiculous."

"Naturally," she said. "You're a top-notch editor."

"Last week the book was turned down by Little Brown.
He had the gall to tell me I had taken the spirit out of the
great work." Langley drained his glass. "He refused to pay
my second installment."

"How unfair!"

"I knew all along that he was a common bounder. But
while I was writing I could tell myself I had a new career,
such as it was, in the same country with my girls. Now
there's no hope. None." His small whimper was the sound
a whipped puppy makes.

She gripped his hand, which was the masculine version
of her own, long and slender.

Langley gazed out at the tangled strip of garden. "I've
been corresponding with Mortimer Franklin-Smith—you
remember him, don't you? He's at Brighton House. An
opening's come up, an excellent one, for a man with my
qualifications."

"In London?" she asked with a shiver. Was she about to
be thrust back into her lonely cell?

Rising, he went into the kitchen. "The way things stand," he said, "I must turn it down. I don't have enough to cover my expenses, much less the fare."

"That's no problem." She followed him. "Curt left me a healthy bank account."

"I can't take your money."

"Daddy, you're being silly. But I do wish you could stay until next month, when he'll be back."

"You know that nothing would please me more than to be here when my first grandchild makes his appearance." The weak, refined features were flattened by desperation. "But a chance like this comes along once in a lifetime."

He seemed to expect an answer, so she nodded.

"Honora," he said, "there's to be no nonsense. I refuse to take a single penny unless it's done as a regular business arrangement, with interest and a note."

The words sounded familiar. During the last debt-ridden year in England hadn't she overheard him snapping them into the telephone? "I'm your daughter," she said.

"It must be a loan, and that's that," Langley said angrily, and did not look at her. "Around a thousand should cover me. Not pounds of course. Dollars."

"A thousand?" she whispered.

"Of course if you can spare more I wouldn't be quite so strapped. Could go second class, not third, and so on."

The largest check she had ever made out was Dr. Capwell's three hundred dollars. How much was left in the account? Imprecise with numbers, she frowned as she tried to recollect her exact bank balance, which was somewhere above twelve hundred dollars. Her father was watching her with that odd, rabbitlike desperation. Curt would be home in a few weeks. She could certainly get by on two hundred plus dollars, couldn't she?

"A thousand is all I can manage." She reddened. Somehow she felt as if she were letting him down.

The following day they were at Union Station hugging goodbye. Both were weeping.

That week Honora's expenses cropped up everywhere. Dr. Capwell insisted she go to a radiologist on the next floor for X-rays. He also referred her to the dentist across the hall, who charged exorbitantly to fill a small cavity. She drove into the nearby Paloverde station and the mechanic told her she was in luck, coming in now: her brakes needed relining. Langley had charged some gift ties on her account at the Broadway. Even so, her withdrawal stubs showed a reassuring balance of a hundred and thirty-five dollars and seventy-three cents.

A tropical rain slashed down on the day the Bank of America envelope arrived with her statement.

Her balance was thirty-five dollars and seventy-three cents!

"They've made an idiotic mistake," she said over the thumping rain, and arranged the canceled checks in the order she had written them.

Unable to think properly, much less add in her head, she used a brown paper grocery bag for scratch paper, reconciling the checks against the stubs five times before she saw her even hundred-dollar mistake in subtraction. She began to cry. After several minutes, her sobs ended and her mind grew hard and clear. She got thoroughly drenched and ruined her cheap loafers on the way to the Western Union office.

For two days she did not leave the apartment, dozing erratically on the sofa and drinking far too many cups of tea as she awaited Curt's reply to her cable.

Each time the baby stirred, clamminess would break out on her forehead. Her first duty lay with this helpless unborn creature, Curt's child, who depended solely on her. Her blind, filial loyalty was gone. *How could I have handed a thousand dollars to Daddy. Crystal never would have given him almost all her money.*

When by the third day there was no reply, she walked through the unpleasantly hot wind—a Santa Ana, Angelenos called it—to the Western Union office. The clerk behind the counter told her the foreign currency exchanges were handled through a bank, suggesting she try her branch. Honora dog-trotted the five blocks to Cahuenga. The assistant manager told her the branch had not been cabled any funds from Lalarhein.

Honora trudged home. Though it was early for the postman, she unlocked her mail box. Inside were three thick envelopes from Curt.

The manager was slowly vacuuming the hall and this was the second of April with the rent unpaid, so Honora stepped outside, her fingers shaking as she opened the thickest letter. She gripped the fluttering pages.

March 15—the Ides

Honora, sweet,

I'll get the bad news over with first. The soil here is more porous than the geological survey indicates. We are having problems. I can't be home before the middle of May at the earliest.

The wind rattled bushes around her and the hard, clear light suddenly seemed excruciatingly bright. She sat on the front step, waves of dizziness washing over her.

19

Honora's hands clenched on the wheel as she passed the wreck. One of the big trucks that plied between Los Angeles and San Francisco had gone off the road, the trailer rolling over on its side while the tall cab remained erect. Curt had told her that the steep grade of the Grapevine was holy hell on the big rig's brakes. The mechanic had relined hers but what if the problem was recurring now?

Her neck ached with a cat's cradle of tensions.

It was two days after she had received Curt's letter. Two days of numbers that constantly plagued her—the sums on her unpaid gas bill, telephone bill, the price stickers on her calcium and Feosal pills, the bright figures in the supermarket.

There had been no response to her pleading telegrams.

Yesterday morning the manager had knocked on her door, her sagging face surrounded by a nest of metal curlers. "It's the fourth, dear," she said, the threat clear beneath her saccharine tones.

"I'm most awfully sorry, but Mr. Ivory's deposit is in a foreign currency and the bank needs time to process it," Honora replied, attempting breeziness. During the Sylvanders' last penurious months in London, she had learned the humiliating art of lying to creditors.

"God knows in your condition I'd let it ride, but the landlord's a Simon Legree about his rents. Seven days overdue and he has me tack up the eviction notice."

Alone, Honora staggered to the couch and lay trembling. Eviction? Where would she go? If only she had, say, an extra hundred dollars she could eke out another month. She ran a shaky hand over her cold, moist forehead. Who would lend her a hundred? What about Crystal? Gideon's threat against Curt remained fresh in Honora's mind and she shook her head as if warding away temptation.

But what about Gideon himself?

How could she humiliate herself—and Curt, too, by inference—by floating a loan from their enemy? Besides, to face Gideon she would have to drive almost five hundred miles each way. How would the journey affect the baby? The pamphlet said that travel, like intercourse, should be restricted.

Could beggars be choosers? Rising unsteadily from the couch, she had searched through Curt's papers for the Texaco map of California.

When, finally, she reached the bottom of the Grapevine she pulled over and walked around the car, filling her lungs with the pervasive sweetness of the mile-square alfalfa fields. Each hour, religiously, she halted for five minutes, hoping that the rests would protect the embryo.

In Bakersfield, she bought Cheez-Its and a carton of milk. She drove and halted until the oncoming headlights became hypnotic, then she pulled over on the shoulder, locking both doors, curling up with difficulty on the seat. Each time one of the big trucks passed, the old coupe shuddered. Late the following morning, she reached San Francisco. While the attendant filled her tank at a Standard station, she used the restroom to wash and change into the freshly ironed smock that she'd placed carefully in the trunk. In the metal mirror, she saw her pale, frightened face.

Parking near Maiden Lane, she climbed stiffly from the car. Her lower body felt heavy, as if the blood had congealed, and for a moment she was terrified about the effects of the long drive on her child. Then she felt a reassuring kick.

The Talbott switchboard operator cast a suspicious, mascaraed eye at Honora's maternity top. "Yes?" she asked.

"I'd like to see Mr. Talbott."

"You have an appointment?"

"No, but—"

"Sorry. That's the rule here. Nobody but nobody gets into Mr. Talbott's office without an appointment."

"He won't mind my popping in. I'm Mrs. Talbott's sister."

"Say, you have even more of that adorable accent. Go on up."

As Honora mounted the uncarpeted staircase, she thought of that afternoon she and Crystal had first visited Langley here. Was it only a year ago? It seemed centuries since the close-knit Sylvander family had begun unraveling.

The second-floor hall was cold and bare, empty of the overflow of drafting tables—additional proof, if she needed any, of the slump.

One of her obsessions on the long drive had been how she would sneak by Gideon's dwarfish, elderly secretary. The woman was away from her desk. Honora opened the frosted glass door with the unobtrusive gold lettering:

G. D. TALBOTT II
President

Gideon was on his feet, his massive shoulders curved over construction plans spread on his desk. Seeing her, he came to attention, a major general abristle with authority.

Conscious of her stiff facial muscles, Honora forced a smile. "Good morning, Gideon."

"How did you get in?" he barked. "That new idiot switchboard girl—"

"Don't blame her." Honora felt dizzy. "I told her I was your sister-in-law."

"Didn't I make that clear? We have no connection."

"You said I mustn't talk to Crystal or Joscelyn and I haven't."

He glared at her. "Well? Why are you here?"

"I need a loan." The words flowed. Why not? Hadn't she rehearsed these sentences all the way up Highway 99? "A hundred dollars. I'll pay whatever interest you decide."

"A loan? Haven't you heard? In this country our charities support homes for women left in the lurch."

"Curt and I are married, Gideon."

"Wear your phony wedding ring and fool the others. But don't lie to me."

"We were married in Tahoe." Her voice was softer, almost a stammer.

He sat in the large leather chair behind the desk, not offering her the seat opposite him. "Then why doesn't your 'husband' handle your financial problems?"

"He's out of the country."

"In Lalarhein, trying to lay out a highway. So you see, I know all about Curt Ivory." As he said the name his eyelids flickered, and momentarily the stern hardness wavered.

She felt a wave of empathy, even sympathy. Her tormenter had rescued Curt from starvation, had endowed him with an education and a profession.

"Gideon," she said, "if it's any consolation, he feels awful about leaving Talbott's. You mean a lot to him."

"No need for soft soap. You're not getting a penny."

She shifted her weight. "I wouldn't be here if I weren't at the end of my rope. Curt left me a quite a lot, but . . . well . . . I was stupid. A hundred dollars would be a huge help."

"You and your father. Throwing away every chance, then come begging."

"Daddy's on his way back to London," she said doggedly. "He's had a top-notch offer."

Gideon gave her a sour look, as if to say he'd believe it when he saw it. "I've done more than enough for Ivory already. I'm not about to support his bastard."

At the word *bastard* anger spurted through her body. White dots scintillated in front of her eyes, and her hands clenched into fists. She had no room for rage or pride, but she could not control herself. How dare this nasty-minded, unforgiving little millionaire who had married her aunt, then her sister, slander her unborn child?

"I'm sorry for you, Gideon," she said in a choked whisper. "The world must always look ugly to you."

"Get out!"

Her breath rasping, she backed from the office. Still suffused and buoyed by rage, she hurried down the stairs. As she reached the bottom landing, the front door opened and closed.

It was Crystal.

The sisters stared at one another through a dusty shaft of sunlight. These moments became an indelible, photographic image etched into their brains: neither would ever manage to exorcise this minuscule fraction of time.

Crystal, halted with one dainty gray ostrich pump pointed forward, was improbably beautiful in a silvery mink coat and matching hat.

Honora held out her hand. "Crys," she murmured. "Crys, I've missed you so much."

Crystal's gaze had been fixed on the maternity smock. The blond head in its fur coronet tilted to the left, an ambiguous gesture that Honora took as condemnation.

"We're m-married," she stammered. "Married. . . ."

Hurrying down the last three steps, she stumbled at the bottom, rescuing herself by grasping the banister, then rushing through the haze of perfume that surrounded her sister.

Up close there was no mistaking Crystal's expression. The incomparable blue eyes held an infuriating, demeaning pity.

Honora stumbled up Maiden Lane, hunching in the dust-covered Ford with her shaking hands covering her wet face.

It was after midnight before she was back in Hollywood. She fell into an exhausted sleep, jerking awake before dawn. She got out her old Edinthorpe skirt, which her father had brought down with him—for some reason it was the only possession of hers that he had packed. The wool was far heavier than people wore in California. Honora used her nail scissors to open the hip seams, resewing them as far to the selvage as possible. By the time she had ironed her stitchery under a damp rag, it was after ten. In the Broadway's Bargain Basement she spent the last of her folding money on a heavy, all-in-one foundation. The boned corset flattened and widened the gentle mound of her stomach, pushing up her enlarged breasts.

In her short, pre–New Look skirt, with her nubby pink sweater pulled down over her hips, she appeared buxom and cheap rather than pregnant.

Scotch-taped inside the window of the Hollywood Boulevard Pig'n'Whistle window was a typed card: *Part-time waitress. Experience necessary. Apply manager.*

She waited while the manager put in a long-distance call to San Francisco. Al Stroud must have given her a good reference. The manager told her that the part-time job was hers.

Thirty-five minutes after Honora entered the cafe she was dressed in a freshly cleaned size fourteen uniform and taking an order.

20

The Pig'n'Whistle was a chain that served food hovering between tea-room delicate and short-order solid: the Hollywood branch opened for breakfast, closing at the hour dictated by California law: two A.M.

Part-time meant that Honora worked five hours in a split shift.

She arrived at seven in the morning, galloping until nine, when the serious breakfasters gave way to the coffee and sweetroll dawdlers. She then took off two hours to return at eleven thirty for the lunch onslaught. At two thirty, when the large side hall was roped off, her workday ended.

During her midmorning off-hours she would stumble the few blocks home to sprawl on the couch with her swollen, white-stockinged feet raised on the armrest. Too exhausted to write letters or read, not permitting herself to nap for fear she'd oversleep, she was easy prey for visions of disaster. Was the all-in-one squashing the baby into deformity? How much longer could she continue on the job? There had been no letters from Curt—had he been injured?

It was almost a relief to force her puffy feet back into her white Naturalizers. The fast turnover of tables at Pig'n'Whistle left her no time to think.

Honora's complexion, though not vivid like Crystal's,

had a natural, creamy luminosity. Now the skin was drab and the Max Factor pancake she used to cover the dark circles under her eyes intensified its lusterless pallor. Yet more depressing was the swelling of her delicate ankles—Curt had often kissed his way up her long, slender legs.

After Dr. Capwell had listened to her stomach through his stethoscope, she asked hesitantly, "Does it mean anything that my ankles are swollen?"

Dr. Capwell did not look up from the dog-eared filing card on which he was scribbling laboriously. "Pregnancy is no time for vanity," he scolded. "What matters is the fetal heartbeat. It's strong and regular."

As she left the office, a very pregnant redhead emerged from the elevator and started along a different corridor. Honora knew a group of obstetricians shared a suite on this floor. She followed the redhead. A prettily furnished waiting room was crowded with women in various stages of pregnancy. She had never seen another pregnant woman in Dr. Capwell's narrow, unbusy waiting room. These premises looked rich, but several of the patients didn't. What would she say to an unknown obstetrician? *Hello, I'm a patient of Dr. Capwell up the hall, and I'm worried about puffy ankles—can the problem be I'm waiting tables in a tight girdle?*

The reception nurse, who was taking a package wrapped in a brown paper bag from the redhead, glanced at her with a tentative, questioning smile.

I can't waste money on a visit. I have to save every penny for when I can't work, and the hospital.

One cloudy afternoon in mid-April Honora sat at a corner booth eating the Daily Special of chicken croquettes, mashed potatoes, carrots and peas that was free to employees—her budgetary conscience forced her to fill up on these starchy meals no matter how tired she was when her shift ended.

At a tap on her shoulder, the minced chicken fell from her fork.

"Hello, stranger," said a familiar voice.

Honora's eyes opened wide. "Vi!"

The last time they were together, it must have been August, Vi had told her a certain somebody had asked her to move to San Berdoo, and it looked like wedding bells again: despite two divorces and a series of disastrous "engagements," Vi remained blithely optimistic when it came to romance. A few days after that Honora had tried to reach Vi at Stroud's and Al told her Vi had quit, leaving no forwarding address.

"Long time no see," Vi grinned.

Tears stupidly brimming in her eyes, Honora instinctively rose to hug her old friend, then sank back in the false leather cushions. Mightn't Vi feel the hard protrusion through the corset?

"Vi . . ."

"Hey, don't choke up on me," said Vi, her own voice none too steady as she slid into the booth opposite Honora.

"I just don't believe it. How can you be here? What about San Bernardino?"

"Mr. San Berdoo was bad news. So here I am, back in the Pig'n'Whistle, my old stomping grounds, on the late shift. I saw the name Honora Ivory on the worksheet. Even if the Ivory didn't fit, not too many Honoras floating around. I came in early for a look-see."

"Now I'm Mrs. Curt Ivory." Honora extended the hand with the wedding ring. Silver showed through the gold plating.

"Hey, congratulations and all." Vi's enthusiasm rang animatedly. "So when can us two get together to catch up?"

"Now." Honora pushed away her nearly full plate. "I live on Cherokee."

Vi drove them in her Chevy.

In the apartment Honora started to pick up the clutter of teacups and throwaway newspapers, but Vi said, "Get a load off, sit down. Bring me up to date."

"Here's my husband." Honora took the stiff, deckle-edged cardboard folder from its place of honor on the coffee table. Curt had needed a picture to send out with his résumé.

Vi whistled. "A real cutie."

"Recognize him?"

Vi peered. "Hey, you could sue the photographer if it's that handsome bozo who came to Stroud's just before you quit."

"It doesn't do him justice, does it?"

"Not one bit. Where's he now? At work?"

"Yes, but out of the country. In Lalarhein—that's near

Saudi Arabia. Building a road—I told you he was an engineer, didn't I?"

"I seem to remember something like that." Vi played with the clasp of her large, fake alligator purse. "Kid, how far along are you?"

Honora felt the blood drain from her face. "What are you talking about?" she asked tartly.

"You used to have a body like Lauren Bacall, slender, tender and tall."

"Can't a girl gain a few pounds once she's married?"

"I saw right away, that's how rotten you look. You poor ignorant mutt. If I'd only known earlier, I could of helped."

"I happen to want the baby, and so does my husband," Honora said coldly.

A muscle jumped near Vi's mouth. "Will you quit with that 'husband' crap?"

"I see that I should have framed the marriage certificate."

"And I'm sick of being high-hatted." Vi's voice rose in that swift, attacking anger. "You think I'm some kind of idiot? You ain't slaving away at the split shift for your health, not when you're in a family way. And I've seen your guy. That kind gives his wife a big house in Bel Air or Beverly Hills and parks a sweet patootie in a dump like this!"

Honora tried to control her tears and failed.

"Hey, listen, you can shack up with Joe Stalin for all I care. I've been through the mill, too, you poor kid." Vi moved to the sofa. "Come to Momma."

Honora let herself be enfolded in Vi's warmth, salty perspiration odors and the cloying scent of lilacs. After a minute of convulsive gasping, her tears ceased.

"Now tell your old pal what's what," Vi comforted.

Honora talked, steadily, sometimes incoherently. "Gideon told me I'm a fallen woman and fired Curt for doing him dirty—as if our private lives were *his* business. And then he turned around and married my sister—I must've told you Crystal's as stunning as a film star. And young enough to be his daughter." She played down Langley's part in the bank account fiasco. She told of the two futile telegrams and the panic she lived with about Curt. She described the long, tense drive to San Francisco, and Gideon's turndown. She fell silent, however, when it came to mentioning that she'd seen Crystal.

Vi dabbed a Kleenex at her eyes and blew her nose loudly. "You always did need a seeing-eye dog to watch over you. But that uncle or brother-in-law or whatever he is—if you'll pardon the French, he's a real prick."

"He saved Curt's life and was generous to me. He's just very straitlaced and Victorian."

"A real prick, so don't invent excuses. Does he realize what a lucky guy he is, this hubby of yours?"

"So you believe we're married?"

"Kid, not even you with all your reading could have invented that cockamamie story."

Honora laughed shakily. "Thank you, Vi."

A few days later four letters came with Arabic stamps. Three were postmarked after she had sent her cables. She scanned Curt's upright handwriting. He had received neither the telegrams nor the letter with her fully fleshed out announcement. But he was safe.

She jerked around the room as she read, unable to keep still. Vi, who labored on the late shift and left the Pig'n'Whistle after two, slept until noon. Though it was only a little past ten Honora dialed her number.

"Whozzit?" Vi grumbled sleepily.

"Me, Honora. Vi, I just got four letters from Curt."

"Next time, for Chrissakes, why don't you wake me with some good news." Vi's voice bubbled. "Hey, kid, I'll pick you up from work and we'll celebrate, really tie one on. Booze for me, milk shake for you and the kid."

Maybe the adrenal rush of undiluted joy depleted Honora. At the height of the lunch confusion, as she stood at the counter calling, "One BLT, one Special," the skin of her head stretched taut as a drum. Sounds reverberated against her ears. Her head seemed to pull away from her body. Then she was toppling into darkness.

She came to almost immediately.

In a disjointed way she was aware that the head fry cook, an enormous Sicilian, had lifted her. From the mobile vantage point of his naked, black haired arms, she was aware of curious eyes and knowing little smirks. She must have passed out again. The next thing she was coughing at the sharp ammonia under her nose. She lay on the narrow cot in the waitresses' lounge with the manager looming over her.

"Honora?"

"Give me a couple of minutes," Honora whispered. Attempting to sit, she made futile, dog-paddling movements with her hands.

"Don't move."

"I have to get back to my station. . . ."

"Kersten and Mary Lu have taken over." Black eyebrows drew together reproachfully. "How could you have done this to me?"

"What?" Honora whispered.

"You know exactly what I mean."

Honora closed her eyes. Even if she weren't pregnant, she would have admitted she was—she would have confessed to murder, that's how weak and demoralized she was.

"Letting me go to the trouble of breaking you in, probably getting me in Dutch with the supervisor."

The manager's heels rang sharply on the linoleum.

I won't be working anymore, Honora thought, and once again numbers began darting in her head. She had $102.53 in her bank account. The $50 rent was due next week. Without her free meals, she would have to buy food. And if Curt wasn't home before her due date she would need money for the hospital: Hollywood Presbyterian's cheapest rate was $25 for four in a room, plus $5 for the baby, and the minimum maternal stay was five days. $150. How would she get it? One thing was certain. She couldn't let Curt's child be born in one of those homes for unwed mothers that Gideon had proposed.

21

"Tell me how I'm meant to feel?" Vi asked. "You drive close to a thousand miles, scared stiff all the way, to beg a few bucks from some no-good, and when I talk a loan, you climb onto your high horse."

"It's different," Honora sighed.

That same afternoon, the Murphy bed was down, and

she lay stretched out in Curt's maroon bathrobe. She had just turned down Vi's offer of a three-hundred-dollar loan.

"You know me, just an American lowlife. Explain the finer points."

"Gideon's one of the family."

"That's what you call a guy who's tossed you out on your can?"

"You're a friend, Vi. I can't borrow from you."

Vi sat on the bed, sagging the springs. "You ain't got much choice, kid," she said quietly. "And your hubby's good for it, so what the hell. It's settled."

Honora reached out and gripped Vi's red, beringed hand.

Honora tried to return to her old regimen without success. The daily two miles was out—her legs were too swollen, and anyway, she was panting by the time she reached the mailbox at the corner. She prepared herself balanced meals—vegetable or fruit, a protein, a starch—but after a few bites she was full, and if she forced down the food she vomited. Yet Dr. Capwell touched the balance of his scales several pounds higher. "You're only at the beginning of your eighth month, and you've put on twenty-nine and three quarter pounds." He frowned as he scribbled on his card. "You must cut down."

"But I've been having trouble eating."

"A prepartum woman metabolizes the food she eats in a more economical manner."

The wedding band cut into her finger: she eased it off with soap, carefully storing it in the top drawer of the walk-in closet. Her sleep was disturbed by the need to pee or by the baby kicking at her chest, yet conversely, two minutes after she opened a book, she dozed.

"You sure seem dragged out," Vi would say.

"I'm sleeping for two."

Or Vi would inspect her worriedly, then say, "You sure don't look good."

"I've stopped wearing pancake, that's all."

"Well, you're seeing a doctor, so I guess it's okay."

In the pre-dawn hours of April 28, Honora awoke with the sensation that a large brick rather than an infant inhabited her stomach.

As she got out of bed, a liquid that was not urine warmed

her thighs. Standing there, the tepid wetness gluing her legs to the loose flannel nightgown that she'd bought at the Junior League Thrift Shop, she realized that this must be what the pamphlet referred to as the "breaking of the water," one of the pamphlet's signals to call her physician.

The baby wasn't due for nearly six weeks!

When the leaking stopped, she washed the rug and herself, then dressed. Giving herself points for remaining calm, she dialed the number taped above her phone, getting Dr. Capwell's exchange. "If you'll spell your name and repeat your number," a contralto voice told her, "the doctor will return your call as soon as possible."

Honora made the bed and swung it up into the wall. She unpacked Curt's small Mark Cross bag to make sure she had the necessities. New red toothbrush, new tube of toothpaste, Jergen's lotion and Mum. Two never-worn shortie nightgowns bought on sale. Two diapers, safety pins, a minute cotton shirt and a tiny yellow silk jacket embroidered with white rabbits that Vi had bought when they shopped together for the minimum layette.

She sat timing the cramps on her watch, consumed with worry about the baby's prematurity.

After a dark, endless hour, she dialed the exchange again. "This is Mrs. Ivory. I put in a call to Dr. Capwell before three and he hasn't called back. I'd like to know if your service was able to contact him," she said politely.

"I gave him your message myself," replied the same contralto.

"Will you please try again? Tell him the pains are seven minutes now."

There was a silence so long that she jumped when the woman finally came back on the line. "Doctor says to go back to bed and call him at the office first thing tomorrow morning."

Honora knew that the average duration of first labor is between sixteen and eighteen hours—*hence there is no need for the first-time father's proverbial panic at the onset of labor*—but she felt she would go crazy alone in the silent apartment. To distract herself she scrubbed and scoured the bathroom and kitchen. It was getting light outside and the pains were coming every five minutes with a strength that made her gasp and rippled sweat between her swollen breasts.

She called Vi. "Young Ivory seems to be putting in a very early appearance."

"Hang in there, kid. Be right over."

Vi arrived in less then ten minutes, black frills of her nightgown showing below her Kelly green coat.

"Is this doctor of yours meeting us at the hospital?"

"I tried to get him twice. The message was to call back when his office opens."

"Jesus Christ! Gimme the number."

Vi screamed into the phone. Finally, Dr. Capwell was on the line. More screaming on Vi's part. Honora was in the midst of a pain when Vi slammed down the receiver. "Pardon my French, but you gotta real turd for a doctor. Well, he's calling over to there. So let's get the show on the road."

At Hollywood Presbyterian, as the stout young OB nurse wheeled her away, Vi shouted, "You keep up the good work, kid, and I'll pace the floor."

Honora was dry-shaved with a blunt blade, given an enema, and taken to a labor room with two other groaning women and their pale husbands. Honora bit blood in her lips to keep from screaming, and a sympathetic nurse said, "You're ready for a shot, but we have no orders from your doctor."

Her cries were skittering down the brightly lit corridor by the time Dr. Capwell arrived. He ordered scopolamine, or twilight sleep, an amnesiac that blocks the memory. Later her only recollection of the birth would be of a blazing, shadowless operating room and a masculine voice shouting furiously, "You're killing her and the baby! If it's the last thing I do in medicine, Capwell, I'll see you're dropped from this hospital, you fucking butcher."

She opened her eyes on sunlight.

Her mouth was dry and when she tried to swallow, she felt as if she had a strep throat. Her stomach hurt, a dull, throbbing ache that was like an infected cut, totally different from the tearing intensity of labor pains. Uncertain whether the baby had been born, she made the effort of lifting her hand. Bandages swathed around her flat stomach.

The door was closed, but she could hear a faraway ripple of feminine laughter. And a strange, punctuated sound that was a cross between buzzing and an insistent bell. Still sedated, it took her about a minute to identify the sound as an infant's wail.

She groped around, finding a black ovoid with a button safety-pinned to her pillow.

She pressed down.

A motherly, gray-haired nurse rustled in. "Ahh, so you're awake, Mrs. Ivory."

"I want to see my baby," Honora whispered hoarsely.

The nurse moved about the bed, straightening the already taut sheets. "The infants are being taken back to the nursery, dear."

"Why can't I see my baby?" Honora was too weak to stop her tears.

"Now, now. Doctor's making his rounds. Let me go find him."

In a couple of minutes a youngish man opened the door, the stethoscope around his neck clicking against a button of his unfastened white coat as he came over to her barred bed. Despite the speed with which he moved, there was a reassuring, almost phlegmatic calm to the long, Lincolnesque face.

"I'm Doctor Taupin, the chief obstetrical resident," he said. "How are you feeling? If that incision hurts, I can order something for the pain."

"Incision? Did I have a cesarean?"

Dr. Taupin blinked and pulled a chair to the bed. "Can you remember anything?"

"Just that I was making an awful fuss," she mumbled apologetically.

"You were having a difficult time," he said, his face carefully composed, his voice expressionless.

"Then there was a bright light and shouting."

He nodded. "The baby was a breech—it was lying crosswise rather than in the right position with the head down. There were complications." He paused. "While you were in the delivery room, I was called in."

"The baby?"

He reached between the bars to grip her hand. "I did everything I could, but the baby was born dead."

"Dead?" She could hear the ridiculous quaver in her voice. "But in the labor room, the intern listened and said he could hear a good, strong heart."

He shook his head. "The complications I told you about, Mrs. Ivory, the breech delivery. I'm sorry, so very sorry." He didn't sound sorry, he sounded angry.

A birch tree outside dappled the sunlight on the opposite wall with moving shadows.

"Mrs. Ivory." Dr. Taupin's fingers warmed her icy flesh. "Death is the most difficult reality to accept, and there's no way to soften it. But at least we saved you."

"What was it?"

"A little boy."

"Was anything wrong with him?"

"Nothing."

"I mean, was he deformed?"

"He was perfect."

"I had to work, I wore a tight girdle."

"Nothing you did hurt the child, none of this was your fault." Again that veiled anger.

"He was premature."

"No, full term."

"But Dr. Capwell said my due date was—"

"He made a miscalculation."

So Gideon was right. Conceived before marriage.

The infants were being returned to the nursery, and she heard the peculiar, thin wailing sound. Her breasts began to ache, and she lifted her hand under the sheet, feeling the moisture that seeped through her hospital gown.

Dr. Taupin saw the gesture. "Mrs. Ivory—okay if I call you Honora?"

"Yes."

"Honora, my opinion is you'll feel a lot better if you're off this floor."

She nodded.

"It helps to cry," he said.

Cry? Desolation and guilt had stripped away the superficial layers of her psyche, the dreaminess people remarked on, the innocence and blind spots, leaving her naked to the truth. She had placed herself in the hands of a medical ignoramus, she hadn't told Curt about his child, she had handed her father the bank account necessary to see her through her confinement, she had flubbed all down the line. And her baby—Curt's son—was dead.

She was wheeled to another private room. During the afternoon visiting hours, Vi bore in a pile of glossy maga-

zines and a bunch of red roses. Her small, bloodshot eyes
were wet.

Honora thanked her in a flat voice.

"I'm sorry, kid, so sorry."

"You've been wonderful, Vi," Honora said.

Vi blew her nose. "What a stinking break."

"Are you paying for the private room?"

"That's the last thing you need to worry about."

"You've been wonderful," Honora repeated. The sore-
ness of her throat and the numbness in her mind made
conversation impossible.

Vi brushed a wisp of hair from Honora's forehead and
clasped her hand. "Kid, listen, I'll buzz along. What you
need is sleep."

Honora nodded, and her eyes closed with an all-encompassing exhaustion.

When she awoke it was night and the room was heavily
shadowed, yet she sensed that somebody was here with her.
She stirred to look around and the incision throbbed
sharply.

"Darling?" A chair scraped against the linoleum. "You
awake?"

"Curt," she said. She felt no surprise that he was here,
standing over her bed.

He grasped the bars, bending to press his cheek to hers.
She could smell toothpaste and weariness.

"Have you seen Vi?"

"Yes. There was a note in the apartment to go to the
Pig'n'Whistle."

"It was a boy," she whispered.

"I know, love, I know," he said. "We'll talk about it
later."

"I should've gone to a proper obstetrician."

"Sweet, you were in a strange city in a strange country,
and this guy came recommended."

"In the back of my mind I knew all along he was no
good, but I'd paid his whole fee and I couldn't afford any
more bills."

"For God's sake, Honora, stop blaming yourself. I'm
blaming *myself* and that's enough."

She looked at Vi's roses. Wilting already, the sweet perfume of their dying battled with the hospital disinfectant.

"I knew you were out of a fairy story, too good for the

real world, I knew better than anyone that people take advantage of you." He was speaking in a peculiarly remote tone she'd never heard him use. "And what did I do? Leave you without friend or family and go off on a job where you can't reach me."

"Is the road finished?"

"A week ago Wednesday," he said. He bent over the bed, and she could feel his breath. "Honora, this is a promise. From here on in, I'll be with you always, I'll look after you, I'll kill anyone who hurts you."

His face contorted, and he sat heavily in the straight chair, hands over his face, his body shaking with hoarse sobs. He had wept once before, when he'd told her about his dreadful childhood, but those had been quiet tears.

22

After Crystal woke from her afternoon nap she lay drowsily admiring the transformation that she and Baynie McHugh had wrought on her bedroom. Those puerile slipper chairs she'd prized last year were replaced with a large, low-slung, creamy-beige, silk sectional couch that matched the velvety wall-to-wall carpet, the gingerbread paneling revered by Matilda Talbott had been demolished in favor of pale, sleekly unadorned ash: instead of the dinky leaded windowpanes, sheets of plate glass admitted the view of the Bay.

Delicious, Crystal thought. And the most delicious aspect of the room was sleeping alone in it. Until five weeks ago, Gideon had shared tenancy with her.

Those jokes about the inadequacies of elderly husbands didn't apply to Gideon. Once—often twice—nightly he lowered himself on her. She lay passive. Wasn't this nocturnal warfare part of the marital bargain she had struck? (Gideon never realized they were pitted in battle. Rather, he viewed his gorgeous young bride's acquiescence as ostentatious proof of affection.) Shuddering beneath her husband's thumping aggression, she loathed him bitterly. The odd part, though, was that by morning her resentment had faded, and when he kissed her goodbye, she would tweak his ear fondly. By late afternoon she found herself anticipating his homecoming. He would tell her about big doings at Talbott's while he drank his ten-year-old scotch and she sipped a companionable Coca-Cola. Since her pregnancy even a drop or so of sherry upset her stomach.

Pregnancy was also the reason she had this room to herself. Gideon, his eyes small beacons of jubilant pride, had decamped to his old room as soon as he learned of her condition.

Crystal arched her back like a satisfied little Persian cat, poising in midstretch as the front door chimes sounded.

The household used the side entry, servants and tradespeople the back. Only guests used the front door. *Must be Imogene dropping over for a cocktail,* Crystal thought. Left at loose ends without Honora, she had joined forces with the thin, sophisticated heiress. The loss of Curt Ivory had turned Imogene into a sharp, flesh-rending piranha of gossip, but this made her wittily amusing.

Irritated with the servants for not summoning her Crystal jumped up from the bed, descending into the vast, dim, entry hall, now a pale monochrome. In the music room, Joscelyn banged out scales as if she had a personal vendetta against the keyboard.

Gideon's office door was ajar and she heard the gravel of anger in his voice. "If you don't leave my house this instant, I'll call the police!"

"Call every cop in the whole goddamn Bay Area. I'm not leaving until I get to the bottom of this. *Did* she or *didn't* she ask you for a loan?"

With the sound of the piano thumping, Crystal didn't immediately place the voice, but after the second sentence she realized that the low, menacing sarcasm belonged to Curt Ivory.

Her long red fingernails clenched into her palms. *How dare he show his face here?*

Crystal felt wretched whenever she thought of Honora running off without a note or telephone call. So much for near-twin closeness, so much for *just us.* In the beginning she could console herself with the thought that living with a man was too consummate a shame for Honorable Honora to confess, but later she had to live with the draining wound that Honora *had* written to Joscelyn. Despite this overt rejection, Crystal had never been able to rouse up an honest animosity toward her sister. It was Curt whom she hated, that smooth wolf, that licentious seducer. He had cut them apart. And the day she had seen Honora at Talbott's, she had been aghast. Actually speechless with distress. The cheesy rayon maternity smock, those sad smudges under the beautiful dark eyes, the timid extension of hand, then the realization that sweet, guileless Honora was bluffing out an illegal pregnancy with a wedding ring.

"I got this third-hand, and I prefer the record straight," Curt was saying. "Did she drive up here to borrow a few bucks?"

"In February or March, yes," Gideon retorted. "And I turned her down. It's time she learned exactly how far her kind of behavior will get her."

"As part of the educational process why didn't you shove her down the stairs?"

"What right have you to accuse me? You're the one who turned the poor, stupid girl into a tramp. After she went to stay openly in your apartment, I explained to her that I'd washed my hands of her."

"Yes, she told me."

Gideon drew a sharp breath. "Was taking advantage of a young girl under my care the way for you to repay me?" His voice rose again. "And since you're talking obligations, what about you? It *is* your child, isn't it?"

Crystal had pushed open the door, but neither man noticed her.

They remained tensed like prizefighters, Gideon, his short legs flexed and pugnacious jaw thrust forward, a massively squat strength, and Curt, arms bent at the elbows, thick, tawny hair windblown, eyes narrowed, a dangerous savage.

Terrific looking, Crystal thought. If she'd had a bottle of sulfuric acid handy, she would have hurled it at his face, destroying his good looks as he'd destroyed her tender gullible sister.

She moved into the room. "What's happened to Honora?" she asked.

Both men jerked.

"Go on back upstairs, dear," Gideon said, his voice suddenly tender. "This is between Ivory and me."

Crystal smoothed the striped taffeta skirt of her hostess gown over her shapely hips, staring at Curt. "Is she all right?"

"She's wonderful," Curt said. "Terrific. Is that what you want to hear?"

"She's my sister."

"Where was that relationship a few months back? Christ, when I think of her slaving in that hash joint so you could prance around in new clothes! And the minute she's desperate for a few measly bucks, you're nowhere in sight."

"How is she?"

"She's alive, the baby isn't."

Crystal felt her throat clog, but she refused to show her sorrow to her enemy. "I'll never forgive you," she said coldly.

He gave a discordant laugh. "That goes double for me. I'll never let myself off the meat hook, either."

"Couldn't you at least have given her enough to see her through?" Crystal demanded.

"That part I *did* take care of. But your father dropped in for a visit. I assume he came to you first?"

Langley had dropped by the house to request a "small loan, I'll pay with interest, of course," so he could return to London, but Gideon had told him point-blank that it was better that he stay in San Francisco, where he had a family to keep an eye on him and his drinking problem.

"So you turned him down," Curt said. "Smart move. She, of course, gave him almost every cent she had, and then tried to get in touch with me, and couldn't." His hands balled into fists and he strode to the window, staring into the gathering darkness. "Being naive, she figured families help each other—the way she'd helped you."

She never came to me, Crystal thought bleakly. "This was hardly Gideon's responsibility," she said.

"Right, right, he couldn't be expected to lend a large fortune of a hundred bucks to a sister-in-law in desperate need, not when he had his own necessities to pay for." Curt glanced at the wall that Baynie had extravagantly covered with pigskin. "She managed handily on her own, stuffing herself into a corset and waiting tables. In the end, she found somebody with means, a well-to-do waitress." The sarcasm was clotted. "There's a possibility she can't have any more children, but thank God she doesn't know *that* yet. If there's any justice, the same'll happen to you."

He said it like a curse, and Gideon moved to Crystal, resting his hand protectively on her shoulder. "All right, Ivory," he said. "I've taken just about enough."

Curt was staring at Crystal. "How could you be such a bitch to her?"

Crystal's beauty made her appear impervious to the emotions twisting like snakes within her, but she was trembling.

"Leave my wife out of this," Gideon snapped. "Ivory, I'm giving you fair warning. From here on in, I'll do anything I can to hurt you."

Another discordant laugh. "How are you going to top this one?"

"You make me ill," Crystal burst out. "Blaming us because you left Honora in the lurch."

"Is that it?" Curt asked. "Set your minds at rest. We were married the day after she left here."

Gideon's thick fingers dug into Crystal's flesh. "No license was issued in your names," he said. "Not in California, Nevada or Arizona."

Curt's fists went up, as if he would deliver the old one-two to the jaw of his former mentor, the man he had revered and loved. "You shit!" For the first time he raised his voice. "You pious, sanctimonious shit!"

The shout appeared to cut some vital wire holding him erect. Abruptly his shoulders slumped, his hands dropped to his sides and he stared around the room, dazed and punchy-looking. Blinking and silent, he left the office. A few moments later, they heard the front door open and close.

Crystal began to weep. Gideon, usually solicitous of her moods—beyond the bed—didn't comfort her. He sank into his desk chair, leaning his head back, his expression showing hurt and bewilderment.

Joscelyn had been desultorily putting in her daily half-hour stint of practice at the new beige piano.

As her skinny fingers arched and banged, she thought of Honora. After her father had slipped her the original letter, she had not heard from her again and for this—as well as for her inner tumult and the omnipresent whispers of abandonment—she blamed Gideon.

Joscelyn no longer admired her uncle cum brother-in-law. She saw him as Crystal's patsy, the aggressive jailer who had cut her off from Honora and usurped her father—another abandonment there.

Her days were a harrowing jumble since Honora had departed. She lived in terror of people, animals, machines, even inanimate objects—a window cornice could topple on you. Her unhappiness showed as arrogant cussedness. She rarely combed her fine, mouse-brown hair, she shoved her uniforms on the closet floor, wearing rumpled blouses and skirts with mussed pleats to her new school, where she earned straight As.

The front door chimed. So *they* had guests. She banged the keyboard antagonistically. As she turned to the page with Minuet in G, she heard Curt's voice.

Her hands hovered, falling with a clashing of notes. *He's come to get me,* she thought.

Rising impatiently, she toppled the piano stool and it fell almost soundlessly to the new beige carpet as she ran to the door.

Gideon boomed angrily. Though she pressed her ear to the crack, entire sentences eluded her. Crystal's high voice joined in the furious conversation. Soon Joscelyn realized that Curt was not here to redeem her but to curse Gideon for not helping Honora.

Honora had had a baby!

The baby was dead.

Joscelyn cringed against the bleached paneling, shivering. A niece or nephew, whose very existence startled her, had died. Her mother had died. Were the Sylvanders as doomed as the inhabitants of Elsinore?

The voices fell silent, the front door opened and closed. Cautiously Joscelyn peered into the hall. Gideon's office was open, and she heard a peculiar, muffled sound. She tiptoed across the space as quietly as possible, opened the side door. From here one could leave the house without being visible from either the office or the kitchen. Easing out, she quietly closed the door behind her.

The blackish blue fog that groped through the dusk blurred Curt's outline as he strode up the hill. Afraid she might be heard inside the house, she didn't call out but charged up the grade after him.

When she reached the crest the fogbank had swallowed him.

Racing helter-skelter downhill through the obscuring dampness, she shouted, "Curt! Curt!"

He turned, halting beneath the aureole of a streetlight. She stopped a couple of feet from him. "Hi," she panted.

His face was slack, and though he nodded she had the sensation that as far as he was concerned, the fog hid her.

"It's me—Joscelyn." She attempted to mimic his easy sarcasm. "Remember? Your esteemed sister-in-law."

"Yeah, sure, Joss."

"It's horrendous, the way they treated Honora."

He shrugged.

"How is she?"

"Dazed."

He looked that way himself, his eyes not quite focusing on her, his mouth lax and vulnerable.

She drew a breath of wet air. "Honora sent a letter inviting me to visit. It seems to me that now's the time to accept. A familiar face would cheer her up." She tried not to sound pleading.

"You know there was a baby?"

"Yes, and I'm very sorry. . . ."

"She hasn't accepted it emotionally."

"Is she in hospital?"

"For another week at least. I've rented a furnished house in Beverly Hills for her to come home to."

Joscelyn shifted her weight from scuffed shoe to shoe. "How many bedrooms?"

"Two."

"Nothing like inviting myself—but don't you agree having somebody in the family around would help bring her out of it?"

For the first time his eyes focused on her. His forehead and high cheeks gleamed, either from the fog's moisture or sweat. "Right," he said. "Come along." And without another word he strode downhill.

She trotted next to him.

On Union Street, the lit sign of a free taxi showed hazily above the headlights. Curt stepped from the sidewalk, lifting his arm. When the cab halted, he said, "The airport."

Fly?

When she was four, living in that farmhouse near Edinthorpe, a Spitfire had crashed in a nearby field. Billows of petrol-smelling smoke, flames, and the odor of broiling meat. Death by roasting.

But fears or no fears, she had the cab door yanked open before Curt could get it for her.

The second Sylvander girl had run from Gideon Talbott's house without so much as a coat to go with Curt Ivory.

23

The fog prevented Curt and Joscelyn's plane from taking off until late the following morning. Curt drove directly from the Burbank airport to Hollywood Presbyterian for the afternoon visiting hours, but Joscelyn was not permitted to accompany him up to Honora's room. Despite their combined arguments, the hospital held firm to the rule that visitors must be over twelve.

So Joscelyn didn't see her sister for ten days.

Curt had rented a pseudo-Spanish bungalow on a narrow, nondescript street south of Wilshire Boulevard in Beverly Hills. After the Clay Street mansion, the rooms seemed minuscule and the heavily varnished Sheraton reproductions low on the social scale. However, Eula Lee, the light-brown, taciturn, elderly maid-cook who drove up each morning in her two-tone Cadillac, was real class. Her meals paid homage to Joscelyn's sweet tooth with fresh baked Tollhouse cookies, flaky-crusted pies, hand-cranked peach ice cream.

At quarter past eight, Curt would depart for McNee's downtown offices—McNee competed with Talbott's and Bechtel for large-scale construction jobs—coming home around six for dinner, then hurrying off to the hospital. On his return, he spread plans or proposals on the dining room table.

Joscelyn wasn't unhappy in the little house. Unlike at Gideon's, nobody fussed at her. It was too near summer vacation to enroll in school, so she explored Beverly Hills' few blocks of neighborhood stores. After that she stayed home, poring over Curt's college engineering text books. At dinner she would question him about stress, thrust, erosion protection, hydraulics, and he, with that half-amused smile, would draw explanatory diagrams on paper napkins. These few minutes were the highlight of her day.

Honora's new specialist sent her home in an ambulance. As the attendants wheeled her up the path, she lifted her head.

"What a lovely street, Curt," she said brightly. "And our house is a regular Alhambra."

"I wouldn't go that far, but it's better than the Hollywood dump."

"And those palms!" She gazed upward at a tall, slender trunk with fronds swaying against the blue sky. "I love them."

Joscelyn, waiting by the open door, had the feeling that this was not her sister, but an actress playing the role of Honora while a director hidden behind the privet hedge called out instructions through his megaphone. Lift head. Look around. Express pleasure. Smile, smile, smile.

The attendants lifted the gantry onto the front patio. "Joss!" Honora cried, lifting her arms.

"Hi." Joscelyn bent down to be hugged.

"How wonderful seeing you. I've missed you so much."

Joscelyn swallowed and her mouth trembled over her armored teeth. "Honora, I'm sorry about—"

"Yes," Honora interrupted. Her face was thin and very pale, which made her eyes seem enormous. "But let them bring me in and then we can catch up."

The attendants couldn't maneuver the stretcher in the narrow hall to the bedrooms, so Curt carried his wife and set her down on newly ironed sheets.

"It's like she's wadded in cotton," Curt said to Joscelyn a week later. "I can't get through to her."

"It's not your fault. You've been terrific."

He had been, too. He brought home small, humorous gifts every night, he told amusing incidents that happened at work, he held her hand when he thought Joscelyn couldn't see. Honora accepted gifts and affection with patently spurious smiles. Joscelyn, too, had tried, talking to her sister about the "old days" in England, the new days in Beverly Hills. Her efforts met with a blank wall of smiles.

Curt said, "She blames herself."

Joscelyn pulled a serious face to be worthy of this adult conversation. "I've never heard her cry. Does she?"

"Not around me. She's always so damn cheerful that *I* want to cry."

"Exactly," said Joscelyn, whose limited patience was wilting under the strain of being perpetually pleasant to the sister who used to mother her.

"Bear with her, Joss, give her time," he said, and a spasm contorted his mouth. "Christ, if only I could do something, anything, to snap her out of it."

Joscelyn glanced out her open bedroom window, which gave onto a small square back garden. Honora knelt before a flowerbed, carefully mounding fertilizer around each little plant. Tender upper lip held by lower teeth, a line drawn between her eyes, she had the dreamy expression of the real Honora.

A few weeks ago, Curt's present had been a flat of zinnias, frail, leafy shoots that looked as if they would wilt immediately in the southern California heat. That same evening Honora had taken the carton of tiny plants into the back garden, planting them a trowel's length apart. Watching, Joscelyn had remembered Honora in outsize trousers, monitor in charge of Edinthorpe's vegetable garden.

Since then Honora had spent most of her time outside, pruning and fertilizing and weeding. In the evening she would sit on the narrow, flagstone patio, as if guarding her flourishing little zinnias.

Honora pulled out a weed, dropping it into the paper grocery sack at her side.

Joscelyn sighed: *Who wants to garden on a hot day like this!*

She herself was dying to be at the beach. The southern California seaside was broad, golden of sand and blaring with records from the hamburger shacks. Curt had bought

Honora a blue Studebaker which looked the same at either end, and in less than fifteen minutes they could be dabbling their toes in the curls of salt foam.

Maybe I can talk her into going after lunch.

Eula Lee served a big spinach salad with bacon and chopped eggs. Honora, showered and wearing a skirt and blouse, ate very little. "What are you doing this afternoon, Joss?"

Joscelyn carefully broke apart her third sweet roll—Eula Lee coiled rich dough around Demerara sugar, pecans and raisins. "I was thinking about the beach."

Honora smiled, and said as if answering a question, "Curt brought me *The Disenchanted* yesterday and I thought I'd start it."

"There's no law against taking books to Santa Monica."

Honora tilted her head as if Joscelyn's words had finally registered. "The beach?"

"Yes, remember? Sand, big waves, cool breezes, etcetera."

"Some other time."

"When?"

Honora rolled her tumbler between her palms, and ice tinkled in the cold, creamed coffee. She smiled absently.

Joscelyn wanted to feel sympathetic, but instead she dropped into the black pit of rejection. "When?" she asked shrilly. "Tomorrow? Thursday week? December 25, 1999?"

"Soon." Honora put down her napkin. "See you later," she said. She moved in that uniquely graceful way from the dining ell, crossing the living room, echoing down the short bedroom hall. A door closed.

Joscelyn sat at the table, picking at her sweet roll as Eula Lee cleared off. After a brief clatter of dishes being stacked, silence descended: the house might have been deserted except for an occasional rustle as the cook turned the pages of the *Los Angeles Times*. It was like this every weekday unless Vi dropped over for lunch.

Into this stillness came silent questions. *Is it such a big deal to drive down to the beach with me? Doesn't she care whether I'm here or not? Will I always be the ugly tagalong who doesn't belong anywhere?*

With a sudden leap, Joscelyn was on her feet, rushing into the back garden.

With disbelieving horror yet unable to stop herself she

began yanking out the bushy little zinnias. The stalks oozed a sourish-smelling gum which stuck in the lines of her palms. It was well over ninety, and by the time every plant was uprooted she was sweating freely. She began a witches' dance, her skinny body circling as her fraying Keds stamped the plants into the Bermuda grass.

The larger bedroom opened onto the rear patio. Intent on wreaking total destruction, Joscelyn didn't hear the creak of the screen door.

Suddenly she was yanked from the trampled plants.

Shaking her, Honora cried, "What have you do-o-one?" The normally soft, low-pitched voice was distorted into a shrieking howl.

Startled, guilty, Joscelyn snapped back, "So the wax-work lady's come to life."

"My poor zinnias!" Honora slapped Joscelyn on the jaw so hard that her braces caught against her flesh. Joscelyn staggered backward, then struck out, raking her dirty, gum-encrusted nails down her sister's creamy cheek. Immediately four angry red lines showed.

"You murderer!" Honora screamed. "You've killed them!"

"Your precious plants! They're more important to you than me. Or Curt!"

Honora dragged her across the lawn to the circular clothesline, then rushed back to sink kneeling by the mound of crushed plants. Violent sobs shuddered below the silk blouse and tears streamed down the scratched oval face onto the mangled zinnias.

Joscelyn's heart began to bang madly. She had no idea how to handle her sister's maniacally out-of-proportion grief.

"My babies, my poor babies," Honora gasped. "I never should have left them. I'm careless, so careless. . . ."

Joscelyn crouched next to her sister, putting her arms around the slim, heaving shoulders. "Honora, please don't. I'm the one who dug them up."

"If I'd taken proper care . . . they'd be alive. . . ."

"No, no."

"Oh, my God. . . ."

"I've always been a monster, you know that, Honora."

"It's me, me . . . my fault." Honora clutched Joscelyn to her muddied blouse.

In the gaudy southern California midday sun, amid the sour odor of uprooted summer flowers, the two sisters knelt on recently mowed grass, clasped together and swaying as they wept for the unalterable, irrefutable truth of death.

That evening when Curt opened the front door, he raised an eyebrow at the scratches on his wife's cheek, the bruise mark on Joscelyn's. "Looks like combat zone."

Joscelyn, in terror lest he dispatch her back to San Francisco, said truculently, "Honora doesn't like my gardening."

"She's dreadful," Honora said with a rueful, genuine laugh. "You'll have to get me some more zinnias."

"I thought it was never going to happen again," Curt said.

Honora pressed his head against her breasts. "I told you two weeks ago Doctor Taupin had given the go-ahead."

"I was waiting for a more enthusiastic invitation."

"Like tonight?"

"Like tonight."

"Do you think Joss heard us?"

"The walls are thick," he said, rubbing, kissing her softness.

24

It was Gideon's habit to visit the nursery before they went out for the evening. On this chilly August night his ponderous tiptoeing on patent pumps was unnecessary.

Gid was awake.

The crib creaked, banging against the wall as the baby jounced back and forth on his hands and knees, snuffling in misery. When his father picked him up, though, his brown eyes widened and he gave his sweet, pink-gummed smile.

"It must be the tooth," said Crystal. A sensual feast in her black chiffon strapless and her cloud of Chanel N° 5 perfume, she remained in the doorway.

Being decades younger than Gideon, Crystal was able to view their child's minor ups and downs with equanimity. At six months, Gid was a solidly healthy specimen who stayed in the precise center of the normal parameters as outlined by his pediatrician. Crystal was filled with maternal affection for her son, and even proud of him, although Gid had inherited his father's burly shoulders and short legs, the small, round, brown eyes.

"Teething?" Gideon shook his head worriedly. "Not with this kind of congestion."

"Piers says it's a tooth, and Piers knows all there is about babies."

Piers, nanny to nobility for a quarter of a century, had been lured from a London registry by a regal salary. This was her every-other-weekend off.

"He's getting slobber all over you." Crystal whipped a clean, initialed diaper from the neatly folded stack to dab at her husband's stiffly starched shirtfront.

"Maybe he's picked up the flu," Gideon said worriedly.

"Gid?" She wiped her son's face and nose. "He's never even had a cold."

"I don't like leaving him."

"Gideon, do you have any idea of how difficult it was to get this invitation?" Crystal asked, smiling prettily. Thomas Wei, a wealthy Chinese-American, was throwing a reception at his San Rafael home to honor a committee from Taiwan, as the Chinese called Formosa. The group was in the United States to select a company to plan and oversee the building of a vast seawall that would ward off the monsoon tidal waves, a never before attempted engineering feat.

To receive an embossed invitation and thus enable Gideon to meet the committee on an informal basis, Crystal had worked her tail off.

Since her marriage, she had joined in a business alliance with her husband, a partnership that she found exciting, deeply satisfying and a beneficial balance to the scales of her horrendous nights. Major construction was emerging from its cyclical slump, and her exquisitely planned entertainments were helping Talbott's win contracts. Gideon, however, nursed uncertainties about his wife's activities: the loans of their new limousine, the lavish weekends at their Monterey house on the golf course, went against his sternly moral grain, even though, as Crystal often pointed out, she was merely following common practice.

Continuing to stroke the back of his son's yellow sleepers, he frowned, his mouth pulling into heavy, downward lines. "You know I don't like pushing my way into people's homes."

"Oh, Gideon! What's so wrong with being a bit friendly?"

"Talbott's has never needed to smear or do favors." His tone was harsh.

"We're going to a party for the Taiwan committee, not buying them each a half dozen singsong girls." She drew a breath. "Gideon, I don't have to remind you that Bechtel and Fluor are offering a free preliminary study. And so is McNee-Ivory. How will you feel if Taiwan awards a contract this size to *them?*"

Curt's successful highway project in Lalarhein had brought McNee several extremely large Mideast jobs: after he was with the company a little over half a year, the elderly George McNee had made him a partner. Gideon was particularly embittered because before their relationship had altered so disastrously he had been considering raising Curt to the same position.

After a moment, Gideon gently laid his son back in his custom-upholstered crib, a gesture of acquiescence. Clear mucus bubbled at Gid's nostrils, and he flailed fat arms and legs, emitting snorting, unhappy wails.

Gideon hastily picked up the baby. "It's all right, Gid, Daddy's here," he soothed.

Crystal squared her shoulders. Her breasts pulled up from her low-cut gown and the dim nursery nightlights danced on the diamonds at her throat. "Gideon, dear," she cooed, "we can't be late. These are Chinamen, they *do* take offense easily, they *never* forgive a loss of face."

Gid sneezed.

Gideon tenderly wiped the baby's nose, then looked up. His jaw was set. "Go ahead without me," he said. When Gideon spoke in this preemptory tone it meant that his mind was closed. He would listen to no argument or pleas.

Settling her white fox stole over her shoulders, Crystal

marched from the nursery and down the stairs to the porte cochere, where the new black Cadillac waited.

As she proceeded through the large, crowded hall with its baroque, curving staircase and into the two-story drawing room, gratifying zephyrs of admiration followed in her wake. Though many of the Chinese-American women were exquisite in their opulent jewelry and their latest Paris creations, Crystal outshone them all with the natural rose of her cheeks, the bright glint of her upswept hair, her firm, magnificent young bosom rising from the swathe of black chiffon. Her host escorted her to the guests of honor. The committee's leader, a tall Manchurian with prominent gold front teeth, must have made some sort of signal. With repetitive bows, his two underlings excused themselves, backing away. Crystal gestured animatedly while she conversed about the real China, as she called Taiwan.

"You are a most knowing lady," said the official in his high-pitched English. "And delightfully beautiful, as befits this house."

Privately, Crystal thought this gabled and towered heap tacky in the extreme. On every wall hung folding screens, the kind of overly gilded horrors you saw in Chinatown store windows: the low, carved Oriental tables were dwarfed by mammoth, antiquated red brocade upholstery. But she smiled her gratitude for the compliment. "Our place can't hold a candle to this, but we do have a rather nice view of the Bay." She tilted her head. "Do you suppose that I could coax you and your friends to see it? My husband was so disappointed he was ill tonight." She had transferred the ailment from Gid to his father. "This dreadful twenty-four-hour flu—San Francisco's having an epidemic."

"We will be delighted to accept," the Chinese said somberly. "But I cannot express my sorriness at Mr. Talbott's unfortunate indisposition. I was so looking forward to have discuss our project congruently with him *and* Mr. Ivory."

"Mr. Ivory?" Crystal's voice rose in shocked surprise.

"Mr. Curt Ivory."

"*Curt* here?"

"Ahh, yes. You did not know that he flies up from Los Angeles for the evening? You have not yet see your brother-in-law?"

"How clever of you to know the relationship," she said in a strangled tone. "Hardly anyone does."

"But you must not be so amazed, Mrs. Talbott," he replied. "This is my obligation, to know about your fine American engineers."

Crystal heard a snap and simultaneously a sharp jolt shot through her arm. Glancing down, she saw that she had broken the stem of her empty champagne goblet. With a little cry, she dropped the two pieces, jumping back as cut glass shattered on the hardwood floor. Nearby guests crowded around to ascertain that Mrs. Talbott's delicate palm was undamaged while servants neatly swept up. In the midst of the hubbub, Crystal lowered her lashes, surreptitiously glancing around. At the far end of the vista of rooms, amid a group of patent-leather glossy heads, she glimpsed a thick mane of dark blond hair.

Her voice high, she assured everyone that no blood had been drawn and she was absolutely all right.

A full glass was placed in her benumbed fingers. She downed it in two gulps.

"Now, where were we?" she asked the committee chief.

"Ahh, yes. I did so want a discussion of these two experts on how to handle the method of sinking the pylons."

"You're talking to a complete idiot about engineering." *Smile,* she told herself. "But hydraulics is my husband's forte."

"So I understand. Already we have decided against the Bechtel and Fluor concepts. But we are most impressed with McNee-Ivory's, and with Talbott's. Thus there is no problem."

"Problem?"

"One family." The gold teeth shone. "Whoever builds our seawall, McNee-Ivory or Talbott's, the other will be glad—or maybe there will be a joint venture."

Crystal again managed a pretty dimple. Setting her empty glass on a passing tray, she reached for a fresh one.

Even at the most raucous cocktail parties, she nursed a single drink. Thus it seemed surprising that the swift consumption of Taittinger did not affect her. She wasn't even slightly tiddled. If she were, would she be able to regale her enchanted audience of one with her recently boned-up-on knowledge of Sino-American politics? From the corner of her eye she again glimpsed Curt, this time with the lesser

two of the delegation. She took another glass—she had difficulty remembering whether it was her fourth or fifth—
launching into accolades for General Chiang Kai-Shek,
whom she knowledgeably called the Gismo. The committee chief responded with his golden smile.

If she were drunk, wouldn't she be verbose, loud, angry,
as her father was when in his cups? Wouldn't her vision
blur? Yes, drunk, she would never see details with this pre-
ternatural clarity. Surrounding conversations drifted in and
out, like a radio being turned on and off, the men talking of
real estate values, the women of servants and children, just
like at a regular Caucasian gathering.

And then all at once Mr. and Mrs. Wei, the roly-poly
host and hostess, were bowing and nodding, inviting their
most honored guest to lead the gathering to the buffet.

Her conquest was borne away. Crystal, feeling drained
by the exertion of her vivacity, decided not to try the thou-
sand-year eggs or shark's fins or whatever other strange
food was being served. As the two-story room cleared, she
glanced toward the rear bay window. Standing alone, Curt
lounged against the arch with that air of relaxed energy
most women seemed to find devastating. Maybe he *had*
married poor Honora, as everyone said, but Crystal bet he
made her life a misery with his chasing.

She inhaled deeply and ran her tongue over her lips.
Pushing her way around two large groups which were me-
andering toward the dining room, she went toward him.

"If it isn't the belle of the ball," he drawled, raising his
highball in a mocking way.

His sardonic grin, or so Imogene said, was sexier than
straight, unadulterated musk, but Crystal considered it
nastily arrogant. His topaz eyes were bloodshot. *He's soz-
zled*, she thought in surprise, and was delighted afresh with
her own sobriety. "Why don't you stay where you belong?"
she demanded.

"The Weis mailed me an invitation." He finished his
drink. "And where's your esteemed husband?"

"You have no right to be in San Francisco," she said
belligerently.

"Oh? Is there a warrant out for my arrest?"

"After what you did to Honora—"

"You don't say her name," he interrupted in a low growl.

"She's my sister." Crystal sounded defiant.

"That," he said, setting down his glass, "is impossible to believe."

"The way you treated her, you deserve to be shot!"

Two women with glossy black chignons turned to look at them.

"Quit shrilling like a two-bit hooker who's lost a trick," Curt hissed.

She was too angry to be intimidated. "Hooker?" Her voice rose yet higher. "Is that what you think of my sister?"

Jerking open a French door, Curt gripped her arm and yanked her outside. The entire first story was surrounded by a pillared porch, and as she stepped onto the painted sequoia planks, she was aware of the chill air, aware that her bare flesh was rising in goosebumps, a discomfort that refreshed her. The summer night was clear, with a full, brilliantly white moon. She felt immortal, clean and strong. She did not need to evade his rough grasp. She was in control, and therefore it was all right to allow him to propel her down the steps to where thick, rattling shrubbery cast impenetrable shadows.

He released her arm and she stared at the man who had reduced her sister to a pathetic, pleading, unwed mother. "You're an animal," she panted. "I can't bear to think of you with poor Honora—"

"You conniving cunt, I told you not to say my wife's name!"

"You've stolen both my sisters." With a stab of sadness she thought of dark-eyed, tender Honora, beloved companion of her girlhood, and of skinny, mean-mouthed little Joscelyn, who suddenly seemed so dear. "My sisters are all that ever meant anything to me," she said. Choking back a sob, she accepted that this unplanned remark was her life's deepest truth: Langley, a charming, boozy loser, had always stood at the periphery of her existence; her elderly, stubborn husband was as inconsequential to her as that dull, sweet infant, her son. Males, all of them. Another species to be wheedled and coaxed and tamed. *My sisters,* she thought, *they're the meaningful part, the mainstay of my life.* Tears of unendurable, irreconcilable loss prickled behind her lashes.

Then, swiftly, her grief converted itself into rage. Rage at Curt, rage at his gender. *Men,* she thought with an all-encompassing blaze of hatred. *Men, with their strong, grasping*

*hands and powerful wrists, men with their ridiculous pride in
that bludgeoning dagger of flesh.*

With a sudden motion she raised her right hand, hitting
below Curt's cheekbone with her full strength. At the loud
report of her hand exhilaration charged through her, and a
slap wasn't enough. The blood drumming deafeningly
against her ears, she used her large, emerald-cut engagement stone as a weapon, catching him close to his left eye,
scratching viciously.

"Bitch!" He grabbed for both her wrists.

There was a long moment when neither moved. By the
reeling, shadowy moonlight she could see that her diamond
had caught his flesh and a droplet of dark blood was oozing
down his high-boned cheek. An incandescent heat flooded
through her and she struggled to mark him again. His
manacling grip tightened. She bared her teeth, hurling herself forward to bite his jaw. He stepped back, and she
lunged again, her stiletto heels catching in the wet grass as
she jerked and swiveled in an attempt to consummate her
animus.

Abruptly he released her wrists. She fell toward him,
flinging her arms around him, a savage wrestler's hold to
crush and annihilate.

In the same enveloping hatred, she reached down for the
fly of his satin-striped trousers.

A convulsive shudder passed through him. Then, bi-
zarrely, unfathomably, they were meshed together, their
locked bodies slowly lowering to the wet, stubby grass in a
gladiatorial embrace. She drew his zipper down sharply, he
shoved up her tulle skirts, exposing white thighs striated by
taut black strips of garter. She was oblivious to the silk cutting into her flesh as he tore at her black panties. Inhaling
the liquor on his breath, the odors of his sweat, she flung
her legs around him.

As he thrust into her she whinnied in triumph.

And then her cherished control left her, and she shook
with violent gasps that rose from the wellspring of her
being.

When awareness returned it was with a buzzing sensation of her extremities—fingers, toes, ears. He was sprawled
with his full weight pressing her into the wet lawn.

Abruptly he pulled away from her and rose to his feet.
Shifting from the painful metal that she recognized as a

sprinkler head that was digging into the small of her back, she stared up at him, a titan swaying over her. The light wavering across his scratched face showed a peculiarly boyish expression of shame.

On the top step he halted to adjust his dinner clothes. Without a glance back at her, he followed the porch around curtained windows, the sound of his footsteps fading.

Dizzily rising to her feet, Crystal suddenly recognized how drunk she was. *Just like Daddy,* she thought. *Uggh.* Bending awkwardly, she shook her full breasts into the wired cups of her Merry Widow, adjusting her strapless bodice, flailing moisture and grass from the diaphanous black folds of her skirt. She was wet through, shivering with the cold. Yet her nerves and muscles felt relaxed, a bone-deep calm. From a distant vantage point above her vertigo and nausea, she wondered whether the shuddering engulfment that she had just experienced was an orgasm.

Holding on to the wood balustrade, she negotiated the steps, halting at the French door. A few groups still clustered in the vast, ugly living room, and it came to her hazily that despite her efforts she probably was exceedingly disheveled. She stumbled along the porch in the same direction as Curt.

Rapping at a side door, she gripped the jamb, waiting. An elderly Chinese maid in a black silk uniform opened up; her wrinkled face showed surprise. Crystal pitched her voice commandingly. "I'm Mrs. Talbott. Bring me my white fox stole, and inform my chauffeur I'm ready to leave."

Waiting for the Cadillac on the gravel driveway, she thought of Curt Ivory's expression as he had stood above her. Young, vulnerable, and hopelessly ashamed.

THREE

1964

Joscelyn

25

A few minutes before seven on a fine morning in March of 1964, Joscelyn pushed open the sliding glass door of her bedroom, stepping onto the terrace, startling a nearby covey of quail. The plump, crested birds rustled heavily from the silver-wet lawn, flying low above the irregular carpets of spring flowers that climbed the canyon wall.

The gardens, Honora's delight and obsession, a loving mixture of landscape styles, were at their best in the dawn stillness. Joscelyn, though, was not paying homage to the beauties of nature, but turning her left hand this way and that so the sun glanced off the facets of Malcolm Peck's tiny round diamond. A softly amorous smile transformed her discreetly madeup, clever face.

It would require the meticulous scrutiny of an archeologist to uncover traces of the deplorably plain child in the woman Joscelyn had become. Those years of orthodontic misery had done the trick of correcting her overbite. Her thick glasses were gone, replaced by contacts that enhanced the clear, pale Cambridge blue of her eyes. The fineness of her hair was an asset for a pixie cut. At just over five nine, she had the Sylvander fine-boned slenderness.

The ugly duckling had turned into a reasonable facsimile of a swan.

Joscelyn's self-identification, however, remained tethered to that homely little girl. No matter how skillfully she fixed herself up, her mirror ultimately reflected a gangly, humiliatingly flat-chested woman. She grudged herself one good feature. Her legs. Long and nicely curved, they were well displayed by her Courrèges minidress.

The forces that had shaped Joscelyn—being motherless and virtually fatherless for her early years, the unsupervised custody of a series of aged, carpingly tyrannical nannies, having two lovely older sisters—had turned her into the harshest of self-critics. In order to feel worthy of the air she breathed, Joscelyn Sylvander must be the best. At Berkeley, one of only twelve female engineering students, she had ferociously honed her keen mind, making Phi Beta Kappa in her junior year, graduating Summa Cum Laude. At Ivory she had arrived early and lugged home a brief-caseful of work: within a year, without the Big Boss lifting a finger, she was promoted to project engineer.

Her career gave her deep satisfaction.

She relished the well-organized, mathematical thinking imposed by engineering. She took pleasure in facing con-crete problems that couldn't be altered by argument—as opposed to the decisions of, say, a psychologist or a lawyer. She enjoyed transferring thought to fact. Her work so im-mersed her that at the conclusion of each project she was overcome by a depression that was almost like a premoni-tion of death. Though she took pride in being successful in a man's world, during her worst moments she would ask herself whether anyone with her drive and discipline could be truly feminine.

Unconsciously her left thumb rubbed her engagement ring, and she smiled. *You're my woman,* Malcolm had said against her ear when he handed her the domed velvet box.

The Ivorys owned a Bel Air canyon whose sides were as steep as those of a bathtub. In the rich, narrow valley nes-tled the house—or rather, a series of structures: Joscelyn's cottage, the servants' quarters, the guesthouse and the seven-car garage were connected to the main building by this winding, pergola-covered walkway. The rambling ar-chitecture with its exposed beams and honey-colored stone had the cozy charm of a miniature Cotswold village. Curt had done the design himself, a complement to the country gardens that Honora had begun planting in 1953, the same year that he had floated an enormous loan to buy out the ailing, septuagenarian George McNee. (Joscelyn admir-ingly saw Curt's acquisition of thirty overpriced Bel Air acres at such a time as illumination of both his openhand-edness and his boundless, optimistic self-confidence.)

She pushed open the glass door of the breakfast room. Her brother-in-law was eating scrambled eggs and bacon at the far end of the rough-hewn Welsh table. The years had served Curt well. A few strands of distinguished white showed in his dark blond hair, which was thick as ever. The grooves in his tanned forehead and smile lines fanning out from his unusual topaz eyes gave him the look of mature strength that is a prerequisite for true power.

Glancing up from the *Los Angeles Times,* he nodded. He disliked early morning conversation, so Joscelyn slipped quietly into her chair, pouring herself coffee.

She was finishing her second cup when Curt, without comment, handed her the financial section.

Glancing down the columns, she saw what he intended her to read: TALBOTT'S FIRST AMERICAN COMPANY TO CONSTRUCT HIGHWAY IN AFGHANISTAN.

"What about the road we built last year out of Kabul?" she asked sourly. "That Crystal!"

Since the foggy evening she had slipped out of the Clay Street mansion's side door, she had seen neither Crystal nor Gideon; she had never laid eyes on their two little boys.

So out of touch were the Talbott and the Ivory ménages that they might have existed in different galaxies, with Langley as the sole space traveler. On his frequent visits to the States, the paterfamilias stayed both in San Francisco and Los Angeles, and on the first of every month he received from the London offices of each of his warring sons-in-law substantial sums that enabled him to reside with an excellent cellar in a large Sloane Square flat, and also to subsidize the delightfully early Victorian offices of Sylvander Press. Sylvander Press had thus far brought out five slender books of avant garde poetry and fiction, losing money on each, but when Langley clinked glasses with the flower of British publishing he was able to drop with casual modesty, "My house did the first Rupert Jacks, y'know." Also he could tell himself that those monthly checks he deposited in his account were sound business investments for his sons-in-law.

Joscelyn scanned the long column about Talbott's other new projects. "She really spews out the hype, doesn't she?"

Curt's eloquent lift of shoulders was as far as he would go in discussing anything connected to his estranged benefactor. He dropped his napkin on the polished old wood. "Tonight's the planning powwow, isn't it?"

Malcolm was coming to dinner so the four of them could discuss wedding plans.

"Tonight's the night," Joscelyn agreed happily.

Curt let himself out the glass door through which she had entered, cutting across an allee of lawn, his shoes leaving dark prints on the dewy grass.

Honora, wearing boots, jeans and a bulky old sweater, emerged from a coppice of wisteria trees. Curt held out his arms and she dropped her trowel, running to snuggle against him. Joscelyn felt a painful catch, reminiscent of the time she'd taken a train across the top of the Andes and her lungs had strained for oxygen in the cold, thin air. She touched her diamond talisman again and her breathing eased.

Malcolm had been invited for seven, and the case clock in the hall was chiming the hour as he buzzed from the wrought-iron electric gates that protected the mouth of the canyon a third of a mile away. Joscelyn buzzed back and went outside to meet him. As Malcolm got out of his gray Volkswagen, she was engulfed by that familiar sense of disbelief. How was it possible that Joscelyn Sylvander had snagged a man this spectacular?

Malcolm's boyish beauty could easily have made him a bit cheap, like a male model, but the gods had seen fit to mitigate his good looks with a few minor aberrations. His dark hair was untamable, rumpling forward to obscure the impeccable widow's peak; his mouth, which was well chiseled and full without being petulant, had a faint white scar bisecting the lower lip, and on the bridge of his straight, masculine nose was a bump, as if a tiny bone had been broken during football scrimmage. The eyes were a pure gray darkened by the porch of his brow. (The deep set of his eyes made Joscelyn see a resemblance between Malcolm and Curt that was invisible to everybody else.) Her betrothed was a fraction over six feet: his wide shoulders, narrow waist and narrower hips made him seem taller.

When not worrying that Malcolm would desert her, Joscelyn fretted about the adverse effects of their age difference. At twenty-four she was two years older—well, actually one year and eleven months.

Last spring, before his graduation from Caltech, Malcolm had been recruited by Ivory, and had become one of the hundreds of beginning engineers swarming through the Spring Street office where she worked. (Ivory, outgrowing its original McNee headquarters, had spread out into various downtown office buildings.) They hadn't met until the fall. On the morning of November 22, when the news first came from Dallas, the corridors had been filled with bewildered, lost-looking people: Joscelyn and Malcolm had comforted one another for the wounding, then the death, of President Kennedy.

Malcolm was smiling as he came up the steps to her. The carriage lamp next to the front door shone on their embrace. Incredibly, he was as deeply in love as she, and far more open about showing it. He called her office several times a day, he brought sandwiches to her cubicle at lunchtime, he spent most evenings with her, and every weekend.

"My geisha, waiting outside," he said, kissing her lingeringly.

Dizzied, she murmured, "Don't get too accustomed to the good treatment, buster. It'll never last."

He nuzzled her cheek. "About tonight, okay if we tell them we want the wedding small and quick?"

"Exactly what I have in mind."

"And soon." He hugged her fiercely. "Christ, am I ready."

Malcolm had an old-fashioned streak. *Joscelyn, hon, I've always dreamed of having a virgin on my wedding night.* And, at the advanced age of twenty-four and a half, she was amazingly that, still a virgin. Not because of moral compunctions or anxiety about unwanted pregnancy, but because neither of her serious boyfriends—soft-voiced Steve Kayloch at Berkeley and Marty Lausch, an electrical engineer at Hughes—had been ready for marriage, and to hop into bed with an uncommitted partner would be one more example of her inferiority to her sisters.

She bit his earlobe gently, murmuring, "How soon is soon?"

"However long it takes to get a license and blood tests."

The dinner table conversation covered everything but the wedding, slipping easily from chances of Ivory doing projects in new third world countries like Zambia and Tanzania to the U.S. involvement in Vietnam to Martin Luther King and the sit-ins in the south, to *Herzog*, which Honora was reading, to who would win the Oscars.

When Malcolm first had started dating Joscelyn he had come to the house wearing his Ivory working uniform, one of two narrow, dark suits with a white, short-sleeved shirt and black knitted tie, but now, like Curt, he had changed to jeans and a checked cotton shirt worn under a sweater. Then, he had said very little, his gray eyes fixed on each as they spoke, giving Honora and Curt's most trivial remarks his devout attention. Now, however, he appeared supremely at ease at the round dining table, laughing, interrupting.

After coffee they adjourned to the family room. Eucalyptus logs snapped and crackled in the enormous fireplace, giving off aromatic odors, and the two couples paired off in the long, chintz-covered flanking couches.

Curt lit a cigarette. "Let's get down to business," he said.

"Yes," Honora said. Her eyes had lost that hint of melancholy and were glowing with excitement. "Have you set a date?"

Malcolm and Joscelyn shook their heads, and Joscelyn started to say that it would be sometime this month, but Honora was raising a cautioning finger.

"One sec," she said. Miniskirt whirling around her slender thighs, she ran to the rolltop pigeonhole desk to fish out a calendar that advertised Westwood Nursery. "How does the last Saturday in May sound?"

"The end of May?" Joscelyn cried.

"Hey, hey, take it easy," Malcolm said.

"But that's nearly three months off!"

"Honest, gang," Malcolm said, grinning. "There is abso-lutely no reason for the big rush."

A flush rose from the bright scarf around Joscelyn's throat.

Honora's creamy skin was pink, too. "I didn't mean to take over," she murmured. "But a wedding does take time, and Curt and I would like to give you a proper send-off."

"Thanks, guys, but no thanks." Joscelyn was still blushing. "All we have in mind is a judge, you two—and Daddy, of course, if he can make it over in time."

Honora murmured, "What about your side, Malcolm?" She knew from Joscelyn that the Pecks had been killed in an automobile accident on the Hollywood Freeway two years ago: Mr. Peck, an executive with Texaco, and Mrs. Peck, a Junior Leaguer, had belonged to Annandale Golf Club; she wore mink, his clothes were tailored at Eddie Harth's, they traveled, they entertained, they had no insurance. Once the debts were paid, including the third mortgage on the large Los Feliz house, their combined estates were scarcely enough to buy burial plots at Forest Lawn. Malcolm had financed his senior year at Caltech by parking cars at a restaurant on Lake Street. "Is there any family?"

"No—well, unless you count cousins in Providence, a dreary bunch I met once when I was ten."

Honora's head tilted sympathetically.

"Not that we don't appreciate the offer," Joscelyn said. "But we've made up our minds."

Malcolm sat back in the couch, his eyes wistful. "Joscelyn, I know this sounds nuts for a guy, but I've always had a yen for the works. Church, flowers, bridesmaids, an enormous cake." He jerked his hand upward, indicating numerous tiers.

His turnabout—his betrayal—hit Joscelyn so hard that her mouth parched and the color drained from her face.

"I'd like my buddies to be there," Malcolm said, adding softly, "I'd like to see you coming down the aisle in a white dress."

"There's a secret desire that never got on the drawing board," she said in a thin voice.

"I'm hardly the one to bring up a huge amount of work," he said quietly. "Not to mention expense."

"Malcolm, quit being an ass," Curt said. "We offered, we meant it."

"We'd really love to." Honora leaned forward. "Our own wedding was small."

"So small," Curt said brusquely, "that it wasn't even recorded. We had to do it over."

Honora consulted her calendar again. "May fifteenth's a Saturday. How does that sound?"

"Great," Malcolm said, looking at Joscelyn. "Okay, hon?"

She touched her diamond. After a long silence she said in a flat tone, "May fifteenth it is, then."

"That's my lady," he said, reaching for her hand, holding it on the chintz as the four of them planned the wedding.

26

"I guess it's true, what they say about men being more sentimental," Joscelyn said, her breath pluming in the chill night air.

Malcolm thrust his hands into his pockets, striding more swiftly uphill.

It was an hour or so later, and at her suggestion they were heading for Honora's new belvedere, which overlooked the city, following the path that zigzagged up the steep slope through the masses of imported bulbs. A hidden spot turned a cluster of tulips, daffodil, iris, into a phosphorescent, voluptuous spring display.

She was matching his strides. "Why didn't you speak up before? Why all the talk about small and quick?"

"I already spelled it out," he said, his voice level. "It's not up to me to toss around other people's money. Besides, anyone could see Honora was dying to do it."

Malcolm was forever ingratiating himself. His hunger for approving affection extended far beyond the Big Boss and the Big Boss's wife. He set out to win every stranger he came in contact with—the supermarket checker, the ticket taker at the movies—and was crushed when he couldn't elicit a heartfelt smile. He put himself out, he flattered, he fitted in. Joscelyn, woefully inadequate when it came to social relationships, adoring him, did not see how inexhaustibly he worked at being liked, only that he *was* liked.

"And what about me? I'm only the bride."

"I guess you feel we shouldn't enjoy any of this." The gigantic shadow of his encircling gesture swept across the trunk of a magnificently pruned sycamore. "Isn't that how your mind works? Forget everything pleasurable and grab for economy?"

Beginning engineers weren't exactly rolling in money,

so she would suggest eating either here or at a Mexican dive before taking in a second-run movie. Joscelyn's hurt was strangling her, and she spoke more acidly than she intended. "Let me see if I've got this straight. The reason you're marrying me is to have a really big show"—she mimicked Ed Sullivan—"in the gardens of the house of Ivory."

"If I were you, Joscelyn, I'd shut up," he snapped. "You've never seen me lose my temper."

"I'm petrified," she said. She was. And fear sharpened her tongue yet more. "Let me tell you, it was really cute down there, you blithering on about what a big deal it is for you to have a real brother and a real sister, how grateful you are to be part of a family. Sure. A real family that happens to be headed by the sole owner of a multinational corporation. You don't honestly believe they were taken in, do you? They're not morons."

"What a cunt you are!"

"If I'm so miserable, why're we engaged, huhh?" Her heart was pounding with terror, but she could not keep quiet. "Fess up. You're marrying this house, these gardens, the boss's sister-in-law."

A gust of cold wind shifted the black shadow that hid his face: for an instant she saw the sudden gleam of sweat on his forehead, the deep-set rage in his eyes.

Both his hands clenched into fists.

Then his right arm shot out.

His blow sank into her stomach. Exhaling in a breathy gasp, she staggered backward from the path into the clumps of iris in a recently cultivated bed. Arms flailing, she somehow managed to stay on her feet.

Then the full force of pain struck her. Bending almost double, she clutched protectively at the heavy, shooting agony below her midriff. Spontaneous tears welled, scalding hot in the night chill.

In movies—Joscelyn had not voluntarily read a novel since she was ten—when a man, even the blackest-hearted of heavies, hit a woman he slapped her with the flat of his palm. Malcolm's blow had been delivered as if she were a mortal, masculine enemy. *Why didn't I shut up? I should've accepted that Joscelyn Sylvander gets the crumbs. Now he hates me. He's so much younger. It's over.*

Still hunched, she tottered back onto the path in the direction of the house, a wounded animal lurching toward the safety of its den.

"Oh, Jesus, hon, Jesus God." Malcolm was in front of her, squatting to peer up into her face, in an attitude of supplication.

Snuffling back her tears, she muttered, "Why didn't you warn me you were a Golden Gloves champ?"

"Did I hurt you bad, hon?" Love and terror shook his voice.

With a repressed grunt she stood erect. "I'll live. But you're the winner by unanimous decision."

He put his arms around her and she leaned into the warmth of his body, rubbing her tears dry on the shoulder of the navy cashmere pullover she'd given him for Christmas.

"Christ, I could kill myself," he said.

"It takes two to tango."

"We're still on then?" he said against her ear.

"Need you ask? I was being a total bitch."

They clung together for a minute, his body heat soothing her raw, aching viscera.

"Better get you back to civilization," he said.

Her first tentative step tore at stomach and pelvic muscles she hadn't known existed. From this point the house was nearly a quarter of a mile down the zigzag path.

"Give me a couple of minutes," she said.

Wincing, she sank on the nearby sequoia log that had been carved to form a bench. The smooth dampness of the wood chilled her through her sheer pantyhose. No lights were placed nearby and the slight, silver trunks of birches showed dimly.

Malcolm's arm tightened around her shoulder. "The thing is," he said in a low voice, "Dad sometimes batted me and Mother around."

Surprised, she turned to him. In this darkness it was impossible to see more than his posture of dejection.

Malcolm always spoke with fond regret of his late mother, but he clearly had idolized his father—and still did. Mr. Peck had taught him to play golf, to sail, to skim on one water ski after a gunning Chris-Craft, to open car doors for frail females. Mr. Peck's record of three homers at the Cub Scouts' father-son picnic had never been broken, a statistic that Malcolm repeated with relish. As a lieutenant

JG, Mr. Peck had been commended for outstanding heroism at the Battle of Midway, and above Malcolm's daybed hung a shadow box of his father's medals centered by the Navy Cross dangling from its blue and white ribbon.

"I can understand swatting a kid, but he hit your *mother?*"

"Not often. Hon, it wasn't his fault."

"Whose was it, then?"

"He had it rough at work. Thatcherson, his superior, was a prissy asshole clerk who'd taken advantage of the war to get a vice presidency. Dad was everything he wasn't, and it goes without saying he kept him down because he was terrified Dad would get *his* job."

Joscelyn managed to keep a look of dopey understanding on her face, but a sinking logic told her that among Mr. Peck's gifts had been a fertile inventiveness when it came to excuses.

"You're saying that when things went sour at the office, your father kicked ass at home?"

"That makes it sound rotten, and it wasn't."

"I didn't mean to knock him, just put it in perspective." She touched the scar at his lip. "Did he do this?"

Malcolm shrugged.

She kissed the tiny ridge. "How?"

"I can't remember," he said. "Not eating my eggs. Dad was all shook because his department was being cut in half."

"Were there stitches?"

"Eight."

Oh, God. "Malcolm, you went to a doctor—"

"The Georgia Street Receiving Hospital."

"Didn't anyone ask how it happened?"

"I said I fell over a sprinkler."

"And this?" Her finger traced the bump on his nose.

"Another guy got Dad's promotion—he'd really worked his tail off, and Thatcherson passed him over. I'd left my two-wheeler in the driveway—it was new, I'd just gotten it for my sixth birthday. When the bandages were off, he took me on my first camping weekend. It was the best time of my life."

"Did he drink?" If Langley had ever laid a finger on her and her sisters, she couldn't remember it, but hectoring and tirades had flown when he was heavily under the influence.

"You've got Dad all wrong, hon. He was a great guy with

a short fuse, that's all. Mother and I knew when things were rough at the office we shouldn't give him any reason to get steamed up."

"But you were only six."

"I don't have to defend him." Malcolm's voice became hard. "He was a fabulous man. Brave, compassionate, with a terrific sense of humor. Mother worshiped him, his friends would do anything for him. I'm sorry I mentioned that crap. Now you've got a distorted picture. Ninety-nine percent of the time Dad was the best there is."

A wonderful father who breaks his six-year-old's nose for not putting away his bicycle, she thought, shivering. The pain in her abdomen had dulled, becoming like a bad, first-day menstrual cramp. "Let's go back," she said.

"You're okay?"

"Good as new," she said, hiding her wince as she stood.

Arms around each other's waists, they walked slowly down toward the lights of the house. Malcolm's mumbled confession had exacerbated Joscelyn's love for him, and she refused to hurt him with further questions, yet she couldn't entirely banish her curiosity about Mrs. Peck—what punishments had been inflicted on her and how had she maintained her adoration during her husband's lapses into despairing rage?

"Joscelyn, look, hitting you like that—"

"It's forgotten," she said firmly.

"You're the one clean, perfect thing in my life. And I want to keep us perfect."

"We *are* perfect," she said, hugging his narrow waist tighter.

Curt and Honora were in the family room, he at the desk going over some preliminary freeway plans, she stretched on the couch with *Herzog* open on her chest.

"Joss didn't want a wedding, did she?" she said.

Curt looked up. "You know our Joscelyn. Above the mundane feminine pleasures."

"I didn't mean to push her into anything."

"She'll get into the swing, if only to please Malcolm."

"It was dear of him, wasn't it, wanting to see her in a white dress?"

"He's really gone on her."

"And she's crazy for him. Curt, does this sound awful? At first I was a bit put off by his good looks."

"As soon as he's in the family, I'll arrange for Quasimodo lessons," Curt said, screwing the top on his pen.

"Did you feel that way?"

"Yeah, a bit. But I figured that was the attraction for Joss. As a kid, she wouldn't have won any prizes."

Honora stared into the fire, her fingers curling upward as if to catch an idea. "The thing is," she said slowly, "she's always been her own person."

"To say the least," Curt chuckled. "And why not? She's got one of the few topflight minds around."

"Do you think Malcolm can handle that?"

"He seems to."

"But what about when they're married, and she keeps being promoted? You've always said she has a big career ahead of her."

"They'll sort it out." Curt was folding his papers into his scuffed maroon Cartier briefcase with the solid gold corners. "Marriage is a gamble."

She smiled. "You sound like you're sorry."

"I'm in despair," he said, pulling her to her feet. His thumb caressed the blue pulse at her narrow wrist.

Distracted from her reservations whether Malcolm, likable and gorgeous but definitely not a first-rate mind, could take Joscelyn's inevitable success, she leaned closer to her husband.

Theirs was the only bedroom in the main part of the house and they were both smiling as they crossed the hall to the big room with the fireplace and beams.

27

Joscelyn and Malcolm were married in St. Alban's, the rustic, stone church opposite UCLA. The bride came down the aisle on her father's arm, looking summery and unusually feminine in a shortsleeved white organza gown.

Most of the dearly beloved gathered here were tied, however tenuously, to Ivory—clients, prospective clients, politicos, board members of the companies with whom Ivory formed consortiums, important men wearing dark, single-breasted suits and expressions of dignified bonhomie. And of the ornamental sprinkle of younger couples, many of the masculine side worked for Ivory, co-workers and comrades of Malcolm and Joscelyn. There were, of course, some old friends. Fuad had flown in from Lalarhein, Vi was there with her new husband, a San Diego building contractor, her red bouffant hairdo rising proudly above her mink stole, the only fur in the church.

Honora, standing in the front pew and holding Curt's hand, thought it should be her husband rather than Langley giving the bride away. After all, who had calmed Joss's juvenile fears and soothed her adolescent crises; vetted her first pimply boyfriends and jokingly steered her away from the rotten eggs? Who had paid her bills and signed the checks for her college expenses; who had been on hand to hug her at her triumphs?

As the bride passed, she gave them a mistily grateful, very un-Joscelyn smile, and all at once Honora thought: *If only Crystal were here.* At not one of the Sylvander girls' weddings had both other sisters been there to embrace and attend the bride.

The long line of cars wound the three miles to the house, where guests were served champagne in the gardens. Great pots of Honora's white cymbidium were everywhere, a luncheon buffet of silver chafing dishes and salads was set under the pergola, and the round tables on the grass were shaded by fringed yellow and white umbrellas. Manny Harmon's band played on the terrace.

Langley led his daughter onto the dance floor for the first dance, an exceptionally dreamy version of "Moon River."

The snug fit of Langley's morning coat over the prosperous little paunch that lately and bulged from his slenderness proved that his attire was not rented but an intrinsic part of his wardrobe; his soft gray hair, cut longer in the English style, was aristocratically rumpled. More than one guest whispered knowingly that the backing of this upper-crust British father-in-law had facilitated Curt Ivory's precipitous climb to the upper reaches of international construction.

Langley, flushed from a combination of the warmth and

a large quantity of French champagne, whirled the bride so that her skirt ballooned out. "I say, Jossie, d'you remember that downpour at Crystal and Gideon's wedding?"

Joscelyn's smile wavered, and she glanced around apprehensively as if the couple might be sitting at one of the circular tables. She had never forgiven Gideon for his holier-than-thou refusal to lend Honora a few bucks in her time of need, had never quite gotten over her childhood rivalry with her overgorgeous middle sister—or her unexpected sense of loss at being cut off from her. "I drew better weather," she said.

Langley broke into laughter. "And a dashed sight better-looking groom. Young Malcolm could be a matinee idol."

Joscelyn's smile blazed. "Oh, I don't think he's *that* spectacular," she lied.

The bride and groom danced to "Call Me Irresponsible."

"Well, does the wedding suit you?" Joscelyn asked.

"It's the best day of my life," Malcolm replied, his cheek touching hers.

"From this day forth I walk three paces behind, kneel when I serve your dinner, speak only when spoken to, wash your back and massage your feet."

"That doesn't sound like my wife," he said, but his smile was young and yearning.

Forgetting that they were alone on the waxed square, and that most people were watching them, she kissed his lips lightly. There was a spattering of applause.

Before their marriage, Joscelyn and Malcolm had co-signed the lease on a brand new apartment in the Wilshire district. They were allotted two parking spaces in the underground security garage and given a key to penetrate the six-foot iron mesh fence surrounding the swimming pool, zealous but necessary precautions. The compensation for living in this petty-crime neighborhood was that barring traffic foul-ups, they were only a ten-minute drive from work. This was a blessing for Joscelyn, who was learning her new avocation of housewifery quite literally from the ground up.

Though Malcolm himself was not particularly neat, he was compulsive about his surroundings being in fastidious order. Joscelyn for the first time in her life had opened herself completely to another person and lived to please him—even though at times his demands seemed excessive. But if he enjoyed having their one-bedroom apartment spic and span, what did it matter that at times she felt herself perpetually stooped over to pick up strewn clothes, Coke bottles, coffee mugs, piles of newspaper, his soggy towels?

Malcolm had an adventurous palate. He bought her heavy, color illustrated copies of *Modern French Culinary Art* and *The Art of Italian Cooking*. Having never cooked, not even as Honora's *sous-chef* in that long-ago San Francisco flat, Joscelyn had not envisioned the time and skilled effort involved, scraping and burning her fingers during the inevitable chopping, grating, blanching, sautéeing and browning. As an engineer she planned with meticulous thoroughness, yet on her Saturday jaunt to the nearby Thriftimart she invariably missed throwing certain vital ingredients into her basket, so it was a rare evening that she did not have to stop on the way home for, say, a half pint of whipping cream or some shallots.

Unlike her, Malcolm was gregarious, but those first few months he seldom suggested they get together with anyone. He, too, wanted to keep their new shared identity inviolably private. The only cloud was his work.

He was in the Petrochemical Division, and his particular unit was planning a $10,000,000 offshore drilling platform that would be built above seventy feet of ocean swells. The client, Paloverde Oil, kept rejecting their construction plans. Each delay cost the Petrochemical Division's profit center dearly, and the twenty-man team, of which Malcolm was a cog, got whiplashed. At these times, he turned moody, biting.

To compound the problem, Joscelyn's project with Los Angeles Gas and Electric was going unexpectedly smoothly.

The utility company was concluding a changeover from 50 to 60 cycles and she was engineer-in-charge of industrial customers.

To familiarize herself with problems in altering to match the new frequency, she took part in the changeover at a sheet-rolling mill. The only woman present, she helped the others inchingly remove a rusty, ancient behemoth of a 1500-hp motor. She placated the thick-accented Hungarian mill owner with promises that he would be back in business in no more than a week, she went to the rewind shop while the stator and rotor were rewound. One week to the day after the motor's removal, at eight twenty-five P.M., the mill roared into operation again. The Hungarian hugged her, slivovitz flowed abundantly, then she sped in her Pinto through dark night streets. She was rushing home to Malcolm and that crazy miracle where their private fantasies merged.

She could see their reflection in the mirror over the dresser, she in her white nylon trousseau negligee, ankles and wrists bound with run-ruined pantyhose, spread-eagled on the bed while he, wearing his striped seersucker pajama bottoms, stared imperiously down at her. They were Pirate and Captive—last night they had played Master and Slave. Though her intellect told her that their games were dumb, dumb, dumb, and though she felt an idiot and not a little self-conscious, she was already moist.

"Malcolm, darling, come down here."

"What do you want me to do?" he asked.

"Fuck me."

"If you beg me for it, beg me right, maybe."

"Please, please."

"Later, then, after I'm finished with that virgin on your ship."

She surged with ridiculous envy for the imaginary untouched damsel. "No, me, please me." She twisted and the Beautyrest mattress springs creaked. "I'm a virgin, too."

"If you're lying, bitch, if you're lying—"

"How will you know?"

"I have a machine."

She began to giggle. "Where did you get it? From a used-pussy lot?"

Malcolm said nothing, waiting until her giggles subsided before he strode to the closet.

"What're you getting?" she asked.

He fished around behind the suitcases.

"Malcolm, remember we agreed? No whips." She craned her neck and saw that he was opening a box to take out a foot-long machine with a soft-looking, beige plastic ball on the tip. "God, what's that?" she cried. "Malcolm, it's a vibrator. Don't you dare. Untie me! Don't you dare—it could be *dangerous.*"

But he was unplugging the lamp on her side of the bed to use the socket. He flicked back the sheer nylon, baring the brown-curled apex of her spread legs.

"No, Malcolm, no!" Her voice rose.

He loomed above the bed, his handsome face glowing with pleasure as she twisted and begged. Was this Malcolm or one of the shadowy terrors of her childhood? She no longer felt that tinge of foolishness at their game, now she was thoroughly frightened, and—oddly—yet wetter.

He switched on the vibrator. The ball whirred and pulsated.

"Malcolm, damn it, untie me! This has gone far enough!"

With an imperious glare, he touched the machine between her legs.

"Oh . . . ahh, Malcolm, darling, stop . . . No, don't stop. Oh, please, please . . . Come down here." She was writhing helplessly, deliriously, a remote corner of her mind clouded with humiliation that he should be staring down at her as she arched herself toward the vibrations, as she gasped and threw back her head, baring her teeth in ecstasy. Her orgasm shook the bed.

Malcolm fell on top of her bound, squirming body, not untying her until afterward. They fell asleep in each other's arms. *A miracle,* she thought as she dropped off. *The crazy way we make love is a miracle. . . .*

28

"The label's dangling from your sweater," Malcolm said.

Joscelyn draped the offending royal blue cashmere over her arm, replying unchagrined, "What's the dif? Tonight's just the four of us."

They should already have been at Curt and Honora's for the barbecue. Malcolm, though, had been held up while a Paloverde representative had pointed out that the construction plans didn't properly utilize the rig's belowdeck space, and on the way home he had been trapped in the rush hour traffic on Wilshire Boulevard, inching through the August heat wave in his unairconditioned VW. Even now, after a hurried shower and wearing khaki Bermudas and white Izod shirt, he looked uncomfortably flushed.

"Only you, me, the top man and his wife," he said.

"I'll mend it later, when I have time."

"You're too damn busy for everything! Except your goddamn work!"

A muscle worked at her eye. Malcolm's moods had shifted dangerously these past few weeks because of the Paloverde job. His flare-ups had increased her anxieties about their age difference, the four levels she was above him, the considerably larger paycheck she deposited in their joint acount. She knew she should keep quiet but discretion was not in her makeup.

"Aren't you getting a mite overwrought about a couple of missing stitches?" she inquired.

Malcolm was transformed into a baleful, critical searchlight, glaring around the room from the rumpled gray linen dress she'd worn to work thrown over the unmade bed to his own sweat-damp suit slung on the chair to the yellow plastic laundry basket piled with unfolded clean wash. "You don't know the first thing about what being a wife means," he snarled.

"All right, I get the message." With cold, stiff fingers, she set down the sweater. "I don't need it anyway, not in this weather."

They took her Pinto because of the air conditioning. Malcolm drove, turning on KRLA fullblast. To the barbaric blare of teenage rock he cut savagely around other cars. She tried not to think about that night he'd slugged her.

It turned out they weren't Curt and Honora's only guests.

The barbecue, built above the house on its own terrace with a covered patio and bar-kitchen was a sort of Petit Trianon where the Ivorys could entertain without servants. Honora wasn't up there yet, but Curt, wielding a long-handled fork, stood presiding over the browning chicken. On a nearby chair lounged an overweight, darkly tanned man with a large nose and bushy black mustache.

"Fuad!" Joscelyn cried happily. "I didn't know you were in Los Angeles. When did you get in?"

"Last night." Rising to his feet, he held out both hands. "I flew ten thousand miles to see my adorable, faithless Joscelyn."

When she was a gawky, unpleasant ten-year-old new to Los Angeles, Fuad Abdulrahman (here on business connected with a highway that Curt had just built in Lalarhein) had vowed she was the exact near nubile maiden for his harem, and since then he'd kept up the innuendos in a fond, avuncular tone. Fuad favored the loudest of American sport clothes—as evidenced by his ample, radically patterned crimson and purple sport shirt, his red slacks— and Joscelyn never could reconcile this taste with Curt's assurances that at home Fuad wore the traditional Lalarheini black robe, the *bisht*, and covered his head with a white *gutra* held in place by a coiled black *agal*. His deep-chested laughter and general air of affectionate optimism made it impossible for Joscelyn not to like him.

"You old faker," she said, hugging his robust body.

Malcolm, who had met Fuad only once, at the wedding, held out his hand. "It's a pleasure to see you again, your highness."

"Among friends, it's Fuad," Fuad said.

"Unless we're doing business." Curt grinned at his friend. "Then kneeling and ring kissing is obligatory."

"You got the contract, didn't you?" Fuad retorted.

In the early sixties oil had been discovered below the Q'ram, Lalarhein's merciless sea of sand, and four companies, including Talbott's, had bid on laying the pipeline and building the five pumping stations that would carry the viscous treasure two hundred and thirty miles to the Persian Gulf. Ivory had been awarded the turnkey contract— that is to say, the company would be in total charge until the installation was complete and ready to go into operation.

"Malcolm, Joss." Honora was coming up from the house. In her loose, flowered Pucci caftan, she seemed to float above the grass. "I was just trying to call you."

"Sorry we're late," Joscelyn said. "The traffic's fierce tonight."

"Excuses, excuses." Malcolm grinned at the others. "My wife! Engineer or no, she's a real gal. You should've seen her in front of the closet deliberating over what sweater to wear. Then, of course, she realized it's too hot to need one."

Joscelyn forced herself to smile as naturally as possible.

During dinner, the discussion centered on the pipeline. Joscelyn was not in the Petrochemical Division and Malcolm was. He said very little, and therefore she found herself blabbing. How did they plan to move and weld the big thirty-inch pipes, where would they house their crews? "Curt, won't you have a big problem getting people to stay on the job?"

"You'd be surprised at the pull of double pay and the tax break that the government gives overseas workers."

"In our division," Malcolm said diffidently, "it's not the money. The guys see the project as an important challenge."

"Challenge?" Fuad's black mustache twitched. "In the Q'ram the challenge is how to take a piss—it comes out hot tea."

"I'd be over there like a shot if I were in the running," said Malcolm. Only engineers and designers above a certain level had the opportunity to go to Lalarhein.

"It really is beastly, Malcolm," Honora said with an apologetic smile at Fuad.

"Oh, I don't know," Joscelyn teased. "Doesn't everybody compare it to the French Riviera?"

"There's no oil in the Riviera," Malcolm said quietly.

They had finished eating. Bright ocher Italian plates clinked as Honora cleared them of heaped up chicken bones and carried them to the small but complete kitchen—later Millie or Paco would come and finish cleaning up.

They relaxed over their coffee in the swift-falling Los Angeles twilight.

"Well, Joscelyn," asked Fuad, "how do you find marriage?"

"It'll pass muster," she said.

"Is that all?" Fuad asked.

"Actually, it's heaven."

"Heaven?" Malcolm smiled at her. "You don't spend much time there."

"We're bogged down with a changeover for a local electrical company," Joscelyn explained to Fuad.

"Joss's being modest," Curt said. "She's way ahead of schedule."

Malcolm stared down at the yellow tablecloth, which the last blaze of sunlight was turning a rufous orange.

Tomorrow being Tuesday, a workday, the Pecks left before ten. Malcolm took Sunset home, silent, handling her car with the same frenetic lack of consideration for other drivers that he had shown on the way over. Joscelyn clutched a striped paper cocktail napkin she'd taken by mistake, staring out the window as the dark shadows of Bel Air then Beverly Hills estates gave way to the brightly lit strip with its artful billboards of singers and entertainers.

By the time they reached the underground garage she could no longer bear the silence between them. Following Malcolm up the cement steps, she said, "Fuad's terrific, isn't he?"

Malcolm had reached the door to the hall. Wheeling, he said with low intensity so she could feel the force of his breath. "You make me want to puke!"

In their apartment he snatched the bourbon from the kitchen shelf, then turned on the TV, taking a long slug from the bottle while Johnny Carson's image came onto the screen. With friends Malcolm might have a couple of drinks, and at dinner he sometimes opened a Heineken. That was the extent of it. To see him slurp from the bottle like an AA going off the wagon made Joscelyn's stomach tense into a hard ball. She scurried into the bedroom.

"This isn't a goddamn barn," he snarled. "Can't you ever shut a door?"

She closed the door quietly.

With a mixture of martyrdom and nerve-tingling dread, she made the bed, hung up their clothes, scrubbed the toilet and washbowl with Ajax, folded the wash, stacking the Jockey shorts and pajama bottoms in Malcolm's side of the bureau. From time to time she went to listen at the closed door. There was only televised laughter and Carson's joking voice kidding her not.

Not until she was ready for bed did she dare go into the living room. Malcolm was slumped in front of the long, walnut "entertainment center" that had been a wedding present from one of Curt's business associates.

"Malcolm, it's after twelve," she said quietly.

He lurched to his feet, coming toward her, his mouth tensed into a distorted smile. He slammed his fist at the left side of her head. She gripped onto the doorjamb to keep herself from falling.

"That's just a taste of what you'll get if you don't lay off me!"

Clasping the side of her head, she staggered to the bed,

collapsing on the monogrammed blanket cover. He slammed the door shut.

Her cheek and ear throbbed hotly and she could hear a resonant whine. The whine didn't let up. Was some delicate part of her ear broken? Should she phone Kaiser Permanente, the medical group to which all Ivory employees belonged? What would she tell the doctor on call? That a Pringle label connected to a sweater by a thread had caused the blow? For by now she was convinced that she was to blame for Malcolm's rage. *If I hadn't acted like a bitch when he was all hot and bothered from the traffic jam, none of this would have happened. I knew how badly things had been going for him at work.* She turned, gingerly lowering her head to the pillow, and to her surprise, dozed off.

She awakened, lifting her head. The whining had been replaced by hoofbeats and a weird, strangled sound that rose, diminished, then rose again.

She jumped from the bed, conscious of the sharp pain cutting across the left side of her ear and jawbone. In the living room an old black and white Western jerked across the screen. Malcolm, his chin slumped on his chest, was wheezing those agonized hoops of sound.

He was crying in his sleep.

Kneeling in front of him, she touched his arm lightly. "Darling, darling, wake up."

His eyes opened and he stared at her, bewildered, frightened. "Joscelyn . . . ?"

"You must've been dreaming."

"A nightmare. I was a kid." He shuddered.

"It's all right." She held his face between her palms, covering his beautiful, damaged mouth and nose with kisses. "Hey, you're fine. Now come inside."

Putting an arm around his narrow, firm waist, she led him into the bedroom.

He stretched out on his back in his Bermudas, and she curved next to him, an arm across his chest. After a minute he turned to her and she patted his shoulders and back, soothing him as if he were a terrified little boy.

"You're not leaving?" he asked.

"Hey, buster, you don't get rid of me that easy."

"Never came up against failure before," he muttered. "That bastard from Paloverde Oil shoots down my every damn idea."

"It's a group project."

"S'my ideas that get shot down."

"You're being too sensitive."

"S'easy for you to say, you're terrific."

"So're you."

"I'll never be a project engineer."

"You will," she said, rubbing between his shoulder blades. "You will."

"Christ, I'd give anything t'be in Lalarhein, a guy could prove 'self in Lalarhein." His words slurred drunkenly, drowsily.

"Shh," she murmured. "It's late."

"Give anything to be there. . . ."

Joscelyn's idea of lunch was to remain in her windowless cubbyhole with a tuna on whole wheat: unless Malcolm dropped by to join her, the sandwich would remain half eaten, giving off a fishy aroma while the crusts turned upward. Two mornings after the barbecue, however, she telephoned Honora, inviting her to lunch at Mike Lyman's.

Joscelyn Sylvander Peck's soul shrank when it came to asking for anything, and she needed a favor from her sister.

The heatwave had not broken and though she had only a short block's walk, her trim, sleeveless navy blouson was damp by the time she plunged into the dimly lit, noisy, steak-odored air of Lyman's. The bar was buried behind businessmen waiting for their tables, but Honora was already seated—the name (Mrs.) Curt Ivory conjured up the magical rustle of five-dollar bills to Los Angeles maître d's.

"Hi," Joscelyn said, and sank down in the leather chair. As she sipped her Tom Collins the oppressiveness of her impending request grew.

The conversation, grouchily truculent on her part, drifted on about the broiling weather, the pruning of Japanese cherry trees, and Fuad's visit until Honora leaned forward, affectionate concern radiating from the dark eyes. "Joss, what's wrong with your cheek?"

Joscelyn pulled back as far as the leather chair permitted. "Nothing."

"You've got a mark here." Honora touched her own cheek near the black wave of her page boy.

Joscelyn had applied triple coats of makeup base to the area, successfully covering the gray-purple of the bruise:

the restaurant's dim lighting, however, brought out the shadows of its slightly raised topography.

"Oh, that. Didn't you notice it Monday night? Over the weekend I decorated myself—I banged the edge of the diving board."

The waiter set down their lunch salads.

The time has come, Joscelyn told herself. Poking at a large shrimp, she muttered, "Honora, listen, there's this thing you can do for me."

"Yes?"

Two couples rose noisily from the next table, and during their forced, clamorous laughter, Joscelyn muttered, "Ask Curt to send Malcolm and me to Lalarhein."

Blinking, Honora stared at her. "I didn't get that."

"Ask Curt about getting Malcolm in on the Lalarheini project." Joscelyn turned from her sister's flabbergasted gaze, breaking a roll, buttering the smaller piece. She could feel the sullen set of her jaw.

Finally Honora said, "Joss, I never interfere in his business, you know that."

"Swell. I really appreciate the help, Honora. Thanks."

Honora's brows drew together in pleading intensity. "D-don't be taken in by the way Fuad acts about your career, Joss." The slight stammer proved her complete misery. "He's lived in America. But Lalarhein's one of the worst Islamic countries as far as women go. They're not allowed to work."

"That's hardly classified information."

"Then . . . You mean you're giving up your career?"

"Obviously."

"But, Joss—you can't! You're a truly talented engineer. Whichever team you're on gets things accomplished—and quickly. Curt's always saying how lucky Ivory is to have you."

The humble tone of Honora's accolades gave Joscelyn a queer shiver of dislocation. *She* had always been the inferior Sylvander girl.

"The company'll survive," she said acidly.

"But what'll you *do* there? Joss, you have no idea what it's like. The mullahs rule every detail. Women stay inside their homes, and if they go out, they're veiled. They aren't allowed to drive. Daralam—the capital—isn't a city, it's a huge, dirty village with no real shops or restaurants, hardly any trees, no proper water system, no garbage collection—

in the photographs it looks picturesque, but it's horrible.
The heat, the flies, the beggars, the smells. Those three days
I was there were enough to last a lifetime. Lalarhein's not a
country, it's an oven, a medieval oven."

Joscelyn chewed her salad. "Working there'll be a giant
boost for Malcolm."

"What about you?"

"I'll keep busy."

Honora's head tilted. "Joss, you aren't preg—"

"God no! I'm not a nineteen-year-old idiot."

Honora's soft upper lip quivered and the lovely eyes
were very bright. *If Curt could see her now, he'd kill me,* Joss
thought. *I deserve to be killed.* Yet she couldn't force herself
to apologize.

After a minute, Honora said, "I'm sure that there's a
project in this country for Malcolm."

"Company policy is to advance people who can handle
the tough assignments in tough places."

A long silence that Joscelyn misconstrued. *She thinks
Malcolm put me up to it.*

"And please don't tell Malcolm about this. He'd murder
me. He gets livid if he thinks the relationship does one iota
for him."

"Oh, Joss, you used to get like this when you were in
trouble at school."

"If you don't want to help Malcolm, just say so!" Joscelyn burst out. The clatter and voices and smells of the busy
lunch hour swam around her. "You've never accepted
him."

"We both like him and have from the beginning." Honora's voice soothed, her eyes reassured.

"Then why are you being so negative about doing this?"

Honora sighed deeply. "If you're sure Lalarhein's really
right for you and Malcolm, of course I'll talk to Curt."

"Thank you," Joscelyn said stiffly. She signaled for the
check, but when Honora had come in she'd told the captain
to put it on Curt's account.

The sisters didn't leave Mike Lyman's together. Joscelyn
was in a rush to get back to the office while Honora's appointment with the tree man on Olympic Boulevard wasn't
until two forty-five.

As Honora watched the tall, pleasantly angular figure
wind around the tables, she was thinking, *Poor Jossie.*

Her reservations about her younger sister's marriage had intensified at the barbecue. For a few moments she had seen beyond Malcolm's endearing, puppyish efforts to please and been aware of another, darker persona. It had been an unnerving revelation.

Did he bully Joss into this? Honora absently formed a triangle of crumbs. *She said no, but methinks she did protest too much. She's really shook up.* Honora, who had no experience with physical abuse, did not consider the possibilities connected to Joscelyn's bruised cheek as she attempted to figure out the unknowable problems surrounding the Pecks' marriage.

She sipped her coffee until only eight or nine tables remained occupied. The busboys were setting up for dinner. She watched them, her mind drifting back to the thin young waitress at Stroud's. Now she was covered by a great slagheap of possessions—furs, jewelry designed for her by Van Cleef and Arpels, the estate in Bel Air and the big house with the boat in Newport Beach, a new flat in London on Upper Brook Street, her garden with its rare plants and trees. She was married to a man she adored and who adored her. She had arrived at the Promised Land. So why did one benign day succeed the next, bland and ultimately empty?

I have my period, that's all, she thought. She had been to specialists here and in New York, suffering a series of painful if minor corrective surgeries, she had tracked her temperature, she and Curt had followed the doctor's orders on when to make love. With paralyzing regularity her periods flowed. Curt reassured her, he said he couldn't even remember telling her that he wanted three children, he needed her and nobody else. *In the old days I might have been poor, sometimes desperate, but I can't recollect feeling utterly useless.*

She pushed sharply away from the table, sloshing iced coffee into the saucer, leaving the now deserted restaurant.

It was Honora and Curt's habit when they dined at home to take an evening stroll in the gardens. As they wound along the lit paths, Honora briefed him about the luncheon and Joscelyn's request.

"Curt . . . is it true that your top people have all worked overseas?"

"So it's a promotion she's after?"

"For Malcolm."

"If that's all there is to it, no big deal. A little nepotism here and there is good for the soul. The levee job I told you about on the Mississippi—I'll send them both."

"She doesn't want to work."

"Joss?" he asked, surprised. "A baby?"

"No," Honora said softly. "Curt . . . well, I don't really understand, but it came to me that maybe she's decided she's too much of a challenge for Malcolm and wants to even things up between them."

"Turn in her ability on his masculine self-respect?"

"Am I getting a bit far out?"

He halted to pick a pale pink hibiscus. "It makes a kind of crazy sense."

"I think they're going through a rough time."

"She told you?"

"You know Joss better than that. No, it's just intuition. She's very intent on Malcolm moving up the ladder."

"And at the barbecue he seemed very intent on Lalarhein. But, Honora, you take on marital problems there, not lose them. We've had several divorces in the few months since the project started."

"She asked me, Curt, she *asked* me, and you know that Joss'd go a hundred miles out of her way rather than ask a simple favor. This Lalarhein job for Malcolm means everything to her."

Curt tucked the hibiscus in his wife's dark hair. "Okay, Sweet Leilani. I'll think about it."

29

The irritating roar of the overburdened air-conditioning unit did not cover the light tap on the plasterboard door. Joscelyn, who had been dozing off with her head propped against the arm of the couch, jumped, and her stationery pad dropped into the pillows behind her. Castigating herself for sinking into yet another unplanned nap, she swung up to a sitting position. "Oh, it's you, Yussuf," she said.

As if it could be anyone else. She was alone in the little house with Yussuf, her Egyptian "boy." It was against Lalarheini mores for a man, no matter how impoverished, to become a servant, and no woman worked outside her home, so household help—and whores, too—were foreign recruits.

Yussuf bowed his white cap and shuffled a few inches forward on feet thrust sockless into oxfords whose backs were stomped down. Spare and short as a gnarled vine, his wrinkled, wood-brown face sprouted a messy gray stubble. "What shall I prepare," he inquired in his soft, heavily accented English, "for the evening meal?"

"I'll take care of things tonight," she said.

Today being Thursday, the eve of Islam's inviolable Friday sabbath, Yussuf would depart and Malcolm would arrive home from the field. Her husband's welcoming meal was planned around a contraband can of ham that had just arrived in one of Honora's care packages. Yussuf was very devout, and Joscelyn—fond of her undemanding fellow prisoner in this air-conditioned prefab—did not insult him by requiring that he prepare foods forbidden by the Koran or serve equally prohibited alcohol, as most of the other Ivory housewives insisted their "boys" do.

"There is still time," he said politely.

"You just run along."

"One hundred thanks to you, madam." He bobbed his head yet deeper. "In the ice box are some good fresh carrots, and a date cake."

Yussuf purchased whatever they required. When Joscelyn had first arrived in Lalarhein, she had looked forward to shopping as the highlight of her day. Arms and legs covered by a long-sleeved blouse and long skirt, she would park in Daralam Square, where for a few coppers a ragged little boy would watch the red Pinto that Ivory had shipped over with the furniture. She would plunge on foot into the labyrinthian, narrow, cloth-covered alleyways that were crowded with beggars, men in robes, the black ghosts of women. At every step a different alien odor had reached her nostrils. The raucous cries of the hawkers mingled in a wild song. The merchants in their tiny, aromatic shops cheated her outrageously, but she would never have abandoned her exotic jaunts because of that. No, it was the pinching. The surreptitious pinching that other Ivory wives immediately informed her was the fate of all unveiled women. She never saw whose unrelenting, anonymous fingers squeezed her flesh. Her buttocks, her thighs, even her small breasts were marked with purplish bruises when she returned home. Malcolm, who had not hit her since the night of the barbecue and was tender of her body, would run his fingers over the welts, horrified. So now Yussuf looped the big, woven, papyrus market basket over the handlebars of his bike and peddled into town.

"Mr. Peck will enjoy them," she said, nodding gravely. "Go ahead, Yussuf. We'll see you on Saturday."

"If Allah wills it, Saturday," he repeated, pressing his palms together for a final bow before he left.

Joscelyn heard the back door squeak as he pushed out his prized, ancient English bike. Going to the window, she opened the Venetian blinds to watch the thin old man swerve past a wagon pulled by a camel and donkey on his way to Daralam. The road, or in Joscelyn's mind, the two-lane, twenty-three-foot-wide wearing surface paved of hot-mix asphaltic concrete, was the first stretch of the job that had so disastrously separated Curt from Honora in the early months of their marriage.

Here, about three miles from town, an Ivory construction crew had assembled identical prefabs, and they stood like Monopoly houses, ten on either side of the road. Given the heat and the exorbitant price of water, it was hardly surprising that there were no attempts at a garden. The yellow weeds straggling below the clotheslines were the sole vegetation.

On the packed, sandy dirt by the Urquharts' front door was a jumble of tricycles, Flexible Flyers and junior bikes with training wheels. Double U, as everyone called Ursula Urquhart, had invited her over. They were endless, these child-infested afternoons when the women smoked like chimneys and drank endless glasses of iced coffee sweetened with rum. (Although alcoholic beverages were illegal in Lalarhein, vast quantities were consumed by the Ivory people.) It would please Malcolm if she wended her way across the street to join the kaffeeklatch. He was perpetually riding her to get into the social swing.

The motivating thrust of Malcolm's life being his search for mass approbation, he ached to have her, his wife, be the popularity kid. Loving him as helplessly as she did, Joscelyn wished she could live up to his expectations. She had, however, never possessed the knack of easy friendship—only at college and then at work did she find a measure of intellectual conviviality. In Lalarhein, trapped five days a week in the enclave with women and children, she felt herself shoved back into that proud, unhappy loneliness of her school days: she was convinced that the other women, hausfraus to the core, despised her as a stuck-up oddball for being an engineer and were hiding their scornful dislike because she was the Big Boss's sister-in-law. (There was a measure of truth in Joscelyn's evaluation but she underestimated the resentment engendered by her sharp, honest tongue.)

From this window she had a view of the camel-colored hills with their scattering of villas built by British officials in the early 1900s when Lalarhein had been a protectorate. Nowadays these houses were owned by the complex family network that was the local royalty. Lacking a hereditary monarchy, the country's leadership shifted from one branch to the other, and at the moment Fuad's older brother, Mohammed Abdulrahman, was Prime Minister.

Joscelyn stared rebelliously through the shimmering heat at the Urquharts' house. *If I go over there I'll have to park my brains and put on a bogus smirk for the II's.* Reducing the women to "II," or Ivory Idiot, relieved a smidge of her sense of rejection.

"Oh, screw it," she muttered aloud, and went back to the couch to finish her letter to Langley.

Just before dusk, the Ivory cavalcade roared along the road. Outside the Pecks' house halted a large, shuddering truck with an elongated flatbed that was specifically designed to carry ninety-three-foot lengths of large-diameter pipe from the Gulf over the incredibly hot Q'ram. (On this job alone Curt had a fortune tied up in heavy equipment: besides several dozen of these pipe carriers, at the site were four enormous Allan Parsons heavy-duty ditching machines, twelve Sideboom tractors, backhoes, tow tractors, bulldozers, cleaning and priming machines, coating and wrapping machines, welding machines, compressors to test the lines, welding trucks and so on.)

Malcolm jumped down from the cab. "Thanks for the lift, Jake, old buddy."

As soon as the front door was closed, he gave Joscelyn an enthusiastic, sweaty hug, and she felt a mindless happiness. *It's been a good week for him,* she thought, spreading kisses along his jaw. When things went well, no nasty squalls rocked their weekend.

"How's my wife?" he asked.

"Good, fine, wonderful." And at this moment, in their clinch, her boring, sleep-squandered days did indeed seem tinged by a roseate light.

"Miss me?"

"Mmm," she said, kissing the flat spot on his nose. "Let me think about it. Want a drink?"

"Later," he said. "Right now I could kill for a bath."

He lounged in the rusty water that cost more than gasoline in Lalarhein while Joscelyn perched on the closed toilet seat, watching his face as he told her about his week's progress on the pipeline.

Her mind automatically analyzed and sorted the information, but her attention was fixed on him. Lighter-brown patches where the skin had peeled on his wide shoulders were the only flaw in his magnificent bronze tan. By contrast the skin covered by his work shorts seemed marble white. Between his shield-shaped pelvic bones floated his penis in its wreath of dark hair.

He pressed his feet hard on the bottom end of the tub—his feet and ankles, being covered by desert boots, were also white. "There's a problem that's come up," he said.

She was used to hearing about problems. Laying pipe requires great skill: once large lines are laid and filled with oil it is nearly impossible for them to be lifted or repaired, which was why Curt had sent experienced people to guide the seven hundred local artisans and laborers. Malcolm, the youngest engineer by ten years on the project, agonized over every decision.

"What is it now?" she asked sympathetically.

"The stretch we're doing, the plans call for burying the pipe. But I'm not sure it should be buried, just not sure at all." There was a boyish appeal in his tone.

"Have you run into rock?" Excavation in rocky ground cost a fortune.

"No, but some geologist sure as hell goofed. Near the ridge the ground's very saline."

"Salt, mmm. Then what choice is there? You can't bury pipe where it'll be corroded."

"But what about Heinrichman?" Heinrichman, in charge of the entire project, thrust out his large belly and questioned every on-site decision made by his engineers in a loud, argumentative voice. "When he finds out he'll hang me out to dry."

"Malcolm, all you have to do is explain to him about the aggressive soil. He'll be grateful."

"Think so?" Malcolm asked uncertainly.

"I'm positive." She was standing. "Ready for me to scrub your back?"

"Be my guest."

She wielded the loofah vigorously to loosen the top layer of skin and engrained sand, then massaged in the soap with her hands, moving slower and more sensually as she worked her way downward to his waist.

"Hey," he said, looking down. "Look at what you've done."

"Time to adjourn to the bedroom," she said, holding out her hand to help him from the bath.

He tugged at her hand. She struggled in his hard grasp a few seconds, then acquiesced, laughing as she splashed atop him. He slipped down her Bermudas and underpants, but left on her dripping shirt. When things were good between them he often initiated one of their crazy games or was adventurous about location and position. They made love like playful seals.

They were at the dinette table eating their ham and carrots au gratin when the phone rang. The instrument sat on the window ledge next to Joscelyn and as she reached for it she was positive she would hear an invitation to one of the liquor-hazed evenings that alternated along the Ivory enclave every weekend. Malcolm shone at these gatherings.

"Is that you, my little turtle dove?" Fuad asked.

She felt warmth surge through her. She had always been crazy about Fuad, and here in Lalarhein she cherished him doubly because he—a Moslem who supposedly saw women as lesser beings—respected her for her engineering expertise while the Ivory men smiled with infuriating tolerance whenever she talked shop. "When did you get home?" she asked. Fuad and his family had been traveling in Europe for much of the time she and Malcolm had been in Lalarhein.

"My little turtle dove, I flew back Monday to be in your arms. Can you and Malcolm come to dinner tomorrow night?"

"It sounds terrific, Fuad, we'd love to."

Fuad's substantial house might have been transported by a djinn from England: crimson brick, numerous prim slate peaks, ornamental chimneys, a plethora of heraldic stained-glass windows, architecture that was at insane odds with the landscape.

The Edwardian interior was overwhelmed by Fuad's collection of Lalarheini carpets, which are widely renowned for the exquisite workmanship of their yellow, rose and indigo floral designs and their graceful arabesques. Every inch of floor was covered, on the walls hung small, subtly faded rugs, the numbers woven into their right-hand corners attesting to their antiquity; lustrous silk rugs covered the low divans. The effect was one of exuberantly colorful opulence.

Fuad came toward them beaming. Joscelyn always needed a minute or so to convince herself that this was indeed Curt's overweight, corny jokester of an old college buddy. In Los Angeles it had been impossible to believe that Fuad was a genuine prince, while here in Lalarhein, wearing his black *bisht* banded with gold to indicate his rank, she found it equally impossible to believe that he was anything other than royalty.

His wife kissed each of them on both cheeks, engulfing them in Jolie Madame.

"Bonsoir, mes chers," she said, although neither of the Pecks knew French. Princess Lelith, or Lelith as she had requested they call her, spoke no English. She concealed herself beneath a black *abeyya* and *gutwah* whenever she stepped beyond the high mud-brick wall surrounding the property, but in her home she preferred her Parisian wardrobe. The short-waisted, short-skirted red Jacques Fath dress made her look like a chubby little girl with protuber-

ant, warmly affectionate eyes, and to complete the impression she wore a bow-shaped diamond barrette to hold back her hennaed hair.

A thin man in his twenties was rising from a divan.

"This is my nephew, Khalid, home from Oxford," Fuad said.

Like his uncle, Khalid wore the traditional garments with the regal band of gilt. His skin was smoothly, tautly pale, his brown mustache appeared painted on with a narrow brush, but it was his eyes that Joscelyn noticed. The left eye moved independently of the right, flashing like his aunt's jewelry.

Fuad draped his stout arm around Joscelyn. "And this is the sister of my dearest American friend, Curt Ivory—Joscelyn Peck."

"It's a pleasure to meet you, Khalid," Joscelyn said.

Khalid averted his gaze from her.

"And this handsome boy, this lucky man, is her husband, Malcolm Peck."

"Your highness," Malcolm said, respectful.

This must be the manner in which Khalid desired to be addressed, for he held out his hand to Malcolm. "Good evening, Mr. Peck," he said, adding tersely, "Mrs. Peck."

Soft drinks were served. Lelith smiled and nodded, as if urging them to converse without her. Fuad sat next to her, from time to time patting her plump, beringed hand.

Khalid said to Malcolm, "So you are building our new petrochemical facilities." His regal tone indicated that the construction was on his property.

"I'm only one of the Ivory people, your highness."

"He's an engineer on the pipeline," Joscelyn added.

Khalid sipped his ginger beer while continuing to look at Malcolm. "In the Trans-Arabian pipeline I've heard the steel was fabricated with carbon, manganese, phosphorus, sulfur. Is that information correct?"

Malcolm nodded, his eyes uncertain. It astonished Joscelyn to realize how little he knew about so similar a project.

"It is," Joscelyn said. "Except we're using a slightly different proportion."

"Joscelyn is an engineer, too," Fuad said. "A Phi Beta Kappa from my old alma mater."

"But of course she's not working on this project, your highness," Malcolm said to Khalid. "Now she's devoting herself to marriage."

Dinner, a six-course banquet, was French in flavor except for the entrée, which was the Lalarheini specialty of baby lamb simmered with dates.

Over the coffee—again French rather than the thick, sweet Mideastern brew, Khalid said, "This oil is a benison for Lalarhein. Now we can have the best of your Western world, yet retain the best of ours."

"Khalid, don't bore our guests with your political views," Fuad said, but his voice was fond. "My nephew, like all you young people, is a bit of an extremist. He believes our legal system should be based solely on the Sharia."

"The same law as the Saudis use," said Joscelyn. Since her immurement here, she had studied about the Mideast with her old schoolgirl intensity, poring over books and newspapers, erudition that wasn't worth a hoot in the Ivory enclave, where people had no interest in the locals. "It's a bit extreme."

"The laws were handed down to Mohammed by Allah," Khalid said.

"But reverting to Sharia would mean scrapping the bulk of your legal system," Joscelyn said.

"A legal system foisted on us by the British," Khalid retorted. "In the West you treat morality and behavior as a private matter. Sharia treats them as a social concern, the responsibility of the entire society. There were over a thousand murders in your Los Angeles County last year, less then fifty in Saudi, which has a slightly larger population." The left eye was flashing wildly.

"Fairly impressive proof of Sharia's superiority," Malcolm said.

Khalid made his first smile. "On the other hand," he said, "your technology is admirable."

"There we agree, Khalid," Fuad said. "Our country needs a sanitary system, more roads, schools, a water supply, possibly a university."

"And don't forget a modern airport," Khalid said. "The Daralam field can't handle the new jumbo jets. Or the new fighter planes."

"Fighter planes . . . ?" Joscelyn asked, her voice trailing off as Malcolm gave her a quick, hard glance.

She picked up her Limoges demitasse cup with trembling fingers, smiling at Lelith.

30

As soon as they were in the house, Malcolm hit her on the hip. It wasn't a hard blow, but like the preliminary jabs a boxer feints at his sparring partner. "Bitch!"

"Okay. So I opened my mouth at a friend's house."

"You're such a fucking genius—don't you know where you are?"

"I'm in a prefab with plasterboard walls, and if you yell any louder, the entire block will tape us."

"You're in the Mideast." Now his pitch was low and dangerous. "That's where you are." He landed another restrained punch on her arm. "You've had your genius nose buried in enough books about the goddamn area, so how come you haven't read someplace that women don't mean shit here?"

"It bugs you that I spoke to that twerpy religious fanatic?"

"It bugs me that you meet one of the royal family and call him by his first name then tell him his religion goes in for barbarism."

"I never said that, I'd die before I hurt Fuad, but since you've brought it up, Sharia does include public whippings and beheadings, lopping off a hand or two."

Another slap. "Khalid—his highness to you—is hot to build an airport. Talbott's has been doing a preliminary plan, and so have we."

"That's no big secret. What I fail to see is the connection with his royal highness."

"I intend to see we get the job."

"Through him?" She gave a snorting laugh. "He just finished college, he's hardly one of the powers that be."

"He's an Abdulrahman."

"Exactly the logic I'd expect from an engineering authority who doesn't know whether to lay pipe above or below the ground."

His eyes glazed, his mouth quivered: he looked like an unjustly whipped child. She sucked in her breath, wishing she could recall her words. Then an angry flush spread across his tanned face to redden his ears. He swung again. This time his blow landed full force in the pit of her stomach. She had no sensation of falling; she was suddenly asprawl on the speckled yellow linoleum. There was no immediate pain. She was too filled with hatred—she had never hated anyone as intensely as she hated Malcolm at this minute.

He went into the kitchen, returning with an unopened bottle of Johnnie Walker. His footsteps reverberated through her, and her sudden fury evaporated.

"Malcolm, please don't go," she whimpered from the floor. "You know what a mean fighter I am. Please?"

He didn't glance at her. The flimsy walls shook as he slammed out. In the reasoning sector of her brain Joscelyn knew her husband had gone to a house identical to his and was ingratiating himself with a group of Americans in various stages of inebriation, but her panicky fear at losing him refused this logic. Was this what she had feared since they had first started dating, the big split?

Struggling to her feet, she lay down on the bed, breathing shallowly so as not to intensify the stabbing pain below her ribs. The fluorescent green hands of the alarm clock were pointing at ten after two when Malcolm got home. She listened to him go to the bathroom, then fall on the daybed in the other bedroom. Only then did she drop into an uneasy, pain-filled sleep.

One of Malcolm's most endearing qualities, though, was an inability to hold a grudge. The following Thursday he arrived home from the Q'ram whistling. He hugged her gently, bending to contritely kiss the broad adhesive that the sweet old English doctor in Daralam Square had taped around her rib cage.

While she was rinsing the dinner dishes, the phone rang. Malcolm took it in the next room. After a minute he pushed open the swinging door.

"That was Khalid," he said, grinning triumphantly. "He'll be here in a half hour."

Kalid brought another guest. Though he himself was
again dressed traditionally, his companion wore cheap
Western clothes that were immensely large for his scrawny
frame. The sleeves of his faded blue shirt were rolled up to
show small, knotty biceps, his trousers belled out around a
waist so thin that he'd wound his belt around twice. Into
the worn leather was thrust a revolver that appeared to be
German army surplus, circa World War I.

"This," Khalid said with a casual wave of his hand, "is
Harb Fawzi."

The one-sided introduction told Joscelyn that skinny
Harb Fawzi was unimportant, probably a servant. She
amended this to be a bodyguard as Fawzi narrowed his
eyes to give her and Malcolm a visual frisk.

Under the intensity of his gaze, Joscelyn frowned uneasily. Then, without a by-your-leave, Fawzi prowled into the
dinky bedroom hall, opening the doors and closets before
going into the kitchen, where he spoke in sharp Arabic to
Yussuf. Joscelyn took a step to rescue her "boy," but Malcolm's glance halted her. She remained by the couch, very
aware of the tight taping around her ribs.

Fawzi returned, nodding. Khalid shot him a flashing
glance and he sat on one of the ladderback dinette chairs,
fingering his gun butt.

Yussuf served coffee, his head bowed respectfully as he
approached Khalid. Joscelyn, as she and Malcolm had
prearranged, took her cup to the bedroom, where through
the thin walls she could hear voices but not words. After
about an hour the big black Lincoln started, purring away
in the direction of the mansion-strewn hills.

Malcolm burst into the bedroom, exhilarated. "Hey,
under that costume Khalid's a regular guy. We got along
fabulously."

"Know something? Outside of the movies, I never saw
anyone wear a handgun tucked into his belt."

"Harb Fawzi, you mean? He's Khalid's driver. At Oxford Khalid gave some speeches and the Zionists got ram-
bunctious. No violence, but ever since Fawzi's played
bodyguard."

"Talk about paranoid. How many Zionists can there be
in Lalarhein?"

"Joss, Khalid's more important than you think. He has
enemies among his own people."

I'll bet he does, Joscelyn thought. "Was there any reason for his visit?" she asked.

"We hit it off the other night." Malcolm spoke a touch too easily. "He likes to shoot the bull, and we're about the same age."

Over the next weeks, Khalid returned five times, and the procedure was always the same: Fawzi, armed and watchful as a lean hound, searched the house while she retired to the bedroom. After the duo left, Malcolm was invariably very up. Joscelyn not only accepted the odd friendship, but exploited it, basking in Malcolm's sunny mood.

Once she heard them laughing, and later asked what it was about. "It cracked him up, how Heinrichman settled that problem at the pumping station site with a judicious smear to the right guys from the slush fund."

A slush fund was kept by every company doing business in the Mideast, where it was the custom to hand out small sums of cash to expedite business and to prevent harassment. While the pilferage at Pumping Station 1 was not major, every piece of supplies had to be shipped in, and the cost of waiting for replacements was monstrous. Heinrichman's solution was to give the workers he suspected of robbery extra wages to be "night watchmen."

As part of their additional benefit package, Ivory employees in Lalarhein had a month's vacation with a travel bonus.

In February, Malcolm took off two weeks. He and Joscelyn flew to Paris. At the Orly airport they rented a sardine-can Citroën and carved leisurely through the winter-struck Loire Valley. Malcolm, who had never been in Europe, studied the red Michelin for starred restaurants, he bought stacks of illustrated guides to châteaux, he learned enough about the local wines to order judiciously.

The second week they returned to Paris, giving up the car and staying in the Hôtel d'Antin, a small, inexpensive place near the Opéra. They strolled, gloved hands entwined, along the Seine embankments, they climbed the steep hills of Montmartre, they gazed entranced at the bright, glowing Impressionist masterpieces in the Jeu de Paume.

After their visit to this small, magnificently endowed mu-

seum, Malcolm invented one of those silly games that
lovers play in Paris, taking Joscelyn into art galleries to
pretend to select a memento of their vacation, a choice they
both knew was vastly out of their range.

One afternoon as they circled the Place de la Concorde
he halted before a window display, a single Impressionist
rendering of wispy plane trees along a canal.

"What do you think?" he asked.

"Malcolm, see that name on the frame? It's a mere Sisley. What about the little Renoir nude you promised me on
the rue St. Honoré?"

"Let's see how cheapo it is," he said.

The stout, cordial salesman told them two hundred
thousand francs—"That is only fifty thousand dollars. It's a
very fine work, Monsieur—Sisley's an excellent investment."

"We'll think about it," Malcolm said gravely.

When they were again on the Place de la Concorde, Joscelyn whooped, "Only fifty thousand dollars!"

"But an excellent investment," Malcolm said, putting his
arm around her waist, squeezing her.

They laughed the rest of the way to the Hôtel d'Antin.

Back in Lalarhein, the khamsin winds blew hot, rattling
the mass-produced windowpanes and setting the nerves on
edge. At first Joscelyn attributed her drowsiness to the
weather, but then her breasts became tender and sourness
churned her stomach. She made an appointment with Dr.
Bryanston, the gray-haired English physician who practiced in his five-story home overlooking Daralam Square.
Dr. Bryanston liked Joscelyn because despite her American
accent she was English born, and Joscelyn liked the doctor
because he had taped her broken rib without a lot of embarrassing inquiries.

Medical men in Lalarhein were obligated to keep two
waiting rooms: she sat amid veiled, heavily scented women
and groaning children impatiently awaiting her turn.

After his examination, Dr. Bryanston said in his quiet
voice, "Mrs. Peck, you have the only happy ailment there
is. You're pregnant."

It must have happened that snowy night in Tours, when
she had forgotten to put in her diaphragm and then hadn't
wanted to leave the cozy *lit matrimonial.*

Driving home, she kept bursting into an off-key rendition of "Yes sir, that's my baby." In the house, though, sipping a ginger ale to quell her nausea, she was abruptly hit by the fact that she and Malcolm had agreed to postpone even talking about a family until his three years in Lalarhein were up. *What if he's angry? In this situation, men have been known to run out on a woman.*

Malcolm arrived home on Thursday with a string of biting questions as to why she hadn't yet planned a party to show the recently returned slides of their trip. She soon realized what had triggered his carping mood: the gathering line he was currently working on had come to an almost complete standstill because of the winds.

The weekend passed in unpleasantness, and she waved goodbye to her husband without having had the right opportunity to tell him the news. After the roar of the trucks faded, the dark sky grew silvery, then pinkened, and Joscelyn knew she would assuredly go bananas if she didn't share her news.

She composed a letter to Honora, concluding with a casual: *By the way, we're having a baby.*

Several times a week a World War II DC-3 bounced between the various Ivory sites to deliver cash for the payroll and slush fund as well as to pick up thick manila envelopes of reports for the main office in Los Angeles. Hitherto Joscelyn had relied on the Lalarheini postal system, which though far improved from a decade earlier still had its vagaries, but now she dispatched Yussuf to the Ivory storefront office on Daralam Square with a request that her letter be included in the pouch.

"Joss," said the soft, familiar voice with faint English intonations.

It was three days later. Roused from her deep postprandial snooze, Joscelyn's first thought was that some pleasant dream of home still engulfed her.

Opening her eyes, she saw her sister. She gasped, unable to believe that Honora was actually here. She seldom embraced anyone other than Malcolm, but now she jumped up to hug Honora. "Why did you materialize?"

"A silly question, after that letter."

"You mean you just hopped on a plane?"

"And hopped and hopped—all those connections. Joss, tell me everything."

"The baby's due on or around November 15—it must've happened when we were in France."

"How are you feeling? I mean, you've never sent anything in the pouch before."

"I didn't mean to shake you up. I'm healthy as a horse—or rather, a camel. Dr. Bryanston says so."

Honora's white teeth bit into her soft upper lip as she gave Joscelyn a caring once-over. "You're sure?"

Joscelyn recollected the bloodily inept licensed quack her sister had gone to. She said reassuringly, "He comes from Dorset. An old dear, and highly qualified. An MD and FRCS not to mention the DPH."

"Malcolm must be walking on air."

Honora's presence had infused Joscelyn with energetic confidence. The problems between her and Malcolm were like historical events, true yet not currently relevant. "He's still in blissful ignorance."

"I've always felt guilty, not telling Curt."

"I only found out for sure last Wednesday. Over the weekend there wasn't a moment—we were so busy. Which reminds me. The gang'll crucify me if I don't have some sort of do to introduce you. And then there's Fuad. That means a separate but equal affair without booze. We'll have him and some of the other Abdulrahman family. Maybe the wives'll come."

"Joss, I promised Curt to meet him in London next Monday. There's so little time, and I thought we'd just relax together."

At this wistful naïveté, Joscelyn's surprisingly hearty laughter exploded. "You're in a country where the parties never stop."

On Friday night couples emerged from the row of prefabs like so many moths drawn to the lights blazing from the Pecks' windows. The wind had died down and quite a few people had braved the road from Ras al Kyn on the Persian Gulf, where Ivory was overseeing the port facility, to pay homage to the Big Boss's wife. Henley Larocha, Ivory's chief Mideast liaison, flew in from Cairo.

A swarm of beggars huddled across the road—kept at their distance by police hired by Malcolm.

The "II's" had come through. Specialties concocted from cans, boxes and foil packets crammed the dinette table while the Urquharts and the Duchamps, who employed "boys" less orthodox than Yussuf, had sent over their servants.

At the start of the evening Malcolm set up an informal reception line: Honora, who stood between him and Joscelyn, was introduced to each new arrival. Having years ago conquered her shyness in large gatherings, she came off as a lovely hybrid between Queen Elizabeth and Dinah Shore hosting the "Chevy Show," calming the guests, many of whom in their nervousness at meeting Mrs. Curt Ivory in the living flesh made unfortunate stabs at levity.

"We're mighty grateful you have a sister here in Lalarhein, ma'am," said a sun-reddened, beefy foreman from Ras al Kyn. "Otherwise how would we have the pleasure of seeing such a beautiful lady?"

"After all the veils," Honora murmured, "all of us must look gorgeous as Sophia Loren."

Everyone in hearing distance laughed.

By eight, guests jammed the prefab, and the air-conditioning units couldn't keep up with the crush: women fanned themselves and dabbed at oozing cosmetics while overtanned men tugged at their wilted collars. Honora convinced Malcolm to take off his jacket, and as the male guests gratefully followed his example a ripe odor of deodorant and sweat rippled through the overheated, smoky rooms.

The last bottle of Johnnie Walker was gone, and then the Smirnoff's. When Joscelyn passed on the bad news to Malcolm, he grinned unperturbed.

"The sign of the best parties, hon, running out."

She kissed his chin, wiping away her lipstick. *As soon as they all leave, I'll tell him.*

With pregnancy her sweet tooth had turned acid, and she warned herself not to take the Pillsbury devil's food cake lavished with frosting, but Letty Toohey, who had baked it, cut her a slab. She took a small mouthful and immediately a wad of sourness rose in her throat. She dashed to the bathroom. The door was locked. She pushed around jovial groups to the service porch, which led onto the side of the house. Outside, she heaved until her healed ribs ached.

The back door opened, and the bare bulb on the service

porch shone on Malcolm's boyishly rumpled black hair. "Joss? That you?"

"I just tossed my cookies."

"Poor honey. Get you a towel."

He returned with a dampened, clean dishcloth and a glass. Gratefully rinsing her mouth out with tepid club soda, she wiped her forehead and her eyes.

"Lucky for *you* there's no more booze," he said.

" 'It's not overindulging, dear,' said she coyly."

He frowned, perplexed. "I don't get you."

"Malcolm, can't you guess?"

One of the "boys" was setting an empty dish on the washing machine, and Malcolm watched, his expression coldly intent. He didn't speak until the service porch was empty.

"Swell, just swell," he said. "I should've figured it. Honora showing up one fine day for no apparent reason. Hell, why shouldn't a future aunt be the first to know?"

"I wanted to tell you, I tried last weekend, but there never seemed a good moment."

"Is that it?" he said. "Or did you figure if she knew you wouldn't have to get rid of the damn thing."

"Oh, Malcolm," she whispered.

"If you'd told me first, I'd've explained that I have enough problems right now. I—do—not—need—a—brat." His hands were clenching and unclenching.

Instinctively Joscelyn clasped her forearms protectively over her stomach.

"Joss?" Honora stood at the door. "Joss, are you out there?"

"Getting a little air," Joscelyn mumbled.

"Both of us," Malcolm said.

"Is everything all right?" Honora asked.

"Our little mama was totally surprising me."

Honora laughed happily. "Isn't it wonderful?"

"She really knocked me for a loop." He put his arm around Joscelyn's waist. "It's the greatest thing that's ever happened to me," he said, and his voice broke.

Turning to gauge whether he was making a play for Honora's good opinion, Joscelyn was astonished to see the glint of tears in his eyes. Real tears. She had done the unthinkable. She had let it seem, however wrongly, that Honora—or anyone else—came before him.

"You're sure?" she whispered.

"I've always wanted a kid," he said.

She kissed his cheek. "You'll be a wonderful papa."

31

After Malcolm's initial outburst, he displayed a poignant, semicomical entrancement with his approaching paternity. He called home on the crackling new telephone lines from the site—sometimes two or three times a day—to check on Joscelyn's well-being. He was tender of her during sex. When the fetal stirrings began he would spend long minutes with his hand curved on her stomach, waiting for a small jolt. Noting the whining, bed-wetting and other disturbances that beset the youngsters cooped up in the compound, he sent away for books on child care, underlining pertinent segments and reading them aloud to Joscelyn—engineer to engineer—as construction plans for a perfect human being.

His pleasure spilled over onto his work. He was no longer so dependent on his superiors' good opinion; he solved the minor problems that came up with reasonable competence. After several Ivory people fell ill during the July inferno and returned home to the States, Heinrichman promoted Malcolm to project manager at Pump Station 5. His immediate pride and pleasure were soon weighed down with fresh attacks of self-doubt that stemmed from lack of knowledge. It was Joscelyn's turn to send for literature. Curt dispatched her all the recent publications on pump stations. A pump station houses mechanically sophisticated means of moving various weights of crude through the pipeline. That long, agonizingly hot summer she passed her days studying, each weekend tutoring her husband with—for her—astonishing tact. Malcolm accepted the lessons willingly, and soon Pump Station 5 was ahead of schedule.

He gave credit to her coaching and to the willing local workers whom Khalid lined up for him.

By the end of October her husband no longer needed her help. It was just as well: Joscelyn's stomach was a large, localized mound, and her due date not far off.

The small, single-story Ivory hospital in Daralam had no facilities for maternity cases, so the company paid the fares for wives returning home to have their babies. Honora, however, suggested that Joscelyn move to the Upper Brook Street flat. She could have her baby in London, six thousand miles nearer to Malcolm than if she went home to California. *Daddy's there,* Honora wrote. *And of course I will come over to be with you.*

On the fifth of November, when Joscelyn landed at Heathrow, she was met by both the Ivorys. Honora, looking like a bewitching, dark-eyed czarina in Curt's latest gift of a creamy Russian lynx maxicoat and hat, carried a sable over her arm. "I'm lending you this," she said. "England's having the strangest weather. It's snowing."

"Snow?" Joscelyn said. "So *that's* what they call the white stuff I saw floating around."

"Pregnancy hasn't turned you sugary, has it?" Curt said, grinning as he kissed her cheek and relieved her of the flight bag.

The unseasonably early snow flurry had ceased by the time they reached the flat. The weather remained foul, though, alternating between sleet and a fine, icy rain. Curt went each day to Ivory's Cadogan Square office, but the sisters ventured out only twice to consult with Sir Harold Jenks, obstetrician to half of the distaff side of Debrett's Peerage. The rest of the days they lounged around the spacious flat. A stream of tiny, androgynously yellow, hand-stitched baby clothes arrived from The White House; Hamley's delivered a soft-furred menagerie. (Honora insisted on buying both toys and layette as a baby gift.) Langley lunched and dined with them, with droll humor making them privy to the literary gossip. Curt's expression remained polite, impervious. Though he sent outrageous monthly checks to his father-in-law, he had neither forgotten nor forgiven Langley's long-ago conning Honora out of her account at the Hollywood Bank of America.

* * *

Though the baby was not due until November the fifteenth, Joscelyn felt thoroughly dragged out by the tenth. That rainy morning she got up late and had just settled her bulk in the deep-cushioned sofa when the Welsh maid brought in the eleven o'clock coffee tray with a Jaeger's parcel addressed to Mrs M Peck. Joscelyn tore open the tissue to find a V-necked pink cashmere pullover.

Honora smiled. "It's from Curt and me."

"A mite warm for Lalarhein," Joscelyn said, shoving the soft wool back in the box. After a few moments she took the sweater out again, stroking it. "And that is just one of my many lovable responses. By now, Honora, you should've learned to curb your generosity."

"At this particular time it's uncurbable," Honora said, pouring the coffee, walking over to give Joscelyn hers before creaming her own. She dipped in a tea biscuit, eating it pensively. "Joss, probably this is ridiculous, so call me an idiot. But ever since you gave up your job I've been a bit worried. Engineering meant so much to you."

"That was premarital," Joscelyn replied. "The pumping station's tough, very, but after Malcolm's paid his dues in Lalarhein, the sky's the limit for him."

"That goes without saying. I was asking about *you.*"

"It's a wife's side of the bargain to help her husband get ahead." *God, I sound like those saccharine advice columns in the women's slicks.*

Carrying her cup and saucer to the window, Honora stared down at the bare, dripping branches of the garden that went with this block of luxury flats. "In the old days you would have been rolling in the aisles if you'd heard that speech."

"Insecurity, that's all. How could I've ever guessed I'd land a gorgeous guy like Malcolm?"

"But you've made an enormous sacrifice. Not only moving to Lalarhein, of all Godforsaken places, but giving up a wonderful career."

"No big deal, Honora, it's standard operating procedure when a gal gets married."

"Curt's always said you're the best there is."

"Shall we put it to music and dance? A wife's obligation is to her husband."

Honora moved from the window, sinking gracefully on the rug in front of the electric fire.

At a sudden twinge, Joscelyn grimaced. "Oh shit, why don't you just come right out and tell me I've turned into a subservient cow."

"I didn't mean to pick on you. You wouldn't be working anymore anyway," Honora soothed contritely. "Not with the Lump." (This had become the family catchphrase for the baby.)

"And anyway," Joscelyn said, "I don't notice you rushing off to do battle brandishing your briefcase."

"I never went to college; I don't have your kind of brain. But I do wish I had some meaningful work that I loved to do." Honora was winding a silky strand of black hair around her finger, and her eyes evoked past griefs.

Joscelyn's expression of defensiveness altered to one of sympathy. "You've forgotten your gardens."

"A hobby." Honora's tone was self-deprecating.

"Sure. Sure. That's why people come from all over to see them."

"Oh, Joss, if you only knew how utterly useless I feel."

Joscelyn could not recollect ever hearing Honora gripe, not even about waiting tables. "What sort of talk is this? Aren't you wrapped in the best bunnyskins? Doesn't Curt kiss you goodbye every morning like he's going to the moon?"

"And I'm cuh-razy about him, too. Joss, do try to understand. He's altering the world—you know the Ivory projects better than I do. He has his work. My entire life is centered around him. He's my everything. It's not fair. If anything goes the least bit wrong between us, he knows I collapse. He's my only resource."

"What some people won't complain about!" Joscelyn said in a determinedly joshing tone. "Being married to a powerful, wildly attractive guy who gives you everything."

"If I were doing something constructive I wouldn't be such a psychological burden."

"Somebody's been stuffing you."

Honora looked strained, anxious. "But you do have a glimmer of what I'm saying?"

"Sure I do, and you might as well know it's not total fulfillment to ponder what would clean the red waterstains out of a Lalarheini toilet trap. But Malcolm's doing fabulously, so it's worth it. And I *am* pregnant." Joscelyn stopped. Honora was yanking at the strand of hair. *Is this whole whine because I'm having a baby?* It was difficult to imagine Honora suffering the pangs of an ignoble emotion like jealousy. *She's flesh and blood,* Joscelyn told herself. After a moment, she asked, "Honora, have you and Curt ever discussed adopting?"

"He's cold on the idea. I think it's got to do with not knowing who he is or where he comes from. He wanted his own children."

"Sometimes life's the pits, isn't it?" As Joscelyn spoke she was hit by the irony that she was about to perform the prime female function, a function that her lovely, rich older sister was incapable of.

Just before seven thirty that night, Joscelyn, Curt and Honora arrived at a spacious early Victorian mansion on Bayswater Road that had been renovated into a private gynecological hospital. A trim, middle-aged Irish nurse stood on the curb, holding an outsize umbrella over a wheelchair. In her lilting voice, she directed Curt and Honora to a graciously proportioned room. On one of the small tables sat a telephone—no institutional wall fixtures to send out tidings of a new member of the ruling class. Curt dialed long distance before sitting back with the latest *Time*: calls to Lalarhein took anywhere from three hours to a day to go through.

They were served tea and small sandwiches that Curt ate hungrily—Joscelyn's pains had canceled dinner. The Irish nurse came to stand in the doorway. "Mrs. Peck would like to see you, Mr. Ivory," she said.

"You mean Mrs. Ivory," Curt replied.

"She asked for you, sir." The song of the Celt. "It will be a short little visit. She's getting her sedation."

Joscelyn's hospital-gowned bulbousness was dammed in by the railings of her narrow bed. The Demerol hadn't taken hold yet, and as Curt came into the labor room she was arching her back, sweat popping out on her distorted face. He reached out and she clutched both of his strongly tendoned hands. When the pain relaxed, she asked, "Honora's not hurt, is she?"

"She understands," he said, raising an eyebrow. "What's up, Joss? What can I do?"

"If anything happens to me—"

"Nothing's going to. Jenks didn't get his knighthood by bungling."

"Let me be dramatic; it's my big moment. Promise if anything happens, you'll keep Malcolm in Ivory?"

"If you're making final requests, try something worthwhile. It's not my habit to go around firing good people." He gave her the less caustic version of his smile. "Joss, Heinrichman's not one to hand out compliments, but he told me Malcolm's completely knowledgeable about pumping stations."

Her seminars had paid off.

Another pain started, but the Demerol was dividing her mind into two compartments. One side was becoming a receptacle for the contraction, absorbing the jagged hurt in the small of her back, the unrelenting pressure that hardened her stomach to concrete, the ripping apart of her rectum. Thanks to the drug, this compartment floated blessedly farther and farther away.

By contrast the other half of her mind jumped with brilliantly edged details. The green walls of the labor room, the persistent hiss of the glinting metal sterilizer, the shadow cast by the scalloped fringe of the drawn blind. She could smell the woodiness of Curt's after-shave—he must have shaved when he came home, before her pains had suddenly crowded together. She noted that the lines on the left side of his forehead were deeper, where his eyebrow went up. His firm grasp generated strength and energy.

Being married to Malcolm is like whirling through space, she thought, not questioning why this had leaped into her mind. *I can be so dizzy with joy that I could die, or I can plummet into the cold void. I'm trapped forever in his gravitational pull.*

A faraway pain clutched her, and another thought blossomed, sharp and clear-edged. *The world threatens Malcolm and he placates everyone but me. He loves me and therefore takes out his fear and frustration on me.*

Curt pushed back her sweaty hair, and she felt the coolness of his fingers on her forehead.

Curt, she thought. *He's not afraid.*

I wish he were the baby's father.

32

"Good morning, Mr. Ivory, Mrs. Ivory," said Sir Harold in a loud, cheerful voice. Wearing blood-streaked surgical greens, he stood in the doorway dangling his mask.

It was ten past six and Honora, who hadn't slept, rose to her feet. Curt, dozing on the couch, came instantly alert.

"You have a beautiful niece, born fifteen minutes ago, at five before six," the titled obstetrician said. "Armistice day, so there'll be no difficulty remembering her birthday. A most perfect little girl."

"And m-my sister . . . ?" Honora coughed to loosen her throat.

"Other than a routine episiotomy, she's as good as new. In a few minutes she'll be coming up—she's still rather drugged, but you can see her for a minute. I congratulate you both." Briskly waving his mask, he disappeared.

Giving a soft little laugh, Honora threw her arms around Curt. "A little girl," she cried. "Isn't it heaven?"

He kissed her on the mouth. "Girls are the best. Damn, why doesn't that call come through!"

A broad little Cockney nurse led them up a floor to Joscelyn's airy room with the three long, narrow windows that overlooked the darkness of Hyde Park. The patient, followed by a small retinue, was wheeled in. Beneath the green blanket Joscelyn looked flat. Her eyes were closed, her pallid face slack.

"Joss?" Honora said.

Joscelyn looked up with a wearily triumphant smile. "A girl!"

"We heard," Honora said. "I'm so happy I'm crying."

"Wait until you see her." Joscelyn's voice was slurred. "She is gorg-ee-ous."

The two orderlies transferred Joscelyn to the bed. As if on cue, the bedside telephone buzzed.

Curt answered. "Hey, Malcolm. Yes, we're here. But let Joss give you the news."

Joscelyn lay back in the pillows, her chin drawn back with worry. "We have a little girl, Malcolm, seven pounds two ounces, twenty-one inches. The most perfect baby. All the nurses raved, and so did Sir Harold. And you know how many babies *they* see. She's an absolute dream." There was a feverish intensity to her drugged voice. After a pause, she said, "I can't quite hear you, darling. Oh, now you're clear. You're sure you don't mind a girl?" Another pause. "Yes, I'm glad, too. Malcolm, not to be gushy, but she has these perfect miniature fingers and toes, the tiniest fingernails." A pause. "No, it's very dark, like yours. I'm calling her Rosalynd Joanna, like we agreed—is that all right? We'll register her with the American Embassy, and—"

"Mrs. Peck, you can talk to your husband later," said the heavyset floor matron. "Now you must sleep."

After her farewells, the phone drooped in Joscelyn's hand and she closed her eyes. Honora touched her lips to her younger sister's slightly clammy forehead. "I'll be back this afternoon. Joss, we're so happy."

Going up in the small elevator to the nursery, Curt said, "That's some mouthful, Rosalynd Joanna."

"She told me before that it's a Peck family name. She sounded apologetic about having a girl, didn't she?"

"The drugs."

"When she told *us* about the baby she was daffy with excitement."

"Maybe Malcolm had his heart set on a Rodney Jeremiah."

They had reached the top floor. Curt tapped on the glassed wall. A capped, masked nurse nodded and went to the farthest canvas cot, carrying her small pink bundle upright to the window.

Rosalynd Joanna Peck's head showed none of the results associated with the arduous journey through the birth canal. Her skin was a luminous, rosy pearl, her button of a nose had a miniature bridge. Her eyes—they had lashes—were closed. As they watched, she opened her well-delineated lips in a prodigious, toothless yawn, then blinked unfocusing. The eyes were a bright blue.

"Joss was right." Curt's voice was low with awe. "She really is something else."

"Exquisite. Curt, except for the coloring, she's the image of Crystal."

"I don't see it." Curt's tone was noncommittal.

"It's so obvious. Look? She even has Crystal's darling cleft in her chin." Honora's cheeks were wet and she accepted that her tears were only in part the product of joy for this niece. She was also weeping for her lost sister, for the unrecapturable past; she was weeping because this baby was not hers.

Three weeks later, Joscelyn and her daughter—whose name had been shortened and softened to Lissie—returned to Lalarhein.

Malcolm's skills as a father amazed Joscelyn. After only one demonstration he knew exactly how to hold Lissie's lovely head while bathing her, he patted her dry, turning her this way and that on the bassinet as he shook the can of Johnson's Baby Powder, he cleaned her miniature, flat-set ears with a Q-Tip, he knew how to burp her after orange juice or water. (Joscelyn was breast feeding, and for the first time in her life had the pleasure of real if minor cleavage.) He didn't even mind changing dirty diapers, a chore that other mothers in the compound assured Joscelyn *their* husbands adamantly refused.

He showed Lissie off to Fuad and Lelith, who gave an antique, hand-knotted silk rug for her room. He carried in the baby for the inspection of Khalid's flashing eye, and even held her out for silent, thin Harb Fawzi to admire. He exulted to the neighbors when she held her silver rattle, staring at it.

"Lissie's got a first-rate mind," he informed Joscelyn. "You better start giving her some mental stimulation."

"Malcolm, she's six weeks old."

"Send away for one of those alphabet mobiles like the Duchamps' kid has dangling over his crib," he said.

On the weekends, Joscelyn would awaken to find him sitting in the nursery rocker, his dark head bent to nuzzle the soft, black down of Lissie's apple-size skull.

"I heard her moving around," he would whisper. "She's not hungry, she just needed a bit of holding."

Lissie was not only exquisite, she was a good baby, seldom crying, eating on a four-hour schedule, sleeping through the night and through every sort of household ruckus and domestic discord. She didn't even have a fussy period.

What did women mean, postpartum blues? For the first time in her entire life, Joscelyn awoke in the morning without that sense that something dreadful might happen to her. She had no need for constant striving. How strange that she, of all women, should glory in motherhood.

But why not? Hadn't she given Malcolm the perfect child?

In March Honora arrived for a visit.

The house had only two bedrooms. "You lucked out, auntie," Malcolm said, only half jestingly. "You get to sleep with my daughter."

This time there were no parties. "I'm only here a few days," Honora said firmly when Malcolm suggested another bash.

"My daughter's the greatest, true," Malcolm retorted. "But you can't sit and admire her the whole time."

"Just watch me," Honora said.

He returned to work early Sunday. Afterward, Honora and Joscelyn, wearing short nylon robes, sat in the living room drinking coffee and talking idly. Lissie lay on the floor, protected by one of her flannel blankets: she lifted up her head to stare soberly at her toy giraffe.

"Have you ever noticed that she doesn't turn at voices, Joss?" Honora asked.

"Our conversation isn't very stimulating."

"She didn't pay any attention to the trucks, and that's a real din. When do they notice noises?"

Joscelyn waved her finger in front of Lissie. The blue eyes followed the movement. "That," she said in an arrogantly authoritative tone, "is what she's meant to do. That's her developmental stage."

But when Honora went to run her rusty bathwater, Joscelyn flew to the bookshelf, flipping through Gesell and Ilg. Infants as young as four weeks respond to sound. Lissie was sixteen weeks.

Joscelyn clapped.

Lissie didn't turn.

Joscelyn clapped so smartly that her palms stung.

Lissie continued rubbing her pretty button nose on yellow-flowered flannel.

Joscelyn picked her up, cuddling her fiercely, kissing the downy black head. The faucet had been turned off. "You were right," she shouted in a gratingly angry voice.

"What?" Honora called back.

"She should hear. She doesn't."

There was a splashing, and Honora flung open the door, a flash of dripping, dazzling white breast and white buttock before she wrapped a blue striped towel around her torso.

She whistled. A long, shrill note.

"Don't you believe me?" Joscelyn demanded. "She—does—not—hear."

"Bring her into the kitchen."

Yussuf averted his gaze, creeping onto the service porch while the towel-clad Honora stood a few inches behind the baby's head, clashing two Revere stainless steel pot covers like cymbals.

Lissie stared straight ahead.

Honora continued her crescendo.

Lissie didn't turn, but began to wail at the tightness of her mother's arms.

"Why don't you stop?" Joscelyn shouted. "She does not hear!"

"We don't know that yet," Honora said, taking the crying baby from her sister's grasp, stroking the child tenderly. "Pretty, pretty. Uncle Curt'll find the best specialist for you, Lissie darling."

33

It took nearly fifteen hours for Honora's call to Los Angeles to go through: Curt's response, however, was instantaneous. Within a few hours two first-class bookings to New

York were waiting at the cramped window of the hot, dirty Daralam airport, the Ivory apartment in the Waldorf Towers was vacated by a pair of vice presidents, an immediate appointment set up at the Weller Pediatric Hearing Clinic where new patients normally waited eight weeks.

The day after Honora, Joscelyn and Lissie landed in New York, they were seated in Dr. Weller's spacious, dark-wood paneled corner office: Joscelyn had been a corporation woman long enough to respect a corner office with windows facing in two directions. The walls were lined with books, and in a prominent space, segregated from the other thick medical tomes by marble bookends, stood five fat volumes imprinted on the spine *Samson J. Weller, MD.*

After the initial questions, Dr. Weller snapped down the hanging type of diagram that one sees in classrooms. "Let's follow the route of sound waves—or, as I like to explain, shook-up air," he said, raising the index finger of his plump white hand to tap at the grossly enlarged ear. "The waves travel through the outer ear, which though pretty much ornamental, does help direct sound waves to the ear canal, here." Tap. "Then our waves travel through the inch of the canal, arriving at the tympanic membrane—the eardrum." He tapped the appropriate area. "The sound waves strike the eardrum with incredibly tiny vibrations, and these infinitesimal sounds reach the middle ear. In the middle ear is a truly remarkable amplification and transmission system called the ossicles. The ossicles are the three smallest bones in the human body...."

Though Dr. Weller was short and outlandishly overweight, he possessed resonant, commandingly rich tonal qualities. Joscelyn let the sonorously spoken words roll over her, pondering whether it was a natural vocal gift or whether he'd taken training to become a radio announcer. She shifted on the rich blue tweed of the couch, rotating her tensed shoulders, careful not to disturb Lissie, who slept in her lap.

Honora touched her arm.

Joscelyn jerked to attention.

"And this is the acoustic nerve," the doctor was saying. He had reached the far end of his diagram, a broad stalk. "The acoustic nerve is where the mechanical energy is encoded in electrical patterns and transmitted to the brain."

At the word *brain,* Joscelyn's eye twitched and her aching shoulders hunched. Was Lissie's brain damaged? An unbearable thought, unbearable. Then she reminded herself that it was impossible. *Lissie's a very quick baby, everyone says so.*

"I think we have the physiology down pat," she said. "Now can we get to the point?"

Honora shot her a reproachful glance. But wasn't it a snap for Honora to remain in control, a perfect lady? Lissie wasn't *her* child.

"In a general way, Mrs. Peck, there are two types of hearing loss. Conductive deafness. Nerve or perceptive deafness. A hearing impairment may be mixed, involving both conductive and nervous apparatus."

"Explain conductive deafness," Joscelyn said, covering her overwhelming fear and the painful twinges of her neck with a Grand Inquisitor act.

"Just what you might guess, Mrs. Peck. The failure of sound waves to be conducted efficiently through the external ear canal, the middle ear or the inner ear." Glossy cloth rattled as he tapped the appropriate patches. "Adequate messages do not reach the inner ear. Conductive impairment, therefore, simply diminishes the loudness of sound. It never causes profound deafness. Conductive deafness can be corrected by surgery."

"Now tell me about perceptive deafness—nerve deafness."

"Again what it sounds like. The nerves are damaged."
"What then?"

Ripples moved across the tentlike white Dacron coat as the doctor sighed deeply. "I'm afraid we have no medical procedure to repair nerves. If the damage is extensive enough, that person can never hear as we do."

Honora's soft upper lip rose, vulnerably.

"Are you saying that modern medicine can't do a damn for nerve deafness?" Joscelyn asked.

"I'm sorry, we can't. But with consistent auditory training and appropriate amplification, that person can learn to develop certain listening skills."

Lissie had been awake several minutes and was sucking her thumb. "It's past her feeding time," Joscelyn said, blinking furiously.

Dr. Weller showed them into a small room.

Lissie was changed and peering alertly at her plush bear

when there was a tap on the door and a young woman came in. Thick red curls framed a face too bony and angular for prettiness: it was the intelligent eagerness of her expression that made her attractive. "What a beautiful little girl," she said, bending her knees to Lissie's level, smiling. "I'm Carole Donovan, the audiologist. We're going to see Dr. Weller."

Joscelyn clasped Lissie to her still oozing breasts. "Are you taking her away?"

"No, Mrs. Peck," Carole reassured. "You and Mrs. Ivory'll be with her in the testing room."

Testing room?

Joscelyn's thighs trembled and she held the baby with tight caution as she went down the short corridor. Dr. Weller sat in a booth like that of a recording studio, his plump fingers playing with knobs and dials that bristled from a console. A large glass window in front of him showed a small interior room.

"Here we go," Carole said, opening the second door.

On this side, the control booth's window was a mirror.

Large, triangular speakers stood in each corner and an oblong speaker descended from the acoustical board ceiling. Toys spilled from two large bins. Lissie, however, reached toward the table: a mechanical monkey held sticks poised over a drum.

"Not that one, Lissie, honey," Carole said, again bending to the child's level. She picked out a yellow rubber whale, squeaking it. "Each of the toys in here makes a different sound."

The rubber fish squeaked again as Lissie thrust its tail into her mouth.

"What Dr. Weller's going to do is play sounds on the various speakers. If Lissie reacts, we reward her by letting my monkey beat his drum."

The speaker behind them gave a high, nearly inaudible whine. Then the rushing roar of surf was all around them. A horn honked stridently. A trumpet blared. Lissie didn't react, the toy monkey remained immobile. The muscles of Joscelyn's shoulders and back were strung so tightly that she worried the baby must sense it. "Here," she said to Honora. "You hold her for a while." Trucks passed through the cubicle, then jets, sirens wailed closer and louder, a jackhammer shuddered mightily. Honora's oval face pulled into a grimacing wince.

Blessed silence.

"As you've noticed, we're at the threshold of pain," Carole said, pressing plugs into her ears. The bright eagerness was gone from her face. "Now you'll pass it."

A cannon blasted, then another. As the cannonade increased unendurably, Joscelyn's eyes involuntarily squeezed shut. Forcing them open, she saw that Lissie, on Honora's lap, had tilted her head fractionally as she continued to placidly mouth the whale.

Silence.

Dr. Weller wheezed as he stepped up into the room with them. His round white face was somber.

"Well?" Joscelyn demanded. "What did your stint at the console prove?"

"Mrs. Peck, we'll talk later. For the next test Lissie must be sedated."

"What are you going to do to her?"

"Nothing that hurts. For the brain stem we prefer the child still, that's all."

"Brain stem?" Joscelyn snatched Lissie from Honora's arms.

"It's nothing ominous," soothed the doctor's fine voice. "We'll attach three electrodes to measure the brain stimulation, then use the bone oscillator, here." He touched behind Lissie's ear, and she gave her lovely, toothless smile. "The brain stem test bypasses the middle ear, which we already know is impaired."

"So at least you did figure out something?"

"Mrs. Peck, it's nearly one. Why don't you and Mrs. Ivory relax, have a bite of lunch? Come back in a couple of hours. Then we'll talk."

And Carole said, "There's a pretty good sandwich counter downstairs in the building."

They ordered an egg-and-pecan salad on whole wheat to split, but neither bit into her overfilled half. In less than fifteen minutes they were back in the Weller Clinic's waiting room.

Two older children with hearing aids were reading, and a pretty teenager wrote in her looseleaf notebook. A little boy, maybe three, sat with his mother near the toy bin. Picking out a ball, he made a strange, high-pitched squeak.

The young mother beamed at him. "Yes, Billy, it's a ball," she said, enunciating carefully. "A big red ball."

The child repeated the squeak. "Baa."

Joscelyn's bladder sent out an urgent signal, and she requested the key to the ladies' room: it proved a false alarm. Honora, silent and pale, sat staring out at the opposite building. Joscelyn flipped through back issues of *The New Yorker,* not seeing the pages. By now her shoulders were so tensed that her neck ached as if from a major whiplash injury.

After an endless two hours the reception nurse told them Dr. Weller was ready.

Next to Dr. Weller's neat desk stood a Portacrib; Lissie slept on her side, angelic, exquisite.

A tiny, middle-aged Oriental woman in a white coat got to her feet. She was dwarfed by Dr. Weller. "This is my chief associate," he introduced. "Dr. Bornstein."

The physician bent her smoothly coiffed, graying head.

"Mrs. Peck." Dr. Weller was looking at Joscelyn, his big white face expressionless. "Our testing can't be entirely accurate because Lissie is so young. However, as you doubtless noticed, she paid very little attention to the loudest sounds. In the low frequencies, two-fifty to five hundred hertz, she has a profound hearing impairment—ninety decibels. And in the high frequencies—a thousand to four thousand—she has no measurable hearing."

"Now say it in English." Joscelyn's voice shook.

"Dr. Bornstein and I concur that your daughter was born with extensive damage in the eighth cranial nerves—I explained earlier those are the receptor mechanisms of the hearing apparatus."

"She has nerve deafness, then," Honora whispered.

"I'm very sorry," Dr. Weller said.

Suddenly it happened. The dark medical library, the prestigious windows, the diagrams of grotesquely outsize ears lurched and spun. Suite 2017 was toppling into Fifty-third Street, the blue couch sinking like a fast elevator, her stomach plummeting. *Earthquake! My God, New York's been hit by a ten on the Richter Scale. Earthquake.* Into her mind swam the precautions every Californian learns: get away from windows, find a doorway with a strong supporting beam. But if the earth was heaving, why were the others calmly watching her as if expecting her to speak?

Honora blew her nose. "What can we do?"

"It's not too soon to start training," Dr. Weller said.

"Most major hospitals have a hearing center, with training and rehabilitation," Dr. Bornstein added. "Mrs. Peck, in Los Angeles you have the John Tracy Clinic. They work with children from infancy to school age, educating the parents and offering them counseling—a hearing-impaired child strains family relationships."

The room continued falling. Joscelyn could scarcely keep her grasp on the blue tweed pillows.

"Why do you keep acting as if she's deaf?" inquired someone. The sound waves must not be vibrating properly, for the words were uttered at least a mile from this quaking, shaking office.

"I'm sorry." Dr. Weller's rotund form bounced like a huge ball. "News like this is difficult to accept, Mrs. Peck. But your daughter is a beautiful, intelligent child, and with the right training, patience, devotion and love, she'll grow into a beautiful, intelligent woman."

"She is not deaf," said the voice, yet farther away.

"When parents find out, they're usually in shock." Dr. Weller's wondrous voice was rich with compassion.

"Here, Joss, you better lie down on the couch."

"She is not . . ."

For the first time in her life, Joscelyn fainted.

Dr. Weller arranged for other opinions. The otolaryngological departments of Baby's Hospital and Beth Israel concurred with his prognosis.

When the limousine left Beth Israel it was dark. Neither woman spoke. In the Waldorf Tower suite, Joscelyn bathed Lissie, crooning as she put her down in the hotel crib while Honora ordered from room service.

Joscelyn took her place opposite her sister in the full-sized dining room.

"Joss," Honora said, "you're leaving tomorrow morning, so tonight we really better make some plans."

Joscelyn pushed at the mealy whiteness of her baked potato. "Doctors! They make me sick! At Berkeley the bright guys were never premed, just the grinds."

"You can't stay in Lalarhein."

"One overweight jerk gives a diagnosis and the others fall in line, backing him up. That's called professional courtesy."

"You really ought to call Malcolm. You haven't phoned him since we got here."

"What's there to say? That an assortment of New York weirdos don't know their asses from hot rocks?"

"Lissie went to the best specialists." Honora's hands were trembling as they curved around her waterglass, yet she spoke with a faint trace of that English remoteness that commanded respect from everyone.

"That obese slob can't be the best."

"The point is that Lissie needs training, and so do you. She's cut off from the normal ways of communicating, so you have to teach her other means—we're lucky she's so very quick—"

"Except in the hearing department. There she's slow."

"Malcolm can be transferred home."

"Why?"

"Oh, Joss, you've never hidden from the truth."

"Since when are you an expert on babies? I've read enough books, I'm a mother. Children develop at different speeds, you know."

"Don't talk to me like that."

"How should I talk to you, when you keep insisting Lissie's defective?"

"You're not ten years old, Joss. The last thing Lissie needs is a mother who snipes at everyone and gives off hateful signals."

"That two-ton quack and his cronies admitted they couldn't be exact. I say Lissie simply hasn't reached the stage where she can respond to their booming and banging and bone oscillating. In her own good time she'll learn."

"Never." Honora's eyes were shadowed and wet. She went around the table to put her arms around her sister's shoulders. "Joss, you've got to accept Lissie's deafness. Otherwise you won't be able to help her."

Joscelyn couldn't take any more. Shrugging away from Honora's embrace, she leaped up, overturning her chair. *"Lissie is not deaf!"* she screamed at the top of her lungs. *"She is not deaf!"*

When Joscelyn arrived at the Daralam airstrip, Francie Duchamp and Mary Curtiss were in the narrow slot assigned to waiting females, both of them waving their covered arms.

As they took the diaper bag, the car seat, the burdensome overnight bag, Joscelyn said quickly, "The kid's fine. Not a thing wrong with her. I guess Malcolm and I were out of line, expecting her to be a genius all the way around. She's just not very quick on the aural side."

At home, she phoned the shack that was field headquarters for Pump Station 5.

Malcolm's first words were: "How's Lissie?"

Joscelyn's throat seemed to close, and air could not get to her brain. She was hyperventilating.

"Joss? You still there?"

"She's fine. I guess we were out of line, expected her to be a genius all the way around," Joscelyn said, repeating by rote. "She's just not very quick on the aural side."

"That's all? It's developmental?"

"Yes," Joscelyn gasped.

"Hey, and I've been too chicken to call and ask about my little sweetheart. Give her a big kiss and tell her Daddy misses her and loves her."

Thursday night, makeup freshened, hair shampooed and blown-dry, Joscelyn hurled herself into her husband's arms.

"Welcome home," he said in a low sexy voice. "Welcome home, baby." He kissed her as if they were lovers, not a married couple.

For a few more seconds she luxuriated in his embrace, then she blurted, "Darling, doctors are such dumb asses."

His body tensed, and his arms fell away from her. "What does that mean?"

"The premeds never were the brightest, remember, just the ones who got the grades—"

"What the fuck did Weller say about Lissie?"

"Please don't shout at me. I can't explain properly when you're this way."

"You better get yourself straightened out, Joscelyn, I'm warning you. If there's something the matter with *my* kid, the last thing I want to hear is your lies."

"It's complicated, Malcolm. They don't know Lissie the way I do. They played with some electrodes and gave her this imbecilic unscientific noise test—*I* couldn't even hear some of the sounds. With a baby this young they aren't sure anyway. I'm the one who knows her, and I can see she's perfectly fine. Sit down, let me fix you a drink—"

He thrust his boyishly handsome face pugnaciously toward her. "What the fuck did they tell you about *my* daughter?" He punched her upper arm.

It was a mean blow, and as she staggered back a step, the

past week's assortment of thin, fat, Jewish, Oriental, didactic and reticent specialists, the biting spells of vertigo, Honora's dark, worried eyes, and Lissie—most of all, Lissie, peacefully sucking on a rubber toy while the last trump sounded—roiled up inside her like vomit.

"You want to know what's wrong, I'll give you what's wrong!" Joscelyn shouted. "She's deaf! Our beautiful, perfect daughter is profoundly deaf!" At this, her first self-admission of Lissie's handicap, Joscelyn's heart was banging against the walls of her chest like a wrecking ball. "She's deaf. Three different sets of specialists said *your* daughter's cold, stone deaf!"

Panting, she awaited physical retaliation. Malcolm bent his head and closed his eyes, standing in his sweat-stained work khakis with enforced stillness. She saw a tear squeeze from his right eye. Had he looked like this when bullied by that monster, his father?

"Darling, I'm sorry, so sorry . . ." She was crying, too. "I shouldn't have yelled it out, but I hadn't let myself believe it before. I've blocked it all the way. Oh God, and she's so perfect otherwise."

"It's permanent?" He didn't look up.

"The eighth cranial nerve is damaged in both ears. The doctors all said the same thing. No hearing in the high frequencies, practically none in the low. There isn't any surgery to correct nerve damage. She'll always be deaf."

His sigh shook.

"The doctors said we ought to go home," Joscelyn said. "The sooner she starts her education, the better. And we both have to learn how to help her."

He wiped his eyes with a grubby knuckle. "There's no deafness in my family," he said in a pleading tone.

"Nor in ours. I feel such a failure."

She reached out to him. They clung together, swaying back and forth in their shared, accepted grief that the child born from the tangling of their imperfect lives was flawed, too.

A few minutes later, after Malcolm had bathed, both Urquharts came over with Double U's inevitable welcome home to Lalarhein, a tuna noodle casserole. Joscelyn, putting Lissie down, could hear their conversation.

"Nothing's really bad with the kid," Malcolm said. "But

she does have a hearing problem that needs a little minor correction, so it's my guess she and Joscelyn will ship home soon. If it were anything major I'd go with them like a shot, but since nothing's vital, I'll stick it out until the pump station's finished. Besides, there's the groundwork I'm doing with Khalid, you know, on the big airport project Ivory's hoping to sew up." Malcolm's voice lowered casually, as it always did when he insinuated he was in the epicenter of big doings, a trick of his performed so ingenuously that most people took his self-aggrandizing hints at face value. "I'll hang in here."

There hadn't been time for them to plan their departure, but Joscelyn had never considered it would not be *en famille*. The air conditioner came on with a blast, and she could not hear them anymore, but she was realizing with a jarring misery that their daughter's handicap was even more unbearable to Malcolm than it was to her.

He's going to try to ignore it, Joscelyn thought. *He's going to lie to himself and everybody else; he's going to act as if her deafness doesn't exist.* She continued to smile down at Lissie, but her hands shook as she tucked the yellow sheet around the baby and her favorite giraffe.

FOUR

1966

Crystal

34

In Taormina, that final week in December of 1966 was like summer.

Crystal, in a white bikini, lay on her back by the pool. Pads called mouse bras covered her eyes. One knee bent, arms at her sides, she shimmered with a cream concocted specifically for her by a Zurich dermatologist who had taken into account the Sicilian latitude when he charted the maximum number of minutes she should expose herself to full sun. No skin-corrugating mahogany tan for Crystal Talbott, but the palest of ambers to honor her fair pigmentation, blond hair and blue eyes.

The pool was a hundred vertical feet from the tile-roofed villa, a polished blue fingernail on the landscaped finger of the little isthmus that jutted out from the cliff halfway to the sea. Steep ledges carved in Roman times led from the house to the pool and thence down to the dock; however, modern inhabitants preferred the glass-enclosed elevator that clung to the rock.

Crystal's timer buzzed.

She slipped on an eyelet beach robe, moving to the shade of a flowered marquee. From here visitors invariably described the view hyperbolically, calling it the most gorgeous in Sicily, Italy, Europe, the world. To her left, the town of Taormina tumbled from the medieval outcropping of Castel Mola to the azure Ionian Sea, a picturesque jumble of red roof tile, pastel stucco, maroon bougainvillea, spired church domes and square gray Crusader towers. Taormina was tethered both to history and the point of the bay by its most eloquent relic, the massive red brick ruin of the Greco-Roman theater. Crystal turned to her right, craning to see the abrupt rise of Mount Etna: a thin curve of smoke feathered above the volcano's uneven cap of snow.

If only the weather holds for the Saudis, she thought. The

Talbotts had invited the Saudi Arabian commission in charge of planning highways to "an intimate weekend" at the beginning of January.

Luxurious entertaining was the villa's purpose.

Crystal, mistress of those artful, seemingly noncommercial friendships that give one the advantage over competitors, last year had determined that their second home, which sprawled along a fairway on Carmel's Seventeen Mile Drive, was too stodgily bourgeois in this jet-set age. So when she heard from her old friend, Imogene Burdetts Lane Steenberg Capelli, that an Italian film star fallen on hard times was selling the spectacular Taormina property at a substantial loss, she flew over. One quick walk through convinced her. The modernization that had retained the villa's eighteenth-century charm, the remnants of the original Roman estate and—most of all—this view would seduce any prospective client. Gideon groused about buying a vacation home in such a remote spot: however, having years earlier accepted his second wife as an indispensable part of his business (because of Crystal, Talbott's had a substantial backlog even during cyclical slumps) he finally agreed to the purchase in his gruffest tone. And Crystal had bargained the desperate actress to an even lower price. The Talbotts had owned the villa ten months and thus far it had already paid for itself twice over with the contract to plan and oversee Egypt's Mitwan Dam, where Gideon had been for the last three days, since the day after Christmas. He was returning to Sicily late this afternoon.

Boisterous masculine laughter rang over the roar of the sea, and a moment later Alexander appeared on the terrace, followed by Gid. Droplets shone on her sons' dark tans, and their hair was plastered down with seawater. Both carried snorkels, fins, masks.

Gid's infant resemblance to Gideon had become more pronounced, the same top-heavy torso and burly calves. His dripping thatch of curly hair was brown, he had Gideon's round brown eyes and the heavy jawline, on which a scattering of zits showed.

The likeness, though, went only skin deep. Gid lacked the self-confident drive, the righteousness of his father. An innately decent, good-natured boy with a mild sense of humor, he kept his thick shoulders slightly hunched, as if to shrug off the adolescent doubts and insecurities that swarmed around him. His even white teeth, now displayed in a disarming smile, were the one feature he'd inherited from his mother.

Alexander, fifteen months younger, had shot up this past year and was an inch or so the taller. He had the long, narrow, Sylvander bone structure. Slight in comparison to his brother, not as physically mature, he moved around the pool toward her with a graceful assurance that made Crystal catch her breath.

Her second son was beautiful, no doubt about it.

His hair, darkened now by seawater, had the same gilded brightness her own had possessed naturally in her teenage years, and he wore it in the longer style of that irritatingly loud musical group from Liverpool, the Beatles. Alexander's nose was fine and tilted slightly, like hers; he held his head at an arrogant backward tilt. His long, tawny eyes presented a continuous if subliminal reminder of Curt Ivory: because Crystal loathed the sire while adoring the son, she never consciously let herself dwell on where Alexander had gotten this particular feature.

Not only in appearance were the two Talbott boys near polar opposites. At Menlo, their prep school, Gid went out for team sports—soccer, hockey, football, baseball in season—while Alexander concentrated on tennis and golf, games that in Crystal's mind would benefit him later. *A* was for Alexander, while Gid earned *C*'s and *B*'s. Gid seldom inhabited the detention room. Alexander was a regular: he had been involved in several prep school scrapes, the most recent involved a marijuana cigarette. Though Alexander had vituperatively and repeatedly denied culpability, Gideon had deprived him of his Vespa for the Christmas break, grounding him over Crystal's protests.

"Mother," Gid said, holding out his large, clenched hand. "I found something near the wreck." This rocky bay had claimed armadas of ships from different millennia. "It's for you."

"Thank you, dear," Crystal said, half rising. Gifts gave her a charge. Gid, knowing this weakness and knowing also that he was bottom man on the fraternal totem pole, spent much of his modest allowance on small presents for her. "Show me."

Gid opened his fingers to display a thin, irregular disk thick with encrustation.

"It's a Roman denarius," Alexander said.

Gid turned. "You told me it was probably a shilling."

"And you believed me? With that junk on it, that shape?" Alexander slapped his towel at Gid. "Put on your eyes, take a look. You can even see a bit of lettering."

Gid retrieved the horn-rims he had set down near his snorkel, peering. "Roman," he sighed, then glared at his brother. "You lied, you shit."

"Gid," Crystal reproved automatically.

"Sorry, Mother," Gid mumbled.

"Hardly a major lie," Alexander said.

"You saw me almost throw it back—you'd have let me, wouldn't you?"

"Then I'd've fished it out, okay?" Grinning, Alexander feinted a mock punch at his brother's navel. "Pow!"

Gid hesitated before his sweet-natured smile appeared. Raising his fists, he lolled his head like a punchy boxer.

The two danced around in a parody of a fight, exuding youthful energy and scattering drops of cold water.

"Can't you do that someplace else?" Crystal asked.

Her shrill note cut through Gid's horseplay. He picked up a towel, rubbing at the coin. "I'll clean it up for you, Mother," he said apologetically.

"If only I had my Vespa," Alexander said, "if only I were allowed out, I'd take it to Montanini's and find out what's what." Montanini, the elderly numismatist on Piazza Municipio, closed at the height of the tourist season because his authentic antique coins were too expensive for the beef-red hordes of English and Germans: he enjoyed showing his ancient treasures to Alexander, who among his other languages commanded fluent Italian. The boy had the knack of easy friendship even with those he scorned. "Welcome to Christmas and New Year's in San Quentin."

Gid rubbed at the metal with terrycloth, scraping his square thumbnail on the verdigris. "A-U-G," he spelled out.

Alexander took the coin. "Caesar Augustus."

"And people say our house in San Francisco is historical," Gid said. "Think. Some poor sailor planned on spending this a thousand years ago."

"Much earlier," Alexander said.

"Wha?"

"Augustus ruled when Christ was born."

"Right, right." Gid good-naturedly slapped at his brother with his towel. "You and that genius IQ."

"Gid, please!" Crystal said. "Go up and dress for lunch, both of you."

She watched them ascend in the elevator. *Sons,* she thought.

The word *sons* was the only manner that her mind lumped the two. She was fond of Gid in a careless maternal way. Alexander she felt closer to than anyone since Honora—indeed, in the ambiguous way that the mind braids past and present, she related his domination of his slightly older brother with her own earlier sibling relationship. A compliment about Alexander warmed her as much as one directed at herself. She argued with Gideon about the punishments he inflicted on the boy. She and Alexander collaborated in keeping secret the constant stream of cash that she slipped him—Gideon idolized the boys; yet, disciplinarian that he was, kept them on pitifully meager allowances.

As the shadows of the resident doves fluttered across the pool, Crystal closed her eyes, returning to her party plans for the Saudis. Unfortunately one of the group was related somehow to Curt Ivory's old college friend, that fat, obnoxious clown, Fuad Abdulrahman, so Ivory had a big edge. Oh, wouldn't it be an ecstatic triumph if Talbott's were awarded the contract?

Gideon landed some four hours late at the seldom used Catania airport, where he was met by one of the squat, swarthy servants who had come with the villa. The drive along the cliffs from Catania to Taormina was long and tortuous, and by the time the Mercedes curved inside the gates it was after eleven. Crystal, on the front step, holding her silk caftan around her in the balmy darkness, laughed softly as the two porters bumbled around their returned master, spouting Italian, which he could not understand, making a big display of their bowing and scraping.

He stumped hastily up the tile steps to her. "How many times do I have to tell them Americans don't go in for that guff?" he asked. "If they're so eager to please me, why don't they get a little work done around here?"

Time, having dealt so generously with Crystal, had cut cruelly at Gideon. His conservative single-breasted suit bulged over a large paunch, the flesh of his chin sagged on his starched collar, his sideburns were completely white.

"That's picturesque Sicily for you, Gideon—kiss the *padrone*'s hand and do *molto* little labor." Crystal pressed her smooth, perfumed cheek to his wrinkled one, catching the sour smell of his weariness. "Was it a horrendous flight?"

"Those Egyptians! They're incapable of getting a plane off the ground on schedule! I for one refuse to believe they can be descendants of the people who engineered Karnak and the pyramids of Giza." A common plaint with him since Talbott's had begun to work on the dam project.

She linked her arm in his as they went up the curving staircase.

"Hey, Dad," Alexander said, emerging from his room. The sound of rock music floated around him, and Crystal detected a faint aroma of cigarette smoke—or was it a more autumnal, illegal odor? Discreetly she closed the door.

"Well, son, what have you been doing?"

"Studying trig like crazy."

The boys had started the Christmas break a few days early: Alexander excelled in math but had antagonized his teacher, so he was given additional trigonometry problems while Gid was meant to make up the lost time with a ten-page essay on the Civil War.

"With that jazz blasting?"

"Jazz was in the twenties, Dad, this is rock," Alexander said, feigning patience. "No, I quit around ten."

Gid emerged from his room, taking off his glasses. "Hey, Dad, you finally made it." He beamed, hesitated, then gripped his father's shoulders in a brief, masculine embrace. "Glad you're back."

Gideon hid his pleasure at the contact by demanding, "What about that history paper? Have you finished?"

"By tomorrow. Been hacking away at it all week."

Gideon turned to Alexander. "Did I smell cigarette in your room?"

"My room?" Alexander replied. "Must've been when Marisa turned down the bed. You know her, a regular chimney." He smiled. "Dad, has Mom told you old Gid gave her a genuine Augustan denarius?"

"A coin?" Gideon asked Gid. "Did you buy it?"

Alexander replied for his brother. "The lucky bast—the lucky guy, he found it by the wreck."

"So you went snorkeling?" Gideon's gray-flecked brows drew together as he turned on Gid. "Do you or do you not remember that I gave you explicit instructions to finish that paper before you went fooling around?"

Swallowing, Gid bent his head. "Sorry, Dad."

Gideon stalked ponderously into his room.

After he showered and put on his robe, he had a belated dinner. Crystal perched next to him, toying with her demitasse cup while he devoured pasta, roast veal and salad. Between mouthfuls, he volleyed a report on the Mitwan Dam. Attention fixed on him, she asked an occasional astute question. A comradely warmth hovered above the round mosaic table.

Gideon wiped his mouth. "Excellent meal, excellent. Just what I needed."

"Coffee, dear?"

"Better not, it's late." He dropped his napkin. "Alexander shouldn't have told on his brother."

"That was a mistake, Gideon, he forgot about Gid's essay. And you know how I feel. This is their vacation. Why keep them cooped up? Besides, if Gid's meant to learn history, where better than Sicily?"

"It's a pattern with Alexander."

Maternal defensiveness swelled through her. "What are you talking about?"

"Whenever I catch him out, he covers up by diverting me to Gid."

"Oh, come on, Gideon!" Crystal's repudiation shook.

"Think about tonight."

"Alexander doesn't have a crafty bone in his body," Crystal cried. "He tried to tell you something nice that Gid had done."

"It's happened over and over." A moth swung around the chandelier above them, throwing blotchy shadows on Gideon's bald, shining pate. "Crystal, I'm his father, I love the boy as much as you do. But I can see him. You, on the other hand, have a blind spot. And believe me, it's no favor to him."

"I do *not* spoil him, he is *not* my pet, so let's not start that again."

"This is for Alexander's good, Crystal. I won't have you ruining him." Gideon, too, had risen. His features were swollen and his eyes were flat brown stones.

He's angry, she thought.

Though remote from physical or mental cowardice, since

the beginning Crystal had nursed a small, healthy fear of her husband: his anger never failed to intimidate her.

She forced a smile. "Let's not argue. I'm too tired," she said, drawing her caftan tightly to her waist, outlining her breasts and hips.

For a few seconds his expression wavered, then softened to beseeching lust.

"Crystal?" he asked huskily. Nowadays he seldom availed himself of his conjugal rights, always asking first.

"Wouldn't you rather wait until tomorrow, when you're not exhausted?"

"I've missed you," he muttered, his eyes still on her breasts.

Her bedroom, which had been occupied by the movie star, was the one excessive room in the villa. Above the huge, circular bed the ceiling was lowered and covered with mirrors.

On the pornographic bed, Gideon immediately initiated his assault. She could see his flabby buttocks pounding away in the dim mirror, and gave thanks for his vigor. In the last two years he'd often been impotent. Sweating buckets, he would caress her frantically, begging her to pull at his limp organ until she felt like an unsatisfactory milk-maid. Generally their combined efforts resulted in nothing. Gideon, apparently believing sex high on her priorities, would apologize for his inadequacy and humbly sneak into his own bedroom.

As his body shook and thwacked against hers, she was wondering: *What made him so dead set against Alexander? Has he guessed the truth?*

35

Crystal avoided introspection about those worrisome matters embedded in the unalterable past, yet when she awoke the following morning and heard Gideon in the connecting room as he dictated to Mitchell, his executive secretary, the dictatorial tone of his barrage reactivated her previous night's trepidations. Gideon had warned her often enough about spoiling Alexander, yet it seemed to her that in the past he had never been so vehement. *Does he suspect?* The horrendous thought reverberated and she rolled onto her back, pressing both palms against the sides of her head.

Gideon was starkly unforgiving when it came to sins of the flesh—witness the way he had cast out Curt, for whom he'd cared deeply, and the way he had denied Honora a few paltry dollars when he believed her illegally pregnant. *If he finds out, it's the end. I'm done for.* With a long, quavering sigh, Crystal reached to press the buzzer set in the elaborately carved headboard.

By the time Anina, the skilled maid who traveled everywhere with her, had brought her breakfast tray, then helped her dress, Gideon's booming had ceased.

Crystal went into his room. Wearing his old bathrobe and holding a sheaf of papers, he slumped in an armchair whose crimson calfskin proved by contrast exactly how weary and ashen his face was.

Alarmed by his appearance, she said, "Gideon, why don't you go back to bed?"

"I'm not in the least tired," he snapped. "While I was gone the reports and other urgent papers piled up."

He was always brusque when reminded of the attritions of time on his physical energy, but Crystal, in her peculiar mood of vulnerability, saw his testiness as aimed at her—and Alexander.

"Would you like some coffee, dear?"

"I'd like to work," he muttered, turning to his papers.

She backed into the sunlit hall, tapping on Alexander's door. There was no answer so she peeked inside. The brass bed was made, the door to the big modern bathroom open—the film of dampness on blue tiles gave evidence of a servant's recent ministrations. It was not yet ten: Alexander, when left to himself on vacations, slept until eleven or later.

She tapped on the adjacent varnished wood door.

"Come on in," Gid called.

Her older son, in rumpled striped pajama bottoms, his curly brown hair wild, sat at his portable electric typewriter. "Morning, Mom." With a broad smile, he brandished a sheaf of laboriously erased, dog-eared, three-hole notebook paper. "It's been a long, tough fight, but the historical masterpiece is ready to type up."

"That's wonderful, dear," she said. "Have you seen Alexander? He's not in his room."

Gid's smile faded a bit. "He got up about a half hour ago. Said he was going to do some laps."

She went down to the pool.

Alexander lay on a multicolored beach towel, smoking. As she emerged from the glass elevator he stubbed the cigarette on a stone, tossing the butt into a hibiscus bush.

In light of their precarious situation, the openness of his misconduct seemed foolhardy, maybe dangerous.

Sitting on a chaise near him, she said, "You shouldn't be smoking."

"What else is there to do in this Italian jail?" The mirrored ovals of his sunglasses reflected the sun, dazzling her.

She wanted it clear that she did not condone Gideon's fuddy-duddy regulations, yet with this new anxiety ruling her mind she also wanted to warn her son that he must tread carefully. "Alexander," she said, "it doesn't mean a thing to me. When I was fourteen I'd puff away whenever I could get my hands on a ciggie." She traced a paving stone with the cork sole of her sandal. "But Dad's home now."

"Screw him and his brilliant punishments." Alexander spoke slowly: his fine mouth had a flaccid quality.

"Haven't you been in enough trouble lately?"

"What else can Gideon the Terr-ible do to Al-ex-an-der the Great? Stret-ch him on the rack or hang him by the thumbs or disembow-el him without bene-fit of clergy?"

"There's no point upsetting him."

Alexander's face looked younger in its sullenness. "How sick to death I am of this whole hip-oh-crit-ical char-ade."

"He's a bit old to have boys your age. He means well."

"More bull-shee-it."

"Why are you talking like that?"

"The four-letter words are part of a nor-mal youth-ful vo-cab-u-lar-ee."

"Slowly, I meant. Stringing out your words."

He sat up so their faces were close, and she could smell the sweetish smoke on his breath.

"You real-ly are out of it, Mother. Your beam-ish boy is ston-ed."

"Oh, Alexander. . . ." Her stomach was a chill, hard ball. She was old enough to find drugs terrifying, lively enough to understand their fascination—and far too straight to risk using the hash or cocaine that Imogene pressed on her.

"Ahh, shee-it." In one smooth, clean motion, Alexander was on his slim, tanned feet and scaling the ladder to the high diving board.

The life-endangering foolhardiness of kids under the influence of drugs flashed warning lights through Crystal. "Alexander!" she shrieked. "Get back down!"

But he ran along the board and performed a perfect jack-knife, his slim, immature body hanging in the brightness, then entering the water with barely a splash. He churned in a butterfly back and forth before hauling himself out.

"Clears the head," he said, toweling his face dry, fingering back his long wet hair, replacing his glasses. "I didn't mean to shake you to your roots, Mom, but it's not the end of Western civilization, smoking a little pot."

She said anxiously, "You must promise me never to again."

"Everybody does grass, Mom. I'll let you in on a secret. Even virtuous Gid indulges now and then."

"He does?" In her surprise, Crystal blurted out, "It's different for him, different entirely."

"Why? The heir apparent can do no wrong?"

"I'm serious, Alexander," she said in a hushed voice. "You are not the same as Gid."

"I was wondering if you'd ever notice," he said lightly. But the impenetrable sunglasses were fixed on her and his mouth was drawn down in a calculating, assessing line. After a moment he said, "You're frightened."

"I am."

"Why?"

Now what? How was she going to communicate her fears without revealing the truth? That would be preposterous. Not only would she tarnish her image, but she would wreak havoc with her beloved son's emotions, doubtless set off a massive identity crisis in him.

The mirrored sunglasses were trained on her. "So," he said slowly. "I'm a sin of your youth."

She had underestimated the quickness of his mind. Her mouth and throat were sandpaper dry. "Don't be ridiculous."

"Then explain how I differ from Gid? Why is it fine for him to bogey a joint and not me?"

The explanations she came up with were so preposterous that they remained trapped in a vacuum behind her tongue. She sought for help in the sea. A long oil freighter lay becalmed on a distant striation of purple.

"I always suspected that my lack of the true blue Talbott righteousness proved something or other," he said. He took off his glasses, and she looked into the pinpoint irises. In this moment his eyes—Curt Ivory's eyes—seemed inimical, ruthless, commanding. If Alexander were thrown into internal confusion, he gave no sign of it in voice or expression.

After a moment she faltered, "I don't want him to have any reason to . . ."

"Disown me?"

"Yes."

"Mom, rest your mind. He doesn't suspect a thing. His wrath and vengeance fall indiscriminately on me and Gid. You're a smart lady, think it through and you'll see I'm right."

All at once the weight fell from her. She said, "He really was furious about poor Gid not finishing his essay, wasn't he?"

"In a hot swivet," Alexander said, imitating Gideon's frown.

Crystal's laughter rang, a high, happy trill of relief.

"So tell me," he asked. "Whose little boy am I?"

Crystal's mind fled back to those wild, alive seconds of lust and hatred on the damp grass while Chinamen chattered behind glass doors a few feet away. "Somebody you don't know," she said.

He replaced the inscrutable glasses. "Well, *un bel dì* you'll tell me. In the meantime we each have our other secrets to share. So quit brooding. From this day forth, I'll be the most virtuous lad the world has ever known." He leaned forward to kiss her forehead, his lips cool on her burning, blushing flesh.

36

Gideon ordered lunch sent up to his room, remaining incommunicado the entire afternoon.

At eight twenty, when Crystal was changed for dinner, she knocked on his door to tell him it was time to go down.

"I have work to finish," he said in a rough tone.

Poised there with the Venetian chandelier casting its soft light on her lovely, worried face, Crystal thought: *He sounds ill.* Although her alarm seemed paradoxical after a morning of biting her nails in anxiety over Gideon's (imaginary) suspicions, the truth was that she brooded heavily about the spells of ill health that her aging husband attempted to hide from her. Gideon was her mentor, her guide, the elderly spouse who cosseted her and showered her with gifts, who thought the sun rose and set above her blond head. Though she might not love him, she was committed heart and mind to their marriage, and dreaded the inevitable day when death would them part.

"Shall I have something brought up?"

"I can buzz for myself. Now will you let me go over these numbers?"

She went slowly down the curving tiled steps to the terrace where the family congregated before dinner.

Padraic Mitchell rose from the low, uneven brick wall, setting down his drink.

Tall, with a cadaverously hollow-cheeked face and a front tooth that jutted out when he smiled, Mitchell was that freakishly rare creature, the perfect employee. At thirty-five, without wife or children, deeply intelligent yet lacking personal ambitions, he served Gideon in much the same way a courtly esquire might once have dedicated himself to his liege lord. Mitchell's goals were whatever advanced the boss's best interests. He composed Gideon's extensive correspondence, fielded important phone calls, played exacting taskmaster to the three lesser secretaries, hopped on planes at no notice, worked weekends and nights. He earned a top-notch salary. The relationship, though, could not be measured by cash on either side. Gideon, for the first time since Curt Ivory, had placed his complete trust in an underling. Consequently Mitchell possessed a comprehensive overview of the diverse and farflung goings-on within each of the divisions; he knew more about Talbott's than any single member of the board.

Mitchell poured Crystal her usual Campari, and she rewarded him with a careless dimple. He was her slave and she knew it. What she did not know was that the vision of her naked, voluptuous blond self—as glimpsed through a crack of the inadvertently left open door to her San Francisco bedroom—was the Venus who presided eternally over his solo amatory rites.

Sipping the bitter aperitif, she said, "Mr. Talbott's too busy for dinner. Wasn't he working all afternoon with you?"

"Just first thing this morning, Mrs. Talbott. I must have left the room around ten fifteen. He hasn't called me in since."

"I saw him this morning, too. He looked very tired. Tonight he sounded ill. How was he in Egypt?"

"He had a terrible case of indigestion one night in Mitwan, but then Egypt's famous for stomach disturbances. After that he said he was fine—but he certainly didn't look it. Still, he went out on the inspections, he attended the meetings with the client, and I'm sure he told you about the reception given for him by President and Mrs. Nasser."

"He overdoes it when he travels," Crystal sighed.

They drank in silence until Alexander and Gid came onto the terrace. Both wore navy blazers and pale gray slacks, but Alexander's outfit draped elegantly around his slight body while Gid looked as if his burly torso would burst the seams in the jacket.

"Victory!" Gid raised his arms as if announcing a winning touchdown. "The masterpiece is typed and finished! Hey, where's Dad?"

"He's working," Crystal said.

"But man, it's eight thirty," Alexander said. "And tonight we celebrate Gid's paper."

"I'll see if he'll come down for five minutes," Gid said, going back into the house.

Alexander lined up Baccarat flutes, pouring chablis into three, glancing at Crystal as he opened a bottle of 7-Up for the other two.

Gid charged back onto the terrace, his heavy features pulled downward in a worried frown. "Mom, Dad's acting really strange. He didn't let me in, so I shouted about the essay being typed. He barked at me to let him work. But there was no light around the door—and his voice was weird, I mean really weird."

Gid's report fused with Crystal's own anxiety. "I better go talk to him," she said.

This time she didn't knock at Gideon's door, but opened it. A sourish odor clung to the blackness.

"Have to finish this by tomorrow," muttered a voice she scarcely recognized.

She pressed the wall switch and couldn't control her breathy gasp.

Gideon lay on the couch as if a giant's foot had squashed him into the crimson cushions. Globules of sweat dripped down his livid face, sweat showed in deep crescents under the armholes of his white-on-white shirt. His tie was pulled open and one hand jerkily massaged at his thick, heaving chest.

"Indigestion," he muttered. "That supper last night. Spicy Italian food. . . ."

She darted to his desk, fumbling with the phone book for the number of the local doctor they used.

That night Mitchell stayed by the downstairs phone, arguing in his strenuously accented Italian with Sicilian operators about putting him through to Rome, to Jidda (he canceled the Saudi weekend), to New York, San Francisco. Before six the following morning, a helicopter carried the patient with his family to Catania Airport, where a private ambulance jet with an American cardiologist aboard was waiting.

When they landed in San Francisco, Gideon was a trace less haggard. He refused to go to St. Mary's.

"The hospital's more convenient for you doctors, that's all," he argued. "I'll be better off in my own home."

Crystal, hearing her husband's more vigorous tone, grew strong with relief. Stationing herself next to the stretcher, she gripped the lax, meaty hand. "You're absolutely right, dear. It's New Year's Eve. Only an idiot goes to the hospital over a holiday—and there's no need for it. Let the hospital come to you."

Gideon's spacious room on Clay Street was transformed with medical equipment. Nurses and technicians moved efficiently through the halls, specialists consulted in the downstairs rooms.

The flowery offerings from all over the world were not yet withered by the time Gideon was sitting up. After a battle with the medical team, he ordered that Mitchell and the lesser secretaries be installed in the guest room across the hall. Gideon Talbott, in his elaborately wired hospital bed, was once again supervising his empire.

He accepted Crystal's offer to be his eyes and voice and legs. She flew in the corporate plane for a quick, unannounced visit to the Colorado mining project for Anaconda Copper, she read his instructive speech at the January 29 meeting of the Talbott's board, she showed up on his behalf at the Anchorage meeting of the consortium investigating the possibly of an Alaska pipeline.

The frantic rush from airport to meeting, the weighty masculine voices adjudicating the lives of thousands of employees, the vastness of the projects, the fortunes asked and spent, made the rest of her days appear to have been wasted on meaningless and trivial games.

She adored every minute of her new life.

If forced to pick the sweetest fruit of those busy weeks, though, she would select the times when Gideon asked her advice.

Perching on his bed, bending her bright head next to his, she surveyed diagrams of a future airport.

"Where do you see the shops?" he asked.

"Lining the corridor after the check-in area." She rested a long nail enameled with stylish silver polish on the thin paper. "Here. And a cluster more here. See? It's where the corridors diverge for the international gates. Then of course you'll have the usual row of duty-frees."

"I asked you *which* shopping area would do best," Gideon asked impatiently.

"All of them, dear. You need all three."

"There's space for *one.*"

"Gideon, this is an international airport. People will be stuck here with hours to kill and their foreign currency. Everybody, given the chance, splurges on last-minute souvenirs and gifts. You've told me yourself over and over how profitable these concessions are."

Gideon's lips puffed out contemplatively.

Her finger moved. "Dear, look at all this lounge space. Think how easily you could design a smaller waiting area with shops surrounding it. Believe me, the airport commission will sing Talbott's praises."

He gave her that stern smile. "If only one of my hundred-thousand-a-year division heads had your common sense," he said.

During that cold January and February, Crystal's crowd clucked that their superlatively lovely friend must be worn out and depressed by her sickroom chores—imagine Gideon getting her to work at such a time! They attempted to inveigle her to luncheons and dinners and cocktail parties. She refused all invitations.

Every weekend the boys came home from Menlo. Alexander, who had been conspicuously free of scrapes since Gideon's coronary, spent hours in the sickroom, reading quietly.

At the end of February, Gideon was recovered enough to be driven for a few hours to the offices on Maiden Lane, whose exterior had been refurbished two years ago under Crystal's supervision. The medical staff and paraphernalia departed, a Talbott's truck came for the secretarial equipment belonging to Mitchell's staff.

Gideon acquired an emerald and diamond necklace that had belonged to Empress Eugenie. "It's nothing compared to what you deserve," he said in his awkward way, fastening the cold weight around her creamy throat. The setting was magnificently crafted, the fiery stones flawless, yet she could summon none of the delight that his previous gifts had evoked.

Her days passed as they had prior to Gideon's illness, when she had considered herself happy and lucky. Now, though, she chafed at the sprawl of aimless golf games, shopping with "her" salespeople, luncheons, teas, those endlessly long and unrewarding telephone conversations. Gid stayed at school because he was goalie on the hockey team. Alexander continued to come home every weekend.

Her son perked her up. They took in movies together or jumped their thoroughbreds in Golden Gate Park. She bought a pair of tickets for a matinee of A.C.T.'s *Little Foxes,* and they lunched first at the nearby Redwood Room in the Clift.

"You really got with that Talbott's crap, didn't you?" he said over the shrimp cocktails.

"It's not crap, Alexander. Your father"—since that morning in Taormina she couldn't prevent an infinitesimal hesitation as she said the word—"is one of the movers and shakers of the earth."

"I wasn't putting Dad down. I'm into Talbott's, too. At least I will be when I leave school." Alexander crushed a few oyster crackers into his leftover red sauce. "Tell me something, Mom. At one time or another Dad's formed consortiums with all of his other major rivals. How come not Ivory?"

Crystal's fingers clamped the small fork and she selected her words carefully. "You have to understand how fond he once was of Curt Ivory. He helped him through school, he gave him a job and promoted him constantly, he invited him to the house with his own friends, he trusted him completely." After the breakup, Gideon refused to discuss Curt, therefore her knowledge of her husband's generosity to his former protégé was limited by the little he had told her and what she had personally witnessed. "And Curt repaid him in the most vicious way possible. We were all living under his roof, his wards more or less, and he seduced your Aunt Honora, then treated her miserably. It's Curt Ivory's fault our family's split apart—before him we were happy and very loving. Your father's right to avoid all contact with him, Alexander. The man's as rotten as they come. Oh, don't get me started on *him.*" Crystal adamantly changed the subject. "I read in the *Chron* that Lillian Hellman says this revival is better than the original."

The performances were indeed superlative and they talked about the play over dinner and until Gideon retired at nine. Then Alexander led the way to the music room. The boy had catholic musical tastes, his record collection ranging from classical, which Crystal found a snore, to rock, which she suffered because of him.

Putting on *Rubber Soul,* his latest Beatle album, he stood

in front of her snapping his fingers, moving his shoulders and narrow hips, an invitation to the dance. Laughing, she rose to her feet. Kicking off her heels, facing Alexander, who was already six inches the taller, she gave herself up to the violent beat, throwing out her arms, bouncing her head.

"Hey, Mom, you're pretty fabulous," he said.

"I used to be considered a good dancer," she said, pushing back a strand of her hair.

"Used? You're no antique. Nobody would guess you were my mother."

"Flattery, flattery."

"I mean it. You don't look old at all."

Delighted, she teased, "Maybe you need glasses like Gid."

"Hey, listen! Why don't we give it a go? Next Saturday Varger's having a party. You could come with me."

"That'd put a damper on the evening. I can remember how welcome parents are."

"I meant as my date." His face was taut with eagerness.

"Come on, Alexander," she said, smiling.

"If you left off the makeup and wore an Indian top or a really neat T-shirt, I say you could pass as my date. Ten dollars, Mom, is it a bet?"

"You'd lose two weeks' allowance," she said.

"I'm serious."

"Do you want to give your father another heart attack?"

"Dad's in bed by nine thirty."

"That's enough, Alexander," she said with no-nonsense, maternal flatness.

But when she met Imogene for lunch Thursday, she couldn't resist boasting about Alexander's bet. "Isn't it idiotic? Imagine me as a teenybopper!"

Imogene's bony face tilted appraisingly. "Never *fourteen*, darling, but then again that gorgeous hunk of yours is advanced. Maybe he goes out with seventeen-year-olds. Without the makeup, hair flapping, yes. . . . Not in *daylight*, of course, but at night maybe. A *definite* maybe." She raised her hand for their waiter and began gathering her gold cigarette case, her glasses, into her Hermes shoulder bag.

"We haven't had our coffee—where are you rushing?"

"Don't you see? This is but *exactly* the boost you need. Since Gideon's heart attack, you've been a *hermit*. It was just too much, the sickroom, never going out, that *dreary* work."

"Imogene, you're mad."

"*Trust* me. Last week Melissa"—one of Imogene's numerous ex-stepchildren—"took me to the most dee-vine thrift shop in the Tenderloin."

37

Crystal's anticipatory pipe dreams about the lark she would share with Alexander bade her adieu as she entered the brown stucco in St. Francis Woods. The Vargers being on a trip to Japan, the kids had the house to themselves.

The less than two decades since Crystal, an English schoolgirl, had burst on the American youth scene could just have easily been a million years, or so it seemed to her. Had these been black Oakland adolescents or hippies from the Haight, she would have been primed for drugs, casual sexual alliances, foul language. But this was Alexander's crowd, private school students, offspring of San Francisco's best people.

They congregated around the crackling eucalyptus fire in the basement playroom, ten of them, male and female alike wearing tight, faded Levi's and a rainbow variety of tops, entertaining themselves by watching their host, Avery Varger, a skinny spider of a boy, studiously roll marijuana in zigzag papers, then handing around the tokes from one to the next, closing their eyes to inhale deeply and appreciatively.

"My mom's such a fucking hypocrite," said a little girl with bare, dirty feet. "She's been dried out a hundred times and all she does is rave on and on about the evils of grass. As far as she's concerned the first goddamn puff sets you on the yellow brick road to being a dope fiend, sticking yourself with needles."

A boy nodded his overlong bush of brown hair in agreement. "I mean, they don't know the first fucking thing about grass, that it's organic and won't hurt you. No, they munch that chemical Miltown shit and guzzle their vodka and fuck their minds and livers, and then dump on us if they discover we're holding."

Crystal could not for the life of her comprehend what pleasure these juveniles derived from nursing on their saliva-slimed marijuana. At first she simply passed on the loathsome thing, but Alexander turned on her. "What's wrong, Cryssie? You chicken?"

His voice shook. A plea? It occurred to her that she was jeopardizing his social life by not entering wholeheartedly into the masquerade.

Resolutely simulating pleasure, she took her turns. But no matter how deeply she dragged or how long she submerged the heavy smoke in her lungs, she felt no effect. Thank God for that. From earliest childhood the mere thought of losing control had filled her with uneasy dread—and that night in San Rafael with Curt Ivory had been an object lesson.

Somebody had put on a record, a grating blast she recognized from Alexander's collection. The redheaded girl with the face of a ten-year-old was skinning off her tie-dye T-shirt to display breasts larger than Crystal's own—although not as shapely. The girl raised her arms, revealing tufts of auburn axial hair as she gyrated her torso to the violent beat, her bulbous nipples rolling like a madman's eyes.

Crystal huddled back in the ancient, dusty-smelling couch. Until now the sexual banter for all its obscenity had a certain innocence—she could remember playing the fraudulent game of sophistication with her dates. But this dance was a defiantly lascivious invitation. The record ended, another began, and the half-naked little slut plopped herself down on the other side of Alexander. Crystal went clammy with horror, envisioning her Alexander coiled in sex with the creature, her Alexander afflicted with VD, about which she knew nothing but imagined as running sores *à la* the finale of the filmed version of *The Portrait of Dorian Gray.*

"Man, this is the best fucking grass," said the boobed wonder. "It from Acapulco, Alexander?"

"Turkey," Alexander retorted tersely.

"Wow, Turkish!" said mine host, the firelight red on his steel braces. "Mellow, Talbott, mellow. Agree, Cryssie?"

Crystal agreed. The one rosy spot about the evening was that she, costumed in her thrift shop finery, hair hanging straight and nearly veiling her face, was accepted as Alexander Talbott's date, Cryssie Saunderson.

The joints seemed to be making the rounds more rapidly.

A huge platter of sandwiches appeared and she devoured four halves before realizing that she detested packaged bologna, and anyway it was loaded with calories.

Varger was pressing his moist, steel-backed lips to hers. She pushed at his scrawny chest with both hands, however, his bologna and smoke tasting tongue continued to foray. She raised her hand in what she intended as a quasi-humorous rebuffing slap. It rang loudly. The others chortled.

"Bitch," Varger snarled. "You're stoned out of your fucking gourd."

"Cut it out, Varger," Alexander said easily. "Let he who's not stoned among us cast the first stone."

Varger shifted to the seminude slut, and Crystal shrank back into the shadows. Vagrant chips of conversation came at her, but her attention was fixed on the orange and yellow flames which rose, writhing like the naked bodies of the damned in an endless sexual torment.

Then Alexander was pulling her to her feet. "Twenty to twelve, Cryssie. Time for the car to pick us up."

"Them and their fucking curfew," she said as an exit line.

The three stories of the Vargers' house descended down the precipitous slope of St. Francis Woods, and this basement room opened onto the back garden. The cold air felt sharp and clean and she reached out her arms to embrace the tulle mist that hid the tops of the pines, tilting her head to catch the faraway, sweetly mournful song of a foghorn.

"This way," Alexander said, leading her along the pine-needle-covered path, his grip firm, his hand considerably larger than her own. "Well?" he said. "Wasn't I right? Nobody guessed, did they?"

"Alexander. . . . That crowd—I didn't like that crowd."

"Face it, being that up front with you proves they accepted you. Mom, you owe me ten."

"Oh, that stupid bet!" she cried. Halting, she fumbled with the clasp of Aunt Matilda's old needlepoint bag, but it got away from her and the contents—mirror, handkerchief, change purse—spilled across exposed bones. Or was it the roots of a tall ponderosa?

As Alexander bent to retrieve her possessions, he said quietly, "It's Curt Ivory, isn't it?"

Certain she'd heard him wrong, she clutched at the empty purse.

He rose to his feet, and she saw nothing but his intent topaz eyes, lion's eyes. "Curt Ivory," he said. "He's my father, isn't he?"

That August night, cold but not foggy like this night, came to her drenched with detail: she could once again feel the wet grass against her naked buttocks, the constricting steel of the Merry Widow, the pounding, furious burden of her sister's husband. She could not properly recall the involuntary, mind-obliterating spasms that were surely hatred—or were they the only orgasm of her life?—but knew she'd experienced them.

"So I'm right," he said softly. Taking the purse from her limp hand, he stuffed in the trivia. "See the steps? Careful, they're sort of uneven."

The shadow of a big Lincoln rose ahead of them. Imogene and her latest, Max, were waiting as promised.

Alexander opened the back door. "The ten bucks is mine!" he announced with adolescent glee. "I mean, two guys hit me for old Cryssie here's phone number and Varger tried to make out. There was one bad moment when my date slugged him, I mean I was shaking she'd announce herself, but she got with it again."

Crystal awoke with a pounding heart and an inflexible premonition of doom. She moved her head cautiously on the mound of tiny pillows: sharp daggers stabbed above her temples. The events and thoughts of the previous evening were blurred together in a monstrous splotch, and she had trouble differentiating between reality and what had transpired within her imagination.

Had Alexander said, *Curt Ivory, he's my father, isn't he?* or were the words as insubstantial as the naked copulating figure she'd glimpsed in the fire?

Anina bore in her breakfast tray. Crystal waved the maid away, mumbling about the flu to excuse herself from eating and from church.

A few minutes later another tap sounded. "Mom, it's me," Alexander called, opening the door.

With his long bright hair flopping over his forehead, white shirt and the pants of his dark suit, he was Christopher Robin grown into naive adolescence.

"Anina tells me you have the bug," he said, closing the door. Approaching the bed, he asked softly, "It's nothing to do with last night, is it?"

"No, I must've been coming down with it."

"That's a relief. No offense, Mom, I didn't mean I want you ill. But that grass Varger got ahold of was Turkish. Top grade. Strong. One thing, you can always count on Varger for good grass."

She held two fingers to her ghastly headache. Hadn't she heard Varger say *Alexander* had procured the dope? Alexander's innocently anxious gaze remained on her. No, her drug-distorted mind must have juxtaposed the remarks.

"I never would've made you go through with it last night if I'd known you were sick."

"I wasn't, not then."

His head tilted and he looked yet younger. "You're sure?"

"It was *fun*, Alexander, the most fun I've had in years. I wish they wouldn't smoke marijuana, or use that kind of language—"

"So what else is new?" he interjected, grinning.

"—but they were very nice, your friends." And as she looked up at her son's beautiful, conspiratorial young face, it did seem to Crystal that the evening had not been a debacle but a bewitched return to the happy harbor of youth.

"Wouldn't it blow their minds if they knew?"

38

Crystal shivered.

Beyond the rain-slashed, breakfast room bay window, deer were taking advantage of the rotten weather to browse on the deserted, sodden golf course, while on the far side of the fairway she could see choppy gray waves breaking and spuming. The barren island rock appeared deserted until a huge bull seal rose up to slither into the morose Pacific.

"I'm sorry about this rain, Daddy," she said. "The worst part is they say it'll keep up through tomorrow."

"Crystal, you grew up an English girl." Langley gave his rueful, charming chuckle. "Have you forgotten our happy breed doesn't melt?"

"Don't let Mom kid you, Grandpa," Gid said. "She ordered the storm to make you feel at home."

They were at the Carmel place for Easter. In honor of the first morning of Langley's visit, Crystal had made an appearance at breakfast. Gideon's place at the head of the maple table was already vacant, its tureen of oatmeal empty, an inch of thin, bluish milk remaining in the cut-glass pitcher—no more tasty over-easy eggs, thick pink rashers of Canadian bacon and hash browns for Gideon Talbott. He couldn't be convinced, however, to alter his practice of working regardless of holidays, and was already immured with Mitchell in the upstairs study.

"Looks like we're stuck inside," Alexander said. "Grandpa, I challenge you to another round of Scrabble."

"Excellent idea." Langley raised his Bloody Mary. "As soon as I finish breakfast."

Before Langley's arrival yesterday afternoon at the small Monterey airport, he had passed two tactfully unmentioned weeks in the Ivorys' Los Angeles house with "my three ladies," as he called Honora, Joscelyn and his baby granddaughter. Curt had been in Singapore, then Washington, D.C. Malcolm was still in Lalarhein.

Gid drained his milk. "This time count me in."

"Good, why not?" Alexander said. "We need a calming influence, don't we, Grandpa? Last night some of those words got pretty imperspicuous, and caliginous, too."

"Hey, what?" Gid said.

"Those're synonyms for esoteric," Alexander retorted.

Gid didn't join the Scrabble game. While Crystal made her calls—she was inviting wives of junketing Congressmen to a bridge luncheon the following day—she heard him clicking balls around the Brunswick pool table. When she finished on the telephone the rain was pelting more fiercely. Reflecting how dear it was of Alexander to entertain his grandfather, she peeked into the den.

"The Rain Fairburn Show" blasted away on the Magnavox while Alexander and Langley leaned across the game table, conversing intently. Seeing her, they stopped talking.

"Don't mind me," Crystal said, turning the set down. "Go on with your game."

"Can't you see my wounds?" asked Langley a shade too heartily. "Trounced by this mere youth. The honor of British publishing destroyed with a kuvasz."

"Kuvasz?" she asked.

"A Hungarian hunting dog," Alexander explained.

"That vocabulary." Crystal smiled indulgently before asking, "What were the pair of you talking about just now? You looked like you were planning World War Three."

"A matter considerably more significant," Alexander said, glancing across the Scrabble board at his grandfather. "We thought after lunch we'd brave the storm and go into Carmel for a movie."

"That sounds perfect," Crystal said. "I've nothing on."

"Grandpa wants *Dr. Zhivago*, Mom. You've seen it."

"So have you."

"It happens I have this big thing for Julie Christie."

"I know when I'm not wanted," she said, a smile covering her sliver of hurt at Alexander's transparent rejection.

The storm lasted that day and the next, when she lunched with the Congressional wives. Thursday, however, the sun was out, drawing ripples of steam from the drying shake rooftops. The ice plant that covered the darkly wet dunes shimmered with wetness; the Pacific was vibrant blues and the fairways a gaudy emerald.

Alexander challenged Gideon to a round of golf.

Alexander had won three gold-plated cups in state teenage tournaments; Gideon swung his clubs with graceless, chopping vigor and seldom broke a hundred. Both played for money—and blood.

When Gideon came in at two, he lay down on his bed, his cheeks an unhealthy purple.

"Didn't you take a cart?" Crystal asked.

"After that storm? You know it'll be at least three days before they allow carts on the course."

"In that case, dear, nine holes is enough."

"I need to brush up on my game, play more, not less. That Alexander's good."

"How much did he win?"

"Seven dollars and thirty-five cents." Gideon scratched his fleshy ear. "Crystal, on the fifth hole his drive landed in the rough, and I'm positive he kicked his ball for a better lie."

Crystal laughed. "You're a bad loser, Gideon."

"Well, if anyone has to beat me, I'm glad it's one of my boys. Gid ought to take it up."

"As far as I can see, Alexander's enough for you."

"Gid wouldn't cheat."

"Stop being idiotic!" she shrilled. Drawing a breath, she said, "Alexander's like you. Competitive."

Later she said to Alexander, "Your father's not well. On the course, go a little easier."

Alexander assumed that unnervingly sullen adolescent expression. "How?"

"Maybe miss a putt now and then."

"Why don't you play with him, then? He can beat you."

Friday the temperature rose to the mid-seventies, and the sky was the clear Saxon blue of Crystal's eyes. Humming, she trotted down the stairs. Gid was watching a pre-season baseball game.

"TV on a day like this?"

"I'm waiting for Grandpa, Mom. We're driving into Carmel."

"With Alexander?"

"Nope. He and Dad had a nine o'clock tee-off time."

Deciding to meet them at the tenth hole and lure Gideon from the course, she drove to the club, hurrying to the tenth tee. From this height she could see beyond the dogleg and formidable sand traps. On the green a thickset figure knelt to line up a putt while a bag-laden caddie and a slender form waited. Raising her hand against the brightness, she ascertained that the twosome was indeed Gideon and Alexander before telling the starter that she wanted to catch up with her husband and son. "Sure thing, Mrs. Talbott, go right head. I'll see nobody hits into you."

By now they were striding toward the next tee. She waved violently to attract their attention, but they were too far away to notice. Seabirds passed overhead in an uneven V. Her cleats dug into the spongy grass and the moisture seeped into her shoes as she descended the dip. Hurrying uphill past the wind-shaped Monterey pines where her third shot often unfortunately landed, she saw them again.

They were walking close together, Alexander's pale, bright hair near the bill of Gideon's cap. A fear without focus washed through Crystal. She began to trot. A foursome of women on the next fairway turned their colorful hats to watch as she charged along, clubless, caddieless.

Alexander was gripping Gideon's arm.

Gideon pulled away, brandishing his iron. Suddenly he dropped the club, swiveling in a half circle, taking two uncertain steps in her direction. His face was white, dazed. He was less than a hundred feet away, but she was positive he did not see her.

Throwing both hands forward as if instinctively to break his fall, he toppled to the emerald-wet grass.

"Gideon!" Crystal screamed. "Gideon!" She raced toward him, her bare knees rising and falling like pistons.

The caddie had dropped the bags, rushing to squat over Gideon. Alexander appeared a frozen onlooker. He did not see her until she almost stumbled over the bags.

"Mom?" he said, his adolescent voice cracking. "Mom, what are you doing here?"

His voice was no more significant than the gulls cawing above them. She dropped to her knees.

Gideon's face was hideously askew. Both eyes were closed.

"What happened?" she panted, bending close to him. "Gideon, your heart?"

The left eye opened and stared up at her. There was a ravaged horror in the brief Cyclops look before the lid came down.

Alexander was also kneeling beside Gideon. "Get a doctor!" she shouted.

But the caddie was already far up the fairway, racing toward the big, white colonial clubhouse.

The Carmel living room, fifty feet long, forty-two feet wide, was further enlarged by the panorama of golf course and Pacific. The upholstery was a stiff cream-colored brocade, the marble tabletops bore burdens of enormous ashtrays precisely where the decorator, Baynie McHugh, had first set them. It was a room intended only for large galas and possibly because of this onerous formality the patient's family had gathered here.

Crystal clasped a sodden handkerchief. With her swollen eyes, lipstick worn away, short, powder blue golf skirt and grass-stained, dimpled knees, she looked a frightened, exquisite little girl dragged from her games to be dealt some as yet unknown but vicious punishment. Near her Gid slumped, his big, boyishly grubby hands dangling between his knees. Pulling a fresh Kleenex from the pack, he blew his nose. Alexander stood by the wall of glass, the sun casting a shimmering path across his hair and highlighting the pale down on his upper lip. There was an alertness about his immobility, something reminiscent of a watchful, half-grown leopard—or Curt. Langley was pouring himself a drink from a Waterford decanter hung with a silver label embossed *Scotch:* his rather petulant lips were set in an expression of righteous satisfaction. (But how could he resist a minor gloat at being in excellent health while that common brother-in-law/son-in-law who thought only of money, money, money, was beset by one medical disaster after another?)

Four doctors—three had been flown in by the Talbott corporate plane from San Francisco—were upstairs in Gideon's room. Mitchell had also contacted London, Houston, New York, and additional specialists, one a renowned vascular surgeon, would arrive tomorrow.

The most recent report from the medical team was that Gideon's condition was "extremely grave." Beyond that they knew he had suffered, in layman's terms, a stroke.

Gid went to the lucite wastebasket. His new handful of wet tissue thumped onto the heap he had deposited earlier. His expression baffled and unhappy, he said, "I just don't understand what caused the stroke."

"We came to his ball. He keeled over," Alexander said. "Shall I go over it again? I mean, maybe some of those present can't understand English."

Gid went back to his chair, his forehead crunched as if he were fighting tears.

"Alexander, that's enough," Crystal said sharply, for once siding with her older son against the younger. "There's plenty to upset us without you being clever."

"Haven't I explained often enough? Everybody knows what happened. Do you all have to keep hacking at me? What do you think, that *I* caused the damn stroke?"

"We don't mean it that way, my lad," Langley soothed. "We're concerned."

"Nobody cares whether *I'*m shook."

"Oh, Alexander," Crystal sighed. "Of course we care."

"Yeah, sure."

"I'd give anything if you hadn't been there when it happened," she said.

Alexander stalked across the room and into the hall. They heard him open a door—probably to the den—and slam it shut.

Langley splashed more scotch into his iceless tumbler. "A thing like this is hard on a lad his age. You can't imagine how keen he is on helping his father. Plans on going into Talbott's."

"Yes, both of us do," Gid said. "We talk about it a lot."

"Alexander's already boning up." Langley gulped at his drink. "Crystal, he begged me not to mention this, but he's been asking about everything from petroleum finds to business rivals."

Crystal felt abruptly cut off from oxygen, as if the warm, ruddy air had been drained from the inhospitable room. *So that's what they've been huddling about, the two of them. Curt Ivory.*

Slow footsteps descended the staircase. Crystal turned pale, and they all stood, watching the hall. Mitchell came down the stairs like an old man, narrow shoulders hunched, one hand clenched hard on the banister, feet coming together on each step. Alexander had emerged into the hall. Nobody spoke as Mitchell crossed the white carpet to where Crystal stood.

"Mrs. Talbott," he said, and then fell silent, his protrudent tooth glinting.

"Is he. . . . Is . . . is he . . . ?" Crystal faltered, discovering she could not utter any of the dread words of finality that had been haunting her thoughts these past hours.

He shook his head. "No. But the doctors think you ought to come up."

"And the boys?" she quavered.

Mitchell shook his head. "Just you."

"We belong, too," Alexander repudiated.

"Alexander," Gid said, tears streaming down his cheeks, his mouth even in grief showing that surprising sweetness, "Mom's the one he really wants."

Crystal had gone limp, and she felt incapable of movement. Mitchell gently took the crook of her arm. Her mind jumped grotesquely: she saw her father in his rented finery leading her down the rose-swagged aisle of Grace Cathedral toward marriage. Now Mitchell was leading her up this Carmel staircase toward widowhood.

She had anticipated a funereal darkness in Gideon's room: instead afternoon sun striped through the open slats of the shutters. A cloth-paneled screen sheltered the high electric hospital bed—Gideon had slept in one since his coronary. Mitchell released her. Ignoring the somber whispers of physicians, feeling disembodied, she slipped toward the screen.

Gideon's thick, veined hands rested lax on the monogrammed silk blanket cover. The colorless flesh of his face sagged back from the broad nose, which was pinched at the nostrils; his deeply shadowed eyes were closed. *He's dead,* Crystal thought. *He died after they sent for me, and not one of them's noticed.*

"Gideon," she whispered urgently. "Gideon."

The right side of his face hung slack in its wrinkles, but the left side contorted with what appeared unendurable effort. Slowly the eyelid raised and he squinted up at her. The earth-colored sclera, dulled iris, lusterless pupil gave the impression that an electric terminal had been doused behind the eye.

He's not dead, but he's dying, dying, Crystal thought, and in the ravagement of the moment her face actually went numb. "Oh, Gideon," she blurted. "I begged you only to play nine holes."

The eye blinked. And to her surprise, watered. Gideon weeping? Her spouse's emotions were formed of hardest rock. Sitting on the chair, she bent close. His fetid breath did not repulse her. "After this, darling, I'm going to play with you. That way I'll be sure you get off when you should."

The left side of his mouth worked and a strange, pinging rumble emerged.

"Shh," she murmured tenderly. "Plenty of time to argue about it later."

He made the sound again, and she knew he was trying to say *Alexander*.

"He wants to come up, and so does Gid." One of the remaining strands of his hair fell over his ear, and she smoothed it back. "Tomorrow, when you're not so tired."

The wetness oozed onto bruise-colored flesh. Another series of facial spasms brought forth a word. "I . . . vry . . . ?"

Hot guilt flooded through her and she could control neither her start nor her blush. *He knows.* In this corrosive moment denials never occurred to her. She could not dishonor this, the solemnest hour of both their lives, with petty prevarication.

Resting her forearms on the pillow so his livid, ugly face filled her vision, she murmured, "Once, darling. It happened once. At that Chinese party in San Rafael. Ever since I've hated him even more. There's never been any other time, Gideon—or anyone else. You've made me very, very happy."

His lips twisted. It flashed through her mind how desperate was her need to be absolved by him—but talk about your hopeless causes. When had Gideon, that soul of Puritanical rectitude, ever forgiven a carnal misstep? Holding her breath, she awaited his dying castigations.

But he was whispering tortuously. "Lo—ove . . . me?"

Yes, she thought in bemused wonder. *I do love him.*

Her love was composed of threads of numerous other emotions: she respected and admired him, she enjoyed his company, she was grateful for the luxuries he provided, she was proud of him and proud that he had introduced her to royal kings and financial princes, and if their relationship had circumnavigated sexual bliss and romantic love, well, she was sensible enough to know that these existed only in disputed and ephemeral mists.

She gripped his cold hand. "Oh, darling, what a question. Of course I love you."

"Me . . . you. . . ."

Forgiveness.

The diminished brown eye closed and Crystal rested her head on the pillow so that their cheeks touched, the faraway roar of the Pacific lulling her. Somebody attempted to draw her from her chair.

She braced herself like steel and shrugged off the hands. Bending to kiss Gideon's dry, foul-smelling mouth, she felt a faint, returning pressure. "I've loved you very much, and I always will," she whispered, and knew she had spoken the truth.

Then she was pulled with forcible gentleness beyond the screen. She could hear two doctors whispering to her, she couldn't hear their words, yet somehow knew they were telling her it wouldn't be much longer. "No," she cried. *No, no, no.*

Her anguish was no longer contained within her but filled the sickroom, like poison gas. Racked with sobs, she ran blindly into their shared dressing room, standing shuddering and gasping with her forehead pressed against Gideon's door for maybe five minutes, devoid of thought or physical sensation, consumed by her singleminded sense of irrevocable loss.

39

When her physical upheaval lessened, Crystal peered around as if unsure of where, exactly, she was. Gradually her tear-blurred attention focused on the beige patterned wool scarf that Gideon had draped over his wooden valet. In her grief the scarf seemed significant evidence of her husband's rock-ribbed loyalty—she had bought it for him in the Haymarket Burberry's a minimum of a dozen years earlier.

She carried it along with three fresh handkerchiefs into her bedroom. Unable to stop crying, she sprawled on the quilted bedspread and held the scarf to her face for tenuous comfort. The cashmere gave off odors of wet wool and Gideon.

Darkness fell, the temperature dropped. She shivered in her lightweight golf outfit, yet didn't move to turn up the thermostat.

The door opened. Lights clicked on.

Alexander.

It was only too clear to her what Alexander had been communicating to Gideon on the tenth and eleventh fairways. Rage, near blinding and sudden and swift, savaged her.

Mindless of everything including the nearby sickroom, she shouted, "Get out!" Never had she yelled at her son—or anyone else—in this intimidating roar.

His composed expression dissolved into shock. "Mom, what's wrong?"

"The sight of you makes me sick!"

He came in, shutting the door behind him, staring at her.

"You viper!" She was on her feet, slashing the scarf ineffectually at his face. "You told him! You told him what you wormed out of me. I hate you! I despise you! You are not my son." Her voice, low now, was yet more blood-curdling.

"Jesus. . . ."

"You got me to that party so you could feed me drugs and find out—"

"Mom. . . ."

"*He*'s never been taken in. He's known all along that behind the brilliance and the charm you're rotten to the core. Sneaky. Dishonest. *He* warned me about you, but I refused to listen."

Flinging the scarf onto the floor, she began to slap his cheeks, alternating sides. Had she ever hit him before? Had anyone?

Alexander didn't duck. He stood with his arms pressed to his sides, the same undefending yet therefore defiant posture with which he had accepted verbal punishments as a toddler. His cheeks and jaw reddened, his head swiveled from side to side with the force of her small, prettily tapered hands. Faced with punishment he had never shown fear or remorse, never apologized, instead he had retreated within himself as if the outrage of adults were a mysterious storm that would pass if he could ride it out. Gideon, exasperated, had always ended up saying there was no getting through to Alexander.

"I've always loved you too much to see you for what you are," she panted.

"Don't you care what a trauma this is for me?"

"Trauma, is that all you have to say?" Suddenly her quivering legs went weak, and she sat on the low, king-size bed. "How did you get to be like this? We must have done something very wrong."

"Wrong?" he asked. The aloof, near smirk was gone from his reddened face, and he rubbed his knuckles across his bewildered eyes. "Mom, I don't understand what you think is so horrible in wanting to know who my real father is."

"How about the way you found out?"

"Does that make me a worthless shit? Why do you—why does everybody—get so uptight about me? Are people jealous? Is it because when I want something I plan how to get it better than other people do?"

Cold chills of suspicion traveled down her spine. "Then you really did calculate on this stroke? You actually intended your father to have a stroke?"

"He's not my father." For a second Alexander again was remote, unreachable. Then he shook his head in bemusement. "I don't know why I told him. Maybe I just wanted to shake him. Maybe I hoped he'd drop dead. Maybe there was no reason. Must there always be a motivation?"

"Oh, Alexander, you have no conscience, none. If you had one you never would have told him."

"Conscience? What does that mean?"

His face was earnest, and she understood the question was an honest request for information.

"Conscience is an interior voice. It doesn't always stop you from being cruel or dishonest, but when you are it punishes you afterward."

He shrugged. "Sounds like a bummer to me."

"If you had one," she said tightly, "you'd feel guilty about what's happened."

"Yeah, sure. But why are you so shook up about his

dying? I mean, he's old, ugly, and you're so great-looking.
You're not like everybody else's mother, you're young,
young like me."

"I care for him," she said. She could hear the thudding of
her heart. "He means everything to me. I *care.*"

He sat on the bed next to her. After a moment he mumbled, "I'm sorry."

Had she ever heard him say this before? She sighed, yet
couldn't stop herself from inquiring, "Sorry? Will sorry
heal a stroke?"

He turned to her, the bedside lamp glowing on his face,
reddened from the slapping. His expression was intent, his
tawny eyes were nakedly unguarded. "That's not what I
meant. I'm not sweating it about him, he's old, he'd die
soon anyway. It's you. I never wanted to hurt you. Mom,
by now you should've realized you're the only person who's
important to me."

The killing rage had gone, she could feel the sweat on her
body and the tingling of her palms. Nothing about the last
few minutes was believable. Who charges one's beloved
son of murder? And what boy not yet fifteen tacitly pleads
nolo contendere?

"You're all I have left," she whispered, holding out her
arms.

Mother and son sat entwined on the edge of her king-size
bed, she weeping, he with his puffed face pulled into lines
of contrition.

A few minutes before midnight, Gideon Talbott died.

40

Crystal, who had always cherished the belief that her brain
cracked the whip over her emotions, found the incapacita-
tion of her grief unbelievable. Mitchell, red-eyed and
shaken, staged a meticulously magnificent funeral. She

somnambulated through it, barely recognizing Governor
Brown or Senator Murphy—and this type of large-scale
function was her métier. Her esophagus closed up when she
tried to eat. She slept heavily for twelve to fourteen hours,
awakening in weary grogginess to imagine she heard ponderous footsteps in the adjoining bedroom. Passing Gideon's small downstairs office, her head would tilt to catch
the gravelly voice. Afternoons, she would yearn for one of
his companionable, dinner-table briefing sessions on the
Talbott projects. The simplest decision—whether to drink
coffee or tea, which shade of pantyhose to wear—became
impossible. A hundred times a day she would think, *I'm not
sure how to do this: better talk it over with Gideon.*

The web of fresh widowhood entrapped her, and she
could not escape.

Honora phoned four times from Los Angeles. Although
Crystal recognized her gentle sister's loving persistence, she
could not pull herself together to take the calls. A condolence letter arrived on stationery embossed *Mrs. Malcolm
Peck.* Joscelyn had written a brief yet elegiac paragraph
about Gideon during the spring and summer that the three
Sylvander sisters had dwelt in his Clay Street house. Crystal's tears splotched the elegant slants of the engineer's
printing: since she could not decently hand over a note
from her own sister to her fussy social secretary for ac-
knowledgment, she dropped it in the wastebasket.

The boys came home each weekend, but even when
Alexander was speaking, even when celebrating his birthday, her attention flickered like a worn-out light bulb.

Most afternoons Mitchell would arrive at the house with
a fresh sheaf of documents. Mesmerized by his quiet, self-
effacing voice, she never grasped his explanations of the
significance of each postmortem paper that she must sign.
She saw the executive secretary as a benign ghost sent by
her dead husband to guide her.

One afternoon in May they sat in the rear drawing room,
he explaining, she staring out the window: the sky was
murky and leaden, turning the choppy Bay a brownish,
elephant-hide gray. She wrote *Crystal Sylvander Talbott* by
his neat exes.

"Mrs. Talbott?"

"Yes, Mitchell?"

Giving a dry, nervous cough, he stacked the signed

legalities in his old, carefully polished leather briefcase. "Something's come to my attention that seems a bit out of the ordinary."

."Oh, handle it however you think best." She managed a listless smile. "I have every faith in you."

Doglike adoration glazed his intelligent eyes. "I don't like bothering you, not now," he said gently, "but I think this is important. The board is meeting on Sunday."

Talbott's eight-man board of directors, composed of the five division heads plus the presidents of Talbott Construction, Inc., Talbott-Arabian Enterprises and Talbott Engineering, Inc., gathered four times a year around the long oval table of the directors' room. In January, while readying her to preside in his place, Gideon had made a rare venture into humor: *No need to be nervous, dear. My bears are quite tame, they'll dance to whatever tune you play.* Since then she had lumped the board that way. The Bears. Each Bear had made a sympathy call, effusively giving reassurances that Talbott's was forging ahead, business-as-usual.

"This isn't the right month," she said. "And anyway isn't Sunday a peculiar day for them to meet?"

"Exactly. And no notification's come for me." He acted as the recording secretary. "Mrs. Talbott, since Mr. Talbott passed on there's been an expression of interest in buying Talbott's."

She had been leaning back in the pillows. Now her spine straightened. "I don't understand. Buy Talbott's?" She peered at him.

"There's been feelers."

"Who is it?" she demanded. "Morrison-Knudsen? Fluor? That damn Ivory?"

"This is all third hand," he said. "It's Woodham."

"Woodham!" Woodham was a large, Illinois-based construction firm with whom Talbott's had often coventured. "Why doesn't Henry Woodham come to *me*? Don't people in the business know that what I don't own outright is in trust for the boys—and that *I* control the trust?"

"I'm certain the disposition of Mr. Talbott's estate is common knowledge."

"So why's Henry Woodham been sniffing around *my* board?"

"I suppose Mr. Woodham believes the directors will make the ultimate decision, and then advise you."

"Hahh!" Crystal's eyes glinted a darker blue. For the first time since Gideon's death her mental processes had regained their normal clarity, precision and immediacy. "Well? And how did they react?"

"I gather with great enthusiasm."

"The whole thing's insane! Alexander—and Gid, too—are looking forward to coming into the business."

"You'd be extremely well recompensed," he said, adding in deliberate slowness, "And so would each board member."

"They're being paid off?"

"They'll receive stock in Woodham. It's traded on the American Stock Exchange."

"I know, I know," she said impatiently. "How much stock?"

"I'm not positive. I believe it's a different amount for each of them. Certainly as a group the board'll receive a substantial block. I gather—again third hand—at this meeting they're going to discuss how to present the Woodham offer to you in its most attractive light."

"How to wheedle me around," she said bitterly.

"Mrs. Talbott, they have no realization of how much you've contributed to the company. They see only the obvious, your beauty, your charm."

Her jaw tightened and she stared across the drab Bay at Alcatraz. "What if I refuse to go along? What will they do?"

His narrow shoulders rose in an eloquent shrug. "The obvious move is for them to resign en masse, or at least threaten to."

"And I'd be out of business."

"Or maybe they'll be more subtle, put you in a position where you'll be forced to go along. We both know how risky construction is. A few large jobs underbid and you'd be in serious financial hot water."

Her face took on that frightening, superhuman beauty as she visualized each director. After a full minute's silence she said, "Redelings, Cline, O'Shea and Masters won't resign or play financial hanky-panky."

"They might *appear* loyal, Mrs. Talbott, but I wouldn't be too sure of them."

"They'll try to coerce me, but they don't want Talbott's going down the tubes," she said. "They're over sixty, they'd never locate another top management job."

Mitchell nodded slowly, respectfully. "That's extremely astute reasoning, Mrs. Talbott. You're right."

All at once Crystal's supporting wires of outrage snapped: small and fragile in her widow's black, she sank back.

"Oh, Mitchell," she sighed shakily. "What's the point of even considering who'll do what? I can't go up against them."

He leaned toward her comfortingly. She could smell the Lifebuoy on him. "Mrs. Talbott, don't underestimate yourself."

"It'll be years before the boys're ready to take over."

"Mr. Talbott often told me how lucky he was to have a wife with a keen mind. And think of during his illness. He couldn't have managed without you. You were a tremendous help to him."

"Help, yes. I ran his errands. But women don't belong in construction," she said. "You won't be sorry for telling me, I'll see to that."

The faintest hint of dismayed reproach showed in the cadaverous face. "Mrs. Talbott, that's not important."

"You're a true friend," she said, floundering about for a nonmercenary reward. With a wan smile, she inquired, "I'm not sure I've heard your Christian name?"

He acknowledged his pleasure by reddening. "Padraic."

"Spelled the Irish way?"

"Yes. My mother's maiden name was Sullivan," he said. "I'd be most grateful if you'd call me Padraic, Mrs. Talbott."

"When we're alone like this, it's Crystal."

"Crystal. . . ."

The next few hours her mind whirled. She would suddenly find herself in the music room, or at her desk, or in her dressing room with no recollection of when she had moved, or why.

Gideon never would have been coerced. But she, by virtue of her sex, was hostage to the Bears. They could put her out of business.

At eleven thirty she found herself dialing long distance.

She convinced an elderly, southern-accented male of her urgent maternal need to speak to Alexander Talbott. Yet when she had her son on the line, she didn't know what to say.

"Alexander . . ." she faltered. "Alexander, are you really interested in going into Talbott's?"

"Come on, Mom, you didn't call after lights out to ask me *that*."

"I have to know."

"It'll be mine, remember?"

"And Gid's."

"Don't worry, Gid'll be there, too."

"Woodham's interested in buying us out."

"Tell 'em to go take a flying fuck."

"Oh, Alexander, be serious."

"Come on, Mom, all the big companies are licking their chops. But the others are waiting a decent couple of months before they rip at you."

"I'm not meant to know."

"Then how do you?"

"Mitchell told me."

"Good old faithful. What's the dope?"

She briefly recapitulated the afternoon's conversation. "And Mitchell says the board'll stop at nothing to make me sell out."

"That's obvious. But you aren't going to."

"What choice do I have? They could easily force me into a corner by threatening to resign. Or by getting me into a financial bind so I'd *have* to sell—and at much worse terms."

"I want Talbott's." He was enunciating carefully.

"I don't know how to handle them." Her voice rose shrilly.

"Let me think," he said.

She clasped the phone tighter. What could be more idiotic than waiting on pins and needles for the advice of a boy who had just had his fifteenth birthday?

"The thing is to get something on each of them," he said finally.

"I don't understand."

"The dirt," he said. "Mom, the dirt."

"Alexander, you know there isn't any. Your father—" She now spoke the word securely. Her confession to Gideon and his forgiveness had released her from the qualms she had always felt about Alexander being a cuckoo in the Talbott nest. "—wouldn't have kept them if he'd seen anything underhanded."

"Ah right—they're an upstanding bunch. Going behind

your back when you're so shook you can't think straight,"
he said with embittered raillery. "There's dirt."

"I just can't believe your father would have—"

"For openers," he interrupted, "try going through their
offices."

"Alexander, you sound so hard."

After the briefest pause, he said, "How should I sound?
Those bastards, I could kill them."

"So could I. With my bare hands."

"Attagirl, Mom. I'm counting on you and so's old Gid."

When she hung up, the force of her headache had eased.
Alexander had not relieved any of her doubts and fears, but
the conversation had settled her mind. He had pointed out
a course of action.

The next afternoon when Mitchell arrived she asked,
"What time is that meeting?"

"Ten thirty. Are you going?"

"I must. The boys are relying on me," she said. "Do you
think I'm being an idiot?"

"No. A brave and courageous lady. I'll be there with
you."

"Thank you, Padraic," she said, and touched his
knuckle. "Tell me if this sounds melodramatic. What if we
wait in Mr. Talbott's office until they're beginning their
meeting, then walk in? Would that give us an advantage?"

"You'll shock the life out of them," Mitchell replied, still
red about the ears from her feather-light touch.

41

Though Crystal had arranged to meet Mitchell at headquarters at ten, her car pulled up on Maiden Lane at a little
before eight—an ungodly early hour for her. Instructing
the chauffeur to return to the house, she poised on the
steps, a badly outnumbered general surveying her bat-

tleground. Talbott's had long ago acquired the two adjacent buildings, and under her guidance the three had acquired a unified Victorian façade.

Her limited supply of confidence faded immediately she unlocked the Pompeiian red door. Across from her, on the staircase wall, hung Gideon's larger than life, full-length portrait. Two narrow windows provided the only light, and the shadows wadding the hall intensified the Rembrandtian chiaroscuro so that the strong, ugly face seemed to jump out at her, a near verbal reminder that whatever influence she might have had on the exterior of Talbott's ceased at this threshold. She was entering Gideon's world—a tough, rapaciously competitive masculine world. In her black Chanel suit with its miniskirt exposing the shapely curves of her thighs, she felt a doll. Frivolous. Breakable. Inadequate. Mindless. A good thing she'd sent the Cadillac away or she would have slunk home.

Incapable of facing the claustrophobic, leather-padded confines of the Otis elevator, she climbed the uncarpeted wooden staircase, her footsteps resounding hollowly. On the second and third floors the interior walls of all three buildings had been removed to form an enormous open space. Low barriers marked the cubicles of project managers, but the impression was of an endless battalion of drafting tables each with an armed light fixture above and a metal stool tucked neatly beneath. She stepped to the nearest table, fingering the safelike equipment that adjusted the mechanical drafting machine. "Gideon bought equipment and engineers," she said. "I can buy them, too." Her high, female voice was smothered by the silence.

The executive offices were on the fourth, the top, floor. As she reached it, a sudden shadow darted. She gasped aloud, then realized the intrusion came from a bird flying above the skylights.

Straightening her shoulders, drawing a deep, calming breath, she moved to the nearest door. The neatly painted lettering read:

A. DONALD MASTERS

Gideon's heavy keys dangled in her hand. This building was hers by inheritance, so why should she be inhibited by this sense of trespassing? *I'd feel a lot less furtive if I believed the Bears are into corruption. But Gideon was shrewd about people and he never would have kept anyone whose morals were questionable.*

Fumbling with the key marked "Masters," she pushed open the heavy door, hurrying through the secretarial antechamber into the domain of the oldest member of the board.

A. D. Masters, a jovial, ruddy-faced man of sixty-two, had risen from piledriver to this large, luxurious office by dint of night school engineering courses and some fancy footwork with San Francisco's edgy labor unions. His unstylishly broad-shouldered suits were always rumpled, his dark tie crooked, his shock of graying hair unkempt. His office showed a similar lack of order.

A car—or maybe it was a truck—rattled up Maiden Lane. Crystal ducked into the corner, waiting until the noisy engine faded before going to the cluttered desk.

She picked up the folded financial page of Friday's *San Francisco Chronicle*. Blue pencil circled *WoCo*, the symbol for Woodham Corporation, which had closed at fifty and a quarter. It didn't take too much brilliance to know that the $100,500 slashed on the margin meant Masters had been offered 2000 shares. *No wonder he's such an eager beaver.* Sitting in the deep, black leather indents of Masters' desk chair, she fished gingerly through his top drawer.

Shoved behind diagrams, she found a wad of department store bills. She frowned at them. Why had these been mailed to the office? Why hadn't they been paid from the big Piedmont house that bony Mrs. Masters kept so immaculate? Crystal laid the receipts in front of her like a fortune-teller's Tarot deck.

Masters had stocked up on inexpensive jewelry and high-priced lingerie.

Crystal's mouth curved in a knowing smile, and her hands moved less hesitantly as she went through the messy drawers. Below a fingermarked volume of specifications was an eight-by-ten glossy. A cheaply voluptuous creature in a minimal bikini posed with a hand on her hip. Across the huge breasts was scrawled: *With all my Heart to Adorable Andy from Your Lucille.* Crystal knew that to everyone, including his prim wife, Masters was A.D.

With a ribald little chuckle, Crystal thought: *Andy, Dandy Andy, what a naughty boy.* "Alexander, you genius," she whispered, and laughed aloud.

She replaced the bills and photographs where she had found them.

O'Shea's office, though identical to Masters', appeared twice the size because it lacked the clutter. In the top drawer of the desk was a manila file typed: *Personal Business.* Inside was a second notice for $8000 due to Loopman's Casino in Reno, and a Western Air Lines round-trip ticket to the same city dated for today.

As she meticulously repositioned the file, the burden of the coming confrontation no longer rested like an intolerable albatross on her shoulders.

Cline's office revealed nothing.

She moved on to Roliu's larger quarters. The head of the Petrochemical Division had not been in on Friday. Crystal flipped through his mail, weighing a heavyish letter with no return address in her hand. After a few moments she carefully worked open the flap with her fingernail tip. A sheet of plain white paper wrapped five one-hundred-dollar bills. *On the take,* she decided, and searched the secretary's desk for glue to reseal the envelope.

LeBaron, at forty-one the youngest director, kept a pair of barbells in the corner. His black datebook lay on the window ledge, opened to this date. The slanted draftsman print was excruciatingly legible. *Meeting 10:30. CT discussion. Luxury loving, vain, conceited woman. Fears losing what she has. Responds to me physically. Offer to personally bring her to the right decision.*

Rage burned through Crystal and she battled a vengeful desire to dig through LeBaron's drawers and cabinets until she came up with evidence of a jailable crime—swindling or liaisons with small boys—however the digital desk clock jumped from 9:17 to 9:18. Every moment she had left must be put to use.

In various other offices she found empty bourbon bottles, a bill for blood tests from a nearby lab on Post Street, a hoard of blurry, revoltingly pornographic Polaroids.

At quarter to ten, after rechecking each of the door locks, she retired to Gideon's domain.

This, the largest office, was furnished with ornate Victoriana that she had ejected from the Clay Street house. On the walls hung framed old sepia photographs. In one the original bushy-bearded Gideon Talbott, the father-in-law who had died decades before her birth, posed at the head of his team of mules. Behind Gideon's desk was a fraying blue banner whose worn gilt letters proclaimed TALBOTT'S WILL BUILD ANYTHING, ANY PLACE, ANY TIME, which remained the company motto.

Having ferreted out secrets that the Bears had managed to keep hidden from Gideon had restored Crystal's confidence. Her hopes for the coming meeting might not be utterly sanguine, but neither were they any longer totally despairing. She sat on the claw-footed black horsehair sofa, her hands folded, her face thoughtful.

When the tiny, faraway sound of the electric bell announced that the front door had been opened, she got to her feet. There was the remote rumble of the elevator then a discreet rap.

"It's me, Padraic."

As she opened the door, the grandfather clock began chiming.

"On the dot," she said.

"I meant to be here first, but then I decided to park a couple of blocks away, where nobody'll see my car."

"Very James Bond," Crystal said with a smile. "I only got here a couple of minutes ago myself."

She trusted Mitchell implicitly, she knew he was with her to the hilt no matter what her methods, but she was not about to let him see her from any unfavorable angle.

When the first car pulled up, they fell silent, glancing at one another. She moved to sit tensely at Gideon's desk.

This office opened directly on the boardroom. By ten thirty the booming of masculine voices and the odor of expensively smuggled Havana cigars seeped around the locked door.

At the smart rapping of a gavel, Crystal's stomach twitched violently. What insanity was this? She, a ninety-three pound woman who had never worked a day in her life, was about to face down a combined ton of masculinity with well over two centuries of experience in heavy building? *Sell out*, her common sense told her. *Take the money and run.* Then she glanced at the silver double frame on the desk. Gid on the right, Alexander on the left. Her younger son's handsome, self-contained face looked out at her. She could hear his voice on the humming, long distance line: *I want Talbott's.*

Clasping the eighteen-carat gold chain of her black alligator purse, she got to her feet, crossing the old-fashioned red Turkey carpet. Mitchell pressed the lock, easing the door open.

She stood in the jamb, lighting up the boardroom like a blazing firecracker—gold hair, flawless English white and rose complexion, small yet exquisite body.

It was like a farcical pantomime the way the men at the long, oval table turned, peering at her through the drifts of cigar smoke, eyes bulging and jaws sagging.

Redelings, with invalid slowness, pushed to his feet. The others followed his example.

Crystal had never before seen any one of the Bears out of his uniform, the anonymous dark suit, fresh white shirt, unpatterned dark tie—the dress code that Gideon had followed and enforced. They might have been in fancy-dress costumes with their sports clothes. A jauntily crushed yachting cap hid Cline's flat, bald pate; LeBaron's short-sleeved knit shirt showed off the meaty biceps produced by those barbells.

Masters, in a beige leisure suit that strained across his ample belly, held the gavel at the head of the long table. After a pause, she moved to him. "Mr. Masters," she said sweetly, "you have my place."

His large, fleshy, windburned face settled into its jovial lines. "Why, Mrs. Talbott," he said. "What a pleasure to welcome you. We know you've been going through a difficult time and—"

"This is where my husband sat," she said resolutely. She knew because she had taken this chair at the January meeting.

Masters weighed the gavel against his palm, continuing to smile at her as if placating a small child. "We're only going over some technical matters today."

"Yes," somebody put in. "It's just dull engineering talk."

"This is my place from now on," she said.

"Mrs. Talbott," Masters said, "there's nothing to interest a lady as lovely as you on our agenda today."

Though she was gazing politely up at Masters' ruddy, genial face, she could sense the others at the table were smirking at his refusal to shift from the presiding officer's chair. "I prefer to be at all the board meetings, as Mr. Talbott was—" She paused several seconds before adding, ". . . Andy."

At the nickname, Masters' heavy flesh sagged and his cheeks puffed in and out as if he were having extreme difficulty breathing.

"Isn't that your place, next to Mr. Roliu?" she asked with one more "Andy?"

"Yes, Mrs. Talbott," he said thickly. "I don't know what got into me. Of course Mr. Talbott's chair is yours, of course you should be at the meeting." He shambled backward unsteadily.

O'Shea spoke up. "Mrs. Talbott, we would have notified you, but there's really no point to your being bored by engineering talk. We've given up our sunny Sunday, but you don't have to."

"It *is* a surprise that you're here, Mr. O'Shea," she said. "I'd heard you'd be in Reno."

O'Shea's small, neat features convulsed. His color drained and he stubbed out his cigar with a trembling hand.

Masters pulled back the head chair for her.

Sitting, she glanced at the small heap of rumpled notes. *Agenda for today: the Woodham proposal.*

"Here, Mr. Masters," she said. "These are yours."

"Thank you, Mrs. Talbott, thank you very much." He grabbed for the papers, crushing them in his big, veined hand. She glanced around the table. She wasn't positive if the other Bears were in on their two colleagues' womanizing and gambling, but from the tense, watchful expressions she could tell that they knew lethal hot buttons had been pressed. Ritter—the consumer of bourbon—had gone white and his left index finger jumped nervously as if he were unwittingly tapping out a Morse code message. Only LeBaron was leaning back in his chair, smiling cockily. The idiot, he really must believe she had a yen for his thick, dumbbell-produced muscles.

"Before we come to order," she said. "I have a few remarks that are off the record. First, I'd like to give you my heartfelt thanks. From the reports that Mr. Mitchell has brought me I know that you've handled Talbott's affairs with efficiency. For this I am extremely grateful. Without your efforts we never would be sailing smoothly through this difficult period of adjustment."

"That's what we're paid for," said LeBaron. The left eyelid came down, a hint of a wink.

She looked steadily down the table at him.

"I mean, we always do our best, Mrs. Talbott," LeBaron said uncertainly.

"Yes," she said. "But, Mr. LeBaron, does that mean I can't tell these other gentlemen that I'm grateful for a short grace period while I adjusted to my deep personal loss?"

Murmurs of sympathy rippled around the table. A cigarette and three cigars were stubbed out.

She kept staring at LeBaron until he mumbled, "No, Mrs. Talbott, of course not."

"Some of you may not know how deep my interest has always been in Talbott's, so maybe you are unaware of the extent that Mr. Talbott relied on my judgment."

They nodded gravely. No more superior smirks.

It was going better than Crystal had anticipated. She had been far more nervous at two thirty this morning as she practiced this speech in front of her bathroom mirror. "I earnestly hope," she went on, "that you will continue to work for me with the same steadfast loyalty that you gave him."

"You bet we will, Mrs. Talbott," Masters said with loud vigor.

A chorus of agreement rang. The four grizzled over-sixty crew spoke most ardently.

"It has come to my attention that certain unscrupulous competitors have decided to prey on Talbott's in what they consider a time of weakness." She allowed her honest bitterness to seep into her tone. "As you must be well aware, Talbott's was started by my late father-in-law over eighty years ago. When my husband inherited the business he expanded our scope beyond the state of California, and today Talbott's is respected worldwide. His sons will carry the same spirit of engineering service and enterprise into the space age." The men gazing at her nodded vigorously. "Until the new generation comes to the helm, however, it is up to me to carry on. I realize that others might hold my sex against me, but I am positive that you on the Talbott's Board of Directors will continue to work with me in the same spirit of generous cooperation that so richly earned my late husband's trust."

"Hear hear!" Masters burst out.

Applause filled the boardroom.

Crystal smiled brightly. "Thank you, gentlemen, for that

informal but heartfelt vote of confidence." She picked up the silver-handled gavel. For the first time since she had entered the boardroom she glanced at Mitchell. His gaze of awed admiration told her how well she had succeeded. She nodded, and he moved to his chair, opening the large black Minutes book.

She rapped the gavel twice. "The meeting will come to order," she said.

FIVE

1969

Joscelyn

42

"Here is Lissie's place mat," Joscelyn said, her expression animated. Sitting at the breakfast table at Lissie's level, she was holding up plastic imprinted with a red train. "Oh, today Lissie has the place mat with the train. What a nice place mat."

The child, who had been watching her mother's mouth with an expression of grave importance, took the shiny oblong, putting it in front of herself, then looked back at Joscelyn. Lissie wore a hearing aid but—in the audiologist's terms—it was to give her sound awareness, for she had little access to the speech spectrum.

"And here is Daddy's place mat," Joscelyn said. "See? Daddy's place mat isn't like Lissie's. Daddy's place mat is blue."

Lissie reached for the woven mat, moving around the table to set it down with a corner turned.

"And here is Mommy's place mat, it is blue, just like Daddy's place mat."

The child placed the second cloth askew opposite the first.

"And here's Lissie's fork. It is a little silver fork."

"Ork," Lissie said in a high, flat inflectionless little squeak.

Joscelyn clapped her hands, beaming. "That's very good speech, Lissie. Fork."

She went through the procedure with the other forks, then the spoons. Almost every child learns to speak easily, by mimicking sound, not by watching incomprehensible facial contortions. Patience was hardly Joscelyn's virtue, yet she discovered a vast, hitherto untapped tolerance when it came to teaching her daughter the means of communication.

When she and Lissie had first come home, while Malcolm was still in Lalarhein, they had stayed with the Ivorys.

Joscelyn and Honora, in order to let Lissie see their faces as they talked, had crawled around yattering to the active baby—both women had constant scabs on their knees. Now, whenever Joscelyn had Lissie's attention, she talked to the child or let her "help," performing her household tasks at a tortoise pace. She sledgehammered the key words thousands upon thousands of times. The rare times in her earlier life that she had ever thought about deafness, she had assumed that with a deaf child one lived in perpetual silence. Instead, she had turned into a nonstop gabber. The habit of talking constantly did not come easily to her: she kept a box of Sucrets for the inevitable sore throat.

"This is Lissie's knife."

She held out the knife. Lissie didn't take it. Instead she ran to the window with a scowl that for some reason Joscelyn found enchanting. The child had an amazing attention span, but she *was* only three and a half, and enough is enough.

Joscelyn swiftly finished setting the table.

"Bu," Lissie said in that odd pitch.

Joscelyn looked out the window at the small back garden. A blue jay was stalking across the patch of recently mowed grass.

"Bu," Lissie repeated, turning to her mother for approval.

Joscelyn clapped. Lissie had learned to understand the concept "bird." "That's very good speech, Lissie, very good. It is a bird, a big bird." She knelt, stroking Lissie's soft black hair. "See his pretty blue feathers, the same color blue as Daddy and Mommy's place mats."

"Mah-mah."

Joscelyn hugged her daughter. What a morning! *Ork* and *bu* and *Mah-mah.* Oh joy! Oh triumph! Yet her natural skepticism never would back down entirely, and that inner voice, her cruelest censor, said: *Three pitifully spoken words that probably only I can recognize.*

Even at her happiest, Joscelyn could never entirely banish that excruciating burden of failure. Didn't it figure? Joscelyn Sylvander Peck couldn't produce a normal kid, one who would learn to communicate without this agony. Lissie was gazing at her with those huge, alert, ultrablue eyes. Joscelyn wouldn't change a silky black hair on the exquisite, clever little head.

Lissie pulled away, rushing into the hall. She had felt the vibrations of Malcolm's footsteps.

Dressed in his charcoal gray suit for work, hair in place from recent water combing, he squatted in front of his daughter—*If you don't get down to her level, all she's going to see is a waggling chin,* Joscelyn kept reminding him. Most of the time he ignored Joscelyn's strictures, treating his daughter as though she were a hearing child. "Hi, Lissie," he enunciated carefully before he hugged her, pulling away so she could see him as he said, "What pretty pink overalls."

Joscelyn smiled down at them. *It's a good day,* she thought.

Lissie knelt on her chair, her small hand hovering near her juice glass until after her father picked up his—Malcolm had a rule that nobody began a meal until they were all seated. She squirmed, vocalizing with inflectionless little cries, tapping with her fingers to attract his attention, but he was absorbed in the sport section.

Malcolm's emotions toward his daughter fluctuated from that early totalitarian devotion to a surliness when, Joscelyn was positive, he did not see Lissie at all, but only three-year-old defective ears. On his very worst days he seemed ashamed of her, and resentful that she occupied such an extensive area of Joscelyn's attention.

Joscelyn swiftly scrambled his eggs and served the bacon from the Roaster-Toaster, handing Lissie two pieces. The child had already taken Cheerios and was picking up the milk pitcher carefully with both hands.

"Very good, Lissie. You're pouring that milk very well," Joscelyn said. Alone with the child, she would have said more, but Malcolm didn't go for a lot of talk at mealtimes.

She sat down to munch a rasher of bacon, remembering how in Lalarhein she had eaten this delicacy only on Yussuf's days off—of course he must have detected the savory odors permeating the kitchen. Her stream of consciousness flowed to Lissie. Poor baby, she sniffed the parental arguments that she was unable to hear, after their bouts becoming either clingily anxious or stamping her small feet in a tantrum.

The Pecks' marriage had yet more rocky spells.

When Malcolm had returned to Ivory headquarters with a two-level promotion, the word *favoritism* had been bruited around: the gossip had wounded him severely and he was determined to commit no blunders, none. He yearned for the affection of the thirty or so men who worked under him. To add to the pressure cooker, since March—and now it was May—he had been in charge of planning a propane deasphalting plant for his old nemesis, Paloverde Oil. He was a tiger at home. He inspected kitchen cabinets and bureau drawers, he insisted meals be served on a stopwatch schedule, he flew into a rage if Joscelyn ironed a near-invisible crease into a shirt collar.

Joscelyn knew exactly what was bugging him, she knew that when he nitpicked her efficient housewifery she should bow her head and keep silent. Generally she managed this, but at times she couldn't contain herself. Since March her records at the Kaiser Permanente Medical Group showed that she'd been treated for cracked rib # 2, had consulted a urologist about blood in her urine, and that her left hand had been stitched—Malcolm had lost control while holding the carving knife.

The pattern was consistent. After Malcolm's explosions he became a contrite lamb. Joscelyn, too, was penitent, accepting her own culpability. Did she have to egg him on? She was older and ought to be above screaming hurtful words. She would swear once again to herself to be an Oriental wife, living to boost his ego.

Lissie had eaten her cereal and was pushing the last soggy Cheerio across her bowl. Joscelyn touched the small wrist, waiting until Lissie looked at her. "Would you like more bacon?" She tilted her head questioningly—in communicating with a small, hearing-impaired child, one becomes quite a thespian. She had held up her own piece to make the message clearer. "More bacon? Do you want more bacon?"

Lissie shook her head.

Malcolm, too, had finished. Dropping the *Times* on the free chair, he leaned toward his daughter. "See you later, Lissie," he said, blowing a path on finespun hair the same true black as his own. Lissie giggled delightedly.

Joscelyn's vision blurred. This was the real Malcolm, tender and loving, the way that nature had intended him to be. She hugged him. "Love you," she murmured.

"Mmm, tonight?"

The sex was no longer wild, kinky or impromptu, but it

was the glue binding them, convincing each of the other's intrinsic love.

"Tonight," she said, and thought: *A very, very good day.*

She was still glowing when his car backed out of the attached garage. Rinsing the breakfast things, she began her endless reinforcement of words to Lissie, who was shoving the stainless steel cutlery into the dishwasher. After the child lost interest and went into her room to play, Joscelyn darted around cleaning, vacuuming, dusting, making beds. She left the bigger bathroom until last. On her hands and knees, she scoured the marks left by Malcolm's heels—the pink marble floor and counter were a bitch to keep clean, however Malcolm took an inordinate, touching pride in this bathroom, which doubled as a powder room. Each time a guest remarked on the coordinating pinks, he told the story of how he had selected the Italian stone at a marble place on Melrose, then had taken along a sample to match the accessories. He had paid a fortune at Sloane's for the large, heavy Venetian glass jar that sat on the counter because the candy-swirled pinks were the exact right shades.

By eight thirty, Joscelyn was buckling Lissie in her car seat. They inched toward the John Tracy Clinic on West Adams Boulevard.

Embedded in rush hour traffic, Joscelyn's warmth toward her husband frayed a little. Malcolm had determined to use the substantial money that had accrued from extra pay and overseas tax advantages for a down payment on a house. Joscelyn had wanted to look in Hancock Park, an island of substantial homes left stranded by the city's tidal movement westward. The area was not only relatively inexpensive but also convenient to both the big new Ivory complex on Wilshire and to the John Tracy Clinic. Malcolm, however, would settle for nothing less than a Beverly Hills address, a geographical snobbery that saddened and irritated Joscelyn—and inconvenienced them all.

Lissie, fortunately, turned drowsy in a car, sleeping most of the excruciatingly slow forty-minute drive.

As they pulled into the parking lot on West Adams, Lissie's friend, Carlos, was jumping from a wheezy pickup. The John Tracy Clinic did not charge for any of its services (Ivory was among the generous corporate donors), so the nursery school drew from all income strata. The two chil-

dren raced into the shade of the enormous Moreton fig tree
that towered over the ramble of beige bungalows. Joscelyn
followed sedately. This was not her day to help at the nursery school; however she planned to observe from the narrow corridor with chairs and a one-way window.

Mrs. Kamp, a trained teacher of the deaf, had lined five
small chairs in front of her, and a group, including Lissie,
sat watching intently as she held up a brown paper sack:
Joscelyn could not hear through the glass barrier, but it was
easy to read the carefully enunciating lipsticked lips. "Can
anyone guess what is in the bag?"

One little girl waved her hand in large circles, and the
other children all turned to her.

"No, Charlene"—Mrs. Kamp's mouth shaped the
words—"it is not a *ball*. But *ball* is a very good guess. Let's
all say *ball*."

Small mouths opened. More squirming, each child turning to the other as he or she spoke.

Lissie was holding up her hand and bouncing. The
teacher turned to her.

Face intent, Lissie formed a sound.

"A doll. Lissie is right. There is a doll in the bag. Come
up here, Lissie, and show us the doll."

Lissie excitedly tore the small, disreputable toy from the
brown paper. The teacher was demonstrating the position
of her tongue, letting Lissie and each child feel her muscles
and breath as she repeated, "Doll."

Mary Jekyll, a small blonde with a pretty, tired face, was
observing, too.

"The world's most impossible task," she sighed. Her
profoundly deaf little boy had entered the nursery group a
month earlier and had yet to say his first word.

Joscelyn, the old hand, said, "We all felt like that at first.
Don't give up the ship."

"Be here tonight?"

On Tuesday nights the clinic held classes to educate the
parents, and there was also a group session with the psychologist where parents could iron out the multifarious
family problems connected with having a deaf child.

"Absolutely," Joscelyn said. "I try never to miss."

"It holds me together, too." Another sigh. "Tonight's
Doug's turn. How I wish we could both make it, but one of
us has to hold down the fort and baby-sit."

Joscelyn's eye twitched. Baby-sitting was not her problem: Honora and Curt had a room furnished for Lissie, and delighted in taking her. Malcolm, though, always used that quintessential masculine excuse, work, to miss the meetings. On Tuesday evenings his briefcase bulged, his inside jacket pocket held scraps of paper jotted with vital phone calls to make. It was, Joscelyn knew from the group's sessions, a classic case of denial. If he avoided John Tracy Clinic, it meant that Lissie was not deaf. "Malcolm lets me come," she said. "He knows how much I need the contact."

Afternoons, Lissie napped for a good three hours. Joscelyn was ironing when the phone rang.

"It's me, hon," Malcolm said. "I've invited the Binchows for dinner."

Ken Binchow was his immediate superior. When Joscelyn had worked downtown at Ivory, she also had worked with Ken, a well-larded man in his early fifties who was devoutly convinced that the female brain came in a lighter density than the male. In Ken's favor, he was a good, solid engineer. She felt neutral toward him. She actively disliked Sandra Binchow, whose pointed, reptilian nose sniffed out areas of human dismay.

"Tonight?" Joscelyn said, sucking in her breath. "But Malcolm, it's Tuesday."

"I don't have time to argue," he snapped. "They're coming at seven thirty. How about that beef Wellington you did last week —and the St. Honoré?"

"Why not? After all, you've given me more than adequate time to market and whip up a three-star feast."

"That's one thing I can always count on—sarcasm from my wife when it comes to helping *me,*" he said, and the phone went dead.

Joscelyn folded the ironing board and went to wake Lissie from her nap. Beef Wellington and a St. Honoré it would be.

43

When Malcolm opened the back door at six twenty-five, Joscelyn was drizzling caramelized sugar over a pyramid of small cream puffs. Propped open on the table was *The Art of French Cuisine*. She never extrapolated a pinch of this or altered ingredients; she followed every recipe with mathematical precision. Her gourmet company meals were not to satisfy herself but to conform to Malcolm's exacting standards.

Lissie stood on a chair, watching. Cookie crumbs and a long drizzle of milk adorned her blouse and pink overalls.

"Want me to put her down?" he asked. Without waiting for a reply, he scooped the child into his arms.

Joscelyn continued drizzling the caramel, twin furrows between her eyebrows. Another sore spot. When they entertained, Malcolm preferred Lissie asleep. He would lead guests into the child's night-lit, beruffled room, beaming at the whispered praise of the beautiful, black-haired little girl sleeping in her youth bed.

Joscelyn was setting the St. Honoré on the top shelf of the refrigerator when she heard the unmusical monotony of Lissie's sobs. She darted into the smaller bedroom. Malcolm sat on the low bed, his daughter clasped between his thighs as he fastened the buttons of her too-short, apple-print Lanz cotton nightgown.

Mucus oozed from Lissie's nose and tears ran down her cheeks. What was she rejecting? Bed? This faded nightie? Malcolm's clamping knees? Lissie had a mind of her own and no means of communicating it.

"I'll finish her," Joscelyn said.

"The Binchows'll be here any minute." He picked Lissie up, flipping her onto the mattress, yanking up the yellow sheet and blanket, pressing down on the squirming child.

Lissie turned to gaze up with tear-reddened eyes. "Mah-mah."

"You're hurting her!"

"That's where you're wrong, Joscelyn. I'm not hurting her. Firmness isn't hurting. She'd be a damn sight better off if you taught her that she can't get away with murder. Now you get yourself the hell ready!"

Having vented his anger on his wife, he rested his cheek next to Lissie's, smiling at her.

Joscelyn retreated to their bathroom, hastily brushing on mascara, penciling eye liner. Maybe she did let Lissie get away with a lot—memories of those domineering, decrepit nannies plagued her still. Malcolm also indulged Lissie. It was only when his anxieties bubbled over that he became a zealous disciplinarian. *If he really takes it out on her, if he ever . . .* Joscelyn thought.

She often went through this litany but had never yet concluded it.

Ken Binchow was wolfing up seconds of pastry-encased beef and duchesse potatoes when Lissie came to the entry of the dining room, half hiding behind the arch. Thumb at her lip, she stared at them with huge, dark blue eyes. *Crystal's eyes,* Joscelyn thought, knowing that Crystal never in her life had gazed with such timid, nakedly yearning beseechment.

"If that isn't the most gorgeous thing," boomed Ken Binchow. "Come on in, little sweetheart."

"She's meant to be asleep," said Joscelyn, her long black hostess skirt rustling across the shag carpet.

"I can't take my eyes off her," cooed Sandra Binchow. "Can't she stay a minute or two?"

"Joscelyn's the strict guy in the family." Malcolm grinned engagingly. "Me, my motto's it doesn't hurt once in a while to let the mice play."

Joscelyn swooped up Lissie.

"Mah-mah?"

At her odd little voice, the Binchows' admiring smiles grew stiff.

"Our Lissie has a minor impediment." Malcolm made his routine explanation.

At this revelation Sandra Binchow's nose twitched. "The sweet booful," she cooed. "What's wrong?"

"Nothing, really," Malcolm said. "A little thing with her inner ear that the doctors'll fix when she's old enough."

Joscelyn carried Lissie to her room, sitting on the bed, gentling the overtired child with long, tender strokes down her back. "Pretty, pretty, pretty," she murmured in the unhearing pink ear that no doctor could fix.

"Joss," Malcolm called. "She isn't sick, is she?"

"A bit feverish," Joscelyn lied.

At this loud parental exchange, Sandra Binchow vowed that a hearing disability could be a blessing: their Scottie had awakened at the least sound.

Over the St. Honoré, Sandra said, "I don't see how you manage a fabulous gourmet meal like this. When Scottie was little, I had my hands full. And it must be so much more time consuming to have a handicapped child."

Joscelyn said, "I loathe the word, handicapped."

"Sandra didn't mean it as an insult," soothed Ken. "But while you were in there with her, Malcolm was telling us how you take her downtown almost every day."

"She goes to John Tracy. A nursery school."

"Sure, but having a kid like Lissie is tough, young lady," said Ken with mock severity. "Tougher than any assignment you ever got handed at Ivory, and don't you ever forget it."

"And I do admire how you're raising her," Sandra put in. "I was rotten on the discipline, wasn't I, Ken? Not that Scottie needed it. You're so normal with her."

"Lissie's hardly a freak."

"I didn't say—"

"She's extremely bright."

"Now, Joss," Malcolm said, turning to Sandra Binchow. "You're right, Sandra, it's a full-time job and I personally don't know how Joscelyn manages everything. Thank God she gets one day off. Honora takes Lissie every Wednesday after school."

At this invocation of the Big Boss's wife, and her relationship, the Binchows both sipped their coffee with chastened expressions.

"God, Malcolm, after you brought up Honora, they tiptoed through dinner. I almost felt sorry for that bitch."

"Christ, what else could I do?" he said morosely. "Your charming habit of insulting everybody I work for."

The Binchows, pleading a weeknight early bedtime, had left less than five minutes ago. It was not yet ten and Malcolm was putting the liquor away in the low cabinet while Joscelyn gathered the dirty glasses and crumpled cocktail napkins on a tray. Although she had been momentarily aggravated at the method of his solidarity against the Binchows, his unexpected alliance had erased her animosity, returning her to this morning's sensuality.

"Malcolm, I was thanking you." She came up behind him, massaging his tensed shoulder muscles. "What did you think of the new potato recipe?"

"Who could notice the food with that kid of yours giving everybody an ulcer? All that blathering you do with her— can't you train her to stay in bed?"

Joscelyn moved away. "If she knew how she embarrassed you, she would never emerge from the covers."

"Can't I make a suggestion without you flying off the handle?"

"So Ken Binchow knows your kid's 'handicapped.' Does that make you a rotten engineer?"

Malcolm took a long drink, his deep-set eyes appearing yet more sunken. "Deaf or not, she's got to learn bedtime means bedtime. If you can't do it, I will. She's going to have to learn to toe the mark."

"Quaint expression, toe the mark. Did you get it from your father?"

"Knowing who's boss never hurt a kid."

"It fucked *you* up for life. Malcolm, I'm warning you. You so much as touch her, I'll . . ."

"You'll what, bitch?"

Without thought, the response came to her. "Tell Curt and Honora."

Among Malcolm's never spelled out yet rigorously enforced husbandly privileges was the sole right to conclude their arguments—not necessarily in an unbenign manner. He might refer to a knock-down-drag-out by kissing her bruises and mumbling sheepishly, "Got a little rough, huhh?" However, let her bring up the bout—even with a humble apology—and he would reopen hostilities. Usually by the time Malcolm extended the olive branch she was too wild with relief for any further sparring. Filled with adoration and irrational hope for the future, she would melt against his strong, perfect, younger body.

Before this, though, Lissie had never been entangled with Malcolm's violent episodes. Oh, certainly the child figured in their scrapping: Joscelyn might try to prove a flaw in Malcolm's character by citing his avoidance of their child's problem, or he, in order to highlight Joscelyn's maternal inadequacy, would bring up one of Lissie's small shows of will. Now for the first time Malcolm's meanness had been directed specifically toward Lissie.

That night Joscelyn slept in the child's room.

At breakfast she served Malcolm his eggs and poured his coffee, otherwise ignoring him. She sat talking to Lissie.

Malcolm sipped the steaming coffee. "This sure hits the spot," he said in a false, buoyant tone—she could actually feel the waves of conciliation flowing from him. "God, I had a load on last night." He looked at her, waiting for her to pick up on his overture, as she always did.

She nodded coldly and continued enunciating. " ... and—today—is—Wednesday. After—school—Lissie—goes—to—help—Auntie—Honora—with—her—gardening."

Lissie wiggled, smiling. "Oo-noo."

"She understands everything," enthused Malcolm.

"Oo-noo," Lissie repeated.

"Hoonoo," Joscelyn said, "is exactly what I used to call Honora when I was a baby. And *I* had hearing."

"Our kid's got real brains." Again that phonily upbeat tone.

He was afraid. After their fights Malcolm was tender, repentant, sometimes self-castigating, but never frightened. Abruptly it came to her that his fear was connected to last night's threat to spill his home behavior to Curt and Honora. That she had the means to punish her husband came as a jolting shock to Joscelyn. *Intolerable,* she thought. It was intolerable for her to possess the power to degrade and diminish him.

"A genius from both sides," she said, putting her hand on his sleeve.

He smiled at her. "I was thinking. Haven't been to the school in ages."

It flashed through Joscelyn's mind that he had never visited, unless one counted sitting on the coarse grass to watch the annual fund-raising show that Walt Disney put on. The negative thought vanished. "Oh, Malcolm, she'd adore it," she said, beaming. "Whenever you can find the time."

"Today," he said.

"Today?"

"Why not?"

He called in sick.

At the nursery school, Joscelyn watched from the one-way window, chuckling for almost the entire three hours. The other two observing mothers in there were laughing, too. Lissie, her black hair whirling, alternated between clinging to her daddy and shoving the other kids away from him. "Malcolm's a fabulous father," said Marlene Leisen. And buxom Kyla Kent said, "Gorgeous, too. Like a black-haired Steve McQueen. Do you fend off poachers with a baseball bat or what?"

After school, the family Peck lunched alfresco at a cement table of a McDonald's, Lissie's favorite eatery.

She held up her hamburger. "Gur."

"Yes, hamburger," Malcolm said.

"Gur," Lissie repeated louder.

The inordinately obese woman at the next table turned, peering with avid curiosity at Lissie. Malcolm, who usually looked in the opposite direction when the child's speech attracted attention, stared down the fat lady until she went back to her malt.

They drove up to Bel Air, depositing a ketchup-smeared, happy, tired Lissie in Honora's arms.

Joscelyn expected Malcolm to drop her off at home and get back to Ivory. As he pulled into the drive, though, he turned off the ignition. "Alone at last," he said meaningfully.

"Hey," she said, her voice catching, "McDonald's must've added Spanish fly to the ingredients between the sesame seed bun."

"Go on, more, deeper," he gasped.

She was kneeling, naked except for the thin platinum chain with the tiny diamond that nestled in the hollow of her exerting throat. He, panting on the redwood patio bench, sat fully dressed with his fly open. *Déjeuner sur l'Herbe* had struck powerful, erotic veins in both of them, and in memory of their Paris trip they had emerged onto the patio for love in the afternoon. A beige-painted, cement-block wall hid them from the alley and neighbor-

ing yards; the nearby houses were also bungalows, so
nobody could look down on them; yet there was an aphro-
disiac element of risk, of danger, doing it *en plein air* and
Joscelyn, ashine with sexual sweat, sucked with electric
bliss.

He gasped dementedly, and came.

When his breathing eased, he said, "Now I'll do you."

"Here?"

"Get on the table," he commanded roughly.

Throwing off his tie, he began his lingual exploration,
soon climbing atop her. Love concluded with a crescendo
of rasping breaths and cries.

Afterward, they heard the neighbor's back door slam.

"Jesus," Malcolm said. "She was listening."

"Oh, let the old bag eat her heart out," Joscelyn said, her
orgasmic flush deeper. "The other mothers at the clinic
were swooning over you."

"No kidding?"

"I could make my fortune, raffling you off—but I'm not
about to."

Chuckling, they went inside to shower together in the
pink bathroom. They had never been more in tune.

Joscelyn could tell from the tension in Malcolm's face,
the sound of his cracking knuckles, that the Paloverde Oil
people were on his back, so she went out of her way to
please him, to run the house perfectly, not to let her incessant oral training extend into the hours he was at home, to
hide herself and be all that he expected of a woman. Yet
the following Saturday night, when they were having two
tables of bridge—the men were on Malcolm's project—his
temper resurfaced, once again focusing on Lissie.

He was playing out a three no-trump hand when the
child edged into the living room. Everyone exclaimed at
her beauty, and Joscelyn jumped to her feet.

Malcolm forestalled her by dropping his cards facedown
at her place. "It's my turn with her." He grinned. "You
play out the hand."

Joscelyn went down one, barely hearing the idiot advice
on how she could have made it, so intent was she on trying
to hear sounds from the bedroom. Finally she mumbled,
"Better go see what's keeping my partner."

The night-light was attached to an outlet at the baseboard, shining upward, casting black, iniquitous shadows of Malcolm as, using both hands, he forced Lissie's stomach to the youth bed. The small, bare feet thrashed in impotent helplessness.

Rage coagulated within Joscelyn: for a moment she was too furious to speak, then she hissed, "Let her go!"

Sensing her presence, Lissie turned and raised her head. "Mah-mah," she bawled.

"Shut the damn door," Malcolm muttered.

Joscelyn slammed it, coming into the dim room. "You shit!"

"That's the thanks I get for doing *your* job."

"What job? Breaking her spirit?"

"If you were one damn bit of a mother, she wouldn't come barging in every time we have company."

"That's what really fries you, isn't it? That they'll know that Mr. Perfect Project Manager has a deaf baby."

"Shout a little louder, why don't you?" he hissed, letting go of Lissie. Lissie sat up. "Now you've done it! All my time in here's shot to hell!"

"Should I weep?" Joscelyn asked. "Or start a fund for you?"

The night-light caught the shine of his clenched knuckles. His arm shot out, catching on the bone between her inadequate breasts.

As his clouts went, the blow was strictly minor league. This, however, was the first time he had hit her in front of Lissie. Gazing from one parent to the other, she cowered back against the headboard of the youth bed.

Joscelyn swept her up, rocking her to and fro. "I warn you. If you ever, ever hurt my baby, I'm telling Curt."

Malcolm drew a shuddering breath as he backed from the beruffled little room.

"Sorry, gang," she heard him say. "The kid must've had a nightmare. Joscelyn'll be right out."

Ten minutes later, when a snuffling Lissie had dropped abruptly into sleep, Joscelyn emerged. The Pecks smiled at one another across the Samsonite card table as if they were the happiest couple in all southern California.

That night proved to be a watershed dividing Malcolm's paternal attitudes. The next few days he treated Lissie as if she were a guest in the house, friendly enough, but with a hint of reserve.

By the following week, he pretty much ignored her, refusing to look when she tried to attract his attention, not taking her small hand when she extended it.

"Malcolm, she's just a baby. She doesn't understand our fights."

"Your idea, Joscelyn—you told me to lay off the kid. And it's just as well. I'm up to my eyeballs earning a living."

"Working and being a father aren't mutually exclusive."

"You go all-out when you entertain, but you haven't noticed who's bringing in the bucks, have you?" (*Is this him or his father speaking?* Joscelyn thought.) "All you can do is whine about needing help with her. I warned you before she'd be a damn sight easier if you laid down a few guidelines."

"She's good, Malcolm, so very good."

"Then you don't need me to play nursemaid, do you?"

Lissie had become their battleground.

The child picked at her food, sucked her thumb, reverted to bed-wetting. She often awoke sobbing.

The child psychologist on the John Tracy Clinic staff invited Joscelyn for a talk. A disarming warmth deepening the wrinkles of her tanned face, she said, "Mrs. Peck, I thought maybe you'd like to talk about any problems you might be having at home."

"Problems?"

"You certainly know by now the strain having a deaf child puts on family relationships."

Joscelyn was consumed with the urge to unburden herself. But wouldn't her psychological salvation come at the price of exposing Malcolm?

"No problems at all," she said brightly. "Why? Is Lissie going through a phase?"

"She's always been so outgoing, and the last month she's pulled into herself. On your days you must have noticed. She doesn't join in with the others."

Oh, my poor Lissie. "She's always hovered when I work."

"Mrs. Peck, please, I'm not accusing you. But I feel it might be a good idea if you and Mr. Peck came in for a visit together."

Fat chance. "He's tremendously tied up at work."

"Yes, we see so little of him."

"He was here not long ago, and Lissie clung to him, too. We were all laughing." *Ho, ho, ho.*

The psychologist sighed and said, "You know where I am if you need me, Mrs. Peck. And thank you for dropping by."

44

On the last Sunday in July the Pecks were invited to early dinner at Honora and Curt's. The only other guest was Senator George Murphy. Malcolm—never before in heady proximity to a star of this magnitude either from the film world or the political scene—was at his best, his conversation light, respectful, yet without the least hint of brown-nose.

While Curt barbecued the thick porterhouses, Lissie sidled up to the stranger, staring at him. The one-time actor was conceded by all who knew him, whatever their views on his talent and/or political persuasion, to be a kindly man.

"Hi, little honey. Ever been told you're very pretty?"

Lissie, before her recent bad times, would have moved closer, but now her thumb migrated to her mouth, and she backed against Joscelyn's knees.

Honora was handing around the pizza that she'd heated in the terrace's little kitchen. "Lissie's hard of hearing, but she's a fabulous lip-reader."

The Senator popped his hors d'oeuvre in his mouth, swallowing as he came across the flagstones to bend his knees in front of Lissie. Her thumb slipped from her mouth and she glanced shyly at him.

He smiled. When she didn't withdraw, he scooped her up. For an instant she stiffened, but then relaxed and let him carry her to his deep patio chair.

"I'll tell you a story," he said. "You feel and watch."

Soon Lissie was her old self, laughing, touching his famous throat, mouth, chest, while he slowly acted out the drama of Goldilocks and the Three Bears.

Joscelyn, Honora and Curt smiled at the twosome. Malcolm did, too, but Joscelyn saw something bereft, mournful, in his smile.

When we're alone, she thought, *I'll make it up to him.*

By the time they left the house, though, his mood had changed and he was spoiling for a fight. "Can't we ever get out alone?" he asked.

"We were at the Binchows' Saturday night." Joscelyn gazed straight ahead lest Lissie, in her car seat behind them, be watching. "But if you're talking about Curt and Honora, no. Lissie's included in the invitation. They're her uncle and aunt, remember?"

"Something you ought to know, Joscelyn. As far as I'm concerned this marriage is going to hell in a bucket."

His low rumble pierced her with sudden doubts. Had she been misinterpreting his foul mood the past weeks? Maybe he wasn't having difficulties with the Paloverde job. Maybe he'd found some nineteen-year-old with enormous boobs like Crystal's and a yoyo brain who acted as if he were Prince Charles.

Her jaw clenched. "I don't find it any bed of roses lately, either," she said.

"You better get on the ball, then. Figure out some way for us to have a life of our own."

She hid her new suspicions and lashed out. "I agree, it's a crying shame that Senator Murphy quit paying attention to you and told Lissie a story. Tell you what. We'll buy one of those records like they have in the new dolls. We'll have it transplanted into Lissie, and the next time we meet a bigtime movie star he'll never guess she's deaf."

He grabbed for her breast, driving one handed, twisting and pinching. During their recent fights it was a point of honor with Joscelyn never to let him know the anguish—mental or physical—that he caused. She could not prevent her harsh groan.

A car with its brights on came toward them, and in the blinding glare, he released her. "That's only a taste of what you'll get if you don't shut up."

At home she carried Lissie, a limp, sleepy weight, into her bedroom. Honora kept a painted wood Surprise Box at her house, and every time Lissie came over there was a present in it, a small toy, a book, something to wear. Tonight Lissie had fished out a new pink nightie. By the time Joscelyn had undressed the drowsy child and put on the new garment, Lissie was asleep. Joscelyn turned on the nightlight and left the door open. Malcolm was sitting on the couch, a bottle of scotch in front of him, his head hunched low between his slumped shoulders. Portrait of dejection.

She sat next to him. "Malcolm, let's not tear at each other. I love you so much."

He drained his glass. "Some way you show it."

"It kills me when we fight."

"Oh, Christ, first you get me thoroughly pussy whipped, then you don't want me around my kid. And now it's a crime to want to take you out swinging occasionally."

"We could swing right here," she said. Since the afternoon of the outsider, they had made love only once. (*Another sign he has somebody else?*)

"You're sure it won't kill you to stay in your own bed one night?" he growled.

"I only go in to Lissie when she has nightmares."

"How you manage to sleep with all the lights on is beyond me."

Lissie's night-light had become their Vietnam. Joscelyn couldn't for the life of her comprehend her husband's vicious guerrilla warfare on the small glow: the closest she could figure was that he saw it as proof that his daughter lacked not only hearing but also courage.

"The light's a necessity. If you'd ever come on a Tuesday night you'd learn a bit about deaf kids—"

"That's a subject I know more than enough about, thanks."

"Lissie has no hearing. If it's all black in her room and she can't see, she's completely cut off."

"The way you swarm over that kid you're turning her into an emotional cripple."

"She's three and a half. And though I know this pains you to hear it, she's profoundly deaf. When she wakes up in the night she needs some sensory input."

"Ahh, what's the use?" Broodingly he poured himself another drink. "You never could listen to a constructive suggestion. You're spoiling her rotten."

She stalked into their bedroom, jabbing on the small television. At this hour, ten, network News wasn't available, so she watched Channel 5. After a few minutes of watching their routine reports of murderous activities in south-central Los Angeles, she turned off the set. Removing her blouse, she went into Malcolm's precious pink bathroom. The mirror reflected a fresh bruise rising like a red-purple sun above her left bra cup.

She was slathering her face with Neutrogena when, over the running water she heard Lissie's sudden shriek of animal panic. Soap on her face, she darted to the other bedroom.

The door had been shut. Flinging it open, she blinked in the darkness. The night-light had been turned off.

She picked up Lissie, cuddling the convulsing little body. Lissie's arms clutched at her neck. "Mah-mah."

"I didn't think she'd wake up before morning." Malcolm, behind her in the hall, spoke in a peculiar, high voice: it was as if he were ventriloquizing the tones of a frightened preadolescent.

"You prick, you unspeakable prick!"

"It's time she learned bed means sleep."

Lissie's wails rang unhappily, yet minus that shrill hack-saw of panic.

"Quit dumping whatever's wrong between us on the poor baby," Joscelyn said, pressing her cheek into her daughter's damp hair. "I don't give a shit if you're humping some secretary."

"Secretary?"

"Lissie tries so hard. She was doing really great until you started in on her. How could you do a remake of your own rotten father?"

"Bitch, shut your mouth about my dad. You're not worthy to say his name. And maybe I *ought* to put it to some other woman. Be a pleasure after you. Go take a look at yourself, titless wonder. Soap all over your face like you're going to shave—what are you, a guy in drag?"

Joscelyn rushed with Lissie into the big pink bathroom. One arm holding the child, whose sobs had lessened to desolate little snuffles, she rinsed her face with the washcloth.

Malcolm burst in. "Tonight, dammit, she's going to bed like every other kid does!"

He reached for Lissie. Joscelyn, feeling the small body tremble, clasped the child more tightly. With her left hand slippery and wet, she couldn't maintain her hold.

Malcolm wrenched Lissie away.

"For God's sake, Malcolm, haven't you terrified her

enough? Give her back." She wrapped both hands around Lissie's waist.

"Fuck off!" Malcolm growled.

Seizing his daughter in a demon grip, he stamped across the bathroom. Joscelyn followed, tugging at the child's soft, boneless-feeling hips.

She could see their mirrored reflection, father, mother, child, united in a swaying, tormented dance across the bathroom. *The Unholy Trinity*.

"Let her go!" Joscelyn screamed. Strengthened by the tiger's milk of maternal protectiveness, she was aware of only one imperative—to get her child away from Malcolm and take her to a safe place, a place where she couldn't be battered as he had been, couldn't have her fragile child's bones broken as his had been.

Malcolm hammered a blow at Joscelyn's bare chest. She staggered back, and a scrap of Lissie's gift nightgown came away in her hands.

"Bastard, give her to me!" she screamed.

Over the rasping of her breath, she could hear Lissie's wailing, but faintly, as if her child were a long way away. Regaining her balance, she charged at her husband.

He struck out at her chest again. This time he missed her. The back of his clenched hand caught Lissie's flailing arm.

The child's mouth opened wide and her body went into a paroxysm as she stored up breath for an onslaught of sound.

At the blow to her daughter's soft flesh, Joscelyn reacted as if a match had been touched to her gasoline-drenched brain. All that lay within the curve of her skull ignited. Redness jumped behind her eyes. An immense roaring drummed against her ears.

Her maddened gaze was attracted by the candy stripes of the useless jar from Venice.

She reached for it. With complete lack of rational thought, she lifted the oversize ornament with both hands, one dry, one wet, raising the heaviness high over her head.

In that instant—it was less time than a heartbeat—Malcolm stared at her. His eyes flickered with something she would never understand. Maybe she momentarily brushed his funny bone, standing without her blouse—*titless wonder*—the heavy, useless ornament above her head, a female Moses set to hurl down the commandments. Maybe he was regretting his cruelty about the night-light. Maybe he was thinking of his punitive, war-hero father. For the rest of her life Joscelyn would attempt to comprehend the thoughts that his deep-set gray eyes reflected.

In a loud, strangled voice, she cried, "I'll teach you to victimize my baby."

The jar seemed to descend mechanically, through no volition of hers, yet her hands remained clasped around the smooth, cool weight.

The blow vibrated through her body. A deep, hollow thump reverberated through the remodeled bathroom. A fraction of a second later the jar slipped from her hands to shatter on pink marble.

Malcolm reeled two small steps. She snatched Lissie from his limp grasp. Then he plunged forward.

He fell amid the still skittering shards. As his forehead hit the marble, another thump sounded, less portentously than the first.

Clutching her daughter, whose body remained tensed in that seemingly eternal paroxysm, Joscelyn stood panting.

Malcolm stretched across the pink floor. Time was infinitely slowed, and in this eternal moment she was able to view him dispassionately. One arm flung forward, the other at his side, his legs slightly apart, she decided that he looked as if he were practicing his Australian crawl. *He's terrific on the first lap,* she thought dizzily. When he challenged Curt he always touched the pool edge first, but after that initial length Curt was the inevitable victor.

Blood was pouring from Malcolm's black hair, rich crimson rivulets that picked up the smaller flecks of rose glass, carrying them like flotsam.

"God, I didn't mean it," she whimpered. "Darling, get up. Please get up."

He didn't move.

She must help him, but how could she put Lissie's bare little feet on this broken glass? She knelt with the child, not noticing the sharpness that pierced her legs and knees. Why was he so still? His eyes were staring.

And then Lissie exploded in the low, sustained howl for which she had been storing breath while Joscelyn had picked up the ornament and crashed it down.

45

The Ivorys were at the front door, arms connubially entwined, watching the red taillights of the Senator's departing car when the phone rang. They exchanged a glance. Nearly eleven, too late for a social call. It was Curt who hurried inside to pick up the extension.

Honora heard him say, "Joss, slow down, I didn't get that." His voice was deepened by that mollifying assertion commonly used to calm hysterics.

Leaving the door open, Honora darted to the library. Curt was hunched around the phone, his cheekbones drawn upward in a frown of pain. "Listen to me. You are not to call anyone until we get there. . . . Joscelyn, do you hear me. . . . No, do nothing. . . . We'll be over pronto."

He slammed down the receiver. "Come along!" he shouted as he ran full speed out the open front door.

Honora, palazzo pants flaring, raced after him along the covered brick walkway to the garage. "What's happened?" she screamed. "Curt, what's happened? Were they in an accident?"

"They're at home. Outside of that I'm not sure of anything except it's bad. Joss was incoherent."

He screeched around the familiar curves of Firenze Road, hitting ninety when he got to Sunset.

As they swerved into the Pecks' drive the door opened. Joscelyn stood in the penumbra of light streaming from the hall.

She wasn't wearing a top. Her chest, white bra and stomach were stained a rusty brown, as was the striped blue and white cotton skirt she'd worn at dinner. Her legs oozed bright scarlet.

Honora, out of the car before Curt, reached the house first, and gagged. The odor summoned a vivid memory from her twelfth year. She had been taking a forbidden novel to read in the stables that belonged to the crenellated house leased by Edinthorpe for the duration and had inadvertently come upon the elderly tenant farmer while he was slaughtering a horse. This identical hot, thick, *animal* smell.

Lissie was crouched under the hall table, rocking back and forth. A streak of brown darkened her new pink nightie, and the ruffled yoke was torn. A trail of splotches crossed the entry's white vinyl tiles, becoming footmarks, long and high arched, at the bedroom corridor.

Curt slammed the front door shut.

"I didn't call anyone," Joscelyn whimpered. Gone was the slight superiority and intelligence that lit her expression, gone the stance of competent engineer and housewife. "I did exactly what you told me."

"Good girl," Curt said quietly.

"Malcolm needs help, please help him?" Her jaw worked, her eyes blinked as if she were about to crumple into tears.

"Joss," Honora murmured, holding out her arms.

Joscelyn stepped aside from the embrace. "He's in the bathroom . . . he's badly hurt."

Curt went down the short hall, halting in the doorframe of the bathroom. He blanched, holding up his palm to keep Honora and Joscelyn back. Firmly closing the door, he moved hastily into Malcolm and Joscelyn's bedroom.

Honora knelt, reaching under the table for Lissie. The child huddled farther into her cave. Honora, coaxingly, formed a *V* with two paired fingers, wiggling bunny ears, an old game, and though Lissie's expression of blank horror didn't alter she permitted herself to be lifted. With a tiny sigh, she rested flaccid against her aunt.

"Let's come in here, Joss," Honora said, leading the way into the living room.

Joscelyn paced around with edgy speed, unnecessarily fluffing a pillow on the sofa, shifting a highball glass from one spot to another, screwing the top on the scotch bottle, unscrewing it. A drop of blood spattered from her legs onto the pale carpet.

Honora could hear her husband in the other room. "Sorry about the time, but we need you right away. It's urgent, Sidney, urgent as hell!" Sidney Sutherland was their friend as well as their personal attorney.

Malcolm's dead, she thought, hugging Lissie more tightly. *Joss must have finally had all she could take.*

Although Joscelyn had never said a word against Malcolm, and although in Honora's presence Malcolm exhibited an unchanging if slightly juvenile uxoriousness, Honora had not been taken in by the evidence of her own eyes. Through the years she had come to recognize the possibility of violence in the Pecks' marriage. Joscelyn's humorous explanations of her string of accidents had never convinced her. Joss might not have been the world's most graceful little girl but she had never been a klutz.

Lissie clung yet tighter. Honora patted her niece's shoulders reassuringly and glanced down. She drew her breath sharply. She had not previously noticed the large, fresh bruise on the child's arm. Although Malcolm avoided the John Tracy Clinic and most of the time attempted—affably, to be sure—to downplay Lissie's deafness, Honora had never had reason to doubt that in other respects her brother-in-law was anything other than as he presented himself, a father so tenderly doting as to be a bit absurd. *To hit the baby? No wonder Joss did whatever she did.*

"Joss, people'll be here soon," she said in a soothing tone. "Let's get you decent and clean up your poor legs."

"People? You mean the ambulance?" Joscelyn shifted the small armchair.

"I'll get you something to wear," Honora said softly.

Still holding Lissie, she edged next to the wall around the closed bathroom door where the red-brown footsteps were darkest. Curt sat on Joscelyn and Malcolm's bed, phone at his ear, waiting. Silent, he shook his head at her, as if to say the worst had happened behind that closed door. Honora pulled a tent dress from the closet, retrieving the sandals Joscelyn had been wearing at the barbecue. In Lissie's bathroom, she juggled the child, clothes, dampened washcloth, mercurochrome bottle. The Band-Aid box fell, spilling plasters adorned with bright stars. Encumbered by Lissie, she picked up a few, leaving the rest scattered.

As she helped Joscelyn on with the loose dress she saw the ugly raised bruise on her sister's breast. Sirens were wailing up the block. Joscelyn, still wearing her blood-stained skirt underneath her dress, darted to the door.

"You have to help my husband!" she shouted as the patrol car halted.

"Joss, come back in here," Honora called.

Joscelyn ran down the three front steps to cry urgently, "My husband needs a doctor!" Two officers, one stocky and dark, the other tall, were hurrying up the path. She clutched the taller cop's arm. "Why didn't they send a paramedic unit?"

"How severely wounded is your husband, ma'am?"

"You have to get him to the hospital right away!"

The two cops glanced at one another and then the dark, stocky partner returned to the car with the blinking yellow and red lights.

Joscelyn led the tall policeman to the bathroom. "I didn't mean to hurt him."

"Joss." Curt swiftly replaced the phone and in one stride gripped her arm. "Keep quiet!" he hissed.

The officer opened the bathroom door.

Joscelyn began to shake. What an indecent amount of blood. She would have followed the cop to kneel by Malcolm's body and obsequiously beg her husband for forgiveness, but Curt was holding her back.

She could hear herself babbling that it was her fault, all her fault. Curt pulled her into the living room where, despite his and Honora's combined efforts to silence her, she continued explaining that she hadn't meant to hurt Malcolm.

One of the policemen was advising her of her rights.

But how could she remain silent? Speech was a barrier to ward off the unfaceable. As long as she was talking there was no need to reconcile the instantaneous swiftness of picking up the ornamental Venetian glass jar with the infinite permanency of death.

The ambulance had arrived plus a paramedic truck; police cars were parked every which way with their lights flashing and their radios metallically blaring calls. The neighbors had clustered across the street. When she emerged between the original tall cop and his partner, the little crowd edged forward.

Sirens howling, Joscelyn zoomed north to the police station in the tall, tile-domed Beverly Hills city hall. That stuff of TV drama, the formalities of violent death, seemed remote yet familiar, like going through a well-rehearsed presentation to a client. She couldn't keep quiet, distressing Curt and his attorney, Sidney Sutherland, who had a foxy-red beard.

First thing tomorrow, Sidney Sutherland promised, she would be out on bail. For tonight, she was locked up.

Beverly Hills is a quiet community, and the other cells were empty. She sank onto the cot, still talking, blabbering a distant prayer from childhood. Finally her sobs came, a flood more violent for having been bottled up, scalding her cheeks, soaking the striped pad.

46

On a bright, warm afternoon in mid-September, Honora was pruning a rosebush on the garden's most secluded terrace while a step away Lissie picked red and yellow zinnia heads.

On the night of Malcolm's death six weeks ago—it seemed eons—Curt had engaged a twenty-four-hour guard service to keep watch at the estate's electric gates. It had been a smart move. The public had latched avidly onto the lurid details of the case—sex, blood, money—and automobiles had jockied between the TV trucks and press cars that clogged the end of the cul-de-sac.

Honora, attempting to succor a shaking, pale Joscelyn through the funeral and the police investigation and at the same time take care of her withdrawn little niece, had not ventured from the estate. An enterprising free-lance photographer had scaled the Ivorys' ten-foot wire mesh wall, scurrying down a swathe of yellow gazania ground cover to aim his zoom at Lissie's exquisite, unhappy face. The photograph, entitled *Millionaire Child of Tragedy,* appeared in hundreds of newspapers and on CBS. Curt had hired additional guards to patrol, and Honora circumspectly kept her charge away from the perimeters of their acreage.

Now, in the pretrial doldrums, only an occasional thrill seeker drove up to the Ivorys' gates to be warned off by shifts of paired Pinkertons stationed in a conspicuous black Lincoln.

Lissie held up her short-stemmed little bouquet. "Mah-mah."

Honora turned. "Do you want to give the flowers to Mama now?" she signed slowly.

The fervid media attention had put an end to Lissie's nursery school. Since signing was not taught at John Tracy Clinic, Honora had engaged an out-of-work young actor—he had hearing but both his parents were profoundly deaf—to give them lessons in American sign language. It was a large philosophical jump to Total Communication, but as Honora had intended, during these hours Joscelyn emerged from the gloomy pressure—and Lissie sometimes smiled.

The child was nodding and reaching for Honora's hand.

She seldom let go of either Honora or Curt, grasping a convenient leg, a nearby hand. Physical contact with them had become a vital necessity to her. If one were seated, she climbed into the lap, quietly looking through an illustrated story book or popping her thumb in her mouth to rest her head against a breast or chest. Unless she was in her human perch she could not swallow her food. Sleep was another problem. She stubbornly refused to drop off unless she was centered in their king-size bed. Honora would sit in the nightlit gloom of the adjacent room—until three years earlier it had been Curt's study, but now the handsome natural cyprus shelves were crammed with dolls and Fisher-Price toys. Lissie's eyelids would tremble closed, her face and body would relax, she would appear solidly in the arms of nod. The instant her aunt tiptoed from the room, though, she would burst into wild, oddly pitched sobs. Joscelyn diverged from her program of canonizing Malcolm long enough to mutter that on the night of the murder he had somehow switched off the night-light, and possibly this was the reason behind Lissie's sleep problems.

Lissie, once a mah-mah's girl, avoided Joscelyn. When Honora suggested she sit in Joscelyn's lap or go to bed in Joscelyn's cottage, Lissie showed that lovely profile, so like Crystal's, averting her gaze from lips and signing hands, transparent evasions that haunted not only her mother, but Curt and Honora as well.

Once in a great while the little girl appeared overcome by a vestigial need to touch home base and see her mother: in Joscelyn's presence, however, the blue eyes would widen, the mouth would quiver, and the child would dart away.

Lissie never said *Daddee*. A young Nisei child psychiatrist had made several house calls: he admitted that it was impossible to know what, exactly, lay in the vivid, isolate landscape of the child's mind, yet he said he felt reasonably certain that she remembered everything.

Hand in hand, Honora and Lissie descended to the house.

As they reached the terrace, a fat ball of reddish fur came yapping toward them—the shelty pup that Curt had brought home for Lissie last week, Kimmy, so christened by his owner.

Kimmy got hold of the lace of Lissie's sneaker and tugged. She dropped the flowers, pushing at him, laughing, yanking at her foot. Failing to get him to release her, she started to run along the terrace. The pup, unable to keep his small, sharp teeth on the shoelace, chased after her, growling and yapping. Suddenly Lissie swerved. She raced up the sloping grass, both arms over her head, her hair spreading behind her like a silky black dandelion puff. The puppy yipped at her heels. She let herself down on the thick grass, propelling herself back down the hill with her arms and legs, rolling over and over. Kimmy stayed close, trying for a grip on her pink sunsuit, her pink hairbow, her socks. On the third roll, she clutched him gleefully.

Honora, laughing, picked up the bedraggled, pungent bouquet, then ran to join the melee.

Joscelyn had emerged from the luxurious cottage that had been hers before marriage to watch them. Though the temperature on the sunlit terrace was well into the eighties, she hugged her cardigan around her. Since Malcolm's death her metabolism had been out of whack: she was constantly cold and had steadily lost weight. A malfunction of her tear glands prevented her from wearing her contacts, and the thick-lensed glasses magnified her pale blue eyes, giving her a blank, remote stare. In her gray sweater and black skirt, without a trace of makeup, she resembled a stern, cancer-ridden schoolmarm.

Gazing broodingly at her daughter and sister, she shivered and stepped back into the comfortable study-sitting-room. The breeze, set up when she slid open the door, had fluttered a few papers out of alignment from the stacks of legal documents that surrounded her desk. Compulsively she straightened them before sitting down with her yellow lined pad.

Her trial was scheduled to be held in Santa Monica Superior Court, where the rare Beverly Hills homicide cases were judged. Her attorneys, readying themselves, had requested a list of provable incidences of Malcolm's physical violence toward her.

A task that she had resisted with vehement unpleasantness.

The many facets of her guilt demanded that she pay—and pay and pay—for her crime. The physical dimension of her grief, her morbid self-horror could never be extirpated, but the full punishment that the California law provided for unpremeditated murder, a life sentence, would be partial atonement. And besides, being the keeper of the flame for her poor, dead love meant she could not blacken him from the witness stand. Curt, on the advice of Sidney Sutherland, had engaged Carter Veerhagen, considered tops in criminal law, to head the legal team for the defense. Accompanied by a phalanx of associates, Veerhagen had escorted Joscelyn to the modest two-bedroom Beverly Hills house (now known to the public as "the swank scene of the crime") where she had walked through the murder. The legal team had solicited statements from neighbors who to Joscelyn's humiliated surprise had been in on the Pecks' marital discord. Five people had signed affidavits that Mr. Peck, normally a charmer, the greatest guy there was, had a violent temper when it came to his wife. The young doctor, summoned from Beverly Hills' emergency room to tweeze glass slivers from her legs, had included torso injuries, both new and faded, in his report. And Honora had informed the police and the attorneys about that fresh bruise on Lissie's arm.

A victim who batted around his wife and deaf little girl? Self-defense, said Veerhagen.

His client at first refused this plea, saying that she did not care to put her dead spouse on trial. In the end, though, Joscelyn capitulated to Curt's logic that she could not let Lissie grow to adulthood with a convicted murderess for a mother.

So here she was, culling her memory for every occasion when proof of Malcolm's temper could be medically corroborated. She wrote: *#5. Lalarhein, December (?) 1964.*

The night they had met Khalid and she, according to Malcolm, had lacked sufficient respect for the princeling. The nice old English doctor in Daralam Square had taped her chest in unquestioning silence, but he must have guessed the cracked rib was the result of marital discord. *Dr. Bryanston,* she wrote.

There was a tap. On the terrace outside her room were Honora, holding Kimmy, and Lissie, clutching her aunt's hand and grasping a fistful of zinnias.

The plate glass separating Joscelyn from the woman and child took on a baleful significance; they seemed forever beyond her reach, untouchable. Mortified as much by her younger-sibling jealousy as by her incipient tears, Joscelyn blinked and went to slide open the door.

Lissie edged in, holding out her sweaty little bouquet. Joscelyn tilted her head questioningly, curving her hands, bringing them toward her chest. "Me?" she asked.

Lissie nodded.

Joscelyn smiled, raising three middle fingers perpendicular to her chin, forming a *W.*

The sign for water. Lissie rushed to the bathroom. Joscelyn swallowed hard. In six weeks shouldn't she have become immunized to Lissie darting away from her? Why each time should she be stricken by this clammy drop of her stomach, as if she were hurtling into a bottomless hole?

Kimmy was whining and struggling to escape Honora's arms.

"Put him down, why don't you?" Joscelyn said.

"With all these papers?"

Joscelyn managed an answering grimace. "She was actually laughing. You're Wonderwoman."

"Come on, Joss—it's been a family project."

"I haven't contributed one thing."

Lissie returned, milk teeth biting on her perfect lower lip, both hands circling the white porcelain toothbrush glass. While Joscelyn arranged the stemless flowers, Lissie ran out on the terrace.

"Take a break, Joss," Honora said. "We're about to have a tea party."

Your friendly family murderess at the feast?

"Veerhagen's after me," she said. "He wants my comments on these." She gestured at the typed statements. "A lifetime job."

Alone, Joscelyn removed her glasses, bending her face in her shaking hands. The instant that it had taken to raise the Venetian glass ornament was a malignant tumor that had spread to destroy all the future moments of her life. But the cancer must have been lying dormant before. When had it begun? With Malcolm's punitive war-hero of a father? With her own parentless childhood and bone-deep inferiorities? Or would they, two immature, insecure people, have had a halfway healthy marriage had Lissie not been born deaf? Unwillingly summoning to mind their ultimate battle and what in retrospect seemed Malcolm's irrational, liquor-hazed attempt to turn their daughter into what she could never be, a child with normal hearing, Joscelyn could feel the tears prickling again. Resolutely she rubbed her eyes with her knuckles, opening a drawer for a looseleaf notebook. Flipping through the pages, she came to a list that she had made during sleepless nights.

REASONS LISSIE IS BETTER OFF WITH HONORA AND CURT. The penciled entries receded from her vision while the ballpoint written ones jumped out.

Curt isn't dead.

Honora isn't a murderess.

There's two of them, the right number of parents.

Lissie adores them.

I terrify her.

She must be worrying I'll crash a large vase over her, too.

The list spilled onto the next page. At the bottom, she wrote: *I am not good enough to be her mother.* Below, she wrote: *I am not good enough,* finishing the sentence with ditto marks.

Curt jerked as Joscelyn touched his shoulder.

Wearing one of his hundred elegantly tailored suits with an incongruous yellow hard hat, Curt squatted next to an enormous hole. Fifty feet below them, earth movers roared and thick, strong-looking men drove or directed heavy equipment. The huge enclosure was shadowed by Ivory's twenty-story Wilshire Boulevard home office. This would be the second phase of the Ivory complex.

He glanced up, saw her and pushed easily to his feet.

"Hi," he said.

Joscelyn, also topped with a hard hat, squinted at the excavation. "That subsoil looks sandy to me."

"Hey, lady, you sound like a pretty good structural engineer."

They were talking loudly over the din rising from the excavation.

"How's about a job?" she said. "When I get out."

"Out? Veerhagen better buy himself a cart and start selling hot dogs if he can't get you *off*. He has enough evidence of previous assault and battery. It's a shoo-in for self-defense—and defense of Lissie."

"We were struggling for her. I egged him on."

"That wasn't to put Malcolm down. If I could raise the dead, I would. I'm talking the law." He paused. "I blame myself for promoting him out of his depth."

She kicked at yellowish adobe soil. "Sorry, Curt. I have dibs on the guilt factor," she said. "If I'm allowed to leave the city, would you give me an assignment?"

He took out his cigarette case. "Is that what you want?"

"Yes. As a matter of fact I'd prefer it be out of the country."

"Then it's settled. The London office. Near your father." His expression, as usual, showed none of his long-range bitterness toward Langley.

"What about a spot on the Mexican refinery project?"

"Me-hi-co?" Sheltering his match, he lit up. "You know that area around Vera Cruz. Hot, muggy, full of bugs. Everyone gets Montezuma's revenge. It's no place for Lissie."

"She'd stay here."

"You want to get away for a while? Great idea. We'll keep her."

"She'll have a lot better chance with you and Honora."

"You're her mother, Joss."

"You bet. And every time she looks at me she sees Mommy bashing in Daddy's skull." She drew a shuddering breath. "Would you adopt her?"

Curt's cigarette fell from his fingers. "Adopt?"

"Sign documents that make you her parents."

He stubbed out the butt with the dusty tip of his British cobbled shoe. The movement was casual, yet Joscelyn knew her brother-in-law well enough to realize that his faculties were tensed, alert.

"No," he said.

"But you just said—"

"I just said we'd keep her. Six months, a year."

"Curt Ivory, one of the richest self-made men in the country—" This had been *Newsweek*'s description of him in their in-depth February 9, 1969, article. "—doesn't want somebody else's child with his self-made name?"

"Let's pretend you didn't say that," he said tightly. "What I *don't* want is for you to rush into anything. You've never been impulsive."

"Say that on the witness stand and there goes Veerhagen's case." She gave a little snort. "Besides, didn't I walk out of Gideon's house without even a coat to chase after you?"

Curt watched a truck filled with dirt grind noisily up the steep incline. "Honora's your sister, why're you asking me about Lissie?"

"That long, sad story begins when I was a nasty little girl and had this big, secret orange crush on you—"

"What makes you think you were so inscrutable?"

"You knew?"

"Joss, you did everything but carve our initials in the table. Hey, no scowls. Stay cool. In those days I was half-baked and conceited enough to enjoy any and all adulation."

"You've always been the only solid, strong male in my life. Remember? I wanted you in the labor room."

"We're talking paternity here," he said stiffly. "We both know that Malcolm performed the rites."

"That night I wanted *you* to help me through."

"Honora and I love Lissie, and you know that we want a child more than anything else. But when somebody's going through hell isn't the time to rush into life decisions."

"I could wait fifty years, but the facts aren't going to change. Her father's dead. I killed him." Joscelyn turned to blow her nose, attempting to hide her tears.

Curt put his hand on her shoulder. "You're serious, aren't you?"

"Yes, and I'm damn sick of begging."

"Let me talk it over with Honora," he said, tightening his grip. He paused, then spoke softly. "And Joss, thank you."

"For what?"

"Giving her to us. You know how crazy we both are about her."

Joscelyn hugged her arms around herself, shuddering as if an icicle had pierced her thin chest.

SIX

1972

Honora

47

It was nearly noon before Crystal replaced the phone. She rotated her shoulders wearily: she had been in her office since before seven for a series of meetings connected with the plant that Talbott's was building for Onyx in Richmond, and her right ear ached from this culminating hour-long conference call to Detroit with the Onyx CEO, Ben Hutchinson. Ben was a demanding perfectionist of a client, rough despite his having eyes for her. (Crystal used her smiles and wiles—but not her widow's bed—to advance Talbott's, viewing her male admirers in much the same light as the enormous contemporary paintings that lined the walls of her Clay Street house: good investments and signs of her net worth that did not touch her emotionally.)

A low grumbling sounded in her stomach. Her lunch meeting wasn't until one.

She pressed the buzzer, and a feminine voice on the other end said, "Yes, Mrs. Talbott?"

"Would you please bring me some coffee. Oh, and ask Mr. Mitchell if he has those notes on the meeting of June 16 with the Onyx people."

Mitchell was there immediately with the file. Arms tight to his narrow body, he smiled approvingly at her light-blue Adolfo suit. "If I may say so, Crystal, your outfit makes it officially summer."

"Why, Padraic, aren't you nice."

She had come to cherish Padraic Mitchell. He was the one employee whose ulterior motives she never need search out; he was staunchly, adoringly on her side. No attack would ever come from him.

After he left, she sipped her black coffee, fanning his neat, precise notes on the cracking tooled leather of Gideon's desk. Not a piece of heavily overcarved Victoriana had been removed from this office. Continuity had the priority over chic. In this same vein, she had kept all of the Bears, more or less taming them. Even with their cooperation, though, Talbott's had had rough sailing—the engineering and construction business is a rockbed of masculinity, no place for a woman to show her prettily powdered nose. The P&L for the quarter ending this month, June of 1972, would be the first to show a profit since Gideon's death.

The door opened without a tap, and she looked up, her frown disappearing as she saw Alexander. He had on the requisite dark suit—another link to the successful past, no relaxation of Gideon's dress code. Except for the suit, though, her son looked out of place in this gloomy office. With his highly shined jodhpur boots, his lean height, his large, tanned features, his sleek, pale hair cut in a long curve, he looked as though he should be strolling across a college quad.

Both boys were at Stanford, Gid an engineering major, Alexander in political science. Crystal, fiercely partisan to her younger son, did not realize that on campus Alexander was widely talked about. After he broke up with Kiki Van Vliet, one of the Van Vliet supermarket heiresses, she crashed her Karmann Ghia into a tree, requiring the services of two orthopedic specialists and a plastic surgeon. In the lecture hall he goaded his professors beyond their endurance, yet turned in flawlessly composed blue books that forced reluctant As from them. He would sequester himself for weeks in the Palo Alto rental that he and Gid shared, then abruptly gather up a crowd, whirling them through chaotic, nonstop partying.

Summers, he (like Gid) worked either here in Maiden Lane or at construction sites around the country: next week he would be on the Colorado Plateau where Talbott's was co-venturing a uranium-processing mill for Union Carbide.

"Word is out," he said bitterly. "Ivory got the contract for the Utah power plant."

"He can't have!" Talbott's, having illegal inside information about the other bids, had gone dangerously low on this quarter-of-a-billion-dollar project.

"I heard less than two minutes ago." His voice was restrained, deliberate, but his eyes were narrow topaz slits.

Crystal was convinced that she understood Alexander. She didn't, not at all. She had briefly glimpsed him on the night of Gideon's death, then banished the memory from her mind. Wishing her brother-in-law and his company nothing but ill, she believed that Alexander had assumed his hereditary burden of the Talbott-Ivory rivalry, and that this was what his embittered expression showed. She had never gauged the full, irrational dimensions of hatred that a bastard might feel for his uncaring natural father.

"Getting a project that size would have helped boost our prestige," she sighed. "You know how we cut our profit to the bone on it."

"That turd Ivory must've gotten to somebody and rigged the bids."

"I don't know about that." Crystal shook her head. "He probably convinced them he's more reliable."

"A shame that when Auntie what's-her-name went on her rampage she didn't clobber him, too."

Crystal played with her coffee cup. She took a certain nasty if human satisfaction in the disaster that had overtaken her brainy, irritating younger sister—Joscelyn had gotten off with two years' probation, and Curt and Honora had taken her poor, defective child—yet at the same time a vestigial Sylvander loyalty made it unpleasant for her to hear anyone, even Alexander, talk about the murder.

"They've got the contract, there's nothing we can do," she said. Alexander's long fingers were tensed, and he splayed them then closed them into his palm several times as if to relax himself. "Mom, okay if before I go to Colorado I take off a week?"

"I told you boys to."

"Gid's keeping his nose to the grindstone, but I'll be using the Mamounia." Talbott's maintained an apartment in the world-famous luxury hotel.

"Marrakesh? At this time of year?"

"Think of it as getting acclimated for working in the Colorado desert."

"Why not go to Cannes?"

"There's that big Pan-Arab Conference in Marrakesh. Since the Ay-rabs won't do business with a woman, what's so wrong with letting them see a male Talbott?"

She tiptoed to kiss his cheek lightly. "Alexander, how lucky I am to have you," she said.

He answered with a smile.

Dingbat . . . gl

Despite the shadows engulfing the crowded, cacophonus alleys of the Marrakesh medina, the heat was so intense that the oddly jutting old houses with their silvery, ancient cedarwood screens wavered and appeared swollen out of proportion. Beneath her long-sleeved, beige cotton midi, Honora was perspiring freely, large drops oozing between her breasts and behind her knees into her linen boots. Even though Morocco had no draconian laws regulating women's clothing, when in Islamic countries she outfitted herself decorously. She had lacked the heart, though, to muffle her six-and-a-half-year-old, so Lissie wore a skimpy white sundress. The child had left her hearing aids at the hotel.

The Ivorys had arrived the evening before. Early this morning Curt—accompanied by the Ivory senior vice president who had made the trip with them—had taken off for a meeting with Fuad and some other Lalarheini ministers here for the Pan-Arabic Conference. Honora had visited Marrakesh several times, but this was Lissie's first time in the Mideast and she was wild with excitement, twisting around to take everything in—the newly dyed cloths hanging between buildings like bunting for a parade, the fat cloth merchant beckoning at them with bright-colored fingers, the skinny little apprentice no taller than she who darted by with a hanging tray of glasses filled with weedy mint tea.

Their short, stringy brown driver, walking a few yards ahead of them as their guide through the maze, had already passed the open space where five alleys met: at this moment the little square appeared empty. The brilliance of the penetrating Sahara sun blinded Honora to the two small, cross-legged figures in the deep shade of a green tile overhang. As her eyes adjusted to the vivid light, she saw them. She first thought they were twin children, then she made out the deep wrinkles carved into the powdery darkness of both faces. One little man caressed a flattish, closed basket. "Madame," he called softly. "Mademoiselle."

Lissie, unable to hear the singsong voice, caught the movement. She halted.

Immediately his comrade lifted a flutelike instrument, playing a slow, sinuous melody. The basket was opened. A cobra—was that what the loathsome snake was?—poked its spoon-shaped head out, rising on its body.

Gasping, Honora stepped backward. But Lissie stared transfixed as the reptile uncoiled. Swiftly, the owner grasped the jewel-faceted skin behind the head, pulling the snake from the basket. In rhythm with the minor-key flute-wail, the creature wrapped symbiotically around the bare, bony arm. The man grinned toothlessly and the snake also parted its jaws, darting its forked tongue.

Honora met the serpent's eyes, brilliant as black sequins in the dim light, an innocent, unknowing projection of evil.

The snake charmer took winding steps toward Lissie. The child let out her high, atonal scream.

Honora lunged, picking up her daughter. "Get away from us!" she shouted, trying to escape into the metal-workers' alley, where the driver had disappeared.

The miniature man forestalled her, darting in front of them. "Mademoiselle?" His hissing burden uncoiled, defying gravity to extend itself toward Lissie.

Honora felt as well as heard the child's rising screams.

Just then a masculine voice snapped a few words in Arabic. The snake charmer backed away, the flute ceased. As Lissie's shrills of terror lessened, Honora looked shakily over her daughter's head at their rescuer.

To her surprise he was the tall young man she had noticed near the massive stone entry arch of the medina. At that time she had thought he could have been stamped *Made in USA*, so much the archetypical young American did he look with his fair hair covering his ears, his long, lean legs encased in faded Levi's, the sleeves of his white shirt casually rolled up. Even the dark glasses curving around his tanned face were the latest style in California. His command of Arabic, though, threw her off. Deciding he must be a French Moroccan, she said breathlessly in her schoolgirl French, *"Merci beaucoup, monsieur."*

"Hey, like it's no big deal," he said in the familiar accent of the far western states. He tossed coins at the pair. "That's how they make a living, snake charmers, terrifying women and little girls."

The driver, having rushed back, was shouting and waving his arms menacingly as the two swarthy little men scurried for the still rolling coins.

Lissie's face remained buried in Honora's shoulder.

"Are you all right, honey?" the young man asked in a gentle tone.

"She can't hear you," Honora said.

Lissie, sensing they were talking about her, lifted her

crimson, tear-splotched face. To hide her embarrassment for her screams, she said, "Nay."

Honora accepted the oddly pitched *Nay* for snake, but few other people would have.

The young man did. "Snakes aren't my favorite either," he said enunciating carefully. He looked at Honora. "Let me introduce myself. I'm Alexander Talbott."

Squiggles of light danced in front of Honora's eyes. The heat, the metallic clamor, Lissie's weight closed in on her and she thought that she might pass out.

"Hey, are you all right?" The concerned male voice seemed battered out of shape.

"N-no. I m-mean, yes," she stammered, giving herself a moment to compose herself by setting Lissie down and straightening the white spaghetti straps of her sundress. "I'm Honora Ivory," she said slowly. "And this is my daughter, Lissie."

The glasses hid his eyes, but his mouth opened in shocked surprise and his cheeks drew in.

"Coincidences," she mumbled.

Alexander took several breaths.

Then he bolted.

The top of his head brushed against a rainbow of dangling cloths, possibly blinding him, and he collided with a porter bent under a load of bright-blue pottery. The dishes fell and the hot air rang with the clamor of shattering plates and cups.

Alexander Talbott had disappeared.

A turbaned merchant had risen from his stool and was pointing a dye-stained finger toward Honora. The crowd in the alley stared at her. She fished out a wad of bills, with no idea to their value, thrusting them at the porter.

When they reached the car, Lissie scuttled inside. On the way to the medina she had bounced around in the air-conditioned Mercedes, talking excitedly about the donkey carts, Djemaa-el-Fna Square, the Koutoubia minaret, the veiled women whizzing by on motor scooters. Now she was silent, snuggling to the comfort of Honora's side as they returned to the hotel.

It wasn't until after the Mamounia's doorman had bowed them into the mercifully cool lobby that Lissie spoke. "Why he run away?"

"Very good speech, Lissie," Honora said, forcing a smile

and waiting until they were in the elevator to kneel at the child's level. "His name is Alexander Talbott." She spelled out the names in the manual alphabet. "Alexander is . . . well, remember, I've told you Auntie Joss and I have another sister?"

"When Grandpa talks about her, he says not to talk about anything to you or Daddy." Lissie's communication was a lively mingling of sound and the manual alphabet. "But you don't mind my knowing Auntie Joss is my real mother, so why should you care about Aunt Crystal? Is he something to do with her, And?"

"Alexander." She spelled out the name again. "He's her son. My nephew, your cousin."

Lissie, lacking older siblings to brag about at Prescott, a small, highly staffed private school for the hearing impaired, had informed her classmates that *she* had two cousins who were grown-up men. "Why he run?" she asked, orally.

Honora shook her head, signing that she wasn't positive. "I think he was surprised to find out who we were."

When Curt returned for lunch Honora told him about snake charmers and the incredible, unbelievable coincidence that their rescuer was her nephew. "I'm afraid I blew it badly when he told us who he was."

"He ran away," said Lissie in her usual mixed media. "He crashed into a man carrying dishes and they spilled."

"Now that is what I call an overreaction," Curt said, signing a slightly different version to his daughter.

Lissie's governess, Miss McEwen, a plump, middle-aged Jamaican with dark freckles covering her broad, café-au-lait face, had landed a plum of a job because of her knowledge of sign language. Honora took care of Lissie, and Miss McEwen's responsibility was an occasional stint of baby-sitting.

At twenty to nine she was performing her function.

The Ivorys were waiting for the maître d' of the Mamounia's Moroccan-style restaurant, which was lit only by pierced metal lanterns. Glancing around, Honora spotted Alexander Talbott. Despite the dimness, he had on his shades: though he was facing in their direction, she couldn't tell whether he saw her or not. She lifted her hand in a tentative wave.

He rose from his pillows, handsome and lean in his white dinner jacket, coming toward her.

"I really made an ass of myself this afternoon, didn't I, Mrs. Ivory?" he said.

Honora was subtle enough to hear the hint of preparation in his apology, yet the nose with the tilt was the masculine version of Crystal's, and there was something of her sister, too, about the lips, certainly in the bright hair. Unlike Crystal, though, he had inherited the Sylvander slender height.

My nephew, Honora thought, a blood knot tying within her. "Do call me Honora," she said warmly. "And I was the one who behaved like an idiot. My only excuse is that the snake petrified me as much as Lissie." She turned to Curt. "This is our rescuer, my nephew, Alexander Talbott. Alexander, this is Curt Ivory."

"I owe you one, Alexander. I can't thank you enough for rescuing my girls from the largest serpent in North Africa." Smiling, Curt extended his hand.

Alexander's dark glasses were fixed on Curt's face. The harem-outfitted entertainer passed them, clapping her tambourine. Alexander continued to stare. Even taking into consideration the family feud and Curt's being Talbott's major rival, the younger man's hesitation seemed disproportionate to Honora. Her heart began to thump and it seemed an endless stretch of time until he at last took Curt's strong, squarish hand.

Honora, impelled to cover the awkwardness, said, "You really do look like Crystal." Her voice went low. "Alexander, how is my sister?"

"Fine, absolutely perfect," he said in a subdued voice. "Nobody believes she can be the mother of two aging lunks."

Alexander had shifted a few feet on the beautiful old rug to stand farther away. Even more flustered, Honora heard herself effusing, "She always was so beautiful that it was unfair. And it's terrific how she's carried on with Talbott's." Though her praise was sincere, it came across as phony. "Alexander, will you join us for dinner?"

"I . . . uhh, what about a rain check? I'm expecting somebody."

The maître d' bustled over, ushering the Ivorys to a large divan by the window jalousies. Sinking into the low, soft pillows, Honora glanced over to where Alexander had been sitting. He was gone.

Curt followed her gaze. "So much for his big date."

"Curt, we're the enemy. He's very young. Meeting us is hard on him."

"I'd say a shade too hard."

Because she had entertained this same thought, she said fiercely, "That's not fair."

"Agreed, when he found out his damsels in distress were his unknown aunt and cousin, he could have been quite naturally shook. But when he came over to talk to you it must've occurred to him he'd have to shake my hand."

"Maybe he takes the rivalry harder than we do."

"And what's he doing here anyway? Talbott's doesn't have any Mideast projects."

"Maybe he's on holiday."

"Maybe he likes a hundred-and-fifteen-degree heat," Curt said acidly. "But wouldn't you say wearing dark glasses in this coal mine is a bit Hollywood?"

"I like him," Honora snapped.

A dark boy in a red fez approached them with the copper pitcher and bowl for handwashing. After the ritual, she sank into gloom. Her son—Curt's son—would have been two years older than Alexander.

48

The following morning, Lissie—influenced by her brush with the snake—suggested staying at the hotel to swim.

As they emerged from the glassed entryway designated for bathers, Honora felt the heat clamp over her like a giant leech and she moved lethargically. Lissie, unaffected by the temperature, zigzagged from side to side on the broad, vine-shaded path, stamping her clogs to leave footmarks on the recently raked earth.

The vast gardens of the Mamounia dated back to the

seventeenth century, and Honora's horticulturally trained eye took in the ancient, gnarled olive trees, the varieties of palms, the rose gardens—a vast harem of blooms ranging from white to palest coral to near-black crimson that spread their wilting petals to give off dense, odalisque perfumes.

Sun-worshiping, out-of-season French tourists rayed around the glinting blue pool while sweating waiters in long white jellabas carried them tall drinks from the open-fronted pavilion. Lissie dashed across the burning deck, arcing into the water, emerging in the center of the pool. Honora cooled off with the breaststroke she'd learned at age five on a summer holiday in Worthing, then sat under a blue and white umbrella, writing postcards. One to Joscelyn, who was living in Georgetown while working on the Washington Metro project, one to Langley, who had just returned from a vacation in Alsace, one with a view of the hotel's ancient ramparts to Mrs. Mel Akers: Vi's third marriage had taken, but at the beginning of the year Mel had died, leaving her a substantial bank account and a garishly furnished condominium overlooking San Diego Bay.

"Hi," said a masculine American voice.

Alexander Talbott stood over her.

The brown, pale-haired length of his legs glowed with sweet-odored suntan oil, and over one broad, bony shoulder was draped a zebra-patterned beach towel rather than the Mamounia's ubiquitous royal blue.

"Good morning," she said, feeling genuine pleasure at the sight of her nephew. With a twinge of alarm lest he take flight again, she slid the postcards into her address book. "So you're at the Mamounia, too?" That zebra-striped terrycloth made her remark rise questioningly.

"We have an apartment here. Not to brag, but it's next door to the sacred Churchill Suite," he said. "From those Olympic Gold Medal dives I'd say Lissie's recovered from the great snake episode."

"Not quite. She wasn't ready to brave outer Marrakesh."

"Smart girl. The thermometer's up ten degrees from yesterday. Am I interrupting?"

"Not at all," she said.

He looked at her.

"It's too hot to write one more card," she said, patting the chaise next to hers.

He stretched out, and they talked idly and easily about

the comparative heat of the Sahara and the Mojave deserts until Lissie dripped her way from the pool. Alexander inquired how to say terrific diver in sign language. After a brief shyness, the child was animatedly teaching him to sign and spell. Honora, watching them, saw the Sylvander inheritance, the same long, fine bone structure. The heat sent the three of them to the pool, where they paddled on bright-blue inflatable rafts. Alexander kept on his mirrored glasses, Lissie continued her instruction.

When they got out, Honora said to her daughter, "That's enough sun for one day."

"No," Lissie said, turning to her cousin. "No! I want to be with Alexander."

He moved his hands, asking Lissie if she would like to go out with him.

"Are you sure you didn't know the manual alphabet before?" Honora asked in astonishment.

"I'm a quick study," he said. "Tomorrow, early, I'm heading for Djemaa-el-Fna Square."

Honora signed this to Lissie.

The little girl smiled up at Alexander, flicking her hands in eager acceptance.

"What about you, Honora?" he asked, patently out of courtesy.

"I think you two can manage on your own."

The following morning about eleven thirty Alexander returned Lissie—flushed and eager to recapitulate the hot, dusty wonders of Djemaa-el-Fna Square. Honora invited him to join them for lunch at the hotel's enclosed veranda cafe. His swift acceptance proved him at loose ends. Honora couldn't help remembering Curt's question: what was Alexander Talbott doing in a Saharan city burdened with heat and crowded with the Pan-Arabic Conference? Her nephew's charm and familial resemblance buried her reservations. After her ice cream Lissie went up to rest. Honora and Alexander moved to the indoor fountains, sitting in the high, peacock-backed chairs amid jovial groups of dignitaries wearing jellabas.

Alexander was well read in a broad swathe of authors; he knew the repertoire of nineteenth century Italian opera, of which she was an ardent aficionado. Although this cool, splashing place was hardly bright, he again kept on his dark glasses. A minor affectation, especially in so young a man, and in Honora's mind one that helped knock down his inhuman sheen of perfection.

The next two days he spent with her and Lissie, either by the pool or sight-seeing. Honora began to hear the sound of cymbals and trumpets. Surely this friendship heralded a reconciliation for the Sylvander sisters.

At eleven o'clock, shortly after Curt had left to attend yet another meeting, a note was delivered to the Ivory suite, where Honora sat reading. (Lissie and Miss McEwen were lunching with Fuad's granddaughter and her nurses: it would have breached etiquette had Honora gone.) The envelope was addressed by hand to Mrs. Curt Ivory. With curiosity Honora slit the paper and pulled out the note.

Honora, if it's not asking too much, could you have lunch with me in the apartment at one thirty? Alone. Alexander.

Honora rang immediately. There was no answer on his phone so she left a message at the desk that she would be delighted to accept Mr. Talbott's invitation.

The Mamounia's air conditioning was not as frigid as in an American hotel. A delightful chill lapped around Honora as she stepped inside the Talbott apartment, which obviously had its own unit: white silk curtains stirred, and the sparse furnishing added to the impression of coolness. Three low, ultramodern couches were set apart Moorish style in an alcove. A taboret held a silver wine cooler, crystal goblets and an earthenware dish covered with a conical lid.

Alexander led her to the central couch. "I ordered a b'stilla sent up."

"How did you guess it's my favorite food?"

"Masculine intuition." He shook out a heavy damask napkin for her. "And Lissie told me." He lifted the cover and steam burst upward. Using three fingers of his right hand in the Arabic way, he skillfully broke apart the round pigeon pie, destroying the diamond mosaic of cinnamon and powdered sugar. He turned the platter toward her—they were eating as the natives did, without dishes or cutlery.

Honora took the jagged piece, closing her eyes to express her pleasure at the first ambrosial bite. Delicate golden flakes drifted onto her napkin. "There's no pastry this light anywhere," she said.

"They drop small pellets of dough until the griddle's covered with a fine tissue and before it browns they peel it onto a plate. One hundred and four layers of pastry go into a b'stilla for twelve."

"Is there *anything* you don't know?"

"I go through these periods when peer-group socializing is like a hair shirt. One time we came here and I hung around the kitchens—that's where I picked up my Arabic. In case you're interested, the b'stilla recipe for twelve calls for three pounds of butter, thirty eggs, six pigeons, a pound of almonds, and I can't remember how much ginger, pimentos, onions, saffron, coriander and sugar."

Honora sensed, as she had several other times, that he'd prepared this speech, so her smile was a trifle forced. "I doubt if I'll fix it anyway," she said. "It sounds a teeny bit complicated."

He concentrated on filling their glasses with chilled Pouilly-Fuissé.

"You really are unique, Honora," he said. "I never knew anyone before who actually doesn't have a mean side—or see anyone else's." He sipped his wine. "I have something deeply Freudian going with Mom, but that doesn't stop me from seeing her faults. She's vain, materialistic—"

"Alexander—"

"—and totally different from you. I mean, I never believed in that word 'lady' before. But you are one."

It seemed to Honora that the thermostat had gone berserk and the cold air rippled with chilly drafts. She knew something bad was about to happen, but she had no idea what it was. "Alexander, let's change the subject."

"Me," he continued after a beat, "I have unexorcisable demons. I do what's necessary to get what I need."

"Your father was a very dominant man," she murmured, then flushed. Until now they had avoided mention of Gideon.

"He wasn't my father."

She peered at Alexander, seeing her distorted, diminutive reflections in his mirrored glasses.

"Gideon Talbott wasn't my father," he repeated. The quietly spoken words seemed to boomerang within the alcove. "I've known who my natural father is since I was fourteen, but I didn't meet him until this week—"

Honora heard the words but her brain refused to accept their meaning. She was on her feet, the napkin slithering to the carpet. "That's enough!" she cried. "I don't want to hear any more."

"—he's Curt Ivory."

"If this is your idea of a joke—" she cried. She was holding out her shaking hands with the palms toward her nephew, a gesture that could be construed either as pleading or barring.

"Why do you think I was so shook at meeting him?" he demanded.

"An act," she said vehemently. "I could see it, he could see it. You were putting on an act."

"Jesus, an act? You prepare yourself, but coming face to face like that—an act? In the medina, when I gaped, then took off, that was an act. Of course I knew who you were. And ever since I've been playing you and Lissie. But when I met him, *that* was no act. My brain went white and flat, as if somebody had wiped away the electrical impulses. There I was for the first time standing next to him and I couldn't think."

Honora couldn't think, either, and a strange little sob welled from her. "Why are you telling me this?"

"My demons, aunt, my demons." The youthful planes of his face sagged with misery. "The thing I regret is that you're such a super lady."

"Whatever Crystal told you, she's a liar!" Honora burst out.

"I don't know how Mom was as a girl, but now she's the tight-ass of all time. Adultery's the last thing she'd dream up."

"She wants to pay me back because Curt's been more successful than Gideon was!" Honora's voice rose to an unaccustomed shrill wail.

For the first time in her presence, Alexander removed his dark glasses, concentrating on folding them before turning to her.

"Look at me," he said.

She forced herself to look into his eyes. Eyes the same slightly Oriental shape as Curt's, the same tawny color. The eyes of love.

Alexander stared back at her. Suddenly she saw the unblinking gaze of the snake.

"So now you believe me," he said quietly.

The strength ebbed from her and a palsied shaking quivered in her legs. "I . . . I'm ill," she muttered. "You'll have to excuse me."

She had forgotten the step of the alcove, lurching down. Alexander watched unhappily while his aunt, in a parody of her usual grace, limped across the fraudulent coolness to let herself out the door.

49

Honora always stamped the Ivorys' hotel suites with her personality—pretty arrangements of local flowers, a small row of her novels, a bright scarf giving color to the couch. Now her efforts at temporary housekeeping jumped out at her as sad reminders of her failures as a wife. Rushing through the sitting room, she dropped onto the wide bed—actually two beds she'd asked the floor boy to push together and make up as one.

In the pit of her stomach a beat pulsed regularly, almost like a misplaced heart.

After a couple of minutes she ran into the lavatory, kneeling over the bowl to vomit up the b'stilla. Dizzy, she supported herself along the wall to the adjacent bathroom. She swirled tap water in her mouth with no consideration for the *Water Not Potable* sign above the sink. She could still taste the soured pigeon pastry, so she brushed her teeth. Unbuttoning her soiled dress, she left the creamy silk heap on the bathroom floor and crept back to the bed in her white bra and bikini underpants.

That odd pulsation of her womb persisted feebly. Curving a hand over her flat stomach, she stared with huge, burned eyes up at the high ceiling.

Curt has a son.

The foundation on which her existence rested was a blind, instinctual belief in Curt's love for her, and now this was shattered.

Oh, stop being ridiculous, she thought in a vain attempt to reassure herself. *You're married to a successful, immensely attractive man. You knew he screwed around before he was married. Who but a naive, gullible idiot expects marital fidelity anyway? Of course he's had a little going on the side. It followeth therefore as night to day that he's fathered a child—children.*

But why Crystal?

Why my own sister?

A lacerating vision presented itself. Curt—as he was now, sturdy with the heavier, visible muscles of maturity—lying naked on his back with Crystal astride him. Crystal, or rather the breathtakingly lush teenager she had been, giving high, excited whinnies as she posted up and down, her sparse golden fuzz of pubic hair engorged by his penis, her firm, honeydew breasts bouncing while Curt gasped out the sweetly erotic obscene compliments that she, Honora, knew well.

A miserable little groan escaped her clenched lips.

Was Curt's nastiness about Alexander to throw me off the track?

Thoughts of her barrenness and the reason for it recurred with thoughts of her ancient rivalry with Crystal and thoughts of Curt's betrayal. She found herself gasping for air at each breath. *Is it still going on?*

Her sense of time had collapsed. She had no idea how much later it was when she heard footsteps beyond her closed door. From the sitting room Lissie squeaked, "Mommy? We're home."

Honora blew her nose, rising on her elbows. "Miss McEwen, explain to Lissie, will you, that I'm not feeling well."

"No wonder," called back the governess's Jamaican lilt. "This heat's too much for anyone. You rest, dear Mrs. Ivory, you rest."

She heard the melodious ripple of Miss McEwen's voice. Then doors closing. These past few days in the oppressive temperature Lissie had reverted to long postprandial naps. A faraway muezzin droned, a masculine voice rang below in the gardens, the insufficient air conditioner clicked off and on, and Honora's thoughts writhed. When the afternoon light flowing between the open shutters had deepened to the color of strong ale, Miss McEwen called out they

were going down for a snack before the veranda room
closed—neither of them had the appetite for a real supper,
dear Mrs. Ivory, not after that midday spread at the little
princess's.

Once the door shut behind them Honora began to sob in
low, uncontrollable howls.

"Honora?"

Curt filled the doorway, a startlingly strong outline back-
lit by the sitting room lamps. Guiltily, as if he had caught
her in flagrante delicto, she passed a sodden Kleenex over
her eyes.

Switching on the bedside lamp, he sat next to her.

"Hey, hey, love. What's wrong?" He caressed her shoulder.

At his touch she flinched. Recognizing her near nudity,
she got up and went to the deep closet.

"I just saw Lissie and Miss McEwen. They told me the
heat had gotten you down."

She reached for her white caftan, pulling it on back to
front. Although the reversed neckline cut against her
throat, she didn't realize her mistake.

"It's not the heat," she said in a hard voice. "I found out
about Alexander."

"Alexander? I know you and Lissie have been seeing
quite a bit of him, but—"

"You don't have to pretend, not now."

"I let you know when I met him how I felt. What was the
point of rubbing it in?"

"I know whose son he is."

He moved swiftly to her, grabbing her by the shoulders.
"What the fuck is going on here?" he demanded. "What
are you talking about?"

She wrenched away from him. "Curt, I am not an idiot,
not anymore."

"Are you trying to tell me he said he was *mine?*"

"He is."

"Gott!" Shocked into the Teutonic intonation of his
early childhood, he crossed the room, his heels making
hard, angry clicks. At the window, he turned to face her.
"Honora, I should've told you this up front, but you and
Lissie were so high on him and he's your nephew. Who was
I to rain on your parade? Men in the business who know
him say the younger Talbott kid is an amoral prick. The
older one's strictly okay. This Alexander is a total shit."

"Curt, no more lies."

"He's spooking you, don't you see?"

"Stop it!" she cried.

Curt came to stand in front of her again. Below his narrowed eyes, the cheekbones stood out like sweat-glossed pillows. "You believe *him*, not me?"

"He has your eyes." This hard, accusatory voice, where had it come from.

"My eyes!"

"Exactly like yours, the color, the shape, everything."

"What a crockful—" All at once Curt's tensed, irate expression went lax. He moved to the nearest chair, slumping into it heavily. He was breathing in ragged gasps.

Fear for him—she knew active, driving men far younger than he who had suffered strokes or coronaries—cut through Honora's tangled fury and despair. "Curt," she asked anxiously. "Are you all right?"

After a moment he looked up. "The time's right," he muttered. "It *is* possible."

The elusive tints of color drained from her face, and her dark, expressive eyes were unbearably mournful.

He turned away. "Possible, is all," he mumbled. "Not probable."

"Is it still going on?"

"Christ, Honora."

"Pretending to be rivals, getting into her—"

"One damn time. One stupid, asshole slip. . . . I don't suppose you'll believe me when I tell you that was my only time with another woman since I met you."

"You're right. I don't believe you."

He curved a hand over his eyes. "Remember that summer I went up to San Francisco to try for the Taiwan seawall contract? There was a big party at Thomas Wei's house and she was there without Gideon. Don't ask me why she was alone. I got drunk. So did your sister. We went into the garden, it was freezing, God knows not the night for a quick roll in the bushes, especially in formal clothes. Looking back, I don't know how it could have happened. She might be a knockout, but she's a hard little alligator. I've never felt anything for her. She grabbed me." He shook his head. "I was drunk, angry, furious at her, furious at Gideon, and guilty about going against him when he had saved my life. Who the hell knows what the hell went on in my mind? I was too loaded to think."

She pulled at the constricting neckline. "Try another excuse," she said bitterly. "My earliest memories are variations on that one."

"I'm only trying to explain what happened," Curt said. "Anyway, why did that miserable shit tell *you?* Why didn't he come to me?"

"He wanted me to know," she said.

"To hurt you? Or because he knows he'd have a tougher sell with *me?* Okay, he found out somehow about that one goddamn drunken bang at the Weis'—what does it prove?"

"He has your eyes!" she screamed, then clamped her hand over her mouth.

Curt had risen from the chair and was pacing up and down the bedroom. His swift strides roused shivers in her; it was as though he were jerking about like an epileptic. She had never before felt any kind of aversion for him. She opened the doors of the balcony, stepping out into the hot desert night. "I can't stay here," she whispered.

Curt followed her. "Sweet, we'll leave tomorrow," he said eagerly. "Tonight if you want. I'll charter a—"

"I'm going alone. Me and Lissie."

"You are not going alone."

"I think I could have borne you having an affair—affairs." Her soft voice faltered. "But with Crystal . . . and to have a son. . . ."

"Will you stop saying that?" he asked heavily.

"Can't you understand?" Her throat had clogged and she had difficulty getting the words out. "This is too much for me to cope with."

"Honora, love, let's just say for the sake of argument that the biological facts are there. So what? As far as I'm concerned that long-haired young prick is somebody I just met. Somebody I don't ever want to see again. *I have no son.*"

All at once she was transported back to that room in the Hollywood Presbyterian Hospital. She could feel the tautness and coarse weave of the linen, see the way that the shadows of leaves bubbled on the wall, smell the perfumed dissolution of Vi's roses, feel the aching of her bereaved, battered, empty body as she mourned for the infant Ivory, male, dead because of her careless, criminally childish pride.

Watching her, Curt took a heaving breath and yanked at

his tie. "Honora, we got some bad news, sure, but we can work it out."

She shook her head. "Maybe you can. For me it's an impossible situation."

"I — am — not — letting — you — go — someplace — by — yourself — to — brood." As emphasis for his separated words, he gripped her upper arms, his fingers burying deep in the flesh.

At the pain she whimpered.

He did not release her. Instead, he pulled her closer, kissing her, an inflexible assault that cut her teeth into her tight closed lips. How strange, being kissed by Curt and feeling not the least fringe of desire, only the pain of his fingers in her biceps and a sickened revulsion. She tried to pull away, but he stayed with her, his tongue thrusting, his hands shifting downward, the widespread fingers splaying around her buttocks as he pressed her against his tumescence. She squirmed, but her attempts to escape increased his obduracy. Curt worked off his tensions athletically, and though her height nearly matched his she was slender, delicately built. Her rejecting struggles were ludicrously inadequate.

Lifting her, he pushed her backward catercorner across the joined mattresses, dropping heavily on top of her. The caftan was caught underneath her so that the reversed neckline cut like a hangman's noose into her windpipe.

Panicked, she kicked and hit frantically.

He was pulling at her panties. She grappled with his hands. He slammed his fist at the base of her hip. The pain brought tears to her eyes, halting her flimsy struggles. *Is this what Joss put up with?* He succeeded in yanking down the panties, the gold of his wedding band cutting into her clenched thighs.

Using his knee to wedge her legs apart, he fumbled with his fly.

As he forced entry, she shrieked.

Sometimes he had taken her caveman style, swiftly and artlessly, and she had responded with wild excitement, dissolving into orgasm as soon as he went into her. Now there was arid pain.

He caressed her flanks, whispering, "Darling . . . love . . . sweet cunt. . . ." His rhythmic pounding swiftened, forcing the breath as if by artificial respiration through the stranglehold of the cotton caftan.

It was over in less than two minutes.

He fell gasping atop her. She squirmed to the far side of the bed, curling around her violated, aching self. His breathing quieted and the springs shifted as he got to his feet.

He turned away from her as he slid down his trousers to straighten his shirt. "That wasn't such a terrific idea, was it?" he asked, half humorously, but his voice broke as he continued. "Okay, Honora, you win. I'll have them make the arrangements for your flight."

"Thank you," she replied leadenly.

"Where are you off to?"

"London," she said, then wondered if the instincts of a mortally wounded animal were directing her to her birthplace.

"London?"

"Please."

"Three seats on the first available flight, then," he said.

"Thank you."

"I don't suppose you want me sleeping in here tonight?" Again that jaunty, sardonic voice.

She said nothing.

"I'll see about another room." Doubtless he could procure one even during the overbooked Pan-Arabic Conference.

"Thank you," she repeated in the same dulled monotone.

He opened the door and went out into the hall. But not before she saw he was weeping.

At a little after one the following day Honora climbed the metal stairs onto the Air France flight from Casablanca to London and Paris. She was carrying a balky, bewildered Lissie while Miss McEwen followed with the hand baggage. Across the landing field, men wearing black robes stood in formation in the broiling sun awaiting the plane of some important sheikh.

As the aircraft took off, Honora was too benumbed to cry. Instead she closed her eyes, feeling as though the distance she was putting between her and Curt had made a concrete fact of her despairing rejection.

50

Curt had arranged for them to be met at Heathrow, but seeing the familiar, hunched figure of the elderly driver, an Ivory employee, caused a return of Honora's pulsing nausea. She sent him away. Lissie and Miss McEwen, perhaps frightened by her stern pallor, didn't question the decision, and neither did the governess comment when, instead of giving the taxi driver the Upper Brook Street address, she said, "The Cumberland."

The name popped out of Honora's childhood memories. She had never stayed at the Cumberland, a large, bustling commercial hotel at Marble Arch—and neither had anyone else she knew. It wasn't until the taxi inched amid the heavy, early evening traffic around Hyde Park Corner that she admitted to herself that her choice had been made because she didn't want any chance of Curt finding them. In her frantic state she was positive that he was in hot pursuit.

The following morning a cold summer rain fell. Cashing travelers checks, Honora gave the governess a small stack of bills to buy herself an all-weather coat and to outfit Lissie in warm clothes and sturdy shoes. As she handed over the money she wondered briefly how she would be able to afford Miss McEwen's considerable wages, but her mind wasn't able to concentrate on more than one problem, and at the moment her concern was to find housing for them. Buying a clear plastic umbrella, the cheapest available in the lobby boutique, she hurried in her lightweight, pale midi to the estate agent around the corner on the Edgware Road. At each splashing step her thigh muscles twinged and the bruise on her hip ached—this morning as she bathed she had gingerly soaped the plum-colored mound.

The agent, a Mr. St. Clair, had a glass eye: its fixed gaze distracted her as she inquired about weekly furnished rentals willing to take children, something nice but inexpensive.

He flipped through a file box, extracting a card. "Just the flat for you. Fifty pounds a week. Brand new. On Great Carrington Place—that's West Kensington." Feeling himself safe with an American who wouldn't be able to differentiate between Kensington and its lesser neighbor, he added, "I'm sure you've heard of West Kensington, it's a tiptop address."

Langley wouldn't be caught dead in West Kensington's unfashionable precincts, and neither would any of the charged, important executives from Ivory's London office.

"Sounds perfect," she said.

He took her in a taxi to see the flat. Great Carrington Place despite its grandiose name proved to be a meager cut above a slum, a cramped brick row that had been flung up at the turn of the century. Three of the depressingly narrow joined houses had been thrown together. As Mr. St. Clair showed Honora through the second-floor flat, her mind kept wandering to Curt and Alexander and she didn't notice the dank odor, the ugly, comfortless furnishings or that the three bedrooms were airless cubicles.

Agreeing to take the place, she further fixed her anonymity by saying, "Oh, and when you speak to the manager, would you tell her I prefer going by my maiden name, Weldon." A dashing monitor in the form above her at Edinthorpe had been called Buzzie Weldon.

"Of course, Mrs. Weldon." The real eye shifted while the artificial fixed its gaze on her. "One week's rent is due in advance."

They moved in that afternoon.

Miss McEwen went through the flat, the freckles showing darkly in her face as if her blood were rising up to bid adieu to deluxe quarters and Arabian princesses. Lissie darted through rooms scarcely larger than those in her playhouse, making her high noises of pleasure.

The rain had stopped but the clouds hung gray and threatening: the governess and Lissie put on their new warm clothes, taking Honora's umbrella when they left on their shopping foray to the nearby shabby high street.

Waving goodbye from the living room's bulbous window, Honora shivered and twisted the radiator knob. There was no answering hiss. Recollecting that Mr. St. Clair had explained that this being summer the central heat was off, she went to her room, the smallest and darkest of the three cubbyholes, opening her suitcase for her beaded stole, the only wrap she had packed for Morocco. Clasping the thin cashmere around her, she returned to sit in the living room. She could feel the prickling of the gray frieze upholstery through her light summer clothing but was too chilled and enervated to move.

Her pity for Curt was profound—those tears on his cheeks—yet her impulsive flight had been totally honest. She could not go back to him.

So how would she manage?

The purse on the plywood bookcase held less than two thousand dollars in uncashed travelers checks. She had never been good with numbers, and now her thoughts rose and fell as if on a roller coaster. The weekly rent of fifty pounds translated into around a hundred and twenty-five dollars. What did it cost nowadays to buy food in London? Certainly she couldn't afford Miss McEwen's salary. Lissie would need private schools and special teachers.

It finally occurred to her that since their marriage Curt had accumulated an immense fortune, and California being a community property state, half was hers.

I'm leaving him, she thought. *I can't take his money.*

Even in her dubious mental state she knew that her ethical code bordered on moronic masochism.

But what did pity and finances have to do with emotions?

So she had a living to earn.

But how? Other than waiting tables, she had never worked. Honora closed her eyes and pressed further into the hard, itchy frieze pillow. She hadn't slept for two nights, and midthought she drowsed.

Nightmare vignettes swooped at her. She was naked in the middle of a snowy street, unable to move as a tank-treaded snowplow bore down on her. Curt, in an SS uniform, was battering at her breasts and pelvis while tears of blood trickled down his face. Alexander Talbott was hissing like a snake at her.

The sound of the door opening jarred her awake.

Lissie, coming in with a white bakery box, saw her mother's alarm. "It's me, Mommy," she said.

"Why, you're shivering so terribly, poor Mrs. Ivory." The governess held a green-woven plastic bag abulge with vegetables and groceries. "You look as if you've caught your death."

She insisted that Honora get into bed while she heated one of the cans she had just bought.

The aromatic steam of Heinz cream of celery soup roused a twitchiness in Honora's stomach. She hadn't eaten anything solid since that ill-fated b'stilla, but Lissie was watching, so she picked up the spoon. Her hand shook, and viscous, greenish liquid dripped onto rental linens.

Miss McEwen went to her room for the thermometer. The mercury stopped at a little over a hundred and two.

"You poor Mrs. Ivory, I best call Mr. Ivory," said Miss McEwen with a heavy note of relief.

"No!" Honora cried.

"But dear Mrs. Ivory, there's many and many strange diseases in Morocco, and I cannot be responsible." She glanced meaningfully at Lissie.

"Get a doctor, then," Honora replied weakly.

The nearby physician, a woman retired from the National Health who still treated private patients, diagnosed flu. She prescribed plenty of fluids, complete bed rest, dropping by the Great Carrington Place flat each morning at eleven.

After a week, Honora's temperature was down to normal. Her wrenched thigh muscles had healed, and the bruise on her hip had faded to a pale but permanent mark. By now she was able to think clearly, and most of her time was spent considering her and Lissie's future.

Joscelyn's taxi turned on Great Carrington Place. Twin rows of horse chestnut trees cast softening shadows on blood-colored brick, but come winter, without this fulmination of leaves, the scrawny attached houses would prove that some Edwardian builder had made obscene profits by cutting corners. As an engineer she noted structural defects, but her professional scorn was tempered by an unwilling remembrance: just before the Sylvanders had left England, Langley's fiscal ineptitudes had condemned them to a street of the same mean construction and red brick. On this sunny August afternoon, however, with London showing her most benevolent face, even this scrungy neighborhood appeared halfway pleasant.

The taxi halted outside a few houses that had been

spruced up into an apartment building. Black paint glittered on spindly iron railings, and potted geraniums with brown edging their leaves flanked the front door.

There were ten buttons. Unhesitatingly Joscelyn pressed the button below the lightly inked *Weldon*.

On the second story a window was thrown up and the black governess's face looked out. "Who is it? Oh, it's you, Miss Sylvander."

Joscelyn, never absolving herself of Malcolm's death, had felt constrained to delete her marital status and legally revert to her maiden name.

A buzzer sounded. She pushed open the door. The narrow staircase was carpeted with a particularly ugly maroon drugget that was obviously new, and the textured, salmon-colored wallpaper as yet showed no fingerprints. The air, however, had an underlying dankness, as if the place had once been opened to the elements, maybe by a buzz bomb, and no amount of cosmetic renovation could exorcise the musty haunting of that long-ago exposure.

Miss McEwen stood on the second floor.

"How happy I am to see you, Miss Sylvander," she said in her Jamaican lilt. "Do come on in."

Joscelyn stepped into a room crowded with an overvarnished dinette set, a wood-armed sofa and chair covered with some gray, hideously textured fabric, a dinky television, which was tuned to some type of British game show.

The governess turned off the set, explaining that she had been killing time while Mrs. Ivory and Lissie were out on a picnic. "They go all over in the tube," she explained, a hardening of her tone condemning both their practice and the plebeian conveyance. "They should be back in a half hour or so. Shall I make you a nice pot of tea while you wait?"

"No, thank you. The tube station's close. I'll go meet them."

Miss McEwen's face fell. Obviously she had been looking forward to a discreet gossip about her employer's current situation. "It's so easy to miss people in a crowd, dear Miss Sylvander."

"If I do, then you'll tell them where I am."

Joscelyn walked briskly in the sun-dappled shade of the horse chestnuts, a tall, thin, bespectacled woman wearing a well-cut sleeveless navy dress of a synthetic-weave linen that would not wrinkle in a suitcase and could be washed without needing the touch of an iron at sites around the world. Her flat-heeled pumps were good for tramping on recently moved earth, but anyone with an eye for quality would notice their elegance—the two vanities Joscelyn permitted herself since Malcolm's death were shoes cobbled by an expensive shoemaker off Via Condotti and ultra-sheer pantyhose. Her hair was cut in a low-maintenance shag and the wispy bangs blew across her forehead as she walked. Her sole jewelry was the gold Cartier watch she had given to Malcolm as a wedding present. Joscelyn had a pleasant, uncluttered breeziness to her, but when she glimpsed her reflection in the Wimpy's window she saw a lamentably plain middle-aged American tourist—possibly an overworked social worker—who had somehow gotten lost from her group.

The tube station was a small one, and she positioned herself between the tiled steps leading downward and the Up escalator.

Although Joscelyn's mathematical mind was poles away from the realm of psychology, she could not dream up any reason other than a sudden mental aberration—a nervous breakdown—that would cause Honora to take off from a husband whom she adored, four large homes, servants, to live in this de facto slum.

Curt had appeared in Washington late yesterday afternoon looking as if he were in the throes of a bad case of hepatitis, his skin yellowish, his eyes streaked with red. Giving her no clues whatsoever, he had commanded, not requested, that she fly immediately to England and find out what was cooking with Honora and Lissie. "Honora had the flu," he had said. "She's been under the weather and I'm too tied up to go over to London." Joscelyn had been shocked to hear that the duo was in London. The last she had heard from Honora was a hastily scrawled two-sentence postcard mailed from Marrakesh: *It's too hot here, so I'm taking Lissie on a holiday. We're not following any itinerary.* Weeks had passed. Her sister's atypical neglect had roused a welter of anxiety, confusion and hurt in Joscelyn. She had phoned Curt in Los Angeles three times to find out where they were, but his secretary had deflected her, saying he was tied up. He had not returned her calls.

With a shrug, Joscelyn partially cleared away her sense of personal rejection.

It was now abundantly obvious that Honora had left Curt.

The question was why.

Honora was the gentlest, most considerate woman. It was impossible to conceive a wrong that Curt could have inflicted on her which would cause her to leave him stewing in his own misery. *And what about me? She drags away my baby, the child I gave to Curt so he could be her father, and she doesn't even drop me a note to say where she is.*

Nothing about Honora's behavior rang true. This reinforced Joscelyn's conclusion: *She must've gone temporarily bonkers.* The important thing was to get her back with Curt.

A cluster of people was coming up on the escalator. Joscelyn, brooding about nervous breakdowns, was startled when she saw her sister, looking healthy and normal, rising smoothly toward her.

Honora's bell-bottom yellow slacks hung loosely, indicating weight loss. Without lipstick, her dark eyes dominating her face, her fine, pale skin slightly flushed by the sun, her thick hair swinging to her shoulders, she looked improbably like a college girl. She held on to the sliding banister, the handle of a green plastic mesh bag looped around her wrist so that the large multicolored ball and thermos inside jounced against each other.

Lissie, in sandals and a grass-stained white sundress, glossy black hair tangled, exquisite indentation of chin smudged with brown that was probably chocolate, gripped Honora's free hand.

It was Lissie who first saw Joscelyn.

For a near immeasurable fraction of a moment that to Joscelyn seemed far longer, the child's eyes widened and the stained mouth trembled. No matter how Joscelyn steeled herself for this millisecond of horror, she could never repress her answering wave of desolation, guilt and loss. An instant later she was consoling herself with the thought that it was far better for Lissie to remember than for that monstrous scene in the pink bathroom to fester in her subconscious.

Then the lovely mouth broke into a smile, showing two large new teeth.

As the escalator steps leveled out, Lissie hurled herself at Joscelyn. Picking up her daughter, Joscelyn buried a kiss in the smooth, chocolate-scented flesh.

Honora spoke over the child's head. "What are you
doing in London?" Her voice shook.

"Nothing like a warm welcome," Joscelyn retorted.

"When did you get in?"

"This morning. I flew BOAC. I'm staying at the Churchill. Anything else you'd like to know?" Joscelyn, replying
to her rejecting sister, one-time surrogate mother, was unable to repress the sullen note. Lissie pulled back to try to
get a drift on what the adults were saying.

"Lissie," Honora said. "Tell Auntie Joss who we saw in
Green Park today."

The child eagerly told about infant royalty and neither
woman needed to say a word as they walked back to Great
Carrington Place.

51

Leaving Lissie to eat supper with Miss McEwen, the sisters
went to the Wheeler's on Duke of York Street—this branch
of the fish restaurants was housed in an extremely narrow,
Dickensian old building. They were seated on the string of
a third floor, where, since it wasn't yet seven o'clock, they
were alone.

As soon as they were settled, Honora demanded, "How
did you know we were in London? How did you get our address?"

In the taxi Joscelyn had thrown up a barrage of small
talk to circumvent the question. Her imperative was for
Lissie's well-being, and this meant repairing the Ivorys'
marriage, a task that needed tact, never her forte. She
played for time. "Let's order first, I'm ravenous. How about
sharing a bottle of wine?"

Honora nodded, seconding the selections Joscelyn gave
their young, fresh-complected waiter. She sat biting her lip
silently until he returned to pour their Liebfraumilch.

As soon as he left, she leaned across the table and repeated, "How did you find us?"

Joscelyn took a long, calming drink of white wine. "Curt told me."

"So he knows. . . ."

"Be realistic, Honora. The man is rich, the man is powerful, the man can find out whatever he wants."

"How? Miss McEwen?"

"I don't know, but as far as I can tell, he's kept perfect tabs on you—you had some sort of bug, right? The real question is why are *you* camping out in that dump?"

"I've left him."

"I'm no moron. But why, Honora? Why?"

Honora turned her head, looking toward the spiral staircase.

Irritated equally by hunger, her sister's stubborn reticence and the murky problems of her self-appointed role, mender of broken marriages, Joscelyn said sharply, "Okay, fine, you've had a major blow-up, for an undisclosed reason. But what about *me?* Why didn't you write or phone *me?* What have I done?"

"You'd have told him where I was."

"Oh, absolutely. Except he hasn't been taking my calls."

Honora looked surprised.

"For God's sake, Honora." Joscelyn drained her glass. "He is dying, dying."

"Dying?" Honora drew a sharp breath. "What do you mean, dying?"

"Oh, you know, in total hell."

"Did he tell you that?"

"Of course not, but it's obvious to anybody who sees him."

Honora looked down at the tablecloth, her hair shadowing her face so Joscelyn couldn't make out her expression. After a minute's silence, she asked in a low voice, "Did he tell you to come here?"

Joscelyn hesitated.

"Did he?" Honora repeated.

"As a matter of fact, yes."

"What're you meant to do? Convince me to go home?"

"He's worried about you."

"The fever's been gone for weeks. I thought he was keeping perfect tabs."

Joscelyn's annoyance flared. "Why are you treating me like I'm some sort of criminal for being here? And why shouldn't Curt want to know what's happening to you and Lissie? Or haven't you stopped to consider that he adopted her, too? That's why I gave her up, so she could have him as her father."

Honora gave a discordant laugh.

"That wasn't intended as humor," Joscelyn barked. "What's with you? I'm the bitchy one here—" She broke off as the waiter returned to slip a half dozen Portuguese oysters in front of each of them.

Joscelyn dabbed hers with horseradish, wolfing two with thin-sliced triangles of buttered brown bread. Honora ignored the food, tapping on the bowl of her wineglass. At each jab, her wedding band, visibly loose, caught the light.

Seeing that the thin fingers were trembling, Joscelyn said in a conciliatory tone, "Try these, Honora, they're marvelous."

"I should've written."

"Honora, look, you're obviously going through a bad time."

"No, it was rotten of me." Her murmured apology shook with sincerity.

"Why don't you talk about it? It helps. And God knows there's no kind of marital problem that'd shock *me.*"

"Do you still think about Malcolm?"

"All the time." Joscelyn blinked rapidly. "Look, Curt's one fabulous, dynamic man. I mean, so what if he's having a little fling?"

Honora stared at her. "What makes you say that?"

"He *is* a terrific guy."

"No, I meant about the affair."

"At first I thought you'd gone a bit crazy, but obviously you haven't, and I can't come up with any other reason for this mess."

"He has a son," Honora said in a whisper.

Joscelyn's fork jerked and an oyster slithered. Bending to catch it with her mouth, she spoke around it. *"What?"*

"I met Crystal's younger boy in Marrakesh—"

Joscelyn couldn't control her shocked gasp. "Our *sister* Crystal's son?"

"Yes—Alexander Talbott. Alexander chanced upon Lissie and me accidentally on purpose in the medina. A snake charmer was scaring us silly—you know how harassing they can get in those countries. Anyway, Alexander sent the men packing. After that he got in with me and Lissie. Oh, we became the very best of friends. It seemed he had some information to give me."

"Are you saying that . . . ?" Joscelyn found herself unable to finish the sentence.

Honora sighed deeply, nodding.

"Alexander Talbott is *Curt's* son?"

"Yes."

"Curt and Crystal?" Joscelyn asked. The horseradish caught in her throat and she began to cough uncontrollably.

Another group had been seated, and the foursome averted their heads with rigid politeness while Honora rose to hit her sister between the shoulder blades. The young waiter rushed over with a glass of water. When Joscelyn's coughing fit finally subsided into throat clearing, her once-broken ribs ached.

Wiping her eyes with a tissue, she asked, "Did Curt admit it?"

"Not at first. He exploded. Told me Alexander was a liar, famous for his sneaky ways. After he cooled down, he admitted it was possible." Honora raised her palms in a melancholy little gesture of helplessness. "Alexander has his eyes. His exact eyes."

"But. . . . With *her?*"

"Joss, I can't talk about it—I get ill even thinking about them together."

"The same old Crystal," Joscelyn said bitterly. "Always borrowing what's not hers." She touched the fragile, trembling wrist. "Honora, is it still going on?"

"He says it only happened that once," Honora said with a little shiver. "Look, call this ridiculous and dramatic, but . . . Joss, it's true, I really do get nauseated when I think about him and Crystal being together. Another affair—affairs—would have crushed me, but I probably could have accepted it. When we started I knew he was sleeping with Imogene—"

"He was?"

"You were too young to realize it then, but he was quite a swinger. Gideon must have really cared tremendously for him to put up with it. I guess that was why he was so hateful later."

"Obviously Gideon never found out about this," Joscelyn said. "Otherwise Crystal would have been a grass widow, not a genuine one."

"I've always felt so ambivalent about her. I love her, I hate her, and I've always graded myself against her, as if our lives were a two-woman competition. If she wins, I lose."

Joscelyn gave a grim little smile of accord. "Well put."

"The only good thing about not seeing her was that the stupid rivalry was laid to rest."

"Ain't it the truth." Joscelyn sighed. "But you, you've always been so together, above the juvenile crap. Generous of heart."

"Never where she's concerned."

"Then you go along with the theory sisters are natural rivals?"

"No," Honora said emphatically. "Joss, I've never, never been like that about you, mixed up, envious, hateful."

Joscelyn, having on occasions suffered these emotions toward Honora, muttered, "Crystal invites it."

"I can't even think. . . ." Honora whispered. "But now do you understand why I ran away from Curt?"

"There was no other choice."

"I couldn't help myself."

"From personal experience," Joscelyn said, "splitting up isn't the worst that can happen."

"If he wants a divorce, certainly I'll understand—tell him that, will you. But I'm still too confused to—"

The waiter was glancing inquiringly at Honora's uneaten oysters, and she nodded that she was finished. Removing her plate and Joscelyn's shells, he served the sole veronique.

"Mmm." Joscelyn sniffed appreciatively. "Any plans at all?"

Honora brightened. "I went to a job broker," she said. "They put me in touch with a London landscaper. A wonderfully talented woman. You wouldn't believe what she can do with a limited space."

"What about financially? Will you be able to make out?"

"Absolutely," Honora said.

Joscelyn, mortified by her animal appetite, ate a mouthful of richly sauced sole and reflected that Honora had always been a soft touch, abysmally generous, a bad money manager. "You'll have quite a bit of expenses."

"Joss, I can't afford Miss McEwen. And she doesn't much like West Ken. She's given her notice for the end of this month."

"Good riddance. But working, you'll certainly need somebody."

"Vi's coming over. Remember? Last January Mel died. She's been at loose ends and likes the idea of London—she's never been in Europe. Mel left her quite well off, so she doesn't have to work. When I'm not around, Lissie'll be with her."

"What about school?"

"I've enrolled her in one where they have these ultra-new auditory trainers, the teachers wear FM microphones and each child has a box strapped onto his chest." She reached for Joscelyn's hand, gripping it tightly. "Joss, Lissie tried one when we went on the interview. She actually heard two or three words!"

"She didn't!"

"She couldn't recognize them as words, of course. Still, it was monumental. I cried."

"I am, too," Joscelyn said, but she was beaming. "It's a miracle." After a moment, she said, "That kind of equipment—it sounds like a very pricey school."

"The tuition's about the same as at Prescott," Honora said quickly. "And Vi'll share all the other expenses."

"Oh, why're we talking like this?" Joscelyn said. "Curt'll give you whatever you need. It's half yours anyway."

Honora said with low vehemence, "I cannot take one thing from him!"

Joscelyn was no longer bewildered that Honora had left Curt, and while Honora was being a bit silly about the financial end, that was understandable, too. Curt had fathered Crystal's son. Could any wrong be greater? (Joscelyn's own hoard of sisterly resentment had been inflated since Crystal, without any kind of training or hard work, had shot to the head of a major engineering company—it was almost as if she had stolen Joscelyn's degree and identity.) She cut into a new potato. "I'll pay the tuition," she said firmly.

Honora shook her head. "Thank you, Joss, but no."

After a few minutes of failed coercion, Joscelyn threw down her napkin. "If you're trying to make me feel like an outsider, you've succeeded."

"I'd rather manage on my own, Joss."

"I *am* her mother."

"We both are." Honora shook her head. "All right, Joss. And thank you. With the school fees things were going to be a bit tight."

It was a lovely moonless night and Joscelyn decided to walk back to the Churchill. Honora went with her as far as Marble Arch.

Outside the tube station, Honora murmured, "You were right, Joss. Curt *is* her father. It's not fair, keeping them apart. Will you work it out with him about his having her during the school holidays?"

"Sure."

They touched each other's cheeks and Honora ran into the brightly lit station, leaving her twisted effort at a smile to linger with Joscelyn.

52

The following afternoon Joscelyn took the TWA flight to Washington. She was asleep in her Georgetown rental when the telephone jolted her awake. Accustomed to late-night calls from the subway site, she switched on the bed-side lamp, reaching for her glasses and notepad before she answered.

"You're back." Curt's accusatory voice.

Joscelyn glanced at the clock. "A couple of hours ago," she said. "You told me you were going home to Los Angeles, so I called the house and left a message."

"Didn't they tell you I was still in Washington?"

"Oh, God, Curt, it was Elena. While I was telling her who I was, she was trying to explain something—but you know me and *Español.*"

"A problem's come up. I'll be right over."

Assuming that he was as usual staying at the Dolley

Madison, the small, luxurious annex to the Madison, that was a fifteen-minute drive away, she half filled the kettle for the Melitta, planning to dress and brush her teeth while the coffee brewed. She was turning on the gas jet as the buzzer sounded. Conscious of a stale taste, she bent over the sink, hastily swirling tepid water in her mouth.

The door shuddered under a barrage of banging. Wiping drops from her chin, she ran to open it. "Hold your horses, Curt. You want to get me kicked out? How did you get here so fast?"

"I was in a phone booth across the street," he said. "There's been a monumental foul-up at the excavation."

"A cave-in?" she asked anxiously.

"Metshtchersky's screwed up, but not that much. A delay."

Relieved, she said, "I need my coffee. No caffeine, no brain action."

She filled the paper cone with MJB, pouring in the boiling water, which steamed up her glasses. While she wiped them, Curt vigorously denounced Andrew Metshtchersky, the short, pompously efficient vice president who was the project manager. The real reason behind his attack was clear to Joscelyn since she sometimes employed this same device herself: he was using anger to avoid bringing up what lay most painfully close to him.

Falling silent, he stared at her.

"I suppose," she said after a moment, "that you're wondering about my jaunt to London?"

He shrugged as though the errand on which he had dispatched her so urgently had become unimportant to him: the wince narrowing his eyes told her that his pose of indifference was maintained only by the utmost mental exertion. "How's Lissie?" he asked.

"Wild about the changing of the guards, and she's fallen in love with clotted cream—can't get enough of it. She sends you her very best—" Joscelyn signed love.

He nodded. The small refrigerator kicked in noisily. It was apparent that he was not going to be the one to bring up the subject of his wife—and equally apparent that he was mad with impatience to hear about her.

"Oh, and Honora's completely recovered from that bug you were worrying about," Joscelyn said.

"I'm very glad to hear that," he said coldly.

"Curt, look, I wish I could think of some snide, clever crack, but I can't. So here it is, straight. Honora's staying over there."

"The return of the native."

"Frankly, I can understand her point of view."

He paced to the window. "So the two of you had a nice, sisterly little chat."

"This isn't taking sides, Curt, but you must understand that you handed her a pretty rough deal. Not having your children is her major cross. And I never knew this, but she's evidently always nourished a string of sisterly resentments toward Crystal." Joscelyn's fingertip traced a dark swirl in the Formica of the breakfast counter. "She was pretty vague about verification. . . ."

"Oh, it's true all right. My wife has her womanly intuition to guide her, but me, I prefer more exact proof than the color of some man's eyes."

"You talked to *Crystal?*"

"Yes, I gave her a buzz. It seems there *is* one co-venture between Ivory and Talbott's." He laughed unpleasantly.

So the impossible was true. Curt was Alexander Talbott's father.

Joscelyn took two pottery mugs from the cabinet, lining them carefully in front of the coffee maker. "Honora would like to work something out so you can have Lissie during school holidays."

"Whatever," he said as if it were irrelevant whether or not he saw the daughter whom he adored. Gazing out the window so his back was to her, he asked cheerfully, "Down to the meat. How much are Mrs. Ivory's solicitors holding me up for?"

How often had he complained, only half humorously, that buying a gift for Honora was impossible? She preferred colored semiprecious stones to diamonds, she wore furs only because he gave them to her, she didn't know one make of car from another—in other words, she was irritatingly unaware of status symbols.

Curt must have construed Joscelyn's hesitation to mean that an inordinate settlement was involved. He turned to squint sourly at her. "She's out to break the bank?" he asked.

Joscelyn could see her sister's thin, trembling fingers as she had burst out that she couldn't take anything from Curt. "She doesn't have a lawyer; she's talking separation, not divorce." The bottom Pyrex was full. "Want some coffee?"

"No."

Joscelyn spooned powdered cream into her mug. "Sure?"

"Shall I say it again and we can dance? I don't want any goddamn coffee." His face was red-splotched and puffy, as if he'd been in a fight. "What's the tariff on a separation, then?"

"Nothing."

"Nothing?" Was that a tremor of disappointment in his voice? Could he have been counting on the frail hope of pulling Honora home by the purse strings?

"You know Honora—she's never been expedient."

"Then she must be planning on going back to her old career. Did you warn her that tips won't pay for her current lifestyle?"

"She has some kind of job, I don't know exactly what, but it's got to do with gardens. Oh, and Vi's going over to stay with her."

"The two of them can rehash old times." He gave another unpleasant laugh. "And what about Lissie? Is she toodling off to the local County Council School?"

"Honora's found a very good place. It sounds like it's more advanced than she had in Los Angeles, with special equipment—Curt, Honora thinks Lissie heard sounds! She's learning to listen!"

For a moment his head tilted in eager interest, then he said studiedly, "Well, that's progress. It's an excellent idea, then, for the two of them to stay over there. The next time you write, tell her that I wish her the best in her new enterprises."

You shit, you nasty shit. "Curt, she's just as miserable about this whole mess as you are."

"Who's miserable?" Curt asked, the false jauntiness buoying his tone.

"Maybe she'll get over it."

"Either she will or she won't." He straddled a high stool, tapping on the empty mug to mark an end to this dubious personal conversation before he returned to Metshtchersky and the imaginary problems besetting the metro project.

At work the following day Joscelyn heard that Curt had left for Lalarhein where Ivory was overseeing the work on a city rising on the sand near Pump Station 5, Malcolm's mark on the desert. The huge increase in oil prices had heaped wealth on the arid little country and there were networks of new roads and lavish aqueducts. Daralam now boasted a Sheraton and a marble-faced Hilton. The beggars were gone, the old British homes of the aristocracy had been replaced with modern palaces. The Daralam airport, completed in 1971, also an Ivory project, was the country's pride, with its magnificent mosaics, restaurants, mini-hotel for laid-over passengers, movie house and swimming pools—one for men, one for women.

A few weeks later she heard that Curt was in Venezuela to inspect the Texaco refinery project. Then he was in Kenya, in Bangkok, in Gabon, in Idaho, in Alaska. Word seeped back from the exotic sites around the globe that the Big Boss was on a rampage.

In November Joscelyn's section of the subway project was completed. She received a note from Australia. Curt's energetic handwriting with the thick downward strokes stood out from the paper as if in bas-relief: *I won't be in Los Angeles, but my house is your house.*

Having given up her furnished single when she went to Washington, she took him up on his offer.

Honora's magnificent camellias along the curving driveway had been disastrously sheared to resemble a privet hedge. Inside, the airy, rambling house sparkled and shone with every kind of polish, so at first Joscelyn couldn't understand why the rooms seemed like roped-off exhibits in a museum. Finally she realized what was missing. Honora. Her sister had spent a lot of time in the little flower room off the kitchen, composing blossoms and greenery from her gardens into loose, pretty arrangements; she had left her books and magazines facedown to mark her place; she had filled bowls with nuts, candy, fruit—she had imbued the house with life.

Each weekday morning at quarter to nine Joscelyn drove to work. At Ivory the engineers in her level were at liberty not to come in at all until they were assigned to a new project. In the past she had spent these inevitable hiatuses with Honora and Lissie. Now she sat in her little glass-walled office on the tenth floor of the new wing of the Ivory complex and read back issues of *Civil Engineering.*

After a week or so of total boredom, she booked herself a round-trip ticket to England.

Making one of her frequent transatlantic calls to Honora, she broached the subject casually. "I'm thinking of taking a holiday."

"Here, Joss?"

"I haven't made up my mind," Joscelyn hedged.

"If you were, it'd be better for Lissie over Christmas. Remember? I told you about the problems she had at first getting accustomed to the auditory trainer. And you know how far English schools are ahead of ours—she's swamped, poor baby. Daddy and I're tutoring her in the literature, and the school gave me the number of a nice young Indian for the maths."

"How're you doing?"

"Mavis"—Honora worked for Lady Mavis Harcomb—"has given me complete charge of a terrace in Belgravia and a garden in Bloomsbury."

"So everything's coming up roses?"

"I'm working seven days a week," Honora said, her soft voice practically inaudible under the hum on the line. "That makes life bearable."

Joscelyn canceled her BOAC flight.

She could never shake the belief that the five indoor servants and seven full-time gardeners were sneering at her for that most shameful of diseases: loneliness. On three successive weekends she took an ocean-view room at the Miramar Hotel, which was less than twenty minutes away in Santa Monica. *Let 'em figure me for the world's most popular houseguest.*

On the third Saturday evening, as she ate her solitary dinner in the hotel dining room, the thought of returning to the impersonal room weighed unbearably on her. Instead of taking the elevator up, she went to the reception desk and checked out. Before nine she was home in Bel Air.

Figuring a brandy would blur her depression, she crossed the dark hall to the family room, where the bar was.

As she pushed open the twin doors, lights blazed at her. It took her a moment to accept the misshapen mound on the area rug as two entwined naked bodies. *The servants are certainly taking advantage,* she thought, backing away.

The female partner had spied her. Blond mermaid hair streaming over improbably large breasts, she sat up and gave Joscelyn an unembarrassed, complicitous smile.

The man rolled over to look at her. It was Curt.

Her brother-in-law's nudity embarrassed Joscelyn so profoundly that she lost all sense of where she was, yet despite the blood flooding her face and roaring behind her ears she found herself noting that Curt was far better endowed than Malcolm had been.

"Aren't you away with friends for the weekend?" His voice had its usual irony.

"Got back early and needed a nightcap. . . ." she mumbled. "When did you get in?"

"Late this afternoon. Be a good girl, will you. Toss us those clothes."

She went to the couch. The air here was tainted with lush perfume, the acridity of sweat and the flat odor of sex. Her clumsy throw strewed garments far short of the rug. The blonde rose on long, shapely legs, bending for a dark, full skirt that she casually put on before tossing Curt his shorts.

As he yanked them on, he said, "Winners of the Jon Hall, Dorothy Lamour look-alike contest. Lindsay, you're too young—"

The girl gave a throaty laugh. She appeared totally at ease half naked. "Sweetie, it's Linda, and Dottie had a wonderful retrospective at the Academy."

"That's right, you told me that you're a member in good standing of SAG. Linda, this is Joscelyn. Joscelyn, Linda."

"Hello, Joscelyn." Linda swung her hair back and raised her hand in a salute.

Inarticulate fury overcame Joscelyn, a sense of being violated, of witnessing some unspeakable orgy that debased not only Honora but Curt as well. She wanted to shake this vain slut until her big, naked breasts fell off. She nodded coldly.

"Now for the drinks. Joss, what's your poison?"

"Changed my mind, thanks." Joscelyn bolted across the room to push open one of the sliding glass doors to the terrace. Linda's actressy chuckle followed her as she ran along the brightly lit pergola to her rooms, where she hugged her arms around herself as if the temperature were below freezing.

53

Sunday morning there was no sign of Curt or Linda, but to avoid any chance of confronting them, Joscelyn had breakfast at Ship's in Westwood, spending the morning in aimless driving, the afternoon at a matinee of *The Godfather,* afterward eating pizza and salad across the street from the movie theater. Darkness was filling the canyon when she arrived back at the house. She had every intention of going directly to her rooms, but as she started along the pergola she realized that Curt was sitting on the terrace.

"Evening," he said.

I can't avoid him forever, she thought. Her knee and hip joints felt stiff as she walked toward him.

He raised his glass. "This is a pretty decent Moselle. Care to sample it?"

"Sure."

She sat on the wrought-iron couch next to him, watching as he took the wine from the Georgian silver cooler and filled one of the half dozen rock-crystal glasses that the servants routinely set out—in Curt Ivory's homes nothing was stinted or done meanly.

"Sorry about last night," he said. "I never figured on you walking in. She's gone, by the way."

Sipping the cool, pale wine, Joscelyn attempted to speak in the same light tone that he had. "I guess now you're home I should find my own place."

"If you're going to be a Fundamentalist about the Lindas of the world, yes," he said.

The setting sun cast its last, most intense, reddish light on the eastern rim of the canyon, where Honora's belvedere stood. Staring up at the airy, octagonal structure, Joscelyn said, "Honora's my sister."

"But these days hardly my wife."

"There's been a parade of Lindas these last few months, hasn't there?"

"Look, last night it was rough, and I apologize. But Joscelyn, facts are facts. I'm a single man nowadays, and I get myself fucked."

He said the last sentence arrogantly, and suddenly she had the feeling that he hoped she would report both this conversation and the Linda incident to Honora.

"I suppose better the Lindas of the world than another co-venture with Crystal," she said, regretting her words immediately.

Prepared for Curt's least pleasant smile and some biting repartee, she glanced through the dusk at him. She was utterly appalled by his expression of guilt-stricken misery.

Joscelyn had always regarded pity as a denigrating emotion, one that lessened the person at whom it was directed. Yet now, looking at her brother-in-law's set profile, she felt a great surge of compassion that in no way diminished her long-term feelings for him.

"Curt," she said softly. "Look, I didn't mean to snipe at you. The truth is I'm very sorry about ... well, the way things turned out with you and Honora. What's the use of keeping up a running battle. You've always been my friend."

"Thanks, Joss," he said, and continued to gaze at the slick dark water of the swimming pool. It seemed to her that his expression and posture were yet more disconsolate.

She set her monogrammed glass on the flagstone and reached over to take his hand, squeezing it comfortingly. He did not draw away, but there was no response from his warm, lax fingers, no answering pressure of palm; she might as well be a woolen glove, yet she found herself incapable of releasing her hold.

Before the breakup of the Ivory marriage, Joscelyn had mentally placed Curt so far off limits that she had never once indulged in a fantasy of them united sexually. He was her brother-in-law, the husband of the adored sister who had taken a mother's place, he was tabu. But on learning of his well-marked liaison with Crystal and seeing at first hand one of his flings, an aperture in her mind had opened. And sitting on the dusk-heavy terrace, feeling the warmth of contact, it seemed to her that the physical aspects of her love might not be so hopelessly unrequitable.

Timidly she began tracing the pulse and strong tendons inside his wrist. He appeared too sunken in his brooding to notice: this casual inattention, rather than frightening off Joscelyn, made her imagine herself his long-married wife consoling him for some ineluctably rotten break.

Out of the depths of her body came a rush of desire, an urgent and pure sensual arousal that she had not experienced since Malcolm's death—indeed, she had decided that this side of her lay buried in Forest Lawn with him.

"Curt," she whispered, in one movement rising to kneel in front of him. Like a supplicant she rested both hands on his thighs. "Ahh, Curt. . . ."

Now her fingers were acting of their own volition, rubbing the white duck fabric over the firm musculature.

He tensed and a shudder ran through his legs. She mistook this tremor for answering passion.

"I can't bear seeing you so miserable," she whispered, her right hand edging upward.

He gripped both of her wrists, wrenching her hands from him.

"I care so much, Curt."

"Oh, Christ, haven't I enough to bear?" he asked in a harsh, strangled whisper. "Joss, please, for God's sake please will you leave me the fuck alone."

At this instant the automatically timed lighting system came on, shining on Curt's expression of revulsion.

She jumped to her feet, in her clumsiness overturning the glass. As it rolled noisily across the uneven flagstones the blood rushed hotly to her face. *It figures, doesn't it?* she thought. *Me, the husband killer, the ugly cockroach Sylvander sister, the one woman alive who turns Curt Ivory off.*

With what appeared a tremendous effort, Curt managed his caustic half smile. "So now you understand about Linda *et al.*, Joss. Women can't keep their hands off me."

She didn't realize until hours later the kindness of his awkward little joke, his attempt to return them to normality. At this moment humiliation was burning in her blood and all she could think of was getting away from him.

"Have a dinner date," she mumbled. "Byee. . . ."

She barged through the house. The next thing she knew she was in the enormous garage, gunning her Porsche, then digging down the driveway. But after the electrified gate doors had swung open for her she slowed. Her mind was

blank of everything except Curt's expression, and she had
no idea of how to escape the horrified topaz eyes. It took
her nearly five minutes to recall that a block or so from the
Miramar was a lively looking bar that she'd never entered.

The place was jumping, obviously a pickup joint for the
young, gorgeously tanned crowd who looked as if in their
combined lifetimes they had experienced not a single rejection. Joscelyn settled into an inconspicuous table in the
corner, ordering several drinks in rapid succession in an
unsuccessful effort to erase that image of Curt.

"Hello there," said a masculine voice.

She looked up. Her vision blurred and she opened her
eyes wide, then squinted to get a proper bead on the man
standing over her. He was even more out of place here than
she, this conservatively dressed business type with his dark
suit, bulging, pregnant belly and thin, lined face. He was
smiling.

She smiled back. "Won't you join me?"

"It's too noisy to get acquainted here," he said. "Maybe
we can find a quieter spot."

"Great idea," she said, opening her shoulder bag for her
American Express card.

But he gallantly insisted on paying her check. When she
stumbled on a curb in the parking lot he put his arm
around her, squeezing her to his soft body as he led her to a
Ford sedan. "It's a rental," he explained. "I'm in LA on
business and staying at the Ramada Inn. What say we adjourn there?"

"Great idea," she repeated. *God, am I ever drunk*, she
thought incredulously. *What am I doing? Better an old slob
who wants me than Curt who doesn't.*

After locking and chaining the hotel door, he embraced
her ardently.

"What's your name?" she asked.

"Ted," he muttered, offering no patronym.

"I'm Joscelyn."

Sober, she would have been uncertain what to do next
with this complete stranger, but being drunk she simply
unzipped her skirt, stepping out of it. He was throwing off
his clothes.

The rolls of flabby chest and big belly were bluish white
and covered with coarse brown hairs except for the smooth,
bald band that marked his beltline. His uncompromising

lack of physical grace pleased her. Here was a man who was suited to her. Hugging, they moved to the bed, and she was overtaken by the blunted desire that liquor imparts. She entered into Malcolm's old call-girl game, making love to a stranger whose name might or might not be Ted, with a cold, clinical explicitness that left both of them gasping and drenched with sweat.

Immediately afterward she fell into a stuporous sleep, jerking awake in the dark with a headache, a vile taste in her mouth, and oppressive thoughts of her dead husband, of her brother-in-law's rejection.

Turning on the bathroom light, she quickly gathered together her clothes. As she bent to adjust her small breasts in the bra, her partner drowsily folded his fat arms under his head. "Know my motto, Joscelyn?" he asked in a self-congratulatory tone. "The nearer the bone the sweeter the meat. The moment I saw you, so thin and prim in your blue outfit, I said to myself, 'Ted, forget all these wild young chicks. The one over there by herself is the girl who'll fuck your brains out.' "

Since this was a compliment, Joscelyn formed a smile as she let herself out. By the time she was back at the Bel Air house her hangover had lessened while conversely that stupid pass she'd made at Curt gnawed yet deeper. To face him again was unendurable.

She turned on her crooknecked desk lamp, methodically composing a letter of resignation on a legal pad, crushing the long yellow sheets four times before she had the right tone, neither recriminatory nor self-abasing, but businesslike. After typing the draft up on her letterhead, she folded it into an envelope, going over to the window.

By now it was light out and the pool was white with Curt's churning strokes. He swam savagely, as if trying to escape something or someone. She stood for several minutes, her cheeks indrawn with thoughtfulness as she watched him do his frantic laps.

He didn't desert me in my terrible time, she thought.

Sighing, she tore the envelope in half, dropping the pieces in her wastebasket.

She joined him for breakfast. Curt, as was his habit in the early morning, spoke very little, but he did inquire, "Good time last night?"

"Super."

They would both ignore the previous evening's incident, although whenever she thought of her hands caressing his thighs she would burn with shame.

That morning on the way to work she rented a brand new, furnished one-bedroom. When she got home that evening the servants informed her that Mr. Ivory had taken off for an unspecified length of time.

SEVEN

1974

Crystal and Honora

54

On the morning of March 22, 1974, at a few minutes past seven, Crystal was stepping cautiously along the planks laid across a corner of the acres of umber mud that had been hardpan when she had arrived yesterday. There had been no clouds then, and there were none now, but during the night she had been awakened by equatorial rain ricocheting against the metal roof of Gid's trailer.

Though she had been told often enough about the humid heat of the Tasi copper and gold mining project in New Guinea, the physical actuality shocked her. The sun was already an electric hot plate relentlessly simmering the muggy air, and adding to the general discomfort were the nonchalant swarms of mosquitoes and the grinding, deafening complaints of heavy machinery.

The Tasi Valley, whose topography was already rearranged by the Talbott crew, lay deep within central New Guinea's Oranje Range—jungle-furred, mineral-veined mountains that had not yet been properly explored. At the cost of nearly a billion dollars in the next decade, this remote isolation would become a gold mine, an open-pit copper mine, smelters, a township. The Tasi was the largest project Talbott's had ever undertaken alone, and Crystal, who popped up at sites to inspire her crews with her beauteous presence, was putting in her first duty visit.

Above her, the grinning, shirtless driver of a Caterpillar circled his hard hat in a wild west salute.

Crystal lifted a hand in response. The mushy ground was softer here, and her movement disturbed her balance. The board beneath her teetered.

Gid grasped her elbow in his large, moist, steadying hand.

"Careful, Mother," he shouted.

Blue eyes narrowed in concentration, she stared at the paved area surrounding temporary headquarters, focusing her attention on the nearest trailer along whose side was a spray-painted poster: WELCOME TO TASI, MRS. TALBOTT. The red letters shimmered in the heat. As her feet encountered the softening blacktop she let out a spontaneous sigh of relief.

Gid and the project leaders, four muscular, tanned men who smelled of sweat and Cutter's insect repellent and wore only khaki shorts with their mud-caked boots, looked expectantly down at her.

"I ought to be used to it by now but I never am," she shouted over the din. "First there's the drawings, then the scale model. But the site itself is always the real miracle."

The engineers beamed.

"Right on, Mom," Gid said with his endearing smile. He jumped up the metal steps to open the trailer door for her.

Then the two of them were alone, surrounded by the blessed air conditioning and the comparative quiet of Gid's living quarters/office. When her sons had completed Stanford, Crystal had started them on their real education, as outlined by Gideon years ago: the two were shifting through the Divisions, and this was Gid's fourth month at the Tasi.

Touching her scented handkerchief to her face, she sat at his desk, which was cluttered with papers, notes, diagrams, empty mugs and a magnificent, creamy orchidaceous bloom in a Pepsi bottle. "What time's that staff breakfast?" she asked.

"Not until seven thirty. You have an entire half hour to recuperate," he said, opening his refrigerator for one of the small Perriers that he had stocked for her.

She took an appreciative swallow. "What's being done about the mosquitoes?"

"We've brought a duster in." Gid had raised his left wrist and was fingering a shiny, unscratched new silver identification bracelet, an adornment that surprised Crystal: Gid lacked all vanity about his appearance. "Mom, tonight at the party there's somebody I've been wanting you to meet."

Crystal, who had been following the flight of a small, iridescently crimson bird of paradise as it looped above the man-made desolation of mud toward the towering, moss-festooned trees of the uncleared jungle, jumped so that mineral water spilled. "Somebody? A girl, you mean?"

"She's of the female persuasion, yes. Don't look so worried, Mom. She's not a Melanesian."

"You know the rule. You and Alexander aren't meant to date employ—"

"She's not one of us Talbott slaves," he interrupted with one of his undisciplined smiles. "But if she were, the hell with rules."

"I hope you don't show that attitude around the men."

"Mom, you know me better than that." His voice softened. "Her name's Anne Hunnicutt, and she's pretty unique."

Crystal's emotion was sharply delineated, recognizable. She was jealous.

Jealous? Of Gid?

Even with her beautiful, brilliant Alexander she'd never been one of those hedgehog mothers who shoot out bristles of antagonism toward every young female. So why should she now feel echoes of the desolation that had engulfed her after Gideon's death?

"Anne's a homegrown product," Gid was saying. "Born and raised in Berkeley."

"Why is she here?"

"Her doctoral thesis is on the Massim and ambilineal descent—you know, am I my mother's son or my father's?"

"You mean she *lives* with the headhunters?"

"There's no unattached heads around here—unless you count some of the rest of the Berkeley team. There's about a dozen of them in a village a few hours from here by jeep."

Crystal formed an image of a thick-legged, earnest-jawed female anthropologist in a pith helmet stalking an immensely rich young bachelor remote from his natural habitat.

Her blouse was sticking to her back like a hot poultice. "I have to get ready," she said peevishly. "And Gid, can't you do something about this desk?"

While she took her second trickly, tepid shower of the morning, she decided that it was up to her to break up this unsuitable attachment. A decision that was translated into self-righteous maternal duty by the time she slipped into gauzy cottons that smelled of fresh ironing—Anina, as always, had accompanied her. Mitchell was already in Tokyo, the next leg of her journey.

Fortunately the Tasi project was ahead of schedule and

under budget so she did not have to pay attention to drawn-out reports and agitated eight-millimeter films of progress. She meted out praise with automatic smiles and spent the time brooding how to sever the relationship between Gid and the hefty, khaki-clad female whom she visualized meeting that night.

The bash was held on the blacktop. The lights strung between trailers dimmed and pulsated whenever the makeshift combo stationed on a flattop truck became unbearably loud. The amateurish, overamplified musicians served one useful purpose: they drowned out barks and alien cries emerging from the jungle. In Crystal's honor, the few women (secretaries, office workers, the wives of the three top men on the project) wore dowdy formals while the engineering and administrative staff had donned dark suits. The "outdoor guys" sweated into checkered sport jackets. Locals padded around barefoot to offer paper plates of tiny, charred hot dogs, Velveeta cheese melted on Ritz crackers and a spicy local concoction made with pork and coconut.

The roar of a Talbott helicopter had announced the arrival of Anne Hunnicutt, who slipped unseen into Gid's trailer to change. Crystal, a pro at such large employee gatherings, permitted everyone to admire her diamonds and black organza Lanvin—her soignée perfection juxtaposed against the primitive site—while she pretended to listen to the booming of Ian Ramsay, the project manager. Her glance kept wandering to the light that glowed behind the curtained windows of the trailer.

Then the girl was in the doorway, glancing around.

Anne Hunnicutt was quite small, and dressed Berkeley style in a Mexican blouse and floor-length patchwork skirt that looked shapeless enough to be homemade. Crystal tightened her mouth, grudging her son's beloved one minor point. Good hair. In this light it gleamed a rich auburn and fell thick and straight almost to her waist.

Gid had gone over to the steps. His back was to Crystal, but she could see his big hand reach out delicately to the girl's narrow waist, where she had tucked the orchidlike bloom from the Pepsi bottle. They stood that way, the lights flooding over them like a benediction, for a few moments before they linked arms, laughing together as they circled the bar table and came across the blacktop. Crystal saw that Anne's left foot came down with eccentric force. The girl limped.

Crystal knew she had a major battle on her hands.

From the beginning Gid's friendships invariably lacked in some dimension—the child was Chinese or Jewish or orphaned or on scholarship—and no matter how Crystal had tried to sway her son, he had stubbornly kept these inappropriate attachments even unto today.

Anne had the inevitable redhead's lavishment of freckles, lighter on her straight nose, sprinkled heavily across her cheeks almost like rouge, an apricot conglomeration on her shoulders and arms.

"Mrs. Talbott, how terrific to finally meet you," she said. Her smile had a warm immediacy. "You've got a great press agent."

"You mustn't believe all you hear," Crystal responded stiffly.

"Oh, I didn't," the girl said, reaching for Gid's hand. "With a son like this, I never believed for a minute that you *were* gorgeous?"

Gid laughed.

"Gid tells me you're an anthropologist," Crystal said.

"Humbly following in Margaret Mead's footsteps."

"Aren't these New Guinea tribes terribly primitive?"

"I know it looks like that from the outside, Mrs. Talbott, but their social structure's elaborate and quite sophisticated. In our village, which is quite small, the men have a ceremonial clubhouse, and none of the younger men are allowed in until after their initiations—it reminds me of the Faculty Club back home."

"It must be fascinating."

Anne laughed. "Mrs. Talbott, you sounded exactly like my mother just then. She thinks I'm insane to be here in New Guinea. If I'd listened to her, I'd be in law school at Berkeley—my father taught at Boalt—picking off a bright young lawyer."

"Instead of a bright young engineer," Gid said. He hadn't taken his eyes off the girl.

"I hate to admit it, Talbott," Anne retorted, "but sometimes Mother's right."

They both chuckled.

Crystal asked, "When're you going home?"

"In a few days." Anne blinked, suddenly looking far softer and younger. Gid reached for her hand. "My grant's run out," she went on, "and my job at the Bancroft Library starts the first of April. While I'm working on my thesis I'll need every cent I can earn."

Couples had begun dancing. Ramsay strode over and in his capacity as big cheese at the Tasi begged Crystal to do him the honor. As he bounded her across the blacktop, Crystal caught glimpses of Gid and Anne facing each other and gyrating, her not ungraceful swoops flaring the patchwork skirt against his gray flannel trousers.

Two mornings later Crystal was getting ready. The company Boeing 727 would take her to Tokyo.

"Mother," Gid said, coming into the trailer bedroom. "You haven't commented."

"I've made so many flattering remarks my throat's sore."

"I meant about Anne."

"You always choose bright girls, dear."

"Go on," he said doggedly.

"She's leaving in a day or so."

"I'll be home in three weeks." Gid's broad, wrestler's shoulders hunched forward, the same stance Gideon had showed when his mind was closed.

And at this moment Crystal understood her unreasonable jealousy. Her husband and her older son had given her the unqualified adoration that provided a seldom noticed but omnipresent substructure to her life. Gideon had deserted her by dying, and now Gid was switching his allegiance. She fought an urge to weep and plead with him to give up the freckled creature, but she was hardheaded enough to accept her tears would serve no purpose other than to make her pitiable in his eyes.

"Gid, have you stopped to think that you're an immensely rich young man?"

"Anne didn't know that until a few weeks ago. And so far the showering of gifts extends to this." He held out the wide, tanned wrist with the new silver identification bracelet.

"Do you really believe that who you are doesn't make any difference to her?"

"Mother, our kind of money has to make a difference to anyone. But money's not everyone's measurement."

"I don't like your tone, Gid."

"I'm happy, Mom, that's all."

"With your father gone somebody has to play devil's advocate," she said. "No matter how admirable Anne is as a person."

"Then you do like her?"

"Of course I do," Crystal lied staunchly.

They went out into the pulsing heat, where Anina was already waiting in the jeep that would take them to the muddy airstrip.

55

Mitchell, climbing aboard the plane on the runway of the Tokyo Airport, was accompanied by a beaming, bowing official who stamped Crystal's passport. As usual, Anina stayed behind to get the baggage through customs.

The Cadillac moved like a majestic liner in the tight-packed river of little Japanese cars, and Crystal closed her eyes, that last defeating conversation with Gid running through her mind. Mitchell did not intrude on her silence until they were inside her Okura Hotel suite.

"Was it a rough flight, Crystal?" he asked sympathetically.

She shook her head.

"You seem tired," he said. "Or worried. I thought the Tasi project's running like clockwork."

"Everything's fine." Though she trusted Mitchell's discretion implicitly, she never discussed family problems with him. "A case of the blues, that's all."

"Is there anything I can do?"

"You're nice, Padraic." She managed a wan smile. "Outside of Mr. Talbott—and my sister when I was young—you're the only real friend I've ever been able to count on."

"Nothing you've said to me has ever made me prouder. Crystal, are you positive there's no way I can help?"

"It's just a mood," she said, unable to repress her sigh.

He sat on the sofa next to her. The bland scent of his cologne comforted her, and after a minute, she rested her head on his shoulder. At this, the first personal physical contact between them, he quivered and his arm encircled her. "I hate to see you unhappy," he said in a low rumble. "You're beautiful and the bravest person I've ever known."

Here again was the unseeking adoration that was an invisible bolster. The Gid/Anne situation had weakened Crystal's confidence and in her desolate need to reaffirm her worth as a woman it seemed the most natural thing to curve his bony hand around her breast. Mitchell's thin body shivered ecstatically. Kneading her softly firm flesh, he snaked his fingers toward the large pearl buttons of her navy Halston. His caresses on her bare flesh aroused nothing physical, yet memories of necking in parked cars and her youthful desires came dimly to her, like quasars from a long-dead star. All at once Mitchell began breathing asthmatically. His body curved against her side, his fingers gouged into her breast. She tugged at the wrist with the steel Rolex, unable to dislodge the hand. He wheezed, gasping. His body arched in a spasm, then went limp.

She did not realize what had happened until the moisture seeped through her dress to her thigh.

Pulling away, she glimpsed the sickly humiliation on his thin face. Through her horror-struck revulsion came the certainty that she must somehow have this incident blow away like smoke; she must leave Mitchell his dignity, otherwise she would lose him. And how could she run Talbott's without his quiet efficiency, his loyalty, his catholic knowledge of the company?

"Padraic, you're right, I am tired, very tired," she said quietly. "But before my meetings we need to go over everything you've learned about the airport commission's plans. Why don't we meet downstairs for breakfast?"

"Nine thirty?" He didn't look at her.

"Ten would be better."

He pushed stiffly to his feet, keeping his back to her as he let himself out of the suite. She ran unsteadily to the bathroom, throwing off her clothes, crushing hosiery, slip and never-before-worn couturier dress into the wastebasket.

She showered, scrubbing at her rounded thigh until the white skin was a vivid pink.

By the time Anina arrived with the baggage, Crystal, wrapped in the hotel kimono, was putting in a call to San Francisco.

On hearing Alexander's voice she felt the hoped-for solace, and quickly invented an excuse for ringing, inquiring again about the Tokyo airport commissioners. Since Alexander's official entry into Talbott's eight months ago he had filled his office wall safe with dossiers on clients and prospective clients. Mr. Okubo's son, he reminded her, was at Harvard: with the stringent government regulations that restricted Japanese from taking money from the country, Okubo would respond favorably to an offer to exchange yen in Tokyo for dollars in Boston. Mr. Kurihara, possessed of a flamboyant Italian mistress, would be swayed by a loan of the Taormina house or the Mamounia suite or the New York apartment at the Sherry Netherland—or all three.

She could contain her unhappiness no longer. "Gid's found the most impossible girl!" she cried.

"Gid? No kidding? One of New Guinea's prettiest highland pygmies?"

"This is nothing to joke about. The girl's a cripple and works as some kind of anthropologist; she's poor as a churchmouse and as much as admitted to me that she's a gold ... digger...." Crystal was unable to hold back her sobs. With a hasty goodbye, she hung up and buried her face in her pillow.

She wept a long time before she fell asleep.

"It's depressing how impossible this Anne Hunnicutt is, Alexander," Crystal said, shifting her pretty legs, which were cramped from being curled under her.

It was the following evening and they were alone in a private, paper-screened room of the Ishibashi Restaurant, which had been on this site for two centuries and accepted reservations only from former clients—or those introduced personally by them. To Crystal's delighted shock, her younger son had strolled into her suite around six, whisking her off to dine here.

"Did you expect old Gid to choose *Princess* Anne?" Alexander asked.

"I told you! This girl's after his money."

"Somebody has to get it." A thin vein of disbelief crept into Alexander's jocular tone. "Mom, I've never seen you shook like this on Gid's behalf."

"He's never given me cause."

Alexander shifted on his cushion, taking off his dark glasses to assess her while the young waitress knelt holding back her kimono sleeve to serve him the last of the enormous strawberries. He ate the berry then glanced at the waitress. *"Okanjo o shite, kudasai."*

Crystal couldn't control a faint smile of pride in his linguistic skill. "What was that?"

"Nothing—I asked for the check."

Crystal returned to her woes. "The worst part is she'll be in Berkeley while he's in the home office."

"Mmm," Alexander said, yawning.

"I do wish you'd take this seriously."

"I'm here, aren't I?"

He paid, their shoes were returned and they were bowed out over the little humpbacked stone bridge that gave the restaurant its name.

It was an unusually warm night for March, and the nearly full moon floated like a great freshwater pearl above the throngs of businessmen in badly cut black suits, younger women in Western clothing and old ladies in kimonos clattering along on getas. Alexander, ordering the limousine to trail them, took her arm, guiding her through the crowd.

"Why not," he said slowly, "put Gid in charge of the Tasi?"

She jerked away from him. "I never heard anything so ridiculous! Gid? For one thing he doesn't have the experience. The Tasi's huge and complicated. Everything's going so smoothly because of Ramsay. While he was on the Kennicott Copper job he learned the ins and outs of this kind of project."

"Didn't you ask my advice?"

"Alexander, I understand what you're getting at: keep Gid away from the little tramp. And you're on the right track." She jumped as a man on a bicycle sped out of a narrow alley in front of them. Alexander took her arm again. She went on. "You know I can't let Gid take over the Tasi. It's a ten-year job."

"Time's in your favor."

"You know exactly what I mean," she said irritatedly. "The next few years you're both moving around. That's how you're learning to run Talbott's."

He beckoned for the car: it pulled up smoothly and the second chauffeur bounced out, opening the door with deep bows.

When they were seated, Alexander continued with his infuriating denseness. "You're worried Gid's too young for the Tasi? What's a bit of chronology when you're talking about the boss's son?"

"You know as well as I the idea's impossible. Stuck in New Guinea, how'll he learn what makes the company tick?" She broke off abruptly.

A shiver was running through her.

That's exactly what Alexander is aiming for, she thought. *To cut Gid out.*

The Cadillac was easing along the brightly lit park that runs parallel to the eastern grounds of the Imperial Palace, and she looked out at the feudal moat and looming fortress walls. *He wants Talbott's for himself.*

She had always known Alexander coveted Talbott's, but had brushed away the thought. Her mind was cluttered with the long, involved clauses in Gideon's will that left his business empire in trust for both boys, with the knowledge that Alexander wasn't a true Talbott, with her own oftimes embattled sense of fair play. Now, gazing at the gray Oriental walls, she accepted her younger son's simple, inexorable logic.

He had flown across the Pacific to suggest she park Gid in New Guinea while he took over.

Why not?

Talbott's rightfully belongs to Gid but so what? Alexander is the heir I want.

What did her rapidly beating heart care for legalities, genetics, ethics, morality? She adored Alexander. (How she had raged at Curt two years earlier when, after ascertaining his paternity, he had made monstrous pronouncements against their son! *A warped psychotic,* he'd called Alexander—oh, hadn't she just gloated with uninhibited joy when Honora had left him!)

"Do you really think if he's separated from this Anne that he'll forget her?" she asked. The quaver in her voice was a signal of capitulation.

In this shapeless moment of illogic and emotion she had joined Alexander in a tacit conspiracy to propel him to undisputed leadership of Talbott's.

"Absolutely. It's pure bullshit that absence makes the heart grow fonder. He'll be too busy to give the gimpy anthropologist a second thought."

". . . can he really manage a project this large?"

"He's a really bitchin' engineer, you know that, Mom. With the Tasi under his belt, he'll be a brilliant one."

"It might not be such a bad idea. . . ." she whispered.

Alexander lounged back, his long body curving into the Cadillac's upholstery as he let out a sighing breath. Crystal realized the tension he'd been under. For all his subtlety at gauging reactions, he hadn't been positive she'd go along.

"What about Ramsay?"

Alexander smiled. "Simple. Promote him."

The following morning he caught the JAL flight back to San Francisco.

Three days later Crystal's meetings with the airport commission were ended. Her time in Tokyo had been rigidly scheduled, so her conversations with Mitchell had of necessity been brief, businesslike.

On the flight home she rectified this. Above the sun-struck clouds she discussed her interest in having Ian Ramsay on the board.

"Who would head the Tasi?" Mitchell asked.

"Gid seems the logical choice, don't you agree?"

She spoke quickly. Mitchell had been aware of Gideon's educational plans for the boys, and what the executive secretary lacked in personal ambition he made up for in intelligence. He squinted down at brilliant clouds, his wary expression proving that he had immediately grasped Gid's future.

The jets hummed. "He's a bit young," Mitchell said finally.

"Yes. That worries me, too. The main thing is that Ramsay would be a tremendous asset on the board." She leaned toward Mitchell, filling his narrow nostrils with freshly applied Jolie Madame. "How would I go about creating a new seat?"

Mitchell itemized the legal steps and the young black steward served them spritzers. As the Boeing sped away from Japan they moved further from possible recriminations about Gid's disinheritance, further from unpleasant memories of the Okura Hotel.

Ian Ramsay, delighted to be offered a vice presidency, packed his clothes and calculators, returning with his full-bosomed, motherly wife to San Francisco.

Six weeks after her first visit to the Tasi, Crystal flew back to New Guinea.

"Somebody has to take over the project. Gid, I'm counting on you."

Rain fusilladed against the metal roof. In this roaring deluge the trailer's air-conditioning unit couldn't function properly, and the miasmic heat clung to the body.

After a long pause, Gid said, "You can't be talking about the whole shooting match."

"Who else can step in for Ramsay?"

"This weather's gotten to you, Mom. It's called jungle fever."

"I didn't fly across the Pacific to make jokes."

"There's maybe a thousand people in Talbott's better equipped than I am."

"Dear, must you always underestimate yourself? You're a natural-born engineer. And the clients"—a Taiwanese company that had been formed with enormous capital of shadowy sources—"insist on you."

"They know I got my degree a year and a half ago?"

"You're a Talbott. For Orientals the important thing is family. With Ramsay gone they're *insisting* on one of the family."

Gid went to the window. She could not see his face, but his shoulders were hunched. "How long into the project do they demand kinfolk?" he asked.

"They didn't mention a date."

"I was counting on getting home."

"I'd never ask this of you, Gid, but I'm in no position to argue. You know they were ready to give Ivory the job until we agreed to take a three million cut in our management fee."

Gid touched the silver identification bracelet with his fingertip, sighing.

"We've never attempted anything this large on our own," Crystal added with a break in her voice.

Resolutely Gid turned to face her. "I'll give it my all," he said.

Crystal dabbed at her eyes. "I knew I could count on you, dear," she said, embracing him.

One evening the following week she was in her sunken tub when the bathroom phone buzzed. It was Gid. "Anne and I're in Port Moresby," he said.

"Anne?" The line was a bad one and her falsetto squeak bounced back at her.

"Congratulations, Mom. You've been a mother-in-law for nearly ten minutes."

She looked down at the still perfect white body. How calm she was. Alexander had spoken the truth. Time does blur emotional responses. When the lively voice of the new Mrs. Gideon Talbott III came through the receiver, Crystal welcomed her into the family with a trill of pretty, echoed laughter.

56

THE ACTIVITIES OF AMERICAN MULTINATIONAL
CORPORATIONS ABROAD

Hearings
before the
SUBCOMMITTEE ON
INTERNATIONAL ECONOMIC POLICY OF
THE COMMITTEE ON INTERNATIONAL RELATIONS
HOUSE OF REPRESENTATIVES
Ninety-fourth Congress

Alexander had strolled the length of his mother's impressive new office to set the green-paper-covered government publication on her desk. Sunlight gleamed on his bright hair as he turned at the windows. The plate glass was streaked, partially obscuring the brilliance of the view of San Francisco and the Bay, but at this height window washing couldn't be at her whim. When the new Talbott Group World Headquarters building in the Financial District was being planned, Crystal had chosen the southeast corner of the thirty-second floor as her own, designing her bailiwick so that visitors walked forty feet to her desk, behind which—like a stern reminder of God—hung the larger than life, chiaroscuro portrait of Gideon.

Frowning, Crystal ruffled the thin, cheap pages with her thumb, and saw that there were over four hundred of them filled with testimony about monies paid out as bribes in foreign countries.

"This kind of garbage makes me ill," she said. She was not using a figure of speech. A queasy sensation shifted through her stomach whenever she read denunciations of overseas payoffs in the newspapers or saw the chastened company officials on the News. "I never heard of anything so insane as this persecution, this witch-hunt. Congress knows how business is done in this country, they come to us for campaign contributions, so hearing that we have to pay through the nose in other places can't be any great shock."

"It's necessary for Congresspersons to revirginate themselves each election year."

"Hypocrites! On one hand they talk about the country needing a good balance of trade, and on the other they talk ethics. Do they think we love paying out *mordida, dash, baksheesh?*"

"Don't get so worked up, Mom. Politicians live on the perfume of sanctity, not the reality of it." He lifted his eyebrows expressively.

Alexander knew about politicians, both American and otherwise. In the two years since that evening in Tokyo he had wooed large, juicy government contracts adeptly as a juggler, smoothly as a magician, setting up an invisible web of intermediaries to distribute a staggering annual $20,000,-000 from three Zurich banks. Talbott's earnings this year, 1976, would be close to a hundred million. The company had climbed far, far from the slump caused by Gideon's death.

Suddenly she clutched the book. "Alexander," she asked

breathily, "you aren't trying to tell me they can trace the Swiss accounts to us?"

"No way," he said. "Our connections are all safe in countries where Congress can't subpoena them."

"Then what's the point of this?" Crystal's diamond flashed blue fire as she tapped the drab, cheap binding.

"I was thinking about the press coverage if there were an investigation of the grease in the Mideast."

The second button on her telephone lit up, but the phone didn't ring: Alexander must have arranged with her secretaries, as he often did, that this conference remain inviolate. Trapped between love of her son and exasperation at his maneuvers, she said, "Alexander, if you're talking about Ivory, just say so."

Hands in his trouser pockets, he strolled back to the desk and took a peppermint from the Ming bowl. "I'm simply pointing out that with the gas prices and the lines outside service stations, the country's not exactly in love with Arabs. The media'll pounce on startling revelations about hanky-panky with them."

"*I've* never heard of Curt using anything more than grease." In numerous countries unless underpaid civil servants were remunerated with small sums—the so-called grease—documents remained unfiled, telephone calls weren't put through, minor but problematical sabotage plagued jobs.

"I happen to know otherwise. There's some Ivory papers ripe to fall into the proper Congressional hands."

"How will *his* being investigated help us?"

The smell of mint spread as Alexander unwrapped the cellophane. "For you Talbott versus Ivory has set rules," he said. "You throw the dice and hope you land on a good space. When Ivory throws his dice, you hope he lands badly."

"Alexander, we aren't talking about Snakes and Ladders."

"No, we aren't." Alexander popped the candy in his mouth. "I want him gone."

"Gone?"

"No longer a player. Out of the game."

She glanced at the window and saw a child's red balloon drift upward and out of sight. Alexander was asking her permission to ruin Curt Ivory, her enemy, her rival. His father. Surely her own goal. So why should her eyes suddenly itch, as if with tears?

Her expression must have showed something of this outrageously misplaced sense of loyalty to the man she hated.

Alexander slumped in one of the Queen Anne corner chairs opposite her. "Forget it," he muttered. "Just forget it."

There was no manipulative artifice in his resentment, only a boyish bitterness. Unwanted came the memory of a foggy night, a pine-odored hill and Alexander's hard hand gripping her arm. She, dressed in teenager's thrift-shop motley and stoned out of her skull, had said aloud what should have remained forever sacrosanct. She told herself that his vindictive tangle lay at her door.

She mustered an unarguable point: "An investigation could easily rebound on us," she said. "You know how the press loves to dig."

He got to his feet, no longer sullen but debonair. "All they'll find in our backyard is the skeleton of a very small mouse."

"And Ivory?"

"What's disinterred will surprise everyone, including the playboy of the Western world."

"Curt? Are you saying he doesn't know what's going on in his own company?"

"He soon will." Alexander came around the desk to kiss her on the forehead. "He soon will."

After he left the office, Crystal pressed a button in the paneling and went into her small sitting room. Her sanctum sanctorum. She stretched on the swan-necked daybed that had graced Empress Josephine's boudoir at Malmaison, pressing icy fingertips to her forehead.

But why should she assume Alexander's plan would boomerang? Hadn't his ideas proved invincible? Hadn't he always anticipated her own goals, and then led her toward them? Witness l'affaire Gid. Gid was doing a bang-up job at the Tasi and Anne was pregnant. Though Crystal dreaded the elevation to grandmotherhood, her raging antipathy to her lively, freckled daughter-in-law had long ago evaporated. She proudly displayed copies of *Ambilineal Descent* by Anne Hunnicutt-Talbott, PhD, on her office desk and in all her homes. When the younger couple came home on leave, she entertained for them, she laughed at their affectionate bantering—indeed, she enjoyed Gid's company far more than she had in his single days.

Why should I be so worried? We have every sort of connection in Congress. President Ford and two of his cabinet are personal friends. And as for Curt, he deserves what he gets, saying that monstrous thing about Alexander, never once approaching him, running around the world with every cheap starlet. God, how he's humiliating poor Honora.

Behind her closed eyelids, she saw her sister's long, tenderly pretty face, her lovely dark eyes.

As Crystal went into the bathroom for a Tylenol, she said aloud, "It might make no sense to me now, but Alexander's a genius at this kind of thing."

57

Honora circled both hands about the bulb's intricate root network as she set the tulip in the ground. Careful of the pointed foliage, she patted the moist, richly mulched earth back into position, then shifted on her damp, mud-encrusted jeans a few inches to her left to measure the length of her trowel and plant the next flower. These black tulips, shipped this morning from Amsterdam by the Jan van der Helst Nursery, weren't black at all of course, but a deep, reddish purple which blended artlessly with the soft blue of ruffled forget-me-nots and the more intense azure of *Iris reticulata* being set in place around the bare-branched wisteria by the two gnarled old gardeners. The small Belgravia garden was romantically informal—or would be when it was completed.

Tentacles of pain rippled from the base of Honora's spine, but she scarcely noticed. When she was doing an installation she was possessed—there was no other word for it—by the necessity of placing each plant in the exact right spot of earth. This wasn't labor but—like singing or dancing—a joy that obliterated all else. Her medium of creation. Though the physical touch of the soil was part of it, she did not normally put in this much stoop labor. One of the workers, a Pakistani, had called in sick—"Drunk, more like it," was Vi's opinion. Honora didn't really mind doing the work. And she would save the Pakistani's pay.

She always needed a bit extra.

In the two years since she had taken over from Mavis, the referrals had flourished gratifyingly, yet the financial inefficiencies of her youth plagued her still. She never could get the hang of adhering to penny and pounds, she never had a clue to the mechanics of budgeting. What were you meant to do when a necessity cropped up? For example, she would set aside a sum for Lissie's clothes: the school had no uniform, so they shopped for hand-knit Irish and Norwegian sweaters, the practical kind that last forever, to wear with warm trousers. Then, sure enough, Lissie would receive a rash of brightly printed invitations, which meant nice gifts and another party frock—the elaborate, fragile garments Curt bought her in California were almost pointedly useless in this colder climate. And how could she mention to Joscelyn the small checks she wrote to Langley's nurses for overtime when her sister was already paying Lissie's walloping school fees? (Honora, who scrimped to pay her half of her father's expenses, guessed that Crystal, too, contributed: Langley, as ever, refused to discuss finances.)

A branch of the Victoria line lay underneath and the ground shuddered as the train went by. Honora didn't falter in her measuring and planting, but her expressive dark eyes saddened.

She was thinking of Curt.

Misty, hazy thoughts. Anguish and ecstasy are equally unrecollectable. In the four years of their separation she had lost exact memory of the mental and physical torment of that final scene at the Mamounia. Neither could she recollect the languorous fever when they made love. The coloration of his voice and expression had faded like the soft Liberty print blouse she wore under her fisherman's sweater. She was left not with a man but with an emotional texture. The shiver of happiness on her skin when they embraced, the protected safety she felt with him, the purpose his energy imparted to her, the warmth she felt during those shared evenings while he worked and she read—ahh, the shared warmth of those evenings.

In the beginning of their separation she had been panicked by the thought that he would come after her, but within six months her fears had changed into a hollow hurt that he had not even made the faintest gesture toward a reconciliation.

Curt avoided publicity, but Mavis, who frequented the ultra-lavish watering spots, occasionally saw him with some highly noticeable girl, and Vi read aloud the gushy sentences in her movie magazines—such and so film princess was dating "a famous international building tycoon." For her friends to pass on the gossip meant that she, Honora, managed a good act of mature indifference. Inwardly her jealousy raged as green as when she was nineteen.

She pushed to her feet, rubbing her lower back. Her soft, full lip drew down, and her glance was calculating as she surveyed the garden. After a minute she nodded decisively. An echo of the tulips was needed in the far corner by the wisteria, and a few additional clumps of both tulip and iris should be worked around the Cotswold stone loggia.

The gardeners, alike as gnarled twins, were knocking off for the day and one offered her the tea remaining in his thermos. She refused. "Rather have coffee, would you?" he said cheerfully, and his mate chimed in, "You Americans!"

In England everyone called her an American. In the United States she had always been thought of as English. Honora perceived this as symbolic. She was a dangling woman. Suspended between countries. Between careers— was she a landscape designer or a day laborer? Between motherhood and fostering. Between marriage and grass-widowhood. Several men had asked her out, and one, a successful barrister married to a child psychologist for whom she'd done an office terrace, had been resolutely persistent, phoning or dropping by the flat. He was a colorful and amusing man, his marriage was one of the open kind—her client had already informed her of that. She was achingly frustrated. So why had she refused his every pass until eventually he gave up?

After the two old men left, while the long English dusk fell and the last light faded, she finished planting the tulips. A few crates of plastic pots stood on the low stone wall, but the outdoor fixtures cast an uncertain, shadowy light and she couldn't make out which plant was needed where. *I'll have to come back tomorrow morning,* she thought and went to wash up in the potting-shed sink, skinning off her filthy, moisture-laden sweater and jeans, putting on a three-year-old trouser suit.

In a jammed tube she lurched to Knightsbridge. At the station's fruiterer she paid two pounds for dusky purple grapes, temporizing the extravagance by telling herself such little luxuries were all her father had left to live for.

A few years ago Langley's liver and kidneys had given way. His doctors had warned him away from alcohol. Though barely past his seventieth birthday, he had become a hunched, yellow-faced, querulous hypochondriac tended by nurses and his elderly manservant.

The central heat in the pricey Sloan Square flat was stifling, yet Langley's chair was pulled close to the drawing room's electric fire; he wore a black woolly vest beneath his dinner jacket, and a plaid mohair rug wrapped his long, spindly legs.

"Hello, Daddy," Honora said, bending to kiss his soft, beautifully combed white hair.

"What d'you have in that bag?" he asked.

She flushed, realizing she had shoved her work clothes into a bag from Marks and Spencer, where Vi searched out bargains with the same enthusiasm she had once pursued tips. Langley considered both the chain and the ex-waitress common beyond redemption.

"Just dirty clothes," Honora said. "I brought you a lovely bunch of grapes—Nurse is washing them."

"I had grapes for lunch; they were quite tasteless," he said. "Well, I suppose now you'll be rushing off."

"Don't be silly, Daddy. I just got here. How are you?"

"My heart was pounding terribly last night. Thump, thump, thump. I would have called, but I don't like worrying you. And I had that cold again, but I took several glasses of hot lemon and cured myself."

"Did you go out?"

"With my cold? In this terrible weather? But it's much worse abroad. There were dreadful rainstorms all across Europe." He paused, peering at her hands. "Honora, your nails."

She curled her fingers, hiding the black rims. "Daddy, tell me what was in this morning's *Times*?"

"You'd have a chance to read it yourself if you weren't a gardener."

"Landscape designer," she murmured.

"I don't understand people anymore. Maybe Curt had no proper background, and I never liked the way he swanked any more than you did, but in my day we stayed married."

Langley's persistence that the Ivorys had split because Curt's riches were too *nouveau* for a Sylvander irritated and stung Honora, but she had long given up correcting him. Clutching her elbows, she sank deeper into the wing chair.

Langley's lips assumed a vestigial hint of his old, whimsical smile. "My poor Portuguese, I always say that you're doing quite your best." And with this he launched into the daily disasters: a hearing into international bribery to be conducted by the United States Congress, an earthquake ravaging Guatemala, crime in Italy, unemployment in the Midlands.

When the buhlwork clock on the mantel chimed seven, she said, "Daddy, I really must be going home."

"When will I see you again?" he asked anxiously.

"Tomorrow at the same time."

He strung out her departure with further tidbits about his ossifying blood vessels, his migratory cold symptoms, the unfolding of a letter from Joscelyn that he'd already read to her twice.

Defeated and guilty, she trudged back to the tube station.

Vi had found them a much larger, nicer flat in a tree-filled, sequestered square in Fulham—oh, how Langley's aristrocratic nostrils had curled. Fulham, indeed!

As Honora climbed the stairs, Lissie, waiting for the vibrations of her footsteps, flung open the door.

Even now, with the bulges and distortions of pre-adolescence, the child remained beautiful. Alas, though, the lively abandon and lack of self-consciousness of her early childhood was gone. Though her oral skills had improved tremendously with the school's elaborate auditory trainers, in the presence of outsiders she held her shoulders tensed as if warding off a question she might have to answer. When she went out she left off her aids and had developed a sad little repertoire of means to avoid conversation with strangers. Telling Honora, who sat carefully in a ponderous straight-back chair, about her day, however, she chattered vivaciously.

The large, squarish room was friendly and pleasant, the heaviness of the department store furniture that Vi had shipped from San Diego having been vanquished by Honora's large, lush houseplants and ferns, her collection of books, the bright posters for art openings that she'd had framed.

Vi padded in from the kitchen. Her orange dye-job was frizzed into an Afro and she had gained eighteen pounds. "Welcome home, stranger," she said cheerfully. "What kept you?"

"I tried to finish the job."

"And then, of course, you dropped in on your pop, right? Kid, some nights why don't you give yourself a break?"

"What smells so wonderful? Fried chicken?"

"Yep, good old Colonel Vi's best. It's in the oven. And you're right to change the subject; when you're beat's not the best time for advice. I'll keep my big mouth shut."

Vi and Lissie, who had already eaten, sat at the table with Honora and soon she forgot her filial guilts, her weariness, her lower back, her loneliness and inadequacies.

She shared the front bedroom with Lissie, and planned to hit bed at the same time as her child. But when Lissie went to brush her teeth, Vi whispered, "I got something to tell you. Private."

Though Lissie couldn't eavesdrop, the child had another sense that telegraphed when they were hiding something. Honora nodded, opening her library copy of *Far Tortuga*.

Vi waited ten minutes after the bedroom door had closed on Lissie. "Today I picked up the American *Time*," she said. To assuage an occasional bout of homesickness, she patronized a news stall that stocked a wide spectrum of American papers and magazines. "Your ex's in it."

"What's he building now?" Honora tried to sound breezy, but to her own ears every remark she made about her estranged husband was tempered by a vague fraudulence.

"Nothing like that. There's going to be another round of them Congressional hearings. He's been called."

"Oh yes, Daddy mentioned something about it. But he didn't say a word about Curt."

"The papers here ain't so hot on our news." Glancing toward the closed bedroom door, Vi extracted the magazine from her large, navy plastic bag. "Page fifty-six."

Honora rustled the slick paper, halting at a column headed "Scandals."

The unmasking of corporate international misbehavior will continue in two weeks, on May 13, when a House subcommittee headed by Oregon Democrat Jason Morrell reconvenes to hear further testimony about American businesses involved in payoffs in the Mideast.

Curt Ivory, who heads the giant Ivory Engineering Company, is among those who have been subpoenaed. There have been rumors that the Morrell committee might question his close friendship with Prince Fuad Abdulrahman, a member of the Lalarheini royal family. Prince Fuad was the minister of finance when Ivory was awarded contracts to build the Lalarheins' Daralam airport, the most grandiose in the Arab world, and the most sophisticated, with its up-to-the-minute American military equipment. Curt Ivory told the Associated Press that he was guilty of no wrongdoing, and welcomed the investigation.

The multimillionaire Ivory lives aboard the *Odyssey*, a 282-foot, 1800-ton yacht, one of the largest, most luxurious private boats afloat. Long separated but not divorced from his wife, who resides with their ten-year-old adopted daughter, Rosalynd, in London, Ivory is a favored escort of young Hollywood beauties.

"Well?" Vi asked.

"It was good of you not to let Lissie see this," Honora said in a stilted voice. "May I?"

"Help yourself."

Paper rasped as Honora tore out the page.

"What do you figure'll happen when he goes to Washington?"

"Nothing."

"What do you mean, nothing?" Vi bristled. "This ain't a picnic. They're gunning for him."

"He's always refused to do business where payoffs were involved, so there's nothing they can find out."

"But this Arab joker—"

"Fuad and Curt have been friends since Berkeley. Vi, my back is killing me. A good long soak is what I need."

"Try Epsom salts, hon," Vi said sympathetically, lumbering across the room to turn on the television.

Ripping the page lengthwise several times, Honora watched the ribbons of print swirl down the toilet. Supine in a scalding bath, she was bludgeoned by envious loathing for those young Hollywood beauties.

God, how those quiet evenings alone with her must have bored him!

58

In 1975, Curt had formed a separate corporation to handle the venture capital, naming the new company Ivory Investments, putting Joscelyn on the board as the only director minus an MBA. The nine members gathered every other month at the Los Angeles headquarters. The other eight, glowing with an excitement that seemed indecently sexual, discussed shelters—oil, cattle, real estate, airplanes. Ignorant of evasive tax action, Joscelyn remained silent. She had an unpleasant sensation of weightlessness. In her social life she had forever formed a large zero, but being a nonperson at work was new to her: she concealed herself behind a yellow legal pad on which she scratched an occasional memo to herself, and had no inkling that the smart money, her confreres, assumed her on the board as a spy for her brother-in-law.

An Ivory Investment board meeting fell ten days before Curt was scheduled to appear before the Morrell Subcommittee. Nobody mentioned it, and this struck Joscelyn as typical of the cautious, money-oriented group—everyone else at Ivory was circulating jokes about the upcoming hearing, and the Conrad cartoon of a thousand-dollar-bill folded like a tusk into an Arabian headgear was pinned to half the office bulletin boards.

The meeting ritually concluded with lunch at the Windsor, whose flawless, high-protein cuisine and generous drinks attracted the expense account crowd. The men drove over in their air-conditioned cars, but Joscelyn always showed her stuff as a hearty outdoor engineer by walking the dozen or so level city blocks to the restaurant. Today Martin Sterret did not continue on the elevator with the others to Ivory's subterranean garage but got off with her, accompanying her down the main steps to the sculpture garden that Honora had planned in happier days.

"My internist," Sterret said, "has ordered more exercise. Mind a little company?"

"If you want," Joscelyn said ungraciously.

"What did you think of that bit in *Time*?" he asked.

"A hatchet job."

"*Newsweek* was worse. They just about called Mr. Ivory a combination of underworld godfather and manipulator of foreign governments."

"I saw it," she said acidly. "Imaginative reporting."

The two deep lines running down Sterret's cheeks were like strings wiggling his jowls. "Joscelyn, this kind of publicity is disaster for a company."

"This isn't a financial corporation," she said pointedly. "In engineering it's strictly a matter of cost and ability."

"We're talking politics here. I don't need mention to *you* how much of Ivory's backlog is in government contracts."

She nodded glumly. "Nearly ten billion, and revenues of over a billion."

"I've denied this until I'm blue in the face, but there's a rumor going around that it's more than smoke that Ivory has paid large sums to the Abdulrahman family."

"I told Curt he ought to sue *Time*—how dare they print that kind of crap! Fuad would no more take a bribe than Curt would offer one."

"*We* know that." They had halted for a red light at Wilshire, and Sterret leaned toward her so close that she could smell the sourness of his breath. *He's frightened,* she thought. "But, Joscelyn, if Mr. Ivory gets the press's full treatment, it won't matter whether he's innocent or not. Whatever comes out at the hearing, he'll be guilty."

"Terrific."

In the smoggy sunlight, she saw the sagging flesh of Sterrett's throat jump as if in a painful hiccup. "I'm not saying this, you understand. But other people have pointed out that it would help if Mrs. Ivory showed up."

"Honora?"

The light changed and they started across the street.

"If she were at the hearing his . . . well, his flamboyance wouldn't be so damaging."

"They're separated," Joscelyn said sharply.

"But not divorced."

"His personal life is his own." A mottled redness appeared on her throat. She was remembering the night she had attempted to enter into that personal life: time had in no way blurred the image of her brother-in-law's revulsed yet pleading expression.

"I don't like saying this, but the press has already found him guilty of a certain amount of, uhh, lax morals."

"If you're talking about his lady friends, why not say so?" Joscelyn snapped.

"With Mrs. Ivory in Washington, people might be more sympathetic—"

"Jesus!"

"Nothing like a good woman standing by her husband. . . ." His words trailed into a muted cough as if, Joscelyn decided, it was coming to him that this particular good woman had stood by her husband and cracked his skull with a large, Venetian glass ornament.

After half a block, Sterret asked, "You're close to him. Do you think he could be convinced to at least talk it over with Mrs. Ivory?"

"There's a subject *I*'d never bring up."

"Having her there would be immensely helpful."

"Then why don't *you* talk to Curt?"

They walked the remainder of the way in silence.

As they turned the corner to the Windsor she saw the rest of the Ivory Investment MBAs gathered beneath the canopy. It was only too obvious that Sterret had been elected spokesman. *If they're so worked up about losing their job, maybe I ought to worry a bit, too,* she thought. Her anxiety was not directed at her own possible unemployment—husband killers don't deserve the luxury of fearing for themselves—but for Curt. The smart money's consensus was that Congress and the media would stretch Curt out like beef drying into jerky. *Are they right? Would Honora's presence make the difference?*

A pot of tea and heel of toasted Hovis smeared with butter, Honora's lunch, waited on a bedside table while she clasped her hands around her knees, drawing her bent legs toward her chest to flatten her spine on the restorative electric heating pad.

It was Saturday, and a few minutes ago Vi and Lissie had bundled in rainclothes to go see a specially captioned matinee of *Sunshine Boys.* Honora had begged off to rest her capricious vertebrae.

It had been a loser of a week on all counts. Chill air from the North Sea had brought icy spring rain whose sibilance now hushed the square. She had shown preliminary sketches to three prospective clients: none had phoned her back. Lissie's Head Mistress had called a parents' meeting to raise funds for a school for the hard of hearing in Zambia: Honora, moved by the black children's plight, had donated a thirty-pound check before realizing that her *bête noire,* an improperly balanced bank account, left her with under five pounds. There wouldn't be any deposits until payments came for her previous two jobs, so she had been forced—once again—to float a loan from Vi. Langley, yet gloomier from being kept indoors, had spouted jeremiads of universal doom. And a particularly copious period had added to her lower-back discomfort.

She straightened her legs, wincing, then rolled cautiously on her side to pour her tea. Picking up her book—she had finished *Far Tortuga* and was starting a yellowing paperback of *Lost Illusions* that she'd picked up at a second-hand stall—she alternately sipped her milky, sweet tea and munched her brown crust.

She was someplace deep in nineteenth-century Angoulême when the doorbell rang. Positive the intruder was a salesman, she stayed put. The bell sounded again and again, a vibrato of irritation. Cautiously she swung her feet down into the flattened fake fur of her slippers, drew her bathrobe sash tighter around her slight waist and went to unlock the front door.

"I'd abandoned all hope," Joscelyn said.

Honora, who had never quite accustomed herself to the way her younger sister dropped in as though she lived nearby in Fulham, pressed her cheek against Joscelyn's icy, rain-scented one.

"What's with you?" Joscelyn asked. "A cold?"

"No, it's nothing. My back's been kicking up a bit, that's all. What brings you to this sunny clime?"

Joscelyn didn't answer. Taking off her raincoat, whose epaulets were dark with wetness, she slung it across her overnight bag. "Let's go where you'll be comfortable."

Honora returned to her room to lie on her comforting heating pad, expecting her sister, after the long flight, to kick off her wet flats and stretch out on Lissie's bed for a chat about their daughter. Instead, Joscelyn paced wordlessly around, crossing and recrossing the scrappy maroon carpet to touch the daffodils Vi had bought yesterday to cheer Honora, to shift a schoolbook on Lissie's shelf. As she adjusted the dressing table mirror, the murky light reflected her as if from a deep pond.

Honora was beginning to get anxious. "Joss, what about some tea? It's no trouble to make fresh."

Joscelyn's eye twitched. "Have anything to drink?"

"Vi just bought some vodka. I'll fix you a Bloody Mary."

"Don't move. In the kitchen?"

"In the cabinet above the sink. The tomato juice is in the fridge."

The sounds of Joscelyn fixing the drink were torturingly slow. She returned, sitting on the dressing table chair, holding the glass with both hands.

Honora's throat felt bruised, but she managed an easy modulation. "Joss, what's wrong?"

"Nothing. Do I always have to be your crippled sparrow?" Joscelyn inquired, exhibiting the perversity that from earliest childhood had disguised her troubles.

"You seem a bit nervy, that's all."

"I'm not in the market for a ministering angel." Joscelyn took a long drink. "But Curt is."

"Curt?" Honora's head jerked up from the pillow. "Is he ill?"

"Fit as a fiddle, whatever that means."

"Is it something to do with this hearing?"

"Yes, and I don't know why you should rush to his support after he's been such a Grade-A shit to you."

"I left him," Honora murmured.

"Who wouldn't, after learning he'd been getting it on

with Crystal and having a kid with her? And what about his whorelets?"

"Did he send you?"

"He'd string me up if he knew I were here. Either that or excommunicate me from my profession."

"But I gather you feel I ought to be helping him."

"I'm ambivalent."

"Joss, there's simply no way I could be any good to him. I've met quite a few Washington people, but he introduced me to all of them and knows them far better than I do—not to mention that he's a major campaign contributor."

"Did I ask you to suborn Congress?"

"Then how on earth could I help him?"

Joscelyn examined her ice cubes. "Remember at the Watergate hearings how Maureen Dean sat behind John, showing the television audience her wardrobe and wifely support? Could a man so beloved be all bad?"

"I understand what you're saying, but you know how things are between us. He didn't even call when Lissie had that bad case of mumps. Believe me, he doesn't want me there."

"They're out to crucify him."

"Do you really believe that?"

"You would too, if you'd been reading American papers, seeing network TV."

"But why?"

"It's an election year and the Morrell Subcommittee will get a circusful of publicity." Joscelyn raised her voice. "Come one, come all, see the sterling electorate body prove that it can cut down to size the billionaire who lives on a world-class yacht with ten, count 'em, ten gorgeous starlets."

Honora shifted on the bed, a furrow biting between the dark, luminous eyes.

Joscelyn kept silent. Though fecklessly incapable of guiding her personal relationships, in business dealings she was a tough cookie: she had learned that silence can be a most effective weapon. She sipped her Bloody Mary.

"Joss," Honora said at last, "let's assume I'm ready to help him, and let's assume that my being with him at the hearing would help. I don't see how I can sit there behind him and prove my loyalty if he doesn't want me around."

"It's my opinion he misses you."

"Oh, absolutely. But when does he find the time from his ten, count 'em, ten gorgeous starlets?"

"Look, I don't blame you if you ignore the whole thing. Why should you spring to his defense? At least poor Malcolm never humiliated me publicly."

"I'm not being punitive."

Joscelyn put her glass on the floor, yawning. "The jetties just hit me," she said.

Kicking off her flats, she stretched on Lissie's bed and pulled the green satin eiderdown up to her collar. In less than a minute her breathing slowed. She was pretending sleep.

Emotions burst wildly through Honora. The pain of Curt's fathering Crystal's son, the crazy yearning to see him, the shame of crawling back to him. She was remembering the loss of self that came over her when her naked body pressed against his, remembering the revulsion that last time when he had raped her. She was visualizing unlined beauties parading on his arm. She was pitying a starving six-year-old. But when had Honora Sylvander Ivory reached her decisions by logical progression?

Her mind was already made up.

59

It was one of those spring days in Los Angeles when the wind has swept away every trace of smog and the distant mountain ranges rear up, their dark ridges showing as a warm, immediate purple. The California sky was a brighter, deeper blue than Honora remembered, and this ravishing color was echoed by the man-made Los Angeles Harbor. Curt's seafaring home was too large to dock at the Marina so he berthed here with commercial vessels.

Reaching the waterfront, Honora's hands clutched the padded leather steering wheel of Joscelyn's sporty, late-model red Corvette: she knew she should make a left, but all at once lacked confidence as to which side of the street she should be on—she had driven only an occasional hired car in five years and was accustomed to traffic flowing on the opposite side. She turned cautiously. An hour of racing along the freeway system had jelled her thighs, tensed the musculature of her neck, and given her an incipient headache to compete with the nagging of her spine. En route she had been too involved in traffic and handling the Corvette to consider her greater anxieties, but only a couple of cars moved along the wharf and she no longer needed to concentrate on driving. In the crisp, clean-smelling ocean breeze, apprehensions rushed at her.

Curt didn't have the foggiest notion she was coming. She hadn't phoned, being positive that either he would hang up or tell her to bug off. And by now she was positive it was crucial that she be at his side at the subcommittee hearing. Her task of convincing him to let her accompany him to Washington had taken on the exalted significance of finding and partaking in the holy grail.

If I only looked more human, she thought.

Never able to properly separate the internal from external truths, Honora took it for granted that her appearance reflected her grungy weariness. Last night she had fallen asleep instantly on the sofa bed in Joscelyn's living room. She had dreamed that she and Curt were young and in a green springtime place where shafts of misty light and jeweled birdsong fell from the newly leafed branches far over their heads. Her conversation had the surrealistic quality of happy dreams when each word one says is true, witty, wise and utterly fascinating to the listener—as far as she could recall on waking, she told him how to prune rosebushes. Smiling, he had cupped her face, leaning forward to kiss her. She'd awakened, her thighs clenched around moist desire. The digital clock had told her she had been in bed less than ten minutes. The remainder of the night she had turned restlessly, dozing briefly just after dawn.

The road curved between massive warehouses, and her pupils took a few seconds to adjust to the deep shadows. She was blinking rapidly as she emerged again into the brightness.

Ahead of her gleamed the *Odyssey.*

After the battered freighters, the yacht seemed yet more preposterous, a sleek floating miracle willed into existence by a magic lantern. The three decks were contoured together; the white paint gleamed as if freshly applied.

She pulled in at the end of a small row of cars. Even while she took calming breaths, traitor memory was repeating details that Lissie had brought back to England. The *Odyssey* carried a custom-built Jensen for Curt, two Chevies for the crew, as well as a Chris-Craft from whose stern Lissie had mastered waterskiing. There was a helicopter pad—Honora could see it extending like an accent mark above the top deck—and an enormous saucer of a satellite system that enabled Curt to dial any number in the world. The master suite had a closet bigger than their whole living room to stash Curt's vast wardrobe, and a bathroom with an enormous, circular, blue marble hot tub. There were four guest staterooms, and Lissie's had a small entry hall and a toy room. The two round, white leather tables in the dining saloon could be joined together by removable leafs to seat twenty for conferences or dining on the Italian chef's specialties.

Intimidated—no, frightened—Honora stumbled as she got out of the low-slung car. She dropped her purse and coins from two countries spilled, as well as a lipstick, a tampon, her paperback novel. She bent her knees, scrabbling for her possessions.

Straightening, she saw Curt.

He was at the point of the bow, his bare arms crossed on the wooden rail. His face and arms were burned dark, the breeze ruffled sunbleached hair.

They gazed at each other across the years and maybe a hundred feet, and in their mysterious joining she felt a warmth pass from her abdomen to her extremities—her fingertips, toes, her ears—the identical sensation of yearning eroticism that had melted her in her dream. Unconsciously, she drew a hand toward her breast.

Abruptly Curt turned. The *Odyssey*'s deck was above the level of the dock and he vanished instantly. Honora was left remembering what time had blurred and softened. Curt's punitive streak. He was helpless before his implacable vindictiveness. He could not control himself from smiting those who wronged him, in whose ranks he must surely place his estranged wife.

You'll pass out if you don't put your head between your

knees, advised an unsympathetic nurse within her. She sat sideways in the car, her feet on the blacktop, her back bowed deeply until the vertigo passed. She walked slowly to the gangplank, which was guarded by an elderly man wearing a navy sweatshirt with *Odyssey* imprinted in white across the chest.

He leaned back in his metal folding chair, resting his magazine on his thighs. "May I help you?"

"I'm Mrs. Ivory," she murmured.

At this he raised and lowered his eyes in what she and Crystal eons ago had called the-once-over-lightly. Was he gauging her against Curt's starlets? Was he wondering whether this old broad in a white silk shirt and flowered skirt bought several summers ago had any authentic connection with the princely vessel he guarded? Honora had never caught on to the aristocratic vibes she gave off, and it shocked her when the man got politely to his feet.

"Yes, Mrs. Ivory," he said. "Go right aboard, ma'am."

Large wicker chairs were clustered in the shade of a noisily flapping cream and white striped awning that matched their upholstery. On a double chaise in direct sunlight lay a girl. She was stretched out on her stomach, the untied straps of her bikini coiling at her sides. Not raising her head, she called, "They're in the main saloon, right through there."

"Who . . . ?"

"Hey, aren't you one of the lawyers?"

"No, I'm . . . uhh . . . Honora Ivory."

The girl sat up, her large, slightly bulging eyes fixed unabashedly on Honora. Her tanned, pancake-shaped breasts with their large, brownish nipples were exposed, and unconcernedly she raised long, thin arms to tie her straps. An elongated, curving Nefertiti neck, a sparely fleshed face, a dominatingly large, lipstickless mouth. She was either beautiful or ugly—or maybe both. She couldn't be much more than twenty, yet there was a hard worldliness about her. Honora felt a powerful surge in her viscera. This, then, was Curt's latest mistress—no. Relationship was the current term.

"I'm Marva Leigh," the girl said, pausing as if for a reaction before going on to enlighten Honora. "I'm this month's *Vogue* cover." Her tone was that of a long-term acquaintance, a friend even.

Honora wondered whether the new mores dictated that

sharing somebody's husband was a tie that bound. Her own churning, outmoded jealousy disturbed her. "Oh yes, I saw it at the airport. With your hair pulled back like this you look entirely different."

Marva Leigh nodded. "Looking different's one of the tricks of the modeling trade. You're divorced, aren't you."

"Separated," Honora corrected, then felt impelled to add, "But it's been a lot of years."

"Yes, sure, Curt told me something or other. Listen, sorry about thinking you were a lawyer, but with this Washington shit they've been swarming aboard for days. I've counted fifty of 'em. The high command's in the saloon right now." She gestured toward the awning: a great curve of windows was coated with a substance that acted as a re-flector.

"Would you mind very much telling . . . uh . . . Curt, that I'm here?"

"He can see you." Marva Leigh was scrutinizing herself in a large round magnifying mirror. Poking her cheek out with her tongue, she frowned. "I adore the sun but it's a bitch on the skin."

". . . Would you mind?"

"You English have all the luck with complexions. Jesus, is that a wrinkle?" Marva Leigh thrust the mirror back in a terrycloth bag. The tendons on the inside of her emaciated thighs stood out like steel as she pushed to her feet. She was at least six feet tall, with broad shoulders, strong burnished knees. "Yeah, sure, Honora. I have to cream up anyway. I'll give him the word."

Her long, bare feet leaving milky prints that slowly faded from the highly varnished, lightwood deck, she pushed through double doors inset with Mondrian-patterned stained glass.

Wavelets lapped against the *Odyssey*. A gull, kept sta-tionary by a gust of wind, descended with owner's arro-gance to perch on the wire strung with lights.

Marva Leigh returned, face and arms gleaming, her streak of ankle-length white linen transforming her boni-ness to enviable chic.

"Curt says he's totally tied up," she said, her tone in-forming Honora of the fraudulence of the message.

Honora felt the blood rush to her face. Pride told her she ought to head for the *Odyssey*'s gangplank. She was, how-ever, imprisoned in her well-sprung wicker chair by psychological chains. *If he has that many lawyers, he must really need my help,* she thought. *Besides, how would I explain leaving to Joss? The truth is that I want to see him; I'm dying to see him.*

"Did he say how long it would be?"

"Look, suddenly he's in one of his moods. Personally, I'd take off and come back later."

"I'll wait," Honora said, her accent and anxiety making her sound remote.

"It's up to you, but he's going to make you sweat it." Resting a hand on her hip, Marva Leigh glanced at her reflection in the mirroring windows. "Don't say I didn't warn you."

Once again she went below.

Honora took out her novel, opening it at random. *Lucien's character made him attentive to first impressions and the most trivial incidents of this evening in society were to have a great effect on him. Like all inexperienced lovers, he arrived so early that Louise had not yet come into the drawing room.*

The words conveyed no meaning, and she did not turn the page. She had forgotten her watch and had no idea how long she waited, but the elderly crew member who had been guarding the gangplank changed places with a short, fat boy—also wearing an *Odyssey* sweatshirt.

Lucien's character made him attentive to . . .

Suddenly the modern glass doors swung open and Curt emerged with his chief lawyers. The soberly clad men made a foil for him, and with his white ducks, open white T-shirt and bare feet thrust into sandals, he looked vital, resiliently energetic.

Honora felt old, dowdy. Awkwardly she got to her feet.

"Hello, Curt," she whispered.

"Honora," he said brusquely, slicing his hand toward each of his legal staff as he named them. Though the five attorneys must have seen her through the coated windows, there was a suggestion of appraisal in their glances as they responded to the introductions with affable politeness.

"Mrs. Ivory, we've met." The shortest man stepped forward, shifting his briefcase so he could extend his right hand. About sixty, his frail, potbellied body in the rumpled dark jacket looked too slight to support his massive bald head. His grip, though, was strong. "Arthur Kohn."

She couldn't remember ever meeting Arthur Kohn, but

she knew him by reputation. He had clerked for Justice Brandeis, he presented important cases *pro bono* to the Supreme Court, he was the senior partner of the prestigious law firm that Curt used as outside counsel in Washington, D.C.

"Certainly, Mr. Kohn. How nice to see you again."

"We're very grateful you're here," he said. The eyes behind the glasses were warm yet speculative. "I'm not going to mince words, Mrs. Ivory. We're hoping you can be with us in Washington for a few days."

The breeze gusted, beating a drumroll on the awning. The lawyers watched her, Arthur Kohn's expressive mouth slightly open, as if he were a teacher encouraging a star pupil to come up with the correct answer.

Before she could respond, Curt said to her, "There you have it. Learned counsel, having no faith in my financial honesty, feel your presence is necessary at the hearings." He went to the rail and lounged against it, staring in the direction of the harbor's rocky entry, into which a freighter was easing.

Her voice came out of her high and stammering. "I'd . . . th-that's why I came back to the States. To help if I can. . . ." Honora couldn't take her eyes from Curt's back.

"We're deeply grateful," said Arthur Kohn, beaming with approbation. "I can't overestimate your importance at the hearing."

"I'm glad to be there, but, well, you're being kind. I'm not vital," Honora replied, still staring at Curt.

"We need as much sympathy as we can muster," said the stoutest lawyer, who bore a vague resemblance to Henry Kissinger.

"Will I have to do anything? I mean . . . testify?"

"No, just attend with us," said Arthur Kohn. "If I may, I'd like to set up a meeting with you in the next day or so."

"Certainly. I'm staying with my sister." She gave him Joscelyn's phone number. Arthur Kohn turned to the youngest member of the team, who took out a small leather book. She repeated the seven digits.

Without a goodbye to any of them, Curt strode inside, and Honora watched the flicker of stained glass as the doors swung in decreasing arcs.

The lawyers shook her hand again and filed off the *Odyssey*.

After a minute, Honora pushed *Lost Illusions* back in her raffia bag. As she followed the others down the gangplank, she was filled with conflicting emotions about Curt. Anger and pity that he felt compelled to behave so rudely toward her. The helpless attraction of a pin to a magnet. Unexpected shock that he had given in so easily—she could not recollect him ever succumbing to unwanted professional advice. *Is he more upset about Congress's probing than he lets on?*

60

A step or so before reaching terra firma, she halted irresolutely. The narrow, ridged boards creaked and shifted gently under her feet, a zephyr flipped a wisp of hair across her lips and she pushed it back absently. The lawyers, caucusing by a large blue car, were glancing circumspectly in her direction, and the pudgy young guard a few yards away peered at her over his wind-riffled *Playboy*.

She barged back up the gangplank precipitately, as if fearing she might change her mind.

In her momentum she took the step onto the deck too hard, a jolt that burned through her spinal column and cut like an excruciating wire down the sciatic nerves of her left hip. Cautiously in her heeled sandals she limped inside. The double doors flapped behind her and the fresh sea air gave way to the flat odor that permeates ships, no matter how luxurious. She could feel a faraway throb of engines—or was the vibration an echo of the drumming of her heart?

Ahead of her, a short flight of elegantly curving steps led upward. To her left was the main saloon.

The three sides of treated windows infused an evenly brilliant light which had the effect of making the space

appear yet more extravagant. The walls, following the
natural contours of the yacht, were covered with silk that
matched the thick white of the carpeting. The couches
and chairs, enormously deep and low slung, were uphol-
stered in white buckskin. The man-size, smoothly abstract
bronze statuary added to the impersonal, masculine sump-
tuousness.

Curt lounged in one of the chairs, sandals kicked off, his
bare feet outthrust, a tall drink in his hand. How could she
have forgotten this near feline quality of his, to seem
charged with energy even when absolutely still.

"Well, if it isn't Mrs. Ivory," he said. "Didn't I just see
you go ashore?"

"I need to talk to you," she murmured, biting her lip.

He stretched out his free hand, opening it as if to say,
You have the floor.

"It's about . . . well, I wanted to explain, to s-say . . ." *My
God, at my age, stammering,* she thought, and her face grew
hot.

He took a long sip, sitting there peering up at her with a
purposefully questioning expression.

"Ab-bout . . ."

"You must be waiting to hear my gratitude," he said.
"Okay, I'm deeply obligated for what you are about to do,
and forever in your debt."

"Don't be like this," she whispered.

"How?"

"S-sarcastic . . . m-mean."

"It's been so long that you must have forgotten," he said.
"You were ever the noble, generous soul in the Ivory family—even if you can't quite get the noble, generous words
out."

She was numbed with misery, not so much for herself as
for him. What had the years done to him that he, never
petty, was reduced to sneering at a minor physical defect?
"Curt, don't. Please don't."

"Don't what?"

"Why can't we talk?"

"Aren't we? Or have I lost the knack of conversing with
you?"

"That's what I mean."

"My learned counsel tell me for their fat fees that I need
a loyal helpmeet at my side when I appear in Washing-

ton—voluntarily, by the way—the story of my subpoena is
incorrect reporting. And you, the high-born UK gardener,
flesh of my flesh, have miraculously appeared. I gather
from your reaction, a simple thank you won't suffice. Now
what? Should I prostrate myself?"

A surge of emotion overcame Honora, and she, who so
seldom lost her temper, was carried by rage. "Do not speak
to me this way!" Her words emerged clear edged and frosty.
"I am not one of your women."

"Baby, you've made *that* abundantly clear," he said with
loud, hectoring sarcasm. "Now do me a favor and get the
hell off my boat."

Once, in a hospital room that smelled of antiseptic and
dying roses he had rubbed his unshaven cheek against hers
and promised to kill anybody who ever hurt her. What if
she called that promise now? Would he commit hari-kari
and get blood all over the white leather and carpet? She
emitted a discordant titter, then tears spurted from her
eyes. Appalled, she turned away from him. A witless move.
He must see how it was with her.

"Honora, sit down," he said in a flat, emotionless voice.

In her humiliation and misery, she pretended not to hear,
fishing in her purse for a Kleenex, dabbing at her eyes as
she headed for the entry.

"You're right," he said quietly. "If we're going to be together in Washington we better get the hostilities ironed
out. Stay a minute or two."

She halted. After estimating the logistics of lowering her
pain-stiffened spine into one of the low, monstrous chairs,
she perched on a high stool at the bronze bar, which curved
sleekly like the statues. Resting her forehead in her palm,
she struggled for control.

When the crying ceased she blew her nose and stared
down at her sodden wad of tissue, wishing disjointedly that
she had remembered to take off her wedding ring.

"How about a drink?" he asked in the same quiet tone.

"Aspirin."

"An Empirin Codeine be all right?"

"Perfect."

He moved behind the bar. She did not look directly at
him, but watched his hands, tanned and strong with beige
hairs tangling on the knuckles, as he shifted ice from the
small refrigerator and poured water at the sink.

He slid the tumbler across to her with a brown prescription phial. She tapped two capsules into her palm.

"They're sixty milligrams," he warned. "Strong stuff."

She nodded, downing both at once with several gulps of water. "My back's been acting up," she explained.

"And my head's been splitting."

"You still have migraines?"

"I have one right now," he said, touching his temple wryly. "Time was when I could take the legal gobbledy-gook in my stride, but not anymore." He poured himself another drink. "The only good thing I can see about getting old is that it beats the other choice."

She smiled.

"Now," he said. "Now, what were you trying to tell me before I drew blood?"

"I'm tired of all the hard feelings."

"I'm not trying to stick it to you again, Honora, but it has been pretty painful, communicating through Joscelyn."

"Better than through Marva Leigh," she said, managing to cover her jealousy with wit.

"Touché," he said. "God, I'd forgotten how you can come back like that."

"Anyway, I guess it was my own failings that made me take it so hard . . . you know, about Alexander." She had intended to further explain that she was ashamed of carrying her grudge so long, but mentioning her nephew alerted the demons that dwelt within her. She shifted her raffia purse in her lap. "Lissie sends her best love."

Curt looked up. "Is she with you?"

"She stayed with Vi. I didn't know what would happen, you know, the hearings. . . ." It wasn't only revelations that she feared. Lissie bore wounds enough from her natural parents' disaster and did not need to be ripped apart by the reverberations of inaudible bombs detonated by her adopted parents' quarrels.

"The last few visits," Curt said, "she's been different. Shy around everybody except me and Joss."

"She avoids talking to people she doesn't know really well."

"Her speech has come along fabulously."

"She's learned to listen quite well with the auditory trainer."

"I have one here, and we've used it," Curt said with a touch of pride.

"She never said a thing to me—but, Curt, she hardly ever mentions things connected to deafness."

"Hey, I figured she was like that with only me. I got a little professional advice about the pre-puberty stage in girls."

She leaned forward in the stool. "I did, too!" This was how she'd acquired for a client the child psychologist whose husband had chased her. "At that age most children question their deafness—Why me? But Lissie's keeping it locked inside. Maybe because of her early traumas."

They discussed their child in the worried, vying tone that separated parents assume. When Curt finished his scotch, Honora slipped from the barstool.

"I borrowed Joss's car," she said. "And I promised faithfully to have it back this afternoon."

Curt walked out on the deck with her. Close up, she saw the imprint of the years. His chestnut tan concealed new lines around his eyes, and deep creases now accommodated the uneven smile. The lightening of his hair was caused as much by the sprinkling of white as by the sun. He was examining her. Her spirits buoyed, she forgot to worry about the revelations strong California light would make on her. Her expression was unguarded and innocent.

He looked suddenly tired, sad. "Honora, this time I mean it," he said quietly. "I appreciate you showing up."

"Are you really sure the committee won't come down hard on you?"

"The one thing going for me is that I've got nothing to hide."

"I know that."

"That's the reason I volunteered to testify."

"It's so unfair to print that you had to be subpoenaed—"

"Ahh, screw them all. At least we're not enemies."

As Honora moved across the asphalt to the Corvette, she felt floaty as silk.

When she turned at the car, she saw Curt and Marva Leigh leaning on the bow rail. Marva Leigh raised her bare arm, a negligent, friendly wave that managed to be narcissistic, as if she were posing for *Vogue*. She rested the hand negligently on Curt's shoulder. Circling his companion's lean waist, he also saluted Honora.

She got in the Corvette. Now she felt drained and wooden. That floatiness, she informed herself, was the effect of the codeine.

* * *

She didn't hear from Curt, however Arthur Kohn took her to lunch at l'Ermitage. Glancing around the nearby booths and tables, which were filled with well-dressed people, he explained in a low voice that she would be protected insofar as possible from the media, and that she and her estranged husband would share a large suite at the Dolley Madison. "You'll have your own quarters, of course, a room, bath and dressing room that can be locked off."

She nodded.

"Mrs. Ivory," he said, his large head averted, "there's the question of clothes. Since they'll be specifically purchased for the hearings, Mr. Ivory wishes them to be charged to him."

"That's quite unnecessary."

"You're already being generous with your time—"

"Mr. Kohn," she interrupted, pushing away her fresh raspberries, "I do support myself."

"He said you'd be touchy."

"And I would feel happier if I weren't discussed behind my back."

"It's a most awkward situation, I appreciate that. But you'll be shopping with someone from my client's public relations firm, so he considers it a business expense. Afterward, you can give the wardrobe away to charity." He watched her, his head tilting and his lips parting in that tutorial expression.

"It's a stupid point to argue, I suppose," she said.

"If you weren't the type of lady that you are, your presence in Washington wouldn't be much use."

"Mr. Kohn, how long do you think this will last? I have my little girl in London, and my business." *But alas no clients.*

"I can't be certain. Surely though he'll be testifying more than once. Two days at the least, four at the most. But of course the committee meets on this coming Thursday, so if it's more than two days you'll be detained for the weekend—" He broke off as the waiter came over.

When Honora arrived back at the apartment Joscelyn's answering machine had recorded a message for her: the New York voice was so deep and raspy that Honora would have been hard put to ascertain its gender if the caller had not explained that she was Mrs. Rickleff, the distaff half of Mr. Ivory's West Coast public relations firm.

The following morning the PR woman—"Call me M.J.,"—took her to Patricia's, chain-smoking thin brown cigarillos while Honora tried on clothes. It had been years since she had bought herself any garment not on a sale rack, and she could not deny the pleasure of sitting in the large, thick-carpeted, mirrored dressing room while pleasant-faced Mrs. Horak, the owner who had waited on her in plusher days, personally carried in outfit after outfit. Yet Honora had been unable to stifle quivers of resentment. This was exactly how she had felt being outfitted for Edinthorpe. The rigidly structured designer clothes that M.J. approved with a raise of her cigarillo were a uniform that had nothing to do with Honora Ivory.

That evening, as she and Joscelyn shared a take-out mushroom pizza in the apartment, she explained her ambivalence.

"You realize don't you," Joscelyn said, "that Curt must be pretty shook to be accepting your help?"

"Of course I know that, Joss. I was trying to explain how *I* felt." She glanced toward the great mound of pale gray boxes adorned with a cerise *Patricia's* in cursive writing.

Joscelyn took another wedge, twisting off the strings of mozzarella. "Well, I'm talking about Curt. Ever since I've known him he's been flamboyant, extrovertish. None of this timid, gray, corporate sobriety. He's never run scared."

"Joss, he's about to have all of his financial and personal life unzipped. Naturally he has a few qualms." *Enough to leave Marva Leigh behind?*

"I thought maybe I'd come along and lend my support, too," Joscelyn said. "Is he staying at the Dolley Madison?"

"Yes—or is it the Madison?"

"The Dolley Madison's the fancy annex of the Madison."

"Oh."

"I'm sure it's a positive move for me to come," Joscelyn said defiantly.

"Absolutely, Joss. You can share my room."

Joscelyn nodded. Her pale blue eyes were not on her sister as she said, "He was at my trial every day."

"Joss, this isn't the same at all. He hasn't done anything. . . ."

"You're saying he's not a murderer?" Joscelyn crunched savagely down on the crust of her pizza. "When the Morrell Committee's finished with him murder'll seem like a minor felony."

EIGHT

1976

Honora, Crystal and Joscelyn

61

Their limousine was halted on Independence Avenue amid the traffic heading toward the Capitol. A vast, threatening umber cloud was covering the city, and office workers carried furled umbrellas while inappropriately light-clad tourists scurried into the castlelike, nineteenth-century red sandstone grotesquerie that was the original Smithsonian Museum.

The Morrell Subcommittee was to meet on the third floor of the Rayburn House Office Building: from this vantage point, a mile or so away, the marble and granite edifice, which had taken on the ominous brownish tones of the sky, seemed dwarfed by the Capitol, yet in actuality the Rayburn Building with its fifty acres of floor space on nine stories was far larger.

Honora glanced at Curt, who was sitting between Joscelyn and herself, a proximity both disturbing and exciting. His hands rested on his dark blue trousers. Then, abruptly, the left index finger rose up, the nail riffling on the immaculate crease. Instinctively she moved to take his hand to comfort him, then she recollected that touch no longer belonged in their vocabulary. Her impulse to murmur a reassurance was inhibited by a near photographic superimposure of Marva Leigh and him leaning entwined on the *Odyssey*'s bow. Natural responses blocked, she stared out the window, spotting a couple of fine old gingko trees and a pond cypress, which was exceedingly rare.

Joscelyn was frowning defiantly at the Capitol dome.

"Hey, ladies," Curt said. His hand was calm now, yet Honora could feel the emanations of his compressed energy. "Go into the hearing looking so grim, and the committee'll figure I'm guilty of more than a bit of grease."

"Grease?" Honora asked. They had been married enough years for her to be intimate with the term, but here was the means of diverting him.

"It's rather like manure in your business," he said.

Joscelyn leaned forward to enlighten Honora in the pedantic cadence of teacher's pet. "If you don't pay off the government clerks, nothing happens. Every corporation overseas has a slush fund to oil the wheels. The Congressional hearings before this have all accepted grease as a routine cost of doing business abroad."

The cars to their left had begun to move, but their line remained stalled.

"We could walk quicker than this," Curt said.

"I couldn't. Not in these beauties." Joscelyn arched her long foot in its elegant, stacked-heel pump.

"Curt, how do you pay the grease money?" Honora asked.

Again Joscelyn answered. "The easiest thing in the world. An intermediary, somebody from the country in question, handles it for you. Most governments demand you hire a native consultant, so you generally use him." She passed her tongue over her pale mouth. "When we were in Lalarhein, Khalid got us a consultant who was terrific at smearing."

"Khalid?" Curt asked.

"Fuad's nephew," Joscelyn said. "Khalid Abdulrahman."

"You've got me baffled," Curt said. "Khalid's never had any connection whatsoever with Ivory."

"He and Malcolm were buddy-buddy."

"I thought Khalid was totally anti-Western," Honora said. Sometime this past winter, maybe it was January, Khalid had been interviewed on the BBC. He had spent about ten minutes denigrating his British education, insisting that it was his years at Harrow and Oxford that had convinced him Islam must turn from Western decadence. His wandering eye had flashed sternly at the cameras when he'd argued that veiled, secluded females were infinitely happier, more secure and lived far more useful lives than their "liberated" Western counterparts. Clips of the program had appeared on the News, there was a to-do in the papers and Prince Khalid attained minor celebrityhood in the United Kingdom.

"Nowadays he certainly is," Curt said. "He refuses to show at any function where there's to be Westerners present—Fuad says Khalid gives him a rough time because he has American friends."

"Khalid always did have the lunatic fringe in love with

him," Joscelyn said. "But I never could figure what Malcolm saw in him. They were about the same age, that's all."

"Well, the consultant he suggested must've been A-okay," Curt said. "As I recall, Malcolm's pumping station finished ahead of schedule."

"By three months," said Joscelyn with sad pride.

The traffic knot loosened. They inched past the enormous grimy glass conservatory that was the Botanic Gardens and the Bartholdi Fountain with its surrounding flowerbeds, going under the Rayburn House Office Building into the gasoline-fumed garage. Their driver halted to let them off near the bank of elevators. A cluster of people waited, all of them wearing colored plastic name tags. The bulgingly fat cameraman with batteries attached to the back of his belt gave them a long, assessing look.

On the third floor more people stared. Honora paid attention to the corridor. The high ceilings gave no sense of grandeur, serving only to amplify the roar of voices and footsteps. Cheap wooden chairs were stacked in pairs outside a Congressman's office.

Arthur Kohn hurried around a corner, greeting them each with a handshake. He was accompanied by two of the partners whom Honora had met aboard the *Odyssey*. Joscelyn was introduced all around and the group fell in step behind Curt.

The media were waiting outside the chamber where the Morrell Subcommittee would meet. Ballpoints and notepads went into action, cumbersome minicams were maneuvered, microphones with call letters were thrust at Curt's face. Reporters shouted questions at him simultaneously.

"Mr. Ivory, what sort of inquiries do you expect?"

"Have you any comment on why you've been called?"

"Is it true that your company has the inside track in the Mideast?"

"Exactly how substantial are Ivory's payments in the Mideast?"

A mike was aimed at Honora's mouth. "Mrs. Ivory, will you comment on why Mr. Ivory has his home on a yacht while you live in London?"

"Mrs. Ivory isn't answering questions," Curt said, gripping Honora's arm.

At the warm strength of his fingers, she swayed spontaneously toward him, then wheeled away, pushing through the crowd. Immediately she realized her purpose in Washington was not to quiver and escape Curt's touch but to establish herself staunchly at his side. She halted in the doorway until he caught up.

In contrast with the behind-the-iron-curtain drabness of the elevators and corridors, the committee chamber showed a somber richness. Portraits of long-dead Speakers of the House gazed down from dark paneling, gold garlands were woven into the crimson carpeting, the looped-back red velvet draperies were fringed with gilt, yet even amid this luxury were incongruous touches of shabbiness—the thick, exposed wiring that tangled near the green-baize-covered witness table and the paper towels placed under each water pitcher.

The five long rows of chairs arranged for visitors were all taken while reporters and camera people bubbled around the pair of press tables at either side of the chamber. The solid curves of desk on the rostrum, however, remained empty. A quartet of aides chattered against the wall while a girl with long, dark blond hair—she looked very little older than Lissie—gravely snapped the subcommittee's names on wooden stands.

Arthur Kohn asked Honora to take the twelfth seat in the front row, which placed her directly behind the witness chair.

The subcommittee began to wander in, a stout, sixtyish woman with elaborately waved blond hair and heavy makeup, a stoop-shouldered man coughing into his palm, a wiry young man who nodded at Curt. The friendly gesture made Honora a bit more sanguine.

The hearing was set for 10:30. At exactly 10:42 the chairman appeared. Representative Jason Morrell was a tall, gray-haired Oregon Democrat who had been in the House for nearly forty years: his jutting jaw gave him a fortuitous resemblance to FDR, a resemblance that he enhanced by wearing small, gold-rimmed glasses and clamping his teeth on a cigarette holder.

Ignoring the cameras with histrionic aplomb, Morrell moved to the center of the rostrum. Two young aides bent over him, he shook his pewter head negatively, then nodded.

Looking around the chamber, including the press and visitors in his somber glance, he rapped his gavel.

"The subcommittee will be in order," he said—he had gone so far as to cultivate a patrician, eastern accent.

"During the past months, charges that American companies have engaged in extensive bribery of foreign public officials have been made and substantiated. The president of the Gulf Corporation has admitted making a three-million-dollar contribution to the last political campaign in the Republic of Korea ... the Northrop Corporation cannot account with accuracy sufficient to satisfy the Securities and Exchange Commission for a thirty-million-dollar fund established and used between 1971 and 1973 ... the Paloverde Oil Company consented to a Securities and Exchange Commission charge that the company had made secret payments totaling four million and a quarter out of corporate funds, overseas. ..."

Honora stared up at the chairman, outrage prickling on her skin. What right did this cheap presidential imitation have to indict Curt by association?

"... before the hearing begins, I wish to say that Ivory and Company is held wholly by Mr. Ivory, which puts him beyond the jurisdiction of the Securities and Exchange Commission, and no charges have been made against him by the Bureau of Internal Revenue. Mr. Ivory is appearing before this committee voluntarily."

"Swell of him to mention it," Joscelyn muttered from the corner of her mouth.

Morrell fitted a fresh cigarette in his holder. "I feel obligated to mention that the Criminal Code, title 18, section 1001, provides that whoever makes a false or fraudulent statement to an agency of the United States Government shall be subject to a ten thousand dollar fine, or imprisonment of not more than five years, or both." He delivered this message sternly, then his politician's smile settled into its creases. "On behalf of the committee, Mr. Ivory, I welcome you."

Cameramen jockeyed for better vantage points as Curt, Arthur Kohn at his side, moved to the witness table. Curt swung his briefcase onto the green baize directly in front of Honora: she could not see his face, but he crossed his ankle on his knee the casual way he did sitting at his desk at home.

Crystal lay on her bed, a mound of small, lacy cushions propping her head as she watched the Six O'Clock News on the Zenith that swung out from her armoire. In her sashed kimono, her bright hair concealed by a scarf, a concoction of her Zurich dermatologist thickly white on her face, she bore more than a passing resemblance to a Japanese Noh actor. Her beauty was being refreshed for an intimate dinner party she was giving. Mitchell and Alexander—he now lived in a bachelor pad on Nob Hill—would enjoy the masterful menu, then tactfully disappear, leaving her alone with Ben Hutchinson: the gruff-voiced grass-widower, head of the Onyx Motor Company, considered himself a beau of hers. Ben was a cautiously belligerent CEO and Crystal was aware that there would be no handshake over the coffee tonight with a go-ahead on the huge Onyx truck factory that was planned for Frankfort, but she was also aware that next month he would read Talbott's proposal with a positive eye.

The anchorman was announcing: ". . . And now we go to Washington for a report from our correspondent, Marcille Whalen."

Crystal's whitened face lifted from the pillows as an attractive young woman wearing a raincoat flashed onto the screen. "This is Marcille Whalen outside the Rayburn House Office Building where the Morrell House Subcommittee is investigating corrupt practices by American business in the Mideast. Curt Ivory was today's witness. Ivory, who heads the multibillion-dollar Ivory engineering and construction firm based in Los Angeles, was accompanied by his wife, here from London, and his sister-in-law, Joscelyn Sylvander, a vice president of his company."

Jumpy shots showed Honora and Joscelyn at Curt's side stonily pushing their way through a crowd of reporters.

"Ivory testified that he had given bribes."

Crystal stiffened as the shot of Curt behind microphones with Honora apparently leaning over his shoulder filled the screen. "Mr. Morrell," Curt said, "in certain countries it is the practice to give gratuities to ministry clerks—their governments aren't as generous as our own with their public servants."

Shot of audience laughing and Morrell rapping his gavel.

"Are you trying to tell this committee, Mr. Ivory, that bribery is practiced by *every* American in those countries?"

"A few tourists might get by without. But if you're conducting business, you'd be in trouble. For example, no building permit is processed without a small amount of cash changing hands."

"How much money do you consider 'small'?"

Close-up of Curt being whispered to by a bulbous-headed man. "My counsel has advised me not to answer," Curt said. "But usually around fifteen bucks."

More laughter. The screen filled with Honora, lips parted, dark, beautiful eyes gazing directly at the camera. Though gentle creases showed here and there, and the oval face seemed thinner, she did not look worn or old. This surprised Crystal. Daddy had said Honora had struggled since she'd left Curt, living in a grim slum with Joss's handicapped little girl, whom she'd adopted, and that coarse, redheaded waitress she'd known at Stroud's all those years ago. She supported herself as a gardener—yes, a gardener! With a surge of warm exasperation that belonged to her youth, Crystal wanted to reach into the color set and shake Honora out of her idiotic impracticality. She was right to leave Curt—staying with him all those years was her mistake—but why on earth hadn't she taken her rightful half of his fortune? And why was she with him in Washington, standing by him? *He must have begged her to,* Crystal thought. *Honora never could resist a cry for help.*

"Curt Ivory will continue his testimony tomorrow. If convicted he faces up to five years' imprisonment. This is Marcille Whalen on Capitol Hill—"

The door to the hall opened and Alexander came in, tieless but wearing dinner clothes. She leaped from the bed, rushing to the bathroom to throw tepid water at her face, scrubbing away the claylike mask. She could not bear to have anyone, especially Alexander, witness the support that her beauty now required.

Revealed, her smooth-pored skin glowed admirably. Rubbing in moisturizer, she returned to the bedroom, where Alexander was sliding the TV back into its recess.

"I didn't hear your car," she said pettishly. "You know dinner's not until eight."

"We need to talk." He closed the doors of the armoire. "On the local news there was a rehash of dear Aunt Joscelyn's misfortunes, and of dear Aunt Honora's peculiar marital situation. Tomorrow morning the papers will be full of it."

"I told you," she said uneasily, "I'm not sure starting this was smart."

"Granted, *he* won a few rounds today, but that's Morrell's routine strategy. He gives the witness enough rope."

Alexander ran his hand through his long blond hair and gave her an ingenuous grin. "Mom, the next step is for us to volunteer to testify."

She had pulled off her scarf. The chiffon wisp fluttered to her bare feet as she gaped at him.

"I never heard of anything so insane!" she cried.

"What's wrong with agreeing with Ivory on the small payola being essential? Everybody else has."

She sat next to him on the window seat. Beneath his cologne, she could detect a faint, hottish smell of excitement. "Alexander, you saw how he was roasted at the witness table?"

"Yes, I saw," he said.

"And you want that to happen to *me*?"

"There's no way we can be connected to anything substantial," Alexander said. "And if you're not up to taking the oath, they'll let me speak for you."

"There's no point even discussing this."

"Gid'll take a leave. We'll present ourselves. The gorgeous little widow who kept the family biz going, her two stalwart, upright sons, the freckled mother-to-be, the four of us reeking with hard work and honesty."

"We are not going to Washington." Her recently creamed hands were unaccountably cold.

"What are you afraid of?" he asked.

"Nothing," she said. But she was afraid. She knew that whoever sat at that green covered table could be stripped naked, be vulnerable to a world of enemies, known and unknown.

62

The following evening, Friday, Honora lay on the couch, head propped, knees bent, a hotel-silver sugar bowl and cream pitcher and a bowl of strawberries ranged on her stomach, her yellowing paperback resting against her thighs. First dipping the pored red tip in the thick cream, then twirling it in sugar, she popped the berry in her mouth, savoring it with a contented sigh.

This was the first time since her arrival in Washington that she had been granted solitude.

At night she had Joscelyn for a roommate. Across the darkness from the other bed flowed a stream of disparaging comments about Morrell and his colleagues, a know-it-all partisanship that baited Honora into defending her foes, Curt's harrying tormenters.

When Joscelyn finally shut up and Honora could sleep, she had orgiastic, embarrassing dreams that she could not dislodge from her memory, adolescent dreams that made it impossible for her to look Curt in the eye. On his part, he had addressed less than a dozen briefly impersonal remarks to her, this even though they had been together two and a half days for most of their waking hours.

Breakfast and dinner were sent up from room service and eaten at the large, reproduction Sheraton dining table with Marvin Callahan, top dog of Curt's PR company, who was in Washington to guide his prestigious client through the hearing, and with Arthur Kohn and two or more of his partners. The flack and the attorneys never deviated from the subject for which they were receiving their bloated fees: Curt and Honora and Joscelyn were instructed what to say and what not to say, when they should smile, even how to walk. Honora toyed with her food, concentrating on their advice. Much as she resented the image-making, she knew she needed the coaching. The face of Honora Ivory had become instantly recognizable. Bits of the hearings were shown on every channel's newsbreak, and there she was, eternally looming behind Curt's shoulder.

She had begun to share the primitive belief that the camera captures the soul. From the minute the limousine drove underneath the Rayburn House Office Building, the flashing Nikons and portable television cameras nibbled away until she felt there was no *her* left. The two days of hearings had degenerated into a rancorous exposé that went beyond political affiliation. Thursday had exhausted the subject of *dash,* as the Arabic world calls petty payoffs. Today, Friday, Curt had presented copies of the company's recent tax returns to the subcommittee. The Honorable Representative from Maryland (D) demanded an interpretation of Ivory Investment's cash flow, Congresswoman Hergesheimer (R) Iowa, was fascinated by deductions Curt had taken for business entertainments aboard the *Odyssey*, Morrell tapped his cigarette holder on the stacked papers, requesting explanations of depreciations until even a financial ignoramus like Honora could see that he was engaged in a fishing expedition.

Dipping another berry, she praised God for giving us Friday.

Over the weekend of course there would be no hearings: the PR man had returned to New York on an afternoon shuttle, Arthur Kohn had escaped to his farm in Delaware. Curt had told the limo's chauffeur to drop him at a Hertz rental agency, leaving Honora with the assumption that he was off to some luxurious private rendezvous with his bony model. Joscelyn, after showering and changing to hip huggers and a new white sweater, had said that she was off to visit her old Georgetown haunts—*her* face was seldom photographed and in a sports outfit and contact lenses she would be incognito. After her sister had left, Honora had expelled a long, trembling breath, like an invalid after a series of grueling medical tests.

The next day, while Lucien was lunching with Coralie, he heard in the quiet street below the brisk rattle of a cabriolet suggestive of an elegant carriage being drawn by a horse whose easy trot—

Without a warning tap, the front door of the suite opened.

Honora jerked involuntarily, swiveling to see who it was.

Curt, dangling the key by its metal tag, stared back at her in equal surprise. "The desk said you and Joscelyn went out."

"Only Joss."

The little jug had toppled and cream was soaking through her old Liberty blouse into her brassiere. She removed her ruined little supper from her torso, a fat strawberry rolling to lodge between her faded jeans and the couch pillow. Recovering it, she scrubbed the whitish patch on the upholstery with her napkin.

"Honora, leave it alone," he said.

"The cream'll stain."

"There's no need to make a major production. I'll pay for the cleaning."

"A little water'll do it," she said, starting for the bathroom.

"Will you for God's sake sit down and quit acting like a Mexican jumping bean?"

"I'm not."

"You've had the itch the entire time in Washington."

He knows about the dreams, she thought. Then told herself it was a sure sign of mental disorder to imagine that another person knows what transpires within your skull. "You're right, I have," she admitted, dropping the napkin. "You know me and my hermit streak."

"The fishbowl's gotten to you?"

"A bit." She shrugged. "Weren't you off for the weekend with Marva Leigh?"

"She has a session in Rome, some big layout for a French magazine," he said. "I drove the hell into Virginia."

"Virginia?"

"Birthplace of presidents," he said. "Now I'm starving. Was that your dinner I made you spill? Come on, you need a bite, too."

She pulled the wet blouse away from herself. A restaurant full of well-dressed Washingtonians ogling them?

"A sandwich or a burger," he said. "You're fine like that."

"What makes you so sure I'm coming?"

"That guilty look," he said, and grinned.

"Have another half," he said.

"I'm stuffed up to here." She touched her throat. "Curt, what on earth possessed you to buy six sandwiches?"

"Memories of a starving youth."

"Several times I've thought about that."

Taking a bite, he looked up at the red light blinking atop the Washington Monument.

Had she presumed too much by referring to a past that he never revealed publicly? She, too, peered at the honey-lit obelisk, which was twinned in the oily blackness of the reflecting pool.

They were sitting on the steps of the Lincoln Memorial, and a chill breeze came off the Tidal Basin. She wore her old, oversize fisherman's sweater, he a gray sweatshirt. The

Washington Post protected their jeans from the cold marble steps, and a large paper bag was open between them. The khaki-clad ranger leaning against one of the Memorial's columns behind them had not intervened, so she assumed it was okay to picnic here.

"I've had a few thoughts of my own," Curt said. "For example, that question about Marva Leigh?"

"It seemed obvious you'd be with her."

"Hmm?"

"It's hardly a secret that you've been getting laid."

"And you have, too?"

In an earlier age an honest response to his question would have crowned her with the virtues of chastity, modesty, self-control. In the final quarter of the twentieth century, though, the truth would make her suspect. Curt could easily believe she had developed lesbian tendencies (Vi?) or turned into a weirdo with onanistic fetishes, or—most shameful—her estrogen level had taken a premenopausal plummet. She gave him what she hoped was a worldly smile.

He peered at her, then said quietly, "Honora, one thing you should know. My major criterion for a female is that she not in any way remind me of you."

A crazy delight wriggled through her. She blew out her breath, and while the cloud evaporated in the floodlit night she cautioned herself that from the beginning Curt'd had a smooth line.

"So there's nobody current?" he asked.

"Talk about being pointed."

"Lissie's never mentioned any uncles," he said.

"So you've got me pegged as a dog?"

"No, not at all. I see you with some tweedy country type, veddy British, who's got you down to Kent to work miracles with the ancestral yews."

"Let us not forget the rhododendrons that Great-Grandpapa brought home from his Himalayan expedition."

They laughed.

"So tell me honestly. Was it only guilt that made you agree to dine *avec moi?*"

A couple was lumbering up the steps. The man, hearing Curt's voice, squinted down at them. His porcine young face pulled into knowing lines, and he put his arm around his girl's fake fur coat, drawing her toward them.

"Hey, you're Curt Ivory, aren't ya?"

Honora stiffened.

"So?" Curt replied.

"Sharp of me to recognize you in them clothes," the intruder said, adding in a confidential tone, "In my opinion you're getting the bum's rush."

"Maybe," Curt said brusquely.

"Let Morrell's crowd come up with something big, that's what I was saying to Shirl here. So you and Mrs. Ivory— Honora—are having a little moonlight picnic, except"—a humorless bray—"there ain't no moon."

Curt shoved their unopened Styrofoam cups back in the deli bag. "Let's have the coffee someplace else," he said, jogging down the steps.

She hurried after him, not catching up until they were behind the Memorial.

"The bastards," he growled. "They see you on TV and they think they own you."

"He was trying to be supportive."

"Supportive my ass. Honora, couldn't you see he was grandstanding for that fat bitch."

He strode in silence to their parking place by the grandiose gilded statues of winged horses given to the country by Italy. Gunning the engine, he dug onto the Rock Creek and Potomac Parkway. When they were passing below the overhang of the Kennedy Center she turned on the radio, switching until she found WGMS, the classical music station. After two solemn chords, she said, "Brahms."

"One."

"No, Three."

The full-bodied orchestra calmed her, and possibly soothed him, too. At any rate, he slowed to a legal speed as he drove through the rustic woods, turning off at Massachusetts Avenue.

Pale glints through the dark trees were the only sign of the well-set-back mansions—this was Washington's embassy row. He turned and turned again. Here there were no sidewalks and the darkness made the narrow road seem deep in the country. Parking on a shoulder overhung with unpruned box, he cut off the motor, turning the key so that the majestic music continued to roll over them.

"The coffee must be iced by now," he said.

"I didn't really want it anyway...."

Her words faded away because Curt had rested his arm on the back of her seat. A VW bus passed, shivering the warm car in its rush of air, and by the beam of headlights she saw his expression, watchful, waiting.

Honora, sweet, look at me.

I love you.

You are love.

That hadn't been a line, but when he'd said it she was nineteen, so maybe she *was* love.

His eyes glinted in the darkness. He was still watching her.

An unbearable tightness constricted her chest: she could hardly breathe yet the lower part of her body was loose and quivery. By some mysterious communion she accepted that Curt would never make the first move, her rejection at the Mamounia had been too all-encompassingly physical for that.

But what about her?

Maybe she was misreading his signal. Maybe all of those erotic dreams had befuddled her. What was sadder than a middle-aged woman making a pass at a man who prefers lolling amid young, gorgeous, firm flesh? Men wore the years with unfair lightness, and he, monstrously rich, in his attractive prime, could have the most beautiful women in the world—he *did* have them. Maybe her semi-ex-husband was hoping she would bring up the subject of divorce.

Rejection would do more than destroy her modest self-esteem. Rejection would annihilate her.

The long, Brahmsian chords had never pulsed more slowly.

"Curt . . ." Leaning forward, she pressed her cheek to his.

His irregular breathing sounded through her, echoing the thud of her heart. She pressed kisses near his ear, along his jaw, and was surprised by the salty wetness on his cheeks. The violence when their lips came together stunned her. Literally. She felt herself losing consciousness and clutched him as if he were a swimmer come to rescue her from the green depths of the ocean—yet she longed to drown in this kiss.

His tongue slid into her open mouth, and at its liquid caress the delicious, itching, wanting, tingling wetness rose through her vagina—empty, oh so empty lo these many years—dissolving the boundaries of her innermost womb, rousing some mysterious level of her being that had nothing yet everything to do with carnality. She reached for his erection, he whispered some wordless endearment. Either she pulled him down or he pressed her back or they were sinking together into the depths of the car seat. She crushed her belly to his, and the separating denim maddened her so she fumbled with her own zipper, squirming as she skinned the jeans and cotton underpants around her knees. Taking his hand, she guided it to the hot, slick wetness.

"Oh Christ . . . Honora . . . love . . ."

She caressed the tendons of his neck, reaching inside the sweatshirt to curve around his shoulders, the well-developed bicep muscles, his nipples. His fingers were rubbing her wet flesh tantalizingly. She unzipped his fly, encircling the hard silkiness of his naked penis, longing for a contortionist's agility to kiss it. Kicking off her pants, spine curved against the door, one foot on the floor of the car, the other lifted, she spread her thighs, helpless before the demanding, blinding approaching torrent that awaited her.

The instant he slid into her, she gasped aloud, a high, surprised cry. "Oh love, Curt . . . love . . . love. . . ."

They lay in the awkward position until their breathing calmed.

"Honora?" he said in her ear. "I haven't done it in a car since I was a kid."

"Thank God it wasn't bucket seats."

They both chuckled in the darkness.

"Your poor back," he said.

"I'm not a kid."

"Thank God for that." The Brahms had just reached the final movement as he shifted from her with a kiss. "I owe you one, so what's say we adjourn to the hotel."

"Somewhere else," she said. Her clenched tone came from beyond her volition. She wanted them back in the green, unknown sea without a past or a future—or a House subcommittee.

63

They drove like adolescents, he with his arm around her, she with her head on his shoulder, surrounded by the marshy smell of sex and the musical selections of WGMS—before they moved out of reception range, the ravishing first-act love duet from *Otello* brought stinging tears to her eyes. Curt turned off I-66 and they traveled on a deserted road, passing dark, scrubby woods marked with haunted names, Manassas, Bull Run. Unwilling to break the spell of their flight from the city, she did not ask where they were going. He turned right onto a graveled drive, braking in front of a trim fretwork sign: THE JEFFERSONIAN.

"I came past here this afternoon," Curt said. "It's one of those new hotel-condominium complexes around a golf course."

"Perfect," she said.

The elderly black desk clerk on late-night duty, apparently impervious to newsprint and TV, read the names Curt printed on the registration card without goggling.

"Nice to have you with us at the Jeffersonian, Mrs. Ivory, Mr. Ivory. You want privacy? Hmmm. . . . 914's vacant. Very quiet out there, if you don't mind a few ducks."

A fancifully antiqued map of the private roads was handed over, and the dark, wrinkled finger pointed the directions.

The three-room condo was lavishly yet not unpleasantly beruffled, everything in the same blue and white cotton. Curt unplugged the television and radio. Honora sat on the print bedspread calling Joscelyn, unsurprised when, after ten rings, the Ivory private line automatically switched to the hotel circuit. Leaving a message that she would be back sometime Sunday, she hung up, yawning and stretching. She was groggy. The engorged urgency of the parked car, the operatic romanticism of the drive had vanished, and from her solar plexus spread a warm, weary, near comradely contentment that Curt and she would soon be sharing this canopied double bed.

"Still sleep with the windows open?" Curt asked.

"Unless Lissie's sick." She covered her mouth for another yawn.

Between the cool, flowery sheets, he put his arms around her. "Zonked?"

"Totally."

"Me, too."

They kissed lightly and in less than five minutes were sleeping as they had their thousands of nights, she curled naked around his naked back, their legs entwined.

"Curt," she said.

He was jerking fitfully and muttering primitive, strangled sounds.

"Curt!" She prodded his shoulder.

He jerked awake. "Wha?"

"You were groaning."

The mattress shifted as he rolled over to face her.

"Nightmare?" She stroked his sweat-drenched hair.

"I've had 'em every night."

"This hearing!"

"No, this woman!" He rubbed his stubbled cheek against her shoulder. "Any idea how polite you've been?"

"I thought I was being biting."

"Polite," he repeated. "In a remote, *distingué* way."

"Flying six thousand miles to force myself on you isn't exactly a sign of indifference."

"In you, Honora, it could be construed as noblesse oblige."

"What was the nightmare about?"

"I have it often. We're at the Mamounia, and it's the lovely, purified and honorable English lady versus the vicious former Austrian guttersnipe grown into major-league SS gauleiter."

"Curt, I never once turned us into stereotypes."

"You asked what *I* was dreaming."

"But it's not fair."

"Since when've nightmares gone in for fair play?" he asked. "Or people, for that matter. Let's face it, love, when you showed up on the *Odyssey*, you can't deny I played the goose-stepping Nazi."

She kissed the coolness of his eye socket. "Mmm, nice."

His fingertip was tracing her collarbones. "I'd forgotten how much silkier your skin is."

Silkier than whose skin? She briefly conjured Marva Leigh—or rather a loony image of Marva Leigh at the head of a long line of shapely girls with crocodile hides. Curt's hand was moving down toward her breasts, and his light, subtle touch started a trembling that afflicted her like a form of paralysis. She could not move, yet her soul seemed to be flowing out in a stream toward his shoulders, his chest, his belly and thighs, his erection.

"Honora?"

"Ahh please, please, please."

The following morning they woke to the drumming of rain. Beyond the looped-back blue and white curtains of the bay window, they could see large drops dancing wildly on the grayness of a man-dredged pond. A half dozen white ducks and their yellow ducklings had clambered beyond the narrow rim of concrete to huddle under the azaleas.

After dressing, they drove through the deluge to a logo marked on the map as Cracker Barrel General Store. Small and brightly lit, its shelves were stocked mostly with exotic, high-priced jars and cans. From the gondola and refrigerator unit Honora selected wholewheat rolls, eggs, bacon, double lamb chops, Boston lettuce, and a "home baked" pecan pie that appeared to be fresh. Curt added Beluga caviar, odd-shaped cans of French pâté de foie gras, glass jars of cornichons, various types of imported crackers and cookies, six quarts of ice cream in various flavors.

"Curt, we're here for a weekend, not a month."

Patting her backside, he said, "You've forgotten my appetite."

He piled in a half dozen bottles of Mumm's, toothbrushes and the new Irwin Shaw novel for Honora.

She never opened the book. Logs were stacked outside the back door, tempting Curt to build a fire that crackled from the moisture.

She sat on the hooked rug, looking into the flames.

" 'What is love? 'Tis not hereafter,' " she recited. " 'Present mirth hath present laughter.' "

"You said it." He stretched out on the hooked rug, his head on her lap.

By lunch the rain had lightened, but it continued the rest of the day.

Sunday morning, though, was a beautiful May day. The sky was clear and the temperature brisk.

Perfect weather, they agreed, for a hike.

Setting out on the gravel road that circled the deserted golf course, they took an unpaved country lane, and soon rich red mud clotted the soles of her sneakers and his loafers. Crossing a one-lane wooden bridge, they came to the white fences of a stud farm. The horses looked like faraway toys grazing up the hill near the white barns. One of the thoroughbred brood mares had wandered down to the road, her carbon-dark colt frisking around her.

Honora picked her way across the scythed grass to the fence, holding out her hand toward the colt. "I wish I had some sugar for Black Beauty," she said. "Think he'll grow up to be a racehorse?"

"A Kentucky Derby winner at least."

"He belongs here, not running his heart out."

"We'll buy him." Curt came to stand next to her. "He'll be Lissie's welcome-home gift."

The breeze chilled the back of Honora's neck. The voluptuous atmosphere of this weekend struggled against the harsher world of reality. "She has her term to finish."

"It's not the end of Western civilization, love, if she misses a couple of weeks. The hearing can't run more than another day or so, then we'll fly over to get her."

"I have two jobs," Honora mumbled. When she had put in her London call Friday morning, Vi had told her excitedly that two of the prospects had telephoned to give the go-ahead.

"That doesn't sound like an insoluble problem. Didn't you start out with a partner? Why not draw up the plans over here and get her to carry them out?"

"I can't work like that. My best ideas come at the installation." She stared at the cavorting colt. "Curt, I suppose we do have to talk about this."

"By all means," he said. "Let's get it on the rug, our long-distance marriage."

"This isn't saying that I didn't miss you while I was in England—I thought I'd die. But there were parts of being on my own that were good. And my work was one of them."

"You're somehow the last woman I'd expect to man—or is it woman?—the barricades with Bella Abzug."

"Don't be snide."

"I didn't mean it that way. Hell, sure I did. You've always had this dreamy quality—that's what attracted me in the first place. I used to think I was protecting a fairy-tale princess."

"And I," she said unhappily, "always felt like a useless china figurine."

He gripped her arm. "Whatever my faults, Honora, I never put you down. I've always told you how much you mean to me. Before you I was hollow, a shell of ice with a terrified, starving kid rattling around inside. You turned me into a human being; you gave me the gift of myself. And this weekend haven't I made it clear how lost I've been without you?"

"This has nothing to do with you, Curt. It's *me*, how *I* feel. Can't you understand?"

"No."

"Think of it this way, then. We Sylvander girls are career-minded." She despised her dumb-little-me conciliatory lightness. "I'm not in Crystal and Joss's league, I'm strictly small time. But I can create gardens. People like my work. And working gives me a tremendous amount of satisfaction."

"I know I'm a money-soiled oaf, but I've always had a problem believing in that art for art's sake crap."

"A major part of the satisfaction is getting paid for what I do. Darling, I'm not saying this to hurt you, only to explain myself."

He picked up a pebble, hurling it over the white split-rail fence. The mare cantered away, the black colt racing gawkily after her.

"You're still holding Alexander against me, aren't you?"

Easy denials flooded to her lips, but the conversation had spawned a feverish need to bring him within the honest circle of her emotions. "I don't blame you, Curt, not anymore. But knowing Crystal had your child made me feel even more extraneous . . . it still does."

"So you're going back to England?"

"Curt, why won't you understand? This has nothing to do with him or with how much I love you—nothing can change my loving you. But you're in business. When you make a commitment you stand by it. Well, I've made a commitment—two commitments."

His pupils seemed to go flat. Her stomach plummeted and she had a sudden, terrifying conviction that his next words would inform her that she must make a choice. *He's going to tell me to pick—it's either love and marriage or my landscaping, my imbalanced checkbook, my shaky independence.*

Instead, he sighed wearily. "It's embarrassing how much I need you."

Weak-kneed with relief, she raised his hand and placed several kisses on his knuckles. "I don't know how to handle this, my work and being with you. The truth is I haven't been thinking at all this weekend."

"That's my wife," he said, either cheerful again or putting on a good act. "Heart is in the right place, below the navel."

"Pretty sure of yourself, aren't you?"

"Why not? You're blushing."

They joined hands, stretching out their arms as they circled either side of a large puddle.

"Thank you," she said.

"For what?"

"Not saying it."

"I don't understand."

"Oh, you could've said something along the lines that it's ridiculous for Mrs. Curt Ivory to occasionally double as a day laborer."

"If there's one thing the past years have taught me, Honora, it's that the accoutrements are my hang-up, not yours." He laughed and said, "So what the hell, we'll commute."

She laughed, too. "Your place or mine?"

"You're different, know that?"

"You've changed, too."

"Yes, but not for the better. And you've become an even more fabulous lady."

Sunday evening they sat on their condominium's curve of flagstone watching the setting sun set fire to the pond. The darkling sky was hung with a slender silver crescent.

"When we were children in England," she said, "we used to wish on a new moon."

"What are you asking for now?"

She smiled and said softly, "To stay here."

He went into the bedroom, and she heard him call the desk to arrange for another night's occupancy. Coming back outside, he said, "If we leave by seven tomorrow morning we'll be at the hotel in plenty of time to dress for the hearing."

They sat in companionable silence for a few minutes.

"Curt, have you seen Alexander?"

"I have only one child," he said. "Lissie."

"That's sophistry."

"I don't want any part of him," Curt said harshly. "He's a psychotic without a twinge of conscience. I've heard rumors about the bribes he dangles—what I've been accused of is along the lines of comparing a piss to the Atlantic Ocean. He seems to have maneuvered his brother—a very competent engineer—into a ten-year exile in New Guinea. He's a master at undermining a rival's credibility—and often does it just for kicks. He came to Marrakesh specifically to break us up."

"Yes. But, Curt, when he told me there was misery, genuine misery, in his voice."

Curt leaned back in the deck chair with a heavy sigh. And Honora knew the furies of that single drunken minute in a San Rafael garden a quarter of a century ago would pursue him through the hours and days of his life.

64

Friday evening Joscelyn had taken a cab to Wisconsin Avenue in Georgetown, to The Jazz Downstairs where the music was deafening and marvelous. She had discovered the basement nightclub when she'd worked on the Washington Metro, and it hadn't changed. Although many of the clientele came alone, it wasn't a place to get picked up, but to share the pleasures of top-notch jazz.

At a few minutes before three she returned to the hotel, exhilarated from the music and a trace high from her split of *vin blanc*. Unlocking the suite door, she stepped quietly into the large bedroom that she shared with Honora. A lamp shone on the neatly turned down beds, each with a green-foil-covered mint chocolate on the pillow.

Joscelyn huddled in the doorway, gawking in ludicrous disbelief at her sister's empty bed.

"Honora! Where are you? *Honora!*" she shouted, then held her hand over her mouth, aghast that she was so distraught as to be yelling in a hotel at three o'clock in the morning. A cursory search revealed the blouse that Honora had been wearing crumpled on the bathroom tiles beneath a towel and washcloth. The open tube of McClean's and a red toothbrush were on the sink counter, the stick deodorant and spray cologne were open. (Among Honora's endearing qualities was a meticulous personal cleanliness combined with reassuring messiness.)

Curt's bedroom opened onto the small foyer, and Joscelyn had passed it in semistoned cheer, but now she saw that the door was ajar. A midnight sepulcher would have been easier to peek into. After that one destructive rebuff she had avoided every questionably sexual area. *If he's in there maybe he'll figure I'm making another pass.*

Indecisively she tiptoed to the foyer. Deep inside Curt's room she could see the triangular gleam of the turned-down linen with the winking green eye of mint.

Of course he was out. He would've heard her yelling.

They're together, she thought. This realization was like plunging into a hidden crevasse. But why the shock? After all, wasn't she the *deus ex machina* who had reunited them? Why should she be experiencing a sense of betrayal because these two people, both of whom she loved, were so obviously in the sack together someplace?

The following morning she was awakened by the discreet buzz of the bedside telephone. There was enough light seeping through the interlined draperies to ascertain that Honora's bed remained empty.

"Joscelyn Sylvander," she said sleepily.

"Miss Sylvander, I'm calling from Mr. Kohn's office," said a feminine voice. "Is Mr. Ivory around?"

"I'm pretty sure he's not, but let me check." She padded to the other bedroom, picking up the extension in there. "Sorry. He's out."

"When'll he be back?"

"He didn't say. When he phones in shall I have him call Mr. Kohn?"

"Yes. Let me give you the number at his farm."

Joscelyn wrote it on the scratchpad and hung up, rubbing her eyes. *How dare they just split?* she thought angrily. *All right, they don't give a damn about me, but what if something comes up about Lissie?*

It was then, finally, that she noticed the glowing red message button. She called down and was given Honora's message.

Around noon Arthur Kohn called himself. Joscelyn explained that Curt was incommunicado for the weekend.

"The whole weekend?" The lawyer's voice crackled.

"I'm sorry. Can I take a message?"

"No, it's a confidential matter that I need to discuss with him. You have my number here at the farm, don't you? Ask him to give me a ring whenever he gets in—no matter what time it is."

Obviously something big and nasty had hit the fan.

Joscelyn's Saturday and Sunday passed in a haze of stale tobacco smoke—she had quit cigarettes cold turkey several years earlier, and her relapse gave her another ground for fury at the absentees. Her back itched, and by Sunday night, when Arthur Kohn called again, the area between her shoulders was scratched raw.

It was after nine on Monday morning when the key sounded in the lock.

Seeing Honora's dark, sparkling eyes and flushed cheeks, Curt's resplendent grin, Joscelyn was crushed between conflicting emotions, but she ached to protect them from whatever perils Arthur Kohn was so anxious to discuss.

She glowered at her sister. "Where've you been?"

"In Virginia—" Honora started.

"You said you'd be back Sunday. You didn't leave any number!"

"Joscelyn." Curt crossed the room to jab off the bright, blabbering television. "This might come as a shock to you, but we don't need your permission to take off."

"Is it Lissie?" Honora asked anxiously.

"If it were, would I be here?" Joscelyn snapped. "It's Arthur Kohn. Curt, he's been trying to get you since Saturday morning."

The tension lines showed around Curt's deep-set eyes. "What's with Arthur?"

"How should I know? It's nothing he'd tell *me.*"

Curt was already dialing.

"Oh, and by the way," Joscelyn said. "The hearing's been postponed until two thirty."

Arthur Kohn's secretary told Curt that Mr. Kohn was away at a meeting, but that he would be at the hearing this afternoon—had anyone given him the message that the hearing would be at two thirty?

They got to the committee room a half hour early. Arthur Kohn was already waiting: the worried way his shoulders were hunched made his head seem yet larger. He and his partners drew Curt into the men's room, the only place they could talk alone, without the press people.

Honora and Joscelyn took their seats in the committee chamber. Honora stared up at the portrait of a goateed, long-dead Speaker. The PR man had stressed that camera crews had a penchant for photographing anxious hands, so she hid her whitened, clenched knuckles under her new scarf.

When Curt came to sit next to her, he whispered into her ear, "Something's up, but Arthur's not sure what. He warned me to go over in my own mind and be ready for anything about Lalarhein that could be incriminating."

Honora, positive that her expression blazed with alarm, smiled.

Before this, the subcommittee had straggled in through various entries: today, at precisely two thirty, they filed in from the anteroom together.

Morrell clenched his cigarette holder with his teeth as he rapped his gavel for silence. "The Committee will be in order. Today we have two new witnesses. Mr. Harold Fish and Lieutenant General Donald Tardikian. Mr. Ivory, we are firm in our belief that your cooperation will continue to be given freely and fully."

Curt, taking this to mean he was to return to the witness table, pushed up from his chair.

Morrell let the jockeying cameramen record this rise before saying in orotund tones, "Let us start with General Tardikian."

The general read a letter on behalf of the Secretary of Defense: the Department had no authority to reveal information in the security classification having to do with United States military assistance.

Morrell called the next witness. Thrusting his pink, Rooseveltian jaw forward, he said into the microphone, "Mr. Harold Fish."

Everyone peered around. A guard descended the few steps to the left of the tiered rostrum, knocking at the anteroom door. It opened. A pair of gray-suited men came up the steps, casing the hearing chamber as if antennae were affixed to their foreheads. After a half minute one turned toward the door.

Harold Fish waddled up the steps.

His swollen body was contained by a navy pin-striped suit nipped in at the waist; his jaw and fat cheeks had the bluish, powdery look imparted by a professional barber's ministrations on a heavy beard; he might have been typecast for the role of prosperous mobster.

Joscelyn felt the breathless disorientation of being suddenly lifted by a great hand from this two-story hearing room on the third floor of the Rayburn House Office Building on Capitol Hill and deposited in a limbo where time and place lost meaning. Was she in 1976 Washington or 1965 Lalarhein? Was she a miserably bored, sometimes abused, sometimes cherished wife of a young engineer living in a prefab on the edge of the desert, or was she a vice president of a multinational company come to offer her support to her brother-in-law the boss? Was this Harold Fish or skinny Harb Fawzi with a naked pistol thrust into a double-wound belt?

As Harold Fish approached the witness chair he glanced at Joscelyn. Indisputably he was Harb Fawzi. She could not catch her breath, and without realizing what she was doing she tugged open the tie of her suit blouse.

"What is it, Joss?" Honora murmured.

"I knew him in Lalarhein," Joscelyn whispered in a choked undertone. "Only his name wasn't Harold Fish then. It was Harb Fawzi. He worked for Khalid, he was Khalid's guard and chauffeur. He always came to the house with Khalid."

Honora's serene expression didn't falter, but Joscelyn could feel her arm tremble.

"First of all, Mr. Fish," Morrell intoned, "we thank you for being here. As you know, this committee is engaged in gathering information that will help us, on behalf of the public of the United States of America, and on behalf of morality and justice, to promulgate certain regulations for the conduct of American businesses in other countries. Mr. Ivory has been hesitant to give certain information about his multinational operation." A lift of Morrell's chin, a flash of smile. "That of course is understandable. And there is no legal obligation for him to place his company in a position of jeopardy."

Curt's brows drew together and one network's camera caught his anger.

"Mr. Fish," Morrell continued, "would you please explain to the committee what your work was in your own country?"

"Honorable sirs and lady, I am in the process of becoming a citizen of the United States. In my *former* country, I was employed as a guard." Fish/Fawzi's heavily accented voice emerged with a sinuous slowness, as if a rope were being unwound from within his stout chest.

Had he always spoken in this peculiar monotone? Joscelyn couldn't remember him opening his mouth. Her image of him was silently searching the house, then sitting at the door, Khalid's lean and hungry hound.

"Will you please tell this committee the name of your former employer?"

"I have already explained to the chairman, honorable sir, that it would be most dangerous to give that information. Indeed, my presence here places me in grave peril, and I appear only because of my duty to my new country."

"We are most grateful." Morrell leaned back in his large, comfortable black leather chair, tapping off an ash. "Mr. Fish, will you please tell the committee your employer's function for Ivory?"

"His services were as liaison between Ivory and the Lalarheini government. He advised Ivory in preparing proposals and explained these proposals to certain ministers."

"Would you please explain that second duty more fully?" Hergesheimer asked.

"Certainly, honorable lady. It is impossible to be knowledgeable about every part of a three-hundred-million-dollar airport with electronic equipment capable of handling aircraft of a very sophisticated nature, and therefore the particular ministers my employer contacted relied totally on what he told them."

"By sophisticated aircraft do you mean bombers?"

"Certainly bombers. And missiles and antimissile devices."

"Were these of American make?"

"Absolutely. And much of the millions for the Daralam Airport came in the form of military aid from the United States."

"To secure this contract did Ivory International make any payments to their Lalarheini consultant above his regular fees?"

"Yes, honorable sir. He received large sums that he passed on to the government ministers."

Curt shook off Arthur Kohn's restraining, long-fingered white hand, jumping to his feet. "That's a lie! The Ivory representative in Lalarhein was and is Prince Fuad Abdulrahman, an American-trained engineer. He received only the routine payment for his services. And nothing above that!"

"Mr. Ivory," Morrell chided.

"Will I have a chance to question this witness?"

"Mr. Ivory, let me reassure you that you aren't on trial."

"The hell I'm not! And I don't care to be perjured or have my friends perjured."

"Mr. Ivory, perjury is a strong word," Morrell said.

"Not strong enough. The general told us Defense refuses to testify. So you're going to rely on what this lying slime tells you."

"It's the committee's task to sift through the evidence," Morrell said. "Mr. Fish, you have made a most serious charge. I trust that you have brought adequate documentation to back it up?"

"I have, in the specific case of the airport." Fish's plump fingers played with the gaudy lock of his new briefcase, and the lid sprang up. "These are copies of receipts that my employer wrote to Ivory International." He took out a sheaf of clipped-together Xeroxes. "Shall I read them?"

Mrs. Hergesheimer said, "Please do."

" 'I have duly received the one hundred thousand cans of peanuts—' "

"Peanuts?"

"It was code for dollars," Fish retorted.

"Please continue."

"Plus a landscape by a French painter called Sisley."

Joscelyn was gulping now, forcing air into the passages to her lungs. That cold winter morning in the Place de la Concorde; she and Malcolm admiring the single exhibit in the exclusive gallery's window, then going inside to ask the price. It had seemed one of the games that lovers play in Paris. But it hadn't been.

Malcolm, oh, Malcolm, those boyish, clubby hints of your work on the airport contract turned out to be true. But you only wanted Curt to think you were a great guy, a real genius, not to destroy him.

"Here are other receipts." Fish held up typed sheets. "They add up to more than five hundred thousand dollars, and are dated in the same week of April 1965, a few months previous to the Lalarheini government's approval of the Ivory designs for the airport."

"Mr. Fish," said Morrell benignly, "we have only your word for the documents' authenticity."

Fish said, "Mr. Ivory's late brother-in-law, Mr. Malcolm Peck, wrote from Paris to my employer suggesting the French painting as a gift to one of the ministers."

The exertion of breathing made Joscelyn's blouse cling to her back, which had begun to itch again. Where had the money come from to buy Impressionists, to make payoffs? *The profit center,* she thought. Yes, the profit center had operated independently, with its own payroll. Malcolm, as project manager, had complete charge of everything, including the cash flow. Khalid, even then considered by some of the fellahin to be the voice of the Prophet, must have convinced his followers to take jobs at very low wages so Malcolm would have large sums left over.

"Mr. Peck's widow is here," said Morrell. "Possibly she will verify the signature."

"Leave her the hell alone," Curt growled, again on his feet.

"Mr. Ivory, if you interrupt the proceedings again, you'll be held in contempt of Congress. Mrs. Peck?"

"Miss Sylvander. I had it legally changed back." Joscelyn's words without amplification trickled out thin and high.

Cameramen edged forward, crouching and kneeling to

focus on Joscelyn. Sinking into wood still warm from Fish's fat rump, she felt exposed, ugly and helpless. How had Curt borne this hour after hour?

"Miss Sylvander, will you examine the letter in question?" asked Congresswoman Hergesheimer after Joscelyn was shown in.

Joscelyn glanced at the yellowing, crumpled sheet, shivering as if her husband's dead hand were touching her as she scanned the large, childish scrawl: *Do you think that X5 would respond to a small Sisley? If not, I'll keep looking.*

"Can you tell the committee if this is your late husband's handwriting?" Again it was Hergesheimer.

"I'm an engineer, not a handwriting expert," Joscelyn retorted, glaring not at the committee but at the elderly Congressional Recorder, who was clicking away to the left of the witness table.

"We appreciate that, Mrs. Peck—"

"Miss Sylvander," Joscelyn corrected.

"I'm sorry, Miss Sylvander. The Committee realizes the evidence cannot be conclusive. Does the signature *appear* to be your late husband's?"

"It has been many years." Her voice shook. "I cannot say."

"Thank you for your cooperation."

Joscelyn had no idea how she got back to her seat. She did not hear Harold Fish say he had met Miss Sylvander, at that time Mrs. Peck, numerous times at her home in Lalarhein.

65

CBS and CNN televised Tuesday's hearing in its entirety: ABC was running promo for a two-hour Sunday Special: "Northrop, Lockheed, Paloverde Oil and Ivory: the Overseas Scandals." Lalarhein, last week unknown to nine hundred and ninety-nine Americans out of a thousand—and to the remaining soul a splotch on the map of the Persian Gulf—was suddenly a household word. *Time* ran a story on the Abdulrahman "dynasty." *Two leaders have emerged. Prince Fuad, a Berkeley-trained engineer, intimate of Curt Ivory, is a pro-American liberal interested in educating his people. His nephew, Prince Khalid, is the* éminence grise *of the militaristic, Islamic fundamentalist radical wing.*

Security was tightened. Guards patrolled the corridors and garage of the Rayburn Building: the entering swarms passed through metal detectors while Capitol police opened purses and briefcases. Lines formed outside the third-floor chamber where the Morrell Subcommittee met.

Wednesday morning, Fish again occupied the witness seat, opening his pristine briefcase to produce a photocopied receipt proving that Malcolm had paid for a safe deposit box in the Bank of Lalarhein.

"It was a 'black account,' " he explained in his accented monotone. "That is the name given to a strongbox for money that is handed out without record."

"Are you saying that the box was for corporate rather than private use?" inquired Congressman Hiroshi Kodama, Hawaii.

"That is exactly right, honored sir."

"Then Mr. Ivory had knowledge of this box?" asked Kodama.

"I cannot say for certain, honored sir, however it *was* for company business."

"Can you give us an idea of how much cash was kept in this, uhh, black account?"

"Sometimes in excess of fifty thousand dollars, but never more than a hundred thousand. I heard Mr. Peck explain to my employer that more than a hundred thousand would be detected by tax auditors."

"Mr. Ivory," Morrell stared at Curt. "The committee would like to hear from you again."

Arthur Kohn whispered, Curt shook his head decisively, moving to the witness table.

"Can you enlighten us about this so-called black account?" asked Congresswoman Hergesheimer.

"I have no knowledge of it," Curt said in a clear, firm voice.

"Then you are reluctant to provide us with information about your slush funds," Hergesheimer persisted.

"Any further information I give you, Mrs. Hergesheimer, would be bleeped on television."

Laughter.

Hergesheimer had the last word. "I can certainly understand your reluctance," she said. "The committee will subpoena the books in question."

As the morning wore on, Joscelyn's left eyelid began to twitch and her attempts to conquer the agitated muscle resulted in a sneerlike grimace that would show on a hundred million television screens. She had suffered a metamorphosis from Mrs.-Ivory's-sister-Miss-Joscelyn-Sylvander-also-at-the-hearing to Mrs.-Joscelyn-Peck-the-widow-of-the-man-who-administered-the-Ivory-slush-fund. Her impolitic slurs against Fish and members of the subcommittee made the front pages, a prematurely gray young woman on the CBS team was assigned specifically to her, the old manslaughter case was disinterred from newspaper morgues.

At eleven thirty-five the clock's second light went on: a recorded vote was being called for on the floor of the House.

Morrell rapped his gavel. "The subcommittee will recess and reconvene at two thirty."

At the noon break they had been invited to use the private Congressional antechambers. Arthur Kohn and his partners had a lunch appointment with another client, as did the two PR men. A breezy young Congressional aide provided them with sandwiches from the cafeteria downstairs and coffee was available from an aluminum urn.

Curt took his paper plate to the large green wing chair, sitting with his ankle crossed over his knee, a relaxed pose belied by his hasty gulping of codeine before he ate.

Honora left her sandwich untasted, wandering to a window. Fish's ugly, droning revelations, the subcommittee's poison-tipped questions, the fetid, smoky air of the hearing room had taken away her appetite. Yet at this minute she was feeling a tentative happiness. Since she had arrived back at the hotel on Monday, her moods had swung up and down, a teeter-totter between joyous relief that she and Curt were back together and terror about her husband's future. (*There's a distinct possibility that Mr. Ivory could face a perjury trial,* Arthur Kohn had said, leaving unspoken the corollary that a jail term might ensue.)

Against the mild blue sky, the Capitol dome was an antique lace bell. Groups strolled on the Hill, fading in and out of dark pools of shade cast by brown-black copper beeches, tall ash, willow oak, ancient sycamore.

She said wistfully, "Even without the cherry blossoms, the trees on the Hill are spectacular."

Curt came to stand next to her. "Let's go take a look."

"Sounds heaven," she said. "But it'll be us and the camera crews."

"Five'll get you ten that our buddies are lunching at the nearest bar. We've set a pattern, skulking in here."

"I for one could use some air," Joscelyn said, depositing her now cold hamburger in a metal wastebasket.

Honora's smile at her sister was masked: she was abandoning her brief vision of an overage Romeo and Juliet wandering hand in hand, alone.

As the trio waited at the Independence Avenue crosswalk, a reporter from the *Denver Post* charged up Capitol Hill in their direction, then halted, shrugging her thick shoulders as if to say: *Enjoy the sunshine.*

All four Talbotts slept in.

Gid and Anne's flight from New Guinea had arrived hours late in San Francisco yesterday, and the family— with Mitchell and Anina—had flown in the company Boeing 727 to Washington, arriving well after midnight at the spankingly trim red brick house in Georgetown.

Alexander rose the latest. It was noon when he jogged down the fanlit staircase. While he decapitated his three-and-three-quarter-minute coddled eggs, the others freshened their coffee, and Anne, smiling and patting the bulge of her pregnancy, helped herself to another pecan schnecke.

"Hey, Alexander," Gid said. "We await final instructions." Their "surprise" visit to the Morrell Subcommittee was planned for this afternoon.

"No changes from what I outlined on the plane. The four of us arrive; Morrell calls me right away. You watch while I wave Old Glory. Then we depart."

"And that encourages business?" Gid asked. "I don't see it."

Crystal set down her Haviland cup carefully in its saucer. She had argued this identical point with Alexander until she was shouting red-faced: *Don't you hear one word? No earthly good can come of this idiotic appearance—and it could so easily rebound on us. Think of the damage, Alexander, think of the damage!* Alexander, as usual, had been able to erode her tenaciousness, but this morning her hands were as tremulous as Langley's had been after a binge.

Alexander salted a spoonful of egg. "At this worldwide media event, prospective clients will learn that dealings with Talbott's are on the up and up, they will learn that our company never will be Congressionally scrutinized, they therefore will entrust us with their major projects."

"Yeah, well, I suppose that puts us ahead of Ivory," Gid said dubiously.

"To demonstrate our corporate honesty, I plan to offer the committee our books."

This was news to Crystal. She could hardly argue whether he was jeopardizing the buried Swiss accounts in front of Gid, his upright father's son. She moved to the mantelpiece, shifting one of the pair of Revere bowls.

"Anybody watch this morning?" Alexander inquired.

The smooth silver bowl slipped in Crystal's hands and she nearly dropped it. The television in her bedroom had been tuned to CBS as she dressed. She had not focused on the fat, greasy Arab, she had ignored the shots of the subcommittee, the close-ups of her enemy, Curt Ivory. Mesmerized, she had waited for glimpses of those two middle-aged women that her sisters had been transformed into. *When Honora has that aloof look it means she's dying inside,* Crystal had thought. *Joscelyn's scowling—she was a mean, tough little girl, always hiding her hurts under nastiness.*

"We didn't," Gid replied. "Listen, there's a couple of hours before we go to the hearing. What say we show Anne a few of the sights?" This was Anne's first visit to Washington.

"This is hardly the time to play tourists," Crystal snapped.

"Where's your spirit, Mom?" Alexander asked, slipping on his dark glasses. "How can we let the kid be born ignorant of our national heritage?"

Anne laughed. "The embryo might consider lunch at the White House prenatal influence enough." The Fords had issued an invitation for tomorrow, Thursday.

"A humbler embryo, maybe," Alexander said. "But never one with Alexander the Great for an uncle."

"Sometimes," Anne said, "I have to pinch myself to believe this family."

Curt in the middle, they strolled beside the Reflecting Pond.

"I should've mentioned Malcolm and Khalid to you, Curt," Joscelyn said, and not for the first time. "I would've, except the whole friendship seemed so unimportant—and dumb. The James Bond way that Fawzi—Fish—cased the joint, then sat guard!"

"There was no way for you to guess what they were up to," Curt said.

"I *was* aware Khalid was very hot for Lalarhein to have a big new airport; he said right in front of me that he wanted the country to have a huge, modern, military installation. And Malcolm was dying to get the contract for you. Poor sweetie, he always wanted you to see him in a good light, and I'm positive he arranged this whole mess so some day he could walk in and surprise you with the information *he* was behind Ivory's getting the contract for the Daralam Airport."

"Joss," Curt said, "there's no point beating yourself."

"I should've caught on," Joscelyn persisted. "The friendship always seemed a bit off kilter. I should've put two and two together and come up with the right answer—that Khalid was using Malcolm for his own ends." Joscelyn's *mea culpas* raced out in an unnerving squeak.

Honora fixed her professional attention on the small banana palms adorning the Capitol's balustrade.

She noticed the young man standing on the balustrade because he was exceptionally tall and elegantly clad, different from the sloppily dressed, overweight tourists moving about him. The breeze ruffled his fair hair around his dark glasses and flapped his charcoal suit jacket.

A millisecond later she thought, *My God, it's Alexander!*

Alexander was pointing out an ornamental ironwork lamppost to a very pregnant redhead who held hands with a shorter, more stockily built young man.

The girl moved. Honora emitted a harsh little grunt as she saw Crystal.

"Honora?" Curt's fingers circled her wrist.

Honora opened her mouth, but no sound came.

The other two followed her gaze.

Curt's fingertips dug convulsively into Honora's pulse. "Oh, Christ, I should've known."

Crystal had turned.

As she and Honora gazed at one another through the soft, yellow sunlight time collapsed and they were once again little English girls in lumpy navy tunics, the dark, dreamy elder sister, the shrewd and lovely younger, clinging together on a narrow dormitory bed, weeping at their half-orphaned state. They were again those innocent selves who could share grief and battle intruders who might laugh at their tears. They were the Sylvander girls.

Pulling from Curt's grasp, Honora ran toward the Capitol's marble stairs.

She met Crystal, halting on the step below her so they were the same height. Panting slightly, they stared at one another. Honora held out her arms. Their hug was charged with unequivocal, childlike love.

Pressing her face to Crystal's warm, perfumed cheek, Honora whispered, "Oh Crystal, Crys. . . . How I've missed you."

"Me you."

Joscelyn had followed Honora up the steps, and now she reached her lanky arms around both her sisters. She was confounded by the electrifying charge of affection for Crystal, cruel tormentor, the envied beauty of the family. Who would have predicted that she, Joscelyn Sylvander, would fall victim to this tribal sentimentality?

Crystal pulled away, her large blue eyes misty. "You're both so much younger than you look on television—but Joss, you are letting yourself go gray."

A prickle of irritation adulterated Joscelyn's pleasure in the reunion. "You're the one," she said with a hint of her old truculence, "who's about to be a granny."

Crystal tossed her bright, exquisitely coiffed head, a gesture reminiscent of her childhood tantrums, but she was smiling. "Isn't it wonderful?" she said sweetly, waving to her family to come.

While Gid matched his pace to the slow off-balance gait of his heavily pregnant wife, Alexander jogged lightly down to them.

"Hello, Aunt Honora, how great to see you again."

Honora's face burned and she could not look into the dark glasses. Did he sleep in them? Did he glue them to his face to hide Curt's eyes from himself? "And you, too, Alexander."

"Is this rubbing salt in wounds? You've been a class act on the tube."

She smiled stiffly. "What brings all of you to Washington?"

"A Presidential invitation," he replied before Crystal could speak. "How's my little coz?"

"Not so little anymore; she's almost five feet," Honora said. "She still talks about you."

"As gorgeous as ever?"

"*I* think so. Joss, let me introduce our nephew. Alexander, this is your Aunt Joscelyn."

"Joscelyn Sylvander, the famous lady engineer, all right!" he said, his enthusiasm perfect, not the least overdone.

Gid and Anne had approached and were waiting behind Crystal—a minor display of solidarity that touched Honora although their familial loyalty was directed against her.

After the introductions, Gid said with guarded courtesy, "It's good to finally meet you, Aunt Honora, Aunt Joscelyn."

As the stilted family greetings made the rounds, Honora glanced down at Curt. He had not moved from the edge of the Reflecting Pond, and was watching them with his usual air of casually leashed energy, but to her he seemed stiff, stonelike, as though an invisible but weighty burden had descended on his shoulders.

66

As they returned through the Capitol gardens, Honora and Joscelyn, both shaken by the meeting, talked rapidly. Honora said that Anne seemed like a terrific person, warm, intelligent, and Joscelyn agreed, pointing out that she limped, a charge Honora denied—"It's being pregnant"—but they concurred on the freckles. Joscelyn grudged that Gid seemed a very decent young man, but didn't Honora think that Crystal's beauty was a bit jelled—you know, as if she'd had work done on her face?

Neither mentioned Alexander.

Curt walked in silence a step ahead. With a long stride, Honora caught up, reaching for his hand: her clasp lacked the pressure of palms, there were no pornographic second-honeymoon vibrations. Her linkage of fingers comforted silently.

"What are they doing here?" he asked.

"A White House invitation, they said."

"I wasn't surprised to see him," Curt said.

"Alexander?" Honora said. "That doesn't make any sense."

"All along I've had a nagging sensation that he's somehow got a hand in this mess."

"Aren't you being a shade paranoid?" Joscelyn asked.

Curt shrugged. "Haven't you wondered how Morrell connected with Fish?"

"Morrell explained that to the press, Curt," Honora said. "Fish presented himself to the committee."

"As his patriotic duty to his new land," Joscelyn added sourly.

"If you believe that, girls," Curt said, "wait until you hear the one about the tooth fairy."

"Maybe he likes being on television," Joscelyn said. "Some people adore it."

"And what about Khalid?" Curt asked. "In Lalarhein a lot of people must know that Fish is Fawzi. And it can't be any secret that Fawzi worked for Khalid."

"You're right," Joscelyn said. "I'm sure Khalid doesn't enjoy having his wheeling dealing about the airport exposed."

"That's exactly my point," Curt said. "Nowadays, or so Fuad assures me, Lalarheinis don't get into Khalid's bad graces—at least not if they hope to remain intact. His disciples are zealots, fanatics; they're on the ready to carry out suicide missions for Khalid."

Honora gripped his fingers. "What you're both saying is that Fish—or Fawzi—is taking a huge chance to come publicly before the committee."

"Yes," Curt said. "And my theory's always been that somebody's paying him. Paying him handsomely. But I never figured out who it was before today."

"Alexander, paying Fish?" Honora's soft voice was skeptical. "How would he even know he existed?"

"Talbott's has quite a network of corporate spies. I believe that Alexander heard that our Harb Fawzi, now known as Harold Fish, was living here. He went to him. Said there'd be a substantial amount of cash, maybe a lifetime supply, if he'd contact Morrell with his information. The more I think about it, the more positive I get that Alexander's behind the hearing. There's no other explanation except a fortune to Fish. For him to take such a risk of angering Khalid, he must be getting very big bucks."

As Honora climbed the seldom used steps of the massive front portico of the Rayburn House Office Building, passing between its enormous, unadorned gray marble pillars, an oppressive clamminess descended on her body and spirit.

Possibly her dismay showed, for when they reached the hearing chamber Curt took her hand, keeping her on the seat next to his and out of the camera's unblinking eye.

The afternoon's witness was Matthias Haugen, an analyst from the Audit Division of the Internal Revenue Service. Honora's nonmathematical mind wandered.

There was a stirring behind her, but having schooled herself to remain immobile without changing her bland expression, she did not turn. Everyone on the rostrum stared at the entry, and a few, Morrell among them, showed wide, expectant smiles.

"Good Christ!" Curt whispered. "It's them."

Honora jerked around.

Crystal stood in the entry. The tall doors, rather than dwarfing her, made her Anglo-Saxon perfection appear yet more jewel-like. Alexander, Gid and Anne were ranged behind her.

Honora's new black alligator purse slipped from her lap. Seeing that she made no move to retrieve it, Arthur Kohn bent, placing the small weight in her numbed hands.

Staring directly at her, Crystal compressed her lovely lips, a defiant expression that back in her aggressive, mischief-filled childhood had meant *Try and stop me*.

Morrell rapped his gavel, silencing the chatter. Cameramen crouched, the other media people hurried back to their tables. "I am certain that Mr. Haugen will yield to our visitor. Mr. Alexander Talbott."

As Alexander walked with springy ease to the witness table, three young, muscular men rose from the rear row, glancing around with watchful wariness.

Crystal slid into the warmed leather between Anne and Gid. A moment ago, when Honora's startled dark eyes had been on her, it had taken all of her self-control not to flee from the complicity within this paneled legislative chamber. Yet looking at this rationally, what was there about Alexander's appearance that could be construed as treacherous to Honora? Her son was merely going to say a few words putting Talbott's in a good light. How did that constitute a betrayal? After all, Honora and Curt had been separated for years, and everybody knew she was in Washington purely as window dressing, an attempt to divert attention from Curt's sea of girls.

Alexander seated himself at the green baize table.

"Mr. Chairman, I'm very grateful for this opportunity to appear before the subcommittee. Our family happened to be in Washington, and my mother, president of the Talbott Group, decided we should use this opportunity to bring some good news to the American public. There has been raised at this hearing, and the others before it, the question of large-scale bribery—I mean really unconscionable bribery. Coming only a few years after Watergate, it's no wonder the country's cynical about government and about big business. My mother feels, and so do my brother and sister-in-law and I, that it is up to companies like ours to set the records straight." By some miracle of vocal pitch he managed to make the rhetoric sound like an easy and casual conversation.

"Thank you, Mr. Talbott—and Mrs. Talbott," Morrell said, beaming at Crystal. The old lecher, when he came asking for campaign contributions he always ogled her breasts. "We are most grateful."

"First of all," Alexander said, "much as I'd like to assure this subcommittee that we of the Talbott Group have never given a bribe of any type, I cannot. Unfortunately what other witnesses and Mr. Ivory have told you is true. Certain countries aren't like our own. If, for example, you have a job going in Indonesia and need to call Jakarta from Surabaya, you must pay the civil service telephone clerks." He turned, glancing at Crystal, as if apologizing for sullying her pretty ears with this information. "Minor bribery is a way of life in these places, and I have to impress on this committee that if our own laws make this type of payment illegal, Americans doing business overseas will be unfairly handicapped."

Morrell raised his cigarette as if dismissing any chance that the Congress would legislate against penny-ante tipping of foreigners.

"That's the purpose of this committee, Mr. Talbott." Hergesheimer's mouth stretched in a near flirtatious smile at the handsome young man. "To discover what is essential to conduct business without unduly hampering our multinational corporations."

Alexander leaned forward, causing a vibrating quiver in the public address system. "A great deal of Talbott's engineering and construction work is done overseas, and we have never sunk to large-scale bribery or illegal political contributions in these countries to get it."

"Has your policy ever hampered you in obtaining business?" asked Hergesheimer.

"A tremendous amount, especially in the area under discussion. We've never done much work in the Mideast. But money's never been the most important thing at Talbott's. My grandfather started with a wagon, a team of mules and a reputation for scrupulous honesty. My father brought us up to respect square dealing; he always told me and my brother that it's up to the top guys to set the ethical standards. My mother now runs the show in Dad and Grandfather's tradition, and so will my brother and I when we take over."

"You don't know how refreshing it is to hear that, Mr. Talbott," Morrell said.

"I'll answer any question you want to put to us to the best of my ability. Our books are open to the committee."

"Today's session is almost ended. Will you return tomorrow?"

"Not in the morning ... we have, uhh, a previous engagement. But in the afternoon, we'd be delighted."

Crystal's lovely features had gone pale under the masterful coat of maquillage.

67

Cheeks drawn in as if she were sucking on a straw, Crystal gazed at the case clock. The old mechanism's ticking sounded loud above the faint, leathery rustle of the trees outside the window, yet the delicate iron minute hand seemed stuck, refusing to move from eleven thirty-seven to thirty-eight.

Alexander was not yet home.

After concluding his testimony, he had pushed his way to the rear of the committee chamber, planting a well-documented kiss on his mother's forehead and another on Anne's freckled brow before he took off. He had not come home in time for dinner. She had moved her food about her plate as if she were on a diet, eating only her sorbet, and before the coffee was served had dispatched Mitchell on meaningless errands to the homes of the three upper-echelon Washingtonians with whom Alexander was thickest. When Gid had tried to buck her up by telling her how great she'd looked on tonight's News, she turned on him irritably. Anne had suffered a siege of yawns, pointing out that their circadian rhythms were attached to another time zone. As their footsteps sounded on the staircase, Crystal snatched up a fashion magazine, riffling the pages.

Her fear that the Morrell Committee might uncover Talbott's dirty tricks was unrelenting. She couldn't cope with Alexander's absence. *Why didn't he tell me we were going back tomorrow? He had it set up with Morrell. What else does he have planned? Where is he?* The answer to her final question popped up immediately. *With some girl.*

Although Alexander hadn't lived on Clay Street for years, she still thought of the inevitable end of his brief affairs as a homecoming—*He always comes back to me,* she would think, taking a complacent attitude toward his sexual vagabondage. Since his adulthood she seldom felt concern about his safety—she was proud of his ability to take care of himself. Tonight, however, she visualized a blazing-eyed husband with a shotgun, some heartbroken ninny snatching up a carving knife, a Latin lover with a dangerous glint of freshly broken glass in his hand. Her head tilted at the sound of a car turning on Q Street. It braked outside, and she ran into the chastely symmetrical hall to fling open the front door.

Mitchell was climbing the black iron steps.

"Oh, it's you, Padraic," she said.

"Sorry I took so long, but I had to wait for Senator Edmunds." As he came inside he added with the deferential tact that so often canceled the need for awkward questions, "There was a small party at the Rogovins'—they'd invited Alexander but he hadn't showed up. He wasn't at the Edmunds' or the Newlins', either."

"He hasn't called, and it's nearly midnight."

He smiled reassuringly. "That's early for Alexander."

"Yes, yes," she sighed. "But he could've gotten 'to a phone."

"It's been a bad day for you."

She agreed. "Horrendous. But at least you're home, and that's a help." With a glance at him, she returned to the living room.

Shutting the door, he sat next to her on the cushioned settee. She shifted closer, resting her head on his shoulder. His jacket felt cool from the night; he smelled of breath mints, a mildly aromatic cologne and something else lightly perfumed, probably a new brand of deodorant. His arm went around her, and after a minute or so the long, thin hand dropped to curve around her breast. Through her blouse and elaborately wired French brassiere she could feel the light, reverent rubbing of his fingertips. Since that time in Tokyo she had occasionally initiated what she persisted in thinking of as a necking session. Though Mitchell's kisses and caresses never bridged the chasm of her frigidity, his worshipful adoration restored a sense of her incalculable worth as a prize, a love object, and thus calmed her mind.

He reached for her top button, but she, anticipating Alexander's return, pushed his hand away. He continued as he had before, and as his temperature rose she caught a whiff of his sexual odor, nowhere near as pungent as Gideon's had been but nevertheless mildly acrid.

He gave a dwindling, convulsive gasp and with a hasty good night, hurried stiff-legged from the room: she heard his footsteps creak on the staircase leading down to the small rooms that had originally been the pantries but now served as additional sleeping quarters. There had never been a repeat of that first repellent leakage.

She washed and creamed herself for bed. Tying the sash of her quilted pink robe, she went into the brightly lit hall to sit on a straight-backed chair, vaguely conscious of the fact that she needed only a rolling pin to complete the time-honored cartoon of a shrew awaiting her errant husband. It was almost one when a car pulled into their garage. Her relief was so intense that she needed to pee. After using the toilet, she stood in her doorway.

Alexander had almost reached the top of the stairs before he saw her.

He elaborated on a courtly bow. "Ahh, the doyenne of this and many other houses waiting to bid me safe return."

He was, she realized, under the influence. God knew what influence—marijuana, cocaine or some trendy new substance she had not heard of. At least when her father had staggered home, they had known the exact nature of the beast that had bitten him.

"You promised today would be the only time we'd be at the hearing!" she burst out.

"Could I help it if the Honorable Morrell demanded a gala repeat of my stirring and patriotic performance?"

"What've you been using?"

"An assortment of the usual."

"If you're going to do drugs"—she used his term—"I wish you wouldn't drive."

He sank down on the top step, shaking his head from side to side. "Mom, do you have any idea how much I hate him?"

She didn't need to be told who *him* was. Sitting on the carpet at his side, she could smell an autumnal sweetness. "Alexander, it was a mistake coming to Washington," she said. "But there's no need for us to go to that hearing. No need at all. Mitchell can go—he'll concoct some sort of excuse and read a statement from us."

"You don't understand me at all, do you?"

"I try to," she said almost humbly. "But this personal crusade, I can't see the sense in it."

"Sense?" He shook his head. "Poor Mom, such a gorgeous, *practical* lady."

"I agree the hearings are turning *his* credibility into a shambles, and it'll take him years to recover. But what's the difference? We'll still have Bechtel, Fluor, Foster-Wheeler—the rest of the competition in the world to contend with."

"Who gives a shit about the others?"

"But how will this help *us?*"

"You're forever trying to impose one form of logic on another. Mom, can't you comprehend that psychological mathematics does not necessarily have to use a base of ten? *My* numbers sometimes have a base of two, or seven."

"Alexander, you better get some sleep."

"Sleep!"

"I understand, darling, I really do. I'm out to hurt him, too. But this hearing could so easily get out of hand."

"I don't want to hurt him. I want him stretched on the wheel until his bones crack, I want to see him groveling, blind, helpless."

"Oh, Alexander. . . ."

He folded his dark glasses, slipping them in his pocket. His eyes were filled with tears. "He has no other son, no other begotten son, and he has never once tried to see me."

She stroked back his hair. "Shhh, darling, he's not worth it."

"I realize this is rough on you, Mom, and I'm sorry. But other than that I have no regrets, not for what I've done or what I'm about to do."

"There's more?" she whispered.

"Yes, indeed. There's more."

She clutched at his arm. "For God's sake, Alexander, tell me what you're going to do!"

"There's a document that connects him with his brother-in-law's bribery operation. It looks exceedingly legit. Even his loving wife will think it's genuine."

"A forgery?"

"A fabulous forgery, by the Rembrandt of forgers."

"Alexander," she said firmly, "we are leaving tomorrow right after the Fords' lunch."

"No way."

"This isn't a game, it's a Congressional hearing."

"I'm aware it's no game. I am hounding Curt Ivory until one of us is in the bosom of eternity."

She shivered. "That's crazy talk."

"Okay. I want him the fuck locked up in Leavenworth, I want his boats and his money and his business down the tubes, I want him destroyed and broken."

She started to remonstrate, but the misery in his glistening eyes silenced her.

Gripping her shoulders, he pressed a long kiss on her mouth. A start of excitement, long missing and presumed dead, tingled through her. She abandoned herself to the reckless pleasure.

Abruptly he released her and sprang to his feet. "Sweet dreams," he said.

As his door closed, she began to shiver so hard that she had to clench her jaw to keep her teeth from chattering. She turned up her bedroom thermostat and left on her quilted robe as she crawled between icy Porthault sheets. She lay there chilled with anxieties about tomorrow's hearing and more than a little frightened by the reverberations of her son's kiss.

68

At this same hour, Joscelyn lay stretched on the unturned-down bed that Honora had occupied last week. She was fully dressed except for her shoes, which were already put away. Her eyes were bloodshot, the lids puffed and the thin brows drawn together in a scowling expression as she attempted to halt the flow of tears. Even during those years of marriage when Malcolm had taken out his unhappy insecurities on her—even in the awful months surrounding his death—she had not been a weeper. Tonight her sobs were uncontrollable. *The kiss of death,* she thought, *that's me.* She knew the structure below Fish's testimony; she knew the role she had played engineering that structure. It was she who had insisted Honora use influence to obtain a managerial position on the pipeline for Malcolm—young and inexperienced but Curt's brother-in-law—and it was through her friendship with Fuad that Malcolm and Khalid had come together. She was responsible for setting in motion the concatenation of forces intent on destroying Curt Ivory. An impossible burden to live with.

She wiped the moisture under her eyes, blew her nose and went to the window, aware of the faint padding sound her stockinged feet made on the thick carpet. Drawing the drapes, pulling aside the white synthetic curtain, she rested her forehead on the cold window glass.

Eight stories below her was the emptiness of M Street.

A peculiar sense of being outside herself came over her. Her breath slowed, filming the glass, her bitter self-recriminations faded and there was only the distant pavement glinting seductively.

Until tonight her infrequent considerations of suicide had always been along succinct, logistical lines. She had seen death by one's own hand as the Big Escape Hatch when faced with painful cancer or inutile old age. But now, gazing down at the shimmery squares of pavement, her normally acute mental processes were distorted and thoughts floated like insubstantial wisps of clouds that could not be grasped.

These are sash windows, she thought with sudden clarity. *It'd be easy to open one.*

She jerked back from the window and stood breathing heavily with her arms crossed over her chest. Her head bent forward. She was crying again.

Joscelyn could not shake the episode of morbid guilt. On the following day when the subcommittee broke for its long midday recess, she insisted Honora and Curt take a stroll on Capitol Hill. She stayed in the anteroom alone. Except for those brief years of marriage, her life had been spent alone. And alone she should be. She was a leper, a plague carrier, she brought death and destruction on those she loved.

At around two, before the subcommittee reconvened, she went into the anteroom's lavatory. A mop and bucket stood in the corner; on the dark wood of one of the two stall doors was taped a penciled note, *Out of order.* Taking off her jacket, she unbuttoned her blouse cuffs, rolling the sleeves above her elbows. For several long minutes she stood at the sink letting cool water flow over her wrists to calm herself.

* * *

When the four Talbotts emerged from the elevator on the third floor of the Rayburn House Office Building, Anne gamely attempted to keep up the pace Alexander was setting in order to avoid the small crowd of media folk hustling in their wake. Before they had traversed the length of the hallway, Anne lifted her hand to the great bulge of her stomach, halting. "Hold up there, Gid," she said.

The other three slowed, as did the press entourage.

"Everything okay?" Gid asked in a low, concerned rumble.

Smiling and wincing, she said, "Our offspring's playing soccer in there. Must be trying to work off the heady gourmet delights of White House cookery."

They had eaten plain broiled chicken—ketchup was available on the side—with unsauced asparagus in the private upstairs dining room with a noted Alabama heart surgeon, a wizened and legendary producer from Hollywood's Golden Age, the cheery, overjeweled wife of a Mexican billionaire and the Presidential couple. A lofty *mise en scène* that should by rights have intimidated Anne into muteness. Instead, she had entertained the long table with her affectionately told tales of the New Guinea ancients whose oral histories she was taping.

Crystal, woozy with lack of sleep and on edge with misgivings about the upcoming afternoon session of the hearings, had nevertheless been pleasantly surprised by her daughter-in-law's success, and now she felt a tug of affectionate concern. "Anne, dear, you and Gid better go on back to the house and rest. We can manage."

"Everything's cool," Anne said. "The thing is, this particular May I'm not in shape for the thousand-meter race."

The cameras were whirring, and Crystal turned her head away. She glimpsed a swarthy, dark-haired man emerge from one of the pedimented doorways, easing along the corridor to slip in and become one of the dozen or so in their retinue. *He doesn't have a press card dangling from his neck,* she thought fleetingly.

"See you in a couple of minutes, then," Alexander said. "Gid, this time you sit between our ladies."

Alexander took Crystal's arm. Trotting at her tall son's side, she fought her irritation with him.

Will he produce that fake document himself? It's not Alexander's style, but then again he's not himself about this whole deal. I hope to God he won't hit out at Curt so that it's obvious what he's doing. I can't bear Honora's huge reproachful eyes again. What does she care anyway? She left Curt ages ago. Why can't it be golden and sweet like it was when we were children, like it was yesterday on the Capitol steps?

Her ankle bent inward. Gripping Alexander's sleeve, she groaned with exaggerated loudness.

"Sorry, Mom," he said *sotto voce.* "But I figured you'd prefer to stay ahead of the vultures." He gripped her elbow, whispering, *"Courage, ma mère, courage."*

"I'll survive," she said with a note of maternal asperity.

"Good. Because we're about to face the foe."

On the far side of the knotted group waiting to be vetted outside the hearing chamber, Curt and Honora were striding along, their long steps synchronized, his arm protectively clasping her shoulders, she bent pliantly toward him. Whatever their marital arguments might have been in the past, it was obvious to Crystal that their reconciliation was not only public but private.

Irrationally Crystal found herself blaming her sister as well as Curt for the mysterious harpies who fed on her son's living flesh. As she moved toward her enemies, she again glimpsed the dark, greasy-looking man. Why was he so intent on Alexander? *Why not?* she asked herself. Everyone else was staring as the paired Ivorys and Talbotts confronted one another at the crush by the committee chamber.

Honora murmured a greeting that was swallowed by the surrounding racket.

"Good afternoon, Aunt Honora," Alexander said. "Mr. Ivory—or should I call you Uncle Curt?"

Father, Crystal thought, and from the pause knew that the four of them were joined in the correction.

More flashes, and pressing forward of snouted motion picture lenses.

The swarthy man had positioned himself three feet or so to their left. He wore a cheap, nondescript brown Dacron suit, white shirt and black knitted tie too narrow for style. Nothing about his clothing or his haircut was unusual. He looked utterly commonplace. So why should her attention be drawn to him? Because, she realized, his was a parody of normalcy. Surrounding him was an aura of wildness that set him apart from the rest of the journalists. His muscles were flexed tauter, heavier moisture gleamed on his Levantine flesh. His eyes protruded a bit, as if being crowded from his head. The pupils, contracted to wary pinpoints, stayed fixed on Alexander.

She gripped her son's arm, feeling the lean muscles, wanting to draw him away from the feral gaze, yet unable to speak.

Did I have time to warn him?

This fine point would haunt her the rest of her life.

She saw the hand reach under the Dacron jacket. A movement swift, yet also incredibly predictable. And she was not surprised when the hand withdrew holding a gun, a smallish pistol, the familiar accoutrement of countless movies and television shows. *So much for all the metal detectors and security,* she thought.

He's aiming at Alexander.

He wants to kill Alexander.

Later, later she would wonder why, if her thoughts drifted so leisurely, she didn't have time to scream a warning.

A body hurled between the gun and Alexander, moving so swiftly that in the blur she didn't realize immediately that it was Curt.

Simultaneously, a sound like a twig cracking. Acrid smoke. Curt's mouth opened, he swayed from side to side and back and forth, like one of those inflatable plastic punching toys that never topple. But he was toppling. Hands reached out to break his fall.

The crowd had the Capitol police pinned near the doorway, and if the dark-skinned assailant had intended to escape he would have had a good chance in the confusion that was eddying outward. Instead, he planted his feet apart, raising his left hand to steady his right wrist as he aimed again at Alexander.

The second shot cracked just before the screaming filled the universe.

"A-a-l-e-e-x-a-a-a-n-d-e-e-e-r. . . ."

69

Honora never saw the gun.

Curt's fingers on her shoulder dug through her clothes and into the flesh for the briefest fraction of time. After that he moved instantaneously. She had no time to register bewilderment or astonishment. Like a defensive fullback, he hurled himself at Alexander. The tackle never made contact. At a sharp, cracking sound Curt halted. He swayed an uneven circle, his face bewildered, his feet not moving. Then his torso sagged.

Adrenaline blazed through Honora, filling her muscles with strength. She grasped his waist, not realizing she was sobbing with the effort of lowering his limp heaviness gently to the marble. She knelt over him.

Still uncertain what had happened, she saw the neatly indented hole just to the left of his top jacket button.

As bright redness oozed onto the dark Italian silk-serge, she pressed the base of her thumb against the slippery fabric, a primitive, instinctive attempt to stay the blood. During the war the upper forms at Edinthorpe had taken Red Cross: now her mind refused to conjure up more of those classes than a vision of the coarse cotton triangles they'd used to tie tourniquets, and the unsubduable, girlish giggles that had accompanied the bluff, gray-haired gym mistress's demonstration of the groin pressure point.

There is a Reaper, whose name is Death, and with his sickle keen he reaps the bearded grain at a breath, and the flowers that grow between.

Why remember poetry and not how to stay the flow of her husband's heart blood?

"Honora. . . ." The struggle of Curt's whisper heaved, slippery, below her hand.

She looked at his face and shivered. How could his

ruddy, vigorous color have drained so quickly? The boat tan overlaid his sudden pallor with the yellowish hue of beef suet bought at a cheap butcher's.

"Honora?" He was staring up at her.

Never before had she been so aware of his eyes, the blackness of the pupils, the brown lines radiating into the topaz iris and the dark brown ring that encircled it. A thin, s-shaped squiggle of redness showed in the left sclera. Moisture clumped his thick, straight lashes.

He had commanded her attention, therefore she dare not distract herself by shouting for a doctor.

In this infinitely stretched moment, she was possessed of a metaphysical certainty, a true religious's fanaticism. Only through her gaze could she infuse Curt with a redemptive life force. The totality of her visual concentration negated her other senses. She didn't hear the cries and stamping of the terrified crowd; she was oblivious to the pushing. She smelled neither the smoky acridity of the gunfire nor the sourish pungency of panic. She scarcely felt the brutal, un-intentional kick between her shoulders, but steadied herself with her hand. Later she would find it impossible to believe that three members of the NBC team, defecting their duty to their network and the public's right to know, had been next to her, circling Curt's recumbent body to protect him from being trampled in the pandemonium. The second and third shots she registered only by Curt's blinks. She never heard Crystal's demented shrieking.

She stared into Curt's eyes as if guiding him through the depths of some dark, primordial forest.

When the sharp sound rang outside in the corridor Jos-celyn was already in the committee chamber. She never would have identified the sudden, dry crack as gunfire if it weren't for the ensuing blast of shouting. She immediately fell prey to her childhood fear that the very worst, either physical or metaphysical, had occurred. Jumping from her chair, she rushed in the direction of the left door.

Frenzied people were thrusting their way inside to escape the shots in the corridor, while many of those inside— either newsmen or spectators fearing that they were trapped and would be mowed down—attempted to push their way out. Over the sounds of panic repetitively came the question: "What's happening?"

Joscelyn was trapped in the crush. As a keening wail rose over the mob sounds, higher, yet higher, Joscelyn elbowed and clawed her way to the exit. Briefly caught against the mahogany jamb, she used her fists to emerge into the corridor.

A lurching, shoulder-held camera partially obscured her vision of Crystal, who was staring down at the floor. The lovely mouth was a wide-open red circle from which came that piercing, blood-chilling shriek. Gid Talbott was shouldering his way through the crowd. Heavy features contorted, he dropped out of Joscelyn's line of vision.

Some radio or TV correspondent was shouting near her ear, "This is awful, awful, oh my God, like Bobby Kennedy's assassination. Blood everywhere. An unknown assassin has shot Alexander Talbott and Curt Ivory. From here it appears both men are dead."

She thrust herself toward a human knot. Three men had linked arms to protect Curt as he lay sprawled on his back. Honora knelt over him, her dark head bent close to his, her expression calm, her lips tender, as if she were about to make love to him.

Jesus, is she ever out of it, Joscelyn thought. She superimposed the vision of another prostrate male body bleeding onto marble that wasn't gray but pink.

Somebody's got to take charge, she told herself.

An exhilarated calm descended on her, a calm made all the more powerful by her fear. Her mind working swiftly, she used her well-developed skills of organization.

"Get a doctor!" she shouted. "Get a doctor over here quickly!"

"There's another body, I think it's the assassin. I hope our camera's picking him up. There's some question whether he was shot by the Capitol's police force or whether he turned his weapon on himself."

"And call for the ambulance!" Joscelyn bawled. She was aware that the security people should already have dispatched this message, but she had learned how often in crises people forgot their jobs. "There's always an ambulance stationed in back of the Capitol."

She ducked below the swaying men who surrounded Curt, and in this crawling position laid her hand on his bloodslick chest. His heart reverberated below her palm. She began to unbutton the soaking shirt. Almost immediately, competent masculine hands took over. "I'm a physician," the man said, squatting next to her as he smartly ripped the Egyptian cotton.

"He's still alive," Joscelyn said.

"We're trying to get our camera through to get a shot of Curt Ivory...."

Joscelyn for the first time focused on Curt's face. The flesh seemed to sag back with the force of gravity. She jumped to her feet again. "Has anybody called that fucking ambulance?" she shouted.

A crew was racing a gurney and equipment along the wide corridor.

"Here!" Joscelyn shouted in a commanding tone to avert the paramedics from tending the other fallen. "Over here!"

"Will you please move back, everybody."

"Mrs. Ivory is kneeling over her slain husband's body—"

"Let us through!"

An ambulance attendant was pushing an oxygen mask over Curt's face while another said, "Gotta rush him over to the Capitol Hospital."

Joscelyn instantly recollected denigrations of that hospital from her stint on the Washington subway. "No," she barked. "The George Washington University Hospital!"

"Ma'am, he's in bad shape, the nearest hospital's the Capitol."

"He'll die for sure there," somebody called out. "Do what the lady says. Take him to George Washington."

"Key figures in the payoff scandal, Alexander Talbott and Curt Ivory, were shot only moments ago by an unknown gunman." The reporter's voice was high and staccato. "Before Capitol police could apprehend the unknown murderer, he turned the gun on himself...."

"Ivory appears to be alive, however Alexander Talbott is dead...."

70

Joscelyn and Honora were in a large, private room at the George Washington University Hospital. Both women had kicked off their shoes; the bloodstained jacket of Honora's new yellow suit had been thrown on the bathroom floor while Joscelyn's navy flannel was neatly hung over the back of a chair. On the bed table was a litter of cups, Lipton's teabags oozing brownly into the saucers. They had been here approximately seven hours, and Curt had been in the operating room all that time.

It was Joscelyn who had inveigled the hospital staff into allowing them to use this room, and coerced them into placing a guard by the nurses' station to prevent intruders; she who had secured tea from the aides. Once three other Ivory vice presidents arrived, however, her executive energy abandoned her and she let the trio take over. They were manning the public phones in the downstairs waiting room and answering the unanswerable queries about Curt's condition that flowed in from around the world. Periodically they came up to speak to Honora, whom only one of them had met before. She looked glazed during their rapid, high-key conversations, which avoided the operating room and centered on the impact of the shooting on the Morrell Hearings. (The consensus was summed up in one remark: "Bad as this is, at least it's broken up the damn committee's momentum.")

Joscelyn's anxieties expelled themselves in hyperkinetic motion. She was forever blinking, rotating her shoulders, straightening her skirt around her narrow flanks, pushing back her hair, pacing around the room.

Honora sat with her hands loosely clasped in her lap: blood had dried on the yellow wool, but she did not see the rusty streaks. Her eyes were focused on some distant, unseeable point. Her abnormal immobility had increased as the hours dragged by.

"Honora," Joscelyn said.

Honora turned reluctantly.

"They said the creep bastard who shot Curt looked like a Mideasterner."

"Mmmm."

"I'm convinced he had some connection to Khalid. The way I see it, Khalid and his bunch were afraid that Alexander was about to spill some very hot beans about Khalid, that he was about to incriminate the Holy One."

Honora's glance begged for silence.

Joscelyn couldn't stop. "Everything fits like a perfectly planned scale model. The assassin's appearance, his killing Alexander, his killing himself, the lack of ID." (A black and white television rested high in the wall opposite the bed, and she had kept switching channels for News Updates, catching repetitious confirmations of Alexander's death and of the assassin's suicide—*Police found no identification on the corpse*—and one cryptic, *Harold Fish, key witness at the Morrell Hearings, could not be reached for comment.* There were many zoom shots of the hospital's exterior—*the George Washington University Medical Center where Curt Ivory, accused of bribery and corruption, hovers near death as doctors attempt to remove a bullet from his heart.* Just before the seven o'clock national news came on, Honora in a strangled voice had requested that the set be turned off.) "And remember what Morley Safer said about Fish being unavailable? I'll bet a million bucks that he's unavailable on a permanent basis."

Honora glanced at her watch. "Five to ten," she whispered.

"Thoracic surgery takes forever, and getting out a bullet is far more complicated than your run-of-the-mill bypass."

Honora closed her eyes.

Her sister's hunger for silence reached through Joscelyn's raw compulsion to speak. *Oh, fuck it,* she thought, biting her lip and scratching ferociously at the itch between her shoulders.

At a tentative rap, they both jumped, simultaneously turning to the door with frightened expectancy.

"Who's there?" Honora whispered at the same instant as Joscelyn said loudly, "Come on in!"

It was Gid. "I hope I'm not intruding," he said.

Honora blinked, shaking her head. "No, not at all, Gid."

His bloodshot eyes appeared small and narrow because of the puffiness of the lids, but otherwise, wearing a collared and striped rugby sweater with shorts that displayed stocky, hairy, tanned legs, he brought into the stale air of the hospital room an almost unbearable reminder of normal, healthy masculine flesh.

"Gid," Honora murmured, "I can't tell you how sorry I am about Alexander."

His Adam's apple worked. After a pause he muttered, "I guess it's always rough, losing a brother, but Alexander and I were so close in age. We spent huge chunks of time together, we were pretty much twins. . . ." His voice wavered.

Honora's hands raised as if to embrace him, then fell to her sides: they had been strangers until yesterday, and her butterfly feeler delicacy informed her that she didn't know this nephew well enough to intrude on his grief. "That's the way Crystal and I were. How is she?"

"The doctor gave her a shot. She's knocked out."

"Poor Crystal. . . ."

"It's very nice of you to drop by," Joscelyn said gruffly. She had seen, as Honora had not, Gid's unabashed sobbing over his brother's body.

"I really appreciate what Mr. Ivory tried to do," he said. "What's happening?"

"He's in the operating room," Honora said thinly.

"Still? We've been worried about him, Anne and I." He gave a funny little smile. "She's here on the third floor— that's maternity."

"The baby's coming?" Joscelyn asked.

"It's a few weeks early. Not quite a month. In a way it's good. We're in New Guinea, and though the Talbott hospital facilities are great for there, better to be a preemie in Washington than at the Tasi." His forehead creased in anxious wrinkles. "At least that's what I tell Anne."

"She'll be fine," Honora murmured. "But shouldn't you be with her, rubbing her back?"

"She ordered me up here to see how Mr. Ivory's doing."

Honora sighed deeply, shaking her head. "We don't know."

"Not a word for hours," Joscelyn said.

"There's no way Mom and I can thank you enough for what he tried to do."

"He saw the gun," Honora said.

"Everybody says he was terrific. The thing I can't figure is what the guy had against Alexander. All Anne and I can guess is that he's a mental case—there's an awful lot of un-boxed nuts around, and—"

Honora returned to her chair. "Gid," she interrupted, "it was dear of you to come, but I know you're in a hurry to get back to the labor room."

"Sure am." He reached for the door handle. "I'll check back later."

After his jogging footsteps faded into the hospital night, Joscelyn ached to discuss the subject their nephew had raised: what had possessed Curt to lay his life on the line for a man he despised? Honora, hands tightly clasped, was absolutely still, her face white, her expression faraway. Joscelyn kept silent.

A half hour later a pair of surgeons slipped into the room's tiny vestibule. They both wore bloodstained, wrinkled scrub suits and green paper boots over their shoes. The taller doctor moved into the room, his shoulders slumped wearily. In a low, sympathetic, southern accent, he explained that they had removed the bullet, repairing as much of the damage to the heart as was possible.

Honora's eyes closed.

"How is he?" Joscelyn demanded.

"His condition's critical."

"How critical?" Joscelyn asked.

The shorter doctor sucked in his fleshy, wrinkled cheeks. "The prognosis is what we call guarded."

"It can go either way?" Joscelyn asked.

"Yes."

Honora gave a little cough. "When can I see him?"

"They'll tell you upstairs in ICU, Mrs. Ivory."

Joscelyn and Honora moved to Fourth Floor North. On the right of the elevators was the windowed reception desk of the Intensive Care Unit. A thin young woman in a white coat shuffled large, blue-covered charts while behind her an orderly was pushing an elaborate piece of equipment down an ominously bright corridor.

The ICU waiting room, a narrow L-shape with a telephone booth in the corner, was empty, but somebody had left a red down jacket on a coat hook.

Honora went to the dark window and stared out at the lit windows of the hospital wings.

When Joscelyn could no longer bear the silence, she said, "I cannot for the life of me imagine what possessed Curt to do it."

A tightening of Honora's shoulders proved she had heard: she did not reply.

"I mean," Joscelyn said, "why on earth would he shove Alexander out of the way of speeding bullets? It's not as if he had any reason to cherish the saintly boy, even if he was his father. I've tried to figure it but I can't."

"It was Curt's fate," Honora said, still gazing into the darkness.

"Fate? Honora, in England have you taken to consulting with gypsies—or is it the druids over there?"

"You asked my opinion."

Honora talking crazily was better than Honora silent, so Joscelyn said, "I don't understand what you mean, fate."

"They're tied together."

"Yes, as father and son."

"It's more complicated than an accident of sperm. Curt tried to reject his fate, but Alexander never did. It's like a Greek tragedy, Sophoclean. Alexander knew he was born to be Curt's nemesis."

"Fate? Nemesis?" Joscelyn shifted uneasily on the lumpy tweed. "Isn't that a bit far out, Honora?"

"Remember when I told you that Alexander admitted to coming to Marrakesh to break us up? It was almost as if he couldn't help himself. You've told me yourself he'd do anything to get a contract away from Ivory. And then there's the hearing."

"That part is pure bull," Joscelyn said loudly.

"Curt believes it."

"Yes, I heard him. But Curt's been under a huge amount of stress and pressure in Washington. Be reasonable, Honora. Nobody, not even our noble-hearted sonny boy, does anyone the dirty by setting up a Congressional hearing, especially when his own company's money is so laundered that it's faded to a light chartreuse." Joscelyn scratched vehemently at her back. "So that's your fate-nemesis theory?"

"I've often wondered why Crystal told him who his real father was, but once she did tell him, the wheels were set in motion—" Honora broke off.

A thin, boyish-looking man had come into the waiting room: purposefully avoiding looking at them, he pulled on the red jacket. After he'd gone down in the elevator Joscelyn tried to revive the conversation, but Honora shook her head wearily.

A sign proclaimed: NO VISITORS BETWEEN 12 P.M. AND SEVEN A.M. At midnight Joscelyn stretched on one of the couches, dozing intermittently. Honora never slept, leaving her chair only once to use the restroom.

A few minutes after seven, as the thin gray morning was oozing through the window at the long end of the waiting room, a chesty nurse wearing scrubs came to the door. "Mrs. Ivory, you can visit now."

Honora was led down the brilliantly lit ICU corridor past glass roomlets where machines beeped noisily and monitoring screens bulged from walls and ceilings.

Her first impression of Curt was that a mad scientist had incarcerated him in a trellis of dripping plastic bottles and ticking robots. His bandaged chest rose and fell rhythmically, a thick, flexible tube strapped to his face disappeared into his mouth. The faint hint of rosiness infusing along his high cheekbones had the duplicity of a mortician's cosmetics.

"He's heavily sedated," said the nurse with a firm tap at his bare shoulder. "Curt. Curt."

Getting not even a flicker of response, she delivered an audible blow.

"Don't," Honora whispered.

The nurse ignored her. Another fly-swatting slap. "Curt, your wife is here."

Curt looked up: his eyes were filmy, bewildered.

Honora leaned over the rail, kissing his forehead. "Darling," she murmured.

His eyes flickered and became less dazed. She gripped his hand, which—lax and passive—didn't feel like his hand at all.

The nurse shook one of the clear plastic bottles that dangled on what looked like a metal coatrack. "Four more minutes, no fudging, Mrs. Ivory," she said pointing to a large Simplex clock that looked homey and familiar amid the proliferation of medical machinery. She moved across the corridor to another patient.

Curt's chapped lips moved around the tube. "Operation . . . ?"

"It's over. They got the bullet out," she said.

He licked his lower lip and muttered, "Thirsty. . . ."

She glanced around but there was no glass. Anyway how could he drink with that tube in his mouth. "I'll get the nurse."

". . . Stay. . . ." His eyes closed.

She stood holding his hand and did not weep until she emerged from the cubicle.

71

Gid Talbott stood with Joscelyn in the waiting room. Their backs were to Honora and she considered sneaking across the hall and hiding behind the swinging door.

Joscelyn turned.

"Honora," she called urgently. "Honora, how is he?"

Honora fought for control, ugly creases forming around her mouth. "He knew me. . . ."

She moved past them to the waiting room window and opened her purse for a handkerchief. "Sorry," she said, looking down into the courtyard. "Gid, how's Anne?"

"Great, fabulous. We've been parents of a son for"—he glanced at his watch—"twenty-nine minutes. Five pounds one ounce, quite a bruiser considering his early arrival. A very funny looking gent—well, he said the same about me."

She used her wet Kleenex again, managing to bestow auntly blessings.

"Aunt Honora?" Gid coughed. "Aunt Joscelyn mentioned that you can only visit once an hour." For reinforcement he glanced across the lobby. On the glass of the ICU window was a sign:

VISITORS ARE LIMITED TO IMMEDIATE FAMILY ONLY
NO MORE THAN TWO FAMILY MEMBERS AT ONE TIME
VISITS ARE PERMITTED FOR FIVE MINUTES OUT OF
EVERY HOUR

He continued, "I realize this is a monstrous imposition, but if I promise to have you back in less than an hour, will you come to the house?"

"*Now?*" The thought of being banished any further from Curt than this waiting room brought tremors to Honora's thighs, and she sank into an armchair.

Joscelyn said flatly, "Impossible."

"This hospital's on Twenty-third, our place is on Twenty-eighth near Q."

"Gid," Joscelyn said sharply. "It's out of the question."

"We're less than five minutes by car," he said doggedly. "In the morning traffic, maybe eight."

"Gid, I can't," Honora said. Looking at his face, she added uncertainly, "Maybe tomorrow."

"Mother needs somebody. I can't help her . . . I, well, I irritate her." He coughed. "She often told us how close you were, and you said so yourself."

"Back in the ice age," Joscelyn put in.

"Until yesterday"—Honora wiped at her eyes, correcting herself—"until the day before yesterday I hadn't seen her in forever."

"The reason we called the doctor last night was because she was banging her head on the wall."

Crystal hammering that gorgeous, *sensible* head against a wall? Honora's mind balked at the vision, then she erupted in fury: how dare Gid Talbott keep up his attempt to tear her from this hospital now, when her every cell—her every molecule—must be focused on Curt?

"Gid," Joscelyn asked, "hasn't she had enough? Or did you bring some nails for her palms?"

Gid flushed, but continued to gaze at Honora. "I swear I'll have you back here in less than an hour—before eight if you want."

"Honora," Joscelyn snapped, "if you're even considering it, stop right now."

"Gid, you don't understand. He might . . ." Honora was unable to utter the word *die*.

Gid slumped into the chair next to hers. "I know how

you feel. I'd never leave Anne," he said. "It's just that Alexander meant everything to Mother."

Honora looked down at her nephew's strong knees and saw the large hands dangling helplessly between them. Sighing, she went to take Joscelyn's navy flannel suit jacket from the wall hook. "Is there a way out of the hospital with no reporters?" she asked.

On the uneven brick sidewalk between the smart, black painted boxes that held ailanthus trees stood a pair of men drinking coffee from large McDonald's containers.

"Our new friends," Gid said.

"Guards?" Honora asked.

"Advance scouts for a Network News car—see those motorcycles? Time for evasive maneuvers." He drove around the corner, swerving down an unpaved alley to park in the rear garage, which was also built of that iron-rich red brick unique to the capital.

As he led Honora through a little garden (even in her helpless, itching impatience, she could not help noting that a row of lovely dogwoods had been atrociously pruned) the back door burst open and a tall, cadaverous man rushed onto the stoop. "Thank heavens you're back!"

"What's wrong, Mitchell?" Gid asked urgently. "Is she worse?"

The man's long upper lip drew back, showing an unfortunate bite. "Anina heard her toilet flush. Since then we've heard her crying and things bumping around, but she keeps the door locked. She didn't even answer when I told her about the baby—"

Gid bolted into the house. Honora followed his pounding footsteps up a fine Federal staircase.

Gid slammed his palm against a door. "Mom, it's me, Gid. *Mom, open up.*"

No sound.

"Anne's had a little boy," he shouted more loudly. "She's fine, and the baby's over five pounds, doesn't need to be in an incubator."

No reply.

"Mom, he's a terrific baby, he has these tiny fingernails." Gid's voice rose, wavering, then cracked like an adolescent's, and he closed his eyes.

Honora made a peculiar little sound, as if gristle were caught in back of her throat.

"Crystal!" she shouted. "It's me. Honora. You let us in, do you hear?"

"Go away!" Crystal shrilled.

"Not before I see you."

"Leave me alone!"

Honora's rapping shuddered against the door. *"I have to be back at the hospital in a few minutes."*

There was a stirring sound. "Just us," Crystal said.

"Just us," Honora repeated their old catchphrase that ensured privacy and secrecy.

The lock clicked and the door opened. Honora slipped inside and gasped.

Every drawer had been yanked open and the contents strewn. The long, louvered closets had been emptied. The clothing had been ripped or cut, then tossed in rich, random heaps across the spacious bedroom. Here an opulence of dismembered silks, there a strew of ripped white organza, on the unmade bed a tender pile of shredded lingerie. Tatters of magnificent blue moiré lay wadded on the dressing table to form nesting places for enormous, glowing, South Sea pearls that had been cut from their knotted string. White sequins were scattered like snowflakes, heels had been pried from tiny, dainty shoes. The deep red of a Cartier purse showed pale, fresh gouges.

Perfume hung heavy in the air, as if it had been thrown like gasoline to ignite a bonfire.

Crystal leaned against the door, pressing the bolt home. The front of her loose, blue satin robe was splotched with perfume, the hem had come undone. Her yellow hair hung in lank strands over her blotched cheeks; her eyes were swollen almost shut, with garish red lines marking the lower lids.

"Well, what's the big deal?" she demanded panting. "What do you have to tell me?"

"You really were rotten just then," Honora said. "Cruel."

"He has a baby, who cares?"

"What a stinking thing to say. He's so dear and proud."

"Shut your stupid face."

"The baby's your own grandchild."

"Are you too soft in the head to understand I don't give a damn!" Crystal shouted, and ran to the bed, one toe catching in a narrow silk strap so she trailed a dismembered froth of lace after her. She flung herself stomach down on

the rumpled blanket cover, her extended foot still dangling
the delicate web. "What are you doing here anyway?"

"Gid asked me to come. He's worried sick—"

"Well both of you can just butt out."

"I should be at the hospital."

"Then go!"

"Will you just look at this room. A bomb could've
struck. You've gone around the bend, Crystal. You're
bats."

"In all these years haven't you learned to mind your own
beeswax?"

As the lingo of their childhood bubbled to their lips, grief
was pulling at their faces.

All at once Crystal pushed up on her elbow, staring
around with a bewildered expression. "What have I done?
You know how careful I am with my things. Oh God, God,
God, who cares about clothes!"

Honora flopped onto the heap of torn lingerie next to her
sister, hugging her. "Crystal ... my poor, darling Crystal...."

"Honora, last night ... they asked me what to do about
the body."

"The *body?*"

"I went all crazy."

"Of course you did, poor darling."

"You're the only one who understands.... My beautiful,
brilliant Alexander...."

Both women were sobbing convulsively.

"My beautiful boy...."

"Ahh, Crystal, humans are so terribly fragile."

"There's never been anybody like him."

"We never realize how fragile until it's too late. When I
think how I've wasted these years away from Curt."

"I lived for him."

"Poor, poor Crys...."

"There'll have to be a funeral, an important one, and I
don't know how to plan it. I'll ask Alexander; he'll tell me
what to do."

Honora stroked the wet blond hair. "Crystal, darling,
what are you saying?"

"I know, I know. But how can my beautiful boy be dead
when I love him so?"

"Hush."

"Curt tried to save Alexander. . . ."

"Of course he did," Honora soothed.

"Is he all right?"

"The doctors don't know. It could go either way. But he's so weak, he looks as if any minute he could . . . Crys, I am such a coward, I can't even say the word."

They wound their arms around each other, pulling as close as they had when, in another decade on another continent, they had once before gasped out their terror and heartbreak in the face of death.

Gid fulfilled his promise, having Honora back in the ICU waiting room before her next visiting time.

Curt's drug-hazed eyes remained open for the entire five minutes and this seemed an improvement. One of the thoracic surgery team—a red-bearded younger man whom she had not met before—came in to examine the dressing on Curt's chest, and when she mentioned the positive omen, he warned her it was far too soon to draw conclusions.

The next visit Curt was delirious, mumbling unintelligibly. His legs and arms twitched and he would have flung himself around on the taut, sweatdamp sheet if it hadn't been for the restraining straps on his legs and arms. Joscelyn, who had accompanied her sister (TWO FAMILY MEMBERS) stood in the corner, covering her face, unable to look, but Honora bent over the bed, murmuring encouragingly as if her husband could comprehend what she said.

The next visiting hour he was weak but lucid.

72

The electric bed was adjusted to tilt up Honora's hips.

Although this July morning was torrid and muggy in Washington, the air conditioning kept the Talbott's

Georgetown house pleasantly cool, and she wore a silky bedjacket over her nightgown. She lay holding the latest *New Yorker*, but her attention had wandered from the short story, first to her omnipresent worries about Curt and then to her luck at being in this comfortable, well-managed house. Crystal, leaving Washington with Alexander's body, had been maddened with grief, incapable of coherent thought, so it was Gid who had suggested to Honora that she stay here rather than the hotel.

Just as well I took him up on his offer, Honora thought, nibbling another graham cracker to quiet her uneasy stomach.

Unbelievably, incredibly, she was pregnant!

After all these years, at her advanced age, having a baby.

Ten days ago, when the urologist whom she had consulted about her symptoms—a pressure on her bladder and a vague but persistent nausea—had referred her to a gynecologist, she had decided that he was shunting a patient suffering from the psychosomatic symptoms of stress onto another medical man. But the tests had proved her condition. The gynecologist had immediately ordered her to bed with her pelvis elevated so that the pull of gravity didn't force the baby out before its term.

In this position she would find herself thinking: *Another chance, another chance,* and laugh out loud. Today, though, her exultation was dimmed by her frantic urge to be at the George Washington University Hospital.

Curt was having another of his fevers.

His tiptop physical condition plus the indomitable strength of his will had resulted in a rapid initial recuperation. Less than three weeks after the shooting he was walking around the floor, vigorously, without any hint of a convalescent shuffle. Then, suddenly and inexplicably, his temperature had shot up to 105. He was pinned to his bed, shivering violently while nurses wrapped him in wet sheets. The baffling fever. It had recurred less violently five times. His team of doctors had pronounced that setbacks had to be anticipated after crucial, delicate thoracic surgery, but when they shook Honora's hand they would hold it a moment too long, subtle proof that they, too, were worried about this immensely rich patient whose medical bulletins went out on Associated Press.

Honora set down the magazine, sighing. Were Curt's relapses somehow connected to the rotten state of affairs at Ivory? Although officers of other multinational corporations now were being roasted in the Morrell Subcommittee's hot seat (the country was gasping over bribes so large that the cash had to be shipped in wooden crates), and although admiration for Curt's act of heroism had been voiced everywhere, several clients had tried to weasel out of existing contracts with Ivory. Worse, there had been no new jobs. Joscelyn and the other Ivory vice presidents flew constantly around the globe, cementing relationships and promoting goodwill, so far without results. Were these rejections weighing on Curt's subconscious, hampering his recovery?

The door opened and Lissie stood there. She and Vi had been in Washington since the day after the shooting, their presence a soothing comfort to Honora.

"Mommy," the child said, and instead of coming to sit on the bed as she usually did, she hung back in the doorway. "There's a lady here to see you."

"Ask one of the maids or Vi to talk to her," Honora signed.

"Vi's out getting her hair done. The lady says she's my aunt. She's very beautiful—"

"Honora?" It was Crystal's high, pretty voice. A moment later she brushed past Lissie into the room.

The sisters had not been together since this room had been strewn with mutilated clothing, and now Honora examined Crystal with that awful morning in mind, noting that her magnificently cut black silk blouse and skirt hung too loosely, faint shadows showed under her eyes, the hollows below her cheeks made the bones seem more pronounced, and her impeccably set hair was somehow softer in color—yes, a few random, pearly white strands showed near the roots. But what Honora found most alarming was Crystal's expression of uncertainty as she glanced around the room. The antithesis of the youthful Crystal who had radiated purposeful assurance.

Then Crystal smiled. "So it's true," she said. "When Joscelyn told me, my mouth dropped open. I told her flat out that I didn't believe her."

Honora beamed back. "What sane person would?"

"It's a total miracle."

"Oh, I'm not all that unique. My doctor says he's safely

delivered several crones older than me." Honora beckoned
to Lissie, and the child came over to stand shyly by the bed.
"Lissie, darling," she said. "This is your Auntie Crystal."

The child signed, "Alexander's mother?"

Honora nodded.

Lissie swallowed several times, clasping her arms around
herself. "Aunt Crystal," she said aloud. "I was very sad
about Alexander. We had fun together in Morocco."

Honora put her arm around the child's shoulders, a hug
of loving approbation. How rare it was nowadays for Lissie
to communicate orally with anyone but Vi and her parents—and this included Joscelyn.

It took Crystal several moments to comprehend Lissie's
speech. The lovely features worked and for a moment
Honora worried that her sister might once again break
down into those awful sobs of maddened grief. But Crystal
said slowly and loudly, "Thank you, dear. I had fun with
him, too."

"What brings you to Washington?" Honora asked. "Do
you have business here?"

"No, Gid's been taking that off my hands." Crystal did
not elaborate further on her presence during the city's least
pleasant season.

"Having you here's a terrific break for me. I'm stuck like
this—not that I'm complaining. But Crystal, this is *your*
house. Stop acting like a visitor—sit down."

Crystal remained at the foot of the bed. "Honora, there's
something I'd dearly love to do while I'm in town, if it's all
right with you. May I visit Curt?"

"Curt? He has a fever right now."

"I haven't thanked him yet for trying to save Alexander," Crystal said, turning to watch the shadows of lilac
branches move on the walls. "But I can understand that
you don't want me seeing him."

Her embarrassment and faint expression of culpability
made Honora realize that Crystal was begging permission
to visit Curt not because she, as wife, was custodian of his
physical condition but because he had fathered Alexander.
Honora's sympathy dimmed. Even now, with her nephew
dead, she could not stifle a nasty, carping quiver of jealousy.

Lissie had been watching them closely, trying to follow
the conversation.

"Lissie," Honora said aloud, giving the little girl another hug before signing, "will you ask the cook to send up some iced tea and lemonade for all of us, and some of those little spritz cookies?"

As the child left, Crystal said, "She's exquisite."

"The black hair's like Malcolm—he was quite the gorgeous man—but except for that, Crys, she's the image of you."

"She is?"

"Don't you see it? The chin, the nose, the mouth, the color of her eyes."

Crystal looked blank. She was gripping the footboard as if she were lost in a fog and desperate to hang on to something.

The compassion Honora felt for her sister was physical, as if a hand had reached into her chest and were roughly squeezing her heart. She touched the bed's control, the mechanism whirred and her head raised a few inches. "Crys," she said softly, "of course it's all right with me if you go to the hospital. But Curt *does* have a fever." She sighed. "He keeps getting them."

"From the shooting?"

"There's no other explanation. He never had fevers before."

"That awful, awful Lalarheini murderer!" Crystal burst out.

Though the so-called "Capitol Murder" remained unsolved, and the identity of the self-slain killer unknown, Crystal had high-up friends in the CIA who were convinced that the assassin had been a disciple of Khalid's. To fortify this belief they pointed out to her that Harold Fish had disappeared on the same day, and despite many weeks of an intensive search, had not been found. It seemed only reasonable to believe that one of Khalid's faithful had given his life to protect his prince's reputation.

"Crys, before you came in I was going to call the hospital to see how he was." Honora reached for the telephone on the bed table. "Let me see if he's up to company."

The male nurse answered, telling her that Mr. Ivory was in the bathroom, his temp was down to a hundred and he was looking forward to seeing Lissie and Vi this afternoon.

During the brief conversation, Crystal was whispering,

"I'll only be there a minute, just long enough to thank him."

"Tell Mr. Ivory he'll have another visitor," Honora said into the instrument. "My sister'll be by before lunch."

As Crystal walked along the recently mopped linoleum of the hospital corridor, she was wishing with all her heart that Alexander were at her side to tell her how to express her gratitude to Curt. That her son had loathed Curt and would have used his best persuasions (and oh, how clever he had been) to prevent her from rendering any such admission was beside the point: Alexander's death had destroyed her inner compass, the part of her which had unerringly pointed toward the attainment of her pragmatic goals. And not only did she have the same indecisiveness that had temporarily plagued her after Gideon's death, but at times she could scarcely function on a physical level. There were days when swallowing food was an impossibility, nights when she slept less than an hour. When she was with people, even Mitchell or Anina, her mind would start to flutter around and then go blank so that she lost the threads of contact. She no longer knew how to behave.

A man with spindly white shanks showing below his bathrobe was glancing at her. She moved more swiftly toward 407. That was the number Honora had given her—or was it? She fumbled in her purse for the slip of paper. Yes, 407.

She pushed open the heavy door.

She had expected to see Curt ill, drained, vanquished, with nurses hovering around him. Instead he was alone, sitting up in the high-propped bed, wearing horn-rim glasses and writing on a set of specifications with his ballpoint pen.

Who was Curt Ivory, her lifelong enemy, to be alive and working prosaically while her beautiful young Alexander lay in a massive bronze coffin beneath the cold, damp earth of San Francisco? A great wave of fury gathered inside her, rising and crashing down, inundating every trace of her gratitude.

"Crystal," he said.

At his old, faintly caustic smile, her heart raced with anger and she had to fight her urges to howl, to rip down the hundreds of get-well cards and telegrams Scotch-taped to the walls, to smash the gift books from the bureau, to hurl down the massed plants and floral arrangements.

"Honora told me you had a high fever and were very ill," she snapped in an accusatory tone.

"Recovering slowly is a better way of putting it. How is my wife? A great pair we are, both of us in hospital beds." Taking off his glasses and folding them, he said with a youthful grin, "A baby, how about that?"

"She *looked* fine," Crystal said.

His eager happiness changed to concern. "There's nothing wrong they're not telling me, is there?"

"It's extremely critical for a woman her age to have a baby," Crystal snapped. "Our mother wasn't nearly as old, and she died having Joscelyn."

"Look, Crystal, if you came here for warfare, you've won. I'm all out of nuclear devices."

"She's my sister," Crystal said coldly. "I'm worried about her."

"I know all the dangers, but there's no point even thinking about them. Honora's absolutely set on having this baby."

He lay back in the pillows. Though he now looked satisfactorily haggard, her fury was unassuagable.

She took several convulsive breaths. Why was she in this hospital room with her bitter rival? Oh, yes. "I came to Washington to thank you for trying to save Alexander," she said in a clenched voice.

"I'd like to take credit," he said. "But it was pure instinct. I saw a Smith and Wesson aimed and I reacted. A reflex action."

"And you'd have done the same if the gun had been pointed at somebody else?"

He squinted at her in an oblique way, as if a space of darkness lay between them. Was he peering down the tunnel of years to that long-ago night in San Rafael, or was he recollecting the insults he had shouted over the phone when she had admitted Alexander was his child?

"I've told you the truth unvarnished. I simply responded. There was a gun. I tried to shove the victim out of range."

"So what you're saying is you'd have done the same for a streetcleaner?" Why was she so impelled to prod out of Curt Ivory what Alexander never had managed to get, a confession of paternal attachment?

"Crystal," he said in a low, weary voice, "for years now I've tried to figure out what I felt for Alexander."

"What a rotten thing to say!" she cried. "He was the most wonderful son in the world."

"I'm feeling pretty punk. We'll talk about it some other time, okay?"

Crystal ignored the plea. Her words tumbled out over the edge of hysteria. "It's *your* loss you never got to know him. There's no guarantee that Honora can have this baby and you've got no other children."

"Lissie's my daughter," Curt whispered, turning his head away. "Crystal, would you step into the hall? There should be a guy out there reading *Track and Field*. He's my nurse. Tell him I need him, will you?"

"Alexander went to Morocco to find you, and you rejected him." Her voice rose to a scream. "How could you have ignored your only son? *You bastard, you unspeakable bastard!*"

Her heart was pounding at an alarming speed. Her chest, legs and stomach—every part of her—throbbed with the banging beat of her pulses. The need to destroy that had come over her on the night of Alexander's death was with her again. She darted to the nearest wall and yanked down a handful of cards.

Abruptly her fury drained. Once again she felt herself drowning in that icy, hideous sea where she was utterly alone, cut off from the rest of humanity. Falling on one of the couches, she broke into desolate sobs. She did not hear Curt get out of bed.

"Don't, Crystal, don't, honey." He sat next to her, his hand moving lightly on her bent head.

"That's . . . why he . . . got this hearing going. . . ." she sobbed. "I warned him . . . but he wanted to pay you back . . . for ignoring him. . . ."

"I wondered why he started it." There was no reproach in Curt's voice, only a heavy sadness.

"How am I going to live without him, Curt? How am I going to live?"

"You Sylvander girls are very strong—believe me, I know." He continued stroking her hair.

"There's nothing left for me . . . nothing."

"You have another son, a grandson."

"They're not . . . Alexander. . . ."

"Christ, Crystal, how sorry I feel for both of us."

Her eyes brimming with tears, she looked questioningly at him.

Frowning in bemusement, he said slowly, "Know something, Crystal? Until this moment I never realized how much I wish I could've saved him."

"Before, you said it was a reflex action."

"But it wasn't."

"Then why did you do it?"

"I have no past. He was my future. My son. . . ." Curt's eyes closed and his face was a mask of misery.

She put her arm around his shoulders. They pressed their cheeks together for a long, mourning moment, and she could feel the heat of his fever.

"I've been running and hiding from the truth of just how much he meant to me ever since I found out about him," Curt whispered. "Honora left me because of him, and I wanted no part of him. But there it was, Crystal. When the chips were down I wanted to save his life."

"Things get buried very deep inside."

"Exactly. Do you believe me when I say if it were possible I'd swap places with him right now?"

"I believe you," she said gently. "It's exactly the way I feel."

"You said you came here to thank me, but there's no reason that you should. I was his father."

Blowing her nose, she went to the door to call his nurse. *If only Alexander were alive,* she thought bleakly, *he would have had what he always longed for—the recognition of his father.*

Epilogue

From *The Wall Street Journal,* Wednesday May 8, 1985.

SAN FRANCISCO—Crystal Talbott, chairman of the board of the Talbott Group, in conjunction with the group's president, Gideon Talbott III, and Curt Ivory, chief executive officer of the Los Angeles headquartered Ivory Corporation, have announced a merger. Talbott-Ivory, like its parent companies, will be privately owned. Last year Ivory booked $8.3 billion, while Talbott's ran a close second with $7.9 billion. The new company will be the world's largest force in engineering and construction.

To celebrate the merger, Crystal threw a small reception. By chance the date she circled on her calendar fell a week before the Clay Street house became the Alexander Talbott Historical Mansion, and so she decided to display her efforts to her guests—the family, Imogene and a few dozen other friends, the senior vice presidents of both companies with their wives.

In the years since Alexander's death, Crystal had dedicated herself with evangelical fervor to building memorials to her slain son. There was an Alexander Talbott Park on a ransom of land in the Financial District—the green and ferny gardens, planned by Honora, had become a favorite place for workers from the surrounding tall office buildings to enjoy their bag lunches. Already under construction was the Alexander Talbott Modern Art Museum in Golden Gate Park, for which Crystal had donated the initial five million. This house, however, sacred to her son's boyhood, was her most hallowed project. For over a year, she had been tracking her size 4AA footprints in the sawdust and getting headaches from the whining saws as she directed European craftsmen in the uncovering of original woodwork that she had disguised.

* * *

Before dinner was served, the chief caterer caught Crystal's eye, giving the meaningful nod that meant the buffet was ready for the traditional hostess inspection. Crystal glanced around. Her hint of hesitancy, like the small lines fanning from her intensely blue eyes and the streaks of white in her natural ash blond hair, added a beguiling softness to her beauty. Mitchell, sensing she might need him, hurried to her side.

As they walked across the hall's magnificent parquet, under carpeting for many decades, he inquired solicitously, "What is it?"

"Everything's so much like the first time I came here when I was churchmouse poor. It's given me the willies."

Mitchell alone fully understood how Alexander's death had unleashed Crystal's prodding devils of self-doubt. "I've never heard so many compliments," he said. "Your dress, the house."

"You don't think I've gone overboard on this global theme?"

"The occasion calls for something unique." His tone deepened respectfully. "If Mr. Talbott were here, he'd tell you so, too."

He opened the side door of the baronial dining room. On either side of the vast Waterford chandelier dangled a pair of enormous floral replicas of the planet earth. One for Ivory, one for Talbott's. Various shades of roses portrayed the continents, and the oceans were blue-dyed marguerites. Both globes bristled with the sprays of white cymbidium that marked the projects of each company. (Ivory had regained its old momentum, and Talbott's, under Gid, had prospered without bid-rigging or any such monkey tricks.)

To carry out Crystal's theme, the menu was international. A turbaned Sikh stood behind a chafing dish of chicken curry, a sushi chef in a hapi coat presided over his art work—Crystal couldn't for the life of her comprehend how anyone could eat seaweed and raw fish wrapped around cold rice, but the younger crowd relished it. There was a veiled lady for the b'stilla and the baby lamb simmered in the Lalarheini manner. In deference to the three little boys, a burly, beaming young black man wearing a Giant's uniform held tongs over hot dogs.

"It's in perfect taste," Mitchell said, smiling down at his employer. "You've outdone yourself."

She patted his thin hand. "Thank you, Padraic."

For years her friends had been after her to break this attachment to Mitchell. Imogene had told her point-blank, "Old men dote on their secretaries, not *gorgeous* things like you. Why, you could *marry* the *cream* of the financial crop." Imogene's argument didn't hold water. Crystal had an enormous fortune of her own. Besides, what would some stranger, who saw only her admittedly ornamental exterior and put-together act, know of her idiosyncratic needs? Padraic had lived in this house with her that dreadful year after Alexander died, he had used a demitasse spoon to feed her purees, he had held her when her whole body trembled with chill.

And after she had moved to the penthouse condominium of a new Nob Hill high-rise, Mitchell had bought a small apartment in the same building to be near her, yet never in all the years had he so much as hinted at marriage or "going all the way." Their relationship suited Crystal to a tee.

Together they admired the length of buffet for another moment, then Crystal smiled at the chief caterer, a signal for him to push back the ornately carved folding doors to the hall.

Over the rippling music of the trio and the party clamor came a child's gleeful whoop that grew louder. One of the boys must be sliding down the highly polished banister.

"And I thought the magician would keep them entertained," Crystal sighed. "I'll bet you anything it's that little devil, Evan. Talk about uncontrollable."

She said it lightly. Like the rest of the family, she considered the child spoiled, and like the others could not condemn the Ivorys. (The truth was they did not overly indulge their son: Evan was Evan, born with an incorruptible strength of will.)

Honora hurried into the hall just as Evan landed on his feet. Crystal could see her sister bending and talking to the child, who replied with a cocky smile that lacked any trace of contrition.

"Evan, Daddy distinctly told you not to do that." Honora's rebuke was ameliorated by a stroking back of dark hair from the boy's domed forehead.

In appearance, Evan Ivory was all Sylvander, with narrow, attenuated bone structure, long face and round-lidded blue eyes—as a matter of fact, he looked very much like his grandfather.

Langley, now ensconced in the Ivorys' Los Angeles house with three shifts of nurses, emerged from his querulous misanthropy only for this grandson. He pronounced Evan a little gentleman. This, Langley's highest compliment, was a misrepresentation if ever Honora had heard one.

Evan shrugged away from her hand. "Didn't you ever slide down when you lived here?" he asked.

"It's a three-story fall from the top—"

"What's going on?" Curt had come into the hall.

"I tried the banister," Evan said.

"Didn't I tell you specifically it was off bounds?"

"What do you think gave me the idea?"

Evan might look like her side, but as he stared up at Curt with that same truculent half smile, Honora knew which parent he honestly resembled.

Unable to stifle his laugh, Curt said, "You'll really get it, buster, if you interrupt my toast."

Most of the guests had congregated in the rear drawing room, with its small-paned but spectacular view of sailboats gliding homeward through the lavender haze of the Bay. Accordingly, Lissie Ivory had seated herself in the music room, sparsely populated, farthest from the crowd. She had flown home for the party from Washington, where she was working toward a masters in psychology at Gallaudet. At nearly five ten, and slim, with long, glossy black hair, the childhood resemblance to Crystal was far less marked. Leaning back on one tanned arm, her legs thrust out in front of the poufed velvet piano bench, she might have been a model posing in the stylish, outsize white pantsuit, even to the expression of hauteur. Lissie raised a wall to prevent strangers from striking up a conversation and thus intruding on her handicap; however, with family and close friends her manner was warm and engagingly uninhibited. Her friendships and the three young men with whom she'd had relationships were all drawn from the lively if silent subculture of the deaf.

Joscelyn was sitting near her.

"What I can't get over," Lissie said, "is that Alexander grew up here. I had sort of a crush on him when I was little—he was the most hip, with-it person I could imagine. And could anything be more old-fashioned than this house?"

"Your aunt's done a fabulous job at restoration, but don't let it fool you." Joscelyn set down her scotch to sign. "This is how the place was when she married Uncle Gideon. Long before Alexander was born she'd changed everything to what we used to call ultramodern in those remote days. Believe it or not, this house was perfect for the Pollocks and de Koonings that are going to Alexander's modern art museum."

"Art, mmm. Auntie Joss, Mother and Daddy showed me some terrific photographs of wildflowers that your friend took." Lissie's arch smile proved what her intonation lacked. "He's quite an artist himself."

Pleasantly embarrassed, Joscelyn glanced toward the center drawing room, where Gid was talking to a robust man with thick, graying hair. "Her friend," as the family called him, was Dr. Jack Steiner, a divorced New York pediatrician whose avocation was photography. She had met him two years ago when she was working on a high-rise project in Manhattan. Dining alone at adjacent tables at a small Columbus Avenue Thai restaurant, they had struck up an acquaintanceship. Joscelyn's unrelenting guilts, not to mention the searing memories of Curt's rebuff, had kept her aloof for a long time. But the doctor had wooed her via long distance calls and by mailing her rare jazz albums and humorously captioned samples of his photography. She had succumbed cautiously. They had shared several bicoastal weekends before she would consent to a vacation at the Mauna Kea. And after Jack had mentioned that he would be in San Francisco for a medical conference on the date of this bash, she had needed to work up a ridiculous amount of courage to invite him.

Jack caught her glance. He smiled, tapping his pipe against his nice square teeth to let her know that he was enjoying himself. Joscelyn half-raised her hand, smiling. *Doubtless Crystal looks down on him because he's Jewish, but so what? God knows he's far more presentable than that creepy secretary of hers.*

"I think he's great," Lissie said. "And so do Mother and Daddy."

"He *is* nice, isn't he?"

"And very interested in you."

"We're just good friends," Joscelyn said, reddening.

Imogene, bone thin and looking like death warmed over from her most recent face-lift, stood in the doorway calling that dinner was *served*.

Joscelyn said to Lissie, "The buffet is officially open. I understand from reliable sources that there's a terrific curry."

A minute later, Vi waddled over to slowly spell out that there was a b'stilla and Lissie should get some now before it was all gone.

Then Honora drifted into the music room. "Lissie, the buffet's open. Wait until you see the sushi."

Lissie glanced in mock dismay at Vi, Joscelyn and Honora. "I'll be fatter than a house, with my three mothers," she said. But it was Honora's hand that she clasped.

When everyone was in the hall or dining room, Gid stood on the staircase, introducing his uncle.

Curt took a glass and Gid handed him the mike.

"I'm going to make two toasts, but I promised Crystal not to let the dinner get ruined, so they'll be short." He raised the tulip-shaped glass. "I give you Talbott-Ivory, a joining of the two best damn engineering outfits the world has ever seen."

With a scattering of hurrahs, the assembly chorused, "To Talbott-Ivory."

"And now let's drink to absent friends." Curt held his glass higher. "I give you Gideon Talbott, my mentor, a man of utmost integrity, an illustrious engineer. He's still with us, and if you don't believe me, take a look out the window and you'll see his bridges." Curt paused, and when he spoke again his eyes were fixed on Crystal. "And I give you Alexander Talbott, whose brilliance was cut short. Many of you here knew Alexander both as a boy and a man." His voice went lower with sincerity. "I envy you."

Crystal's guests drank her vintage French champagne, but she did not. She was weeping, and so was Gid, who had his arm around her.

The crowd milled toward the buffet.

Curt drew Honora a few steps up the staircase. "Listen, you didn't mind my mentioning Alexander?"

"I'm glad you did."

"Time was when you couldn't cope with that particular situation."

"Neither of us could," she said. The years had healed her wounds and now she was able to think of Alexander as her dead nephew. And as for Curt, after that confrontation with Crystal in his hospital room, his fevers (and paternal resentments) had ceased.

For Honora, the dark nooks and corners, the ornate bulges and heavily fringed velvet upholstery were crowded with youthful ghosts. Filled with a desire to recapture that time when life was lit by a younger, rosier star, she set down her half-eaten curry, murmuring an excuse to Gid and Anne, who were sharing a chair next to hers. She slipped across the hall into the circular room, the *Salon Oriental.*

She was alone and as she closed the door, she could hear, actually hear, the hushed, bickering English voices. Her ears tingled, growing warm. She sank down on the huge, voluptuous central ottoman, remembering, remembering.

As the door opened she glanced up with a hint of annoyance. But the intruder was Crystal, a flutter of fog-gray chiffon, the other half of her memories.

"So you weren't able to resist either," Crystal said. "Can't you just see the pair of us in our City of Paris marked-down bargain hats?"

"It's sheer magic, Crystal, the way you've turned back the clock."

Absurdly delighted by Honora's approval, Crystal laughed. "Do you remember how you fought against coming?"

"I never did have your good sense."

Crystal took this sincere compliment for a sisterly dig, possibly about Padraic Mitchell: though she clung obstinately to him, she was extremely sensitive about the relationship, seeing criticism everywhere. "If it hadn't been for my so-called good sense," she retorted, "what sort of lives would we have had?"

"Exactly what I was thinking when you came in. Crystal, Gideon was so very good to us."

Though mollified, Crystal couldn't help adding another prod. "You never would've met Curt."

"Crystal . . . have you ever stopped to think that we're

each connected to him by our children? I have Evan. Joscelyn asked him to adopt Lissie. And there was . . ." Her voice faded. Crystal's lovely mouth had curved down. Honora put an arm around the small, square shoulders. "Crys, do you still miss him so terribly?"

"Every day—every single day—I wake up thinking, 'This morning I'll see Alexander.' " Crystal paused, continuing in a determined voice, "Curt tells me you're doing a reflecting garden for the Norock Museum."

Honora held up her crossed fingers. "Hoping to." Pregnancy had put an end to her London landscaping career. However, Evan, after his first two years, had steadfastly battled off any attempt at high-caliber mothering so Honora had begun working again, this time from an office in her Bel Air house: she had more than enough jobs to keep her busy. "They're making their decision next week."

The door opened again.

"Crystal, Honora," Joscelyn said.

As her sisters turned toward her, Joscelyn couldn't control a dart of that old, childish misery. *They never thought of asking me to come in here with them.* Would she ever shake this sense of being barred from their closeness, cut off from their enviably popular, more beautiful lives? "Why're you hiding?"

"We both felt drawn," Crystal said with a hint of annoying mystery.

"To what?" Joscelyn demanded.

"This room. It's where we were put to wait for Gideon the first time we visited," Honora explained, smiling and making a circular, invitational gesture with her arm. "Come be nostalgic with us."

Feeling part of the Sylvander sisterhood again, Joscelyn sat on the ottoman with them. "What point in the memoirs have you reached?"

Crystal said, "We'd just started."

"The first time *I* saw the place I can remember quite distinctly thinking that there couldn't be a man richer or more lavish than Gideon."

"He was always tremendously generous," Honora put in.

"Looking back, in our cases maybe a bit much so," Crystal said thoughtfully. "He gave us too much too soon."

"Especially me," Joscelyn chuckled. "God, the amount of cake I gorged at those Open Houses!"

"It must've been pretty dreary for a child," Honora excused. "No wonder the food seemed the best thing to you."

The sentimentality that Joscelyn normally kept incarcerated had been released. "Not the best thing," she said a bit shakily. "I know I kept it well hidden, but having you two for sisters was the best thing—and it still is."

"Same here," Honora and Crystal said at the same moment.

Misty-eyed, the sisters wound their arms around one another, a joint hug like the embraces that the Sylvander family had shared long ago.

Joscelyn pulled away first.

They began dredging up recollections of those long-ago months when they had lived under this immense slate roof, interrupting one another as the memories flooded.

Curt had come to the door, which Joscelyn had left ajar. He stood for maybe a minute watching the three women on whose lives he had made such an indelible imprint. "Don't get too close to the nitty-gritty, gals," he said, his flippant tone marred by a slight huskiness. "You have an eavesdropper."

As they looked toward him, each remained immersed in the past.

Crystal inevitably thought of the hideous speck of time when he had flung himself between a gun and all that she held dearest on this earth.

Joscelyn's mind jumped to a thin, homely, painfully bright little girl falling for this same teasing smile—oh, how Curt had molded her life.

Honora's thoughts were softer and fuzzier than those of her sisters: she was trying to recapture the magic of that love-at-first-sight moment by the bric-a-brac covered piano.

He came over to link his arm in hers. "I hate like hell to break this up," he said, "but in case you've forgotten there's a party going on."

His smile included them all.

The three women smiled back, but as they left the circular room with him their eyes were again moist.